Alexander Balloch Grosart, Henry More

The Complete Poems of Dr. Henry More,1614-1687

For the first time collected and edited: with memorial-introduction, notes and

illustrations, glossarial index, and portrait, &c.

Alexander Balloch Grosart, Henry More

The Complete Poems of Dr. Henry More,1614-1687
*For the first time collected and edited: with memorial-introduction, notes and illustrations,
glossarial index, and portrait, &c.*

ISBN/EAN: 9783337402679

Printed in Europe, USA, Canada, Australia, Japan

Cover: Foto ©Andreas Hilbeck / pixelio.de

More available books at **www.hansebooks.com**

Chertsey Worthies' Library.

THE
COMPLETE POEMS

OF

Dr. Henry More

(1614-1687)

FOR THE FIRST TIME COLLECTED AND EDITED:
WITH MEMORIAL-INTRODUCTION, NOTES AND ILLUSTRATIONS,
GLOSSARIAL INDEX, AND PORTRAIT, &c.

BY

THE REV. ALEXANDER B. GROSART, LL.D., F.S.A.

ST. GEORGE'S, BLACKBURN, LANCASHIRE.

PRINTED FOR PRIVATE CIRCULATION.

1878.

CONTENTS.

N.B.—In Nos. IV. and V. there are quotations from his other Poems ; but it was deemed well to give them—being so short—as the Author did, viz. in his Poems-proper and in his Prose.

. The Portrait of More is to go before the general Title-page, and the Plate of Diagrams, etc., between pages 148 and 149.

MEMORIAL-INTRODUCTION.

I.—BIOGRAPHICAL.

RICHARD WARD, A.M., 'Rector of Ingoldsby, in Lincolnshire,' has written the 'Life' of our Worthy in a considerable volume.[1] Of it the Rev. BENJAMIN STREET, B.A., now of Barnetby-le-Wold (Lincolnshire), in his 'Historical Notes on Grantham and Grantham Church,'[2] says— 'His [More's] Life is in the Vestry Library, written by a Rector of Ingoldsby, who achieved in it the difficult task of writing a Biography without giving any information respecting his hero' (p. 155). Unfortunately this drastically-put verdict is ill-warranted by the Critic's own notices; for notwithstanding that from local advantages—as being resident in Grantham—he might have added to our information, he does not one iota, and blunders, *e.g.*, he turns Alexander More into Sir Alexander More, Knt. (repeatedly), and our Dr. Henry More himself into 'Sir Henry More.'[3] More justly, but still too severely, has PRINCIPAL TULLOCH said of the quaint discursive old book : 'Ward's Life is interesting, but vague, uncritical, and digressive, after the manner of the time.'[4] I feel in-clined to soften, or at least explain away, each adjective. The uneventfulness outwardly of the 'Life' accounts for the few facts given, and so for a certain 'vague' element. 'Un-critical' betrays, I fear, hasty reading; for it is superabundant in its criticism, albeit perchance not very careful or sifting in its selection of points. Then as to its being 'digressive,' I for one am thankful, seeing that—as in De Quincey later—it is in the digressions the best *bits* are met with. No one who will leisurely and with becoming sympathy study Ward's 'Life' will regret it. It is further to be remembered that the Biographer left behind him an additional Manuscript, wherein he discusses more fully, and with all his first enthusiasm of reverence, the manifold Works of More.[1] Besides these, More has written a kind of Autobiography in the 'Prefatio Generalissima' of his 'Opera Omnia' (1679), and earlier in his 'Apology' (1664), giving a 'General Account' of the *motif* and purpose of his writings—the former as notable as Herbert of Cherbury's for its supreme self-estimate. The 'Biographia Britannica' (1760)—those noble old folios, matterful and painstaking,

---

[1] The Life of the Learned and Pious Dr. Henry More, Late Fellow of Christ's College in Cambridge. To which are an-nex'd Divers of his Useful and Excellent Letters. By Richard Ward, A.M. Rector of Ingoldsby in Lincolnshire. London, Printed and Sold by Joseph Downing in Bartholomew Close near West Smithfield. 1710. 8vo, 12 leaves [unpaged] and pp. 366.
[2] Grantham, 1857. 1 vol. 8vo, pp. 164.
[3] I have to thank Mr. Street for kind attention to my in-quiries, so that it is a pain to need thus to retort his harsh words on Ward.
[4] Rational Theology, etc., vol. ii. p. 304.

[1] Principal Tulloch inadvertently states that this Manuscript was in the possession of *John* Crossley, Esq. It is in the good keeping of my bookish and scholarly friend James Crossley, Esq., F.S.A., Manchester—to whom I venture to iterate Pro-fessor Mayor's appeal in Notes and Queries ('2d Series, vii.' 59 : pp. 249, 50), that he will make this MS. public, annotated like his Worthington's Diary. The published 'Life' and this MS. should be most acceptable additions to the very valuable series of the Chetham Society's books.

and putting to shame the literary scambling of to-day—has also a Life of him ; and elsewhere you come on notices that show the *grip* he took of his contemporaries, and especially his swift readiness to write 'weighty and powerful' letters even when the inquirer who turned to him for counsel was of the oddest.

Some day—may it be soon—a capable son of Cambridge will address himself to reproducing worthily the collective Works of that remarkable group of Thinkers whereof HENRY MORE was the most potential. For it cannot be that the University Presses will reprint such empty and effete 'Collective Works' as our shelves groan under, and continue to neglect them (except JOHN SMITH), — RALPH CUDWORTH, BENJAMIN WHICHCOT, RUST, GLANVILL, CRADOCK, PETER STERRY, JOHN NORRIS.[1] PRINCIPAL TULLOCH'S most masterly and thorough 'Rational Theology and Christian Philosophy in England in the Seventeenth Century,'[2] like young ALFRED VAUGHAN'S 'Mystics,'[3] only exacerbates one's longing for accessible critical texts of the Works. When these Works are thus revived, it will be recognised that these Thinkers and noble Livers—each meet follower of Him, 'the first true gentleman that ever breathed '[4] —have shaped and coloured our highest and purest thought and feeling to an extent that your so-called 'Histories of Philosophy' —whether home or foreign—only shallowly estimate.[5]

My little task is a much humbler one. I have first of all to give the ascertained outward facts of my Worthy's 'Life ;' and thereafter examine suggestively, rather than exhaustively, his Poetry, as now for the first time brought together.

The earliest of the name—variously spelled earlier and later Moore and More—was a WILLIAM MOORE of Lichfield, co. Stafford (buried at Grantham 27th November 1587). His son RICHARD MOORE is found at Grantham, married to Goditha, a daughter of John Green of Uppingham, co. Rutland (she was buried at Grantham 26th September 1608[1]). He was a Justice of the Peace for the Parts of Kesteven in 1584: M.P. for Grantham in the Armada year, 1588 : Receiver for co. Lincoln 1591-2. He died 10th, and was buried at Grantham 11th August 1595 (Will dated 29th March 1595, sealed 3d April, and proved 29th October 1595). The eldest son of this RICHARD MOORE[2] was Alexander Moore of Grantham. He was aged 25 at his father's death.[3] He married Anne, daughter of William Lacy

---

1 It is invidious to go into minute detail, but surely BRAGGE on the Parables, etc., and BISHOP PATRICK'S Works (9 volumes ! !) might have been long-delayed to say the least.

2 2 vols. 8vo.   1872 (Blackwood).

3 2 vols. cr. 8vo, 2d edn.

4 Thomas Dekker.

5 See Principal Tulloch's remonstrance with the University of Cambridge and its Pitt Press (Preface, p. xii., note 1) ; but he is mistaken (*meo judicio*) in imagining that Henry More's Works are 'forgotten' and without living influence. Students of them increase, and will. Professor Mayor is indicated by the Principal as *the* man to whom the noble task ought to be confided. All who know his immense erudition and 'collections,' and almost morbid painstaking, will agree.

---

1 An Elizabeth More was buried at Grantham May 1568. She was daughter of a Gabriel Armstrong. She was the first wife of Richard. Goditha Green was his second wife. She bore him Alexander in 1570.

2 Besides Alexander there were the following :—(*a*) Richard More, second son, living 12th October 1652, and had a son Adam baptized at Grantham 28th May 1603 : living 12th October 1652. (*b*) Thomas, third son, living 29th March 1595—to be apprenticed. (*c*) Gabriel Moore, D.D., fourth son : baptized at Grantham 18th April 1585 : Prebendary of Westminster, installed 8th March 1631-2 : died at his lodgings in Clement's Lane, Westminster, 17th, and buried in Westminster Abbey 29th October 1652 : Will dated 12th October, and proved 2d November 1652. (*d*) Elizabeth, married at Grantham, 1583, Francis Everingham of Barton-on-Humber—not named in her father's Will. (*e*) Susan, baptized at Grantham 10th October 1582 : married Sir Richard Green, Clerk of ye Check of ye Gent. Pensioners : dead 12th October 1652—his Will, as of Dixley Grange, co. Leicester, dated 10th December 1637, and proved by her 9th February 1637-8. (*f*) Robert, baptized 22d January, and buried 1st February 1586-7 at Grantham. (*g*) Ursula, living 1595, wife of John Fisher, with daughter Martha. (*h*) Mary, unmarried 29th March 1595 : but apparently contracted to Raphael Wiseman, Silkman in Cheapside.

3 As the 'Philosophical Poems' were dedicated to him in 1647, he was then living ; but the Register at Grantham from October 5, 1644 to March 27, 1652 has no burial entries. So Canon Clements informs me.

of Deeping, co. Lincoln (marriage-settlement dated 1st March 1594-5).

These were the parents of our HENRY MORE. The father was Alderman of Grantham in 1594, and Mayor in 1617, and onward repeatedly. The mother's family, by intermarriages, linked on our Poet and Philosopher to many illustrious names — and we must pause to note some of them. Besides his daughter Anne (our More's mother) William Lacy had two sons and three daughters. Two of these brought about the relation and associations I have intimated. *First*, Robert, one of the sons, who is described as of Washingborough (which is a parish close to the city of Lincoln and within its ancient 'Liberty'), married Cassandra, daughter of Thomas Ogle of Pinchbeck, co. Lincoln. This lady's mother was Jane Welby, sister of Henry Welby the celebrated recluse;[1] and her Grandmother Beatrice, the wife of Richard Ogle, was a sister of Sir Anthony Cooke of Gidea Hall in Essex, sometime Tutor of Edward the Sixth. Her father was thus first cousin to Mildred Cooke, who, as second wife to Lord Burghley, was mother to Robert, Earl of Salisbury. Robert Lacy died without issue, and his widow Cassandra married, secondly, Sir Francis Beaumont, who was uncle on the mother's side to George Villiers, Duke of Buckingham, and Crashaw's friend and convert, Susan, Countess of Denbigh. Sir Francis Beaumont was buried at Washingborough in 1625, and his widow Cassandra in 1632, leaving no issue.

Secondly—Elizabeth, one of the daughters of William Lacy—and aunt of course to our Worthy—became the wife of Henry Chol-

meley, founder of that branch of the family now residing, as baronets, at Easton, near Grantham. Henry Cholmeley was knighted and died in 1620, leaving a son and heir— our Poet's first cousin—of whose alliances we find the following account in Burke and the usual authorities:—'Henry Cholmeley succeeded to the estate of Easton, and died in 1632. He married Elizabeth Sondes, the daughter of Sir Richard Sondes of Throwley, and sister of George Sondes, who, in consideration of his loyalty to Kings Charles I. and II., was created by the latter monarch Earl of Feversham. . . . The mother of Elizabeth Sondes . . . was Susan Montague, daughter of Sir Edward Montague, Baronet,[1] by Elizabeth Harrington, daughter of Sir James Harrington of Exton, maternally descended from the Sydneys. Henry Cholmeley and Elizabeth Sondes had issue Montague Cholmeley of Easton, who died in 1652. He married Elizabeth, daughter of Sir Edward Hartopp, Bart., and maternal grand-daughter of Sir Erasmus Dryden, Bart., and therefore first cousin to "glorious John."'

These details are somewhat of the Dr. Dry-as-dust school, some reader may exclaim. But 'an' it please' him, others will be interested thus to connect the names of SYDNEY, SIR THOMAS MORE, HARRINGTON, DRYDEN, and our POET LAUREATE, with our HENRY MORE.[2] Returning from this genealogical excursion, it thus appears that our More was the seventh son of Alexander More of Grantham, by his wife Anne, daughter of William Lacy. He was baptized at Grantham (in Lincolnshire) on October 10th, 1614 (*not* born 12th October, as Ward

---

[1] Henry Welby, 'the Phœnix of these times, who lived at his house in Grub Street forty and four years, and in that space was never seen by any,' married Alice, daughter of Thomas White of Tuxford in co. Nottingham, by Anne Cecil, sister of Lord Burghley. He left an only daughter and heiress, who married Sir Christopher Hildyard of Winstead, co. York (Marvell's birthplace). Tennyson is lineally descended from this alliance.

[1] Sir Edward Montague's mother was Helen or Eleanor Roper, sister to that William Roper of Eltham who married Margaret More, daughter of the great Chancellor, . . .

'who clasp'd in her last trance
Her murdered father's head.'

[2] I am indebted to my good friend, the Rev. J. H. Clark, M.A., Vicar of West Dereham, for most of these details; but see 'Burke's Peerage and Baronetage,' and similar reference-works.

and all hitherto).[1] He probably drew his Christian name from *Henry* Cholmeley (as *supra*.[2])

It was something for a Poet to have had for birthplace so renowned a spot. Every one knows that few small towns (speaking comparatively) have so venerable and lustrous a history to recount. 'Royalism' must have interpenetrated its very atmosphere, though to-day—if we may subordinate Queens Editha, Maud, Eleanor—its most memorable historical incident is the victory of one ' Colonel Cromwell ' over far-outnumbering troops of the King (Charles I.). In Literature it must ever hold a place of honour ; for besides Henry More, JOHN STILL (Bishop), author of that drollest and quaintest of our elder English Comedies, ' Gammer Gurton's Needle ' (1575), was also born in Grantham. Supremest of all, to its School—from neighbouring Woolsthorpe—came Isaac Newton, as earlier Sir William Cecil. Its great church is the cynosure of pilgrim-visitants from all lands.

I know of only a single allusion to his mother by More—that she, like his father, was a Calvinist. Of his father he has frequent notices. The Epistle-dedicatory of his Poems to his father (p. 4) may be at this point advantageously turned to. WARD— after characterising the son as ' this Eximous [= eximious, excellent] Person,' says of the father, that he was ' one of excellent understanding, probity, and piety ; and of a fair estate and fortune in the world, remembered yet with esteem in the place where he liv'd ' (p. 22). The elder Mores were, like most of the Puritans, accepters of the theological system known as Calvinism—the Calvinism of the youthful ' Institutes ' rather than of the later Commentaries and Letters of John Calvin. In the outset, I fear the home-discipline and teaching were over-stern and exacting. Yet it is to be pleasantly remembered that the rigid family-training of these our forefathers was based on gravity born of an abiding sense of the presence of Almighty God everywhere and always ; nor less so that evidence remains that there were breaks of humour and sparkles of wit and the warble of quiet laughter, among the staid and thoughtful men and women of the type of the Mores. I like to recall that it was to his father Master Henry owed his bookish tastes and his introduction to Spenser's 'Fairy Queen.'

The Registers of the famous School of

---

[1] Authority—Parchment Roll at Grantham, entitled ' A true Certificate of all such as were baptized in the Parish Church of Grantham, Anno Domini 1614.' The entry is thus :—' October 10. Henry the sonne of Mr. [Alexander] More' (Folio Register Parchment)— Rev. Benjamin Street, as before, and Canon Clements, to me.

[2] I relegate to a foot-note the other members of the household as follow :—(*a*) Richard, baptized at Grantham 18th December 1597 : admitted to Gray's Inn 3d March 1617-18, as son and heirapparent. (*b*) Alexander More, baptized at Grantham 17th December 1598 : admitted to Gray's Inn 15th March 1619-20 : Councillor of Law of Gray's Inn 1634 : M.P. for Grantham 1628 : ob. v.p. Buried at Grantham 5th January 1635-6, as Alexander More the younger, Esquire. He married Catharine, daughter of Richard Oliver of Shire Lane, co. Middlesex ; (she married, secondly, Peregrine Mackworth, second son of Sir Thomas Mackworth of Normanton, co. Rutland, first baronet : married at Grantham 17th February 1652-3 : ob. s.p.). The children of Alexander More were (1) Richard, first son and heir, æt. 6 years and 2 months at father's death ; probably died young : (2) Gabriel More, baptized at Grantham 26th October 1634 : second son, and heir of his brother : heir and executor of his great-uncle, Gabriel, whose Will be proved, 1652 : died 21st February, and buried at Grantham 1st March 1698-9 : Will dated 16th October 1697 : proved 16th June 1699 : last of his Family, and left his estates to charitable uses. See more onward. (3) Anne, baptized at Grantham 26th December 1630. (4) Catherine, living 12th October 1652. (5) Jane, baptized at Grantham 14th January 1635-6 (a posthumous child). (*c*) William, baptized at Grantham, 27th March, and buried there 21st August 1602. (*d*) John, baptized at Grantham 4th December 1603. (*e*) Gabriel, baptized at Grantham 24th July 1608, and buried there 27th February 1652-3. (*f*) William, baptized at Grantham 10th July 1609, buried there 5th November 1657. (*g*) Henry—is our Worthy. (*h*) Elizabeth, baptized at Grantham 1st June 1600 ; married Henry Calverley of Calverley, co. York : apparently dead in 1634, ob. s.p. (*i*) Jane, baptized at Grantham 21st June 1612 : married there 23d September 1634, to John Colby of Nappa (see Dugdale's Yorkshire, p. 47). (*j*) Catherine, baptized at Grantham 27th October, November, or December 1596. (*k*) Goditha, buried at Grantham 15th September 1596. (*l*) Anne, baptized at Grantham 1st January 1604-5, and buried there 21st June 1607. For these and other entries I have to give thanks, mainly, to my always well-furnished and always obliging friend, Dr. Chester of Bermondsey. I have also to acknowledge help on the same lines from Arthur Larken, Esq., through the Rev. J. H. Clark, as before, and Canon Clements, Vicar of Grantham.

Grantham—founded by Bishop RICHARD Fox, founder of Corpus Christi College, Oxford, and confirmed and enlarged by Edward VI.—have perished ; but there can be no doubt that young More received his early education in it. I question if he were well-grounded in this School ; for his Latin Prose is not of the purest, and his Latin and Greek Verse somewhat faulty.[1] His School Exercises sorely exercised his Masters with admiration (= wonder). ' And yet,' observes his Biographer, ' the Dr. hath been heard to say, that the wonder and pleasure with which he and others would sometimes read them, elated him not ; but that he was rather troubled and asham'd ; as not knowing whether he could do so well another time ' (p. 22). I shall have occasion to return on this characteristic trait. His progress at Grantham School, 'his anxious and thoughtful genius from his childhood' (*ibid.*) struck his paternal uncle ; and he took him in charge. He was sent in his thirteenth or fourteenth year to Eton.[2] Thither he certainly carried an old man's head on very young shoulders. For in his ' Prefatio ' (as before) he informs us that even thus early he had rebelled against the teaching (as he understood or misunderstood it) of his father on Predestination. His uncle threatened him with the birch if he did not acquiesce in the family orthodoxy. It is easy to cry out against the threat ; but doubtless it was directed against the pertness and 'answering-back' as much as against the impugnment of the specific opinion. *Certes* such matters were 'too high' for the lad, and he had been a healthier man every way had he not so prematurely 'intermeddled ' with the *metaphysic* of this prodigious postulate, not of Calvinism or of the

Bible merely, but of universal nature and human nature. Here is his own narrative, than which few more remarkable are to be read : [1]—

' For the better Understanding of all this, we are to take (*saith he*) our Rise a little higher ; and to premise some things which fell out in my *Youth* ; if not also in my *Childhood* it self : To the End that it may more fully appear, that the things which I have written, are not any borrowed, or far-fetch'd Opinions, owing unto *Education*, and the *Reading of Books* ; but the proper Sentiments of *my own* Mind, drawn and derived from my most *intimate Nature* ; and that every *Humane Soul* is no *abrasa tabula*, or *mere Blank Sheet* ; but hath *innate Sensations* and *Notions* in it, both of *good* and *evil*, *just* and *unjust*, *true* and *false* ; and those very strong and vivid.

' Concerning which Matter, I am the more assur'd, in that the *Sensations* of my own Mind are so far from being owing to *Education*, that they are directly contrary to it ; I being bred up, to the almost 14th *Year* of my Age, under *Parents* and a *Master* that were great *Calvinists* (but withal, very pious and good ones) : At which Time, by the Order of my *Parents*, persuaded to it by my *Uncle*, I immediately went to *Æton* School ; not to learn any new Precepts or Institutes of *Religion* ; but for the perfecting of the *Greek* and *Latin* Tongue. But neither there, nor yet any where else, could I ever swallow down that hard Doctrine concerning *Fate*. On the contrary, I remember, that upon those Words of *Epictetus*, Ἄγε με ὦ Ζεῦ καὶ σύ ἡ πεπρωμένη, *Lead me, O Jupiter and thou Fate*, I did (with my *eldest Brother*, who then, as it happened, had accompanied my *Uncle* thither) very stoutly, and earnestly for my Years, dispute against this *Fate* or *Calvinistick Predestination*, as it is usually call'd : And that my *Uncle*, when he came to know it, chid me severely ; adding menaces withall of Correction, and a Rod for my immature Forwardness in *Philosophizing* concerning such Matters : Moreover, that I had such a deep Aversion in my Temper to this Opinion, and so firm and unshaken a Perswasion of the *Divine Justice* and *Goodness* ; that on a certain Day, in a Ground belonging to *Æton* College, where the Boys us'd to play, and exercise themselves, *musing* concerning these Things with my self, and recalling to my mind this Doctrine of *Calvin*, I did thus seriously and deliberately conclude within my self, *viz. If I am one of those that are predestinated unto Hell, where all Things are full of nothing but Cursing and Blasphemy, yet will I behave*

---

[1] In the Cambridge University MSS. (G g vi. 11, art. 1, pp. 2-33) is a correspondence (1671-2) between More and H. H., wherein the latter corrects More's Latinity.

[2] The Rev. Dr. GOODFORD writes me that there is no record at Eton of our More's attendance at the celebrated School. The sooner his name is added to its great roll the better.

---

[1] Ward, as before, pp. 5-8.

*my self there patiently and submissively towards God ;
and if there be any one Thing more than another, that
is acceptable to him, that will I set my self to do with a
sincere Heart, and to the utmost of my Power :* Being
certainly persuaded, that if I thus demeaned my self,
he would hardly keep me long in that Place. Which
Meditation of mine, is as firmly fix'd in my Memory,
and the very place where I stood, as if the Thing
had been transacted but a Day or two ago.

' And as to what concerns the *Existence* of GOD :
Though in that Ground mentioned, walking, as my
Manner was, slowly, and with my Head on one Side,
and kicking now and then the Stones with my Feet,
I was wont sometimes with a sort of Musical and
Melancholick Murmur to repeat, or rather humm to
my self, those Verses of *Claudian :*

> *Sæpe mihi dubiam traxit sententia mentem ;
> Curarent Superi terras ; an nullus inesset
> Rector, & incerto fluerent Mortalia casu.*

[*Oft hath my anxious Mind divided stood ;
Whether the Gods did mind this lower World ;
Or whether no such Ruler (Wise and Good)
We had ; and all things here by Chance were hurld.*]

Yet that exceeding hail and entire *Sense* of GOD,
which *Nature* her self had planted deeply *in me,*
very easily silenced all such slight and *Poetical Dubi-
tations* as these. Yea even in my first *Childhood,*
an *inward Sense* of the *Divine Presence* was so strong
upon my Mind ; that I did then believe, there could
no Deed, Word, or Thought be hidden from him :
Nor was I by any others that were older than my
self, to be otherwise persuaded. Which Thing since
no distinct Reason, Philosophy, or Instruction taught
it me at that Age ; but only an *internal Sensation*
urg'd it upon me ; I think it is very evident, that
this was an *innate Sense* or *Notion* in me, contrary
to some witless and sordid *Philosophasters* of our
present Age. And if these cunning *Sophisters* shall
here reply ; that I drew this Sense of mine *ex Tra-
duce,* or by way of *Propagation,* as being born of
Parents exceeding *Pious* and *Religious ;* I demand,
how it came to pass, that I drew not *Calvinism* also
in along with it ? For both my *Father* and *Uncle,*
and so also my *Mother,* were all earnest followers
of *Calvin.* But these Things I pass ; since men
Atheistically disposed cannot so receive them, as
I from an inward Feeling speak them.'

These and kindred revelations impress me
with the awfulness—and I use the word
deliberately—of the responsibility of the
Head-master of a great School such as Eton,
or indeed any School, in the knowledge that
just such agitated young minds are constantly
being placed under their supervision and
influence.

Coincident with his rejection of the paternal Calvinism, *in re* predestination, was a
like rejection of paternal plans for his life-
occupation. Not only his opinions but his
career he decided for himself. His father
evidently wished him to enter on some active
work-a-day profession, as a road to wealth
and position. But the son answered—as we
learn from the Epistle-dedicatory of his
Poems—

' Your early Encomiums of Learning and Philosophie did so fire my credulous [= believing] Youth
with the desire of the knowledge of things, that your
After-advertisements, how contemptible Learning
would prove without Riches, and what a piece of
Unmannerlinesse and Incivility it would be held to
seem wiser then them that are more wealthy and
powerfull, could never yet restrain my mind from
her first pursuit, nor quicken my attention to the
affairs of this World. But this bookish disease, let it
make me as much poor as it will, it shall never make
me the lesse just.'—(p. 4.)

His father evidently acquiesced ; and,
indeed later, when he visited his son at
Christ's College and saw him surrounded
with his books, he told him he was occupied
in ' an angelical way.' Nor need there have
been any shadow of fear of poverty. From
the outset he was well-provided for, and
onward inherited a considerable fortune. So
that self-dedicated to ' high thinking ' and
noble-living, as with Wordsworth in an after-
generation, he found abundant and unexpected friends and means, without need of
the greater Poet's ' Stamp-office ' drudgery,
in person or by deputy. He never had—
any more than Wordsworth—a doubt of the
rightness of the mode of life he had chosen.

He remained three years at Eton. He then
proceeded—in 1631—in his seventeenth
year, to Cambridge University. His admis-
sion-entry to Christ's College there, runs
thus :—

'Decemb. 31°. 1631

Henricus More, filius Alexandri, natus Grant-
hamiæ in agro Lincolinensi, literis institutus Etonæ
a Mᵣᵒ Harrison, anno ætatis 17°. admissus est
Pensionarius minor sub Mᵣᵒ Gell.'[1]

The word 'pensionarius' meant one who
paid a *pensio* or rent for rooms in College,
as distinguished from the higher 'noblemen'
and 'fellow-commoners,' and the humbler
'sizars.'

It is to be noted that JOHN MILTON was
still in attendance at this College; so that a
memorandum in one of More's Works, in the
Vestry Library at Grantham, is doubtless
true, that 'he was acquainted with Milton.'

His tutor was William Chappell—who had
also the distinction of having acted in a like
capacity to the great Hebraist, JOHN LIGHT-
FOOT, and others of after-repute. [2]

We are again enabled to see him at this
period from his 'Præfatio,' as follows :[3]—

'Endued as I was with these Principles, that is
to say, a firm and unshaken Belief of the *Existence*
of GOD, as also of his *unspotted Righteousness* and
perfect Goodness, that he is a God *infinitely Good*, as
well as *infinitely Great ;* (and what other would any
Person, that is not doltish or superstitious, ever admit
of) at the Command of my *Uncle*, to whose Care my
Father had committed me, having spent about *three*
Years at *Æton*, I went to *Cambridge ;* recommended
to the Care of a Person both *learned* and *pious*, and,
what I was not a little sollicitous about, not at all a
Calvinist ; but a *Tutour* most *skilful* and *vigilant :*
Who presently after the very first Salutation and
Discourse with me, ask'd me, whether I had a *Dis-
cernment of Things Good and Evil ?* To which,
answering in somewhat a low Voice, I said ; *I hope
I have :* When at the same Time I was Conscious to
my self, that I had, from my very Soul, a most
strong *Sense* and savoury *Discrimination*, as to all

1 The Rev. Dr. Cartmell, Master of Christ's College, was
good enough to favour me with this, as also with the long Latin
Epitaph by More (see the Poems, p. 206). By the way, the
authority for assigning this epitaph to More is Ward, p. 192,
where he names several of his Pupils, among others, Sir John
Finch and Sir Thomas Bains, herein celebrated.

2 *e.g.* Robert Gouge (Calamy's Account, *s. n.*), Dr. Clark
(Turnor's Grantham, p. 176), Owen Stockton (Sam. Clarke's
Lives, 1683, p. 186). See Appendix A to this Introduction for
notice of Chappell and Milton.   3 Pages 8-11.

those Matters. Notwithstanding, the mean while,
a mighty and almost immoderate Thirst after *Knowledge* possess'd me throughout; especially for that
which was *Natural ;* and above all others, that which
was said to dive into the deepest Cause of Things,
and *Aristotle* calls *the first* and *highest Philosophy*, or
Wisdom.

'After which when my prudent and pious *Tutour*
observed my Mind to be inflam'd, and carried with
so eager and vehement a Career ; He ask'd me on a
certain Time, *why I was so above Measure intent upon
my Studies ;* that is to say, for what End I was so ?
Suspecting, as I suppose, that there was only at the
Bottom a certain Itch, or Hunt after *Vain-glory ;* and
to become, by this means, some Famous *Philosopher*
amongst those of my own Standing. But I answered
briefly, and that from my very Heart ; *That I may
know. But, young Man, What is the Reason*, saith
he again, *that you so earnestly desire to know Things ?*
To which I instantly return'd ; *I desire, I say, so
earnestly to know, That I may know*. For even at
that Time, the *Knowledge* of *natural* and *divine*
Things, seem'd to me the highest *Pleasure* and *Felicity* imaginable.

'Thus then persuaded, and esteeming it what was
highly Fit, I immerse my self over Head and Ears
in the *Study* of *Philosophy*, promising a most *wonderful Happiness* to my self in it. *Aristotle* therefore,
Cardan, Julius Scaliger, and other *Philosophers* of
the greatest Note, I very diligently peruse.   In
which, the Truth is, though I met here and there
with some things wittily and acutely, and sometimes
also solidly spoken ; yet the most seem'd to me
either so *false* or *uncertain*, or else so *obvious* and
trivial, that I look'd upon my self as having plainly
lost my time in the Reading of *such Authors*.   And
to speak all in a Word, Those almost whole *Four
Years* which I spent in Studies of this kind, as to
what concern'd those Matters which I chiefly desired
to be satisfied about, (for as to *the Existence of a God*,
and the *Duties* of *Morality*, I never had the least
Doubt) ended in nothing, in a manner, but mere
Scepticism.   Which made me that, as my manner
was, (for I was wont to set down the present State of
my Mind, or any Sense of it that was warmer or
deeper than ordinary, in some short Notes, whether
in *Verse* or *Prose ;* and that also in *English, Greek*,
or *Latin*) it made me, I say, that as a perpetual
Record of the Thing, I compos'd of eight Verses,
which is call'd 'Aπoριa, and is to be found inserted
in the end of my Second *Philosophical Volume*, viz.

Οὐκ ἔγνων πόθεν εἰμὶ ὁ δύσμορος, οὐδὲ τίς εἰμι, &c.
[To this purpose, as *translated* admirably by the
Author himself.]

Nor whence, nor who I am, poor Wretch! know I:
Nor yet, O Madness! Whither I must goe;
But in Grief's crooked Claws fast held I lie;
And live, I think, by force tugg'd to and fro.
Asleep or wake all one. O Father Jove,
'Tis brave, we Mortals live in Clouds like thee.
Lies, Night-dreams, empty Toys, Fear, fatal Love,
This is my Life: I nothing else do see.

'And these things happen'd to me before that I
had taken any *Degree* in the *University.*'

He took his degree of A.B. in 1635: proceeded A.M. in 1638: was chosen Fellow
and Tutor—gaining pupils who later distinguished themselves: was ordained Deacon
same year, and Priest in 1641.   In 1642
he was instituted and inducted to the living of Ingoldsby in Lincolnshire — the
'living' being the property of his father.   His
name occurs once — and I believe only
once—in the Ingoldsby Register; so that
he was non-resident.   In his own stately
way he admitted that whether from his
'inward voice' or otherwise, he was not
one for the Pulpit or to sway an audience
lesser or larger by personal address.   He
returned from Ingoldsby almost immediately
after his institution, to his College of Christ's;
and there undisturbed by the commotions
of the Civil War, as uninterfered with by the
Government of Cromwell, he serenely lived
out his appointed term as a life-long student.

The dates and data furnished, cover
nearly the entire Facts—apart from his successive books—of his ' Life,' so much was he
a recluse and meditator rather than actor.

Of his 'manner of life' in training and
disciplining himself we are once more in-
formed in his ' Præfatio' thus :[1]—

'After taking my *Degree*, to pass over and omit
abundance of things ; I designing not here the
Draught of my own Life (though some, and those
very Famous Men too, have done that before me ;
and *Cardan* hath given so exact an Account of his
own Writings, that he hath not so much as omitted
those that were spoiled by the Urine of a Cat) but
only a brief Introduction for the better Understand-

[1] Pages 11-15.

ing the Occasion of writing my First Book ; It fell
out truly very *Happily* for me, that I suffer'd so great
a *Disappointment* in my *Studies*.   For it made me
seriously at last begin to think with my self ; whether
the *Knowledge* of things was really that *Supreme Felicity* of Man ; or something *Greater* and *more Divine*
was : Or, supposing it to be so, whether it was to be
acquir'd by such an *Eagerness* and *Intentness* in the
reading of Authors, and *Contemplating* of Things ;
or by the *Purging* of the *Mind* from all sorts of Vices
whatsoever: Especially having begun to read now
the *Platonick* Writers, *Marsilius Ficinus, Plotinus*
himself, *Mercurius Trismegistus;* and the *Mystical
Divines;* among whom there was frequent mention
made of the *Purification* of the *Soul,* and of the
Purgative Course that is previous to the *Illumina-
tive;* as if the Person that expected to have his
Mind *illuminated* of God, was to endeavour after
the *Highest Purity.*

' But amongst all the Writings of this kind there
was none, to speak the Truth, so pierced and affected
me, as that *Golden little Book*, with which *Luther* is
also said to have been wonderfully taken, *viz. Theo-
logia Germanica:* Though several Symptoms, even
at that time, seem'd ever and anon to occur to me,
of a certain deep *Melancholy ;* as also no slight
Errors in Matters of *Philosophy.*   But that which
he doth so mightily inculcate, viz. *That we should
thoroughly put off, and extinguish our own proper
Will; that being thus Dead to our selves, we may live
alone unto God, and do all things whatsoever by his
Instinct or plenary Permission ;* was so Connatural,
as it were, and agreenble to my most intimate *Reason*
and *Conscience,* that I could not of any thing whatsoever be more clearly or certainly convinced.   Which
Sense yet (that no one may here use that dull and
idle Expression, *Quales legimus, Tales evadimus, Such
as we read, Such we are*) that truly *Golden Book* did
not then first implant in my Soul, but struck and
rouz'd it, as it were, out of Sleep in me : Which it
did verily as in a Moment, or the twinkling of an
Eye.   But after that the *Sense* and *Consciousness* of
this *great* and plainly *Divine Duty,* was thus awakend
in me ; Good God! what Struglings and Conflicts
follow'd presently between this *Divine Principle* and
the *Animal Nature!*   For since I was most firmly
perswaded, not only concerning the *Existence of God,*
but also of *His Absolute* both *Goodness* and *Power,*
and of *His* most real *Will* that *we should be perfect,
even as our Father which is in Heaven is perfect ;*
there was no room left for any *Tergiversation ;* but a
necessity of immediately entring the Lists, and of
using all possible Endeavours, that our *own Will,* by
which we relish our selves, and what belongs to us,

in things as well of the *Soul* as of the *Body*, might be *oppos'd, destroy'd, annihilated* ; that so the *Divine Will* alone, with the *New Birth*, may *revive* and *grow up* in us. And, if I may here freely speak my Mind, before this *Conflict* between the *Divine Will*, and our *own* proper *Will* or *Self-Love*, there can no certain *Signs* appear to us of this *New Birth* at all. But *this Conflict* is the very *Punctum saliens*, or *First Motion* of the *New Life* or *Birth* begun in us. As to other Performances, whether of *Morality* or *Religion*, arising from mere *Self-Love*, let them be as Specious or Goodly as you please, they are at best but as *Preparations*, or the more refin'd *Exercises* of a sort of *Theological Hobbianisme*.

'But there is nothing that the *Animal Man* dreads so much as *this Conflict*: And he looks upon it as a piece of mere *Folly* and *Madness*, to attempt any thing that is not for his own *Self-Interest* ; or that is not to be accomplish'd by his own proper Strength and Reason. And therefore the *Old Man*; while it doth but exercise, all this time, its own nature divers ways, and adjusts it self to outward multifarious *Opinions* and *Practices* in *Religion*, and bends and winds it self about this way and that way ; is still a mere *Serpent*, the mere *Old Man*; as a Dunghil, turn it into what Shapes and Postures you will, still remains a Dunghil. The *Divine Seed* alone is that which is acceptable unto God ; and the sole invincible *Basis* of all *true Religion*. The *Revelation*, through the *Divine Grace*, of which *Heavenly* and *sincere Principle* in my self, immediately occasion'd, that all my other *Studies*, in comparison of *this*, became vile and of no Account : And that insatiable Desire and Thirst of mine after the *Knowledge* of things was wholly almost extinguish'd in me ; as being sollicitous now, about nothing so much as a more full *Union* with this *Divine* and *Cœlestial Principle*, the inward flowing Well-spring of *Life eternal* : With the most fervent Prayers breathing often unto God, that he would be pleas'd thoroughly to set me free from the dark Chains, and this so sordid Captivity of my *own Will*.

' But here openly to declare the Thing as it was ; When this inordinate Desire after the *Knowledge* of things was thus allay'd in me, and I aspir'd after nothing but this sole *Purity* and *Simplicity* of *Mind*, there shone in upon me daily a greater *Assurance* than ever I could have expected, even of those things which before I had the greatest Desire *to know*: Insomuch that within a few Years, I was got into a most *Joyous* and *Lucid* State of *Mind*; and such plainly as is *ineffable* ; though, according to my Custom, I have endeavoured to express it, to my Power, in another *Stanza* of Eight *Verses*, both in

Sense and *Title* answering in a way of direct Opposition unto the Former ; Which is call'd (as that 'Ἀπορία, *Inviousness* and *Emptiness*, so this) Εὐπορία, *Fulness* and *Perviousness*.'

It is impossible altogether to pass by this urgent and most sincere writing but none the less egregiously misdirected treatment of himself. So to denounce this body of ours— God's own temple—and so to deem it right and obligatory to 'oppose, destroy, annihilate' our own Will—God's magnificent dower to man—was to err in fundamentals, whilst to thus calumniate even fallen human nature as 'dunghill,' and all the rest of his false-witness against himself, was to be led captive by mere theological (not Scriptural) figments. One marvels that whilst More resisted the error—as he regarded it—of his father's Predestination, he should have so abjectly accepted vulgar inferences (not exegeses) from misunderstood and mutilated texts. It is a sorrowful, a tragical spectacle altogether ; and, nevertheless, so splendid was the aspiration and actual attainment that we cannot altogether condemn.

The flower of his finest, subtlest, most inner thought and emotion went into his Verse. His little Epigrams (so called) of 'Ἀπορία and Εὐπορία seem to have been written when he was in his teens. Among his 'Occasional Poems' are contributions in 1632, 1633, 1635,[1] 1637, 1638, 1640, 1641, to the University Collections. It is noteworthy that within a year of his entry at Christ's College he contributed to the 'Anthologia in Regia Exanthema,' and to ' Rex Redux' the year after. Still more noteworthy that he was one of the verse-mourners for Edward King, the 'Lycidas' of Milton. These were merely 'Occasional.' But in 1640 he girded up himself for a great

---

[1] Since his Occasional Poems were issued, a friend has sent us others from an overlooked University Collection. They will be found in Appendix B to this Introduction.

utterance of what was deepest in him, as he thus tells : [1]—

'But to reach now at length the Scope I drive at ; Not content with this short *Epigram*, I did afterwards, about the Beginning of the Year 1640, comprise the chief *Speculations* and *Experiences* I fell into, by persisting in the Enterprise before mention'd, in a pretty full *Poem* call'd *Psychozoia*, or the *Life of the Soul :* Stir'd up to it, I believe, by some *Heavenly Impulse* of *Mind ;* since I did it at that time with no other Design, than that it should remain by me a private Record of the *Sensations* and *Experiences* of my own *Soul.*'

His Biographer continues : [2]—

'This was the *Occasion* of his Writing that *first Part* of his Book of *Poems.* Which that it might lie the better conceal'd, he tells us next, how *darkly* and *obscurely* it was in several respects composed by him. And afterwards he gives an Account of his adding the rest, some at one time, and some at another ; and then proceeds to a short *List* of all his *Writings* whatsoever, with the *Times* and *Occasions* of them. Which with the entire *Preface* would be highly worth the Knowledge of the *English Reader*, if proper to be given in this Place.'

Somewhat excursive and discursive certainly is WARD's further account—half-translating, half-supplying—yet to the sympathetic reader it has a fascinating interest. Accordingly I venture to give it *in extenso:* [3]—

'I shall only advertise the *Reader* farther, That though this first Poem of the *Life of the Soul* was written in the Year 1640, when the Author was between 25 and 26 Years of Age ; yet with some more that he added concerning the *Immortality*, and both against the *Sleep* and *Unity* of *Souls*, it came not out till 1642, and then he tells us, at the *Instigation* of some *Learned* and *Pious Friends*, to whom he had in private *accidentally* shew'd them. Nay, for that *first Piece*, he several times, it seems, thought of *burning* it, *lest it should fall into the Hands of others.* But *Providence* design'd not that such a Jewel, with the rest that follow'd, should be lost to the World ; and so ordered the Matter, as we have seen, otherwise. And these were to be the *First-fruits*, or *Primordia* of his *Studies ;* and a *Pledge* of his *future Performances.*

'If any shall be here curious to enquire into the more particular extent of his *intra paucos Annos*, or those *few Years* wherein he arriv'd to so admirable a Degree both of *Life* and *Knowledge*, and such a *Divine* State of *Joy* consequent upon them ; I can assure him on very good Grounds, or from the *Author* himself, that it was the Space of between 3 and 4 Years. This *short* time of *Holy Discipline* and *Conflict*, let him in, it seems, to wonderful *Communications ;* and open'd, as it were, the Gates of *Paradise* to Him.

'Concerning which matter, it is not, I conceive, for any that have not had some very considerable *Experiences* of this kind to make a true Judgment : Nor will I my self pretend to a sufficient *Knowledge* or *Experience* of it. But it is not, I should think, difficult to apprehend ; That a Man having once rescued himself from the *Obliquity* and *Captivity* of his own *Self-will* and *Self-love*, and got, so far as even *this* Life suffers, from the *Bondage of Corruption*, into the *Glorious Liberty of the Children of God ;* into a high State of *Virtue* and *Divine Purity*, with a most Free, Noble, Intelligent, and Universal *Love* of God, and of the whole Creation : I say, it is not difficult to conceive, that the *Life* of such a Person, especially of a Person of the *Doctor's* Parts and Constitution, must needs be very highly *Joyous* and *Blessed.* A Heart loosed from it self, is like a Ship sailing in the midst of the Seas : And we having recovered our selves into the due *Love of God*, and of *one another*, to a State of *Freedom* and *Innocency ;* what remains, but to live in a most unspeakable *Peace, Liberty* and *Felicity* for evermore ?

'Such will *exult* in GOD, in this *Divine Life* communicated to them, and in *all Creatures :* Whose *Numbers, Orders, Happinesses*, and *Extent*, with the *Works of Providence* in the *Universe* at large, are unspeakable and unknowable ; but will be shrewdly guess'd at, and most magnificently conce:v'd of, by Men of *this Character :* And indeed even *Philosophy* it self doth present us with admirable and astonishing Prospects of them.

'This then was the *Blissful* and *Glorious* Issue of the *Doctor's* so *sincere* and *Heroical* Enterprise, in the freeing of his *Soul* from *Sin* and *Self ;* it was *excellent Wisdom ;* and that *sudden*, in a manner, and *unexpected ;* a clear *Æthereal* sort of Temperament of *Body* and of *Mind ;* a gladsome and even *Enthusiastick* Sense of *Joy*, in the *Nature, Works* and *Providence* of GOD ; with a most stable *Truth* and *Rectitude* of *Nature* as to *himself.* Nor can any deny, but that all these are the *noblest Fruits* and *Attainments* of *Religion ;* the *highest* and most *perfect Exercises* of it ; and that, according to our

---

[1] Page 16.   [2] Page 17.   [3] Pages 17-21.

Powers, we are all of us oblig'd to aspire after this *Sincerity* and *Virtue.*

' Let me only add now, with respect to that *Poetical* Description of his, touching the so high *Conflict* and *Victory* in Himself (which to its useful and pious Seriousness hath all the Art and Elegancy added, that an incomparable Piece of *Divine Poetry,* writ in that way, can be embelish'd or adorn'd with) what he speaks of that matter in another Place thus.

' But being well advis'd, both by the Dictates of my own *Conscience,* and clear Information of those *Holy Oracles* which we all deservedly reverence ; that God reserves his *choicest Secrets* for the *purest Minds* ; and that it is *Uncleanness* of *Spirit,* not *distance* of *Place,* that dissevers us from the *Deity ;* I was fully convinc'd, that *true Holiness* was the only safe Entrance into *Divine Knowledge.* And having an unshaken Belief of the *Existence of God,* and of *his Will* that *we* should be *holy* even as *he* is *holy ;* Nothing that is truly Sinful, could appear to me unconquerable, assisted by such a Power : Which urged me therefore seriously to set my self to the Task. Of the *Experiences* and *Events* of which Enterprise my *2d* and *3d Canto* of the *Life of the Soul* is a real and faithful *Record.*

' So that this *Great Person* hath, we see, in a Measure, and in some of the most concerning Instances of it, presented his own *Life* and Picture to the World. Which though he hath done in little, or, as it were, in *Miniature,* and could not be prevail'd upon to enlarge ; yet am I glad, for my part, that he hath drawn the *Effigies* so far as he hath. And we may perceive by his *Lætissimum, Lucidissimumque Anima statum, & plane ineffabilem,* his *most lucid, joyous, and unspeakable State of Mind,* with such other Intimations up and down in his Writings, that there was assuredly something not a little *Extraordinary* in His *Character.* For the rest ; Whoever would obtain a more complete *Draught* of Dr. *More,* he must have it from his *Works ;* as those that are the truest *Pourtraicture* of his *Spirit.* It was his own Expression indeed, that *if any Man had written, his Works would best shew to all intelligent Readers what he was.* And perhaps never Person wrote more the Sentiments of his own Mind, or hath more truly represented the free and absolute Results of his own Reason and Conscience to the World than He himself hath done.

' *I have writ,* saith he, *after no Copy but the Eternal Characters of the Mind of Man, and the known* Phænomena *of Nature.* And again ; *I borrow'd them not from Books, but fetch'd them from the Nature of the thing it self, and indelible Ideas of the Soul of Man.* And once more ; In his Epistle Dedicatory before

the *Immortality of the Soul,* he tells that noble Lord, that *He can without vanity Profess, that what he offers to him, is the genuine Result of his own anxious and thoughtful Mind, no old Stuff purloin'd or borrow'd from other Writers.*

Throughout I am reminded of a still greater man and poet of our own era ; for nowhere so much as in HENRY MORE do we find that self-contained and almost preterhuman sense of the grandeur of the human intellect as exemplified in himself, that exposed WILLIAM WORDSWORTH to misconstruction as though it were poor vanity or conceit. ELLIS YARNALL (of America) has put the thing admirably in his 'Reminiscences,' where he describes the great Poet's reading Professor Reed's Introduction to his 'Selections' from his Poems. 'He made,' he says, 'but little comment on your notice of him. Occasionally he would say, as he came to a particular fact, "That's quite correct ;" or, after reading a quotation from his own works, he would add, "That's from my writings." These quotations he read in a way that much impressed me ; it seemed almost as if he was AWED BY THE GREATNESS OF HIS OWN POWER, THE GIFTS WITH WHICH HE HAD BEEN ENDOWED.'[1] The same impression is inevitable in reading More, even in his casual sayings, and deepeningly as you ponder his Poetry. Of the former, take this from WARD with his own elucidatory words :[2] —

' The *Doctor* in his Book of *Ethicks* speaks of some that, by a *Divine Sort of Fate,* are *Virtuous* and *Good ;* and this is to a very great and *Heroical* Degree. And the *same* may seem by him to be intimated elsewhere, as coming into this World rather for the *Good of others,* and by a *Divine force,* than through *their own proper fault* or any necessary and immediate *Congruity* of their *Natures.* All which is agreeable to that Opinion of *Plato : That some descend hither to declare the* Being and Nature *of the Gods ;*

---

[1] Grosart's Wordsworth's Prose Works, vol. iii. p. 484 (3 Vols. 8vo, 1876).

[2] Page 34.

and for the greater Health, Purity, *and* Perfection *of this* Lower World.

'I will not say, that the *Great* Person I here write of, was of this sort: But this, I think, may notwithstanding be affirm'd; that he seem'd to act or appear as one of these. And it was once his own Expression (yet free and unaffected) of himself; *That he had as a fiery Arrow been shot into the World; and he hoped, that he had hit the Mark.* And certainly that noble *Zeal* and *Activity* which was in him, was not a little Extraordinary. He was truly in his time *a burning* and *a shining Light:* And there were not a few that *did* and *do rejoice in it.*'

Be it noted that in the preceding, the rebel against his father's theological 'Predestination' affirms an ethical predestination.

Again:[1]—

'The Dr. had always a great care to preserve His *Body* as a well-strung Instrument to His *Soul,* that so they might be *both* in Tune, and make due Musick and Harmony together. *His Body,* he said, *seem'd built for a Hundred Years, if he did not over-debilitate it with his Studies.* But with respect to *these* I have also heard him say, *That it was almost a Wonder to him at times, that he had not long before then fired,* (as he express'd it) *his little World about him:* And that he thought, *there were not many that could have born that high Warmth and Activity of Thoughtfulness, and intense Writing, that he himself had done;* Or to that purpose. And there was one Thing farther Observable, which he would sometimes speak of; *That after all his Study, and Depth of Thought in the Day-time; when he came to sleep (more especially when* Young) *he had a strange sort of* Narcotick *Power* (as his Word was) *that drew him to it; and he was no sooner, in a manner, laid in his Bed, but the Falling of a House would scarce wake him:* When yet early in the Morning he was wont to awake usually into an immediate unexpressible Life and Vigour; with all his Thoughts and Notions *raying* (as I may so speak) about him, as Beams surrounding the Centre from whence they all Proceed.'

Once more:[2]—

'I say (*breaks he out in a Place of it*) that a *Free, Divine, Universalis'd Spirit* is worth *all.* How *lovely,* how *Magnificent* a *State* is the *Soul of Man* in, when the *Life of God* inactuating her, shoots her along with himself through Heaven and Earth; makes her *Unite* with, and after a Sort feel her

self *animate* the whole World, &c. This is to be become *Dei-form,* to be thus suspended, (not by Imagination, but by Union of Life; Κέντρον κέντρῳ συνάψαντα, *joining Centres* with God) and by a sensible Touch to be held up from the clotty dark Personality of this Compacted Body. Here is *Love,* here is *Freedom,* here is *Justice* and *Equity* in the *Super-essential Causes* of them. He that is here looks upon All things as One; and on himself, if he can then Mind himself, as a part of the Whole.

'And after much more both of *Zeal* and *Triumph,* he goes on thus;

'Nor am I out of my Wits, as some may fondly interpret me in this *Divine Freedom.* But the *Love of God* compell'd me. Nor am I at all, *Philalethes, Enthusiastical.* For God doth not ride me as a Horse, and guide me I know not whither my self; but converseth with me as a *Friend;* and speaks to me in such a *Dialect* as I understand fully, and can make others understand, that have not made Shipwrack of the Faculties that God hath given them, by *Superstition* or *Sensuality:* For with such I cannot converse, because they do not converse with God; but only pity them, or am angry with them, as I am Merry and Pleasant with Thee. For God hath permitted to me all these things; and I have it under the Broad Seal of Heaven. Who dare Charge me? God doth acquit me. For he hath made me full Lord of the Four Elements; and hath constituted me Emperour of the World. I am in the *Fire* of *Choler,* and am not burn'd; in the *Water* of *Phlegm,* and am not drown'd; in the *Airy Sanguine,* and yet not blown away with every blast of transient Pleasure, or vain Doctrines of Men; I descend also into the sad *Earthly Melancholy,* and yet am not buried from the Sight of my God. I am, *Philalethes,* (though I dare say thou takest me for no Bird of Paradise) *Incola Cæli in Terrâ,* an *Inhabitant* of *Paradise* and *Heaven* upon *Earth.*—I sport with the Beasts of the Earth; the Lion licks my Hand like a Spaniel; and the Serpent sleeps upon my Lap, and stings me not. I play with the Fowls of Heaven; and the Birds of the Air sit Singing on my Fist.—All these things are true in a Sober Sense. And the *Dispensation* I live in, is more *Happiness* above all measure, than if thou could'st call down the Moon so near thee, by thy *Magick* Charms, that thou mayst kiss her, as she is said to have kiss'd *Endymeon;* or couldst stop the Course of the Sun; or which is all one, with one Stamp of thy Foot stay the Motion of the Earth.

'I will conclude with a Passage he hath before.

'He that is come hither, God hath taken him to be his own *Familiar Friend:* And though he speaks to others aloof off, in Outward Religions and

---

[1] Pages 41-42.   [2] Pages 48-51.

Parables; yet he leads this Man by the Hand, teaching him intelligible Documents upon all the Objects of his *Providence;* speaks to him plainly in his own Language; sweetly insinuates himself, and possesseth all his *Faculties,* Understanding, Reason and Memory. *This* is the Darling of God; and a Prince amongst Men; far above the *Dispensation* of either *Miracle* or *Prophesie.*'

Further :[1]—

'*HE had spent,* he said to one, *many* Happy Days *in his Chamber; And* that *his* Labours *were to him often in looking back upon them, as an* Aromatick *Field.* So sweet and pleasing a Fruit did they yield to him; and so satisfied was his Mind in the Contemplation of them.

'And it is here worthy of special Remark, what He said likewise, upon another Occasion, of Himself; as I had it from those that were then present. When some in the Company were speaking with Regret of the Time they had lost, or how they would act if it was to be all pass'd over again; He replied, (and it was not many Years before he died) *That if he was to live his whole time over again, he would do* just, *for the main, as he had done.* Which is such an egregious *Attestation* to his *Piety* and *Conduct;* and such an *Applause* of *Conscience* to its own *Actions,* and that for a whole Life; as is not, I believe we shall all agree, to be easily met with.

'*There were some,* as he expressed it, *amongst the* Spiritualists, *that would have had him, he thought, to go up upon a Stall, and from thence preach to the People.* But in the telling of this, he broke out into this High and Extraordinary *Expression; I have measured my self from the* Height *to the* Depth *; and know what I can do, and what I ought to do, and I do it.* But the *Air,* the Person told me, and *Gesture* with which he said it, was so Noble and Unaffected; that he knew not which most to admire, the Thing it self, or the Manner of speaking it.

Again :[2]—

'It was not for nothing that Extraordinary Expression fell so *Emphatically* from his Pen, *Enthus. Triumph.* Numb. 53. *I profess, I stand amaz'd, while I consider the ineffable* Advantage *of a Mind thus submitted to the* Divine Will; *how* calm, *how* comprehensive, *how* quick *and* sensible *she is, how* free, *how* sagacious, *of how* tender *a* Touch *and* Judgment *she is in all things.*'

Finally here :[3]—

---

[1] Pages 77-78.   [2] Pages 78-79.   [3] Pages 89-90.

'FOR *Purity;* Doubtless he had arrived to the *Highest* Measures and degrees of it. You may see his *Description* of *this Virtue* also in his *Enthusiasmus Triumphatus,* as well as in the Place of his *Mystery of Godliness* before referr'd to. *Understanding* by it a *due* Moderation *and Rule over all the* Joys *and Pleasures of the* Flesh ; *bearing so* strict *an* Hand, *and having so* watchful *an* Eye *over their Subtil* Enticements *and* Allurements, *and that firm and loyal* Affection *to that* Idea *of* Cœlestial Beauty *set up in our* Minds, *that neither the* Pains *of the* Body, *nor the* Pleasures *of the* Animal *Life, shall ever work us below our* Spiritual *Happiness, and all the competible* Enjoyments *of that Life that is truly* Divine.

'And this undoubtedly was his own most true *State,* His *Body* was for its part not Unsuitable to his Mind, *Temperance* and *Devotion, Charity* and *Humility,* seem to have refined his *Nature* and inmost *Spirits,* to an Extraordinary Pitch of *Sanctity* and *Purity. This,* saith he to *Eugenius,* (speaking of the State of *Virtue* he was under) *is that true* Chymical *Fire, that hath* purged *my* Soul, *and* purified *it; and hath* Chrystaliz'd *it into a bright Throne, and shining Habitation of the* Divine Majesty.'

Turning similarly to his Poetry, the most casual reader will be struck by touches of self-portraiture declarative of the same Wordsworthian consciousness of his largeness of soul and intellectual strength. *Ad aperturam libri,*—let these speak for themselves :—

'The just and constant man, a multitude
Set upon mischief cannot him constrain
To do amisse by all their uprores rude ;
Not for a tyrants threat will he ere stain
His inward honour. The rough Adrian
Tost with unquiet winds doth nothing move
His steddy heart. Much pleasure he doth gain
To see the glory of his Master Jove,
When his drad darts with hurrying light through all do rove.

'If Heaven and Earth should rush with a great noise,
He fearlesse stands ; he knows whom he doth trust,
Is confident of his souls after joyes,
Though this vain bulk were grinded into dust.
Strange strength resideth in the soul that's just,
She feels her power how't commands the sprite
Of the low man, vigorously finds she must
Be independent of such feeble might,
Whose motions dare not 'pear before her awfull sight.'
(p. 84. st. 12. 13.)

Again :—

'But sooth to say though my triumphant Muse
Seemeth to vaunt as in got victory,

And with puissant stroke the head to bruize
Of her stiffe foe, and daze his phantasie,
Captive his reason, dead each faculty :
Yet in her self so strong a force withstands
That of her self afraid, she'll not aby,
Nor keep the field.   She'll fall by her own hand
As *Ajax* once laid *Ajax* dead upon the strand.'
                                    (p. 87, st. 39.)

Once more :—

' Hence, hence unhallowed ears and hearts more hard
Then winter clods fast froze with Northern wind.
But most of all, foul tongue I thee discard
That blamest all that thy dark strait'ned mind,
Cannot conceive : But that no blame thou find ;
Whate're my pregnant Muse brings forth to light,
She'll not acknowledge to be of her kind,
Till Eagle-like she turn them to the sight
Of the eternall Word, all deckt with glory bright.

' Strange sights do straggle in my restlesse thoughts,
And lively forms with orient colours clad
Walk in my boundlesse mind, as men ybrought
Into some spacious room, who when they've had
A turn or two, go out, although unhad.
All these I see and know, but entertain
None to my friend but who's most sober sad ;
Although, the time my roof doth them contain
Their presence doth possesse me till they out again.'
                                    (p. 91, st. 1, 2.)

Further :—

' Yet doth the soul of such like forms discourse,
And finden fault at this deficiency,
And rightly term this better and that worse ;
Wherefore the measure is our own *Idee*,
Which th' humane soul in her own self doth see.
And sooth to sayen when ever she doth strive
To find pure truth, her own profundity
She enters, in her self doth deeply dive ;
From thence attempts each essence rightly to descrive.'
                                    (p. 111, st. 39.)

Thus realizing within himself the 'height
and depth' of the human soul—his own, the
measure and type of both to himself—
HENRY MORE combined withal a touching
personal humility, and was eager to 'serve'
and to communicate.   I think of him in
Christ's College and in the University as a
Knight of the Red-Cross shield, leading a
pure white life unstained and unstainable as
the light.   It is well that so many sat at his
feet and welcomed his books ; for if ever
man has been a saint on earth and the in-

carnation of his own ideal, it was this Mystic
and Christian-Platonist.

I do not attempt so much as an enumera-
tion of his manifold PROSE Writings.   That
were out-of-place in an Introduction to his
Verse.   Suffice it that they grew out of two
main things, (*a*) His Meditativeness on
human nature—with himself in all the
subtleties of a natively subtle intellect and
emotional temperament, for text ; (*b*) His
omnivorous reading and learning—as miscel-
laneous and odd as ROBERT BURTON'S, and as
varied and unexpected as THOMAS FULLER'S,
though, sooth to say, without either's fusing
and transfusing faculty.   From the former
—as I think—you have in his most fantastic
speculations and inferences, substantive
additions to high philosophical thought and
darts of insight into intellectual and spiritual
problems that are like intuition.   From the
latter, you have throughout, if not learning
in the highest and exactest sense, extraordinary extent of reading and recollection.
One must smile at his Cabbalistical-Hebraistic
lore and credulous interpretation of ' pro-
phecies' and 'visions,' as of the Apocalypse ;
but you will never read a book of his without
coming on original thinking illustrated by recondite quotations.   His much 'reading'
(or learning) was drawn on inevitably from
his manifold attacks and opponents—as
Descartes—Dr. Joseph Beaumont—John
Butler, B.D.—Thomas Vaughan—H. Stubbe
—Sir Matthew Hale—Richard Hayter.   His
'Cabbalistical' reveries (not to call them
'vagaries') sent him a-searching in wasteful
places.   Many a forgotten folio had the
dust blown from it by this eager inquirer.
Must it be owned that he saw through his
spectacles in all such reading, rather than
through his own 'cleare eyen'?

That our Worthy sequestered himself so
absolutely was of his own choice ; for he
had abundant opportunities of acquiring
important and influential public positions.

Ward tells us this garrulously yet with fine touches, as thus :[1]—

'Truly what, if we consider it, was his *Whole Life* spent in, but in a Course of *Retirement* and *Contemplation* ; in the *Viewing* of the Works of *God* and *Nature*, and a *rejoycing* at the *Happiness* of the *Creatures* that have been made by Him ; in doing *Honour* unto *God*, and *Good* to *Men* ; in *Clearing* up the *Existence of God*, and his *Attributes* ; and *shewing* the *Excellency* and the *Reasonableness* both of *Providence* and of *Religion* ; more especially in *Asserting* the *Christian Religion*, and *Magnifying*, after the justest manner, Him who is the *Author* and *Finisher* of it ; in the *Illustrating* of our *State* Present and Future ; and in a very particular *Discovery* of the two Grand *Mysteries* both of *Godliness* and *Iniquity* ; in the *Clearing* up of *Truth* and *Dissipating* of *Errour* ; and in a most diligent *laying open* the *Visions* and *Prophesies* of *Holy Scripture* ; in a word, in a universal *Promoting* the Interests of *Peace* and *Righteousness* in the *Earth* ; and *giving* in general an *Example* of *Prudence* and *Piety*, of *Charity* and *Integrity* amongst Men ? It was sometimes his Expression amongst his Friends, *That he should not have known what to have done in the World, if he could not have preach'd at his Fingers Ends*. His Voice was somewhat inward ; and so not fit for that of a Publick Orator.

'FOR the being *Preferr'd* to any Great Dignities ; He was so far from Coveting, that he particularly *Declin'd* it ; Making good here that Expression of a Father ; *Totus ei Mundus possessio est, qui toto co quasi suo utitur*. The whole *World is the* large *Possession* of him *that useth* and enjoys *the whole as his own*.

'I have seen Letters from an *Honourable* Person to him, Courting him to accept of very great *Preferments* in *Ireland* ; and assuring him, that the Interest was actually made, and the Way smooth'd to his Hands with the Lord Deputy. The *Deanary* of *Christ-Church*, said to be worth 900*l. per Annum*, was one ; and the *Provostship* of *Dublin College* with the *Deanary* of St. *Patricks* was another. And these were but by way of Preparation to something Greater : For there were withal two *Bishopricks* in view offer'd to his Choice ; of which one was said to be valued at no less then 1500*l. per Annum*. And that *Noble* Person added this Piece of Pleasant and Friendly Instigation ; *Pray be not so Morose, or Humoursome, as to refuse all things you have not known so long as* Christ-College.

1 Pages 57-60.

'Nay farther, to shew his Temper in these Matters, I have been inform'd from such as had it from himself ; that a very good *Bishoprick* was procur'd for him once in this our own Kingdom ; and that his Friends had got him on a Day as far as *White-Hall*, in order to the Kissing of the *Royal* Hand for it ; But when he understood the Business, he was not upon any account to be perswaded to it.

'These things he refus'd not from any Supercilious Contempt ; but from the pure Love of *Contemplation*, and *Solitude* ; and because he thought that he could do the *Church of God* greater Service, as also better enjoy his *own* Proper Happiness, in a *Private* than in a *Publick* Station : Taking great *Satisfaction*, the mean while, in the Promotion of many Pious and Learned Men to these Places of Trust and Honour in the Church ; (To whom he heartily *congratulated* such Dignities) and being exceeding Sensible of the *Weight* as well as the *Honour* of them ; and how Necessary it was to have them fill'd with Able and Worthy Persons.

'Once indeed, and that about 12 Years before he died, he *accepted* of a *Prebend* in the Church of *Gloucester* ; given him by the Right Honourable the Earl of *Nottingham*, then Lord Chancellour of *England* : But he soon made a shift, (not without, I believe, such an original Intent) *to resign* it again ; Procuring it at the same time for one of his *Worthy Friends*, now himself a Right Reverend *Bishop* of our Church : To whom, when he would have reimburs'd him his Charges, he pleasantly said, *That if he would not accept it upon his own Terms, he might let it alone*. And though he thus desir'd Nothing for himself ; yet was he Happily instrumental in the doing Signal Services unto others : Nor was any one more *ready* to serve a Friend, or more *Active* therein, than He was, whenever there was a good Opportunity offer'd him.'

And so he 'liv'd and died a private Fellow of Christ's College in Cambridge ;' having troops of friends and disciples, and such correspondents among others as DESCARTES and VAN HELMONT, but shrinking from the ostentation and noise of the world outside. Nevertheless he had quick and practical sympathies with the poor and the suffering. His Biographer tells us— 'His very Chamber-Door was a Hospital to the Needy' (p. 85).

PRINCIPAL TULLOCH has well summed up his retired life—'Such a life as More's necessarily presents few points of contact with the great events of his time. "He was so busy in his chamber with his pen and lines as not to mind much the bustles and affairs of the world without." He did not occupy any party position, even in that indefinite sense in which Whichcote and Cudworth may be said to have done. He had no relations with the statesmen of the civil war and the Commonwealth, and never made, like his friends, any prominent public appearance. Educated in a Calvinistic although not a Puritan home [?], he turned aside very early from all that could have connected him with the religious parties dominant in his youth. His ideal was the Church of England as it existed before the times of disturbance—the Church of the Reformation and of Hooker' (II. pp. 335-6). The same Writer, with shrewd outlook and insight, reminds us of a modern parallel, as eloquently thus :—'If More's life as a student kept him retired from the world, it greatly stimulated his productivity as an author. Probably, also, it contributed in some degree to the endless prolixity and repetitions of his writings. We feel especially with him—as more or less with all the Cambridge school, except Which-cote—that we are conversing with a mind too little braced by active discipline, and the prompt, systematic, compact habits which come from large intercourse with men, and the affairs which stir men to powerful movement or great ambitions. The air of a school, which was after all confined to a narrow if influential sphere, is more pervading in his writings than in any of the others. Christ College, with its books, is never far out of sight ; and all the sweetness and seclusion of Ragley, "the solemness of the place, its shady walks and hills and woods, where he lost sight of the world and the world of him' (Ep. ded. to *Immortality of the Soul*) did not help to let the light of day or the breath of the common air into his

"choice Theories," however they may have assisted him in "finding them out" and elaborating them. In this respect we have been reminded more than once of an analogy betwixt him and the leaders of the modern High-Church school in its original development. Oxford and Hursely Parsonage may not inaptly be compared to Cambridge and Ragley ; and the enervating force of a wilful seclusion from the world is certainly not less conspicuous in Keble and Newman— although in a different direction—than in our author. It may be pleasant to keep away from the "bustles and affairs of the world without," as it is pleasant to contemplate the peculiar beauty and serenity of character which ripens amidst such retirement, but, after all, no man can escape from his fellow-men, and the rough facts of ordinary human life, without spiritual and intellectual injury. The product may be finer that is grown in solitude, but it will neither be so useful, nor, in many respects, so true and good' (II. pp. 339, 340).

I must now leave WARD to give his account in his own lingering and loving and loveable way, with innumerable personal traits and characteristics, of 'the end':[1]—

'I AM brought now at length to give an Account of his *Death* and *Last Illness:* Which I shall do *chiefly* from one that was a faithful Attender on him in it ; and who, as he ever honour'd him with a very Particular Honour, so did he *signally* shew it upon this Occasion. A very Great Person in our Church, and no less Friend to the *Doctor*, was pleas'd to say ; That he never observ'd a greater Instance of *Friendship* in any Person, than in *this* Party at that Time. And to my Knowledge it was very *Extraordinary ;* and no less Grateful and Serviceable to his Dear Friend the *Doctor :* Who would several times tell him ; *That he was a mighty* Cordial *and* Refreshment *to him.* To my self he express'd *how greatly he was oblig'd to him for his Company ; and that he should not have known what almost to have done without him.* From this *Worthy* and *Reverend* Person, my *Honoured* Friend Dr. *John Davies,* it is (I say) *mainly,* that I

---

1 Pages 213-227.

shall with all Faithfulness give the *Reader* an Account of that Cloud and Weakness, which after some time carried off the *Doctor* from this to a Better Life.

'He enjoy'd in the general (though Checquer'd with some Illnesses, and what he call'd, I remember, once a *Valetudinarian State*) an excellent Habit both of Body and of Mind ; as may sufficiently be collected (amongst other things) from the Nature and Frequency of his *Writings*. But for some time before his Last Sickness, he found himself to be often pretty much out of Order ; and had particularly many times every 3*d* or 4*th* Turn an intermitting Pulse ; and once for Six Hours together (though he seem'd otherwise to be well, and went into the Hall) no Pulse at all. He was taken one Night after Supper very Ill in the Fellows Room, and swooned away ; He complained afterwards, *That his Distemper was Wind, but he hoped it would not carry him away in a Storm.* This was about a Year before he died. And the Summer before this, for many Nights together, he felt himself in a perfect Fever : But it going off again after a few Hours, and he sleeping well the rest of the Night, and finding himself at Ease, and fit for Study in the Morning, with an Appetite for his Meat, Dinner and Supper, he took no farther notice of it.

'But it had been much *Happier* in all Probability (I say not for *himself*, but for the *Church* and *Publick*) if he had given some more heed to these Friendly *Items* of *Nature*. But immoderate Studies past (not to say, and present too) the Breakings and Weaknesses of Age, with some Trouble in Affairs more than Ordinary from without (which yet could never, I am perswaded, have made that Impression upon his Mind at any other Season) meeting altogether with an actual Indisposition, drew him at length into a sort of Sadness and Deficiency of Spirits : Insomuch that my Friend writing to me about that time, gave me this Account. *He seems to labour under a Divine Melancholy ; from whence notwithstanding he promiseth to himself a very great* Advantage *in the End.* And in that same Letter again, speaking of the *Decays of Strength* he was under, he adds this upon it : *But his Mind is Vigorous within ; and breaths, beyond what I can express, after* GOD *and Virtue.*

'This was in *November* before his Death : And much to the same purpose was that which he wrote the Month following ; *Our most Excellent Friend is still held in a Doubtful State, as to the Recovery of his Health : But he aspires, with an incredible Ardour of Mind, after that which is* Best. And a while after he was pleas'd to send me the ensuing Relation ; *That he had been let Blood, and seem'd after it much better than before ; yet it had a great deal of black Melancholy in it, though other Parts of it were very Florid and Sanguine : That though before the Writing*

of this Letter, at his sitting down to Dinner, he look'd dispirited, yet it was also with an Appearance of approaching Health ; but before he had dined, and after Dinner, I never saw (saith he) *more vigorous Emanations from him, nor the Air of his Face Stronger or Chearfuller.*

'Yet after all this promising Appearance, the Sun began soon to be clouded afresh ; and the dark sullen Vapours, as glad to take him at so great an Advantage, to be multiplied upon him ; till weary with struggling, this envelop'd Star yielded at length to their Force and Power ; and was carried away by them from its State here into another Region ; yet in *this* Case not *to lose*, but *to increase* (as I said) his *Lustre* in that New World.

'As his Body had been out of Tune, for some time, so had his Mind in a sort, before his great Illness ; I speak as to that deep and *Plastick* sense (to use his own term) he had been under usually in *Divine* Matters : Insomuch that he complained on a certain time to his Friend, *That he had for a long Season been in as good a Way as he could almost wish ; but he knew not, how he came to be* whimm'd *off from it* (as his Expression was). And he noted again afterwards, *how the* Plastick *went one way, and his* Intellective *another. If he was to live, he could fetch them both up together* (he said) *again ; but for that, he left it wholly to the Will and good Providence of God.* And perhaps his over-great Endeavours to do this, in the State he was in, prov'd still but the more Injurious to him. He was (if possible) for making all *Vital* and *Unison* anew (with respect, I mean, both to *Body* and *Mind*) and for the rendring of his *Affections* and *Passions*, as well as *Reason* and *Understanding*, Joyous and Divine. He took notice once, looking on his Hands, *That his Body* (as he express'd it) *was strangely run out.* His meaning, I conceive, was, Things were not so Compact and Spiritous in it as they had formerly been.

'Even this *Wonderful Man* (saith my Friend to me, in another of his Letters) *repents him of several things that are past ; and complains, that he hath not been in all things so closely united to the Will of God, as a Faithful and Perfect Servant of Christ ought to be.* And he said to him another time ; *That* Repentance *was a sweet thing.* And yet it is certainly *True*, what he spoke to this same Person many Years before, as we have above remark'd ; *That he did not remember of a long time, that he had done any thing that was really Evil.* In all which, if rightly understood, there is nothing, as I conceive, either of vain Boast or of Contradiction : And there may be a Difference between the not doing things truly Sinful, and the not doing all the Good that was possible ; or that might tend to a greater Perfection.

'He was twice (as I take it) after that first time let Blood again ; and then there appear'd nothing of that black Melancholy in it : But yet still it avail'd not to a Recovery.

'In *June* I my self saw him ; and twice waited on him. He was the *first* time much indispos'd ; as much almost, my Friend told me, as he had seen him any time of his Illness. Weaker indeed he was afterwards ; but little more disorder'd : *The Calamity* (he was pleas'd to tell me) *of his Condition had been exceeding great ; that for many Weeks together he had liv'd almost a perpetual* Pervigilium (*with little or no Sleep at all*) *So that it was a Wonder, and the great Mercy of God to him, that he had not been perfectly Distracted.* Yet *that Day* he walked abroad ; and *Prudent*, *Pious*, and even *Pleasant* things would come from him.

'He had a *Melancholy*, and some unruly *Ferment* of *Nature* about him. It was his own Reflection more than once to his Friend ; *That his Body was out of Order ; but that as to his Mind, it was in its right Frame, and fix'd on God.* He said, *He thought he should have dyed Laughing ;* but was sensible now how much the Scene was chang'd with him, and repeated twice (as I remember) *That he was as a Fish out of its Element, and that lay tumbling in the Dust of the Street.* And at another time he said, *That he was but the Remains of an Ordinary Man.*

'He was very Sensible of the State he was in, and the Occasion it might give the World to discourse ; and that some possibly might be prone to make an ill Use of it to the Prejudice of his *Writings:* But then he pleasantly observ'd upon it this ; *That he had read of a Person, an excellent Mathematician, that at last came to doat ; but none* (saith he) *will say, that any of his former Demonstrations were ever the worse for all that.* Than which I know not what could have been said more *solidly* or *ingeniously* by any person.

'The *second* time I saw him, he was in an extraordinary Calm and Easy temper. I was expressing my Hopes to see him perfectly recover'd. He replied, *That* GOD *alone knew that ; to* whom, *through our Lord* Jesus Christ, *he entirely resign'd all that concern'd him ; and that* there was his Anchorage, *and his* Rest : *Not doubting of the Remission of all his Sins, through him that had dyed on the Cross for them.* To which he added, *That never any person thirsted more after his Meat and Drink, than He, if it pleas'd God, after a Release from the Body:* Professing withal, *that he had deserv'd greater Afflictions from the Hands of God, than those he had met with.*

'I took an Occasion to say ; That he might indeed be the willinger to die, because he seem'd to have done the great Work that God had sent him into the World for. His Answer was, *That he hoped he had not spent his Time in Vain ; and that his* Writings *would be of Use to the* Church of God, *and to* Mankind. It was his Expression (it seems) some Years before this ; *That it was to him a very great Pleasure, to think that, when he was gone out of the World, he should still converse with it by his* Writings. As he added also farther at this time to my self ; *That it was a great Satisfaction to him, to consider that he was going to those, with whom he should be as well acquainted in a quarter of an Hour, as if he had Known them many Years.* And this was the Last Time I had the Honour and Happiness to see him, being much Pleas'd to leave him so Easy and in so Hopeful a way, as I thought, of Recovery.

'But the *Divine Foresight* had not decreed his Stay here. His Weakness continued, and advanced upon him. Yet as a Wise Person, both living and dying, and to add now at last to all the rest of his Pious and Prudent Reflections, he said this to his Friend towards the End of his Sickness ; "It is the frequent Trick of some of the *Romanists*, when they speak of Men that have writ more than Ordinarily against them, to give out, that they alter'd their Minds before they died : Therefore do you tell all my Friends, that I have the same Sense of the *Church of Rome*, and of all the *Great Points* of *Religion* now, that I had when I wrote : And farther, if any one shall pretend, that he ever heard me speak any thing that is Contrary to my Publick Writings ; assure them again, They are my true Sense ; and that to them I stand.

'He was not (as likewise most other Persons at that time) without a due Sense, and Sollicitous Foresight, of what seem'd so plainly coming on us in a late Reign. *We had a very Prudent Power* (he said) *over us.* Such was his own Prudent and *Cautious* Expression that he used to my self. And he added somewhat at that time ; *That he hoped, he should be ready for whatever it should please God to cut out for him.* But to his Faithful Friend and Attender he said more particularly, and at large, thus ; *That if he were to be called out to a Stake, he could speak little to the People in that Condition : But this* (saith he) *I think, would be sufficient ; to let them know, that my Sense, as to* all Points *in Controversy between us and the Church of Rome, was in my Publick Works ; and that I was there come to seal it with my Blood.* And certain it is, that a very small time before his Death, he seem'd with some Concern to express it ; *That he should not do that Service to the Truth, as to die or suffer in Testimony of it : But however, he having writ so very freely, and thereby having so much expos'd himself to it, and being ready in Mind, as he had often declared himself to be ; it might not be without its Use.*

'And this reminds me now of another Passage in the *Doctor*, which he likewise spake of (and I tell it here, on Condition it may not be mis-interpreted by any) *viz.* That some time before his *Illness* (on what Occasion I know not) he was making at a leisure time (by way of *Diversion* or *Experiment*) an *Anagram* of his Name, *Henricus Morus Cantabrigiensis.* It was falling otherwise at first; but not hitting thoroughly, it settled it self at length with these significant and exact Words; *Insignis Heros curnam se curabit?* (Why should this Eximious *Heros* be Sollicitous for himself?) Which he soon naturally interpreted as a sort of gentle Reprehension from Providence *for it:* As it could not also, at the same time, but serve as greatly to fortifie his Mind *under it.* Certain it is, as well the *Character* as the *Sense* was very highly Applicable to both the *Person* and the *Season.*

'He profess'd with Tears in his Eyes; *That he had with great* Sincerity *offer'd what he had written to the World;* and added this afterwards, *That he had spent all his* Time *in the State of those* Words, Quid Verum sit, & quid Bonum, quæro, & rogo; & in hoc Omnis sum: *That what is good, and what is true, were the two great things that he had always sought and* enquir'd after, *and was* wholly *indeed* taken up *with them.* Which is not much unlike that of *Siracides*, at large taken notice of in his *Preface general;* and which he there affirms *to be the* Bent and Scope *of all his* Writings *whatsoever;* and shews it by a particular Application to be so. *Quid est Homo? &c. What is man, and whereto serveth he? What is his Good, and what is his evil? And then he adds this;* Whoso affects *Niceties*, or *unprofitable Curiosities*, let him seek them elsewhere: What *Fruit*, or *Entertainment* this my own Garden affords, I have sufficiently by this inform'd the *Reader.*

'This calls to my Remembrance a Saying of *Lactantius; Primus Sapientiæ Gradus, &c.* The first *Degree of* Wisdom *is, to understand the things which are* false; *the* second, *those that are true; than which there can no greater* Pleasure *appertain to Man.* As *Tully* again hath very *Heroically* asserted; *That there was no* better Gift *ever yet given unto* Mankind, *No, nor ever shall be, than the Knowledge of* Philosophy. Which, if it be understood of the Highest *Wisdom* and *Philosophy* indeed, both *Natural* and *Reveal'd*, is most True and Sacred according unto that of *Philotheus* in the *Dialogues; For my Part, I look upon the* Christian Religion *rightly understood, to be the* deepest *and* choicest Piece *of* Philosophy *that is.* And how much be undervalued all *Other Philosophy* in comparison of *this*, or when void of the *Virtues* and *Graces* of it, may at large be seen, *Dial.* 3. *Numb.* 3.

'*Demosthenes* is said to have griev'd at his Death, after having liv'd 107 Years, that he should go out of the World, *When he was but just beginning to grow Wise.* The *Doctor*, on the contrary, had been long acquainted both with *Natural* and *Divine Wisdom;* and died Contentedly in the full, and even antient Embraces and Possessions of them: And this to *that* Degree, that it puts me in mind of *that* Notable Saying of one of the *Philosophers; Cum Homo copulatus fuerit Intellectui per Scientiam omnium Rerum complet, tunc est Deus in Humano Corpore hospitatus. i.e.* When a Man shall be joined to *Intellect*, or *Understanding*, by a sort of Complete Knowledge of all things, then a *God* (or, as I would interpret it, an extraordinary *Heroe*) may be said to sojourn in a Human Body.

'Let me conclude here with that of the *Poet;* and which, I confess, I take to be the *Doctor's* Character in a distinguishing manner.

Felix, qui potuit Rerum cognoscere Causas;
Atque Metus omnes, & inexorabile Fatum,
Subjecit pedibus, strepitumque Acherontis avari!

To this Sense.

Happy the Man, that knows the Causes deep
Of Things; and all dread Fears can under keep;
Tread upon Death's inexorable Claws,
And slight the Roar of Acheron's *rav'nous Jaws.*

But here I have run out, I fear, unseasonably. To return to the *Doctor*, and to the Close of this Account I am giving of him; He broke out, but a short time before he Died, thus: *Doctor* (saith he) *I have marvellous things to tell you.* Sir, replied the other, *You are full*, I suppose, *of Divine Joy.* He answer'd with a most deep Sense, *Full.* It is Pity but that Reverend Person had ask'd him a little more particularly about it; namely, what those *Marvellous Things* were: But he saw him extreme Weak; and so it pass'd over.

'The Day before he died, his Nephew *Gabriel More*, Esq., came to him; being sent for out of the Country by a Messenger on Purpose; Whom though some things had pass'd that were far from being Grateful or Easy between them, (as the Publick since hath been sufficiently acquainted) he made his Sole *Executor*, and left a very large Addition of Estate to him; saluting him at his coming very affectionately, and saying, *Nephew, You are kindly Welcome.*

'He said particularly to a Party some time before his Death, *that he was throughly reconciled to him:* And when some admir'd at his *Candour*, He replied; *There was something that drew a Man's* Affections *in such Cases almost whether he would or no.*

'With respect to his being sent for, and the State the *Doctor* was then in, I had this Account. "After this he was in a clammy Sweat, and his Pulse almost gone : Death seem'd to sit on his Countenance ; and I thought he would have gone off. Asking him what I should say to his Nephew ; He told me, that he was exceeding Weak, and must refer him to my own Informations ; *but*, said he very affectionately and plainly, though also very weakly, *my kind hearty Love to him.* When I ask'd him positively afterwards, whether I should *send* for him, he seem'd unresolv'd ; saying, that he was *Melancholick* and *Suspicious*, and might think that we play'd tricks with him, if he should continue thus *at trot*, and *loll*, and *hang on.*' This Person since is dead himself ; and left the main of all that he had (as the *Doctor* had also once intended to do) to Charitable Uses.

'About 3 of the Clock the Day before he died, he called for a Glass of Sack ; and seem'd somewhat reviv'd ; his Face lost its Cloud, and his Pulse came a little better, but very Weak. As his Friend was speaking to him as a Dying Man should be spoken to, he express'd his Sense of Death in those *first Words* of that famous Sentence of *Tully's* ; *O Præclarum illum Diem !* The whole is to this Purpose ; *O most Blessed Day ! when I shall come to that Company of Divine Souls above, and shall depart from this Sink and Rout below.*

'That last Night of all, his Passionate Friend and Lover, seeing him so extreme Weak, wish'd him a *Good Night* with a more than Ordinary *Pathos* and Affection : To whom he replied as deeply and affectionately ; *Good Night, Dear Doctor.* And it was the last time he ever saw him alive : For the next Morning, between 4 and 5 of the Clock, being the *First* of *September*, 1687, and the 73d Year of his Age (his *Body* as well as *Mind* being now Fit for it) immediately before his Friend came into the Room, and while his Steps were heard upon the Stairs, *the Doctor departed this Life ;* in so *Easy* a manner, and with so *Calm* a Passage, that the Nurse with him was not sensible of it.'

There is added this :[1]—

' He was *Buried* decently by his Executor, *Sept.* 3. and lies Interr'd in the Chapel of that *College*, to which he had been so long an *Egregious Ornament.* He died indeed a *Present* and *Future Honour*, not only to the *College* and *University* at large ; but to the whole *Church* and *Kingdom*, the very *Age* he liv'd in, and to the *Race of Mankind.*'

In accord with this in the College Chapel, within the altar rails, is a slab of marble, forming part of the floor, with the following inscription : —

[1] Page 227.

[Arms.]

Here lyeth ye Body of Dr. Ralph Cudworth late Master of Christ Colledge about 34 years Hebrew Professor, & Prebendary of Gloucester he died ye 26th of June 1688 in ye 71st year of his Age.

[Arms.]

As also :—

The Body of Dr. Henry Moore late fellow of this College he died ye 1st of Sept. 1687 in ye 73d year of his Age.

On the Eastern Wall of the Chapel is a small plain tablet, with a Latin inscription commemorative of DR. JOSEPH MEDE, MORE, and CUDWORTH.[1]

We take this summary 'Description of his Person' from Ward :[2]—

'IT remains now to give a brief Touch upon the *Description* of his *Person*. He was, for *Stature* inclining to Tallness ; of a thin *Body*, but of a Serene and Vivacious *Countenance* ; rather pale in his latter Years than florid of *Complexion* ; yet was it Clear and Spirituous ; and his *Eye* hazel, Vivid as an Eagle. One that knew him in his more middle Age, when he was somewhat swarthy, compared him to the Appearance of *a duskish Diamond*. He had an extraordinary *Purity* and *Tenuity* of *Spirits* (if it need to be repeated) which appear'd in the very Looks and Air of his *Face* ; in which *Seriousness* and *Pleasantness*, *Gravity* and *Benignity*, seem'd to seat themselves by turns ; or rather, in a sort, to reside together. His *Temper* was *Sanguine* ; yet with a due Quantity of Noble *Melancholy* that was mix'd with it : As it was *Aristotle's* Observation, *That all Persons* eminent, *whether in* Philosophy, Politicks, Poetry, *or any other* Arts, *do partake pretty much of the* Melancholick *Constitution.* And the Reason seems evident ; for that nothing of these can be Extraordinary, without a certain Weight and Depth of Thoughtfulness in the

1 From the Rev. Dr. Cartmell, as before. The mural inscription may find a place here :—

> Ut admoneantur Posteri
> Sepultos fuisse in hoc sacello
> Josephum Mede S. T. B. Socium
> Henricum More S. T. P. Socium
> Radulphum Cudworth S. T. P. Magistrum
> Collegii Academiæ Ecclesiæ Anglicanæ
> Olim Lumina
> Hanc Tabulam ponendam curarunt
> Magister et Socii
> A.D. MDCCCXXVIII.

It would seem that the three occupy one grave.
2 Page 228, 229, 230.

Frame and Complexion of Man. IIis *Body* was, in the general, well proportion'd ; and his *Person* Fair and Agreeable. In short, *Nature* had not fitted amiss the *Case* to the *Jewel*, the *Body* to the *Soul*. . . . . His *Picture* was twice drawn, and prefix'd to his *Writings*. The *first* of these Draughts, placed before the *Theological* Volume, was not happily perfected : It had not the true Air, or Spirit of his Countenance. The *Motto's* underneath it are a much truer Representation of him. The *second* (by *Loggan*) was more lucky and exact ; and contains in a sufficient Measure the real Air and Visage of the *Doctor* : So that Posterity may be justly gratified with the *outward* as well as *inward* Pourtraicture of him.'

It is the latter that has been reproduced for us ; and of it PRINCIPAL TULLOCH writes penetratively, thus :[1]—'There is indeed, as all who have seen his portrait by Loggan will admit, a singularly vivid elevation in his countenance—with some lines strongly drawn round the mouth, but with ineffable sweetness, light and dignity in the general

expression. As he is the most poetic and transcendental, so he is upon the whole the most spiritual-looking of all the Cambridge divines.' To me there are lines and shadows in the face that explain—with all his 'sweetness and light' and tenderness—his egregious gibes and almost ribaldry in his controversy with Thomas Vaughan ('Eugenies Philalethes') twin-brother of Henry Vaughan the Silurist, and are declarative of an ultimate conquest indeed, yet of a hard struggle of the 'spirit' with the 'flesh,' or of the 'flesh' with the 'spirit' as he himself puts it. It has been thus with many. Saintly PHINEAS FLETCHER and GEORGE HERBERT and RICHARD BAXTER and JOHN BUNYAN have admitted passionately—like St. Paul—that only by higher might and control than their own did they find themselves walking in obedience at once to their own conscience and to the One supreme Lord of conscience.

---

[1] As before, 11. 347-8.

II.—CRITICAL.

I LIMIT myself here to the Poetry of our Worthy. The preceding portion of our Memorial-Introduction has made it clear that it was to 'sing' his Philosophy that he became a Poet, and that his Poetry was designed as the vehicle of his highest reach of attainment as a Philosopher. Nevertheless it is not for its philosophy *per se*, but for its imaginative qualities and vividness of fancy and exquisite nicety of expression of the most gossamery thinking and feeling, and its pre-Raphael-like studies of nature, and now and again—alas ! at long intervals, and mainly in the minor Poems—wonderfulness of rapture and aspiration, that we hold the Poetry of HENRY MORE to be worthy of prolonged

study. Regarding him broadly, Dr. George MacDonald, in his 'England's Antiphon,'[1] has written judicially and eloquently ; and so far as his Philosophy in his Verse goes, I know not that I need to do more than leave him very much to speak for me. 'Whatever,' he says, 'may be thought of his theories, they belong at least to the highest order of philosophy ; and it will be seen from the poems I give that they must have borne their part in lifting the soul of the man towards a lofty spiritual condition of faith and fearlessness. The mystical philosophy seems to me safe enough in the hands of a poet : with

---

[1] In Sunday Library for Household Reading (Macmillan).

others it may degenerate into dank and dusty materialism' (p. 223). 'Dank *and* dusty' is an odd combination; but I suppose the meaning is that, unconsecrated by high personal devoutness, mysticism is apt to 'degenerate' into sensuism, if not sensualism. He next quotes 'Resolution,'[1] and thus expounds the two lines :—

> 'Those too officious beams discover
> Of forms that round about us hover.'

—'It is the light of the soul going out from the eyes, as certainly as the light of the world coming in at the eyes, that makes things seen.' Reverting to the close of 'Resolution'[1] —and let every reader turn and return on the entire poem,—he observes—'This is magnificent as any single passage I know in literature' (p. 226). He continues :—'Is it lawful, after reading this, to wonder whether Henry More, the retired, and so far untried, student of Cambridge, would have been able thus to meet the alternations of suffering which he imagines? It is one thing to see reasonableness, another to be reasonable when objects have become circumstances. Would he, then, by spiritual might, have risen indeed above bodily torture? It is *possible* for a man to arrive at this perfection ; it is absolutely *necessary* that a man should some day or other reach it ; and I think the wise doctor would have proved the truth of his principles. But there are many who would gladly part with their whole bodies rather than offend, and could not yet so rise above the invasions of the senses. Here, as in less important things, our business is not to speculate what we would do in other circumstances, but to perform the duty of the moment, the one true preparation for the duty to come. Possibly, however, the right development of our human relations in the world may be a more difficult and more important task still than this condition of divine alienation. To find God in others is

better than to grow *solely* in the discovery of Him in ourselves, if indeed the latter were possible' (pp. 226, 227). He next quotes 'Devotion,'[1] and 'The Philosopher's Devotion,'[2] and 'Charity and Humility,'[3] and thus criticises them and all—'There are strange things, and worth pondering, in all these. An occasional classical allusion seems to us quite out of place, but such things we must pass. The poems are quite different from any we have had before. There has been only a few of such writers in our nation, but I suspect those have had a good deal more influence upon the religious life of it than many thinkers suppose. They are in closest sympathy with the deeper forms of truth employed by St. Paul and St. John. This last poem, concerning humility as the house in which charity dwells, is very truth. A repentant sinner feels that he is making himself little when he prays to be made humble : the Christian philosopher sees such a glory and spiritual wealth in humility that it appears to him almost too much to pray for.

✗ 'The very essence of these mystical writers seems to me to be poetry. They use the largest figures for the largest spiritual ideas —*light* for *good*, *darkness* for *evil*. Such symbols are the true bodies of the true ideas. For this service mainly what we term *nature* was called into being, namely, to furnish forms for truths, for without form truth cannot be uttered. Having found their symbols, these writers next proceed to use them logically ; and here begins the peculiar danger. When the logic leaves the poetry behind, it grows first presumptuous, then hard, then narrow, and untrue to the original breadth of the symbol ; the glory of

---

[1] Minor Poems, page 176.
[2] *Ibid.*, pages 178-80. On l. 7, 'and this eye has multiplied,' he annotates 'suns, as centres of systems,' and on l. 10, 'Toucheth each,' etc. Intransitively used. 'They touch each other': on l. 30, '*back*'=go back : a verb.
[3] *Ibid.*, page 181.

---

[1] Minor Poems, pages 175, 176.

the symbol vanishes; and the final result is a worship of the symbol, which has withered into an apple of Sodom. Witness some of the writings of the European master of the order—Swedenborg: the highest of them are rich in truth; the lowest are poverty-stricken indeed' (pp. 231-232). Bating the pagan hopelessness of its close, GEORGE GILFILLAN has also well *generalised* the character of More, as follows :—' More's prose writings give us, on the whole, a higher idea of his powers than his poem. This is not exactly, as a recent critic calls it, "dull and tedious," but it is in some parts prosaic, and in others obscure. The gleams of fancy in it are genuine, but few and far between. But his prose works constitute, like those of Cudworth, Charnock, Jeremy Taylor, and John Scott, a vast old quarry, abounding both in blocks and in gems—blocks of granite solidity, and gems of starry lustre. The peculiarity of More is in that poetico-philosophic mist, which, like the autumnal gossamer, hangs in light and beautiful festoons over his thoughts, and which suggests pleasing memories of Plato and the Alexandrian school. Like all followers of the Grecian sage, he dwells in a region of 'ideas,' which are to him the only realities, and are not cold, but warm; he sees all things in Divine solution; the visible is lost in the invisible, and nature retires before her God. Surely they are splendid reveries those of the Platonic school; but it is sad to reflect that they have not cast the slightest gleam of light on the dark, frightful, faith-shattering mysteries which perplex all inquirers. The old shadows of sin, death, damnation, evil, and hell, are found to darken the "ideas" of Plato's world quite as deeply as they do the actualities of this weary, work-day earth, into which men have, for some inscrutable purpose, been sent to be, on the whole, miserable,—so often to toil without compensation, to suffer without benefit, and to hope without

fulfilment.'[1] It will be noted that the minor Poems—More's most absolute workmanship —are overlooked by Gilfillan in his criticism as in his 'Specimens.' The brief notices of CAMPBELL and SOUTHEY fitly close this *general* aspect of More as a Poet. The former thus picturesquely and succinctly sums up his verdict :—' As a poet he has woven together a singular texture of Gothic fancy and Greek philosophy, and made the Christiano-Platonic system of metaphysics a ground-work for the fables of the nursery. The versification, though he tells us that he was won to the Muses in his childhood by the melody of Spenser, is but a faint echo of the Spenserian tune. In fancy he is dark and lethargic. Yet his Psychozoia is not a commonplace production : a certain solemnity and earnestness in his tone leaves an impression that he "believed the magic wonders which he sung" [Collins]. His poetry is not, indeed, like a beautiful landscape on which the eye can repose, but may be compared to some curious grotto, whose gloomy labyrinths we might be curious to explore for the strange and mystic associations they create.'[2]

The latter writes to a friend :—' He was a most odd fellow, the veriest believer in ghosts, goblins, vampires. But I have not done full justice to him as a poet. Strange and sometimes uncouth as he is, there are lines and passages of the highest poetry and most exquisite beauty.'[3]

I have now to bring before the student-reader of this remarkable Poetry certain things in it that deserve and will reward prolonged thought :—

---

[1] Specimens, with Memoirs, of the Less-known British Poets, vol. ii. pp. 221-2 (in Nichol's Poets—3 vols. 8vo, 1862). *En passant*, it seems right to notice that Mr. Gilfillan inadvertently spells Van Helmont's name (twice) as Van Helment, and also confounds the son with the father.

[2] 'Specimens,' p. 297 : 1 vol. 8vo, 1844. Campbell, like Gilfillan, leaves unnoticed More's minor poems—in both suggestive.

[3] Quoted in the Sotheby MSS. in Chetham Library, *s.n.*

(a) The words and workmanship.
(b) Personal opinions and characteristics.
(c) His love of nature.
(d) His assurance of ‘fit readers.’

(a) THE WORDS AND WORKMANSHIP.—In his Epistle to the Reader of his ‘Philosophical Poems’ (1647), he thus makes his Apology (in the old sense) :—

‘If I seem too bold in presenting my self again so suddenly to publick view, let it excuse me, at least in part, that there is not so much boldnesse in this, as in my first adventure. For whereas I had then no encouragement but mine own well meaning, and carelessenesse of the opinions of men ; I have now (beside that resolv’d neglect of mens hasty censures) the experience (though unexpected) of the favourable acceptance of the bravest and best improved spirits.

‘For whose sakes, and as many else as are at leasure a while to lay aside the pleasure or trouble of the world, and entertain their minds with thoughts of a greater compasse then the fetching in of a little wealth or honour ; I have taken the pains to peruse these Poems of the soul, and to lick them into some more tolerable form and smoothnesse. For I must confesse such was the present haste and heat that I was then hurried in (dispatching them in fewer moneths then some cold-pated-Gentlemen have conceited me to have spent years about them, and letting them slip from me so suddenly while I was so immerse in the inward sense and representation of things, that it was even necessary to forget the œconomie of words, and leave them behind me aloft, to float and run together at randome (like chaff and straws on the surface of the water) that it could not but send them out in so uneven and rude a dresse. Nor yet can I, (I professe) ever hope to find leasure or patience so exquisitely to polish them, as fully to answer mine own curiosity, if I would be also humorous, or the delicacy of some Lady-wits that can like nothing that is not as compos’d as their own hair, or as smooth as their Mistresses Looking-glasse. But may these emendations prove but acceptable to the more generous and manly Genius : I shall please my self enough, if I prove but tolerable to those female phansies.’   (p. 6.)

Again—in his ‘Interpretation Generall’ he pleads—

‘If any man conceive I have done amisse in using such obscure words in my writings, I answer, That it is sometime fit for Poeticall pomp sake, as in my Psychozoia : Otherwise time necessitie requires it,

Propter egestatem linguæ, & rerum novitatem,

as Lucretius pleads for himself in like case. Again, there is that significancie in some of the barbarous words (for the Greeks are barbarians to us) that, although not out of superstition, yet upon due reason I was easily drawn to follow the Counsel of the Chaldee Oracle, Ὀνόματα

βάρβαρα μή ποτ’ ἀλλάξης, Not to change those barbarous terms into our English tongue. Lastly, if I have offended in using such hard names or words, I shall make amends now by interpreting them.’   (p. 159.)

Most characteristic too is his consideration for the ‘common people.’   Thus :—

‘Nothing else can be now expected for the easie and profitable understanding of this Poem, but the interpretation of the names that frequently occurre in it. Which I will interpret at the end of these Books ; (as also the hard terms of the other Poems) for their sakes whose real worth and understanding is many times equall with the best, onely they have not fed of husks and shels, as others have been forced to do, the superficiary knowledge of tongues. But it would be well, that neither the Linguist would contemne the illiterate for his ignorance, nor the ignorant condemn the learned for his knowledge, For it is not unlearnednesse that God is so pleased withall, or sillinesse and emptinesse of mind, but singlenesse and simplicity of heart.’   (p. 12, col. 2 fin.)

So too in his Poetry itself, *e.g.* :—

. . . ‘So hath my muse with much uncertaintie
Exprest herself, so as her phantasie
Strongly enacted guides her easie pen ;
I nought obtrude with sow’r anxietie,
But freely offer hints to wiser men :
The wise from rash assent in darksome things abstain.’

With lowlier candour still, in his ‘Cupid’s Conflict’—one of the most memorable of the minor poems—he admits his unskilfulness and obscurity and ‘barbarous words,’ as against mellifluous love-lays that he might have sung, *e.g.* :—

. . . ‘now thy riddles all men do neglect,
Thy rugged lines of all do ly forlorn.
Unwelcome rhymes that rudely do detect
The Readers ignorance. Men holden scorn
To be so often non-plus’d or to spell,
And on one stanza a whole age to dwell.

‘ Besides this harsh and hard obscurity
Of the hid sense, thy words are barbarous
And strangely new, and yet too frequently
Return, as usuall plain and obvious,
So that the show of the new thick-set patch
Marres all the old with which it ill doth match.

‘ But if thy haughty mind, forsooth would deign
To stoop so low as t’hearken to my lore,
Then wouldst thou with trim words not disdeign
To adorn th’ outside, set the best before.
Nor rub nor wrinkle would thy verses spoil,
Thy rhymes should run as glib and smooth as oyl.’
          (pp. 171, 172.)

He is nevertheless resolved to keep to his own way, as thus :—

> . . . 'what thou dost Pedantickly object
> Concerning my rude rugged uncouth style,
> As childish toy I manfully neglect,
> And at thy hidden snares do inly smile.
> How ill alas ! with wisdome it accords
> To sell my living sense for livelesse words.
>
> ' My thought's the fittest measure of my tongue,
> Wherefore I'll use what's most significant,
> And rather then my inward meaning wrong
> Or my full-shining notion trimly skant,
> I'll conjure up old words out of their grave,
> Or call fresh forrein force in if need crave.
>
> ' And these attending on my moving mind
> Shall duly usher in the fitting sense
> As oft as meet occasion I find.
> Unusuall words oft used give lesse offence ;
> Nor will the old contexture dim or marre,
> For often us'd they're next to old, thred-bare.
>
> ' And if the old seem in too rusty hew,
> Then frequent rubbing makes them shine like gold,
> And glister all with colour gayly new.
> Wherefore to use them both we will be bold.
> This lifts me fondly with fond folk to toy,
> And answer fools with equall foolery.
>
> ' The meaner mind works with more nicetie
> As Spiders wont to weave their idle web,
> But braver spirits do all things gallantly
> Of lesser failings nought at all affred :
> So Natures carelesse pencill dipt in light
> With sprinkled starres hath spattered the Night.'
> (p. 172, cols. 1, 2.)

Then with touch of pathos in the recognition of the ebbing out of his ' fine phrensy' that suffused his barest words to himself with light of glory—as the sun transfigures into the radiance of a diamond a *bit* of delf on a ploughed hill-side—and his infinite short-coming from his ideal—we have this :—

> ' Right well I wot, my rhymes seem rudely drest
> In the nice judgement of thy shallow mind
> That mark'st expressions more than what's exprest,
> Busily billing the rough outward rinde,
> But reaching not the pith. Such surface skill's
> Unmeet to measure the profounder quill.
>
> ' Yea I alas ! my self too often feel
> Thy indispos'dnesse ; when my weakened soul
> Unstedfast, into this Outworld doth reel,
> And lyes immerse in my low vitall mold.
> For then my mind, from th' inward spright estrang'd
> My Muse into an uncouth hew hath chang'd.

' A rude confuséd heap of ashes dead
My verses seem, when that cælestiall flame
That sacred spirit of life's extinguished
In my cold brest. Then gin I rashly blame
My rugged lines : This word is obsolete ;
That boldly coynd, a third too oft doth beat

' Mine humerous ears. Thus fondly curious
Is the faint Reader, that doth want that fire
And inward vigour heavenly furious
That made my enrag'd spirit in strong desire
Break through such tender cob-web niceties,
That oft intangle these blind buzzing flies.

' Possest with living sense I inly rave,
Carelesse how outward words do from me flow,
So be the image of my mind they have
Truly exprest, and do my visage show ;
As doth each river deckt with Phebus beams
Fairly reflect the viewer of his streams.'

(p. 177.)

These and other admissions will win for More forgiveness—such as Spenser had to ask in his 'Shepherd's Calendar,' because of his Chaucerian and older words—for inevitable obscurantism and irritating neologies. Many of the new words and new 'ideas' were as hierogylphs rather than expressions of his thoughts, intelligible or semi-intelligible to himself, but hidden to the multitude.

Notwithstanding all this, when you compare the little volume of 1642 with the larger of of 1647, you find that he did more than merely enlarge. In our quotation from the 'Epistle to the Reader,' it is to be observed that he professes—' I have taken the pains to peruse these Poems of the soul, and to lick them into some more tolerable form and smoothnesse ;' and the reader who will emulate the Author's 'pains' to peruse and re-peruse, and compare, will be interested with the marks of revision and nicety of labour in the most unlooked-for places. But so far as I have discovered, the more 'tolerable form and smoothnesse' belong rather to the additional stanzas inserted throughout, so as to give a firmer *nexus*, and a less abrupt succession to the philosophising and fancies. I have been struck with the untouched perfection of all that arrests you in reading, when the portions are common to both the editions. Not verbal but structural and constructural were his endeavours 'to lick them' into shape. Thus in the 'Argument of Psychozoia,' Canto I., except in slight changes in spelling, 1642 and 1647 are identical; but in Canto II., for the 79 stanzas of 1642, in 1647 we have no fewer than 148; *i.e.* in 1647, after st. 56 come st. 57 to 125 now, and st. 126 as st. 57 of 1642, and therein st. 57 to 79 represent st. 126 to 148. The other additions the Author's own Epistles and Notes point out. Seeing that there is little or nothing of Herrick's or Herbert's earlier, or Wordsworth's or Tennyson's later, re-working of epithet and turn, it does not seem expedient to dwell on them. That More had an ear for the melody of versification, and an eye for the colouring of choice words, many and many a stanza in his 'Philosophical Poems,'—as finely wrought in workmanship as gem from Holland,—goes to demonstrate. I can only cull a few flowers from the rich Garden, and like Alexander Wilson's little friend say, 'The woods are full of them,' the book will yield well-nigh innumerable such. I leave them without italicizing, to commend themselves.

THE SON OF GOD.

'His beauty and His race no man can tell :
His glory darkeneth the Sunnes bright face ;
Or if ought else the Sunnes bright face excell,
His splendour would it dim, and all that glory quell.'

(p. 14, st. 8.)

THE EAGLE.

'The fulvid Eagle with her sun-bright eye.'—(p. 13, st. 3.)

DAWN OF DAY AND SUNSET.

'There you may see the eyelids of the Morn
With lofty silver arch displaid i' th' East,
And in the midst the burnisht gold doth burn ;
A lucid purple mantle in the West
Doth close the day, and hap the Sun at rest.
Nor doth these lamping shewes the azur quell,
Or other colours : where 't beseemeth best
There they themselves dispose ; so seemly well
Doth light and changing tinctures deck this goodly veil.

'But 'mongst these glaring glittering rows of light,
And flaming Circles, and the grisell gray,

And crudled clouds, with silver tippings dight,
And many other deckings wondrous gay,
As *Iris* and the *Halo ;* there doth play
Still-pac'd *Euphrona* in her Conique tire ;
By stealth her steeple-cap she doth assay
To whelm on th' earth : So School-boyes do aspire
With coppell'd hat to quelme the Bee all arm'd with ire.'

(p. 15, st. 24-5.)

THE SUNBEAMS.

'Then let us borrow from the glorious Sun
A little light to illustrate this act,
Such as he is in his solstitial Noon,
When in the Welkin there's no cloudy tract
For to make grosse his beams, and light refract.
Then sweep by all those Globes that by reflexion
His long small shafts do rudely beaten back,[1]
And let his rayes have undenied projection,
And so we will pursue this mysteries retection.'

(pp. 19-20, st. 7.)

MNEMON.

'With that his face shone like the rosie Morn
With maiden blush from inward modesty,
Which wicked wights do holden in such scorn :
Sweet harmlesse Modesty a rose withouten thorn !'

(p. 36, st. 36.)

THE SHREW-WIFE.

'So through her moody importunity
From downright death she rescues the poore man :
Self favouring sense ; not that due loyaltie
Doth wring from her this false compassion,
Compassion that no cruelty can
Well equalize. Her husband lies agast ;
Death on his horrid face so pale and wan
Doth creep with ashy wings. He thus embrac'd
Perforce too many dayes in deadly wo doth wast.'

(p. 37, st. 41.)

SPRING.

'Fairly invited by Sols piercing ray
And inward tickled with his chearing spright,
All plants break thorough into open day,
Rend the thick curtain of cold cloying night,
The earths opakeness, enemy to light,
And crown themselves in sign of victory
With shining leaves, and goodly blossoms bright.
Thus called out by friendly sympathy
Their souls move of themselves on their *Centreitie.*'

(p. 49, st. 31.)

---

[1] I know only one finer working out of a kindred comparison of the sun-beams—that of Marlowe in Tamburlane the Great (iv. 2):—

'I will persist, a terror to the world,
Making the meteors (that, like armèd men,
Are seen to march upon the towers of Heaven)
Run tilting round about the firmament,
And break their burning lances in the air
For honour of my wondrous victories.'

HORSES.

. . . 'coursers strike the grassie ground
With swift tempestuous feet . . .' (p. 49, st. 32.)

A NYMPH.

' Thus wrapt in rufull thought through the waste field
I staggeréd on, and scatteréd my woe,
Bedew'd the grasse with tears mine eyes did yield,
At last I am arriv'd with footing slow
Near a black pitchy wood that strongest throw
Of starry beam no'te easily penetrate :
On the North side I walkéd to and fro
In solitary shade. The Moons sly gate
Had cross'd the middle line : It was at least so late.

' When th' other part of night in painfull grief
Was almost spent, out of that solemn grove
There issuéd forth for my timely relief,
The fairest wight that ever sight did prove,
So fair a wight as might command the love
Of best of mortall race ; her count'nance sheen
The pensive shade gently before her drove,
A mild sweet light shone from her lovely eyne :
She seem'd no earthly branch but sprung of stock divine.

' A silken mantle, colour'd like the skie
With silver starres in a due distance set,
Was cast about her somewhat carelesly,
And her bright flowing hair was not ylet
By Arts device ; onely a chappelet
Of chiefest flowers, which from far and near
The Nymphs in their pure Lilly hands had set,
Upon her temples she did seemly weare ;
Her own fair beams made all her ornaments appear.

' What wilfull wight doth thus his kindly rest
Forsake? said she, approaching me unto.
What rage, what sorrow boils thus in thy chest
That thou thus spend'st the night in wasting wo?
Oft help he gets that his hid ill doth show.
Ay me! said I, my grief's not all mine own ;
For all mens griefs into my heart do flow,
Nor mens alone, but every mornfull grone
Of dying beast, or what so else that grief hath shown.

' From fading plants my sorrows freshly spring ;
And thou thy self that com'st to comfort me,
Would strong'st occasion of deep sorrow bring,
If thou wert subject to mortality :
But I no mortall wight thee deem to be,
Thy face, thy voice, immortall thee proclaim.
Do I not well to wail the vanity
Of fading life, and churlish fates to blame
That with cold frozen death lifes chearfull motions
tame?'   (p. 53, st. 10-14.)

BODY AND SOUL.

' But low'st 'gins first to work, the soul doth frame
This bodies shape, imploy'd in one long thought
So wholy taken up, that she the same
Observeth not, till she it quite hath wrought.

So men asleep some work to end have brought
Not knowing of it, yet have found it done :
Or we may say the matter that she raught
And suck'd unto her self to work upon
Is of one warmth with her own spright, & feels as one.

' And thus the body being the souls work
From her own centre so entirely made,
Seated i' th' heart,—for there this spright doth lurk,—
It is no wonder 'tis so easily sway'd
At her command. But when this work shall fade,
The Soul dismisseth it as an old thought,
'Tis but one form ; but many be display'd
Amid her higher rayes, dismist and brought
Back as she list, & many come that ne're were sought.'
          (pp. 67-68, st. 15, 16.)

THE VISIBLE AND INVISIBLE : SOUL AND SENSE.

' So eyes and ears be not mere perforations,
But a due temper of the *Mundane* spright
And ours together ; else the *circulations*
Of sounds would be well known by outward sight,
And th' eare would colours know, figures & light.
So that it's plain that when this bodie's gone,
This world to us is clos'd in darknesse quite,
And all to us is in dead silence drown :
Thus in one point of time is this world's glory flown.

' But if 't be so, how doth *Psyche* hear or see
That hath nor eyes nor eares? She sees more clear
Then we that see but secondarily.
We see at distance by a *circular*
Diffusion of that spright of this great sphear
Of th' Universe : Her sight is tactuall.
The Sun and all the starres that do appear
She feels them in herself, can distance all,
For she is at each one purely presentiall.

' To us what doth *diffusion circular*,
And our pure shadowed eyes, bright, crystalline,
But vigorously our spright particular
Affect, while things in it so clearly shine?
That's done continually in the heavens sheen.
The Sun, the Moon, the Earth, blew-glimmering Hel,
Scorch'd Ætna's bowels, each shape you'l divine
To be in Nature, every dern cell
With fire-eyed dragons, or what else therein doth dwel :

' These be all parts of the wide worlds excesse,
They be all seated in the *Mundane* spright,
And shew just as they are in their bignesse
To her. But *circulation* shews not right
The magnitude of things : for distant site
Makes a deficience in these *circulings*.
But all things lie ope-right unto the sight
Of heavens great eye ; their thin-shot shadowings
And lightned sides. All this we find in Natures springs.'
          (p. 68, st. 20-23.)

I would specify ' Exorcismus ' (pp. 177-8)
as in every way marvellously worked out.

Others of his minor Poems already named and noticed are equally exquisite in adaptation of word to 'idea.' His 'Hymns'—strong, severely simple, hearty—I place far above the effusive sentimentalisms of our popular Hymnology. It is a scandal and a sorrow that some of them have not long since been used in the Churches.[1]

(*b*) PERSONAL OPINIONS AND CHARACTERISTICS.—I have already stated and illustrated More's Wordsworthian self-scrutiny and lofty self-estimate. The most cursory reader will be struck with his ingenuity in working into his arguments his own experiences and likings. No one will confound this characteristic with the petty vanity of your small nature, that is constantly exemplifying the old fable of the fly on the chariot wheel. 'Personal as these details are,' observes Principal Tulloch, 'there is nothing egotistical in them. They are naturally and simply told, after the manner of the time. Such moods are for the most part left untold. The reserve of after-years and many experiences seldom permits the veil to be lifted up on the early secrets of the soul. But More, both as a boy and as a man, was singularly transparent in his deepest nature. His communings and ecstasies have not the slightest taint of morbid self-elation. They are the natural carriage of his strangely-gifted spirit. "From the beginning all things in a manner came flowing to him;" and his mind—according to his own saying—"was enlightened with a sense of the noblest Theories in the morning of his days"' (ii. pp. 307-8).

Of his personal opinions and characteristics revealed in his Poetry, I value inestimably his catholicity. He was a clergyman of the Anglican Church, and he 'defended' her with courage and force when she was on the losing side. He is full of tart and even sarcastic rebuke of the infinite factions and fractions of Nonconformity who broke off from the National Church. But he rose far above mere Churchism, and estimated a man's religion by what the man was and did, not by the Church-name he bore. Thus common-sensely does he put the matter in his 'Epistle to the Reader:'—

'I have also enlarged the second Canto of *PSYCHO-ZOIA*, and have added (that I might avoid all suspicion of partiality) to *Psittaco* and *Pithecus* diverse other persons, *Pico*, *Corvino*, *Graculo*, and *Glaucis*, but am so sensible of that sober precept in *Josephus*, which he affirms to be out of Moses, Μηδεὶς βλασφημείτω οὓς ἀλλαὶ πόλεις νομίζουσι Θεούς, that I would be very loth to be so farre mistaken as to be thought a Censurer or Contemner of other mens Religions or Opinions, if they serve God in them in the simplicity and sincerity of their hearts, and have some more precious *substratum* within, then inveterate custome or naturall complexion. All that I mean is this: That neither eager promoting of Opinion or Ceremony, nor the earnest opposing of the same, no not the acutenesse of Reason, nor yet a strong, if naked conceit, that we have the Spirit of God, can excuse a man from being in any better condition then in the Land of Brutes or in the mere animal nature. Which conclusion I thought worth my labour to set off with such Artifice and Circumstance as I have; the gullery and deceit therein, if not avoided, being of so great and evil consequence. For if we can but once entitle our opinions and mistakes to Religion, and Gods Spirit, it

---

[1] I would record here certain Author's and Editor's oversights for correction by the Reader: p. 17, st. 43, for 'hiddenlie' read 'hidden lie'; p. 35, st. 21, l. 5, for 'lives' read 'lies': p. 64, st. 17, l. 8, for 'truths' read 'truth's': p. 84, st. 5, l. 8, for ''tis' read ''ts': p. 121, st. 20, l. 3, for 'over oft' read 'overmost': p. 122, st. 36, l. 7, for 'of' read 'to': p. 176, Aphroditus, l. 4 (from end), put comma after 'Haec': p. 139, 3, for st. 59 read 49: p. 150, Canto ii., fill in '2' after 'Stanz.': p. 156, *b*, l. 36, for 'omnipotency' read 'omnipresency.' Specially correct the following:—p. 20, st. 17, l, 2, for 'foul' read 'soul': p. 21, st. 27, l. 8, put: after 'up-bray': p. 26, st. 77, l. 7, delete second 'the': p. 38, st. 59, l. 4, for 'lift' read 'list:' and so too in p. 172, *b*, st. 1, l. 5, for 'lifts' read 'lists': p. 81, st. 56, l. 5, for 'switnesse' read 'swiftnesse.' Occasionally I ought perhaps to have now added to and now changed the Author's punctuation.

I have further to ask kind attention to the following:—In the Section 'From Prose Works' (pp. 191-3) No. I. is repeated from p. 128, *ante* (Præexistency of the Soul, st. 101-2); No. III. from p. 175, *ante* (being extracted from 'Resolution'); No. IV. from pp 180-1 *ante* ('The Philosopher's Devotion'—with slight variations); No. II. is from Spenser's 'Faerie Queene,' B. II., c. vi. st. 1. No. VI. is from George Sandys' Version of the Psalms—the first 20 lines from the beginning of Psalm xcii., and the remainder from the end of Psalm xcvi. No. V. I have not elsewhere met with. It is of course a paraphrase of Revelation xv. 3, 4. It need scarcely be pointed out that the Latin Poems which follow the English set are translations of the last four of them.

is like running quicksilver in the back of a sword, and will enable us to strike to utter destruction and ruine. But it would prevent a great deal of bloud and bitternesse in the Christian world, if we reserved the flower and strength of our zeal for the undoubted Truth of God and His immutable Righteousnesse, and were more mildly and moderately affected concerning the Traditions and determinations of the Elders.'—(p. 6, *b.*)

In accord with this are his rebukes of all mere Church-authority, *e.g.* :—

'Say on said *Psittaco*. There 's a third, said I,
Nor reason nor unreasonablenesse hight.
Here *Graccus*. The disjunction you deny.
Then I, there is a third ycleep'd Gods spright
Nor reason nor unreasonablenesse hight.
Corvino straight foam'd like his champing jade
And said I was a very silly wight,
And how through melancholy I was mad
And unto private spirits all holy truth betray'd.

'But I nould with like fury him invade
But mildly as I mought made this reply.
Gods Spirit is no private empty shade
But that great Ghost that fills both earth and sky,
And through the boundlesse Universe doth ly,
Shining through purgéd hearts and simple minds
When doubting clouds of thick hypocrisie
Be blown away with strongly brushing winds ;
Who first this tempest feels the Sun he after finds.

'Thus wise and godly men I hear to teach,
And know no hurt this doctrine to believe.
Certes it much occasion doth reach
To leave the world and holily to live.
All due observance to Gods laws to give.
With care and diligence to maken pure
Those vessels that this heavenly dew receive.
But most in point of faith sleep too secure
And want this bait their souls to goodnesse to allure.

'For they believen as the Church believes
Never expecting any other light,
And hence it is, each one so loosely lives,
Hopelesse of help from that internall spright.
Enough ! said *Graculo*, *Corvino's* right.
Let 's hear, dispute in figure and in mood.
And stifly with smart syllogismes fight
That what thou wouldst may wel be understood,
But now thou rovest out, and rav'st as thou wert wood.

'Reason I say all Scripture sense must judge
Do thou one reason 'gainst this truth produce :
Reason, said I, in humane things may drudge
But in divine thy soul it may seduce.
Gr. Prove that. *Mn.* I prove it thus. For reasons use
Back'd with advantage of all sciences,
Of Arts, of tongues, cannot such light transfuse
But that most learnéd men do think amisse
In highest points divided as well you know, I wisse.'

(p. 27, st. 90-94.)

Again :—

'If then, said he, the spirit may not be
Right reason, surely we must deem it sense.
Yes, sense it is, this was my short reply.
Sense upon which holy Intelligence
And heavenly Reason and comely Prudence
(O beauteous branches of that root divine !)
Do springen up, through inly experience
Of Gods hid wayes, as he doth ope the ey'n
Of our dark souls and in our hearts his light enshrine.

'Here *Graculus* did seem exceeding glad
On any terms to hear but reason nam'd,
And with great joy and jollity he bad
Adew to me as if that he had gain'd
The victory. Besides *Corvino* blam'd
His too long stay. Wherefore he forward goes
Now more confirm'd his Nutshell-cap contain'd
What ever any living mortall knows.
Ne longer would he stay this sweet conceit to loose.

'Thus *Psittaco* and I alone were left
In sober silence holding on our way,
His musing skull, poor man ! was well nigh cleft
By strong distracting thoughts drove either way ;
Whom pittying I thus began to say,
Dear *Psittaco* what anxious thoughts oppresse
Thy carefull heart and musing mind dismay ?
I am perplexed much I must confesse
Said he, and thou art authour of my heavinesse.

'My self *Corvino's* Church-Autority
No certain ground of holy truth do deem.
And Scripture the next ground alledg'd by me
By *Graco* was confuted well, I ween,
But thou as in these points farre deeper seen
Than either *Corvin* or *Don Graculo*
Yea than my self, assent doth almost win
That Church nor Scripture, cast in reason too
Can to our searching minds truth's hidden treasures show.

'Wherefore a fourth, sole ground of certainty
Thou didst produce, to weet, the Spirit divine.
But now, alas ! here is the misery,
That left to doubt we cannot well enjoyn
Nor this nor that, nor Faith-forms freely coyn
And make the trembling conscience swear thereto,
For we our selves do but ghesse and divine
What we force other men to swear is true,
Untill the day-star rise our eyes with light t' embew.

'Which gift though it be given to me and you,
Mn. (Not unto me, courteous *Don Psittaco !*)
Ps. Yet certainly there be but very few
That so sublime a pitch ascend unto.
Mn. My self, alas ! a silly Swain I know
So far from solving these hard knots, said I,
That more and harder my ranck brain o'regrow
And wonder that thy quick sagacity
Doth not winde out a further inconveniency.

If light divine we know by divine light
Nor can by any other means it see
This ties their hands from force that have the spirit.
How can, said *Psittaco*, these things agree?
For without force vain is Church-Polity ;
Mn. But to use force 'gainst men that thing to do
In which they've not the least ability
May seem unjust and violent ; I trow,
'Gainst reason, 'gainst Religion, 'gainst all sence and law.'
(p. 28, st. 99-105.)

Once more :—

' Not rage, nor mischief, nor love of a sect,
Nor eating irefulnesse, harsh cruelty
Contracting Gods good will, nor conscience checkt
Or chok'd continually with impiety,
Fauster'd and fed with hid hypocrisie ;
Nor tyranny against perplexèd minds,
Nor fore'd conceit, nor man-idolatry,
All which the eye of searching reason blinds,
And the souls heavenly flame in dungeon darknesse
binds.

' Can warres and jarres and fierce contention,
Swoln hatred, and consuming envie spring
From piety? No. 'Tis opinion
That makes the riven heavens with trumpets ring,
And thundring engine mur'drous balls out-sling,
And send mens groning ghosts to lower shade
Of horrid hell. This the wide world doth bring
To devastation, makes mankind to fade :
Such direfull things doth false Religion perswade.

' But true Religion sprong from God above
Is like her fountain full of charity,
Embracing all things with a tender love,
Full of good will and meek expectancy,
Full of true justice and sure verity,
In heart and voice ; free, large, even infinite,
Not wedg'd in strait particularity,
But grasping all in her vast active spright,
Bright lamp of God! that men would joy in thy pure
light!' (p. 63, st. 4-6.)

Of his own devoutness and 'walking with
God,'—as walked the two of Emmaus,—
there are everywhere heart-stirring evidences.
The Reader will find himself taken captive by
these ; nor will he seek to abate one word of
Principal Tulloch's tribute :—' More himself
is at once the most typical and the most
vital and interesting of all the Cambridge
School. He is the most Platonicall of the
Platonic sect, and at the same time the most
genial, natural, and perfect man of them all.
We get nearer to him than any of them, and
can read more intimately his temper, character, and manners—the lofty and serene
beauty of his personality—one of the most
exquisite and charming portraits which the
whole history of religion and philosophy
presents' (II. 303).

As the corollary of all this, the student-
Reader will be half-awed half-touched by the
pervading sanctity of the man and of the
Poet. With beaming eye and tremble in his
voice he thus greets ' virgin youth as yet immaculate : '—

' Dear lads! How do I love your harmlesse years
And melt in heart while I the Morning-shine
Do view of rising virtue which appears
In your sweet faces, and mild modest eyne.
Adore that God that doth himself enshrine
In your untainted breasts ; and give no eare
To wicked voice that may your souls encline
Unto false peace, or unto fruitlesse fear,
Least loosened from your selves Harpyes away you bear.'
(p. 30, st. 124.)

He utterly rejects ' naked Faith disjoyn'd
from Purity' (p. 30, st. 116). He scourges
the ' froward hypocrite '—'That finds pretexts to keep his darling sinne ' (p. 85, st. 23).
Here is his rightly-based ecstasy :—

' But O ! how oft when she her self doth cut
From nearer commerce with the low delight
Of things corporeall, and her eyes doth shut
To those false fading lights, she feels her spright
Fill'd with excessive pleasure, such a plight
She finds that it doth fully satisfie
Her thirsty life. Then reason shines out bright,
And holy love with mild serenity
Doth hug her harmlesse self in this her purity.'
(p. 72, st. 28.)

Again :—

' But the clean soul by virtue purifi'd
Collecting her own self from the foul steem
Of earthly life, is often dignifi'd
With that pure pleasure that from God doth streem,
Often's enlighten'd by that radiant beam,
That issues forth from his divinity,
Then feelingly immortall she doth deem
Her self, conjoynd by so near unity
With God, and nothing doubts of her eternitie.'
(p. 113, st. 12.)

Once more :—

' Like to a light fast-lock'd in lanthorn dark,
Whereby, by night our wary steps we guide

In slabby streets, and dirty channels mark,
Some weaker rayes through the black top do glide,
And flusher streams perhaps from horny side.
But when we've past the perill of the way
Arriv'd at home, and laid that case aside,
The naked light how clearly doth it ray
And spread its joyfull beams as bright as Summers day.

'Even so the soul in this contracted state
Confin'd to these strait instruments of sense
More dull and narrowly doth operate.
At this hole hears, there smels ; But when she's gone from
   hence,
Like naked lamp she is one shining sphear,
And round about has perfect cognoscence
Whatere in her Horizon doth appear :
She is one Orb of sense, all eye, all airy ear.'
            (p. 128, st. 101-2.)

Further :—

'Thus have I stoutly rescuéd the soul
From centrall death or pure mortalitie,
And from the listlesse flouds of Lethe dull,
And from the swallow of drad Unitie.
What now remains, but since we are so sure
Of endlesse life, that to true pietie
We bend our minds, and make our conscience pure,
Lest living Night in bitter darknesse us immure.'
            (p. 134, st. 40.)

Again :—

'This proves the soul to sit at liberty,
Not wedg'd into this masse of earth, but free
Unloos'd from any strong necessity
To do the bodies dictates, while we see
Clear reason shining in serenity,
Calling above unto us, pointing to
What's right and decent, what doth best agree
With those sweet lovely Ideas, that do show
Some glimps of their pure light. So Sol through clouds
   doth flow.'   (p. 74, st. 40.)

Once more :—

SOCRATES.

'Als Socrates, when (his large *Intellect*
Being fill'd with streaming light from God above)
To that fair sight his soul did close collect,
That inward lustre through the body drove
Bright beams of beauty. These examples prove
That our low being the great Deity
Invades, and powerfully doth change and move.
Which if you grant, the souls divinity
More fitly doth receive so high a Majesty.'
            (p. 112, st. 4.)

Finally here :—

'Thrice happy he whose name is writ above,
And doeth good though gaining infamy ;

Requiteth evil turns with hearty love,
And recks not what befalls him outwardly :
  Whose worth is in himself, and onely blisse
  In his pure conscience that doth nought amisse.

'Who placeth pleasure in his purgéd soul
And virtuous life his treasure doth esteem ;
Who can his passions master and controll,
And that true lordly manlinesse doth deem,
  Who from this world himself hath clearly quit,
  Counts nought his own but what lives in his sprite.

'So when his spright from this vain world shall flit
It bears all with it whatsoever was dear
Unto it self, passing in easie fit,
As kindly ripen'd corn comes out of th' ear.
  Thus mindlesse of what idle men will say
  He takes his own and stilly goes his way.'
      (p. 172, st. 5, 4, 3, from bottom col. 2.)

It is questionable if any man is complete, or of kin to the highest, who has no humour. The finest Humourists of all literatures have had the largest and strongest intellect. Shakespeare is so utterly supreme and exceptional all round, that it needeth not to adduce him. But apart from him, I know none of the mighties who lacked this element. JOHN MILTON and WILLIAM WORDSWORTH are vulgarly supposed to have been without it. It is a 'Vulgar Error.' I was glad in studying More to discern, amid all his restraint and gravity, sufficient indications that he had humour and pleasantry of wit. None but a genuine Humourist could have drawn these portraits :—

'All the nice questions of the School-men old
And subtilties as thin as cobwebs bet,
Which he wore thinner in his thoughts yrold.
And his warm brains, they say, were closer set
With sharp distinctions than a cushionet
With pins and needles ; which he can shoot out
Like angry Porcupine, where e're they hit.
Certes a doughty Clerk and Champion stout
He seem'd and well appointed against every doubt.

'The other rod on a fat resty jade
That neighed loud. His rider was not lean.
His black plump belly fairly outward swai'd
And pressed somewhat hard on th' horses mane.
Most like methought to a Cathedrall Dean.
A man of prudence and great courtesie
And wisely in the world he knew to glean.
His sweaty neck did shine right greasily
Top heavy was his head with earthily policy.'
          (p. 26, st. 76-77.)

Again :—

'Brethren ! said he, (and held by holy belt
Corvino grave, ne did his hands abhor't
When he the black silk rope soft fimbling felt
And with his fingers milked evermore
The hanging frienge) one thing perplexeth sore
My reason weak and puzled thoughts, said he.
Tell then, ye learned Clerks, which of these foure
To weet, from Scripture, Church authority,
Gods Spirit, or mans Reason is Faiths Certainty.'

(p. 26, st. 83.)

Once more, how capitally drawn is this likening of Graculo to a daw !—

'Here Graculo leaning up with one eye
View'd the broad Heavens long resting in a pause
And all the while he held his neck awry
Like listning daw, turning his nimble nose,
At last these words his silent tongue did loose.
What is this spirit, say what's this spirit, man !
Who has it, answer'd I, he onely knows.
'Tis the hid Manna and the graven stone.'
He canteth, said Corvino, come Grac, let's be gone.'

(p. 28, st. 95.)

Has your Materialist ever been more keenly ridiculed than here ?—

'For then our soul can nothing be but bloud
Or nerves or brains, or body modifide.
Whence it will follow that cold stopping crud,
Hard moldy cheese, dry nuts, when they have rid
Due circuits through the heart, at last shall speed
Of life and sense, look thorough our thin eyes
And view the Close wherein the Cow did feed
Whence they were milk'd ; grosse Pie-crust will grow wise,
And pickled Cucumbers sans doubt Philosophize.'

(p. 127, st. 90.)

Again :—

'Wherefore who thinks from souls new souls to bring
The same let presse the Sunne beams in his fist
And squeez out drops of light, or strongly wring
The Rainbow, till it die his hands, well-prest.
Or with uncessant industry persist
Th' intentionall species to mash and bray
In marble morter, till he has exprest
A sovereigne eye-salve to discern a Fay :
As easily as the first all these effect you may.'

(p. 127, st. 87.)

There is more than humour, there is the condensation of wit,—which is as lightning to light,—as thus :—

'But most of all Corvin and Psittaco
Prudentiall men and of a mighty reach

Who through their wisdome sage th' events foreknow
Of future things ; and confidently preach
Unlesse there be a form which men must teach
Of sound opinions (each meaning his own)
But t' be left free to doubt and counter-speech
Authority is lost, our trade is gone
Our Tyrian wares forsaken, we, alas ! shall mone.

'Or at the best our life will bitter be :
For we must toyle to make our doctrine good.
Which will empair the flesh and weak the knee.
Our mind cannot attend our trencher-food,
Nor be let loose to sue the worldly good.
All's our dear wives, poore wenches ! they alone
Must ly long part of night when we withstood
By scrupulous wits must watch to nights high Noon
Till all our members grow as cold as any stone.

'Heaps of such inconveniences arise
From Conscience-freedome, Christian liberty.
Beside our office all men will despise
Unlesse our lives gain us Autority.
Which in good sooth a harder task will be.
Dear brethren ! sacred souls of Behiron !
Help, help as you desire to liven free
To ease, to wealth, to honour, and renown
And sway th' affrighted world with your disguized frown.'

(p. 26, st. 79-81.)

Yet could he speak too with a Seer's splendid passion :—

'A deep self-love, Want of true sympathy
With all mankind, Th' admiring their own heard,
Fond pride, a sanctimonious cruelty
'Gainst those by whom their wrathfull minds be stird
By strangling reason, and are so afeard
To lose their credit with the vulgar sort ;
Opinion and long speech 'fore life preferr'd,
Lesse reverence of God then of the Court,
Fear, and despair, Evill surmises, False report.'

(p. 34, st. 14.)

Soft though pungent is this of 'grave ignorance :'—

'Now let's go on (we have well-cleard the way)
More plainly prove this seeming paradox
And make this truth shine brighter then midday,
Neglect dull sconses mowes and idle mocks.
O constant hearts, as stark as Thracian rocks,
Well-grounded in grave ignorance, that scorn
Reasons sly force, its light slight subtile strokes.
Sing we to those wast hills, dern, deaf, forlorn,
Or to the cheerfull children of the quick-ey'd Morn ?'

(p. 80, st. 41.)

No grim ascetic, no misanthropic recluse, but a whole-hearted, clean-conscienced man was Henry More. I like him all the better that he manfully avowed his love of the nut-brown ale of his College, and that he did not believe in 'Fasting'—for everybody.

'I have heard,' says Ward, 'from some, that when he was first about to be chosen Fellow, they were afraid of him as a melancholy man ; till some that knew him better rectified the mistake, and assur'd them of his being more than ordinarily pleasant, as well as studious and serious; and that he was indeed, in his way, one of the merriest Greeks they were acquainted with' (p. 120).[1]

One feels certain he spoke truly when he exclaimed :—

> . . . 'my felicity
> Is multiply'd, when others I like happy see.'
> (p. 84, st. 6.)

It could scarcely have been otherwise, for his conception of our common Fatherhood and Brotherhood was Christ-like, as thus[2] :—

> 'His good Art
> Is all to save that will to Him return,
> That all to Him return, nought of him is forlorn :
>
> 'For what can be forlorn, when his good hands
> Hold all in life, that of life do partake ?
> *O surest confidence of Loves strong bands !*
> *Love loveth all that's made ;* Love all did make :
> And when false life doth fail, it's for the sake
> Of better being.'
> (p. 13, st. 6-7.)

Again :—

> 'The highest improvement of this life is love.'
> (p. 171, col. 1, st. 1.)

---

[1] Among Ward's anecdotes and sayings—of which there are not a few capital ones—take this :—'He said after the finishing of some of his writings, and a long and wasting studiousness, humourously and pleasantly (as he was lucky in putting things into an elegant and sententious posture), ' Now for these three months, I will neither think a wise thought, nor speak a wise word, nor do an ill thing' (p. 144).

[2] Very noble is his rejection of current conceptions of God that exalt the Almightiness above the Fatherhood. I regret that I can only refer to these among other matterful arguings-out of alike the loftiest and deepest problems: p. 85, st. 15, 17, 18, 19, 21 : p. 94, st. 36 : p. 165, closing demonstration. That he had no common reasoning faculty if without the music of Sir John Davies in his kindred arguments, let the student judge by turning to p. 49, st. 38 : p. 62, st. 33 : p. 67, st. 6-7 : p. 68, st. 15-16 : p. 72, st. 21-2 : p. 73, st. 35-6 : p. 74, st. 40-50 : p. 85, st. 19 : p. 96, st. 60 : p. 127. Note reason above sense, p. 57, st. 5 : p. 60, st. 10. Present-day burning questions, p. 86, st, 29, 31, *et alibi.*

Finally here :—

> 'The Good is uniform, the Evil infinite.'
> (p. 39, st. 71.)

'While More, in short,' says Principal Tulloch, ' was no hero, either in thought or deed,—his speculations were too transcendental, and his life too retired for this,—he yet comes before us as a singularly beautiful, benign, and noble character—one of those higher spirits who help us to feel the divine presence on earth, and to believe in its reality' (II. 350). Even his darkness was as of a holy place.

(*c*) His Love of Nature.—This comes out very much as in the great ancient Painters, whose backgrounds of portraits or sacred personalities rather than land-scape, or sea-scape, or sky-scape proper, assure us that they had eyes to look into, and not merely on, this so radiant and beautiful earth of ours. That is to say, you have nothing of the later Wordsworthian clarity and intuition of seeing, that *humanizing* of ' the meanest flower that blows,' which is part of Wordsworth's measureless gift to our English-speaking race. But you have snatches of description, elect *traits* of the visible and audible, dainty epithet and interblended perception and emotion. And so you have him crying out with a great joy :—

> 'How sweet it is to live ! what joy to see the Sunne.'
> (p. 16, st. 32.)

Similarly in his Preface to the Mystery of Godlinesse,' in speaking of the ' contemplation of this outward world,' he tells us that its ' several powers and properties touching variously upon my tender senses, made to me such enravishing musick, and snatch'd away my soul into so great admiration, love, and desire of a nearer acquaintance with their principle from whence all these things did flow ; that the pleasure and joy, which frequently accrued to me from hence, is plainly unutterable ; though I have attempted to

f

leave some marks and traces thereof in my Philosophical Poems.'

I venture to italicise a few lines here and there in these illustrative quotations :—

BEIRAH.

' When we that stately wall had undercrept,
We straightway found our selves in *Dizoie :*
The melting clouds chill drizzeling teares then wept ;
The mistie aire swet for deep agony,
Swet a cold sweat, and loose frigiditie
Fill'd all with a white smoke ; pale *Cynthia*
Did foul her silver limbs with filthy die,
Whiles wading on she measured out her way,
And cut the muddy heavens defil'd with whitish clay.

' No light to guide but the Moons pallid ray,
And that even lost in mistie troubled aire :
No tract to take, there was no beaten way ;
No chearing strength, but that which might appear
From *Dians* face ; her face then shin'd not clear,
And when it shineth clearest, little might
She yieldeth, yet the goddesse is severe.
Hence wrathfull dogs do bark at her dead light :
Christ help the man thus clos'd and prison'd in drad
Night.'

(p. 33, st. 3, 4.)

VISIONS OF EARTH.

' Fresh varnish'd groves, tall hills, and gilded clouds
Arching an eyelid for the glaring Morn ;
Fair clustred buildings which our sight so crouds
At distance, with high spires to heaven yborn ;
Vast plains with lowly cottages forlorn,
Rounded about with the low wavering skie,
Cragg'd vapours, like to ragged rocks ytorn ;
She views those prospects in our distant eye :
These and such like be the first *centres* mysterie.'

(p. 68, st. 25.)

THE SUNBEAMS.

' If not the same, then like to flowing stream
You deem the light that passeth still away,
New parts ever succeeding. The Sun-beam
Hath no reflexion then, if it decay
So fast as it comes forth : Nor were there day ;
For it would vanish 'fore it could arrive
At us. But in a moment Sol doth ray.
One end of his long shafts then we conceive,
At once both touch himself and down to us do dive.'

(p. 71, st. 16.)

THE CREATOR.

' Better the indigent be mov'd, then he
That wanteth nought : He fills all things with light
And kindly heat : through his fecundity
Peoples the world ; by his exciting sprite
Wakens the plants, calls them out of deep night.

They thrust themselves into his fostring rayes,
Stretch themselves forth, stird by his quickning might.
And all the while their merry roundelayes
As lightsome fancies deem) each Planet spritely playes.'

(p. 77, st. 16.)

TERROR.

' Certes such knowledge is a vanity,
And hath no strength t' abide a stormy stour ;
Such thin slight clothing, will not keep us dry
When the grim heavens, all black and sadly soure
With rage and tempest, plenteously down shower
Great flouds of rain. Dispread exility
Of slyer reasons fails : Some greater power
Found in a lively vigorous Unity
With God, must free the soul from this perplexity.'

(p. 84, st. 10.)

MARS.

. . . 'Mars rangeth in a round
With fiery locks and angry flaming eye.'

(p. 93, st. 22.)

SUNS.

' These with their suns I severall worlds do call,
Whereof the number I deem infinite :
Else infinite darknesse were in this great Hall
Of th' endlesse Universe ; For nothing finite
Could put that *immense shadow into flight.*
But if that infinite Suns we shall admit,
Then infinite worlds follow in reason right,
For every Sun with Planets must be fit,
And have some mark for his farre-shining shafts to hit.'

(p. 93, st. 26.)

GOD AND CREATION.

' That God is infinite all men confesse,
And that the Creature is some realtie
Besides Gods self, though infinitely lesse.
Joyn now the world unto the Deity.
What ? is there added no more entity
By this conjunction, then there was before ?
Is the broad-breasted earth ? the spacious skie
Spangled with silver light, and burning Ore ?
And the wide bellowing Seas, whose boyling billows roar,
Are all these nothing ?'

(p. 94, st. 34-5.)

THE MIND.

' Adde unto these, that the soul would take pains
For her destruction while she doth aspire
To reach at things (that were her wofull gains)
That be not corporall, but seated higher
Above the bodies sphere. Thus should she tire
Her self to 'stroy her self. Again, the mind
Receives contrary forms. *The feverish fire*
Makes her cool brooks and shadowing groves to find
Within her thoughts, thus hot and cold in one she binds.'

(p. 65, st. 23.)

WILD FANCY.

'Then the wild phansie from her horrid wombe
Will senden forth foul shapes.   O dreadfull sight!
Overgrown toads fierce serpents thence will come,
Red-scaléd Dragons with deep burning light
In their hollow eye-pits : With these she must fight ;
Then thinks her self ill-wounded, sorely stung.
Old fulsome Hags with scabs and skurf bedight,
Foul tarry spittle tumbling with their tongue
On their raw lether lips, these near will to her clung.

'And lovingly salute against her will,
Closely embrace, and make her mad with wo :
She'd lever thousand times they did her kill,
Then force her such vile basenesse undergo.
Anon some Giant his huge self will show,
Gaping with mouth as vast as any Cave,
With stony staring eyes, and footing slow :
She surely deems him her live-walking grave,
From that dern hollow pit knows not her self to save.

'After a while, tost on the Ocean main
A boundlesse sea she finds of misery :
The fiery snorts of the Leviathan
(That makes the boyling waves before him flie)
She hears, she sees his blazing morn-bright eye :
If here she scape, deep gulfs and threatning rocks
Her frighted self do straightway terrifie ;
Steel-coloured clouds with rattling thunder knocks,
With these she is amaz'd, and thousand such like mocks.'
          (p. 116, st. 43-45.)

INNOCENCE.

'O happy they that then the first are born,
While yet the world is in her vernall pride :
For old corruption quite away is worn
As metall pure so is her mold well-tride.
Sweet dews, cool breathing airs, and spaces wide
Of precious spicery wafted with soft wind :
Fair comely bodies, goodly beautifi'd,
Snow-limb'd, rose-cheek'd, ruby-lip'd, pearl-teeth'd,
     star-eyn'd :
Their parts, each fair, in fit proportion all combin'd.'
          (p. 100, st. 99.)

THE STARS.

'Thus nothing's lost of Gods fecundity.
But stretching out himself in all degrees
His wisedome, goodnesse and due equity
Are rightly rank'd, in all the soul them sees.
O holy lamps of God ! O sacred eyes
Filléd with love and wonder every where !
Ye wandring tapers to whom God descryes
His secret paths, great *Psyches* darlings dear !
Behold her works, but see your hearts close not too near.'
          (p. 120, st. 10.)

A WOODLAND STREAM.

'The labouring brook did break its toilsome way.'
          (p. 170, col. 2, st. 2.)

NIGHT.

'It was the time when all things quiet lay
In silent rest ; and Night her rusty Carre
Drawn with black teem had drove above half way.
Her curbed steeds foaming out lavering tarre
And finely trampling the soft misty air
With proner course toward the West did fare.'
          (p. 178, Ins. Phil. st. 1.)

THE EAGLE.

'But above these birds of more sightly plume
With gold and purple feathers gayly dight
Are rank'd aloft.   But th' Eagle doth assume
The highest sprig.   For his it is by right.
Therefore in seemly sort he there is pight
Sitting aloft in his green Cabinet
From whence he all beholds with awfull sight.
Who ever in that solemne place were met,
At the West end for better view, right stately set.'
          (p. 24, st. 61.)

BIRDS' WAYS.

'After a song loud chanted by that Quire
Tun'd to the whistling of the hollow winde
Comes out a gay Pye in his rich attire
The snowie white with the black sattin shin'd,
On's head a silken cap he wore unlin'd.
When he had hopped to the middle flore
His bowing head right lowly he inclin'd
As if some Deity he did adore,
And seemly gestures make courting the Heavenly powr.

'Thus cring'd he toward th' East with shivering wings
With eyes on the square sod devoutly bent.
Then with short flight up to the Oak he springs
Where he thrice congied after his ascent
With posture chang'd from th' East to th' Occident.
Thrice bowed he down and easily thrice he rose ;
Bow'd down so low as if't had been's intent
On the green mosse to wipe his swarthy nose.
Anon he chatters loud, but why himself best knows.

'There we him leave, impatient of stay
My self amaz'd such actions to see
And pretty gestures 'mongst those creatures gay :
So unexpected Uniformitie,
And such a semblance of due piety :
For every Crow as when he cries for rain
Did Eastward nod ; and every Daw we see
When they first entered this grassie Plain
With shaking wings and bended bills ador'd the same.'
          (p. 25, st. 62-64.)

THE SNAIL.

'And that particular Lives that be yborn
Into this world, when their act doth dispear,
Do cease to be no more then the snails horn,
That she shrinks in because she cannot bear
The wanton boys rude touch, or heavie chear
Of stormy winds.   The secundary light
As surely shineth in the heavens clear,

As do the first fair beams of Phœbus bright,
Lasting they are as they, though not of so great might.'
(p. 56, st. 5.)

SPIDER.

' Beside the senses each one are restraind
To his own object : so is Phantasie.
That in the spirits compasse is containd ;
As likewise the low naturall memory.
But sooth to say, by a strong sympathy
We both are mov'd by these, and these do move.
As the light spider that makes at a fly,
Her selfe now moves the web she subt'ly wove,
Mov'd first by her own web, when here the fly did rove.

' Like spider in her web, so do we sit
Within this spirit, and if ought do shake
This subtile loom we feel as it doth hit ;
Most part into adversion we awake,
Unlesse we chance into our selves betake
Our selves, and listen to the lucid voice
Of th' *Intellect*, which these low tumults slake :
But our own selves judge of whatere accloyes
Our muddied mind, or what lifts up to heavenly joyes.'
(p. 75, st. 53-4.)

FINE REPETITIONS.

' Therefore those different hews through all extend
So farre as light : Let light be every where :
And every where with light distinctly blend
Those different colours which I nam'd whilere
The Extremities of that farre shining sphear.
And that far shining sphear, which Centre was
Of all those different colours, and bright chear,
You must unfasten ; so o'respred it has,
Or rather deeply fill'd with Centrall sand each place.'
(p. 20, st. 11.)

The student will not neglect his *fantastique* of faith in tree-life so quaintly argued and illustrated (p. 47, st. 14-15: p. 48, st. 26: p. 50, st. 49). Is this an anticipation of the Telephone? 'so the low Spirit of the Universe, though it go quite through the world, yet it is not totally in every part of the world; Else we should heare our Antipodes, if they did but whisper' (p. 10, col. 1).

(*d*) His Assurance of 'Fit Readers.'—In his verse-address 'To the Reader'—originally prefixed to the volume of 1642—More,—though when he wrote it he was only in his twenty-sixth year,—claims the purest and wisest for his readers.

He separates himself from the 'prevailing' Poets of the day :—

' Expect from me no Teian strain,
No light, wanton, Lesbian vein :
Though well I wot the vulgar spright
Such Harmony doth more strongly smite.'

His is a *moral* purpose as well as intellectual :—

' Silent Secesse, wast Solitude
Deep searching thoughts often renew'd,
Stiffe conflict 'gainst importunate vice,
That daily doth the Soul entice
From her high throne of circuling light,
To plunge her in infernall Night :
Collection of the mind from stroke
Of this worlds Magick, that doth choke
Her with foul smothering mists and stench,
And in Lethæan waves her drench :
A daily Death ; drad Agony,
Privation, dry Sterility.'

The like-minded and like-experienced alone would he have 'nearly view' his 'open Book : '—

' *Who is well entred in those wayes*
Fitt'st man to read my lofty layes.
But whom lust, wrath, and fear controull,
Scarce know their body from their soul.
If any such chance hear my verse,
Dark numerous Nothings I rehearse
To them : measure out an idle sound,
In which no inward sense is found.'

All such are in grievous error, and he 'sings' not for them :—

' Thus sing I to cragg'd clifts, and hils,
To sighing winds, to murmuring rills,
To wastefull woods, to empty groves :
Such things as my dear mind most loves.
But they heed not my heavenly passion,
Fast fixt on their own operation.
On chalky rocks hard by the Sea,
Safe guided by fair Cynthia,
I strike my silver-sounded lyre,
First struck my self by some strong fire ;
And all the while her wavering ray,
Reflected from fluid glasse doth play
On the white banks. *But all are deaf
Vnto my Muse, that is most lief
To mine own self. So they nor blame
My pleasant notes, nor praise the same.
Nor do thou, Reader, rashly brand
My rythmes 'fore thou them understand.'* (p. 8.)

We have need of the same passionate rebukes to-day ; for to-day while there is not —as a rule—the earlier grossness, there is a deplorable abundance of Verse that has no '*inward* sense,' no message, no apocalypse, mere word-art, and bearing no higher relation to true poetry than the trivialities of Sèvres or other porcelain-painting to nature, or to painting itself. I am thankful to have More's avowal of a 'purpose' and disavowal of purpose-less-ness. His manly words come across our mephitic atmosphere with the freshness of a salt wind blown across the sea. That he should win such Readers as he coveted, and not be forgotten, be was tranquilly assured. He tells his honoured father—'I am not indeed much solicitous how every particle of these poems may please you. In the meantime, I am sure that I please myself in the main; which is, the embalming of his name to immortality, that next under God, is the Author of my Life and Being' (p. 4). Elsewhere he declares that that on which the 'wizards of old time' had 'divers conceits,' and that he himself was to 'inquire' after, he 'would set forth *in an eternal rhyme*' (p. 47, st. 10). And so when he has demolished his antagonists in controversy, he recalls himself :—

> ' But I'll break off ; My Muse her self forgot,
> Her own great strength and her foes feeblenesse.'
> (p. 66, st. 29.)

With a self-respect — again reminding of Wordsworth—that partakes of grandeur, he looks around on the men and ways of the Present into the Future :—

> ' To cleanse the soule from sinn, and still diffide
> Whether our reasons eye be clear enough
> To intromit true light, that fain would glide
> Into purg'd hearts, this way's too harsh and rough :
>   Therefore the clearest truths may well seem dark
>   When sloathfull men have eyes so dimme and stark.
> ' These be our times. But if my minds presage
> Bear any moment, they can ne're last long ;
> A three branch'd Flame will soon sweep clean the stage
> Of this old dirty drosse and all wex young.
>   *My words into this frozen air I throw*
>   *Will then grow vocall at that generall thaw.*'

While he had this calm confidence in and for himself, his was no absurd magnifying of

his poetic gift. He had sung because he must sing. Interrogated how it was his 'busie Muse' was moved 'such fruitlesse pains to prove'—fruitless by the world's verdict—he answers :—

> ' *No pains but pleasure to do th' dictates dear*
> *Of inward living nature.* What doth move
> The Nightingall to sing so sweet and clear?
> The Thrush, or Lark that mounting high above
>   Chants her shrill notes *to heedlesse ears of corn*
>   *Heavily hanging in the dewy Morn.*' (p. 173 *b*, st 5.)

Finelier still—and on the same level, not height—is his opening of 'Psychathanasia':—

> ' Whatever man he be that dares to deem
> True Poets skill to spring of earthly race,
> I must him tell, that he doth misesteem
> Their strange estate, and eke himselfe disgrace
>   By his rude ignorance. For there 's no place
>   For forcéd labour, or slow industry
> Of flagging wits, in that high fiery chace :
>   *So soon as of the Muse they quickned be,*
> *At once they rise, and lively sing like Lark in skie.*'
> (p. 43, st. 1.)

That is his highest claim ; 'rais'd upon' the Muse's 'spreaden wing,' he—

> . . . 'softly playes, and warbles in the wind,
> And carols out the inward life and spring
> Of overflowing joy.' (p. 43, st. 3.)

There is nothing of the spasmodic or ambitious in all this. He knows that he sang 'true' alike to himself and the truth ; and in his lowly sphere, he recognises his Verse as having the stuff of imperishableness in it ; and so as with the Meteor—according to the old belief—'whose materiall is low unwieldy earth, base unctuous slime,' but having 'its inward spright' fired of 'great Phœbus lamp :'—

> . . . 'then even of it self doth climb ;
> That earst was dark becomes all eye, all sight.'

he sees his Poetry as a—

> 'Bright starre, that to the wise, of future things gives
>   light.' (p. 43, st. 2.)

And now I ask for the Poetry of Henry More new and sympathetic Readers and Students. I have no hesitation in affirming substantive additions to philosophic thought and opinion in his Prose. Were it for no more than his strenuous assertion of the ethical, as well as intellectual, side of all truth, and his wise scorn of any attempt to 'intermeddle' with either ethical or divine things without a clear and purified spiritual vision, and his co-equal rejection of any religion that rested on mere dogma and creed and untouched of aspiration as of action, and above all, his self-introspection as an exemplar of a human soul—as lovingly and lingeringly as anything in 'The Prelude' itself—I should so regard his Prose. Because of this, your Historians of Ethical-metaphysical Philosophy must imitate WHE-WELL'S and COLERIDGE'S and MAURICE'S appreciation, not MACKINTOSH'S and LEWES' and BAIN'S, and others' neglect. But as furnishing his complete Poems, I am naturally most of all concerned to win readers for them. Granted that there is much barbarous and uncouth wording, recondite and obscurant speculation, hard and barren controversy, and all too often absence of finished art and consequent discords — granted every abatement, there nevertheless remains in these Poems—in nearly all the minor, and in well-nigh every page of the larger—ample to vindicate their revival, and to reinscribe the venerable name of Henry More among our real Makers and Singers to the full extent of his own modest claim. It will fitly close this Memorial-Introduction to read John Norris's 'Ode to Dr. More'[n]— as follows :—

To Dr. MORE ; *An ODE Written by the Ingenious and* Learned *Mr.* Norris.

I.

G O *Muse*, go hasten to the *Cell* of *Fame*,
  (Thou know'st her reverend aweful Seat ;
  It stands hard by your Blest Retreat)
Go with a brisk Alarm, assault her Ear ;

---

[1] Collection of Miscell. consisting of Poems, &c., p. 73 : quoted in Ward's Life after the Preface.

Bid her her loudest Trump prepare,
To sound a *more* than *Humane* Name,
  A *Name* more *Excellent* and *Great*
  Than She could ever publish yet :
Tell her ; She need not stay till *Fate* shall give
A *License* to his *Works*, and bid them *live ;*
His Worth *now shines* through Envy's base Alloy ;
'Twill *fill* her widest Trump, and *all* her Breath employ.

II.

Learning, which long, like an *Enchanted Land,*
  Did *Human Force* and *Art* defie,
And stood the *Virtuoso's* best Artillery,
  Which nothing *mortal* could subdue,
Has yielded to *this Hero's Fatal* hand ;
By him is *conquer'd, held,* and *peopled* too.
  Like Seas that border on the Shore,
The *Muses Suburbs* some *Possession* knew ;
But like the deep Abyss their *inner* Store
Lay *unpossess'd,* till seiz'd and own'd by *You :*
  Truth's Outer Courts were trod before ;
Sacred was her *Recess ; that* Fate reserv'd for MORE.

III.

Others in *Learning's Chorus* bear their part ;
  And the great *Work distinctly* share :
Thou our great *Catholick Professor* art ;
All Science is annexed to thy *unerring Chair.*
  Some lesser *Synods* of the *Wise*
The *Muses* kept in *Universities ;*
  But never yet, till in *thy Soul,*
Had they a *Council Oecumenical.*
  An *Abstract* they'd a mind to see
Of all their *scatter'd Gifts,* and *summ'd* them up in *Thee.*
  Thou hast the *Arts* whole *Zodiack* run ;
  And fathom'st all that *here* is known.
  Strange restless *Curiosity !*
  Adam himself came short of *Thee.*
He *tasted of the Fruit,* Thou *bear'st away the Tree.*

IV.

  Whilst to be *Great* the *most* aspire,
Or with *low Souls* to raise their *Fortunes higher ;*
Knowledge the *chiefest Treasure* of the *Blest,*
  Knowledge, the *Wise* Man's *best Request,*
Was made *thy Choice :* For *this* thou hast declin'd
A *Life* of *Noise, Impertinence* and *State ;*
  And whate'r'e else the *Muses* hate ;
And mad'st it thy own *Business* to *Enrich* thy *Mind.*
How *Calm* thy *Life,* how *Easie,* how *Secure,*
  Thou *Intellectual Epicure !*
Thou, as another *Solomon,* hast try'd
All Nature through ; and nothing thy Soul *deny'd.*
  Who can two *such* Examples shew ?
He All things try'd *t' enjoy,* and *you* All things *to know.*

V.

By *Babel's* Curse, and our *Contracted Span,*
Heaven thought to check the swift Career of Man :

And so it prov'd till *now;* Our Age
Is much too *short* to run so *long* a Stage :
And to learn Words is such a vast *Delay,*
That we're *benighted* e're we come half way.
   Thou with *unusual Hast* driv'st on ;
And dost even *Time* it self *out-run.*
No Hindrance can retard *thy* Course,
Thou rid'st *the Muses winged Horse ;*
Thy Stage of *Learning* ends e're that of *Life* be done.
There is now no Work left for *thy* Accomplish'd Mind,
But *to survey* thy *Conquests,* and *inform Mankind.'*

I cannot close this Introduction without returning publicly my heartfelt thanks to G. H. WHITE, Esq. of Glenthorne, St. Mary Church, Torquay, for his most pains-taking co-operation with me in preparing the full Glossarial Index ; and which I rejoice to announce he is continuing for Davies of Hereford, and Nicholas Breton. I have also to thank my manifold-gifted friend, the Rev. J. W. Ebsworth, M.A., of Molash Vicarage, for his engraving of the plate of diagrams.

              ALEXANDER B. GROSART.

TREMYNFA,
   PENMAENMAWR,
      NORTH WALES,
       16th July 1878.

APPENDIX.

A.—CHAPPELL, MORE'S TUTOR. P. xv.

Chappell was Milton's first tutor, and according to Aubrey, quarrelled with and 'flogged' him. He would please More as anti-Calvinist, *e.g.,* 'Lately there sprung up a new brood of such as did assist Arminianism, as Dutch Tompson of Clare Hall, and Mr. William Chappell, Fellow of Christ's College ; as the many pupils that were arminianized under his tuition show' (Quoted (from whom ?) in Masson's Life of Milton, vol. i. p. 105). Chappell was Provost of Trinity College, Dublin (Professor Dowden to me).

B.—P. xvii.

From 'Carmen Natalitium ad Cunas Illustrissimae Principis Elisabethae.' 1635.

Εἰς τὴν καλλίστην καὶ θεοειδεστάτην Ἡρωίνην
      Ποσειδ. γεγεννημένην.

Νὸξ μακρὴ καὶ χεῖμα, ὅταν τὰ πρῶτ' ἐπεφάνθη
  Φῶς τεὸν ἢ ζαθέη, δέσποτι, καλλοσύνη.
Γυμνὴ, πότνια γαῖα ἐὸν κλέος ἀνθρώποισιν
  Ἔκρυβεν, ἢ χιόνος λειρ' ἀμειψαμένη.
Εἰαρινὴ δέσποινα, τὸ λείριον οὔ σε καλέσσω,
  Παντοδαπῶν δ' ἀνθῶν καὶ χαρίτων πεδίον.
Φεῦ ! ποίην θήσουσι περιπλόμενοί σ' ἐνιαυτοί,
  Ἢ καιροὺς κρῖναι, καὶ βρέφος ὂν, δύνασαι ;

Εἰς τὴν τῆς ΜΑΡΙΑΣ τῆς μακαριωτάτης βασιλείας
      πολυτεκνίαν.

Ἄλλῳ ἄλλος ἀριθμὸς ἀρεσκέτω· αἴθε δὲ μύστας
  Τὰν ὀρφνὰν σκεδάσαι δᾷδα ἐπισχόμενος.
Αὐτάρκης μονάς ἐντι, καὶ ἄλλων ἀρχὰ ἀριθμῶν.
  Ὦ τᾶς ἀρχαίων θεσπεσίω σοφίας !
Ἐντι μονὰς κρέσσων δυάδος, τριάδος δυάς, ἐντι
  Πεμπτάδος ἁ τετράς, τᾶς τετράδος δὲ τριάς.

Ταῦθ' ὁ γέρων Σάμιος. τί δέ σοι δοκεῖ Ὦ βασίλισσα.
  'Ὦ θαλέων ἱερὰ ῥίζα διοτρεφέων ;
Εἶπ' ἴθι, καὶ μονάδ' ἀμφαγαπᾷς· ἄγε, μήτι ταραχθῇς,
  Τίκτε δὲ σῷ γαμέτῃ μυριάδας μονάδων.
                 'Ἑρρῖκος ὁ Μοροῦ, ἐκ Χριστοῦ.

In tepidam humidamque tempestatem circa natalitia Serenissimae Principis natae 5 Cal. Jan.

Quæ vis repressit flamina Thracia ?
Aut quæ, Decembris tristia frigora
  Compescuit ? non mitis imber
    Jane tuas decuit Calendas.

Dic, Qui tepores Caucasias nives,
Quinam fugarunt Sarmaticum gelu ?
  Crystallinas quinam calores
    Tam subitò soluère gemmas ?

Gemmam stupendis artibus omnium
Mater polivit molliter, & suam
  Pulcherrimam mirata prolem
    Pectore sollicitam favillam

Concepit ; arsit ; jussaque nubibus
Vultu severo dixit. At illius
  Parebat universa moles
    Legibus, atque operi favebat.

Sudabat aër, quod sacra pignora
Algore posset lædere : quòd nive
  Possent suâ nocere, densæ
    In lacrymas abière nubes.

Cæleste germen, machina cui favet
Immensa, quantam Cynthia circuit,
  Lætare, gaude, vive ; Χαῖρε
    Quæ populo sine voce dixti.

              Hen. More, è Christi.

I.—PHILOSOPHICAL POEMS.

NOTE.

Of the original and later editions of the 'Philosophical Poems' of More, see the Memorial-Introduction. Our text is the second edition of 1647, whose general and separate title-pages are given in their respective places. The only change made is one of a slightly differing arrangement of the Author's Notes and Commentaries. These we remove collectively to the close of the Poems to which they refer, rather than to the end of the volume. The Greek and Latin quotations are extended from their somewhat curious contractions, and very many errors have been corrected. Our own Notes and Illustrations and Glossarial Index will be added at the conclusion of the whole of the Poems. Throughout, the Author's own orthography and capitals and italics and punctuation have been reproduced in integrity, save in obvious errors, over and above the considerable errata-list drawn up by himself.—G.

PHILOSOPHICALL
POEMS,

BY

HENRY MORE:

Mafter of Arts, and Fellow of

CHRISTS COLLEDGE

IN

CAMBRIDGE.

Hinc · Lvcem · et · Pocvla · Sacra.

Avia Pieridum peragro loca, nullius ante
Trita solo, juvat integros accedere fontes. Lucr.

CAMBRIDGE,
Printed by ROGER DANIEL
Printer to the UNIVERSITY.
1647.

To his dear Father

ALEXANDER MORE

ESQUIRE.

SIR,

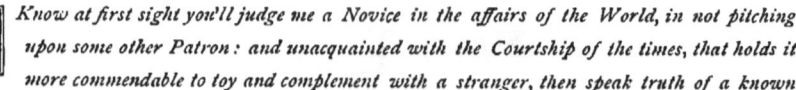 Know at first sight you'll judge me a Novice in the affairs of the World, in not pitching upon some other Patron: and unacquainted with the Courtship of the times, that holds it more commendable to toy and complement with a stranger, then speak truth of a known friend. But I am meditating no Stage-play of ordinary Apish Civility, but sober Truth: Nor intend this an act of worldly discretion and advantage, but of Justice and Gratitude. For I cannot hope that ever any man shall deserve so well of me as your self has done. Besides what hath hitherto commended you to all that know you; your Faithfulnesse, Uprightnesse, Sedulity for the publick Welfare of the place wherein you live, your generous Opennesse and Veracity. Nor can ever that thick cloud you are now enveloped with, of melancholized old Age, and undeserved Adversity, either dark the remembrance of your pristine Lustre, or hide from me the sight of your present Worth. Sir, I could wish my self a stranger to your bloud, that I might with the better decorum set out the noble-nesse of your spirit. But to speak modestly; You deserve the Patronage of better Poems then these, though you may lay a more proper claim to these then to any. You having from my childhood tuned mine ears to Spencers rhymes, entertaining us on winter nights, with that incomparable Peice of his, The Fairy Queen, a Poem as richly fraught with divine Morality as Phansy. Your early Encomiums also of Learning and Philosophy did so fire my credulous Youth with the desire of the knowledge of things, that your After-advertisements, how contemptible Learning would prove with-out Riches, and what a piece of Unmannerlinesse and Incivility it would be held to seem wiser then them that are more wealthy and powerfull, could never yet restrain my mind from her first pursuit, nor quicken my attention to the affairs of the World. But this bookish disease let it make me as much poor as it will, it shall never make me the lesse just. Nor will you, I hope, esteem me the lesse dutyfull, that without your cognoscence I become thus thankfull. For I never held my self bound to ask leave of any man to exercise an act of Virtue. And yet am I conscious to my self, there may have some juvenile Extravagancies passed my pen, which your judgement and gray hairs will more slowly allow of, and my self may haply dislike by that time I arrive to half your years. But let it be my excuse, that that which was to be made common for all, could not be so exactly fitted for any one Age or Person. I am not indeed much solicitous, how every particle of these Poems may please you. In the mean time I am sure that I please my self in the main; which is, The embalming of his name to Immortality, that next under God, is the Authour of my Life and Being.

Your affectionate Sonne,

HENRY MORE.

A

𝔓latonick 𝔖ong

of the

S O U L ;

Treating

Of
- *The Life of the Soul,*
- *Her Immortalitie,*
- *The Sleep of the Soul,*
- *The Vnitie of Souls, and*
- *Memorie after Death.*

Nullam majorem afferre solet ignaris inscitia voluptatem
quam expeditum fastidiosumq; contemptum. Scal.

CAMBRIDGE,
Printed by ROGER DANIEL Printer
to the Universitie. 1647.

To the Reader.

Upon this second Edition.

Reader,

F I seem too bold in presenting my self again so suddenly to publick view, let it excuse me, at least in part, that there is not so much boldnesse in this, as in my first adventure. For whereas I had then no encouragement but mine own well meaning, and carelessenesse of the opinions of men ; I have now (beside that resolv'd neglect of mens hasty censures) the experience (though unexpected) of the favourable acceptance of the bravest and best improved spirits.

For whose sakes, and as many else as are at leasure a while to lay aside the pleasure or trouble of the world, and entertain their minds with thoughts of a greater compasse then the fetching in of a little wealth or honour ; I have taken the pains to peruse these Poems of the soul, and to lick them into some more tolerable form and smoothnesse. For I must confesse such was the present haste and heat that I was then hurried in (dispatching them in fewer moneths then some cold-pated-Gentlemen have conceited me to have spent years about them, and letting them slip from me so suddenly while I was so immerse in the inward sense and representation of things, that it was even necessary to forget the œconomic of words, and leave them behind me aloft, to float and run together at randome (like chaff and straws on the surface of the water) that it could not but send them out in so uneven and rude a dresse. Nor yet can I, (I professe) ever hope to find leasure or patience so exquisitely to polish them, as fully to answer mine own curiosity, if I would be also humorous, or the delicacy of some Lady-wits that can like nothing that is not as compos'd as their own hair, or as smooth as their Mistresses Looking-glasse. But may these emendations prove but acceptable to the more generous and manly Genius ; I shall please my self enough, if I prove but tolerable to those female phansies.

But as I would not industriously neglect these, so I hope I have more solidly gratifi'd the other, by the enlargement of this Poem. For besides the Canto of the INFINITY of WORLDS, I have also added another of the PRÆEXISTENCY of the SOUL, where I have set out the nature of SPIRITS and given an account of APPARITIONS and WITCH-CRAFT, very answerable I conceive to experience and story, invited to that task by the frequent discoveries of this very Age. Which if they were publickly recorded, and that course continued in euery Parish, it would prove one of the best Antidotes against that earthly and cold disease of Sadducisme and Atheisme, which may easily grow upon us, if not prevented, to the hazard of all Religion, and the best kinds of Philosophy.

I have also enlarged the second Canto of PSYCHOZOIA, and have added (that I might avoid all suspicion of partiality) to Psittaco and Pithecus diverse other persons, Pico, Corvino, Graculo, and Glaucis, but am so sensible of that sober precept in Josephus, which he affirms to be out of Moses, Μηδεὶς βλασφημείτω οὓς ἄλλαι πόλεις νομίζουσι Θεούς, that I would be very loth to be so farre mistaken as to be thought a Censurer or Contemner of other mens Religions or Opinions, if they serve God in them in the simplicity and sincerity of their hearts, and have some more precious substratum within, then inveterate custome or naturall complexion. All that I mean is this : That neither eager promoting of Opinion or Ceremony, nor the earnest opposing of the same, no not the acutenesse of Reason, nor yet a strong, if naked conceit, that we have the Spirit of God, can excuse a man from being in any better condition then in the Land of Brutes or in the mere animal nature. Which conclusion I thought worth my labour to set off with such Artifice and Circumstance as I have ; the gullery and deceit therein, if not avoided, being of so great and evil consequence. For if we can but once entitle our opinions and mistakes to Religion, and Gods Spirit, it is like running quicksilver in the back of a sword, and will enable us to strike to utter destruction and ruine. But it would prevent a great deal of bloud and bitternesse in the Christian world, if we reserved the flower and strength of our zeal for the undoubted Truth of God and His immutable Righteousnesse, and were more mildly and moderately affected concerning the Traditions and determinations of the Elders.

Furthermore, I have added Notes for the better understanding, not onely of my *Psychozoia*, but of the Principles of *Plato's* Philosophy. In both which I would be so understood, as a Representer of the Wisdome of the Ancients rather then a warranter of the same. Contemplations concerning the dry essence of the Deity are very consuming and unsatisfactory. 'Tis better to drink of the bloud of the grape, then bite the root of the vine, to smell of the rose then chew the stalk. And blessed be God, the meanest of men are capable of the former, very few successefull in the latter. And the lesse, because the reports of them that have busied themselves that way, have not onely seem'd strange to the vulgar, but even repugnant with one another. But I should in charity referre this to the nature of the pigeons neck, rather then to mistake or contradiction. One and the same Object in Nature affords many and different φαινόμενα. And God is as infinitely various as simple. Like a circle, indifferent, whether you suppose it of one Uniform line, or an infinite number of Angles. Wherefore it is more safe to admit all possible perfections in God, then rashly to deny what appears not to us in our particular posture.

I have also adjoined some few scattering notes to the second part of the *Song of the Soul.* Where I have also, beside some subtil considerations concerning *ATOMS* and *QVANTITY*, set out very plainly, the *Hypothesis* of *Pythagoras*, or *Copernicus* concerning the *MOTION* of the *EARTH*, as also opened the mystery of the *FLVX* and *REFLVX* of the *SEA.* Which two contemplations are not inferiour to any, for either pleasantnesse in themselves, or conduciblenesse for the finding out of the right frame of Nature.

Finally, I have cast into this second Edition severall smaller Poems, of which together with all the rest that I have published I would give this generall Advertisement, *Est pictura Poesis.* Every poem is an Idyllium. And a Poet no more sings himself, then a Painter draws his own picture. Nor can I by these assume to my self the honour of being a Platonist, no more then Virgil incurre the suspicion of being an Epicurean by his Silenus, whom notwithstanding Alexander Severus thought good to style *poetarum* Plato.

As for a more determinate decision of those many speculations which I have set on foot in these writings, though I made some kind of promise that way in my first, I must crave leave a while to deferre it, till I find the thing it self of more consequence, and my self at better leisure. However without that, there is so great accession made to this second Edition that I easily hope, that of as many as I was received favourably before, that I shall now be received with much more favour.

As for others, whom sensuall immersion or the deadnesse of Melancholy have more deeply seiz'd upon, I must acknowledge that in my own judgement I can seem no better to them then a piece of highly inacted

folly, they obstinately preferring that sad ground of incredulity before any thing lesse then a Demonstration. For whose satisfaction *Mounsieur des Chartes* hath attempted bravely, but yet methinks on this side of Mathematicall evidence. He and that learned Knight our own Countryman had done a great deal more if they had promised lesse. So high confidence might become the heat and scheme of Poetry much better then sober Philosophy. Yet he has not done nothing, though not so much as he raiseth mens expectations to. And if he had performed lesse, it had been enough to souls that have well recovered that divine sagacity and quick sent of their own Interest. If this sweet ethereall gale of divine breathing do not quicken and enliven the sent and relish of such arguments as Reason, Nature, and story will afford, they will all prove weak and uselesse : Especially to exercised Wits that have so written and wrested their phansies that they can imagine or disimagine any thing, so weakened it that it is born down as wel with the smallest as greatest weight : so crusted and made hard their inward κριτήριον by overmuch and triviall wearing it, that that delicate discrimination and divine touch of the soul is even lost, in so much that it would be safer to ask the judgement of young lads or Countrey idiots concerning the force of Arguments for Gods existence or the Souls immortality, then those lubricous Wits and overworn Philosophers. And surely if we will but admit of Providence and her eye to be placed upon man, and this world to be his instruction, together with the undistorted suggestions of his own heart, these easie hints and pointings will be found no fallacious directions. And true opinion is as faithfull a Guide, as Necessity and Demonstration.

That obvious conceit of the nature of light and colours, though perhaps false in it self, yet is an easie and safe conductour to that grand Truth of the divine Hypostases held up by the whole Christian world for these many hundred years and by more then have acknowledged themselves Christians. How naturally are we invited from the appearing of men deceased, to think the soul survives the body, though we may perversely suppose that those Apparitions are but our own imaginations, or that some sportfull or over officious spirit puts himself in the form and fashion of the deceased party? But what was the first and most easie suggestion, is such a truth as all Ages and Nations without intermission have embraced it. Nor yet will this be for a Demonstration and winne undoubted assent with austere and melancholick tempers. Nor is reason unback'd with better principles mathematically satisfiable in matters of this kind. Nor am I offended that it is not. For would it not be an overproportionated engine, to the again endangering of Cleombrotus neck, or too forcibly driving men to obedience if they had their immortality as demonstrable as ; That the three angles in a triangle are equall to two right angles. Besides it would prevent that fitting triall of the soul, how she would be affected if there were nothing to come ; whence she would not be able so sensibly to discover to her self her own Hypocrisie or sinceritie. Lastly, that loving adherence and affectionate cleaving to God by Faith and divine sense, would be forestall'd by such undeniable evidence of Reason and Nature. Which though it would very much gratifie the naturall man, yet it would not prove so profitable to us, as in things appertaining to God. For seeing our most palpable evidence of the souls immortality is from an inward sense, and this inward sense is kept alive the best by devotion and purity, by freedome from worldly care and sorrow, and the grosser pleasures of the body (otherwise her ethereall vehicle will drink in so much of earthy and mortall dregs, that the sense of the soul will be changed), and being outvoted as it were by the overswaying number of terrene particles, which that ethereal nature hath so plentifully imbib'd and incorporated with,

she will become in a manner corporeall, συμπαθοῦσα καὶ ὁμοδοξοῦσα τῷ σώματι, as Jamblichus speaks, and in the extremity of this weaknesse and dotage will be easily drawn off to pronounce her self such as the body is, (dissolvable and mortall) ; therefore it is better for us that we become doubtfull of our immortall condition when we stray from that virgin-purity and unspottednesse, that we may withdraw our feet from these paths of death, then that Demonstration and Infallibility should permit us to proceed so farre, that our immortality would prove an heavy disadvantage. But this is meant onely to them that are lovers of God and their own souls. For they that are at enmity with Him, desire no such instructions, but rather embrace all means of laying asleep that disquieting truth ; that they bear about with them so precious a charge as an immortall Spirit.

To the Reader.

Eader, sith it is the fashion
    To bestow some salutation,
    I greet thee ; give free leave to look
    And nearly view my open Book.
But see then that thine eyes be clear
If ought thou wouldst discover there.
Expect from me no Teian strain,
No light wanton Lesbian vein :
Though well I wot the vulgar spright
Such Harmony doth more strongly smite.
Silent Secesse, wast Solitude
Deep searching thoughts often renew'd,
Stiffe conflict 'gainst importunate vice,
That daily doth the Soul entice
From her high throne of circuling light
To plunge her in infernall Night :
Collection of the mind from stroke
Of this worlds Magick, that doth choke
Her with foul smothering mists and stench,
And in Lethæan waves her drench :
A daily Death, drad Agony,
Privation, dry Sterility ;
Who is well entred in those wayes
Fitt'st man to read my lofty layes.
But whom lust, wrath and fear controule,

Scarce know their body from their soul.
If any such chance hear my verse,
Dark numerous Nothings I rehearse
To them : measure out an idle sound,
In which no inward sense is found.
Thus sing I to cragg'd clifts, and hills,
To sighing winds, to murmuring rills,
To wastefull woods, to empty groves :
Such things as my dear mind most loves.
But they heed not my heavenly passion,
Fast fixt on their own operation.
On chalky rocks hard by the Sea,
Safe guided by fair Cynthia,
I strike my silver-sounded lyre,
First struck my self by some strong fire ;
And all the while her wavering ray,
Reflected from fluid glasse doth play
On the white banks. But all are deaf
Unto my Muse, that is most lief
To mine own self. So they nor blame
My pleasant notes, nor praise the same.
Nor do thou, Reader, rashly brand
My rythmes 'fore thou them understand.

                        H. M.

PSYCHOZOIA,

OR

The firſt part of the Song

of the

SOUL,

Containing

A Chriſtiano-Platonicall diſplay of

LIFE.

By *H. M.* Maſter of Arts, and Fellow of Chriſts
Colledge in *Cambridge.*

*Tot vitæ gradus cognoscimus, quot in nobis met-
ipsis expedimus.* Mars. Ficin.

CAMBRIDGE,
Printed by *Roger Daniel,* Printer to the
Universitie. 1647.

TO THE READER,

Upon the firſt Canto of

PSYCHOZOIA.

His first Canto, as you may judge by the names therein, was intended for a mere Platonicall description of Universall life, or life that is omnipresent, though not alike omnipresent. As in Noahs Deluge, the water that overflowed the earth was present in every part thereof, but every part of the water was not in every part of the earth, or all in every part ; so the low Spirit of the Universe, though it go quite through the world, yet it is not totally in every part of the world ; Else we should heare our Antipodes, if they did but whisper : Because our lower man is a part of the inferiour Spirit of the Universe.

Ahad, Æon, and *Psyche* are all omnipresent in the World, after the most perfect way that humane reason can conceive of. For they are in the world all totally and at once every where.

This is the famous Platonicall Triad : which though they slight the Christian Trinity do take for a figment ; yet I think it is no contemptible argument, that the Platonists, the best and divinest of Philosophers, and the Christians, the best of all that do professe religion, do both concur that there is a Trinity. In what they differ, I leave to be found out according to the safe direction of that infallible Rule of Faith, the holy Word.

In the mean time I shall not be blamed by any thing but ignorance and malignity, for being invited to sing of the second Unity of the Platonicall Triad, in a Christian and Poeticall scheme, that which the holy Scripture witnesseth of the second Person of the Christian Trinity. As that his patrimony is the possession of the whole earth. For if it be not all one with Christ, according to his Divinity ; yet the Platonists placing him in the same order, and giving him the like attributes, with the Person of the Sonne in Christianity, it is nothing harsh for me to take occasion from hence to sing a while the true Christian *Autocalon,* whose beauty shall adorn the whole Earth in good time ; if we believe the Prophets.

For that hath not as yet happened. For Christ is not where ever his Name is : but as he is the Truth, so will he be truly displayed upon the face of the whole Earth. For God doth not fill the World with his Glory by words and sounds, but by Spirit, and Life, and Reality.

Now this Eternall life I sing of, even in the middest of Platonisme : for I cannot conceal from whence I am, *viz.* of Christ : but yet acknowledging, that God hath not left the Heathen, *Plato* especially, without witnesse of himself. Whose doctrine might strike our adulterate Christian Professors with shame and astonishment ; their lives falling so exceeding short of the better Heathen. How far short are they then of that admirable and transcendent high mystery of true Christianisme? To which *Plato* is a very good subservient Minister ; whose Philosophy I singing here in a full heat ; why may it not be free for me to break out into an higher strain, and under it to touch upon some points of Christianity ; as well as all-approved *Spencer,* sings of Christ under the name of *Pan ?* Saint *Paul* also transfers those things that be spoken of *Jupiter,* to God himself, Arat. φαινόμενα.

Πάντη δὲ Διὸς κεχρήμεθα πάντες·
Τοῦ γὰρ καὶ γένος ἐσμέν.

Those latter words he gives to the Christian God, whom he himself preached. I will omit the usuall course of the Spirit of God in Holy Writ, to take occasion from things that have some resemblance with Divine things under them to speak of the true things themselves.

And that I may not seem rather forcibly to break out here out of Platonisme into Christianisme, then to be fairly and easily led into this digression by the fit similitude of things, or at least very near correspondency of Names, which should imply agreement of nature ; I have thought good to exhibite to the Readers eye the grounds of this my deviation founded in this Parallelisme of Titles, belonging to the second Unity of each Triad.

Platonic.		Christian.
The Sonne of the Good.	1	The Sonne of God.
Τὸ αὐτοκαλὸν τὸ φῶς.	2	Ἀπαύγασμα τῆς δόξης τοῦ
Τὸ γὰρ εἶδος φῶς. *Plotin.*		πατρός.
Λόγος καὶ εἶδος	3	Λόγος. *John* 1.
Ἰδέα	4	Ἡ ἀλήθεια
Ὁ νοῦς ἡ σοφία	5	Ἡ σοφία. *Proverbs.* 8.
Æon.	6	Eternall Life.
Τὸ ὂν, ἡ ἀληθινὴ σοφία οὐσία	7	Ὁ ὢν καὶ ὁ ἦν, καὶ ὁ
καὶ ἡ ἀληθινὴ οὐσία σοφία.		ἐρχόμενος.
Plot. p. 547.		or יהוה

For indeed the Greek ὁ ἦν, καὶ ὁ ὢν καὶ ὁ ἐρχόμενος
is but a Periphrasis of יהוה which contains in ה ו י
the future present, and time past, as Criticks observe.

I might adde further correspondencies betwixt the
Platonick Triad, and diverse passages of Scripture
according to the interpretations of no contemptible
Authours. As Gods making the World by his Word,
which is very reasonable, He being the wisedome of God
or the Intellectuall World ; the Idea of the visible and
naturall Creature. And that he is the Redeemer of the
laps'd World, *viz.* Mankind, while he reduceth the
right shape and image again into man, wisedome and
righteousnesse.

Take in the whole Trinity, you shall find a strange
concordance and harmony betwixt the nature of each
Hypostasis in either of their order. *Atove* or *Ahad*, is
simply the first Principle of all beings, the Father of
all existences, and the Universall Creation is but his
Family ; and therefore hath he a full right of imposing
Lawes on the whole Creature.

θεμιστεύει δὲ ἕκαστος

Παίδων ἠδ' ἀλόχων. As *Aristotle* observes out of
the Poet. The naturall Creature (as *David* also bears
them witnesse) keepeth this Law. But Man breaketh
it : however the Law is still propounded to him, which
when it doth take hold upon him, strikes him with
dread and horrour. Hence will he extrinsecally shape
and proportion his actions according to that outward
Rule through fear and force as it were : As if a man
should impresse any character, or stamp upon wax,
paste, or any such like matter. And this I conceive is
to be under the Law that makes nothing perfect, and
may be called φώτισμα τοῦ νόμου, which is signified also
by *Diana* in the third Canto of Psychozoia. This
God vouchsafes sometime to second with the gift of
his Sonne, who is ὁ ὀρθὸς θεοῦ λόγος πρωτόγονος
υἱός as *Philo* the Platonist calls him. He once come
sits not so much on the surface of the soul, as dives
and divides to the depth of the Spirit, and rooting himself there worketh out from the very bottome all
corruption and filth, cleanseth us throughly from our
sins, and healeth us of our infirmities, shapes us from
an inward vitall Principle, (even as the *Ratio seminalis*
figures out a tree) into a new life and shape, even into
the Image of God ; that is, inward Living Righteousnesse and Truth, instructing us continually, and guiding

us with his eye : For he is properly Wisedome and
Intellect. And this may be termed φώτισμα τοῦ λόγου,
even of the Sonne of Righteousnesse. See *Philo
Judæus, pag.* 390. 391. 403, 407. as also in his περὶ τοῦ
Κάϊν, *pag.* 76.

Of this λόγος *Trismegist* calling him νοῦς, writeth
thus οὗτος δὲ ὁ νοῦς ἐν μὲν ἀνθρώποις θεός ἐστι διὸ καί
τινες τῶν ἀνθρώπων θεοί εἰσι. The same which *John*
intimates : As many as receive him become the sons of
God. And a little after, he tells us that this Universall
Intellect as it doth συνεργεῖν cooperate with all things ;
so it doth also, ἀντιπράσσειν, resist and oppose the
souls of men hurried on to pleasure and passion by this
disadvantagious union with the body.

Ὅσαις ἂν οὖν ψυχαῖς ὁ νοῦς ἐπιστατήσῃ, ταύταις φαίνει
ἑαυτοῦ τὸ φέγγος, ἀντιπράσσων αὐτῶν τοῖς προλήμμασιν,
ὥσπερ ἰατρὸς ἀγαθὸς λυπεῖ τὸ σῶμα προειλημμένον
ὑπὸ νόσου, καίων ἢ τέμνων· τὸν αὐτὸν τρόπον καὶ ὁ
νοῦς ψυχὴν λυπεῖ ἐξυφαιρῶν αὐτῆς τὴν ἡδονὴν ἀφ' ἧς
πᾶσα νόσος ψυχῆς γίνεται· νόσος δὲ μεγάλη ψυχῆς
ἀθεότης.—*Trismeg.* περὶ νοῦ κοινοῦ πρὸς Τάτ.

But now being thus healed, purged, and illuminated
by this Baptisme of the living Word or Intellect, which
is Christ, we are no longer under the Law, nor the
terrour thereof, but serve willingly, as from a vitall
Principle in us, under Christ. Wherefore such ones as
are thus eminently good and virtuous in themselves,
even according to the judgement of *Aristotle, Politic.
lib.* 3. are not under the Law. Κατὰ τῶν τοιούτων
οὐκ ἔστι νόμος, αὐτοὶ γάρ εἰσι νόμος. *Against such
there is no Law, for they themselves are a Law.* The
very same with the words of the Apostle. *Gal. cap.* 5.
vers. 24. *Rom.* 2. *vers.* 14. 15. And a little before,
Ὥσπερ γὰρ θεὸν ἐν ἀνθρώποις εἰκὸς εἶναι τὸν
τοιοῦτον and therefore not to be under the Law, no
more then a Deity can be under their Law, Παραπλήσιον
γάρ, κἂν εἰ τοῦ Διὸς ἄρχειν ἀξιοῖεν, μερίζοντες ἀρχάς.
For 'tis as if they should take upon them to rule Jupiter
himself, and share his kingdome. See *Aristot. Politic.
lib.* 3.

The last accomplishment of all, and the highest perfection as the Apostle witnesseth, is Love, and this
is ever referr'd to the Holy Ghost, whom *Peter* Lombard
contends to be Love, *lib.* 1. *distinct,* 17. And this
agrees *ad amussim* with *Uranore* or *Psyche,* whom
Plotinus calls οὐρανίαν ἀφροδίτην the celestiall *Venus,*
out of which is born the heavenly *Cupid,* the divine
Love. The same is also *Juno* the sister and wife of
Jove ; that is, of the Divine Intellect, as the same
Philosopher observes. And the Greek name of *Juno*
doth fitly agree to this purpose, *viz.* Ἥρα παρὰ τοῦ
ἐρᾶν, her name implying Love. And a further signe
that *Juno* and *Venus* are all one, is, that Astronomers
have noted one and the same Starre by both their
names. Μεθ' ὃν ὁ τοῦ Φωσφόρου, ὃν Ἀφροδίτης οἱ δὲ
Ἥρας προσαγορεύουσιν. *Aristot. de Mundo.* See
Plotin. Ennead. 3 *lib.* 6.

So then the proper effect of this third Hypostasis in either Trinity is Love, which completeth the circle, and reduceth us again to the first Principle of all, the simple and absolute good which we enjoy by this single Act or Energie of the Soul, *viz.* divine Love : and this is φώτισμα τοῦ πνεύματος, to be baptized with the Holy Ghost.

This trinall effect or spirituall influence on the Soul is experientially true : But this threefold Hypostasis, *viz.* *Ahad*, *Æon*, and *Psyche*, cannot be known by experience, but is rather concluded by collection of reason. Nor indeed is reason it self able sufficiently to confirm or confute it, sith it can conceive that one single Essence can perform many and various functions as doth the Soul, that being one, enfolds her self into varieties of operations.

Yet have the Platonists established their Triad upon no contemptible grounds which I will not be so tedious as here to relate : but give the Reader leave to peruse *Plotinus* at his leisure. And I must confesse that that mystery seems to me a thing of it self, standing on its own Basis, and to happen rather to agree with some Principles of Christianisme, then to be drawn from the holy Scripture.

But the best is, that the happinesse of man is not the Essence, but the Influence of the Divinity; and to be baptized in the name of the Father, Son, and Holy Ghost, of more consequence then to read and understand all the curious and acute school-tracts of the Trinity. For this may be permitted to the Divell : that is the priviledge onely of the good and pious man. Nor is it any wonder at all.

For be it so that the contemplation of these things is very sublime and subtile, yet well I wot they are nothing satisfactory to the soul. For the exile Theories of the Infinity of God and Trinity, are but as it were the dry measuring and numbering of the Deity, and profit as much to the soul devoid of charity, as the Diametre of the Sunnes body, or the remembrance of that trinall property in *Lux Lumen* and Calefaction can warm a man in a cold frosty night.

But if any man would be sufficiently initiated into these mysteries, he must repair to the ever living Word of God, that subtile and searching fire, that will sift all the vanities of dreaming Philosophers, and burn up the vain imaginations of false Christians, like stubble.

All this out of a tendernesse of mind, being exceeding loth to give any man offence by my writings, For though knowledge and theory be better then any thing but honesty and true piety, yet it is not so good as that I should willingly offend my neighbour hy it.

Thus much by way of preparation to the first Canto of this Poem. I will now leave thee to thine own discretion, and judgement.

Vpon the second Canto.

THis second Canto, before we descend to particular lives, exhibits to our apprehension, by as fit a similitude as I could light upon, the Universe, as one simple uniform being from Ahad to Hyle, no particular strained being, as yet being made ; no earth or any other Orb as yet kned together. All homogeneall, simple, single, pure, pervious, unknotted, uncoacted, nothing existing but those eight universall orders.

There God hath full command, builds and destroyes what he lists.

That all our souls are free effluxes from his essence. What follows is so plain that the Reader wants no direction

Vpon the third Canto.

THere is no knot at all in this last Canto, if men do not seek one. I plainly and positively declare no opinion, but shew the abuse of those opinions there touched, crouding a number of enormities together, that easily shroud themselves there, where all sinfulnesse surely may easily get harbour, if we be not yet well aware of the Devil, that makes true opinions oftentimes serve for mischief.

Nothing else can be now expected for the easie and profitable understanding of this Poem, but the interpretation of the names that frequently occurre in it. Which I will interpret at the end of these Books ; (as also the hard terms of the other Poems) for their sakes whose real worth and understanding is many times equall with the best, onely they have not fed of husks and shels, as others have been forced to do, the superficiary knowledge of tongues. But it would be well, that neither the Linguist would contemne the illiterate for his ignorance, nor the ignorant condemn the learned for his knowledge, For it is not unlearnednesse that God is so pleased withall, or sillinesse and emptinesse of mind, but singlenesse and simplicity of heart.

H. M.

The Argument of

PSYCHOZOIA,

Or

The life of the Soul.

CANT. I.

This Song great Psyches parentage
With her fourefold array,
And that mysterious marriage,
To th' Reader doth display.

1

Or Ladies loves, nor Knights brave martiall
deeds,
　　Ywrapt in rolls of hid Antiquitie ;
　　But th' inward Fountain, and the unseen
　　　　Seeds,
From whence are these and what so under eye
Doth fall, or is record in memorie,
Psyche, I'll sing. *Psyche !* from thee they sprong.
O life of Time, and all Alterity !
The life of lives instill his nectar strong,
My soul t' inebriate, while I sing *Psyches* song.

2

But thou, whoe're thou art that hear'st this strain,
Or read'st these rythmes which from Platonick rage
Do powerfully flow forth, dare not to blame
My forward pen of foul miscarriage ;
If all that's spoke, with thoughts more sadly sage
Doth not agree. My task is not to try
What's simply true. I onely do engage
My self to make a fit discovery,
Give some fair glimpse of Plato's hid Philosophy.

3

What man alive that hath but common wit
(When skilfull limmer 'suing his intent
Shall fairly well pourtray and wisely hit
The true proportion of each lineament,
And in right colours to the life depaint
The fulvid Eagle with her sun-bright eye)
Would wexen wroth with inward choler brent
Cause 'tis no Buzard or discolour'd Pie ?
Why men ? I meant it not : Cease thy fond obloquie.

4

So if what's consonant to Plato's school
(Which well agrees with learned Pythagore,
Egyptian Trismegist, and th' antique roll
Of Chaldee wisdome, all which time hath tore
But Plato and deep Plotin do restore)
Which is my scope, I sing out lustily :
If any twitten me for such strange lore,
And me all blamelesse brand with infamy,
God purge that man from fault of foul malignity.

5

Th' Ancient of dayes, Sire of Eternitie,
Sprung of himself, or rather no wise sprong :
Father of lights and everlasting glee,
Who puts to silence every daring tongue
And flies man's sight, shrowding himself among
His glorious rayes, good *Atove*, from whom came
All good that *Pedia* spies in thickest throng
Of most desireables, all's from that same,
That same, that *Atove* hight, and sweet *Abinoam*.

6

Now can I not with flowring phantasie
To drowsie sensuall souls such words impart,
Which in their sprights, may cause sweet agony,
And thrill their bodies through with pleasing dart,
And spread in flowing fire their close-twist heart,
All chearing fire, that nothing wont to burn
That *Atove* lists to save ; and his good Art
Is all to save that will to him return,
That all to him return, nought of him is forlorn :

7

For what can be forlorn, when his good hands
Hold all in life, that of life do partake ?
O surest confidence of Loves strong bands !
Love loveth all that's made ; Love all did make :
And when false life doth fail, it's for the sake

Of better being. Riving tortures spight,
 That life disjoynts, and makes the heart to quake,
 To good the soul doth nearer reunite :
So ancient *Atove* hence all-joyning *Ahad* hight.

8

This *Ahad* of himself the *Æon* fair
 Begot, the brightnesse of his father's grace :
No living wight in heav'n to him compare,
 Ne work his goodly honour such disgrace,
 Nor lose thy time in telling of his race.
 His beauty and his race no man can tell :
 His glory darkeneth the Sunnes bright face ;
 Or if ought else the Sunnes bright face excel',
His splendour would it dim, and all that glory quell.

9

This is that ancient *Eidos* omniform,
 Fount of all beauty, root of flowring glee,
 Hyle old hag, foul, filthy, and deform,
 Cannot come near.   Joyfull *Eternity*
 Admits no change or mutability,
 No shade of change, no imminution,
 No nor increase ; for what increase can be
 To that that's all ? and where *Hyl'* hath no throne
Can ought decay? such is the state of great *Æon.*

10

Farre otherwise it fares in this same Lond
 Of Truth and Beauty, then in mortall brood
 Of earthly lovers, who impassion'd
 With outward forms (not rightly understood
 From whence proceeds this amorous sweet flood,
 And choice delight which in their spright they feel :
 Can outward Idole yield so heavenly mood ?)
 This inward beauty unto that they deal
That little beauteous is : Thus into th' dirt they reel.

11

Like to Narcissus, on the grassie shore,
 Viewing his outward face in watery glasse ;
 Still as he looks, his looks adde evermore
 New fire, new light, new love, new comely grace
 To's inward form ; and it displayes apace
 It's hidden rayes, and so new lustre sends
 To that vain shadow : but the boy, alas !
 Unhappy boy ! the inward nought attends,
But in foul filthy mire, love, life, and form he blends.

12

And this I wot is the Souls excellence,
 That from the hint of every painted glance
 Of shadows sensible, she doth from hence
 Her radiant life, and lovely hue advance
 To higher pitch, and by good governance
 May wained be from love of fading light
 In outward forms, having true Cognizance,
 That those vain shows are not the beauty bright
That takes men so, but what they cause in humane spright.

13

Farre otherwise it fares in *Æons* Realm,
 O happy close of sight and that there's seen !
 That there is seen is good *Abinoam,*
 Who *Atove* hight : And *Atuvus* I ween,
 Cannot be lesse then he that sets his eyen
 On that abysse of good eternally,
 The youthfull *Æon,* whose fair face doth shine
 While he his Fathers glory doth espy,
Which waters his fine flowring forms with light from high.

14

Not that his forms increase, or that they die :
 For *Æon-land,* which men *Idea* call,
 Is nought but life in full serenity,
 Vigour of life is root, stock, branch, and all
 Nought here increaseth, nought here hath it's fall :
 For *Æons* Kingdomes alwayes perfect stand,
 Birds, Beasts, Fields, Springs, Plants, Men and
     Minerall,
 To perfectnesse nought added be there can :
This *Æon* also hight *Autocalon* and *On.*

15

This is the eldest sonne of *Hattove* hore :
 But th' eldest daughter of this aged Sire,
 That virgin wife of *Æon, Vranore.*
 She *Vranora* hight, because the fire
 Of *Æthers* essence she with bright attire,
 And inward unseen golden hew doth dight,
 And life of sense and phansie doth inspire.
 Æther's the vehicle of touch, smell, sight,
Of taste, and hearing too, and of the plastick might.

16

Whilome me chancèd (O my happy chance !)
 To spie this spotlesse pure fair *Uranore :*
 I spi'd her, but, alas ! with slighter glance
 Beheld her on the *Atuvæan* shore :
 She stood the last ; for her did stand before
 The lovely *Autocal.* But first of all
 Was mighty *Atove,* deeply covered o're
 With unseen light. No might imaginall
May reach that vast profunditie, [or raise its pall.]

17

Whiles thus they stood by that good lucid spring
 Of liuing blisse, her fourefold ornament
 I there observ'd ; and that's the onely thing
 That I dare write with due advisèment.
 Fool-hardy man that purposeth intent
 Far 'bove his reach, like the proud Phaeton,
 Who clomb the fiery car and was ybrent
 Through his fond juvenile ambition ;
Th' unruly flundring steeds wrought his confusion.

18

Now rise, my Muse, and straight thy self addresse
 To write the pourtraiture of th' outward vest,
 And to display its perfect comlinesse :
 Begin and leave where it shall please thee best.

Nor do assay to tell all, let the rest
Be understood. For no man can unfold
The many plicatures so closely prest
At lowest verge. Things 'fore our feet yrold,
If they be hard, how shall the highest things be told?

19

Its unseen figure I must here omit :
For tbing so mighty vast no mortall eye
Can compasse ; and if eye not compasse it,
The extreme parts, at least some, hidden lie :
And if that they lie hid, who can descry
The truth of figure? Bodies figurèd
Receive their shape from each extremity.
But if conjecture may stand in truths stead
The garment round or circular I do aread.

20

As for it's colour and materiall,
It silken seems, and of an azure hiew,
If hiew it have or colour naturall :
For much it may amaze mans erring view.
Those parts the eye is near give not the shew
Of any colour ; but the rurall Swains,
O easie ignorance ! would swear 'tis blew,
Such as their Phyllis would, when as she plains
Their Sunday-cloths, and the washt white with azure
stains.

21 ✓

But this fair azure colour's fouly stain'd
By base comparison with that blew dust.
But you of *Uranore* are not disdain'd,
O silly Shepherds, if you hit not just
In your conceits, so that you'r put in trust
You duly do attend. If simple deed
Accord with simple life, then needs you must
From the great *Uranore* of favour speed,
Though you cannot unfold the nature of her weed.

24

For who can it unfold, and reade aright
The divers colours, and the tinctures fair,
Which in this various vesture changes write
Of light, of duskishnesse, of thick, of rare
Consistences : ever new changes marre
Former impressions. The dubious shine
Of changeable silk stuffs, this passeth farre.
Farre more variety, and farre more fine,
Then interwoven silk with gold or silver twine.

23

Lo what delightfull immutations
On her soft flowing vest we contemplate !
The glory of the Court, their fashions,
And brave agguize with all their Princely state,
Which Poets or Historians relate
This farre excels, farther than pompous Court
Excels the homeliest garb of Countrey rate :
Unspeakable it is how great a sort
Of glorious glistring showes, in it themselves disport.

24

There you may see the eyelids of the Morn
With lofty silver arch displaid ith' East,
And in the midst the burnisht gold doth burn ;
A lucid purple mantle in the West
Doth close the day, and hap the Sun at rest.
Nor doth these lamping shewes the azur quell,
Or other colours : where 't beseemeth best
There they themselves dispose ; so seemly well
Doth light and changing tinctures deck this goodly veil.

25

But 'mongst these glaring glittering rows of light,
And flaming Circles, and the grisell gray,
And crudled clouds, with silver tippings dight,
And many other deckings wondrous gay,
As *Iris* and the *Halo;* there doth play
Still-pac'd *Euphrona* in her Conique tire ;
By stealth her steeple-cap she doth assay
To whelm on th' earth : So School-boyes do aspire
With coppell'd hat to quelme the Bee all arm'd with ire.

26

I saw pourtrai'd on this sky-coloured silk
Two lovely Lads, with wings fully dispread
Of silver plumes, their skins more white then milk,
Their lilly limbs I greatly admired,
Their cheary looks and lusty livelyhed :
Athwart their snowy brest, a scarf they wore
Of azur hew ; fairly bespangeled
Was the gold fringe. Like Doves so forth they fore:
Some message they, I ween, to *Monocardia* bore.

27

O gentle Sprights, whose carefull oversight
Tends humane actions, sons of Solyma.
O heavenly Salems sons ! you fend the right,
You violence resist, and fraud bewray ;
The ill with ill, the good with good you pay.
And if you list to mortall eye appear,
You thick that veil, and so your selves array
With visibility : O myst'ry rare !
That thickned veile should maken things appear more
bare !

28

But well I wot that nothing's bare to sense,
For sense cannot arrive to th' inwardnesse
Of things, nor penetrate the crusty fence
Of constipated matter close compresse :
Or that were laid aside, yet nathelesse
Things thus unbar'd to sense be more obscure.
Therefore those sonnes of Love when they them dresse
For sight, they thick the vest of *Vranure*,
And from their centre overflow't with beauty pure.

29

Thus many goodly things have been unfold
Of *Uranures* fair changing ornament :
Yet farre more hidden lye as yet untold ;
For all to tell was never my intent,

Neither all could I tell if I so meant.
For her large robe all the wide world doth fill:
It's various largenesse no man can depaint:
My pen's from thence, my Book my Ink; but skill
From *Uranuret* own selfe down gently doth distill.

30

But yet one thing I saw that I'll not passe:
At the low hem of this large garment gay
Number of goodly balls there pendant was,
Some like the Sun, some like the Moones white ray,
Some like discoloured Tellus, when the day
Discries her painted coat: In wondrous wise
These coloured ones do circle, float and play,
As those farre shining Rounds in open skies:
Their course the best Astronomer might well aggrize.

31

These danc't about: but some I did espie
That steady stood, 'mongst which there shinèd one,
More fairly shineth not the worlds great eye,
Which from his plenteous store unto the Moon
Kindly imparteth light, that when he's gone,
She might supply his place, and well abate
The irksome uglinesse of that foul drone,
Sad heavie Night; yet quick to work the fate
Of murd'red travellers, when they themselves belate.

32

O gladsome life of sense that doth adore
The outward shape of the worlds curious frame!
The proudest Prince that ever Sceptre bore
(Though he perhaps observeth not the same)
The lowest hem doth kisse of that we name,
The stole of *Vranore*, these parts that won
To drag in dirty earth (nor do him blame)
These doth he kisse: why should he be fordone?
How sweet it is to live! what joy to see the Sunne!

33

But O what joy it is to see the Sun
Of *Æons* kingdomes, and th' eternall Day
That never night o'retakes! the radiant throne
Of the great Queen, the Queen *Vranura!*
Then she gan first the Scepter for to sway,
And rule with wisdome, when Atuvus old;
—Hence Ahad we him call,—did tie them tway
With nuptiall charm and wedding-ring of gold:
Then sagely he the case gan to them thus unfold:

34

My first born Sonne, and thou my Daughter dear,
Look on your aged Sire, the deep abysse,
In which and out of which you first appear;
I *Ahad* hight, and *Ahad* onenesse is:
Therefore be one (his words do never misse)
They one became. I *Hattove* also hight,
Said he; and *Hattove* goodnesse is and blisse:
Therefore in goodnesse be ye fast unite:
Let Unity, Love, Good, be measures of your might.

35

They straight accord: then he put on the ring,
The ring of lasting gold on *Uranure;*
Then gan the youthfull lads aloud to sing.
Hymen! O Hymen! O the Virgin pure!
O holy Bride! long may this joy indure.
After the song *Atove* his speech again
Renews. My Son, I unto thee assure
All judgement and authority soveraign;
He spake as unto one: for one became those twain.

36

To thee each knee in Heaven and Earth shall bow,
And whatsoever wons in darker cell
Under the Earth: If thou thy awfull brow
Contract, those of the Æthiopian hell
Shall lout, and do thee homage; they that dwell
In Tharsis, Tritons fry, the Ocean-god,
Iim and Ziim, all the Satyres fell
That in empse Ilands maken their abode:
All those and all things else shall tremble at thy rod.

37

Thy rod thou thalt extend from sea to sea,
And thy Dominion to the worlds end;
All Kings shall vow thee faithfull fealty,
Then peace and truth on all the earth I'll send:
Nor moody Mars my metalls may mispend,
Of Warlike instruments they plow-shares shall
And pruning hooks efform. All things shall wend
For th' best, and thou the head shalt be o're all:
Have I not sworn thee King? true King Catholicall!

38

Thus farre he spake, and then again respired;
And all this time he held their hand in one;
Then they with chearfull look one thing desired,
That he nould break this happy union:
I happy union breake? quoth he anon:
I *Ahad?* Father of Community?
Then they: That you nould let your hand be gone
Off from our hands: He grants with smiling glee:
So each stroke struck on earth is struck from these same
  three.

39

These three are *Ahad, Æon, Uranore:*
Ahad these three in one doth counite.
What so is done on earth, the self-same power
(Which is exert upon each mortall wight)
Is joyntly from all these. But she that hight
Fair *Uranore*, men also *Psyche* call.
Great *Psyche* men and Angels dear delight,
Invested in her stole ætchereall,
Which though so high it be, down to the earth doth fall.

40

The externall form of this large flowing stole,
My Muse so as she might, above displaid:
But th' inward triple golden film to unroll,
Ah! he me teach that triple film hath made,

And brought out light out of the deadly shade
Of darkest Chaos, and things that are seen
Made to appear out of the gloomy glade
Of unseen beings : Them we call unseen,
Not that they're so indeed, but so to mortall eyen.

41

The first of these fair films, we Physis name.
Nothing in Nature did you ever spy,
But there's pourtraid : all beasts both wild and tame,
Each bird is here, and every buzzing fly ;
All forrest-work is in this tapestry :
The Oke, the Holm, the Ash, the Aspine tree,
The lonesome Buzzard, th' Eagle and the Py,
The Buck, the Bear, the Boar, the Hare, the Bee,
The Brize, the black-arm'd Clock, the Gnat, the butterflie.

42

Snakes, Adders, Hydraes, Dragons, Toads and Frogs,
Th' own-litter-loving Ape, the Worm, and Snail,
Th' undaunted Lion, Horses, Men, and Dogs,.
Their number's infinite, nought doth't avail
To reckon all, the time would surely fail :
And all besprinkled with centrall spots,
Dark little spots, is this hid inward veil :
But when the hot bright dart doth pierce these knots,
Each one dispreads it self according to their lots.

43

When they dispread themselves, then gins to swell
Dame *Psyches* outward vest, as th' inward wind
Softly gives forth, full softly doth it well
Forth from the centrall spot ; yet as confin'd
To certain shape, according to the mind
Of the first centre, not perfect circ'lar-wise,
It shoots it self : for so the outward kind
Of things were lost, and Natures good device
Of different forms would hiddenlie in one agguize.

44

But it according to the imprest Art
(That Arts impression's from *Idea-Lond*)
So drives it forth before it every part
According to true Symmetry : the bond
And just precinct (unlesse it be withstood)
It alwayes keeps. But that old Hag that hight
Foul Hyle mistresse of the miry strond,
Oft her withstands, and taketh great delight
To hinder *Physis* work, and work her all despight.

45

The self same envious witch with poyson'd dew,
From her foul eben-box, all tinctures stains,
Which fairly good be in hid *Physis* hew :
That film all tinctures fair in it contains :
But she their goodly glory much restrains.
She colours dims ; clogs tastes ; and damps the sounds
Of sweetest musick ; touch to scorching pains
She turns, or baser tumults ; smels confounds.
O horrid womb of hell, that with such ill abounds.

19

46

From this first film all bulk in quantity
Doth bougen out, and figure thence obtain.
Here eke begins the life of Sympathy,
And hidden virtue of magnetick vein,
Where unknown spirits beat, and *Psyche's* trane
Drag as they list, upon pursuit or flight ;
One part into another they constrain
Through strong desire, and then again remit.
Each outward form's a shrine of its magnetick spright.

47

The ripen'd child breaks through his mothers womb,
The raving billows closely undermine
The ragged rocks, and then the seas intomb
Their heavy corse, and they their heads recline
On working sand : The Sunne and Moon combine,
Then they're at ods in site Diametrall :
The former age to th' present place resigne :
And what's all this but wafts of winds centrall
That ruffle, touze, and tosse Dame *Psyche's* wrimpled
veil?

48

So *Physis.* Next is Arachnea thin,
The thinner of these two, but thinn'st of all
Is *Semele*, that's next to Psyches skin.
The second we thin *Arachnea* call,
Because the spider, that in Princes hall
Takes hold with her industrious hand, and weaves
Her dainty tender web ; far short doth fall
Of this soft yeilding vest ; this vest deceives
The spiders curious touch, and of her praise bereaves.

49

In midst of this fine web doth *Haphe* sit :
She is the centre from whence all the light
Dispreads, and goodly glorious Forms do flit
Hither and thither. Of this mirour bright
Haphe's the life and representing might,
Haphe's the mother of sense-sympathy ;
Hence are both Hearing, Smelling, Taste, and Sight :
Haphe's the root of felt vitality ;
But *Haphe's* mother hight all-spread Community.

50

In this clear shining mirour *Psyche* sees
All that falls under sense, what ere is done
Upon the Earth ; the Deserts shaken trees,
The mournfull winds, the solitary wonne
Of dreaded beasts, the Lybian Lyons moan,
When their hot entralls scorch with hunger keen,
And they to God for meat do deeply groan ;
He hears their cry, he sees of them unseen ;
His eyelids compasse all that in the wide world been.

51

He sees the weary traveller sit down
In the waste field oft-times with carefull chear :
His chafed feet, and the long way to town,
His burning thirst, faintnesse, and Panick fear,

C

Because he sees not him that stands so near,
Fetch from his soul deep sighs with count'nance sad,
But he looks on to whom nought doth dispear :
O happy man that full persuasion had
Of this I if right at home, nought of him were y'drad.

52

A many sparrows for small price be sold,
Yet none of them his wings on earth doth close
Lighting full soft, but that eye doth behold,
Their jets, their jumps, that mirour doth disclose.
Thrice happy he that putteth his repose
In his all-present God.   That Africk rock
But touch't with heedlesse hand, Auster arose
With blust'ring rage, that with his irefull shock
And moody might he made the worlds frame nigh to rock.

53

And shall not He, when his Anointed be
Ill handled, rise, and in his wrathfull stour
Disperse, and quell the haughty enemy,
Make their brisk sprights to lout and lowly lowr ?
Or else confound them quite with mighty power ?
Touch not my Kings, my Prophets let alone,
Harm not my Priests ; or you shall ill endure
Your works sad payment and that deadly lone ;
Keep off your hand from that high holy Rock of stone.

54

Do not I see ? I slumber not nor sleep.
Do not I hear ? each noise by shady night
My mirour represents ; when mortals steep
Their languid limbs in Morpheus dull delight,
I hear such sounds as Adams brood would fright.
The dolefull echoes from the hollow hill
Mock howling wolves : the woods with black bedight
Answer rough Pan, his pipe and eke his skill,
And all the Satyr-routs rude whoops and shoutings shrill :

55

The night's no night to me : What ? shall the Owl
And nimble Cat their courses truly steer,
And guide their feet and wings to every hole
So right, this on the ground, that in the air ?
And shall not I by night see full as clear ?
All sense doth in proportion consist,
Arachnea doth all proportions bear ;
All sensible proportions that fine twist
Contains ; all life of sense is in great *Haphes* list.

56

Sense and concent, and all abhorrency,
Be variously divided in each one
Partic'lar creature : But antipathy
Cannot be there where fit proportion
Strikes in with all things in harmonious tone.
Thus *Haphe* feels nought to her self contrair :
In her there's tun'd a just Diapason
For every outward stroke : withouten jarre
Thus each thing doth she feel, and each thing easly bear.

57

But *Haphe* and *Arachne* I'll dismisse,
And that fourth vest, rich *Semele* display :
The largest of all foure and loosest is
This floting flouring changeable array.
How fairly doth it shine, and nimbly play,
Whiles gentle winds of Paradise do blow,
And that bright Sun of the eternall day
Upon it glorious light and forms doth strow,
And *Ahad* it with love and joy doth overflow.

58

This all-spread *Semele* doth *Bacchus* bear,
Impregn'd of *Jove* or *On*. He is the wine
That sad down-drooping senses wont to rear,
And chearlesse hearts to comfort in ill tine.
He 'flames chast Poets brains with fire divine ;
The stronger spright the weaker spright doth sway ;
No wonder then each phansie doth incline
To their great mother *Semel*, and obey
The vigourous impresse of her enforcing ray.

59

She is the mother of each Semele :
The daughters be divided one from one ;
But she grasps all.   How can she then but see
Each Semels shadows by this union ?
She sees and swayes imagination
As she thinks good ; and if that she think good
She lets it play by't self, yet looketh on,
While she keeps in that large strong-beating floud
That makes the Poet write, and rave as he were wood.

60

Prophets and Poets have their life from hence,
Like fire into their marrow it searcheth deep,
This flaming fiery flake doth choak all sense,
And binds the lower man with brazen sleep :
Corruption through all his bones doth creep,
And raging raptures do his soul outsnatch :
Round-turning whirlwinds on Olympus steep
Do cast the soul that earst they out did catch :
Then stiller whispering winds dark visions unlatch.

61

But not too farre, thou bold Platonick Swain :
Strive not at once all myst'ries to discover
Of that strange School ; More and more hard remain
As yet untold.   But let us now recover
Strength to our selves by rest in duly houre.
Great *Psyches* Parentage, Marriage, and Weeds
We having song according to our power,
That we may rise more fresh for morning deeds,
Let's here take Inne and rest our weary sweating steeds. ✕

The Argument of

P S Y C H O Z O I A,

Or,

The life of the Soul.

CANT. II.

Here's taught how into Psychanie
Souls from their centrall sourse
Go forth, Here Beirons ingeny
Old Mnemon doth discourse.

1

Sang great *Psyche* in my former song,
Old *Atoves* daughter, sister unto *On*,
Mother of all that nimble Atom-throng
Of winged Lives, and Generation.
When *Psyche* wedded to *Autocalon,*
They both to *Ahad* forthwith straight were wed :
For as you heard, all these became but one,
And so conjoyn'd they lie all in one bed,
And with that four-fold vest they be all overspred.

2

Here lies the inmost Centre of Creation,
From whence all inward forms and life proceed :
Here's that aereall stole, that to each fashion
Of Sensibles is matter for their weed.
This is the ground where God doth sow his seed
And whilest he sows with whispering charms doth
   bid
This flourish long, and that to make more speed,
And all in order by his Word doth rid :
So in their fatall round they 'pear and then are hid.

3

Beginning, End, Form and Continuance
Th' impression of his Word to them doth deal,
Occurrences he sees, and mindeth chance :
But chance hath bounds. The Sea cannot o're swell
His just precincts. Or rocky shores repell
His foming force ; or else his inward life
And Centrall rains do fairly him compell
Within himself, and gently 'pease the strife,
Or makes him gnaw the bit with rore and rage full rife.

4

So fluid chance is set its certain bound,
Although with circling winds it be y tost ;
And so the pilots skill doth quite confound
With unexpected storms, and men have lost
Their time, their labour, and their precious cost.
Yet ther's a Neptune Soveraign of this Sea,
Which those that in themselves put not their trust
To rude mischance did never yet betray :
It's He, whom both the winds and stormy Seas obey.

5

Now sith my wandring Bark so far is gone,
And flitten forth upon the Ocean main,
I thee beseech that just dominion
Hast of the Sea, and art true Soveraign
Of working phancie when it floats amain
With full impregned billows and strong rage
Enforceth way upon the boyling plain,
That thou wouldst steer my ship with wisdome sage,
That I with happy course may run my watery stage.

6

My mind is mov'd dark Parables to sing
Of *Psyches* progeny that from her came,
When she was married to that great King,
Great *Æon*, who just title well may claim
To every soul, and brand them with his name.
Its He that made us, and not our own might :
But who, alas ! this work can well proclaim ?
We silly sheep cannot bleat out aright
The manner how : but that that giveth light is light.

7

Then let us borrow from the glorious Sun
A little light to illustrate this act,
Such as he is in his solstitial Noon,
When in the Welkin there's no cloudy tract

For to make grosse his beams, and light refract.
Then sweep by all those Globes that by reflexion
His long small shafts do rudely beaten back,
And let his rayes have undenied projection,
And so we will pursue this mysteries retection.

8

Now think upon that gay discoloured Bow :
That part that is remotest from the light
Doth duskish hew to the beholder show ;
The nearer parts have colour farre more bright,
And next the brightest is the subtle light ;
Then colours seem but a distinct degree
Of light now failing ; such let be the sight
Of his farre spreaden beams that shines on high :
Let vast discoloured Orbs close his extremitie,

9

The last Extreme, the farthest off from light,
That's Natures deadly shadow, *Hyle's* cell.
O horrid cave, and womb of dreaded night ?
Mother of witchcraft, and the cursed spell,
Which nothing can avail 'gainst *Israel.*
No Magick can him hurt ; his portion
Is not divided Nature ; he doth dwell
In light, in holy love, in union ;
Not fast to this or that, but free communion.

10

Dependance of this All hence doth appear,
And several degrees subordinate.
But phancie's so unfit such things to clear,
That oft it makes them seem more intricate :
And now Gods work it doth disterminate
Too farre from his own reach : But he withall
More inward is, and farre more intimate
Then things are with themselves. His Ideall,
And Centrall presence is in every Atom-ball

11

Therefore those different hews through all extend
So farre as light : Let light be every where ;
And every where with light distinctly blend
Those different colours which I nam'd whilere
The Extremities of that farre shining sphear.
And that far shining sphear, which Centre was
Of all those different colours, and bright chear,
You must unfasten ; so o'respred it has,
Or rather deeply fill'd with Centrall sand each place.

12

Now sith that this withouten penetrance
Of bodies may be done ; we clearly see
(As well as that pendent subordinance)
The nearly couching of each Realtie,
And the Creatours close propinquitie
To ev'ry creature. This be understood
Of differentiall profunditie.
But for the overspreading Latitude ;
Why may't not equally be stretch'd with th' Ocean floud ?

13

There *Proteus* wonnes and fleet *Idothea*,
Where the lowest step of that profunditie
Is pight ; Next that is *Psyche's* out-array :
It *Tasis* hight : *Physis* is next degree :
There *Psyche's* feet impart a smaller fee
Of gentle warmth. *Physis* is the great womb
From whence all things in th' University
Yclad in divers forms do gaily bloom,
And after fade away, as *Psyche* gives the doom.

14

Next *Physis* is the tender *Arachnee.*
There in her subtile loom doth *Haphe* sit :
But the last vest is changing *Semele :*
And next is *Psyches* self. These garments fit
Her sacred limbs full well, and are so knit
One part to other, that the strongest sway
Of sharpest axe, them no'te asunder smite.
The seaventh is *Æon* with Eternall ray :
The eighth *Atove,* steddy Cube, all propping *Adonai.*

15

Upon this universall Ogdoas
Is founded every particularment :
From this same universall Diapase
Each harmony is fram'd and sweet concent.
But that I swerve not far from my intent,
This Ogdoas let 'be an Unitie
One mighty quickned Orb of vast extent,
Throughly possest of lifes community,
And so those vests be seats of Gods vitality.

16

Now deem this universall Round alone,
And rayes no rayes but a first all-spred light,
And centrick all like one pellucid Sun ;
A Sun that's free, not bound by Natures might,
That where he lists exerts his rayes outright,
Both when he lists, and what, and eke how long,
And then retracts so as he thinketh meet.
These rayes be that particular creature-throng :
Their number none can tell, but that all-making tongue.

17

Now blundring Naturalist behold the spring
Of thy deep-searching foul, that fain would know
Whether a mortall or immortall thing
It be, and whence at first it 'gan to flow ;
And that which chiefest is where it must go.
Some fixt necessity thou fain wouldst find :
But no necessity, where there's no law,
But the good pleasure of an unty'd mind :
Therefore thy God seek out, and leave Nature behind.

18

He kills, He makes alive ; the keys of Hell
And Death he hath. He can keep souls to wo
When cruell hands of Fate them hence expell :
Or He in *Lethe's* lake can drench them so,

That they no act of life or sense can show.
They march out at His word, and they retreat ;
March out with joy, retreat with footing slow
In gloomy shade, benumm'd with pallid sweat,
And with their feeble wings their fainting breasts they
beat.

19

But souls that of his own good life partake
He loves as his own self ; dear as His eye
They are to him : He'll never them forsake :
When they shall dye, then God himself shall die
They live, they live in blest Eternity.
The wicked are not so ; but like the dirt,
Trampled by man and beast, in grave they lye.
Filth and corruption is their rufull sort :
Themselves with death and wormes in darknesse they
disport.

20

Their rotten relicks lurk close under ground ;
With living wight no sense or sympathy
They have at all ; nor hollow thundring sound
Of roring winds, that cold mortality
Can wake, ywrapt in sad Fatality.
To horses hoof that beats his grassie dore
He answers not : The Moon in silency,
Doth passe by night, and all bedew him or'e
With her cold humid rayes ; but he feels not Heavens
power.

21

O dolefull lot of disobedience !
If God should souls thus drench in Lethe lake
But O unspeakable torture of sense,
When sinfull souls do life and sense partake,
That those damn'd Spirits may them anvils make
Of their fell cruelty, that lay such blows
That very ruth doth make my heart to quake
When I consider of the drery woes,
And tearing torment that each soul then undergoes.

22

Hence the souls nature we may plainly see :
A beam it is of th' Intellectuall Sun,
A ray indeed of that Æternity ;
But such a ray as when it first out shone,
From a free light its shining date begun.
And that same light when 't list can call it in ;
Yet that free light hath given a free wonne
To this dependent ray : Hence cometh sin ;
From sin dred Death and Hell these wages doth it win.

23

Each life a severall ray is from that Sphear
That Sphear doth every life in it contain.
Arachnee, Semel, and the rest do bear
Their proper virtue, and with one joynt strain

And powerfull sway they make impression plain,
And all their rayes be ioyned into one
By Ahad : so this womb withouten pain
Doth flocks of souls send out that have their won
Where they list most to graze ; as I shall tell anon.

24

The countrey where they live Psychania hight,
Great Psychany, that hath so mighty bounds,
If bounds it have at all. So infinite
It is of bignesse, that it me confounds
To think to what a vastnesse it amounds.
The Sun Saturnus, Saturn the Earth exceeds
The Earth the Moon ; but all those fixed Rounds ;
But Psychany, those fixed Rounds exceeds,
As farre as those fix'd Rounds excell small mustard-seeds.

25

Two mighty Kingdomes hath this Psychany,
The one self-feeling Autæsthesia ;
The other hight god-like Theoprepy,
Autæsthesy's divided into tway :
One province cleped is great Adamah
Which also hight Beirah of brutish fashion ;
The other Providence is Dizoie ;
There you may see much mungrill transformation,
Such monstrous shapes proceed from Niles foul inunda-
tion.

26

Great Michael ruleth Theoprepia,
A mighty Prince. King of Autæsthesy
Is that great Giant who bears mighty sway,
Father of Discord, Falshood, Tyranny,
His name is Dæmon, not from Sciency,
Although he boasteth much of skilful pride ;
But he's the fount of foul duality,
That wicked witch Duessa is his bride :
From his dividing force this name to him betide.

27

Or for that he himself is quite divided
Down to the belly ; there's some unity :
But head, and tongue, and heart be quite discided ;
Two heads, two tongues, and eke two hearts there be.
This head doth mischief plot, that head doth see
Wrong fairly to o'reguild. One tongue doth pray,
The other curse. The hearts do ne're agree
But felly one another do upbray
An ugly cloven foot this monster doth upstay.

28

Two sons great Dæmon and Duessa hath :
Autophilus the one ycleeped is ;
In Dizoie he worketh wondrous scath ;
He is the cause what so there goes amisse,
In Psyches stronger plumed progenies.
But Philosomatus rules Beirah.
This proud puft Giant whilom did arise,
Born of the slime of Autæsthesia,
And bred up these two sons yborn of Duessa.

29

Duessa first invented magick lore,
And great skill hath to joyn and disunite ;
This herb makes love, that hearb makes hatred sore
And much she can against an *Edomite;*
But nought she can against an *Israelite,*
Whose heart's upright and doth himself forsake.
For he that's one with God no magick might
Can draw or here or there through blind mistake.
Magick can onely quell natures *Dæmoniake.*

30

But that I may in time my self betake
To straighter course, few things I will relate,
Of which old *Mnemon* mention once did make.
A jolly swain he was in youthfull state,
When he mens natures gan to contemplate,
And kingdomes view : But he was aged then
When I him saw ; his years bore a great date ;
He numbred had full ten times ten times ten :
There's no *Pythagorist* but knows well what I mean.

31

Old *Mnemons* head and beard was hoary white,
But yet a chearfull countenance he had :
His vigorous eyes did shine like starres bright,
And in gond decent freez he was yclad,
As blith and buxom as was any lad
Of one and twenty cloth'd in forrest green ;
Both blith he was, and eke of counsell sad :
Like winter-morn bedight with snow and rine
And sunny rayes, so did his goodly Eldship shine.

32

Of many famous towns in *Beïrah,*
And many famous Laws and uncouth Rites
He spake : but vain it is for to assay
To reckon up such numbers infinite.
And much he spake where I had no insight,
But well I wot that some there present had ;
For words to speak to uncapable wight
Of foolishnesse proceeds or phrensie mad.
So, alwayes some, I wis, could trace his speeches pad.

33

But that which I do now remember best,
Is that which he of *Psittacusa* lond
Did speak. This *Psittacuse* is not the least,
Or the most obscure, Countrey, that is found
In wastefull *Beïron :* it is renown'd
For famous Clerks yclad in greenest cloke,
Like Turkish Priests, if *Amoritish* ground
We call 't, no cause, that title to revoke.
But of this Land to this effect old *Mnemon* spoke.

34

I travelled in *Psittacusa* Lond :
Th' Inhabitants the lesser *Adamah*
Do call it ; but then Adam I have found
It ancienter, if so I safely may

Unfold th' antiquity. They by one day
Are elder then old Adam, and by one
At least are younger then Arcadia.
O' th' sixth day Adam had's creation ;
Those on the fifth, the Arcades before the Moon.

35

In this same Land as I was on the rode,
A nimble traveller me overtook :
Fairly together on the way we yode.
Tho I gan closely on his person look,
And eye his garb : He straight occasion took
To entertain discourse, though none I raught,
But unprovok'd he first me undertook :
So soon as he gan talk, then straight I laught :
The Sage himself represt, but thought me nigh distraught.

36

His concave nose, great head, and grave aspect,
Affected tone, words without inward sense,
My inly tickled spright made me detect
By outward laughter ; but by best pretence
I purg'd my self, and gave due reverence.
Then he gan gravely treat of codicils,
And of Book-readings passing excellence,
And tri'd his wit in praysing gooses quills :
O happy age ! quoth he, the world Minerva fills.

37

I gave the talk to him, which pleas'd him well :
For then he seem'd a learned clerk to been,
When none contrary'd his uncontrolled spell,
But I, alas ! though unto him unseen,
Did flow with tears, as if that onyons keen
Had pierc'd mine eyen. Strange vertue of fond joy :
They ought to weep that be in heavie teen.
But nought my lightsome heart did then annoy :
So light it lay, it mov'd at every windie toy.

38

As we yode softly on, a Yongster gent
With bever cock't, and arm set on one side
(His youthfull fire quickly our pace out-went)
Full fiercely pricked on in madcap pride,
The mettle of his horses heels he tri'd,
He hasted to his countrey *Pithecuse.*
Most haste, worst speed : still on our way we ride,
And him o'retake halting through haplesse bruize ;
We help him up again, our help he nould refuse.

39

Then gan the learn'd and ag'd *Don Psittaco,*
When he another auditour had got,
To spruse his plumes, and wisdome sage to show,
And with his sacred lore to wash the spot
Of youthfull blemishes ; but frequent jot
Of his hard setting jade did so confound
The words that he by paper-stealth had got,
That their lost sense the yongster could not sound.
Though he with mimicall attention did abound.

40

Yet some of those faint winged words came near,
Of God, of Adam, and the shape divine,
Which Adams children have; (these pierc'd his care)
And how that man is lord of every kind
Of beasts, of birds, and of each hidden mine
Of natures treasures. He to Adams sonne
The wide world for his kingdome doth designe :
And ever naming God, he lookd aboven :
Pithecus straight plac'd God a thought above the Moon.

41

Pithecus, so they call this gentle wight,
The docible young man eas'ly could trace
His masters steps, most quick and expedite.
When *Psittaco* look'd up to holy place,
Pithecus straight with sanctimonious grace
Cast up his eyes ; and when the shape divine,
Which Adam had from God, he gan to praise,
Pithecus draws himself straight from that line,
And phansies his sweet face with heavenly hiew to shine.

42

He pincht his hat, and from his horses side
Stretch forth his russet legs, himself inclin'd
Now here, now there, and most exactly eyed
His comely lineaments, that he might find
What ever beauty else he had not mind
As yet in his fair corse. But that full right
And vast prerogative did so vnbind
His straighted sprights, that with tyrannick might
He forc'd his feeble beast, and straight fled out of sight.

43

Then I and *Psittaco* were left alone ;
And which was strange, he deeply silent was :
Whether some inward grief he from that son,
Conceiv'd, and deemed it no small disgrace
That that bold youngster should so little passe
His learned speech ; or whether nought to sain
He had then left ; or whether a wild chase
Of flitting inconsistent thoughts he than
Pursu'd, which turn'd and toy'd in his confused brain.

44

Or whether he was woxen so discreet,
As not to speak till fit occasion.
(To judge the best, that Charity counts meet)
Therefore that Senior sad I gan anon
Thus to bespeak : Good Sir, I crave pardon
If so I chance to break that golden twist
You spin, by rude interpellation,
That twist of choicest thoughts. No whit I miss'd
The mark I aimed at ; to speak he had great list.

45

So then his spirits gan to come again,
And to enact his corps and impart might
Unto his languide tongue, and every vein
Received heat, when due conceived right

I did to him ; and weend he plainly see't
That I was toucht with admiration
Of his deep learning, and quick-shifting sight,
Then I gan quire of the wide *Behiron*.
Behiron, quoth that Sage, that hight *Anthropion*.

46

Anthropion we call't ; but th' holy tongue
(His learning lay in words) that *Behiron*
Which we *Anthropion*, calls, as I among
The Rabbins read : but sooth to say, no tone,
Nor tongue, or speech, so sweet as is our own,
Or so significant. For mark the sense :
From ἄνω ἀθρεῖν is *Anthropion* ;
And we are all of an upright presence ;
Nor I'll be drawn from this conceit by no pretence.

47

I prais'd his steddy faith and confidence,
That stood as fast as trunk or rock of stone ;
Yet nathelesse, said I, the excellence
Of stedfastnesse is not to yield to none,
But stiff to stand till mov'd by right reason ;
And then by yielding, part of victory
To gain. What fitnesse in *Anthropion ?*
Baboons, and Apes, as well as th' *Anthropi*
Do go upright, and beasts grown mad do view the sky.

48

Then marken well, what great affinitie
There is twixt Ape, mad Beast, and Satyrs wild,
And the Inhabitants of *Anthropie*,
When they are destitute of manners mild,
And th' inward man with brutishnesse defil'd
Hath life and love and lust and cogitation
Fixt in foul sense, or moving in false guile ;
That holy tongue the better nomination,
So farre, I know, may give : 'Tis ghesse, not full
perswasion.

49

Therefore, O learned Sir, aread aright,
What may this word *Behiron* signifie ?
He wondrous glad to shew his Grammar-might,
This same word *Behiron* doth signifie
The brutish nature, or brutallitie,
Said he : and with his voice lift up his front.
Then I his skill did gaily magnifie,
And blest me, I an idiot should light on't
So happily, that never was a scholar count ;

50

And said, Then holy tongue is on my side :
And holy tongue is better then profane.
He angry at his courtesie, reply'd,
That learned men ought for to entertain
Discourse of learned tongues, and countrey swain
Of countrey 'fairs. But for to answer thee,
This I dare warrant surely to maintain,
If to contrair the holy tongue should be
Absurd, I find enough such contrariety.

51

Then I in simple sort him answered thus,
I ken not the strange guize of learned Schools,
But if Gods thoughts be contrair unto us,
Let not deep wonderment possesse our souls,
If he call fools wisemen, and wisemen fools.
If rich he poore men term, if poore men rich,
If crafty States-men, silly countrey gulls,
Beasts men, men beasts, with many other such :
God seeth not as man seeth, God speaks not in mans
     speech.

52

Straight he to higher pearch, like bird in cage,
Did skip, and sang of etern Destiny,
Of sight and foresight he with count'nance sage
Did speak, and did unfold Gods secresie,
And left untoucht no hidden mystery.
I lowly louting held my cap in hond :
He askt what meant that so sudden coursie.
I pardon crave, said I, for manners fond ;
You are Heavens Privy-Counsellour I understond,

53

Which I wist not before : so deep insight
Into the hidden things of God who can
Attain unto, without that quickning spright
Of the true God ? Who knows the mind of man
But that same spright that in his brest doth won ?
Therefore the key of Gods hid secresie
Is his own spright, that's proper to the Son,
And those of that second nativity,
Which holy Temples are of the Divinity.

54

Therefore as th' sacred Seat o' th' Deity,
I unto you seemly behaviour make,
If you be such as you may seem to be.
It is mans nature easily to mistake.
My words his mind did quite asunder break :
For he full forward was all to assume
That might him gild with glory, and pertake
With God ; and joyed greatly in vain fume,
And prided much himself in his purloined plume.

55

So that full loth he was for to undo
My fairly winded up conclusion ;
Yet inwardly did not assent unto
My premises : for foul presumption
He thought, if that a private idiot man
By his new birth should either equallize,
Or else outstrip the bookish nation.
Perhaps some foul deformities disguise
Their life : tush ! that to knowledge is no prejudice.

56

But he nould say so : for why ? he was bent
To keep the credit which he then had got,
As he conceiv'd : for it had been yblent ;
It might have hazarded half of his lot,

To wit his god-like hue withouten spot,
If so be such deep knowledge could consist
With wicked life : but he nould lose one jot
Of his so high esteem, nor me resist.
So I escap'd the souse of his contracted fist.

57

And here I think we both as dumb had been
As were the slow-foot beasts on which we rode
Had not Don *Psittaco* by fortune seen
A place which well he knew though disallow'd :
Which he to me with earnest countenance show'd
Histing me nearer ; nearer both we go
And closely under the thick hedges crowd,
Which were not yet so thick but they did show
Through their false sprays all the whole place and
     persons too.

58

It was to weet, a trimly deckéd Close
Whose grassie pavement wrought with even line
Ran from the Morn upon the Evening-close.
The Eastern end by certain steps they climbe
To do their holy things, (O sight divine !)
There on the middle of the highest flore
A large green turf squar'd out, all fresh and fine
Not much unlike to Altars us'd of yore
Right fairly was adorn'd with every glittering flower.

59

At either end of this well raised sod
A stately stalk shot up of Torchwort high
Whose yellow flames small light did cast abroad
But yet a pleasant shew they yield the eye.
A pretty space from this we did descry
An hollow Oak, whose navell the rough saw
Long since had clove : so standing wet and dry
Around the stumped top soft mosse did grow
Whose velvet hue and verdure cushion-like did show.

60

Within the higher hedge of thickn'd trees
A lower rank on either side we saw
Of lesser shrubs even-set with artifice.
There the wood-queristers sat on a row
And sweetly sung while Boreas did blow
Above their heads, with various whistling,
As his blasts hap to break (now high, now low)
Against the branches of the waving Pines
And other neighbour plants, still rocking with the winds.

61

But above these birds of more sightly plume
With gold and purple feathers gayly dight
Are rank'd aloft. But th' Eagle doth assume
The highest sprig. For his it is by right.
Therefore in seemly sort he there is pight
Sitting aloft in his green Cabinet
From whence he all beholds with awfull sight,
Who ever in that solemne place were met,
At the West end for better view, right stately set.

62

After a song loud chanted by that Quire
Tun'd to the whistling of the hollow winde
Comes out a gay Pye in his rich attire
The snowie white with the black sattin shin'd,
On's head a silken cap he wore unlin'd.
When he had hopped to the middle flore
His bowing head right lowly he inclin'd
As if some Deity he did adore,
And seemly gestures make courting the Heavenly powr.

63

Thus cring'd he toward th' East with shivering wings
With eyes on the square sod devoutly bent.
Then with short flight up to the Oak he springs
Where he thrice congied after his ascent
With posture chang'd from th' East to th' Occident,
Thrice bowed he down and easily thrice he rose ;
Bow'd down so low as if't had been's intent
On the green mosse to wipe his swarthy nose.
Anon he chatters loud, but why himself best knows.

64

There we him leave, impatient of stay
My self amaz'd such actions to see
And pretty gestures 'mongst those creatures gay :
So unexpected Uniformitie,
And such a semblance of due piety :
For every Crow as when he cries for rain
Did Eastward nod ; and every Daw we see
When they first entered this grassie Plain
With shaking wings and bended bills ador'd the same.

65

O that the spirit of *Pythagoras*
Would now invade my breast, dear *Psittaco !*
Said I. In nature he so cunning was
As both the mind of birds and beasts to know,
What meant their voyces and their gestures too.
So might we riddle out some mystery
Which lieth hid in this strange uncouth show ;
But thy grave self may be as wise as he
I wote. Aread then *Psittaco* what sights these be.

66

Certes, said he, thine eyes be waxen dim
These be the people of wide *Adamah*
These be no birds, 'tis true, they're sons of sin
And vessels of Heavens ire, for sooth to say
They have no faith, I fear nor ever may,
But be shap'd out for everlasting shame,
Though they deride us of *Psittacusa :*
Yet well I wot, we have the onely name
Above, and though all foul yet there devoyd of blame.

67

And that green spot which thou maist deem a Close
It is to them no Close but holy place
Yeleep'd a Church, whose sight doth well dispose
Approaching souls. The rest thy self maist trace

By true analogy, But I'll not passe
One thing remarkable, said he to me :
It was Don *Pico* took the preaching place
A man of mighty power in his own See ;
A man, no bird, as he did fondly seem to thee.

68

Mn. Tell then Don *Psittaco*, what *Pico* ment
By his three bowings to the setting Sun
And single obesance toward th' Orient.
What ! were they postures of Religion ?
If so ; why had those yellow flames but one ?
The Eagle three ? That th' Eagle was his God
It is, said he, a strong presumption,
Whom he first slightly in that holy sod
After ador'd more fully with a triple nod.

69

Certes, quoth I, such Majesty divine
And seemly graces in the Eagle be
That they the gentle heart may well incline
To all respect and due civility.
But if that worship civill be, said he,
Certes, Don *Pico* can not well excuse
Himself from fault of impious flattery
His holy gestures streightway thus to use
To mortall man, redoubling thrice the bold abuse.

70

But well observe, said I, the motion.
While he draws lowly back his demure bill
Making it touch the mossie cushion,
His moving Karkas shrinketh nearer still
Toward the sacred sod.
What then, quoth he, was it in *Pico's* mind
That solemn service with four ducks to fill
But one before, the other three behind.
My duller wit, said I, the mystery cannot find.

71

Ps. But I can find it. Superstition
And flattery, have made Don *Pico* blind.
These interfare in fond confusion.
But both conspire to hold up his swoln mind
In supercilious pride and wayes unkind.
For he doth dominere o're *Psittacuse.*
Dear *Psittacuse !* when shalt thou once outwind
Thy self from this sad yoke ? who brings the news
Of Sions full release from scorn and foul abuse ?

72

O had we once the power in our hands
How carefully the youth wee'd catechise,
But bind Gods enemies in iron bands
(Such honour have his Saints) and would devise
Set forms of Truth, on Discipline advise
That unto both all men must needs conform.
Mn. But what if any tender heart denies ?
Ps. If he will his own fortunes overturn
It cannot well be holp, we must be uniform.

73

Mn. Good reason too, said I. Don *Pico* grave
The self same doctrine preacheth as I hear.
But Reverend *Psittaco*, let me freedome crave
To ask one question, Is't because 't's so clear
That who so shall dissent shall pay so dear.
Or will you in those things you do not know
But be uncertain, certain mischief bear
To them that due assent cannot bestow?
It is in such, said he, that we for certain know.

74

But how know you those things for certainty?
By Reason, Scripture, or the Spirit divine,
Or lastly by Churches Authority?
With that Don *Psittaco* cast up his eyen
Brim ful of thoughts to solve this knot of mine.
But in the fall of his high-gazing sight
He spide two on the rode he did divine
To be of his acquaintance, them we meet,
Forthwith Don *Psittaco* the strangers kindly greet.

75

And he them both seemly salutes again.
The one on a lean fiery jade did sit
And seem'd a wight of a right subtile brain.
Both cloth'd as black as jet. But he was fit
With a dry wall-nut shell to fence his wit.
Which like a quilted cap on's head he wore
Lin'd with white taffity, wherein were writ
More trimly than the Iliads of yore
The laws of Mood and Figure and many precepts more.

76

All the nice questions of the School-men old
And subtilties as thin as cobwebs bet,
Which he wore thinner in his thoughts yrold.
And his warm brains, they say, were closer set
With sharp distinctions than a cushionet
With pins and needles ; which he can shoot out
Like angry Porcupine, where e're they hit.
Certes a doughty Clerk and Champion stout
He seem'd and well appointed against every doubt.

77

The other rod on a fat resty jade
That neighed loud. His rider was not lean.
His black plump belly fairly outward swai'd
And pressed somewhat hard on th' horses mane.
Most like methought to a Cathedrall Dean.
A man of prudence and great courtesie
And wisely in the world he knew to glean.
His sweaty neck did shine right greasily
Top heavy was his head with earthily policy.

78

This wight *Corvino*, *Psittacus* me told
Was named, and the other *Graculo*.
They both of his acquaintance were of old
Though so near freindship now they did not owe.

But yet in generalls agreed, I trow,
For they all dearly hug dominion,
And love to hold mens consciences in awe
Each standing stiff for his opinion
In holy things, against all contradiction.

79

But most of all *Corvin* and *Psittaco*
Prudentiall men and of a mighty reach
Who through their wisdome sage th' events foreknow
Of future things ; and confidently preach
Unlesse there be a form which men must teach
Of sound opinions (each meaning his own)
But t' be left free to doubt and counter-speech
Authority is lost, our trade is gone
Our Tyrian wares forsaken, we, alas ! shall mone.

80

Or at the best our life will bitter be :
For we must toyle to make our doctrine good.
Which will empair the flesh and weak the knee.
Our mind cannot attend our trencher-food,
Nor be let loose to sue the worldly good.
All's our dear wives, poore wenches ! they alone
Must ly long part of night when we withstood
By scrupulous wits must watch to nights high Noon
Till all our members grow as cold as any stone.

81

Heaps of such inconveniences arise
From Conscience-freedome, Christian liberty.
Beside our office all men will despise
Unlesse our lives gain us Autority.
Which in good sooth a harder task will be.
Dear brethren ! sacred souls of *Behiron !*
Help, help as you desire to liven free
To ease, to wealth, to honour, and renown
And sway th' affrighted world with your disguized frown.

82

This is the Genius of *Corvino* sage
And *Psittaco* falls little short in wit,
Though short he fall of old *Corvino's* age,
His steppings with the other footsteps fit.
And heavens bright eye it will aware of it,
But now me lists few passages to show
Amongst us foure when we together met
Occasion'd first by hardy *Psittaco*
Who *Corvin* did accost and nutshell *Graculo*.

83

Brethren ! said he, (and held by holy belt
Corvino grave, ne did his hands abhor't
When he the black silk rope soft fimbling felt
And with his fingers milked evermore
The hanging frienge) one thing perplexeth sore
My reason weak and puzled thoughts, said he.
Tell then, ye learned Clerks, which of these foure
To weet, from Scripture, Church authority,
Gods Spirit, or mans Reason is Faiths Certainty.

84

For, well I wot, our selves must fully assent
To points of Faith we rigidly obtrude
On others, else there is no punishment
Due to gainsayers. *Corvin* here indewd
With singular gravity this point pursu'd,
Saying that all belief is solv'd at last
Into the Church, ne may the people rude
Nor learned wit her honour dare to blast
Nor scrupulous thoughts, nor doubtfull queres out to
cast.

85

Strait *Graculo* with eyes as fierce as Ferrit
Reply'd : If all mens faith resolved be
Into each Church, all nations shall inherit
For ever their Ancestours Idolatry.
An Indian ever shall an Indian be
A Turk a Turk. To this *Corvin* anon ;
I give not this infallibility
To every Church, but onely to our own
Full witnesse to her self of all the truths she'll own.

86

Gr. That then is truth what she will say is true.
But not unlesse her the true Church thou hold.
How knowst thou then her such, good *Corvin* shew.
Friend *Graculo* in talk we be too bold.
Let's go, I fear my self and horse take cold.
But t' answer to that question, 'fore we go
The Church is true as she her self me told.
A goodly answer said Don *Graculo.*
You dispute in a Circle as all Logicians know.

87

Here *Psittaco* could not but inly smile
To see how *Graculo Corvin* did orecrow,
And fair replying with demeanance mild,
The truth, said he, the Scriptures onely show.
Streight nimble *Graculus ;* But who can know
The sense of Scripture without reason found ?
The Scripture is both key and treasure too
It opes it self (so said that Clerk profound)
This place with that compar'd. This is the strongest
ground.

88

Gr. But what with judgement doth them both compare ?
Is't reason or unreasonablenesse, I pray.
To which grave *Psittacus*, you so subtill are,
I list not with such cunning wits to play.
Here I stept in and thus began to say
Right worthy Clerks, for so you be I ween,
Your quaint discourse your breedings doth bewray,
Long time you have at learned Athens been
And all the dainty tricks of Art and Science seen.

89

If me a stranger wight it may beseem
But homely bred, as yet unripe in years,
Who conscious of his weaknesses doth deem
Himself unfit to speak among his peers,

Much more unfit for your judicious ears
Whom Age and Arts do equally adorn
And solemne habit no small semblance bears
Of highest knowledge, might I be but born
A word or two to speak, now would I take my turn.

90

Say on said *Psittaco.* There's a third, said I,
Nor reason nor unreasonablenesse hight.
Here *Graccus.* The disjunction you deny.
Then I, there is a third ycleep'd Gods spright
Nor reason nor unreasonablenesse hight.
Corvino straight foam'd like his champing jade
And said I was a very silly wight,
And how through melancholy I was mad
And unto private spirits all holy truth betray'd.

91

But I nould with like fury him invade
But mildly as I mought made this reply.
Gods Spirit is no private empty shade
But that great Ghost that fills both earth and sky,
And through the boundlesse Universe doth ly,
Shining through purged hearts and simple minds
When doubling clouds of thick hypocrisie
Be blown away with strongly brushing winds ;
Who first this tempest feels the Sun he after finds.

92

Thus wise and godly men I hear to teach,
And know no hurt this doctrine to believe.
Certes it much occasion doth reach
To leave the world and holily to live.
All due observance to Gods laws to give.
With care and diligence to maken pure
Those vessels that this heavenly dew receive.
But most in point of faith sleep too secure
And want this bait their souls to goodnesse to allure.

93

For they believen as the Church believes
Never expecting any other light,
And hence it is, each one so loosely lives,
Hopelesse of help from that internall spright.
Enough ! said *Graculo, Corvino's* right.
Let's hear, dispute in figure and in mood,
And stifly with smart syllogismes fight
That what thou wouldst may wel be understood,
But now thou rovest out, and rav'st as thou wert wood.

94

Reason I say all Scripture sense must judge
Do thou one reason 'gainst this truth produce :
Reason, said I, in humane things may drudge
But in divine thy soul it may seduce.
Gr. Prove that, *Mn.* I prove it thus. For reasons use
Back'd with advantage of all sciences,
Of Arts, of tongues, cannot such light transfuse
But that most learned men do think amisse
In highest points divided as well you know, I wisse.

95

Here *Graculo* learing up with one eye
View'd the broad Heavens long resting in a pause
And all the while he held his neck awry
Like listning daw, turning his nimble nose,
At last these words his silent tongue did loose.
What is this spirit, say what's this spirit, man !
Who has it, answer'd I, he onely knows.
'Tis the hid Manna and the graven stone.
He canteth, said *Corvino*, come *Grac*, let's be gone.

96

But *Grac* stayd still this question to move.
Doth not, said he, reason to us descry
What things soever reasonable prove?
Not so. For the whole world that ope doth lie
Unto our sight, not reason but our eye
Discovers first, but upon that fair view
Our reason takes occasion to trie
Her proper skill and curiously pursue
The Art and sweet contrivance Heauen and Earth do
    shew.

97

There's no man colour smels, or sees a sound,
Nor sucks the labour of the hony-bee
With's hungry lugs, nor binds a gaping wound
With's slippery ey-balls. Every faculty
And object have their due Analogy,
Nor can reach further than it's proper sphear.
Who divine sense by reason would descry
Unto the Sun-shine listens with his ear.
So plain this truth to me, *Don Graco*, doth appear.

98

How then, said *Graco*, is the spirit known
If not by reason : To this I replyde,
Onely the spirit can the spirit own.
But this, said he, is back again to slide
And in an idle Circle round to ride.
Why so, said I, Is not light seen by light?
Streight *Graculo* did skilfully divide
All knowledge into sense and reason right.
Be't so, said I, *Don Graco*, what's this reasons might.

99

If then, said he, the spirit may not be
Right reason, surely we must deem it sense.
Yes, sense it is, this was my short reply.
Sense upon which holy Intelligence
And heavenly Reason and comely Prudence
(O beauteous branches of that root divine !)
Do springen up, through inly experience
Of Gods hid wayes, as he doth ope the ey'n
Of our dark souls and in our hearts his light enshrine.

100

Here *Graculus* did seem exceeding glad
On any terms to hear but reason nam'd,
And with great joy and jollity he bad
Adew to me as if that he had gain'd

The victory. Besides *Corvino* blam'd
His too long stay. Wherefore he forward goes
Now more confirm'd his Nutshell-cap contain'd
What ever any living mortall knows.
Ne longer would he stay this sweet conceit to loose.

101

Thus *Psittaco* and I alone were left
In sober silence holding on our way.
His musing skull, poor man ! was well nigh cleft
By strong distracting thoughts drove either way ;
Whom pittying I thus began to say.
Dear *Psittaco* what anxious thoughts oppresse
Thy carefull heart and musing mind dismay?
I am perplexed much I must confesse
Said he, and thou art authour of my heavinesse.

102

My self *Corvino's* Church-Autority
No certain ground of holy truth do deem.
And Scripture the next ground alledg'd by me
By *Graco* was confuted well, I ween.
But thou as in these points farre deeper seen
Than either *Corvin* or *Don Graculo*
Yea than my self, assent doth almost win
That Church nor Scripture, cast in reason too
Can to our searching minds truth's hidden treasures show.

103

Wherefore a fourth, sole ground of certainty
Thou didst produce, to weet, the Spirit divine.
But now, alas ! here is the misery,
That left to doubt we cannot well enjoyn
Nor this nor that, nor Faith-forms freely coyn
And make the trembling conscience swear thereto,
For we our selves do but ghesse and divine
What we force other men to swear is true,
Untill the day-star rise our eyes with light t' embew.

104

Which gift though it be given to me and you,
Mn. (Not unto me, courteous *Don Psittaco !*)
Ps. Yet certainly there be but very few
That so sublime a pitch ascend unto.
Mn. My self, alas ! a silly Swain I know
So far from solving these hard knots, said I,
That more and harder my ranck brain o'regrow
And wonder that thy quick sagacity
Doth not winde out a further inconveniency.

105

If light divine we know by divine light
Nor can by any other means it see
This ties their hands from force that have the spirit.
How can, said *Psittaco*, these things agree ?
For without force vain is Church-Polity ;
Mn. But to use force 'gainst men that thing to do
In which they've not the least ability
May seem unjust and violent ; I trow,
'Gainst reason, 'gainst Religion, 'gainst all sence and law.

106

For 'tis as if the King of Arragon
Who was well skilled in Astronomy,
Should by decree deprive each Countrey Clown
Of life, of lands, or of sweet liberty
That would not fully avow each star in sky
Were bigger then the Earth. Here *Psittaco*
Though what I said did not well satisfie
His grave judicious self, yet he did know
Of whom this talk much 'plause would gain and kind-
  nesse too :

107

And straight gan say, Dear *Glaucis!* hadst thou been
At this discourse, how would thy joyous spright
Have danc'd along. For thou art or well seen
In these queint points, or dost at least delight
Exceeding much to hear them open'd right.
And, well I wot, on earth scarce can be found
So witty girl, so wily female wight
As this my *Glaucis*, over all renown'd ;
I mean for quicker parts, if not for judgment sound.

108

How fit an Auditour would she then prov'd
To thee, young *Mnemon ?* how had she admired
Thy sifting wit, thy speech and person lov'd,
Clove to that mouth with melting zeal all fired,
And hung upon those lips so highly inspired?
Mn. Certes she'd been a bold immodest wight
To come so near when not at all desired.
Ps. Alas I good *Mnemon* you mistake me quite
I meant no fond salutes, but what is just and right ;

109

Her due attention on thy wise discourse,
Though what thou deemst, and more then thou didst
  deem
May fit you too. For why? by Natures course
Like joyn with like : wherefore, right well I ween,
Mought I but make the match't would well beseem.
For your conspiring minds exactly agree
In points, which the wide world through wrath and teen
Rudely divide, I mean free Liberty.
Be't so, said I, yet may our grounds farre different be.

110

For might I but repeat without offence
What I have heard, ill symtomes men descry
In this thy *Glaucis*, though the nimble wench
So dexterously can pray and prophecy,
And lectures read of drad mortality,
Clasping her palms with fatall noise and shreeks,
Inculcating approching misery
To sad afflicted houses, when she strikes
With brushing strokes the glassic doors and entrance
  seeks.

111

Nor doth her solemne looks much like her Sire
Or native zeal which she did once derive
From thee grave *Psittaco !* exalt her higher
Then Earth and Nature : For men do conceive
Black sanguine fumes my spouse do thus deceive
Translating her into fools Paradise
And so of sense and reason her bereave,
And that that melting love which doth so please
Her gulled soul, the thawing is of her own grease.

112

The naturall spright it self doth sweetly hug
In false conceit and ill-deceiving guile,
Sucking fond solace from it's own dear dug,
Like the mistaken Cat that lick'd the file
And drawing bloud, uncessantly did toyl
To suck that sweet, as if there Moses rock
Had swet new milk. Thus *Glaucis* doth beguil
Her likorish taste, als' doth delude her flock,
Teaching them suck themselves, their empty souls to
  mock.

113

Thus they intoxicate with their own bloud
Mistaken Elves ! deem it no worse a thing
Then pure Ambrosian Nectar fresh and good,
In golden streams that from great Jove did spring :
And count themselves His onely choice Ofspring
Upon no count but that their count is so.
O sweet conceit ! full joy ! Soul-ravishing
Delight ! Pure faith ! Self-love keep close thereto.
Allow but this to us, we'll any thing allow.

114

Besides the fixednesse of th' eternall Fates
And Adamantine laws of Gods decree
Whereby immutably he loves and hates
May prove new grounds of *Glaucis* liberty.
No danger then nor detriment can be
To his own people whom of old he chose
From the out-goings of Eternity.
No infecting poyson may them ill dispose.
What worthlesse wit of man this puzling knot may loose.

115

Did not I tell thee what a wily lasse,
Said *Psittaco*, my daughter *Glaux* would prove ?
And well perceiving how averse I was
From her strange manners, left all suits of love,
And straight gan show me how she did improve
Her principles to lewdnesse and excesse :
Secure, no fault, no filth can ever move
Her Maker to dislike, no unrighteousnesse
Can hurt her soul, ne sorrow needs she to expresse.

116

Thus in the wicked wench rank fields do grow
Of Rapine, Riot, Lust, and Covetize,
Of Pride, of Sacriledge, and a thousand moe
Disorders, which no mortall can devise,

Said I, from ought, but that mistake t' arise
Of naked Faith disjoyn'd from Purity,
So with full bitter words he did chastise
His absent child ; but whether zeal it be,
Or deep conceived hatred, I no'te well descry.

117

Nor stopt he here, but told me all her guise
How law-lesse quite and out of shape she's grown
Affecting still wilde contrarieties,
Averse from what for good all others own.
Preposterous Girl ! how often hast thou thrown
Thy self into dark corners at Mid-day,
And then at dead of Night away art flown
To some old barn, thereon to preach and pray
Ending thy dark devotions just at Break of day.

118

When others sleep or weep, then dost thou sing
In frosty night on neighbours chimney set,
When others fast 'ginst thou thy revelling ;
Thy lustfull sparrows greedily dost eat,
Which thou by bloud and violence dost get.
When others eyes plainly can nothing see,
Then thy prodigious lamps by night unwet
And unblown-out, can read right readily
Withouten spectacles, the smallest prints that be.

119

If chance or free election ever brings
Thee to our Churches, then with hooting wild,
Thou causest uproars, and our holy things
Font, Table, Pulpit, they be all defil'd
With thy broad mutings and large squirtings vilde.
Mn. Phy ; *Psittaco !* hide such infirmities
From stranger wight : Who would his own dear child
Thus shamefully disgrace ? With mine own eyes
Have I thy *Glaucis* seen, and better things surmise.

120

Good sooth, methinks, she is not so defac'd
And all mishapen, and grown out of square,
But that my self most evidently trac'd
Thy comely feature in her visage bare.
Spare then thy self, if her thou wilt not spare,
Ill may it seem what thine own strength begot
With foul reproach and shame thus to besmear,
And through thy zeal thine owne great name to blot :
To two so worthy wights befall some better lot.

121

Thus in my youth, said *Mnemon*, did I use
With Reverend Ignorance to sport and toy,
Aud slily would obnoxius Age abuse ;
For I was a crank wit, a brisk young boy ;
But naturally abhorr'd hypocrisie,
And craft the upshot of experienc'd Age ;
And more then life I lov'd my liberty,
And much suspected all that would engage
My heart to their own sect, and free-born soul encage.

122

For I ev'n at those years was well aware
Of mans false friendship, and grown subtilty,
Which made me snuf the wind, drink the free aire
Like a young Colt upon the mountains high,
And turning tail my hunters all defie.
Ne took I any guide but th' innate light
Of my true Conscience, whose voice to deny,
Was the sole sting of my offended spright :
Thus God and Nature taught their rude Cosmopolite.

123

I mean not Natures harsh obdurate light,
The shamelesse eye-brows of the Serpent old,
That arm'd with custome will not stick to fight
With God and him affront with courage bold :
But that sweet temper we may oft behold
In virgin Youth as yet immaculate,
And unto drudging Policy unfold,
Who do without designe, now love, now hate
And freely give and take withouten price or rate.

124

Dear lads ! How do I love your harmelesse years
And melt in heart while I the Morning-shine
Do view of rising virtue which appears
In your sweet faces, and mild modest cyne.
Adore that God that doth himself enshrine
In your untainted breasts ; and give no eare
To wicked voice that may your souls encline
Unto false peace, or unto fruitlesse fear,
Least loosened from your selves Harpyes away you bear.

125

Abstain from censure, seek and you shall find,
Drink your own waters drawn from living well,
Mend in your selves what ill elsewhere you mind,
Deal so with men as you would have them deal,
Honour the Aged that it may go well
With you in Age : For I my self indeed
Have born much scorn for these pranks, I you tell,
By boyes oft bearded, which I deem the meed
Of my abusive youth.   But now I will proceed.

126

By this we came into a way that did
Divide it self into three parts ; the one
To *Leontopolis ;* that in the mid
Did lead straight forth out of wide *Beïron,*
That was the way that I mought take alone ;
The third way led unto *Onopolis,*
And thitherward *Don Psittaco* put on.
With both these towns *Alopecopolis*
Is in firm league, and golden *Myrmecopolis.*

127

For nothing they attempt without the aid
Of these two Cities.   They'll not wagen war,
Nor peace conclude nor permit any trade,
Nor make decrees, nor shake the civil jar,

Nor take up private wrongs, nor plead at bar,
Nor Temples consecrate, nor Mattins say ;
They nought begin divine or secular,
But they advisen with those Cities tway.
O potent Citizens that bear so great a sway !

128

No truth of justice in *Beïrah* lond :
No sincere faith void of slie subtility,
That alwayes seeks it self, is to be found ;
But law delusion and false Polity,
False Polity that into Tyrannie
Would quickly wend, did not stern Fear restrain
And keep in awe. Th' *Onites* Democracy
Is nought but a large hungry tyrant-train :
Oppression from the poore is an all-sweeping rain.

129

A sweeping torrent that beats down the corn,
And wasts the oxens labour, head-long throws
The tallest trees up by the root ytorn,
Its ranging force in all the land it shows ;
Woods rent from hence, its rowling rage bestows
In other places that were bare before,
With muddied arms of trees the earth it strows ;
The list'ning shepherd is amazed sore,
While it with swift descent so hideously doth rore.

130

Such is the out-rage of Democracie,
When fearlesse it doth rule in *Beïrah :*
And little better is false Monarchy,
When it in this same countrey bears the sway.
(Is't not a part of *Autæsthesia* ?)
So to an inward sucking whirlpools close
They change this swelling torrents surquedry,
Much treasure it draws in, and doth inclose
In 'ts winding mouth, but whither then, there's no man
  knows.

131

O falsest *Beironites*, what gars you plain
One of another, and vainly accuse,
Of foul offence ? when you all entertain
Tyrannick thoughts. You all alike do muse
Of your own private good, though with abuse
Of those you can tread down with safety,
No way to wealth or honour you refuse.
False *Onople* doth grudge, and grone, and cry,
Because she is denied a greater tyranny.

132

Two of that City whylom on the way,
With languid lugs, and count'nance gravely sad,
Did deeply sigh, and rudely rough did bray
'Gainst *Leontopolis.* The equall pad
Of justice now, alas ! is seldome trad,
Said they ; The Lions might is law and right.
Where's love or mercy now ? with that out strad
A little dog, his dames onely delight,
And ran near to their tails, and bark'd with all his might.

133

The surly irefull *Onopolitan*
Without all mercy kickt with yron heel
The little bawling curre, that at him ran ;
It made his feeble corse to th' earth to reel,
That was so pierc'd with the imprinted steel,
That it might grieve a heart of flinty stone.
No herbs, no salves the breach could ever heal ;
The good old wife did then keep house alone,
False hearted carles, is this your great compassion ?

134

There's no society in *Behirah*
But beastlike grazing in one pasture ground.
No love but of the animated clay
With beauties fading flowers trimly crown'd,
Or from strong sympathies heart-striking stound,
No order but what riches strength and wit
Prescribe. So bad the good eas'ly confound.
Is Honesty in such unruly fit
That it's held in no rank ? they 'steem it not awhit.

135

But I am weary of this uncouth place ;
If any man their bad condition
And brutish manners listeth for to trace ;
We may them read in the creation
Of this wide Sensible ; where every passion
Of birds and beasts distinctly do display
To but an ord'nary imagination,
The life and soul of them in *Behirah :*
This *Behirah* that hight the greater *Adamah.*

136

The swelling hatefull Toad, industrious Ant,
Lascivious Goat, Parrot, or prating Py,
The kingly Lion, docil Elephant,
All-imitating Ape, gay Butterfly,
The crafty Fox famous for subtilty,
Majestick Horse, the beast that twixt two trees
(A fit resemblance of foul gluttonny)
When he hath fil'd his gorge, himself doth squeeze
To feed afresh, Court Spaniels, and politick Bees ;

137

With many more which I list not repeat ;
Some foul, some fair : to th' fair the name they give
Of holy virtues ; but 'tis but deceit,
None in *Beiron* virtuously do live ;
None in that land so much as ever strive
For truth of virtue, though sometimes they wont,
As Swine do Swine, their own blood to relieve.
Beiron's all bruits, the true manhood they want,
If outward form you pierce with phansic fulminant.

138

So having got experience enough
Of this ill land, for nothing there was new,
My purpose I held on, and rode quite through
That middle way, and did th' extremes eschew.

When I came near the end there was in view
No passage : for the wall was very high,
But there no doore to me it self did shew :
Looking about at length I did espy
A lively youth, to whom I presently gan cry.

139

More willing he's to come then I to call :
Simon he hight, who also's cal'd a Rock :
Simon is that obedientiall
Nature, who boysterous seas and winds doth mock ;
No tempest can him move with fiercest shock ;
The house that's thereon built doth surely stand :
Nor blustring storm, nor rapid torrents stroke
Can make it fall ; it easily doth withstand
The gates of Death and Hell, and all the Stygian band.

140

When I gan call, forthwith in seemly sort
He me approch'd in decent russet clad,
More fit for labour then the flaunting Court.
When he came near, in chearfull wise he bad
Tell what I would : then I unto the lad
Gan thus reply ; alas! too long astray
Here have I trampled foul *Behirons* pad :
Out of this land I thought this the next way,
But I no gate can find, so vain is mine assay.

141

Then the wise youth, Good Sir, you look too high :
The wall aloft is rais'd ; but that same doore
Where you must passe in deep descent doth lie :
But he bad follow, he would go before.
Hard by there was a place, all covered o're
With stinging nettles and such weedery,
The pricking thistles the hard'st legs would gore,
Under the wall a straight doore we descry :
The wall hight *Self-conceit ;* the doore *Humility.*

142

When we came at the doore fast lockt it was,
And *Simon* had the key, but he nould grant
That I into that other land should passe,
Without I made him my Concomitant.
It pleas'd me well, I mus'd not much upon't,
But straight accord : for why? a jolly Swain
Methought he was ; meek, chearfull, and pleasant.
When he saw this, he thus to me again,
Sir, See you that sad couple ? Then I ; I see those
    twain.

143

A sorry couple certainly they be.
The man a bloudy knife holds at his heart
With chearlesse countenance, as sad is she.
Or eld, or else intolerable smart,
Which she can not decline by any Art,
Doth thus distort and writh her wrinkled face ;

A leaden Quadrate swayes hard on that part
That's fit for burdens ; foulnesse doth deface
Her aged looks ; with a strait staff her steps she stayes.

144

Right well you say, then said that lusty Swain :
Yet this poore couple be my Parents dear ;
Nor can I hence depart without these twain :
These twain give life to me, though void of chear
They be themselves.   Then let's all go yfere.
The young mans speech caus'd sad perplexity
Within my brest, but yet I did forbear,
And fairly ask'd their names.   He answered me :
He *Autaparnes* hight ; but she *Hypomone.*

145

I *Simon* am the son of this sad pair,
Who though full harsh they seem to outward sight ;
Yet when to *Dizoie* men forth do fare,
No company in all the land so meet
They find as these.   Their pace full well I weet,
Is very slow, and so to youthfull haste
Displeasing, and their counsels nothing sweet
To any *Beironite ;* but sweetest taste
Doth bitter choler breed, and haste doth maken waste.

146

Nor let that breast impierc'd with weeping wound,
An uncouth spectacle, disturb your mind.
His blood's my food : If he his life effund
To utmost death, the high God hath design'd
That we both live.   He in my heart shall find
A seat for his transfused soul to dwell ;
And when that's done, this death doth eke unbind
That heavie weight that doth *Hypom'ne* quell,
Then I *Anantæsthetus* hight, which seems me well.

147

So both their lives do vanish into mine.
And mine into *Atuvus* life doth melt,
Which fading flux of time doth not define,
Nor is by any *Autæsthesian* felt.
This life to On the good *Atvvus* delt ;
In it's all Joy, Truth, Knowledge, Love and Force ;
Such force no weight created can repel't.
All strength and livelyhood is from this sourse,
All Lives to this first spring have circular recourse.

148

A lecture strange he seem'd to read to me ;
And though I did not rightly understand
His menning, yet I deemed it to be
Some goodly thing, and weary of that land
Where then I stood, I did not him withstand
In his request, although full loth I were
Slow-footed eld the journey should command ;
Yet we were guided by that sorry pair,
And so to *Dizoie* full softly we do fare.

The *Argument* of

P S Y C H O Z O I A,
Or,

The life of the Soul.

Strange state of Dizoie Mnemons skill
Here wisely doth explain,
Ida's strong charms, and Eloim-hill,
With the drad dale of Ain.

1

Ut now new Stories I 'gin to relate,
  Which agèd *Mnemon* unto us did tell,
  Whiles we on grassie bed did lie prostrate
  Under a shady Beach, which did repell
The fiery scorching shafts which *Uriel*
From Southern quarter darted with strong hand.
No other help we had ; for *Gabriel*
His wholesome cooling blasts then quite restrain'd :
The Lions flaming breath with heat parch'd all the Land.

2

Here seemly sitting down, thus gan that Sage,
Last time we were together here ymet,
Beïrah wall, that was the utmost stage
Of our discourse, if I do not forget.
When we departed thence the Sun was set,
Yet nathelesse we past that lofty wall
That very Evening.   The Nights nimble net
That doth encompasse every opake ball,
That swim's in liquid aire, did *Simon* nought apall.

3

When we that stately wall had undercrept,
We straightway found our selves in *Dizoie :*
The melting clouds chill drizzeling teares then wept ;
The mistie aire swet for deep agony,
Swet a cold sweat, and loose frigiditie
Fill'd all with a white smoke ; pale *Cynthia*
Did foul her silver limbs with filthy die,
Whiles wading on she measured out her way,
And cut the muddy heavens defil'd with whitish clay.

4

No light to guide but the Moons pallid ray,
And that even lost in mistie troubled aire :
No tract to take, there was no beaten way ;
No chearing strength, but that which might appear
From *Dians* face ; her face then shin'd not clear,
And when it shineth clearest, little might
She yieldeth, yet the goddesse is severe.
Hence wrathfull dogs do bark at her dead light :
Christ help the man thus clos'd and prison'd in drad
    Night.

5

O'rewhelm'd with irksome toyl of strange annoyes
In stony stound like senselesse stake I stood,
Till the vast thumps of massie hammers noise,
That on the groning steel laid on such lode,
Empierc'd mine ears in that sad stupid mood.
I weening then some harbour to be nigh,
In sory pace thitherward slowly yode,
By eare directed more then by mine eye,
But here, alas ! I found small hospitality.

6

Foure grisly Black-smiths stoutly did their task
Upon an anvile form'd in Conick wise.
They neither minded who, nor what I ask,
But with stern grimy look do still avise
Upon their works ; but I my first emprise
Would not forsake, and therefore venture in.
Or none hath list to speak, or none espies,
Or hears ; the heavy hammers never blin ;
And but a blue faint light in this black shop did shine.

7

There I into a darksome corner creep,
And lay my weary limbs on dusty flore,
Expecting still when soft down-sliding sleep
Should seize mine eyes, and strength to me restore

E

But when with hovering wings she 'proch'd, e'remore
The mighty souses those foul knaves laid on,
And those huge bellows that aloud did rore,
Chac'd her away that she was ever gone
Before she came, on pitchy plumes, for fear yflone.

8

The first of those rude rascals *Lypon* hight,
A foul great stooping slouch with heavie eyes,
And hanging lip : the second ugly sight
Pale *Phobon*, with his hedghog-hairs disguise.
Aelpon is the third, he the false skies
No longer trusts ; The fourth of furious fashion
Phrenition hight, fraught with impatiencies,
The bellows be ycleep'd deep *Suspiration :*
Each knave these bellows blow in mutual circulation.

9

There is a number of these lonesome forges
In *Bacha* vale (this was in *Bacha* vale)
There be no Innes but these, and these but scourges ;
In stead of ease they work much deadly bale
To those that in this lowly trench do trale
Their feeble loins. Ah me ! who here would fare ?
Sad ghosts oft crosse the way with visage pale,
Sharp thorns and thistles wound their feeten bare :
Yet happy is the man that here doth bear a share.

10

When I in this sad vale no little time
Had measurèd, and oft had taken Inne,
And by long penance paid for mine ill crime ;
Methought the Sunne it self began to shine,
And that I'd past *Diana's* discipline.
But day was not yet come, 'twas perfect night :
I *Phœbus* head from *Ida* hill had seen ;
For *Ida* hill doth give to men the sight,
Of *Phœbus* form, before *Aurora's* silver light.

11

But *Phœbus* form from that high hill's not clear
Nor figure perfect. It's invelopèd
In purple cloudy veil ; and if't appear
In rounder shape with skouling dreryhed,
A glowing face it shows, ne rayes doth shed
Of lights serenity, yet duller eyes
With gazing on this irefull sight be fed
Best to their pleasing ; small things they will prise
That never better saw, nor better can devise.

12

On *Ida* hill there stands a Castle strong,
They that it built call it *Pantheothen.*
(Hither resort a rascall rabble throng
Of miscreant wights ;) but if that wiser men
May name that Fort, *Pandœmoniothen*
They would it cleep. It is the strong'st delusion
That ever *Dæmon* wrought ; the safest pen
That e're held silly sheep for their confusion :
Ill life and want of love, hence springs each false con-
clusion.

13

That rabble rout that in this Castle won,
Is irefull-ignorance, Unseemly zeal,
Strong-self-conceit, Rotten-religion,
Contentious-reproch-'gainst-Michael-
If-he-of-*Moses*-body-ought-reveal-
Which-their-dull-skonses cannot-eas'ly-reach,
Love-of-the-carkas, An Inept appeal-
T' uncertain papyrs, a-False-formall-fetch-
Of-feignèd-sighs, Contempt-of-poore-and-sinfull-wretch.

14

A deep self-love, Want of true sympathy-
With all mankind, Th' admiring their own heard,
Fond pride, a sanctimonious cruelty
'Gainst those by whom their wrathfull minds be stird
By strangling reason, and are so afeard
To lose their credit with the vulgar sort ;
Opinion and long speech 'fore life preferr'd,
Lesse reverence of God then of the Court,
Fear, and despair, Evill surmises, False report.

15

Oppression-of-the-poore, Fell-rigourousnesse,
Contempt-of-Government, Fiercenesse, Fleshly lust,
The-measuring-of-all-true righteousnesse
By-their own-modell, Cleaving unto-dust,
Rash-censure, and despising-of the just-
That-are-not-of-their-sect, False-reasoning-
Concerning-God, Vain-hope, needlesse mistrust,
Strutting-in knowledge, Egre slavering-
After hid-skill, with every inward uncouth thing.

16

These and such like be that rude Regiment,
That from the glittering sword of *Michael* fly :
They fly his outstrech'd arm, else were they shent
If they unto this Castle did not hie,
Strongly within its walls to fortifie
Themselves : Great *Dæmon* hath no stronger hold
Then this high Tower. When the good Majesty
Shines forth in love and light, a vapour cold
And a black hellish smoke from hence doth all infold.

17

And all that love and light and offer'd might
Is thus chok'd up in that foul Stygian steem :
If Hells dark Jawes should open in despight,
And breath its inmost breath, which foul'st I deem ;
Yet this more deadly foul I do esteem,
And more contagious, which this charmèd tower
Ever spues forth, like that fell Dragons steem
Which he from poyson'd mouth in rage did poure
At her, whose first-born child his chaps might not
devour.

18

But lest the rasher wit my Muse should blame,
As if she did those faults appropriate
(Which I even now in that black list did name)
Unto *Panthcothen ;* The self same state

I dare avouch you'll find, where ever Hate
Back'd with rough zeal, and bold for want of skill,
All sects besides its own doth execrate.
This peevish spright with wo the world doth fill,
While each man all would bind to his fierce furious will.

19

O Hate! the fulsome daughter of fell Pride,
Sister to surly Superstition,
That clear out-shining Truth cannot abide,
That loves it self and large Dominion,
And in false show of a fair Union
Would all encroch to 't self, would purchase all
At a cheap rate, for slight Opinion.
Thus cram they their wide-gaping Crumenall :
But now to *Ida* hill me lists my feet recall.

20

No such enchantment in all *Dizoie*   .
As on this hill ; nor sadder sight was seen
Then you may in this rufull place espy.
'Twixt two huge walls on solitary Green,
Of funerall Cypresse many groves there been,
And eke of Ewe, Eben, and Poppy trees :
And in their gloomy shade foul grisly fiend
Use to resort, and busily to seize
The darker phansièd souls that live in ill disease.

21

Hence you may see, if that you dare to mind,
Upon the side of this accursèd hil,
Many a dreadfull corse ytost in wind,
Which with hard halter their loathd life did spill.
There lives another which himself did kill
With rusty knife, all roll'd in his own blood,
And ever and anon a dolefull knill
Comes from the fatall Owl, that in sad mood
With drery sound doth pierce through the death-
  shadowed wood.

22

Who can expresse with pen the irksome state
Of those that be in this strong Castle thrall ?
Yet hard it is this Fort to ruinate,
It is so strongly fenc'd with double wall.
The fiercest but of Ram no'te make them fall :
The first *Inevitable Destiny*
Of Gods Decree ; the other they do call
Invincible fleshie Infirmitie :
But Keeper of the Tower's *unfelt Hypocrisie.*

23

What Poets phancies fain'd to be in Hell
Are truly here, A Vulture *Tytius* heart
Still gnaws, yet death doth never *Tityus* quell !
Sad *Sisyphus* a stone with toylsome smart
Doth roul up hill, but it transcends his art,
To get it to the top, where it may lye,
On steddy Plain, and never backward start :
His course is stopt by strong Infirmity,
His roul comes to this wall, but then back it doth fly.

24

Here fifty Sisters in a sieve do draw
Thorough-siping water : *Tantalus* is here,
Who though the glory of the Lord ore-flow
The earth, and doth incompasse him so near,
Yet waters, he in waters doth requere.
Stoop *Tantalus* and take those waters in !
What strength of witchcraft thus blinds all yfere
Twixt these two massie walls, this hold of sinne ?
Aye me ! who shall this Fort so strongly fencèd win !

25

I hear the clattering of an armèd troup,
My ears do ring with the strong prancers heels.
(My soul get up out of thy drowsie droop,
And look unto the everlasting Hills)
The hollow ground, ah ! how my sense it fills
With sound of solid horses hoofs.   A wonder
It is, to think how cold my spirit thrills,
With strange amaze. Who can this strength dis-
  sunder ?
Hark how the warlike Steeds do neigh, their necks do
  thunder.

26

All Milkwhite Steeds in trappings goodly gay,
On which in golden letters be ywrit
These words (even he that runs it readen may)
True righteousnesse unto the Lord of might.
O comely spectacle ! O glorious sight !
'Twould easily ravish the beholders eye
To see such beasts, so fair so full of spright,
All in due ranks to prance so gallantly,
Bearing their riders arm'd with perfect panoply.

27

In perfect silver glistring panoply
They ride, the army of the highest God.
Ten thousands of his Saints approchen nie,
To judge the world, and rule it with his rod.
They leave all plain whereever they have trod.
Each rider on his shield doth bear the Sun
With golden shining beams dispread abroad,
The Sun of righteousnesse at high-day noon,
By this same strength, I ween, this Fort is easily wonne.

28

They that but hear thereof shall straight obey ;
But the strange children shall false semblance make,
But all hypocrisie shall soon decay,
All wickednesse into that deadly lake,
All darknesse thither shall it self betake.
That false brood shall in their close places fade.
The glory of the Lord shall ne're forsake
The earth again, nor shall deaths dreadfull shade
Return againe. Him praise that this great day hath
  made.

29

This is the mighty warlick *Michaels* host,
That easily shall wade through that foul spue
Which the false Dragon casts in every coast,
That the moon-trampling woman much doth rue
His deadly spaul ; but no hurt doth accrew
To this strong army from this filthy steam.
Nor horse nor man doth fear its lurid hew.
They safely both can swim in this foul stream ;
This stream the earth sups up cleft ope by Michaels
     beam.

30

But whiles it beareth sway, this poysons might
Is to make sterill or prolong the birth,
To cause cold palsies, and to dull the sight
By sleepy sloth ; the melancholic earth
It doth increase, that hinders all good mirth.
Yet this dead liquor dull *Pantheothen*
Before the nectar of the Gods preferr'th.
But it so weakens and disables men,
That they of manhood give no goodly specimen.

31

Here one of us began to interpeal
Old *Mnemon, Tharrhon* that young ladkin hight,
He prayed this agèd Sire for to reveal
What way this Dragons poysonous despight,
And strong *Pantheothens* inwalling might,
We may escape. Then *Mnemon* thus gan say ;
Some strange devise, I know, each youthfull wight
Would here expect, or lofty brave assay :
But I'll the simple truth, in simple wise convey.

32

Good Conscience, kept with all the strength and might
That God already unto us hath given ;
A presse pursuit of that foregoing light
That egs us on 'cording to what we have liven,
And helps us on 'cording to what we have striven,
To shaken off the bonds of prejudice,
Nor dote too much of that we have first conceiven ;
By hearty prayer to beg the sweet delice
Of Gods all-loving spright : such things I you advise.

33

Can pity move the hearts of parents dear,
When that their haplesse child in heavie plight
Doth grieve and moan ! whiles pinching tortures tear
His fainting life, and doth not that sad sight
Of Gods own Sonne empassion his good spright
With deeper sorrow? The tender babe lies torn
In us by cruell wounds from hostile might :
Is Gods own life of God himself forlorn ?
Or was he to continuall pain of God yborn ?

34

Or will you say if this be Gods own Sonne,
Let him descend the Crosse : for well we ween
That he'll not suffer him to be fordonne
By wicked hand, if Gods own Sonne he been.

But you have not those sacred mysteries seen,
True-crucifying Jews ! The weaker thing
Is held in great contempt in worldly eyen :
But time may come when deep implerced sting
Shall prick your heart, and it shall melt with sorrowing.

35

Then you shall view him whom with cruell spear
You had transfix'd, true crucified Sonne
Of the true God, unto his Father dear,
And dear to you, nought dearer under Sun :
Through this strong love and deep compassion,
How vastly God his Kingdome would enlarge
You'll easily see, and how with strong iron
He'll quite subdue the utmost earthly verge.
O foolish men ! the heavens why do you fondly charge ?

36

Subtimidus, when *Tharrhon* sped so well,
Took courage to himself, and thus gan say
To *Mnemon ;* Pray you Sir vouchsafe to tell
What *Autaparnes* and *Hypomone*
And *Simon* do this while in *Dizoie.*
With that his face shone like the rosie Morn
With maiden blush from inward modesty,
Which wicked wights do holden in such scorn :
Sweet harmlesse Modesty a rose withouten thorn !

37

Old *Mnemon* lov'd the Lad even from his face,
Which blamelesse blush with sanguin light had dyed ;
His harmlesse lucid spright with flouring grace
His outward form so seemly beautified.
So the old man him highly magnified
For his so fit inquiry of those three ;
And to his question thus anon replyed,
There's small recourse (till that Fort passèd be)
To *Simon Autaparnes* or *Hypomone.*

38

For all that space from *Behirons* high wall
Unto *Pantheothen,* none dares arise
From his base dunghill warmth ; such Magicall
Attraction his flagging soul down ties
To his foul flesh : 'mongst which, alas ! there lyes
A little spark of Gods vitality,
But smoreing filth so close it doth comprize
That it cannot flame out nor get on high :
This Province hence is hight earth-groveling *Aptery.*

39

But yet fair semblances these *Apterites*
Do make of good, and sighen very sore,
That God no stronger is : False hypocrites !
You make no use of that great plenteous store
Of Gods good strength which he doth on you pour.
But you fast friends of foul carnality,
And false to God, his tender sonne do gore,
And plaud your selves, if't be not mortally
Nor let you him live in ease, nor let you him fairly dy.

40

Like faithlesse wife that by her frampared guize,
Peevish demeanour, sullen sad disdain,
Doth inly deep the spright melancholize
Of her aggrieved husband, and long pain
At last to some sharp sicknesse doth constrain
His weakned nature to yield victory;
His scorching torture then counts death a gain.
But when Death comes, in womanish phrensie
That froward femall wretch doth shreek and loudly cry.

41

So through her moody importunity
From downright death she rescues the poore man :
Self favouring sense ; not that due loyaltie
Doth wring from her this false compassion,
Compassion that no cruelty can
Well equalize. Her husband lies agast ;
Death on his horrid face so pale and wan
Doth creep with ashy wings. He thus embrac'd
Perforce too many dayes in deadly wo doth wast.

42

This is the love that's found in *Aptery*
To Gods dear life. If they his Son present
Half live, half dead, handled despightfully,
Or sunk in sicknesse, or with deep wound rent,
So be he's not quite dead they'r well content,
And hope sure favour of his Sire to have.
They have the signes how can they then be shent ?
The God of love for his dear life us save
From such conceits, which men to sin do us inslave.

43

But when from *Aptery* we were ygone,
And past *Pantheothens* inthralling power ;
Then from the East chearfull *Eous* shone,
And drave away the Nights dead lumpish stour :
He took by th' hand Aurora's vernall hour ;
These freshly tripp'd it on the silver hills,
And thorow all the fields sweet life did shower :
Then gan the joyfull birds to try their skills ;
They skipt, they chirpt amain, they pip'd, they danc'd
    their fills.

44

This other Province of *Dizoia*
Hight *Pteroessa*. On the flowry side
Of a green bank, as I went on my way
Strong youthfull *Gabriel* I there espide,
Courting a Nymph all in her maiden pride,
Not for himself : His strife was her to win
To *Michael*, in wedlock to be tide :
He promised she should be *Michaels* Queen,
And greater things then eare hath heard, or eye hath seen :

45

This lovely Maid to *Gabriel* thus replide,
Thanks, Sir, for your good news ; but may I know
Who *Michael* is, that would have me his Bride ?
Its *Michael*, said he, that works such woe

To all that fry of Hell ; and on his foe
Those fiends of darknesse such great triumphs hath :
The powers of sin and death he down doth mow.
In this strong Arm of God have thou but faith,
That in great *Dæmons* troups doth work so wondrous
    scath.

46

The simple Girl believed every word,
Nor did by subtile querks elude the might
And proferr'd strength of the soul-loving Lord ;
But answered thus. Good Sir, but reade aright
When shall I then appear in *Michaels* sight ?
When *Gabriel* had won her full assent,
And well observ'd how he had flam'd her spright,
He answered, After the complishment
Of his behests, and so her told what hests he ment.

47

She willingly took the condition,
And pliable she promised to be ;
And *Gabriel* sware he would wait upon
Her Virginship, whiles in simplicity
His masters will with all good industry
She would fullfill. So here the simple Maid
Strove for her self in all fidelity,
Nor took her self for nothing ; but she plaid
Her part, she thought, as if Indentures had been made.

48

For she did not with her own self gin think
So curiously, that it is God alone
That gives both strengths when ever we do swink :
Graces and Natures might be both from one,
Who is our lifes strong sustentation.
Impossible it is therefore to merit,
When we poore men have nothing of our own :
Certes by him alone she stands upright ;
And surely falls without his help in per'lous fight :

49

But we went on in *Pteroessa* lond :
The fresh bright Morning was no small repast
After the toil in *Aptery* we found,
So that with merry chear we went full fast :
But I observed well that in this haste
Simon wax'd faint, and feeble, and decay'd
In strength and life before we far had past :
And by how much his youthfull flower did fade,
So much more vigour to his parents was repai'd.

50

For that old crumpled wight gan go upstraight,
And *Autaparnes* face recovered blood !
But *Simon* looked pale withouten might,
Withouten chear, or joy, or livelyhood :
Cause of all this at last I understood.
For *Autaparn* that knife had from him cast,
And almost clos'd the passage of that flood.
That flood, that blood, was that which *Simons* taste
Alone could fit ; if that were gone the lad did waste.

51

And his old mother, call'd *Hypomone*,
Did ease her back from that down-swaying weight,
That leaden Quadrate, which did miserably
Annoy her crasie corse ; but that more light
She might fare on, she in her husbands sight
Threw down her load, where he threw down his blade,
And from that time began the pitious plight
Of sickly *Simon :* so we them perswade
Back to retreat, and do their dying son some aid.

52

Though loth, yet at the length they do assent :
So we return unto the place where lay
The heavy Quadrate, and that instrument
Of bleeding smart. It would a man dismay
To think how that square lead her back did sway ;
And how the half-clos'd wound was open tore
With that sharp-pointed knife : and sooth to say
Simon himself was inly grievèd sore,
Seeing the deadly smart that his dear parents bore.

53

So we remeasure the way we had gone,
Still fareing on towards *Theoprepy.*
Great strength and comfort 'twas to think upon
Our good escape from listlesse *Aptery*,
And from the thraldome of *Infirmity.*
Now nought perplex'd our stronger plumèd spright,
But what may be the blamelesse verity :
Oft we conceiv'd things were transacted right :
And oft we found our selves guld with strong passions might.

54

But now more feeble farre we find their force
Then erst it was, when as in *Aptery*
To strong *Pantheothen* they had recourse :
For then a plain impossibility
It was to overcome their cruelty.
But here encouragèd by *Gabriel*
We strongly trust to have the victory.
And if by chance they do our forces quell ;
It's not by strength of armes, but by some misty spell.

55

So bravely we went on withouten dread,
Till at the last we came whereas a hill
With steep ascent highly lift up his head :
To th' agèd hoof it worken would much ill
To climb this cliff ; with weary ach 't would fill
His drier bones. But yet it's smoooth and plain
Upon the top. It passeth farre my skill
The springs, the bowers, the walks, the goodly train
Of faire chaste Nymphs that haunt that place, for to explain.

56

I saw three sisters there in seemly wise
Together walking on the flowry Green,
Yclad in snowy stoles of fair agguize.
The glistring streams of silver waving shine,
Skilfully interwove with silken line,
So variously did play in that fair vest,
That much it did delight my wondring eyne :
Their face with Love and Vigour was ydrest,
With Modesty and Joy ; their tongue with just behest :

57

Their locks hung loose, A triple coronet
Of flaming gold and star-like twinkling stone
Of highest price, was on their temples set :
The Amethist, the radiant Diamond,
The Jasper, enemy to spirits won,
With many other glorious for to see.
These three enameld rimmes of that fair Crown
Be these : the first hight *Dicæosyne*,
Philosophy the next, the last stiff *Apathy.*

58

I gaz'd and mus'd and was well nigh distraught
With admiration of those three maids,
And could no further get, ne further saught ;
Down on the hill my weary limbs I laid,
And fed my feeble eyes, which me betray'd
Unto Loves bondage. *Simon* lik'd it not
To see me so bewitch'd, and thus assay'd
By wisest speech to loose this Magick knot ;
Great pity things so fair should have so foul a spot :

59

What spot, said I, can in these fair be found ?
Both spot in those white vests, and eke a flaw
In those bright gems wherewith these Maids be crown'd,
If you'll but lift to see, I'll eas'ly show.
Then I, both Love of man and holy law
Exactly's kept upon this sacred hill ;
True fortitude that truest foes doth awe,
Justice and Abstinence from sweetest ill,
And Wisedome like the Sun doth all with light o're spill,

60

Thanks be to God we are so well arriv'd
To the long-sought for land, *Theoprepy.*
Nay soft good Sir, said *Simon*, you'r deceiv'd,
You are not yet past through *Autæsthesy :*
With that the spot and flaw he bad me see
Which he descry'd in that goodly array.
The spot and flaw self-sens'd *Autopathy*
Was hight, the eldest Nymph *Pythagorissa*,
Next *Platonissa* hight ; the last hight *Stoicissa.*

61

But this high Mount where these three sisters wonne,
Said *Simon*, cleepèd is, *Har-Eloim.*
To these it's said, Do worship to my Sonne :
It's right, that all the Gods do worship him,
There's none exempt : those that the highest climbe
Are but his Ministers, their turns they take

To serve as well as those of lower slime.
What so is not of Christ but doth partake
Of th' *Autæsthesian* soil, is life *Dæmoniake.*

62

His words did strangely work upon my spright,
And wean'd my mind from that I dearly lov'd ;
So I nould dwell on this so pleasing sight,
But down descended, as it me behov'd,
And as my trusty guide me friendly mov'd.
So when we down had come, and thence did passe
On the low plain, *Simon* more clearly prov'd,
That though much beauty there and goodnesse was,
Yet that in *Theoprepia* did farre surpasse.

63

So forward on we fare, and leave that hill,
And presse still further, the further we go,
Simon more strength, more life and godly will,
More vigour he and livelyhood did show ;
But *Autaparnes* wox more wan and wo :
He faints, he sinks, ready to give up ghost,
And ag'd *Hypom'ne* trod with footing slow,
And stagger'd with her load ; so ill dispos'd
Their fading spirits were, that life was well nigh lost.

64

By this, in sight of that black wall we came,
A wall by stone-artificer not made :
For it is nought but smoke from duskish flame,
Which in that low deep valleys pitchy shade
Doth fiercely th' *Autopathian* life invade,
With glowing heat, and eateth out that spot.
This dreadfull triall many hath dismaid ;
When *Autaparnes* saw this was his lot,
Fear did his sense benum, he wox like earthly clot.

65

In solem silence this vapour rose
From this drad Dale, and hid the Eastern sky
With its deep darknesse, and the Evening-close
Forestall'd with Stygian obscurity ;
Yet was't not thick, nor thin, nor moist, nor dry ;
Nor stank it ill, nor yet gave fragrant smell,
Nor did't take in through pellucidity
The penetrating light, nor did't repell
Through grosse opacity the beams of *Michael.*

66

Yet terrible it is to *Psyche's* brood,
That still retain the life *Dæmoniake ;*
Constraining fear calls in their vitall flood,
When the drad Magus once doth mention make
Of the deep dark Abysse ; for fear they quake
At that strong-awing word : But they that die
Unto self-feeling life, naught shall them shake ;
Base fear proceeds from weak *Autopathy.*
This dale hight *Ain*, the fumes hight *Anautæsthesy.*

67

Into this dismall Dale we all descend,
Here *Autaparnes* and *Hypomone*
Their languid life with that dark vapour blend.
Thus perishèd fading vitality,
But nought did fade of Lifes reality.
When these two old ones their last gasp had fet,
In this drad valley their dead corps did lie ;
But what could well be sav'd to *Simon* flet.
Here *Simon* first became spotlesse *Anautæsthet.*

68

When we had waded quite through this deep shade,
We then appear'd in bright *Theoprepy :*
Here Phœbus ray in straightest line was laid,
That erst lay broke in grosse consistency
Of cloudy substance. For strong sympathy
Of the divided natures Magick band
Was burnt to dust in *Anautæsthesie :*
Now there's no fear of Death's dart-holding hand :
Fast love, fix'd life, firm peace in *Theoprepia* land.

69

When *Mnemon* hither came, he leanèd back :
Upon his seat, and a long time respired.
When I perceiv'd this holy Sage so slack
To speak (well as I might) I him desired
Still to hold on, if so he were not tired ;
And tell what fell in blest *Theoprepy ;*
But he nould do the thing that I required :
Too hard it is, said he, that kingdomes glee
To show ; who list to know himself must come and see.

70

This story under the cool shadowing Beach
Old *Mnemon* told of famous *Dizoie :*
To set down all he said passeth my reach,
That all would reach even to infinity.
Strange things he spake of the biformity
Of the *Dizoians ;* What mongrill sort
Of living wights ; how monstrous shap'd they be,
And how that man and beast in one consort ;
Goats britch, mans tongue, goose head, with monki's
    mouth distort.

71

Of *Centaures, Cynocephals,* walking trees,
Tritons, and *Mermayds,* and such uncouth things ;
Of weeping Serpents with fair womans eyes,
Mad-making waters, sex-transforming springs ;
Of foul *Circean* swine with golden rings,
With many such like falshoods ; but the streight
Will easily judge all crooked wanderings.
Suffice it then we have taught that ruling Right,
The Good is uniform, the Evil infinite.

PSYCHATHANASIA

OR

The fecond part of the Song

of the

SOUL,

Treating

Of the Immortality of Souls, efpecially

MANS SOUL.

By *H. M.* Mafter of Arts, and Fellow of Chrifts
Colledge in *Cambridge.*

Φύσις οὐδενός ἐστιν
Ἀλλὰ μόνον μίξις τε διάλλαξις τε μιγέντων,
Empcdoclcs.

Omnia mutantur, nihil interit,
Ovid.

Πᾶν ἄρα ζῶον ἀθάνατον· πάντων δε μᾶλλον ὁ ἄνθρωπος ὁ καὶ τοῦ θεοῦ
δεκτικὸς, καὶ τῷ θεῷ συνουσιαστός. Trismegist.

CAMBRIDGE,
Printed by *Roger Daniel,* Printer to the
Univerfitie. 1647.

The Preface to the Reader.

He very nerves and sinews of Religion is hope of immortality. What greater incitement to virtue and justice then eternall happinesse? what greater terrour from wickednesse, then a full perswasion of after-judgement and continuall torture of spirit? But my labour is superfluous, Men from their very childhood are perswaded of these things. Verily, I fear how they are perswaded of them when they become men. Else would not they whom the fear of hell doth not affright, die so unwillingly, nor wicked men so securely; nor would so many be wicked. For even naturall-providence would bid them look forward.

Beside some men of a melancholick temper (which commonly distrust and suspicion do accompany) though otherwise pious, yet out of an exceeding desire of eternall being, think they can never have security enough for this so pleasing hope and expectation, and so even with anxiety of mind busie themselves to prove the truth of that strongly, which they desire vehemently to be true. And this body, which dissolution waits upon, helpeth our infidelity exceedingly. For the soul not seeing it self, judgeth it self of such a nature, as those things are to which she is nearest united: Falsely saith, but yet ordinarily, I am sick, I am weak, I faint, I die; when it is nought but the perishing life of the body that is in such plight, to which she is so close tyed in most intimate love and sympathy. So a tender mother, if she see a knife struck to her childs heart, would shreek and swound as if her selfe had been smit; whenas if her eye had not beheld that spectacle, she had not been moved though the thing were surely done. So I do verily think that the mind being taken up in some higher contemplation, if it should please God to keep it in that ecstasie, the body might be destroyed without any disturbance to the soul, for how can there be or sense or pain without animadversion.

But while we have such continuall commerce with this frail body, it is not to be expected, but that we shall be assaulted with the fear of death and darknesse. For alas! how few are there that do not make this visible world, their Adonai, their stay and sustentation of life, the prop of their soul, their God? How many Christians are not prone to whisper that of the Heathen Poet,

> Soles occidere & redire possunt;
> Nobis cùm semel occidit brevis lux
> Nox est perpetua una dormienda.
> The Sunne may set and rise again;
> If once sets our short light,
> Deep sleep us binds with iron chain,
> Wrapt in eternall Night.

But I would not be so injurious, as to make men worse then they are, that my little work may seem of greater use and worth then it is.

Admit then that men are mostwhat perswaded of the souls immortality, yet here they may read reasons to confirm that perswasion, and be put in mind, as they reade, of their end, and future condition, which cannot be but profitable at least.

For the pleasure they'll reap from this Poem, it will be according as their Genius is fitted for it. For as Plato speaks in his Io, Ὁ μὲν τῶν ποιητῶν ἐξ ἄλλης Μούσης, ὁ δὲ ἐξ ἄλλης ἐξήρτηται, or according to the more usuall phrase κατέχεται, &c. The spirit of every Poet is not alike, nor his writings alike suitable to all dispositions. As Io, the reciter of Homers verses, professeth himself to be snatcht away with an extraordinary fury or ecstasie at the repeating of Homers Poesie, but others so little to move him that he could even fall asleep. So that no man is rashly to condemn another mans labour in this kind, because he is not taken with it. As wise or wiser then himselfe may.

But this is a main piece of idolatry and injustice in the world, that every man would make his private Genius an universall God; and would devour all mens apprehensions by his own fire, that glowes so hot in him, and (as he thinks) shines so clear.

As for this present song of the Immortality of the soul, it is not unlikely but that it will prove sung *Montibus & Sylvis* to the waste woods and solitary mountains. For all men are so full of their own phansies and idiopathies, that they scarce have the civility to interchange any words with a stranger. If they chance to hear his exotick tone, they entertain it with laughter, a passion very incident upon that occasion, to children and clowns. But it were much better neither to embosome nor reject any thing, though strange, till we were well acquainted with it.

Exquisite disquisition begets diffidence; diffidence in knowledge, humility; humility, good manners and meek conversation. For mine own part, I desire no man to take any thing I write, upon trust, without canvasing; and would be thought rather to propound then to assert what I have here or elsewhere written. But continually to have exprest my diffidence in the very tractates themselves, had been languid and ridiculous.

It were a piece of injustice to expect of others, that which I could never indure to stoop to my self. That knowledge which is built upon humane authority, is no better then a Castle in the Aire. For what man is αὐτόπιστος or at least can be proved to us to be so? Wherefore the foundation of that argument will but prove precarious, that is so built. And we have rather a sound of words signifying the thing is so, then any true understanding that the thing is so indeed.

Whatever may seeme strange in this Poem, condemne it not, till thou findest it dissonant to Plato's School, or not deducible from it. But there be many arguments, that have no strangenesse at all to prove the Souls immortality so, that no man that is not utterly illiterate shall lose his labour in reading this short Treatise.

I must confesse I intended to spin it out to a greater length; but things of greater importance then curious Theory, take me off; beside the hazard of speaking hard things to a multitude.

I make no question, but those that are rightly acquainted with Platonisme, will accept of that small pains, and make a good construction of my labours. For I well assure thee (Reader) that it will be nothing but ignorance of my scope, that shall make any do otherwise. I fly too high to take notice of lesser flaws. If thou seest them, I give thee free liberty to mend them. But if thou regardest not lesser trifles, we be well met.

Farewell.

H. M.

The Argument of
PSYCHATHANASIA,
Or
The Immortality of the Soul.

Struck with strong sense of Gods good will
The immortality
Of Souls I sing ; Praise with my quill
Plato's Philosophy.

1

Hatever man he be that dares to deem
   True Poets skill to spring of earthly race,
   I must him tell, that he doth misesteem
   Their strange estate, and eke himselfe dis-
grace
By his rude ignorance. For there's no place
For forcèd labour, or slow industry
Of flagging wits, in that high fiery chace :
So soon as of the Muse they quickned be,
At once they rise, and lively sing like Lark in skie.

2

Like to a Meteor, whose materiall
Is low unwieldy earth, base unctuous slime,
Whose inward hidden parts ethereall
Ly close upwrapt in that dull sluggish sime,
Ly fast asleep, till at some fatall time
Great Phœbus lamp has fir'd its inward spright,
And then even of it self on high doth climb ;
That earst was dark becomes all eye, all sight,
Bright starre, that to the wise of future things gives light.

3

Even so the weaker mind, that languid lies
Knit up in rags of dirt, dark, cold, and blind,
So soon that purer flame of Love unties
Her clogging chains, and doth her spright unbind,
Shee sores aloft ; for shee her self doth find
Well plum'd ; so rais'd upon her spreaden wing,
She softly playes, and warbles in the wind,
And carols out her inward life and spring
Of overflowing joy, and of pure love doth sing.

4

She sings of purest love, not that base passion
That fouls the soul with filth of lawlesse lust,
And Circe-like her shape doth all misfashion ;
But that bright flame that's proper to the just,
And eats away all drosse and cankred rust
With its refining heat, unites the mind
With Gods own spright, who raiseth from the dust
The slumbring soul, and with his usage kind
Makes t' breath after that life that time hath not defin'd.

5

So hath he rais'd my soul, and so possest
My inward spright, with that unfainèd will
He bears to *Psyche's* brood, that I nere rest
But ruth or ragefull indignation fill
My troubled veins, that I my life near spill
With sorrow and disdain, for that foul lore
That crept from dismall shades of Night, and quill
Steep'd in sad Styx, and fed with stinking gore
Suckt from corrupted corse, that God and men abhorre.

6

Such is thy putid muse, Lucretius,
That fain would teach that souls all mortall be :
The dusty Atoms of Democritus
Certes have fall'n into thy feeble eye,
And thee bereft of perspicacity.
Others through the strong steem of their dull bloud,
Without the help of that Philosophy,
Have with more ease the truth not understood,
And the same thing conclude in some sad drooping mood.

7

But most of all my soul doth them refuse
That have extinguish'd natures awfull light
By evil custome, and unkind abuse
Of Gods young tender work, that in their spright

He first gins frame. But they with heddy might
Of over-whelming liquour that life drownd,
And reasons eye swell up or put out quite.
Hence horrid darknesse doth their souls confound ;
And foul blasphemous belch from their furd mouth re-
    sounds.

8

Thus while false way they take to large their spirit
By vaster cups of Bacchus, they get fire
Without true light, and 'cording to demerit
Infernall blasts blind confidence inspire :
Bold heat to uncouth thoughts is their bad hire.
Which they then dearly hug, and ween their feet
Have clombe, whither vulgar men dare not aspire.
But its the fruit of their burnt sootie spright :
Thus dream they of drad death, and an eternall night.

9

Now in the covert of dame Natures cell
They think they'r shrowded, and the mystery
Of her deep secrets they can wisely spell ;
And 'pprove that art above true piety ;
Laugh at religion as a mockery,
A thing found out to aw the simpler sort :
But they, brave sparks, have broke from this dark tie :
The light of nature yields more sure comfort.
Alas ! too many souls in this fond thought consort.

10

Like men new made contriv'd into a cave
That ne're saw light, but in that shadowing pit,
Some uncouth might them hoodwink hither drave,
Now with their backs to the dens mouth they sit,
Yet shoulder not all light from the dern pit :
So much gets in as Optick art counts meet
To shew the forms that hard without do flit.
With learned quære each other here they greet :
True moving substances they deem each shadow slight :

11

When fowls flie by, and with their swapping wings
Beat the inconstant air, and mournfull noise
Stirre up with their continuall chastisings
In the soft yielding penitent ; the voice
These solemn Sages nought at all accoyes.
'Tis common ; onely they philosophize,
Busying their brains in the mysterious toyes
Of flittie motion, warie well advize
On'ts inward principles the hid *Entelechies :*

12

And whereabout that inward life is seated,
That moves the living creature, they espie
Passing in their dim world. So they'r defeated,
Calling thin shadows true realitie,
And deeply doubt if corporalitie,
(For so they term those visibles) were stroy'd

Whether that inward first vitalitie
Could then subsist. But they are ill accloy'd
With cloddie earth, and with blind duskishnesse annoy'd.

13

If roaring Lion or the neighing Horse,
With frisking tail to brush off busie flies,
Approch their den, then haply they discourse
From what part of these creatures may arise
Those greater sounds. Together they advise,
And gravely do conclude that from the thing
That we would term the tail, those thund'ring neyes
Do issue forth : tail of that shadowing
They see then movèd most, while he is whinneying.

14

And so the Lions huge and hideous roar
They think proceeds from his rugg'd flowing mane,
Which the fierce winds do tosse and tousell sore ;
Unlesse perhaps he stirre his bushie train :
For then the tail will carrie it again.
Thus upon each occasion their frail wit
Bestirres itself to find out errours vain
And uselesse theories in this dark pit :
Fond reasoning they have, seldome or never hit.

15

So soon new shadows enter in the cave,
New *entelechias* they then conceive
Brought forth of nature : when they passèd have
Their gloomy orb (false shades eas'ly deceive)
Not onely they that visible bereave
Of life and being, but the hidden might
And moving root, unliv'd, unbeen'd they leave
In their vain thoughts : for they those shadows slight
Do deem sole prop and stay of th' hidden motive spright.

16

This is that awfull cell where Naturalists
Brood deep opinion, as themselves conceit ;
This Errours den wherein a magick mist
Men hatch their own delusion and deceit,
And grasp vain shows. Here their bold brains they
    beat,
And dig full deep, as deep as *Hyle's* hell,
Unbare the root of life (O searching wit !)
But root of life in *Hyles* shade no'te dwell.
For God's the root of all, as I elsewhere shall tell.

17

This is the stupid state of drooping soul,
That loves the body and false forms admires ;
Slave to base sense, fierce 'gainst reasons controul,
That still itself with lower lust bemires ;
That nought believeth and much lesse desires
Things of that unseen world and inward life,
Nor unto height of purer truth aspires :
But cowardly declines the noble strife
'Gainst vice and ignorance ; so gets it no relief.

18

From this default, the lustfull Epicure
Democritè, or th' unthankfull Stagarite,
Most men preferre 'fore holy Pythagore,
Divinest Plato, and grave Epictete :
But I am so inflam'd with the sweet sight
And goodly beauty seen on *Eloim-hill*,
That maugre all mens clamours in despight
I'll praise my *Platonissa* with loud quill ;
My strong intended voice all the wide world shall fill.

19

O sacred Nymph begot of highest Jove !
Queen of Philosophie and virtuous lear !
That firest the nobler heart with spotlesse love,
And sadder minds with Nectar drops dost chear,
That oft bedrencht with sorrows while we're here
Exil'd from our dear home, that heavenly soil.
Through wandring wayes thou safely dost us bear
Into the land of truth, from dirtie foil
Thou keepst our slipping feet oft wearied with long toil.

20

When I with other beauties thine compare,
O lovely maid, all others I must scorn.
For why ? they all rude and deform'd appear :
Certes they be ill thew'd and baser born :
Yet thou, alas ! of men art more forlorn.
For like will to its like : but few can see
Thy worth ; so night-birds flie the glorious morn.
Thou art a beam shot from the Deitie,
And nearest art ally'd to Christianitie.

21

But they be sprung of sturdie *Giants* race,
Ally'd to *Night* and the foul *Earthy clay*,
Love of the carcase, Envie, Spight, Disgrace,
Contention, Pride, that unto th' highest doth bray,
Rash labour, a *Titanicall assay*
To pluck down wisdome from her radiant seat,
With mirie arms to bear her quite away.
But thy dear mother *Thorough-cleansing virtue* hight :
Here will true wisdome lodge, here will she deigne to
    light.

22

Come, Gentle Virgin, take me by the hand,
To yonder grove with speedie pace we'll hie :
(Its not farre off from *Alethea land*)
Swift as the levin from the sneezing skie,
So swift we'll go, before an envious eye
Can reach us. There I'll purge out the strong steem
Of prepossessing prejudice, that I
Perhaps may have contract in common stream ;
And warie well wash out my old conceived dream.

23

And when I've breath'd awhile in that free air,
And clear'd my self from tinctures took before,
Then deigne thou to thy novice to declare
Thy secret skill, and bid mysterious lore,
And I due thanks shall plenteously down poure.
But well I wote thou'lt not envassall me :
That law were rudenesse. I may not adore
Ought but the lasting spotlesse veritie.
Well thewed minds the mind do alwayes setten free.

24

Free to that inward awfull Majestie
Hight *Logos*, whom they term great sonne of God,
Who fram'd the world by his deep sciency,
The greater world. Als' makes his near abode
In the lesse world : so he can trace the trod
Of that hid ancient path, whenas he made
This stately Fabrick of the world so broad.
He plainly doth unfold his skilfull trade,
When he doth harmlesse hearts by his good spright
    invade.

25

O thou eternall Spright, cleave ope the skie,
And take thy flight into my feeble breast,
Enlarge my thoughts, enlight my dimmer eye,
That wisely of that burthen closely prest
In my strait mind, I may be dispossest :
My Muse must sing of things of mickle weight ;
The souls eternity is my great quest :
Do thou me guide, that art the souls sure light,
Grant that I never erre, but ever wend aright.

The Argument of

PSYCHATHANASIA,

Or,

The Immortality of the Soul.

BOOK I. CANT. 2.

What a soul is here I define,
After I have comparèd
All powers of life: That stamp divine
Show that brutes never sharèd.

1

Ow I'll address me to my mighty task,
    So mighty task that makes my heart to
       shrink,
    While I compute the labour it will ask,
And on my own frail weaknesse I gin think.
Like tender Lad that on the rivers brink,
That fain would wash him, while the Evening keen
With sharper air doth make his pores to wink,
Shakes all his body, nips his naked skin,
At first makes some delay but after skippeth in:

2

So I upon a wary due debate
With my perplexèd mind, after perswade
My softer heart. I need no longer wait.
Lo! now new strength my vitals doth invade
And rear again, that earst began to fade,
My life, my light, my senses all revive
That fearfull doubts before had ill apaid.
Leap in, my soul, and strongly 'fore thee drive
The fleeting waves, and when thee list to th' bottome
    dive.

3

For thou canst dive full well, and flote aloft,
Dive down as deep as the old *Hyle's* shade,
Through that slight darknesse glid'st thou sly and soft,
Through pitchy cumbring fogs strongly canst wade,
Nor in thy flight could'st thou be ever staid,
If in thy flight thou flewest not from him,
That for himself thine excellent might hath made.
Contract desire, repulse strong Magick steem,
Then even in foul *Cocytus* thou mayest fearlesse swim.

4

Like that strange uncouth fish *Lucerna* hight,
Whose wonne is in the brackish Seas, yet fire
She eas'ly carries and clear native light
In her close mouth: and the more to admire,
In darkest night when she lists to aspire
To th' utmost surface of the wat'ry Main,
And opes her jawes, that light doth not expire,
But lively shines till she shut up again:
Nor liquid Sea, nor moistned Aire this light restrain.

5

Or like a lamp arm'd with pellucid horn,
Which ruffling winds about do rudely tosse,
And felly lash with injury and scorn,
But her mild light they cannot easily crosse:
She shines to her own foes withouten losse:
Even so the soul into her self collected,
Or in her native hew withouten drosse,
In midst of bitter storms is not dejected,
Nor her eternall state is any whit suspected.

6

As Cynthia in her stouping Perigee,
That deeper wades in the earths duskish Cone,
Yet safely wallows through in silency
Till she again her silver face hath shown,
And tells the world that she's the self-same Moon:
Not now more listlesse then I was whileare
When I was hid in my Apogeon,
For I my self alike do always bear
In every circling race: blind ignorance breeds fear.

7

Nor being hid after my monthly wane,
Long keppen back from your expecting sight,
Dull damps and darknesse do my beauty stain;
When none I show then have I the most light,

Nearer to Phœbus more I am bedight
With his fair rayes. And better to confute,
All vain suspicion of my worser plight,
Mark aye my face, after my close salute
With that sharp-witted God, seem I not more acute?

8

This is the state of th' evermoving soul,
Whirling about upon her circling wheel ;
Certes to sight she variously doth roll,
And as men deem full dangerously doth reel,
But oft when men fear most, her self doth feel
In happiest plight conjoy'nd with that great Sun
Of lasting blisse, that doth himself reveal
More fully then, by that close union,
Though men, that misse her here, do think her quite
    undone.

9

But lest we rashly wander out too farre,
And be yblown about with wanton wind,
Withouten stern, or card, or Polar starre,
In its round little list so close confin'd :
Let the souls nature first be well defin'd :
Then we'll proceed. But all the while I crave
When e're I speak 'cording to Plato's mind,
That you my faultlesse drift do not deprave,
For I the free-born soul to no sect would inslave.

10

Divers conceits the wizards of old time
Have had concerning that we here inquire,
And would set forth in an eternall rhyme ;
But we list not our dainty Muse to tire
In such foul wayes, and plunge her in the mire.
Strange dreams their drowsie scholars they have taught,
The *heart*, the *heart-bloud*, *brains* fleet *aire*, hot *fire*
To be the thing that they so prestly sought,
Some have defin'd, some *temper*, some *atomes*, some
    nought.

11

But I must needs decline this wandring path ;
For well I wote errour is infinite,
But he that simple truth once reachèd hath
Needs not with every single shade to fight :
One stroke will put all falsities to flight.
So soon as Sol his fiery head doth rear
Above the eastern waves his glowing sight
As angry darknesse so long rule did bear,
Straight all night-trifling sprights doth chase away with
    fear.

12

Long have I swonk with anxious assay
To finden out what this hid soul may be,
That doth her self so variously bewray
In different motions. Other we her see

When she so fairly spreads the branching tree ;
Other when as sh' hath loos'd her self from ground,
And opes her root, and breaths in heaven free,
And doth her wants in the wide air resound,
Speaks out her joy, no longer whispers under-ground.

13

Such is the noise of chearfull chirping birds,
That tell the sweet impressions of the spring ;
Or 'fore some storm, when their quick sprights be stird
With nearer strong appulse and hid heaving,
That fills their little souls, and makes them sing,
Puft up with joy and o'rflowing delight :
Eftsoons with ratling winds the air doth ring,
The sturdy storm doth make them take their flight
Into thick bush or hedge to save them from heavens spight.

14

From this same sourse of sense are murmuring moans
Of bellowing bullocks, when sharp hunger bites ;
Hence whining dog so pittifully groans
Whenas with knotted whip his Lord him smites ;
And every beast when with Deaths pangs he fights.
But senslesse trees nor feel the bleaker wind,
That nip their sides, nor the Suns scorching might,
Nor the sharp ax piercing their ruggid rind ;
Yet have they soul, whose life in their sweet growth we
    find.

15

So plants spring up, flourish and fade away,
Not marking their own state : they never found
Themselves, when first they 'pear'd in sunny day ;
Nor ever sought themselves, though in the ground
They search full deep : Nor are they wak'd by wound
Of biting iron ; to nought are attent
That them befalls, when cold humours abound
And clog their vitall heat, or when they're brent
With Sirius flame, or when through eld they waxen faint.

16

Or whatsoever diseases them betide
That hasten death, they nought at all regard :
But when to plantall life quick sense is ti'd,
And progging phansie, then upon her guard
She gins to stand, and well her self to ward
From foes she plainly feels, pursues her joy,
Remembers where she well or ill hath far'd,
Or swiftly flies from that that doth annoy,
Or stoutly strives her fierce destroyer to destroy.

17

Thus have we run thorow these two degrees
Of the souls working seen in beast and plant ;
Reason's the third, of common qualities
The best. Of this the humane race doth vaunt
As proper to themselves ; But if we skan't
Sans prejudice, it's not in them alone ;
The Dog, the Horse, the Ape, the Elephant,
Will all rush in striving to make up one,
And sternly claim their share in use of right reason.

18

But whether brutes do reason and reflect
Upon their reasoning, I'll not dispute ;
Nor care I what brisk boyes will here object :
Long task it were all fondlings to confute.
But I'll lay down that which will better sute
With that high heavenly spark, the soul of man ;
His proper character (I would he knew't)
Is that which *Adam* lost by wily train
Of th' old sly snake that *Eve* beguil'd with speeches vain.

19

This was the Image of the highest God,
Which brutes partake not of. This Image hight
True Justice, that keeps ever th' even trod,
True Piety that yields to man the sight
Of heavenly beauty, those fair beams so bright
Of th' everlasting Deity, that shed
Their sacred fire within the purer spright,
The fruit of Eden wherewith souls be fed,
Mans awfull majesty of every beast ydred.

20

Nor is that radiant force in humane kind
Extinguisht quite, he that did them create
Can those dull rusty chains of sleep unbind,
And rear the soul unto her pristin state
He can them so inlarge and elevate
And sprenden out, that they can compasse all,
When they no longer be incarcerate
In this dark dungeon, this foul fleshly wall,
Nor be no longer wedg'd in things corporeall :

21

But rais'd aloft into their proper sphere,
That sphere that hight th' Orb *Intellectuall*,
They quiet sit, as when the flitting fire
That Natures mighty Magic down did call
Into the oyly wood, at its own fall
Grows full of wrath and rage, and gins to fume,
And roars and strives 'gainst its disquietall,
Like troubled Ghost forc'd some shape to assume ;
But it its holding foe at last doth quite consume.

22

And then like gliding spright doth straight dispear,
That earst was forc'd to take a fiery form :
Full lightly it ascends into the clear
And subtile aire devoid of cloudy storm,
Where it doth steddy stand, all-uniform,
Pure, pervious, immixt, innocuous, mild,
Nought scorching, nought glowing, nothing enorm,
Nought destroying, not destroy'd not defil'd ;
Foul fume being spent, just 'fore its flight it fairly smil'd.

23

Thus have I trac'd the soul in all her works,
And severall conditions have displaid,
And show'd all places where so e'r she lurks,
Even her own lurking's of her self bewray'd,

In plants, in beasts, in men, while here she staid :
And freed from earth how then she sprends on high
Her heavenly rayes, that also hath been said.
Look now, my Muse, and cast thy piercing eye
On every kind, and tell wherein all souls agree.

24

Here dare I not define't, th' *Entelechie*
Of organized bodies. For this life,
This centrall life, which men take souls to be,
Is not among the beings relative ;
And sure some souls at least are self-active
Withouten body having *Energie.*
Many put out their force informative
In their ethereall corporeity,
Devoid of heterogeneall organity.

25

Self-moving substance, that be th' definition
Of souls, that 'longs to them in generall :
This well expresseth that common condition
Of every vitall centre creaturall.
For why? both what hight form *spermaticall*
Hath here a share, as also that we term
Soul sensitive, I'll call't form bestiall,
It makes a beast added to plantall sperm ;
Adde rationall form, it makes a man, as men affirm.

26

All these be substances self-moveable :
And that we call virtue magneticall
(That what's defin'd be irreprovable)
I comprehend it in the life plantall :
Mongst trees ther's found life *Sympatheticall ;*
Though trees have not animadversive sense.
Therefore the soul's *Autokineticall*
Alone. Whatere's in this defining sense
Is soul, what ere's not soul is driven far from hence.

27

But that each soul's *Autokineticall,*
Is easly shown by sifting all degrees
Of souls. The first are forms *Spermaticall,*
That best be seen in shaping armèd trees.
Which if they want their fixt *Centreities,*
By which they fairly every part extend,
And gently inact with spred vitalities
The flowring boughs. How Natures work doth wend
Who knows? or from what inward stay it doth depend?

28

Forthy let first an inward centre hid
Be put. That's nought but Natures fancie ti'd
In closer knot, shut up into the mid
Of its own self : so our own spirits gride
With piercing wind in storming Winter tide,
Contract themselves and shrivell up together,
Like snake the countrey man in snow espi'd,
Whose spright was quite shrunk in by nipping weather.
From whence things come, by fo-man forc'd they back-
ward thither.

29

The rigid cold had forc'd into its centre
This serpents life ; but when the rurall Swain
Plac'd her upon warm hearth, and heat did enter
Into her nummèd corps, she gan to strain
And stretch herself, and her host entertain
With scornfull hisse, shooting her anchor'd tongue,
Threatning her venom'd teeth ; so straight again
She prov'd a living snake, when she along
Her corse free life had drove from centre steddie strong.

30

So doth the gentle warmth of solar heat
Eas'ly awake the centre *seminall*,
That makes it softly streak on its own seat,
And fairly forward force its life internall.
That inward life's th' impresse *imaginall*
Of Natures Art, which sweetly flowreth out
From that is cleep'd the *Sphere spermaticall :*
For there is plac'd the never fading root
Of every flower or herb that into th' air doth shoot.

31

Fairly invited by Sols piercing ray
And inward tickled with his chearing spright,
All plants break thorough into open day,
Rend the thick curtain of cold cloying night,
The earths opakenes, enemy to light,
And crown themselves in sign of victory
With shining leaves, and goodly blossomes bright.
Thus callèd out by friendly sympathy
Their souls move of themselves on their *Centreitie.*

32

But it's more plain in animalitie,
When fiery coursers strike the grassie ground
With swift tempestuous feet, that farre and nigh
They fill mens ears with a broad thundering sound :
(From hollow hoof so strongly it doth rebound)
What's that that twitcheth up their legs so fast,
And fiercely jerks them forth, that many wound
They give to their own mother in their hast ?
With eager steps they quickly mete the forrest wast.

34

That outward form is but a neurospast ;
The soul it is that on her subtile ray,
That she shoots out, the limbs of moving beast
Doth stretch straight forth, so straightly as she may.
Bones joynts and sinews shap'd of stubborn clay
Cannot so eas'ly lie in one straight line
With her projected might, much lesse obey
Direct retractions of these beamès fine :
Of force, so straight retreat they ever must decline.

35

But yet they follow in a course oblique,
With angular doublings, as the joynts permit :
So go they up together, not unlike
An iron candle-stick the smith hath fit

With many junctures, whom in studious fit
Some scholar set awork : but to return,
Lest what we aim'd at we unwares omit ;
If souls of beasts their bodies move and turn,
And wield at phansies beck, as we describ'd beforn :

36

Then be the souls of beasts self-moving forms,
Bearing their bodies as themselves think meet,
Invited or provok'd, so they transform
At first themselves within, then straight in sight
Those motions come, which suddenly do light
Upon the bodies visible, which move
According to the will of th' inward spright.
In th' inward spright be anger, hate and love :
Hence claws, horns, hoofs they use the pinching ill
t' amove.

37

Thus have I plainly prov'd that souls of beasts
And plants do move themselves. That souls of men
Should be more stupid, and farre lesse releast
From matters bondage, surely there's none can
Admit of, though but slightly they do scan
The cause. But for to put all out of doubt,
Let's take again the same way we have ran,
Break down all obstacles that hinder mought
Our future course to make all plain all clear throughout.

38

If there be no self-motion in mans soul,
That she nor this nor that way can propend
Of her own self, nor can no whit controll
Nor will of her own self, who can offend ?
For no mans self (if you do well perpend)
Guiltie's of ought when nought doth from him flow.
Whither do learning, laws, grave speeches tend ?
Speaks the rude Carter to the wagon slow
With threat'ning words, or to the beasts that do it
draw ?

39

Surely unto the beasts that eas'ly go :
For there's the principle of motion,
Such principle as can it self foreslow,
Or forward presse by incitation :
Which though it mov'd by commination
So stifly strives, yet from it self it strives,
Bears it self forth with stout contention,
And ever and anon the whip revives
That inward life, so bravely on the Rustick drives.

40

Again, all that sweet labour would be lost
That Gods good spirit takes in humane mind,
So oft we courted be so often cross'd :
But nor that tender amorous courtship kind

G

Hath any place where we no place can find
For a self-yielding love ; Or if self-will
Be not in us, how eas'ly were declin'd
All crosses ? None could happen us untill,
How will I want, and want no crosse passeth my skill.

41

Besides when reason works with phantasie,
And changeable conceits we do contrive,
Purging and pruning with all industrie,
What's dead or uselesse, lesse demonstrative,
What's dull or flaccid, nought illustrative,
Quenching unfitted phantasms in our brain,
And for our better choice new flames revive ;
The busie soul thus doth her reason strain
To write or speak what envious tongue may never stain.

42

Or when quite heedlesse of this earthie world
She lifts her self unto the azure skie,
And with those wheeling gyres around is hurld,
Turns in herself in a due distancie
The erring Seven, or a stretch'd line doth tie
O' th' silver-bowèd moon from horn to horn ;
Or finds out Phœbus vast soliditie
By his diametre, measures the Morn,
Girds the swoln earth with linear list, though earth she
    scorn.

43

All this is done, though bodie never move :
The soul about it self circumgyrates
Her various forms, and what she most doth love
She oft before herself stabilitates ;
She stifly stayes't and wistly contemplates,
Or lets it somewhat slowlier descend
Down to the nether Night ; she temperates
Her starrie orb, makes her bright forms to wend
Even as she list : Anon she'll all with darknesse blend.

44

Thus variously she doth herself invest
With rising forms, and reasons all the way ;
And by right reason doth herself devest
Of falser fancies. Who then can gainsay
But she's self-mov'd when she doth with self-sway
Thus change herself, as inward life doth feel ?
If not, then some inspiring sprights bewray
Each reasoning. Yet though to them we deal
First motion, yet our selves ought know what they reveal.

45

But if nor of our selves we movèd be
At first, without any invasion
Of stirring forms that into energie
Awake the soul ; nor after-motion
From its own centre by occasion
Doth issue forth ; then it's not conscious
Of ought : For so 'twill want adversion.
But nothing can animadvert for us :
Therefore all humane souls be self-vivacious.

46

Thus have I prov'd all souls have centrall motion
Springing from their own selves. But they'll object
'Gainst th' universalnesse of this clear notion,
That whiles self-flowing source I here detect
In plants, in brutes, in men, I ought reject
No soul from wishèd immortalitie,
But give them durance when they are resect
From organizèd corporeitie :
Thus brutes and plants shall gain lasting eternitie.

47

'Tis true, a never fading durancie
Belongs to all hid principles of life ;
But that full grasp of vast *Eternitie*
'Longs not to beings simply vegetive,
Nor yet to creatures merely sensitive :
Reason alone cannot arrive to it.
Onely souls *Deiform* intellective,
Unto that height of happinesse can get ;
Yet immortalitie with other souls may fit.

48

No force of Nature can their strength annoy.
For they be subtiler than the silken air,
Which fatall fire from heaven cannot destroy :
All grossenesse its devouring teeth may shear,
And present state of visibles empare ;
But the fine curtains of the lasting skie,
Though not of love, yet it perforce must spare,
If they could burn, each spark from flint would trie,
And a bright broad-spread flame to either Pole would
    hie.

49

But if all souls survive their bulks decay,
Another difficultie will straight arise,
Concerning their estate when they're away
Flit from this grosser world. Shall Paradise
Receive the sprights of beasts? or wants it trees,
That their sweet verdant souls should thither take ?
Who shall conduct those stragling colonies ?
Or be they straightway drench'd in Lethe lake ?
So that cold sleep their shriveld life from work doth
    slake.

50

Or if that all or some of them awake,
What is their miserie ? what their delight ?
How come they that refinèd state forsake ?
Or had they their first being in our sight ?
Whither to serve ? what is the usefull might
Of these spirituall trees ? doth fearfull hare
Flie the pursuing dog ? doth soaring kite
Prey upon silly chickins ? is there jarre,
Or be those sprights agreed, none to other contraire ?

51

If some contraire ; then tell me, how's their fight ?
What is the spoil ? what the stout victor's meed ?

No flesh, no bloud whereon to spend their spight,
Or whereupon these hungry souls may feed.
Or doth the stronger suck the aiery weed
Wherewith the other did itself invest?
And so more freshly deck itself at need?
An aierie prey for aierie spright is best?
Or do they want no food, but be still full and rest?

52

Die they again? draw they in any breath?
Orbe they sterill? or bring forth their young?
Beat their light feet on the soft aierie heath?
Expresse they joy or sorrow with their tongue?
Enough! whoere thou art that thus dost throng
My tender Muse with rough objections stout,
Give me but leave to tell thee thou art wrong,
If being of a thing thou call'st in doubt
Cause its more hid conditions shine not clearly out.

53

Who questions but there is a quantitie
Of things corporeall, a trinall dimension,
Of solid bodies? yet to satisfie
All doubts that may be made about extension
Would plunge the wisest Clerk.   I'll onely mention
That quære, of what parts it doth consist,
Whether of Atoms; or what strange retention
Still keepeth so much back, that if God list
He could not count the parts of a small linear twist.

54

For his division never could exhaust
The particles, say they, of quantitie.
O daring wit of man that thus doth boast
Itself, and in pursuit of sciencie
Forget the reverend laws of pietie.
What thing is hid from that all-seeing light?
What thing not done by his all-potencie?
He can discern by his clear-piercing might
The close couch'd number of each bignesse comes in
    sight:

55

And so can count them out even part by part;
In number, measure, weight, he all things made;
Each unite he dissevers by his Art;
But here this searching reason to evade,

Each quantum's infinite, straight will be said,
That's against sense.   If it be infinite
Of parts, then tell me, be those parts outspread?
Or not extent? if extended outright
Each flie in summer-Even is higher then Heavens height.

56

If not extended, then that quantum's nought,
Some be extended, others not extent
Already (answers a vain shifting thought)
But those potentiall parts, how be they meint
With those that now be actually distent?
Even thus you grant, that those that actuall be
Be plainly finite, against your intent,
Grant me but that, and we shall well agree,
So must sleight Atoms be sole parts of quantitie.

57

But if't consist of points, then a Scalene
I'll prove all one with an Isosceles:
With as much ease I'll evince clear and clean
That the crosse lines of a Rhomboides
That from their meeting to all angles presse
Be of one length, though one from earth to heaven
Would reach, and that the other were much lesse
Then a small digit of the lowest of seven
So as she 'pears to us, yet I could prove them even.

58

And that the moon (though her circumference
Be farre more strait then is the earthie ball)
Sometime the earth illumineth at once
And with her grasping rayes enlights it all;
And that the Sunnes great body sphericall
Greater then th' earth, farre greater then the moon,
Even at midday illumines not at all
This earthy globe in his Apogeon;
So that we in deep darknesse sit, though at high noon.

59

Of will, of motion, of divine foresight,
Here might I treat with like perplexitie.
But it's already clear that 'tis not right
To reason down the firm subsistencie
Of things from ignorance of their propertie.
Therfore not requisite for to determ
The hid conditions of vitalitie
Or shrunk or sever'd; onely I'll affirm
It is, which my next song shall further yet confirm.

The Argument of

PSYCHATHANASIA

Or

The Immortality of the Soul.

BOOK 1. CANT 3.

Orewhelm'd with grief and pitious wo
For fading lifes decayes ;
How no souls die, from Lunar bow,
A Nymph to me displayes.

1

N silent night, when mortalls be at rest,
And bathe their molten limbs in slothfull
    sleep,
My troubled ghost strange cares did straight
    molest
And plung'd my heavie soul in sorrow deep :
Large floods of tears my moistned cheeks did steep,
My heart was wounded with compassionate love
Of all the creatures : sadly out I creep
From mens close mansions, the more to improve
My mournfull plight, so softly on I forward move.

2

Aye me ! said I, within my wearied breast,
And sighèd sad, wherefore did God erect
This stage of misery ? thrice, foure times blest
Whom churlish Nature never did eject
From her dark womb, and cruelly object
By sense and life unto such balefull smart ;
Every slight entrance into joy is checkt
By that soure stepdames threats, and visage tart :
Our pleasure of our pain is not the thousandth part.

3

Thus vex'd I was 'cause of mortality :
Her curst remembrance cast me in this plight,
That I grew sick of the worlds vanity
Ne ought recomfort could my sunken spright,
What so I hate may do me no delight,
Few things (alas) I hate, the more my wo,
The things I love by mine own sad foresight
Make me the greater torments undergo,
Because I know at last they're gone like idle show.

4

Each goodly sight my sense doth captivate
When vernall flowers their silken leaves display,
And ope their fragrant bosomes, I that state
Would not have changèd but indure for aye ;
Nor care to mind that that fatall decay
Is still recured by faithfull succession.
But why should ought that's good thus fade away ?
Should steddy Spring exclude Summers accession
Or Summer spoil the Spring with furious hot oppression !

5

You chearfull chaunters of the flowring woods,
That feed your carelesse souls with pleasant layes,
O silly birds ! cease from your merry moods :
Ill suits such mirth when dreary deaths assayes
So closely presse your sory carkases :
To mournfull note turn your light verilayes,
Death be your song, and winters hoary sprayes,
Spend your vain sprights in sighing Elegies :
I'll help you to lament your wofull miseries.

6

When we lay cover'd in the shady Night
Of senselesse matter, we were well content
With that estate, nought pierc'd our anxious spright,
No harm we sufferèd, no harm we ment ;
Our rest not with light dream of ill was blent :
But when rough Nature, with her iron hond,
Pull'd us from our soft ease, and hither hent,
Disturbing fear and pinching pain we found,
Full many a bitter blast, full many a dreadfull stound.

7

Yet lifes strong love doth so intoxicate
Our misty minds, that we do fear to dy.
What did dame Nature brood all things of hate
And onely give them life for misery ?
Sense for an undeservèd penalty ?
And show that if she list, that she could make

Them happy ? but with spightfull cruelty
Doth force their groaning ghosts this house forsake?
And to their ancient Nought their empty selves betake !

8

Thus in deep sorrow and restlesse disdain
Against the cankerèd doom of envious fate,
I clove my very heart with riving pain,
While I in sullen rage did ruminate
The Creatures vanity and wofull state ;
And night that ought to yield us timely rest,
My swelling griefs did much more aggravatè :
The sighs and groans of weary sleeping beast
Seem'd as if sleep itself their spirits did molest :

9

Or as constrain'd perforce that boon to wrest
From envious Nature. All things did augment
My heavie plight, that fouly I blam'd the hest
Of stubborn destiny cause of this wayment.
Even sleep that's for our restauration ment,
As execrable thing I did abhorre,
Cause ugly death to th' life it did depeint:
What good came to my mind I did deplore,
Because it perish must and not live evermore.

10

Thus wrapt in rufull thought through the waste field
I staggerèd on, and scatterèd my woe,
Bedew'd the grasse with tears mine eyes did yield,
At last I am arriv'd with footing slow
Near a black pitchy wood that strongest throw
Of starry beam no'te easily penetrate :
On the North side I walkèd to and fro
In solitary shade. The Moons sly gate
Had cross'd the middle line : It was at least so late.

11

When th' other part of night in painfull grief
Was almost spent, out of that solemn grove
There issuèd forth for my timely relief,
The fairest wight that ever sight did prove,
So fair a wight as might command the love
Of best of mortall race ; her count'nance sheen
The pensive shade gently before her drove,
A mild sweet light shone from her lovely eyne :
She seem'd no earthly branch but sprung of stock divine.

12

A silken mantle, colour'd like the skie
With silver starres in a due distance set,
Was cast about her somewhat carelesly,
And her bright flowing hair was not ylet
By Arts device ; onely a chappelet
Of chiefest flowers, which from far and near
The Nymphs in their pure Lilly hands had set,
Upon her temples she did seemly weare ;
Her own fair beams made all her ornaments appear.

13

What wilfull wight doth thus his kindly rest
Forsake? said she, approching me unto.
What rage, what sorrow boils thus in thy chest
That thou thus spend'st the night in wasting wo ?
Oft help he gets that his hid ill doth show.
Ay me ! said I, my grief's not all mine own ;
For all mens griefs into my heart do flow,
Nor mens alone, but every mornfull grone
Of dying beast, or what so else that grief hath shown.

14

From fading plants my sorrows freshly spring ;
And thou thy self that com'st to comfort me,
Wouldst strongst occasion of deep sorrow bring,
If thou wert subject to mortality :
But I no mortall wight thee deem to be,
Thy face, thy voice, immortall thee proclaim.
Do I not well to wail the vanity
Of fading life, and churlish fates to blame
That with cold frozen death lifes chearfull motions tame ?

15

Thou dost not well, said she to me again,
Thou hurt'st thy self and dost to them no good.
The sighs thou sendest out cannot regain
Life to the dead, thou canst not change the mood
Of stedfast destiny. That man is wood
That weetingly hastes on the thing he hates :
Dull sorrow chokes the sprights, congeals the blood,
The bodies fabrick quickly ruinates.
Yet foolish men do fondly blame the hasty fates.

16

Come, hasty fates, said I, come take away
My weary life, the fountain of my wo :
When that's extinct or shrunk into cold clay,
Then well I wote that I shall undergo
No longer pain. O ! why are you so slow :
Fond speech, said she, nor chang'd her countenance,
No signe of grief or anger she did show ;
Full well she knew passions misgovernance,
Through her clear breast fond passion never yet did lance.

17

But thus spake on, Sith friendly sympathy
With all the creatures thus invades thy brest,
And strikes thine heart with so deep agony
For their decay, 'cording to that behest
Which the pure sourse of sympathy hath prest
On all that of those lovely streams have drunk,
I'll tell thee that that needs must please thee best,
All life's immortall ; though the outward trunk
May changèd be, yet life to nothing never shrunk.

18

With that she bad me rear my heavie eye
Up toward heaven, I rear'd them toward th' East,
Where in a roscid cloud I did espy
A Lunar rainbow in her painted vest ;

The heavenly maid in the mean while surceast
From further speech, while I the bow did view :
But mine old malady was more increas'd,
The bow gan break, and all the gawdy hiew
Dispearèd, that my heart the sight did inly rue.

19

Thus life doth vanish as this bow is gone,
Said I. That sacred Nymph forthwith reply'd,
Vain showes may vanish that have gaily shone
To feeble sense ; but if the truth be tri'd,
Life cannot perish or to nothing slide :
It is not life that falleth under sight,
None but vain flitting qualities are ey'd
By wondring ignorance. The vitall spright
As surely doth remain as the Suns lasting light.

20

This bow, whose breaking struck thy troubled heart,
Of causelesse grief, I hope, shall thee recure,
When I have well explain'd with skilfull Art
By its resemblance what things must indure,
What things decay and cannot standen sure.
The higher causes of that coloured Ark,
Whate're becomes of it, do sit secure ;
That so (the body falling) lifes fair spark
Is safe, I'll clearly show if you but list to mark.

21

There be six Orders 'fore you do descend
To this gay painted bow : Sols centrall spright
To the first place, to th' next we must commend
His hid spread form, then his inherent light,
The fourth his rayes wherewith he is bedight,
The fifth that glistring circle of the Moon,
That goodly round full face all silver bright,
The sixth be beams that from her visage shone ;
The seventh that gawdy bow that was so quickly gone.

22

The fluid matter was that dewy cloud,
That faild as faithlesse Hyle wont to fail :
New guest being come, the old she out doth croud :
But see how little Hyle did prevail,
Or sad destruction in this deemèd bale !
Sols spright, hid form, fair light and out-gone rayes,
The Moons round silver face withouten veil
Do still remain, her beams she still displayes,
The cloud but melt, not lost, the bow onely decayes.

23

This number suits well with the *Universe :*
The number's eight of the Orbs generall,
From whence things flow or wherein they converse,
The first we name *Nature Monadicall,*
The second hight *Life Intellectuall,*
Third *Psychicall ;* the fourth *Imaginative,*
Fifth *Sensitive,* the sixth *Spermaticall,*
The seventh be fading forms *Quantitative,*
The eighth *Hyle* or *Ananke* perverse, coactive.

24

That last is nought but potentiality,
Which in the lower creature causeth strife,
Destruction by incompossibility
In some, as in the forms *Quantitative.*
All here depend on the Orb *Unitive,*
Which also hight Nature *Monadicall ;*
As all those lights and colours did derive
Themselves from lively Phœbus life centrall.
Nought therefore but vain sensibles we see caducall.

25

And that the first *Every-where-Unitie*
Is the true root of all the living creatures,
As they descend in each distinct degree,
That God's the sustentacle of all Natures ;
And though those outward forms and gawdy features
May quail like rainbows in the roscid sky,
Or glistring Parelies or other meteors ;
Yet the clear light doth not to nothing flie :
Those six degrees of life stand sure, and never die.

26

So now we plainly see that the dark matter
Is not that needfull prop to hold up life ;
And though deaths engins this grosse bulk do shatter
We have not lost our Orb conservative,
Of which we are a ray derivative,
The body sensible so garnishèd
With outward forms these inward do relieve,
Keep up in fashion and fresh lively-hed ;
But this grosse bulk those inward lives stands in no sted.

27

Nor can one inward form another slay,
Though they may quell their present energy,
And make them close contract their yielding ray
And hide themselves in their *centreity,*
Till some friendly appulse doth set them free,
And call them out again into broad day :
Hence lives gush not in superfluity
Into this world, but their due time do stay,
Though their strong centrall essence never can decay.

28

In Earth, in Aire, in the vast flowing Plain,
In that high Region hight Æthereall,
In every place these Atom-lives remain,
Even those that cleepèd are forms *seminall.*
But souls of men by force *imaginall*
Easly supply their place, when so they list
Appear in thickned Aire with shape externall,
Display their light and form in cloudy mist,
That much it doth amaze the musing Naturalist.

29

Whereof sith life so strongly sealèd is,
Purge out fond thoughts out of thy weary mind,
And rather strive that thou do nought amisse,
Then God to blame, and Nature as unkind

When nought in them we blamable can find.
When groaning ghosts of beasts or men depart,
Their tender mother doth but them unbind
From grosser fetters, and more toilsome smart.
Bless'd is the man that hath true knowledge of her Art.

30

And more for to confirm this mysterie,
She vanish'd in my presence into Aire,
She spread her self with the thin liquid sky ;
But I thereat fell not into despair
Of her return, nor wail'd her visage fair,
That so was gone. For I was woxen strong

In this belief. That nothing can empair
The inward life, or its hid essence wrong.
O the prevailing might of a sweet learnèd tongue !

31

By this the Suns bright waggon gan ascend
The Eastern hill, and draw on chearfull day ;
So I full fraught with joy do homeward wend
And fed my self with that that Nymph did say,
And did so cunningly to me convey,
Resolving for to teach all willing men
Lifes mysterie, and quite to chase away
Mind-mudding mist sprung from low fulsome fen :
Praise my good will, but pardon my weak faltring pen.

The *Argument* of

P S Y C H A T H A N A S I A

Or

The Immortality of the Soul.

BOOK I. CANT. 4.

That Hyle or first matter's nought
But potentialitie ;
That God's the never-fading root
Of all Vitalitie.

I

Hat I was wisely taught in that still Night,
That *Hyle* is the Potentialitie
Of Gods dear Creatures, I embrace as right,
And them nigh blame of deep idolatrie
That give so much to that slight nullitie,
That they should make it root substantiall
Of nimble life, and that quick entitie
That doth so strongly move things naturall,
That life from hence should spring, that hither life should
      fall.

2

For how things spring from hence and be resolv'd
Into this mirksome sourse, *first matter* hight,
This muddy myst'rie they no'te well unfold.
If it be onely a bare passive might
With Gods and Natures goodly dowries dight,
Bringing hid Noughts into existencie,

Or sleeping Somethings into wide day-light,
Then *Hyle's* plain potentialitie,
Which doth not straight inferre certain mortalitie.

3

For the immortall Angels do consist
Of out-gone act and possibilitie ;
Nor any other creature doth exist,
Releast from dreary deaths necessity ;
If these composures it so certainly
Ensuen must. If substance actuall
They will avouch this first matter to be,
Fountain of forms, and prop fiduciall
Of all those lives and beings cleeped Naturall ;

4

Then may it prove the sphear *spermaticall*
Or *sensitive* (if they would yield it life)
Or that is next, the Orb *Imaginall*,
Or rather all these Orbs ; withouten strife
So mought we all conclude that their relief
And first existence from this sphear they drew
And so our adversaries, loth or lief
Must needs confesse that all the lore was true
Concerning life, that that fair Nymph so clearly shew ;

5

And that particular Lives that be yborn
Into this world, when their act doth dispear,
Do cense to be no more then the snails horn.
That she shrinks in because she cannot bear
The wanton boys rude touch, or heavie chear
Of stormy winds.   The secundary light
As surely shineth in the heavens clear,
As do the first fair beams of Phœbus bright,
Lasting they are as they, though not of so great might.

6

So be the effluxes of those six orders,
Unfading lives from fount of livelihood :
Onely what next to strifefull *Hyle* borders,
Particular visibles deaths drearyhood
Can seiz upon.   They passe like sliding flood.
For when to this worlds dregs lives downward hie,
They 'stroy one th' other in fell cankred mood,
Beat back their rayes by strong antipathie,
Or some more broad-spread cause doth choke their
      energie.

7

But to go on to that common conceit
Of the first matter : What can substance do,
Poore, naked substance, megre, dry, dull, slight,
Inert, unactive, that no might can show
Of good or ill to either friend or foe,
All livelesse, all formlesse ? She doth sustain.
And hath no strength that task to undergo ?
Besides that work is needlesse all in vain :
Each *centrall* form its rayes with ease can well up-stayen.

8

What holds the earth in this the fluid aire ?
Can matter void of fix'd solidity ?
But she like kindly nurse her forms doth chear.
What can be suck'd from her dark dugges drie ?
Nor warmth, nor moistnesse, nor fast density
Belong to her.   Therefore ill nurse I ween
She'll make, that neither hath to satisfie
Young-craving life, nor firmnesse to sustein
The burden that upon her arms should safely lean.

9

Therefore an uselesse superfluity
It is to make *Hyle* substantiall :
Onely let's term't the possibility
Of all created beings.   Lives *centrall*
Can frame themselves a right compositall,
While as they sitten soft in the sweet rayes
Or vitall vest of the lives generall,
As those that out of the earths covert raise
Themselves, fairly provok'd by warmth of sunny dayes.

10

And thus all accidents will prove the beams
Of inward forms, their flowing energy ;
And quantity th' extension of such streams,
That goes along even with each qualitie.
Thus have we div'd to the profundity
Of darkest matter, and have found it nought :
But all this world's bare *Possibility*.
Nought therefore 'gainst lifes durance can be brought
From *Hyles* pit, that quenchen may that pleasant
      thought.

The Argument of

PSYCHATHANASIA,

Or

The Immortalitie of the Soul.

Mans soul with beasts and plants I here
Compare; Tell my chief end
His immortality's to clear;
Show whence grosse errours wend.

1

But hitherto I have with fluttering wings
But lightly hover'd in the generall,
And taught the lasting durance of all springs
Of hidden life. That life hight *seminall,*
Doth issue forth from its deep root centrall,
One onely form entire, and no'te advert
What steals from it. Beasts life *Phantasticall*
Lets out more forms, and eke themselves convert
To view the various frie from their dark wombs exert.

2

But mans vast soul, the image of her Maker,
Like God that made her, with her mighty sway
And inward *Fiat* (if he nould forsake her)
Can turn sad darknesse into lightsome day,
And the whole creature 'fore her self display :
Bid them come forth and stand before her sight,
They straight flush out and her drad voice obey :
Each shape, each life doth leapen out full light,
And at her beck return into their usuall *Night.*

3

Oft God himself here listeth to appear,
Though not perforce yet of his own frank will
Sheds his sweet life, disprends his beauty clear,
And like the Sun this lesser world doth fill,
And like the Sun doth the foul *Python* kill
With his bright darts, but cheareth each good spright.
This is the soul that I with presser quill
Must now pursue and fall upon down-right,
Not to destroy but prove her of immortall might.

4

Nor let blind Momus dare my Muse backbite,
As wanton or superfluously wise
For what is past. She is but justly quit
With Lucrece, who all souls doth mortalize :
Wherefore she did them all immortalize. ;
Besides in beasts and men th' affinity
Doth seem so great, that without prejudice
To many proofs for th' immortality
Of humane Souls, the same to beasts we no'te deny.

5

But I herein no longer list contend.
The two first kinds of souls I'll quite omit,
And 'cording as at first I did intend
Bestirre me stifly, force my feeble wit
To rescue humane souls from deaths deep pit ;
Which I shall do with reasons as subtile
As I can find ; slight proofs cannot well fit
In so great cause, nor phansies florid wile ;
I'll win no mans assent by a false specious guile.

6

I onely wish that arguments exile
May not seem nought unto the duller eye ;
Nor that the fatter phansie my lean style
Do blame : it's fittest for philosophy.
And give me leave from any energie
That springs from humane soul my cause to prove,
And in that order as they list to flie
Of their own selves, so let them freely rove :
That naturally doth come doth oft the stronger move.

7

Self-motion and centrall stability
I have already urg'd in generall ;
Als' did right presly to our soul apply
Those properties, who list it to recall

Unto their minds ; but now we'll let it fall
As needlesse.   Onely that vitality,
That doth extend this great Universall,
And move th' inert Materiality
Of great and little worlds, that keep in memory.

8

And how the mixture of their rayes may breed
Th' opinion of uncertain quality,
When they from certain roots of life do spreed ;
But their pure beams must needs ychangèd be
When that those rayes or not be setten free,
Thinly dispers'd, or else be closely meint
With other beams of plain diversity,
That causeth oft a strong impediment :
So doth this bodies life to the souls high intent.

9

The lower man is nought but a fair plant,
Whose grosser matter is from the base ground ;
The Plastick might thus finely did him paint,
And fill'd him with the life that doth abound
In all the places of the world around.
This spirit of life is in each shapen'd thing,
Suck'd in and changèd and strangely confound,
As we conceive :   This is the nourishing
Of all ; but *spermall* form, the certain shapening.

10

This is that strange-form'd statue magicall,
That hovering souls unto it can allure
When it's right fitted ; down those spirits fall
Like Eagle to her prey, and so endure
While that low life is in good temperature.
That a dead body without vitall spright
And friendly temper should a guest procure
Of so great worth, without the dear delight
Of joyous sympathy, no man can reckon right.

11

But here unluckly Souls do waxen sick
Of an ill surfeit from the poison'd bait
Of this sweet tree, yet here perforce they stick
In weak condition, in a languid state.
Many through ignorance do fondly hate
To be releas'd from this imprisonment,
And grieve the walls be so nigh ruinate.
They be bewitch'd so with the blandishment
Of that fresh strumpet, when in love they first were meant.

12

Others disdain this so near unity,
So farre they be from thinking they be born

Of such low parentage, so base degree,
And fleshes foul attraction they do scorn.
They be th' outgoings of the *Eastern morn*,
Alli'd unto th' eternall Deity,
And pray to their first spring, that thus forlorn
And left in mud, that he would set them free,
And them again possesse of pristine purity.

13

But seemeth not my Muse too hastily
To soar aloft, that better by degrees
Unto the vulgar mans capacity
Mought show the souls so high excellencies,
And softly from all corporeities
It heaven up unto its proper seat,
When we have drove away grosse falsities,
That do assault the weaker mens conceit,
And free the simple mind from phansies foul deceit.

14

The drooping soul so strongly's colourèd
With the long commerce of corporeals,
That she from her own self awide is led,
Knows not her self, but by false name she calls
Her own high being, and what ere befalls
Her grosser bodie, she that misery
Doth deem her own : for she her self miscalls
Or some thin body, or spread quality,
Or point of quality, or fixt or setten free.

15

But whether thin spread body she doth deem
Her self dispersèd through this grosser frame ;
Or doth her self a quality esteem,
Or quient complexion, streaming through the same ;
Or else some lucid point her self doth name
Of such a quality in chiefest part
Strongly fix'd down ; or whether she doth clame
More freedome from that point, in head nor heart
Fast seated ; yet, saith she, the bodies brat thou art.

16

Thence thou arose, thence thou canst not depart :
There die thou must, when thy dear nurse decayes :
But these false phansies I with reason smart
Shall eas'ly chace away, and the mind raise
To higher pitch.   O listen to my layes,
And when you have seen fast seald eternity
Of humane souls, then your great Maker praise
For his never fading benignity,
And feed your selves with thought of immortality.

The *Argument* of

PSYCHATHANASIA,

Or,

The Immortality of the Soul.

BOOK II. CANT. 2.

Sense no good judge of truth: What spright,
What body we descry:
Prove from the souls inferiour might
Her incorp'reitie.

1

Hile I do purpose with my self to sing
The souls incorporeity, I fear
That it a worse perplexitie may bring
Unto the weaker mind and duller ear ;
For she may deem herself 'stroyd quite & clear
While all corporeals from her we expell :
For she has yet not mark'd that higher sphear
Where her own essence doth in safety dwell,
But views her lower shade, like boy at brink of well ;

2

Dotes upon sense, ne higher doth arise
Busied about vain forms corporeall ;
Contemns as nought unseen exilities,
Objects of virtue *Intellectuall,*
Though these of substances be principall.
But I to better hope would fainly lead
The sunken mind, and cunningly recall
Again to life that long hath liggen dead :
Awake ye drooping souls ! shake off that drousihead !

3

Why do you thus confide in sleepy sense,
Ill judge of her own objects ? who'll believe
The eye contracting Phœbus Orb immense
Into the compasse of a common sieve?
If solid reason did not us relieve,
The host of heaven alwayes would idle stand
In our conceit, nor could the Sun revive
The nether world, nor do his Lords command :
Things near seem further off ; farst off, the nearst at hand.

4

The touch acknowledgeth no gustables ;
The tast no fragrant smell or stinking sent ;

The smell doth not once dream of audibles ;
The hearing never knew the verdant peint
Of springs gay mantle, nor heavens light ylent
That must discover all that goodly pride :
So that the senses would with zeal fervent
Condemne each other, and their voice deride
If mutually they heard such things they never try'd.

5

But reason, that above the sense doth sit,
Doth comprehend all their impressions,
And tells the touch its no fanatick fit
That makes the sight of illustrations
So stifly talk upon occasions.
But judgeth all their voyces to be true
Concerning their straight operations,
And doth by nimble consequences shew
To her own self what those wise Five yet never knew.

6

They never knew ought but corporealls :
But see how reason doth their verdict rude
Confute, by loosening materialls
Into their principles, as latitude
Profundity of bodies to conclude.
The term of latitude is breadthlesse line ;
A point the line doth manfully retrude
From infinite processe ; site doth confine
This point ; take site away its straight a spark divine.

7

And thus unloos'd it equally respects
The bodies parts, not fixt to any one.
Let 't be diffused through all.   Thus it detects
The soul's strange nature, operation,
Her independency, loose union
With this frail body.   So 's this unity
Great, but without that grosse extension,
Exceeding great in her high *energie,*
Extended far and wide from her non-quantity.

8

If yet you understand not, let the soul,
Which you suppose extended with this masse,

Be all contract and close together roll
Into the centre of the hearts compasse :
As the suns beams that by a concave glasse
Be strangely strengthned with their strait constraint
Into one point, that thence they stoutly passe,
Fire all before them withouten restraint,
The high arch'd roof of heaven with smouldry smoke
    they taint.

9

But now that grosnesse, which we call the heart,
Quite take away, and leave that spark alone
Without that sensible corporeall part
Of humane body : so when that is gone,
One nimble point of life, that's all at one
In its own self, doth wonderfully move,
Indispers'd, quick, close with self-union,
Hot, sparkling, active, mounting high above,
In bignesse nought, in virtue like to thundring Jove.

10

Thus maugre all th' obmurmurings of sense
We have found an essence incorporeall,
A shifting centre with circumference,
But she not onely sits in midst of all,
But is also in a manner centrall
In her outflowing lines. For the extension
Of th' outshot rayes circumferentiall
Be not gone from her by distrought distension,
Her point is at each point of all that spread dimension.

11

This is a substance truly spirituall,
That reason by her glistring lamp hath shown :
No such the sense in things corporeall
Can ere find out. May this perswasion,
O sunken souls! slaves of sensation!
Rear up your heads and chase away all fear
How (when by strong argumentation
I shall you strip of what so doth appear
Corporeall) that you to nought should vanish clear.

12

The naked essence of the body's this
Matter extent in three dimensions
(Hardnesse or softnesse be but qualities)
Withouten *self-reduplications*
Or *outspread circling propagations*
Of its own presence. These be corporall,
And what with these in such extension
Singly's stretch'd out, is form materiall.
Whether our soul be such now to the test we'll call :

13

If souls be bodies, or inanimate
They be, or else endowed with life. If they
Be livelesse, give they life? if animate,
Then tell me what doth life to them convey?
Some other body? Here can be no stay.
Straight we must ask whether that livelesse be

Or living. Then, what 'lives it. Thus we'll play
Till we have forc'd you to infinity,
And make your cheeks wax red at your Philosophy.

14

Again, pray tell me, is this body grosse
Or fluid, and thin you deem the soul to be ?
If grosse, then either strongly it is cross'd
From entring some parts of this rigid tree
And so of life they'll want their 'lotted fee :
Or if it penetrate this bulk throughout,
It breaks and tears and puts to penalty
This sory corse. If't thin and fluid be thought,
How pulls it up those limbs and again jerks them out ?

15

Besides, if stretchen corporeity
Longs to the soul, then Augmentation
Must likewise thereto appertain. But see
Th' absurdities that this opinion
Will drag on with it : for effluxion
Of parts will spoil the steddy memory,
And wash away all intellection,
Deface the beauty of that imagery
That once was fairly graven in her phantasie.

16

But oft when the weak bodie's worn and wasted
And far shrunk in, the nimble phantasie
(So far she's from being witherèd and blasted)
More largely worketh, and more glitterandly
Displayes her spreaden forms, and chearfully
Pursues her sports. Again, the greater corse
Would most be fill'd with magnanimity :
But oft we see the lesse hath greater force,
To fight, or talk ; the greater oft we see the worse.

17

All which if weighèd well, must ill agree
With bodies natures, which merely consist
In a dull, silent, stupid quantity,
Stretching forth mirksome matter, in what list
Or precincts no man knows. No Naturalist
Can it define, unless they adde a form
That easly curbs the thing that no'te resist,
And after her own will can it inform :
It still and stupid stands and thinks nor good nor harm.

18

The man is mad, that will at all agree
That this is soul. Or if forme bodily
Non-replicate, extent, not setten free,
But straight stretch'd out in corporeity
(Betwixt these two there's that affinity)
As little wit that man will seem to have.
Which I shall plainly prove by th' energie
Of sense, though that same force seem not so brave,
Yet for the present I'll not climbe to higher stave.

19

If Souls be substances corporeall,
Be they as big just as the body is?
Or shoot they out to th' height Æthereall?
(Of such extent are the sights energies)
If they shoot out, be they equally transmisse
Around this body? or but upward start?
If round the body, Nature did amisse
To lose her pains in half of the souls part,
That part can finden nought that through the earth doth
 dart.

20

Or will you say she is an hemisphere?
But a ridiculous experiment
Will soon confute it : list you but to rear
Your agill heels towards the firmament,
And stand upon your head ; that part is bent
Down through the earth, that earst did threat the skie :
So that your soul now upward is extent
No higher then your heels, yet with your eye
The heavens great vastnesse as before you now discry.

21

You'll say, this souls thin spread exility
Turns not at all. How doth it then depend
Upon this body? It has no unity
Therewith, but onely doth of cur'sy lend
It life, as doth the worlds great lamp down send
Both light and warmth unto each living wight ;
And if they chance to fail and make an end,
Its nought to him, he shineth yet as bright
As ere he did. This showes the soul immortall quite.

22

But if the soul be justly coextent
With this straight body, nought can bigger be
Then is our body, that she doth present ;
'Cording to laws of Corporeity
So must she represent each realty.
Thus tallest Gyants would be oft defied
By groveling Pigmees : for they could not see
The difference, nor mete his manly stride,
Nor ween what matchlesse strength did in his armes
 reside.

23

For they must judge him just as their own selves
Of the same stature, of the self-same might :
All men would seem to them their fellow Elves ;
Nor little curs would tremble at the sight
Of greater dogs ; nor hawks would put to flight
The lesser birds. Th' impression of a seal
Can be no larger then the wax ; or right
As big, or lesse it is. Therefore repeal
This grosse conceit, and hold as reason doth reveal.

24

Again, if souls corporeall you ween ;
Do the light images of things appear

Upon the surface, slick, bright, smooth and sheen
As in a looking glasse? Or whether dare
They passe the outside and venture so farre
As into the depth of the souls substance?
If this ; then they together blended are
That nought we see with right discriminance :
If that, the object gone, away those forms do glance.

25

Thus should we be devoid of memory,
And be all darknesse, till the good presence
Of outward objects doth the soul unty
From heavy sleep. But this experience
Plainly confutes. For even in their absence
We do retain their true similitude :
So lovers wont to maken dalliance
With the fair shade their minds do still include,
And wistly view the grace wherewith she is endude.

26

But now new reasons I will set on foot,
Drawn from the common sense, that's not extense
But like a centre that around doth shoot
Its rayes ; those rayes should be the outward sense
As some resemble't. But by no pretence
Would I the outward senses should be thought
To act so in a spread circumference
That the seat of their forms should be distrought,
Or that by reach of quantities dead arms they wrought.

27

For see how little share hath quantitie
In act of seeing, when we comprehend
The heavens vast compasse in our straitned eye ;
Nor may the Ox with the Eagle contend,
Because a larger circle doth extend
His slower lights. So that if outward sense
In his low acts doth not at all depend
On quantity, how shall the common-sense,
That is farre more spirituall, depend from thence?

28

But still more presly this point to pursue ;
By th' smelling, odours ; voices by the ear ;
By th' eye we apprehend the coloured hew
Of bodies visible. But what shall steer
The erring senses? where shall they compear
In controversie? what the difference
Of all their objects can with judgement clear
Distinguish and discern? One common-sense :
For one alone must have this great preeminence.

29

And all this one must know, though still but one ;
Else't could not judge of all. But make it two ;
Then tell me, doth the soul by this alone
Apprehend this object that the sense doth show,
And that by that ; or doth it by both know
Both objects? as this colour and that sound.
If both knew both, then nature did bestow
In vain one faculty, it doth redound :
But if this that, that this, what shall them both compound?

30

And by comparison judge of them both?
Therefore that judge is one. But whether one
Without division, let's now try that troth.
If it be any wise extent, you're gone
By the same reason that afore was shown.
Suppose't a line the least of quantity.
Or sound is here, there colour, or each one
Of the lines parts receive them both. If we
Grant that, again we find a superfluity.

31

If this part this, and that part that receive,
We are at the same losse we were afore,
For one to judge them both, or we bereave
Our souls of judgement. For who can judge more
Than what he knows? It is above his power.
Therefore it's plain the common sense is one,
One individed faculty. But store
Of parts would breed a strange confusion,
When every part mought claim proper sensation.

32

If not, nor all could exercise the Act
Of any sense. For could a power of sense
Arise from stupid parts that plainly lack'd
That might themselves. Thus with great confidence
We may conclude that th' humane souls essence
Is indivisible, yet every where
In this her body. Cause th' intelligence
She hath of whatsoever happens here :
The aking foot the eye doth view, the hand doth cheer.

33

What tells the hand or head the toes great grief,
When it alone is pinch'd with galling shooes?
Do other parts not hurt call for relief
For their dear mates? Ill messenger of woes
That grieveth not himself. Can they disclose
That misery without impression
Upon themselves? Therefore one spirit goes
Through all this bulk, not by extension
But by a totall *Self-reduplication.*

34

Which neither body, nor dispersèd form,
Nor point of form dispersèd e'r could do.
And bodies life or sprite for to transform
Into our soul, though that might this undo,
Yet to so rash conceit to yield unto
Cannot be safe : for if it propagate
It's self and 'ts passions, yet they free may go
Unmark'd, if sense would not them contemplate.
So doth the *Mundane* sprite not heeded circulate.

35

Besides, if from that spirit naturall
The nurse of plants, you should dare to assert
That lively inward *Animadversall*
To springen out, it would surely invert

36

The order of the Orbs from whence do stert
All severall beings and of them depend.
Therefore the Orb *Phantastick* must exert
All life *phantasticall ; sensitive* send
The life of sense ; so of the rest unto each end.

36

There's nought from its own self can senden forth
Ought better then it self. So nought gives sense
That hath not sense it self, nor greater worth
Then sense, nor sense, nor better springs from thence.
Nor that which higher is can have essence
Lesse active, lesse *reduplicate*, lesse free,
Lesse spiritall, then that's amov'd from hence,
And is an Orb of a more low degree.
Wherefore that centrall life hath more activitie,

37

And present is in each part totally
Of this her body. Nor we ought diffide,
Although some creatures still alive we see
To stirre and move when we have them divide
And cut in twain. Thus worms in sturdie pride
Do wrigge and wrest their parts divorc'd by knife ;
But we must know that Natures womb doth hide
Innumerable treasures of all life ;
And how to breaken out upon each hint they strive.

38

So when the present actuall centrall life
Of sense and motion is gone with one part
To manage it, strait for the due relief
Of th' other particle there up doth start
Another centrall life, and tries her art :
But she cannot raigne long, nor yet recure
That deadly wound. The plantall lifes depart,
And flitten or shrunk spright, that did procure
Her company, being lost, make her she'll not endure.

39

And so at last is gone, from whence she came,
For soon did fade that sweet allurement,
The plantall life, which for a while did flame
With sympathetick fire, but that being spent
Straight she is flown. Or may you this content ?
That some impression of that very soul
That's gone, if gone, with plantall spirit meint
The broken corse thus busily may roll.
Long 'tis till water boild doth stranger heat controul.

40

Thus have we prov'd 'cording to our insight
That humane souls be not corporeall
(With reasons drawn from the sensitive might)
Nor bodies, nor spread forms materiall,
Whether you substances list them to call
Or qualities, or point of these. I'll bring
Hereafter proofs from power rationall
In humane souls, to prove the self same-thing.
Mount up aloft, my Muse, and now more shrilly sing.

The *Argument of*

PSYCHATHANASIA,

Or,

The Immortality of the Soul.

The souls incorporeitie
From powers rationull
We prove ; Discern true pietie
From bitternesse and gall.

1

Ike Carpenter entred into a wood
  To cut down timber for some edifice
  Of stately structure, whiles he casts abroad
  His curious eye, he much perplexèd is
(There stand in view so many goodly trees)
Where to make choice to enter his rugg'd saw :
My Muse is plung'd in like perplexities,
So many arguments themselves do show,
That where to pitch my wavering mind doth yet scarce
  know.

2

One taller then the rest my circling eye
Hath hit upon, which if 't be sound at heart
Will prove a goodly piece to raise on high
The heavenly structure of that deemèd part
Of man, his soul, and by unerring art
Set his foundation 'bove the bodies frame
On his own wheels, that he may thence depart
Intire, unhurt. So doth the Scythian swain
Drive his light moving house on the waste verdant plain.

3

I'll sing of piety : that now I mean
That Trismegist thus wisely doth define,
Knowledge of God. That's piety I ween,
The highest of virtues, a bright beam divine
Which to the purer soul doth sweetly shine.
But what's this beam ? and how doth it enlight ?
What doth it teach ? It teacheth to decline
Self-love, and frampard wayes the hypocrite
Doth trample in, accloy'd with dirt and dismall night.

4

Not rage, nor mischief, nor love of a sect,
Nor eating fretfulnesse, harsh cruelty
Contracting Gods good will, nor conscience checkt
Or chok'd continually with impiety,
Fauster'd and fed with hid hypocrisie ;
Nor tyranny against perplexèd minds,
Nor forc'd conceit, nor man-idolatry,
All which the eye of searching reason blinds,
And the souls heavenly flame in dungeon darknesse
  binds.

5

Can warres and jarres and fierce contention,
Swoln hatred, and consuming envie spring
From piety ? No. 'Tis opinion
That makes the riven heavens with trumpets ring,
And thundring engine mur'drous balls out-sling,
And send mens groning ghosts to lower shade
Of horrid hell. This the wide world doth bring
To devastation, makes mankind to fade :
Such direfull things doth false Religion perswade.

6

But true Religion sprong from God above
Is like her fountain full of charity,
Embracing all things with a tender love,
Full of good will and meek expectancy,
Full of true justice and sure verity,
In heart and voice ; free, large, even infinite,
Not wedg'd in strait particularity,
But grasping all in her vast active spright,
Bright lamp of God ! that men would joy in thy pure
  light !

7

Can souls that be thus universalis'd,
Begot into the life of God e're dy ?

(His light is like the sun that doth arise
Upon the just and unjust) can they fly
Into a nothing? and hath God an eye
To see himself thus wasted and decay
In his true members? can mortality
Seize upon that that doth it self display
Above the laws of matter, or the bodies sway?

8

For both the body and the bodies spright
Doth things unto particulars confine,
Teaching them partiall friendship and fell spight.
But those pure souls full of the life divine :
Look upon all things with mild friendly eyne
Ready to do them good. Thus is their will
Sweetly spread out, and ever doth incline
The bent of the first Goodnesse to fulfill.
Ay me ! that dreary death such lovely life should spill !

9

Besides this largenesse in the will of man
And wingèd freenesse, now let's think upon
His understanding, and how it doth scan
Gods being, unto whom religion
Is consecrate. Imagination
That takes its rise from sence so high ascent
Can never reach, yet intellection
Or higher gets, or at least hath some sent
Of God, *vaticinates,* or is *parturient.*

10

For ask her whether God be this or that,
A body infinite, or some mighty spright,
Yet not almighty, such vain speech she'll hate.
Whether all present, or in some place pight,
Whether part here part there, or every whit
In every point, she likes that latter well :
So that its plain that some kind of insight
Of Gods own being in the soul doth dwell
Though what God is we cannot yet so plainly tell.

11

As when a name lodg'd in the memory,
But yet through time almost obliterate,
Confusely hovers near the phantasie :
The man that's thus affected bids relate
A catalogue of names. It is not that,
Saith he, nor that ; that's something like to it,
That nothing like, that's likst of all I wot.
This last you nam'd it's not like that a whit ;
O that's the very name, now we have rightly hit.

12

Thus if't be lawfull least things to compare
With greatest, so our selves affected be
Concerning Gods high essence : for we are
Not ignorant quite of this mystery,
Nor clearly apprehend the Deity,
But in mid state, I call't *parturient,*

And should bring forth that live Divinity
Within our selves, if once God would consent
To shew his specious form and nature eminent :

13

For here it lies like colours in the night
Unseen and unregarded, but the sunne
Displayes the beauty and the gladsome plight
Of the adornèd earth, while he doth runne
His upper stage. But this high prize is wonne
By curbing sense and the self-seeking life
(True Christian mortification)
Thus God will his own self in us revive,
If we to mortifie our straitned selves do strive.

14

But can ought bodily Gods form receive ?
Or have it in it self potentially ?
Or can ought sprung of this base body heve
It self so high as to the Deitie
To clamber ? strive to reach infinity ?
Can ought born of this carcase be so free
As to grasp all things in large sympathie ?
Can lives corporeall quite loosened be
From their own selves, casheering their *centreity ?*

15

These all ill suit with corporeitie :
But do we not amisse with stroke so strong
All to dispatch at once? needed we flie
So high at first ? we might have chose among
The many arguments that close do throng
And tender their own selves this cause to prove
Some of a meaner rank, and then along
Fairly and softly by degrees to move.
My Muse kens no such pomp, she must with freedome
rove.

16

And now as chance her guides, compendiously
The heads of many proofs she will repeat,
Which she lists not pursue so curiously,
But leaves the Reader his own brains to beat,
To find their fuller strength. As the souls meat,
Of which she feeds, if that she fed at all ;
She is immortall if she need not eat ;
But if her food prove to be spirituall,
Then can we deem herself to be corporeall ?

17

The souls most proper food is verity
Got and digest by Contemplation.
Hence strength, enlargement, and activity
She finds, as th' body by infusion
Of grosser meats and drinks (concoction
Well perfected) our limbs grow strong by these ;
The soul by reasons right perswasion :
But that truths spirituall we may with ease
Find out : For truth the soul from bodies doth release.

18

Next argument let be abstraction,
Whenas the soul with notion precise
Keeps off the corporall condition,
And a nak'd simple essence doth devise
Against the law of Corporeities,
It doth devest them both of time and place,
And of all individualities,
And matter doth of all her forms uncase,
Corporeall wight such subtile virtue never has.

19

Now shall the indivisibilitie
Of the souls virtues make an argument.
For certainly there's no such qualitie
Resideth in a body that's extent.
For, tell me, is that quality strait pent
Within a point of that corporeall ?
Or is it with some spreaden part distent ?
If in a point, then 'longs it not at all
To th' body : in spread part ? then 'tis extentionall.

20

But that some virtue's not extentionall
May thus be provèd. Is there no science
Of numbers? Yes. But what is principall
And root of all : have we intelligence
Of Unities ? Or else what's sprong from thence
We could not know : what doth the soul then frame
Within her self ? Is that Idea extense?
Or indivisible ? If not, we'll blame
The soul of falshood, and continuall lying shame.

21

Again, if we suppose our intellect
Corporeall, then must we all things know
By a swift touch : what ? do we then detect
The truth of bignesse, when one point doth go
Of our quick mind ? (It need not be o'reflow
For infinite parts be found in quantitie)
Or doth it use its latitude ? If so
Remember that some things unspreaden be,
How shall it find them out ? Or if 't use both we'll see.

22

That both be unsufficient I prove.
A point cannot discern loose unity
Freed from all site. That latitude must move
On all the body that it doth descry.
So must it be upstretch'd unto the skie
And rub against the Stars, surround the Sun
And her own parts to every part apply,
Then swiftly fridge about the pallid Moon :
Thus both their quantities the mind hath strangely won.

23

Adde unto these, that the soul would take pains
For her destruction while she doth aspire
'To reach at things (that were her wofull gains)

That be not corporall, but seated higher
Above the bodies sphere. Thus should she tire
Her self to 'stroy her self. Again, the mind
Receives contrary forms. The feverish fire
Makes her cool brooks and shadowing groves to find
Within her thoughts, thus hot and cold in one she binds.

24

Nor is she chang'd by the susception
Of any forms : For thus her self contraire
Should be unto her self. But Union
She then possesseth, when heat and cold are
Together met : They meet withouten jarre
Within our souls. Such forms they be not true
You'll say. But of their truth lest you despair,
Each form in purer minds more perfect hew
Obtains, then those in matter we do dayly view.

25

For there, they're mixt, soild and contaminate,
But truth doth clear, unweave, and simplifie,
Search, sever, pierce, open, and disgregate
All ascititious cloggins ; then doth eye
The naked essence and its property,
Or you must grant the soul cannot define
Ought right in things ; or you must not deny
These forms be true that in her self do shine :
These be her rule of truth, these her unerring line.

26

Bodies have no such properties. Again,
See in one cluster many arguments
Compris'd : She multitudes can close constrain
Into one nature. Things that be fluent,
As flitting time, by her be straight retent
Unto one point ; she joyns future and past,
And makes them steddy stand as if present :
Things distant she can into one place cast :
Calls kinds immortall, though their singulars do waste.

27

Upon her self she strangely operates,
And from her self and by her self returns
Into her self ; thus the soul circulates.
Do bodies so ? Her axle-tree it burns
With heat of motion. This low world she spurns,
Raiseth her self to catch infinity.
Unspeakable great numbers how she turns
Within her mind, like evening mist the eye
Discerns, whose muddy atomes 'fore the wind do fly.

28

Stretcheth out time at both ends without end,
Makes place still higher swell, often creates
What God nere made, nor doth at all intend
To make, free phantasms ; laughs at future fates,
Foresees her own condition, she relates
Th' all comprehension of eternity,
Complains she's thirsty still in all estates,
That all she sees or has no'te satisfie
Her hungry self, nor fill her vast capacity.

19   I

29

But I'll break off ; My Muse her self forgot,
Her own great strength and her foes feeblenesse,
That she her name by her own pains may blot,
While she so many strokes heaps in excesse,
'That fond grosse phansie quite for to suppresse
Of the souls corporal'tie. For men may think
Her adversaries strength doth thus her presse
To multitude of reasons, makes her swink
With weary toyl, and sweat out thus much forcèd ink :

30

Or that she loves with trampling insultations
To domineere in easie victory.
But let not men dare cast such accusations
Against the blamelesse. For no mastery,
Nor fruitlesse pomp, nor any verity
Of that opinion that she here destroyes
Made her so large. No, 'tis her jealousie
'Gainst witching falshood that weak souls annoyes,
And oft doth choke those chearing hopes of lasting joyes.

The Argument of

PSYCHATHANASIA,

Or

The Immortality of the Soul.

BOOK III. CANT. I.

The souls free independency ;
Her drery dreadfull state
In hell ; Her tricentreity :
What brings to heavens gate.

I

WEll said that man, whatever man that was,
That said, what things we would we straight
believe
Upon each slight report t' have come to
passe :
But better he, that said, Slow faith we give
To things we long for most. Hope and fear rive
Distracted minds, as when nigh equall weights
Cast on the trembling scales, each tug and strive
To pull the other up. But the same sleights
By turns do urge them both in their descents and heights :

2

Thus waves the mind in things of greatest weight ;
For things we value most are companied
With fear as well as hope : these stifly fight :

The stronger hope, the stronger fear is fed;
One mother both and the like livelybed.
One object both, from whence they both do spring.
The greater she, the greater these she bred,
The greater these, the greater wavering
And longer time to end their sturdy struggeling.

3

But is there any thing of more import
Then the souls immortality ? Hence fear
And hope we striving feel with strong effort
Against each other : That nor reason clear
Nor sacred Oracles can straight down bear
That sturdy rascall, with black phantasies
Yclad, and clouded with drad dismall chear ;
But still new mists he casts before our eyes,
And now derides our prov'd incorporieties,

4

And grinning saith, That labour's all in vain.
For though the soul were incorporeall,
Yet her existence to this flesh restrain,
They be so nearly link'd, that if one fall
The other fails. The eare nor hears our call

In stouping age, nor eye can see ought clear ;
Benumming palsies shake the bodies wall,
The soul hath lost her strength and cannot steer
Her crasie corse, but staggering on reels here and there.

5

So plain it is (that though the soul's a spright,
Not corporall) that it must needs depend
Upon this body, and must perish quite
When her foundation falls.   But now attend
And see what false conceits vain fears do send :
'Tis true, I cannot write without a quill,
Nor ride without an horse.   If chance that rend
Or use make blunt, o're-labouring this kill,
Then can I walk not ride, not write but think my fill.

6

Our body is but the souls instrument ;
And when it fails, onely these actions cease
That thence depend.   But if new eyes were sent
Unto the agèd man, with as much ease
And accuratenesse, as when his youth did please
The wanton lasse, he now could all things see.
Old age is but the watry blouds disease.
The soul from death and sickness standeth free :
My hackney fails, not I ; my pen, not sciencie.

7

But as I said, of things we do desire
So vehemently we never can be sure
Enough.   Therefore, my Muse, thou must aspire
To higher pitch, and fearfull hearts secure
Not with slight phansie but with reason pure.
Evincing the souls independency
Upon this body that doth her immure ;
That when from this dark prison she shall flie
All men may judge her rest in immortality.

8

Therefore I'll sing the *Tricentreity*
Of humane souls, and how they wake from sleep,
In which ywrapt of old they long do lie
Contract with cold and drench'd in Lethe deep,
Hugging their plantall point.   It makes me weep
Now I so clearly view the solemn Spring
Of silent Night, whose Magick dew doth steep
These drowsie souls of men, whose dropping wing
Keeps off the light of life, and blunts each fiery sting.

9

Three centres hath the soul ; One plantall hight :
Our parents this revive in nuptiall bed.
This is the principle that hales on Night,
Subjects the mind unto dull drowsyhed :
If we this follow, thus we shall be led
To that dark straitnesse that did bind before
Our sluggish life when that is shrivellèd
Into its sunken centre, we no more
Are conscious of life : what can us then restore?

10

Unlesse with fiery whips fell Nemesis
Do lash our sprights, and cruelly do gore
Our groning ghosts ; this is the way, I wisse,
The onely way to keep 's from Morpheus power.
Both these so dismall are that I do showr
Uncessant tears from my compassionate eyes :
Alas ! ye souls ! Why should or sleep devour
Sweet functions of life ? or hellish cries
To tender heart resound your just calamities ?

11

Thus may you all from your dead drowsinesse
Be wak'd by inward sting and pinching wo,
That you could wish that that same heavinesse
Might ever you o'represse, and Lethe flow
Upon your drownèd life.   But you shall glow
With urging fire, that doth resuscitate
Your middle point, and makes itself to gnaw
Itself with madnesse, while 't doth ruminate
On its deformity and sterill vexing state.

12

Continuall desire that nought effects,
Perfect hot-glowing fervour out to spring
In some good world : With fury she affects
To reach the Land of life, then struck with sting
Of wounding memory, despairs the thing,
And further off she sees her self, the more
She rageth to obtain : thus doth she bring
More fewell to her flame that scorchèd sore
With searching fire, she's forc'd to yell and loudly rore.

13

Thus she devours her self, not satisfies
Her self ; nought hath she but what's dearly spun
From her own bowels, jejune exilities :
Her body's gone, therefore the rising sun
She sees no more, nor what in day is done,
The sporting aire no longer cools her bloud,
Pleasures of youth and manhood quite are gone,
Nor songs her eare, nor mouth delicious food
Doth fill.   But I 'll have this more fully understood.

14

Three centres hath mans soul in Unity
Together joynd ; or if you will, but one.
Those three are one, with a Triplicity
Of power or rayes.   Th' high'st intellection,
Which being wak'd the soul's in Union
With God.   If perfectly regenerate
Into that better world, corruption
Hath then no force her blisse to perturbate,
The low'st do make us subject to disturbing fate.

15

But low'st 'gins first to work, the soul doth frame
This bodies shape, imploy'd in one long thought
So wholy taken up, that she the same

Observeth not, till she it quite hath wrought.
So men asleep some work to end have brought
Not knowing of it, yet have found it done :
Or we may say the matter that she raught
And suck'd unto her self to work upon
Is of one warmth with her own spright, & feels as one.

16

And thus the body being the souls work
From her own centre so entirely made,
Seated i' th' heart,—for there this spright doth lurk,—
It is no wonder 'tis so easly sway'd
At her command. But when this work shall fade,
The soul dismisseth it as an old thought,
'Tis but one form ; but many be display'd
Amid her higher rayes, dismist, and brought
Back as she list, & many come that ne're were sought.

17

The soul by making this strange edifice,
Makes way unto herself to exercise
Functions of life, and still more wakèd is
The more she has perfected her fine devise,
Hath wrought her self into sure sympathies
With this great world.   Her ears like hollow caves
Resound to her own spright the energies
Of the worlds spright.   If it ought suffered have,
Then *presentifick circles* to her straight notice gave.

18

We know this world, because our soul hath made
Our bodie of this sensible worlds spright
And body.   Therefore in the glassie shade
Of our own eyes (they having the same might
That glasse or water hath) we have the sight
Of what the *Mundane* spirit suffereth
By colours, figures, or inherent light :
Sun, stars, and all on earth hath sight
To each point of itself so far as 't *circuleth*.

19

And where he lighteth on advantages,
His *circulings* grow sensible.   So hills
That hollow be do audible voices
Resound.   The soul doth imitate that skill
In framing of the eare, that sounds may swell
In that concavitie.   The crystall springs
Reflect the light of heaven, if they be still
And clear ; the soul doth imitate and bring
The eye to such a temper in her shapening.

20

So eyes and ears be not mere perforations,
But a due temper of the *Mundane* spright
And ours together ; else the *circulations*
Of sounds would be well known by outward sight,
And th' eare would colours know, figures & light.
So that it's plain that when this bodie 's gone,
This world to us is clos'd in darknesse quite,
And all to us is in dead silence drown :
Thus in one point of time is this worlds glory flown.

21

But if 't be so, how doth *Psyche* hear or see
That hath nor eyes nor eares?   She sees more clear
Then we that see but secondarily.
We see at distance by a *circular*
Diffusion of that spright of this great sphear
Of th' Universe : Her sight is tactuall.
The Sun and all the starres that do appear
She feels them in herself, can distance all,
For she is at each one purely presentiall.

22

To us what doth *diffusion circular*,
And our pure shadowed eyes, bright, crystalline.
But vigorously our spright particular
Affect, while things in it so clearly shine?
That's done continually in the heavens sheen.
The Sun, the Moon, the Earth, blew-glimmering Hel,
Scorch'd Ætna's bowels, each shape you'l divine
To be in Nature, every dern cell
With fire-eyed dragons, or what else therein doth dwel :

23

These be all parts of the wide worlds excesse,
They be all seated in the *Mundane* spright,
And shew just as they are in their bignesse
To her.   But *circulation* shews not right
The magnitude of things : for distant site
Makes a deficience in these *circulings*.
But all things lie ope-right unto the sight
Of heavens great eye ; their thin-shot shadowings
And lightned sides.   All this we find in Natures springs.

24

The worlds great soul knows by *Protopathie*
All what befalls this lower sprite, but we
Can onely know't by *Deuteropathie*,
At least in sight and hearing.   She doth see
In our own eyes, by the close unitie
Of ours and the worlds life, our passion ;
Plainly perceives our *Idiopathie*,
As we do hers, by the same union ;
But we cannot see hers in that perfection.

25

Fresh varnish'd groves, tall hills, and gilded clouds
Arching an eyelid for the glowing Morn ;
Fair clustred buildings which our sight so crouds
At distance, with high spires to heaven yborn ;
Vast plains with lowly cottages forlorn,
Rounded about with the low wavering skie,
Cragg'd vapours, like to ragged rocks ytorn ;
She views those prospects in our distant eye :
These and such like be the first *centres* mysterie.

26

Or if you will the first low energie
Of that one centre, which the soul is hight,
Which knows this world by the close unitie

Concorporation with the *Mundane* sprite ;
Unloos'd from this she wants a certain light,
Unlesse by true regeneration
She be incorporate with God, unite
With his own spright ; so a new mansion
Sh' has got, oft saught with deepest suspiration.

27

But robb'd of her first clothing by hard fate,
If she fall short of this, wo's me ! what pains
She undergoes ? when this lost former state
So kindled hath lifes thirst, that still remains.
Thus her eternitie her nothing gains
But hungry flames, raging voracitie
Feeding on its own self.   The heavens she stains
With execrations and foul blasphemie :
Thus in fell discontent and smoth'ring fire they frie.

28

Vain man that striv'st to have all things at will !
What wilt thou do in this sterilitie ?
Whom canst thou then command ? or what shall fill
Thy gaping soul ? O depth of miserie !
Prepare thy self by deep humilitie :
Destroy that fretting fire while thou art here,
Forsake this worlds bewitching vanitie,
Nor death nor hell then shalt thou need to fear :
Kill and cast down thy self, to heaven God shall thee rear.

29

This middle *centrall essence* of the soul
Is that which still survives asleep or waking :
The life she shed in this grosse earthly moul
Is quite shrunk up, lost in the bodies breaking :
Now with slight phantasms of her own fond making
She's clad (so is her life drie and jejune)
But all flit souls be not in the same taking :
That state this lifes proportion doth tune,
So as thou livest here, such measure must ensuen.

30

But they whose souls *deiform* summitie
Is waken'd in this life, and so to God
Are nearly joyn'd in a firm Unitie
(This outward bodie is but earthie clod
Digested, having life transfus'd abroad,
The worlds life and our lower vitalitie

Unite in one) their souls have their aboad
In Christs own body ; are eternally
One with our God, by true and strong communitie.

31

When we are clothèd with this outward world,
Feel the soft air, behold the glorious Sunne,
All this we have from meat that's daily hurld
Into these mouths.   But first of all we wonne
This priviledge by our first union
With this worlds body and diffusèd spright.
I' th' higher world there's such communion :
Christ is the sunne that by his chearing might
Awakes our higher rayes to joyn with his pure light.

32

And when he hath that life elicited,
He gives his own dear body and his bloud
To drink and eat.   Thus dayly we are fed
Unto eternall life.   Thus do we bud,
True heavenly plants, suck in our lasting food
From the first spring of life, incorporate
Into the higher world (as erst I show'd
Our lower rayes the soul to subjugate
To this low world) we fearlesse sit above all fate.

33

Safely that kingdomes glory contemplate,
O'reflow with joy by a full sympathie
With that worlds sprite, and blesse our own estate,
Praising the fount of all felicitie,
The lovely light of the blest Deitie.
Vain mortals think on this, and raise your mind
Above the bodies life ; strike through the skie
With piercing throbs and sighs, that you may find
His face.   Base fleshly fumes your drowsie eyes thus
    blind.

34

So hath my Muse according to her skill
Discoverèd the soul in all her rayes,
The lowest may occasionate much ill,
But is indifferent.   Who may dispraise
Dame Natures work ? But yet you ought to raise
Your selves to higher state.   Eternitie
Is the souls rest, and everlasting dayes :
Aspire to this, and hope for victorie.
I further yet shall prove her immortalitie.

The *Argument of*

PSYCHATHANASIA

Or

The Immortality of the Soul.

Book III. Cant. 2.

From many arguments we show
The independencie
Of humane souls : That all Lives flow
From a free Deitie.

1

Hree apprehensions do my mind divide
Concerning the souls preexistencie,
Before into this outward world she glide :
So hath my muse with much uncertaintie
Exprest her self, so as her phantasie
Strongly inacted guides her easie pen ;
I nought obtrude with sow'r anxietie,
But freely offer hints to wiser men :
The wise from rash assent in darksome things abstein.

2

Or souls be well awake but hovering,
Not fixt to ought, but by a Magick might
Drawable here and there, and so their wing
Struck with the steem of this low *Mundane* sprite
May lower flag and take its stooping flight
Into some plantall man, new edified
By his own plastick point. Or else (deep Night
Drawn on by drooping phansie) she doth slide
Into this world, and by her self that skill is tried ;

3

Makes to her self this fleshly habitation ;
For this worlds spirit hath provok'd these rayes :
Then drown in sleep she works that efformation
Of her own body, all its parts displayes,
As doth the senselesse plant. The two next wayes
Are these : A reall *tricentreitie*.
First centre ever wakes, unmov'd stayes,
Hight *Intellect*. The next in sleep doth lie
Till the last *centre* burst into this open skie.

4

And then the middle wakes. But the last way
Makes but one centre, which doth sleep likewise
Till its low life hath reach'd this worlds glad day.
A fourth we'll adde that we may all comprise :
Take quite away all preexistencies
Of humane souls, and grant they're then first made
When they begin this bodies edifice,
And actually this outward world invade :
None of these wayes do show that they must ever fade.

5

The first way might be well occasionèd
By what the soul in her self feels and tries.
She works sometime as though she quite had fled
All commerce with these low carnalities,
Yet falls she down at last and lowly lies
In this base mansion, is so close contract
That sleep doth seise her *actualities*,
Retains no memory of that strange fact,
Nor of her self that soar'd in that high heavenly tract.

6

The second way that makes the soul *tricentrall*,
The highest awake, the other with sleep drownd,
May spring from hence. None would vouchsafe the entrall
Into this life, if they were but once bound
To that vast *centre* where all things are found,
Hight *Intellect*. The lowest is not awake,
Therefore the midst lies close in sleep upwound.
Three *centres* made, that souls may quite forsake
This baser world when union with the lowest they break.

7

Again, because this bodie's fashionèd
Without our knowledge, reason doth suggest

That it could no wise be thus figurèd
From our own *centre*, and yet we not prest
To any adversion. Therefore we are drest
With this grosse clothing by some plantall spright
Centred in Nature. So that glorious vest
The *Deiform intellect* by our own might's
Not made, but we have rayes which each of these will fit.

8

Ardent desire, strong breathing after God,
At length may work us to that better place,
Body or clothing, that high sure abond
That searching weather nor time can deface.
But to go on in our proposèd race,
The third and fourth way have the same foundation,
Not multiplying beings to surpasse
Their use. What needs that numerous clos'd *centra-
tion,*
Like wastefull sand ytost with boisterous inundation?

9

Let wiser Clerks the truth dare to define
I leave it loose for men to muse upon,
View at their leasure : but yet this call mine ;
Though we should grant the souls condition
Before her deep incorporation
Into dull matter, to be nothing more
But bare *potentiality*, yet none
Can prove from thence that she must fade therefore,
When to its earth this earth the trusty fates restore.

10

For though she and her body be at once,
Yet of her body she doth not depend
But it of her : she doth its members branch,
Pierce, bind, digest, and after makes it wend
At her own will, when she hath brought to end
Her curious work, and hath consolidate
Its tender limbs which earst did feebly bend
Through weaknesse ; then this world she contemplates,
And life still blazing higher seeks an heavenly state.

11

Breaths after the first fountain of all life,
Her sweet Creatour, thither doth aspire,
Would see his face ; nor will she cease this strife
Till he fulfill her thirsty fierce desire :
Nothing can quench this so deep rooted fire
But his own presence. So she 'gins despise
This bodies pleasures, ceaseth to admire
Ought fair or comely to these outward eyes :
Or if she do, from hence she higher doth arise.

12

But can she higher rise then her own head?
Therefore her spring is God : thence doth she 'pend,
Thence did she flow, thither again she's fled.
When she this life hath lost, and made an end
Of this low earthly course, she doth ascend,

Unto her circles ancient *Apogie,*
Lifted aloft, not again to descend,
Nor stoups nor sets that Sunne, but standeth free
On never-shaken pillars of Æternitie.

13

But still this truth more clearly to evince,
Remember how all things are from one light,
It shall thy reason forceably convince
That nought but God destroyes a *centrall* spright.
If be sucks in his beams, eternall night
Seiseth upon that life, that it no'te flow
In actuall efflux, hath no being quite
But Gods own power. He lets his breath out go,
The self-same things again so eas'ly doth he show.

14

Let be Noon day, the welkin clear, the Moon
I' th' nether world, reflecting the Suns rayes
To cheer the irksome night. Well ! That being done,
Call out some wondrous might, that listlesse stayes
In slower phansies. Bid't break all delayes ;
Surround with solid dark opacity
The utmost beams that Phœbus light displayes,
Softly steal on with equall distancy,
Till they have close clapt up all his explendency.

15

All's now in darknesse : tell me, what's become
Of that infinity of rayes that shone?
Where second centres from whence out did come
Other faint beams? what be they all quite flone?
All perish'd quite? You stiflers now be gone.
Let fall that smoring mantle. Do not straight
All things return? The nether world the Moon,
The Sun enlightens us. The self same light
Now shines, that shone before this deep and dismall
Night.

16

If not the same, then like to flowing stream
You deem the light that passeth still away,
New parts ever succeeding. The Sun-beam
Hath no reflexion then, if it decay
So fast as it comes forth : Nor were there day ;
For it would vanish 'fore it could arrive
At us. But in a moment Sol doth ray.
One end of his long shafts then we conceive,
At once both touch himself and down to us do dive.

17

Beside, this air is not the sustentation
Of spreaden light ; for then as it did move
The light would move. And sturdy conflictation
Of struggling winds, when they have fiercely strove,
Phœbus fair golden locks would rudely move
Out of their place ; and Eastern winds at morn
Would make more glorious dayes, while light is drove
From that bright quarter : Southern blasts do burn
From midday sun, but yet Northwinds like light have
born.

18

What then must be the channell of this river,
If we'll have light to flow as passing stream?
So plain it is that Nature doth dissever
The light and th' air, that th' air the Suns bright beams
Doth not uphold as the warmth of his gleams
Or heat that lodgeth there. From this firm might
Nought leaning on the Air, well may we't deem
Some subtile body, or some grosser spright
Depending of fair Phœbus, of no other wight.

19

And when these rayes were forcèd to retire
Into their fountain, they were not so gone
But that the same sprong out from the first fire.
So fine spun glittering silk crumpled in one
Changeth not 'ts individuation
From what it was, when it was gaily spread
In fluttering winds to th' admiration
Of the beholder. Thus is nought so dead
But God can it restore to its old livelyhed.

20

For all the creature's but the out-gone rayes
Of a free sunne, and what I meanèd most,
Of him alone depend. He deads their blaze
By calling in his breath. Though things be tost
And strangely chang'd, yet nought at all is lost
Unlesse he list. Nor then so lost but he
Can them return, In every thing compost
Each part of th' essence its *centreity*
Keeps to it self, it shrinks not to a nullity.

21

When that compounded nature is dissolv'd,
Each *centre's* safe, as safe as second light
Or drove into the Sun, or thence out-rol'd.
So all depend on th' Universall spright
From hight to depth, as they are rankèd right
In their due orders. Lifes full pregnancy
Breaks out when friendly sympathy doth smite.
The higher rank the higher energie
From natures lowly lap to Gods sublimity:

22

But well may man be call'd the epitome
Of all things. Therefore no low life him made.
The Highest holds all in His capacity,
Therefore mans soul from Gods own life outray'd,
His outgone *Centre's* on that centre staid.
What disadvantage then can the decay
Of this poore carcase do, when it doth fade?
The soul no more depends on this frail clay,
Then on our eye depends bright Phœbus glist'ring ray.

23

But in this argument we'll no longer stay,
Consider now the souls conversion
Into her self. Nought divisible may
Close with it self by revolution.

For then or part in this reflection,
Is drove into a part, or part to th' whole,
Or whole to part, or near compression
The whole into the whole doth closely roll:
But easily all these wayes right reason will controll.

24

If part turn into part, part into whole,
Whole into part, the thing doth not convert
Into itself; the thing itself is all
Not part of 't self: if all to all revert,
Each part then into each part is insert.
But tell me then how is their quantity
If every part with each part is refert?
Thus swallowed up, they'l have no distancy;
So you destroy suppos'd divisibility.

25

Wherefore that thing is individuous
Whatever can into it self reflect,
Such is the soul as hath been prov'd by us
Before, and further now we do detect
By her foure wheels: The first hight Intellect,
Wherewith she drives into her Nature deep
And finds it out; next Will, this doth affect
Her self found out. Her self then out doth peep
Into these acts, she into both doth cas'ly creep.

26

But this conversion's from the body free;
Begins not thence, nor thither doth return:
Nor is the soul worse then her energie,
If in her acts she be far higher born
Then they should 'pend on this base corse forlorn:
Then also she hath no dependency
Upon this body, but may safely scorn
That low condition of servility,
And blame all that averre that false necessity.

27

If she should issue from this nether spring,
Nearer she kept to her Originall
She were the stronger, and her works would bring
To more perfection; but alas! they fall
They fail by near approch. The best of all
Wax weak and faint by too close union
With this foul fount. Might intellectuall
Grows misty by this strait conjunction;
The will is woxen weak, its vigour quite is gone.

28

But O! how oft when she her self doth cut
From nearer commerce with the low delight
Of things corporeall, and her eyes doth shut
To those false fading lights, she feels her spright
Fill'd with excessive pleasure, such a plight
She finds that it doth fully satisfie
Her thirsty life. Then reason shines out bright,
And holy love with mild serenity
Doth hug her harmlesse self in this her purity.

29

What grave monitions and sure prophesie
Have men in sicknesse left? a true testation
Of the souls utter independency
On this poore crasie corse. May that narration
Of Aristotles move easie perswasion
Of his Eudemus, to whom sick at Phere
While sleep his senses bound, this revelation
A gentle youth did bring with goodly chear,
And jolly blith deportment, chasing needlesse fear.

30

Told him that sicknesse would not mortall prove,
He should grow well er'e long, but deaths drad power
On that towns tyrant should be shortly droxe,
Swift vengeance on his cursèd head should showᴛ:
Both provèd true. I could in plenty poure
Such like examples, as of Pherecyde,
Calanus, him of Rhodes, and others more;
But it is needlesse, 'tis a truth well tried,
The higher works the soul the more she is untied.

31

Then quite set loose from this her heavy chain
Shee is in happiest plight, so far she is
From being nought or perishing. Again,
We find such utter contrarieties
Betwixt the bodies and her qualities
That we can no wayes think she 'pends at all
Of that with which she has such repugnancies.
What thing doth fight with its Originall?
The spring and stream be alwayes homogeneall.

32

But the high heaven-born soul sprung out from Jove
Ever is clashing with the foolery
Of this dull body, which the sense doth love,
And erring phansie. It were long to try
In every thing: O how 'twould magnifie
The hight of pleasures that fall under sense:
This well describ'd would prove its Deity.
A vast round body cloth'd with th' excellence
Of glorious glistring light through the wide aire extense:

33

Bravely adorn'd with diverse colours gay,
Even infinite varieties that shine
With wondrous brightnesse, varnish'd with the ray
Of that clear light, with motion circuline:
Let turn about and stir up sounds divine,
That sweetly may affect th' attentive ear.
Adde fragrant odours waft with gentle wind,
Adde pleasant taste, soft touch to Venus dear;
This is the bodies God, this is its highest sphear.

34

But from far higher place and brighter light
Our reason checks us for this vanity,
Calls to us, warns us that that empty sight
Lead not our soul unto Idolatry,

Make us not rest in easie falsity.
If thou be stirrèd up by working fire
To search out God, to find the Deity;
Take to thy self not what thine eyes admire
Or any outward sense, or what sense can desire.

35

Behold a light far brighter then the Sun!
The Sun's a shadow if you them compare,
Or grosse Cimmerian mist; the fairest Noon
Exceeds not the meridian night so far
As that light doth the Sun. So perfect clear
So perfect pure it is, that outward eye
Cannot behold this inward subtile starre,
But indisperst is this bright Majesty,
Yet every where out shining in infinitie;

36

Unplac'd, unparted, one close Unity,
Yet omnipresent; all things, yet but one;
Not streak'd with gaudy multiplicity,
Pure light without discolouration,
Stable without circumvolution,
Eternall rest, joy without passing sound;
What sound is made without collision?
Smell, taste, and touch make God a grosse compound;
Yet truth of all that's good is perfectly here found.

37

This is a riddle unto outward sense:
And heavie phansie, that can rise no higher
Then outward senses, knows no excellence
But what those Five do faithfully inspire
From their great God, this world; nor do desire
More then they know: wherefore to consopite
Or quench this false light of bold phansies fire,
Surely must be an act contrary quite
Unto this bodies life, and its low groveling spright.

38

Wherefore the body's not Originall
Of humane soul when she doth thus resist
That principle: which still more clearly shall
Be provèd. Oft when either drowsie mists
Provoke to sleep, or worst of senses lists
To ease his swelling veins, or stomach craves
His wonted food, that he too long hath mist,
Or our dry lungs cool liquor fain would have,
Or when in warre our heart suggests the fear of grave:

39

Yet high desire of truth, and deep insight
Into Gods mystery makes us command
These low attractions; and our countries right
Bids march on bravely, stout and stifly stand
In bloudy fight, and try't by strength of hand.
Thus truth and honesty so sway our will,
That we no longer doubt to break the band
Of lower Nature, and this body kill
Or vex, so we the Laws of reason may fulfill.

40

This proves the soul to sit at liberty,
Not wedg'd into this masse of earth, but free
Unloos'd from any strong necessity
To do the bodies dictates, while we see
Clear reason shining in serenity,
Calling above unto us, pointing to
What's right and decent, what doth best agree
With those sweet lovely Ideas, that do show
Some glimps of their pure light. So Sol through clouds
  doth flow.

41

How oft do we neglect this bodies life,
And outward comely plight, for to adorn
Our soul with virtuous ornaments? and strive
To fat our mind with truth, while it's forlorn,
Squalid, half-nasty, pallid, wan, deform?
Can this desire from the base body spring?
No sure such brave atchievements be yborn
Within the soul, tend to her perfecting,
See th' independent mind in her self circuling!

42

Best plight of body hinders such like acts.
How doth she then upon the body pend?
To do those subtle, high, pure, heavenly facts?
What? doth the Sun his rayes that he out-sends
Smother or choke? though clouds that upward wend
May rais'd be by him, yet of those clouds
That he doth congregate he no'te depend.
Nor doth the soul that in this flesh doth croud
Her self, rely on that thick vapour where she's shroud.

43

But still to prove it clearer : If the mind
Without the bodyes help can operate
Of her own self, then nothing can we find
To scruple at, but that souls separate
Safely exist, not subject unto fate,
Nothing depending on their carcases,
That they should fade when those be ruinate.
But first perpend well both their properties
That we may better see their independencies.

44

The living body where the soul doth 'bide
These functions hath, phansie, sense, memory.
How into sense these outward forms do glide
I have already told, and did descry
How *presentifick circularity*
Is spread through all : there is one *Mundane* spright
And body, vitall corporality
We have from hence. Our souls be counite
With the worlds spright and body, with these herself
  she has dight.

45

Our body struck by evolution
Of outward forms spread in the worlds vast spright,

Our listning mind by its adversion
Doth notice take, but nothing is empight
In it. Of old Gods hand did all forms write
In humane souls, which waken at the knock
Of *Mundane* shapes. If they were naked quite
Of innate forms, though heaven and earth should rock
With roring winds, they'd hear no more then senselesse
  stock.

46

Phansy's th' impression of those forms that flit
In this low life : They oft continue long,
Whenas our spright more potently is hit
By their incursions and appulses strong,
Like heated water, though a while but hung
On fiercer fire, an hot impression
Long time retains ; so forms more stoutly flung
Against our spright make deep insculption ;
Long time it is till their clear abolition.

47

Hence springeth that which men call memory,
When outward object doth characterize
Our inward *common spright ;* or when that we
From our own soul stir up clear phantasies
Which be our own elicited *Idees,*
Springing from our own centrall life, by might
Of our strong *Fiat* as oft as we please.
With these we seal that under grosser spright,
Make that our note-book, there our choisest notions
  write.

48

But sith it is not any part of us,
But 'longeth unto the great world, it must
Be chang'd ; for course of Time voraginous
With rapid force is violently just,
Makes each thing pay with what it was in trust.
The common life sucks back the common spright,
The body backward falls into the dust ;
It doth it by degrees. Hence phancie, sight,
And memory in age do not their functions right.

49

Often disease, or some hard casualtie
Doth hurt this spirit, that a man doth lose
The use of sense, wit, phansie, memory ;
That hence rash men our souls mortall suppose
Through their rude ignorance ; but to disclose
The very truth, our soul's in safety
In that distemper, that doth ill dispose
Her under spright. But her sad misery
Is that so close she's tied in a prone Unitie,

50

Leans on this bodies false security,
Seeks for things there, not in herself, nor higher,
Extremely loves this bodies company,
Trusts in its life, thither bends her desire :
But when it gins to fail, she's left i' th' mire.
Yet hard upon us hangs th' *Eternall* light

The *ever-live-Idees*, the lamping fire
Of lasting *Intellect*, whose nearnesse might
Illumin, were our minds not lost in that frail spright.

51

That spright and we are plain another thing ;
Which now I'll clearly show that we may see
Our independency on his existing,
Which prove I must from eithers property.
That spright hath no perceptibility
Of his impressions : Phantasie nor sense
Perceive themselves ; often with open eye
We look upon a man in our presence,
And yet of that near object have no cognoscence.

52

And so of Phansies that be fresh enough,
Even deeply seald upon that lower spright,
Unlesse we seek them out and pierce them through
With aiming *animadversion*, they in night
Do lurk unknown to us, though they be bright
In their own selves. Again, some object may
In its great vigour, lustre, sweying might
This spirit wound by its fierce riving ray ;
Our sight is hurt by th' eye of the broad blasing day.

53

Beside the senses each one are restraind
To his own object : so is Phantasie.
That in the spirits compasse is containd ;
As likewise the low naturall memory.
But sooth to say, by a strong sympathy
We both are mov'd by these, and these do move.
As the light spider that makes at a fly,
Her selfe now moves the web she subt'ly wove,
Mov'd first by her own web, when here the fly did rove.

54

Like spider in her web, so do we sit
Within this spirit, and if ought do shake
This subtile loom we feel as it doth hit ;
Most part into adversion we awake,
Unlesse we chance into our selves betake
Our selves, and listen to the lucid voice
Of th' *Intellect*, which these low tumults slake :
But our own selves judge of whatere accloyes
Our muddied mind, or what lifts up to heavenly joyes.

55

All the five senses, Phansie, Memorie,
We feel their work, distinguish and compare,
Find out their natures by the subtiltie
Of sifting reason. Then they objects are
Of th' understanding, bear no greater share
In this same act then objects wont to do.
They are two realties distinguish'd clear
One from the other, as I erst did show.
She knows that spright, that spright our soul can never know.

56

Sense, Phansie, Memorie, as afore was said
Be hurt by stronger objects, or be spoild

By longer exercise : Our soul ne're fades,
But doth her spright commiserate long toild
With agitation, when she feels it moild
Descends to comfort it, and gives it rest ;
But she grows quicker, vaster, never foild
With contemplations that this spright molest :
The inward soul's renew'd as cannot be exprest.

57

How soul and spright be severèd we see,
But how't works by it self is not yet shown ;
I mean without this sprights assistencie,
Though not quite by her self. High light doth crown
Her summitie, when sleep that spright doth drown
Rapt into highest heavens in ecstasie
She sees such things as would low life confound,
Enrage with a tumultuous agonie,
Burst this pent spright for want of fit capacitie.

58

Then is she joynd with the *Eternall Idees*,
Which move our souls as sights do here below :
Joynd with the spright of God we gaze on these,
As by the *Mundane* spright th' *Out-world* we know :
Our soul hangs twixt them both, and there doth go
Where either spright doth snatch her. Either raise
Her inward forms, which leap out nothing slow
When sympathie them calls. Thus she displaces
Her inward life, God's light views with her wakened rayes.

59

When we confute a pregnant falsitie
Cloth'd with strong phantasmes in our snarèd mind,
As this suppose : The earths stabilitie,
What help can we in our low phansie find,
Possest of this impression ? what shall bind
This stubborn falshood so inveterate ?
That spright so stifly set can't be inclin'd
By ought but by the soul that contemplates
Truth by her self, brings out her forms that be innate ?

60

Flies she to sense ? sense pleads for Ptolemee.
Flies she to her low phansie ? that's so swayd
By sense, and fore-imprest Astronomie,
By botch'd inculcate paradigmes made
By senses dictate, that they'll both perswade
That Philolaus and wife Heraclide
Be frantick both, Copernicus twice mad.
She cannot then this question well decide.
By ought but her own forms that in her self reside.

61

Which she calls out unto her faithfull aid,
Commands deep silence to fond phantasie,
Whose odious prating truth hath oft betraid,
And in her stead brought in rash falsitie,
Seated in sowr inert stupiditie.
Then farewell sense, and what from sense hath sprong
Saith she, I'll contemplate in puritie,
And quit my self of that tumultuous throng :
What then she finds shall be unfold in my next song.

The Argument of

PSYCHATHANASIA,

Or

The Immortality of the Soul.

BOOK III. CANT. 3.

That th' earth doth move, proofs Physicall
Unto us do descrie ;
Adde reasons Theosophicall,
Als adde Astronomic.

1

Lest souls first Authors of Astronomie !
Who clomb the heavens with your high
reaching mind,
Scal'd the high battlements of the lofty skie,
To whom compar'd this earth a point you find ;
Your bodies lesse, what measure hath defin'd ?
What art that mighty vastnesse ? Such high facts
The ancient Giants swoln with raging wind
Could not effect. A subtile Parallax,
A dark Eclipse do quite obscure their braving acts.

2

O the great might of mans high Phantasie !
Which with a shade or a divided line,
That nought, this but a thin exilitie,
Can do farre more then strength enrag'd with tine,
Hoysted with haughty pride. That brood combine
To clamber up to heaven. Hill upon hill,
Ossa upon Olympus doth recline :
Their brawnie arms redoubled force doth fill,
While they their spirits summon t'effect their furious
will.

3

But all in vain, they want the inward skill.
What comes from heaven onely can there ascend.
Not rage nor tempest that this bulk doth fill
Can profit ought, but gently to attend
The souls still working, patiently to bend
Our mind to sifting reason, and clear light,
That strangely figur'd in our soul doth wend
Shifting its forms, still playing in our sight,
'Till something it present that we shall take for right.

4

The busie soul it is that hither hent
By strength of reason, the true distancies
Of th' erring Planets, and the vast extent
Of their round bodies without outward eyes
Hath view'd, told their proportionalities,
Confounded sense by reasons strange report
(But wiser he that on reason relies
Then stupid sense low-sunken into dirt)
This weapon I have got none from me may extort.

5

O You stiff-standers for ag'd Ptolemee,
I heartily praise your humble reverence
If willingly given to Antiquitie ;
But when of him in whom's your confidence,
Or your own reason and experience
In those same arts, you find those things are true
That utterly oppugne our outward sense,
Then are you forc'd to sense to bid adieu,
Not what your sense gainsayes to holden straight untrue.

6

Though contraire unto sense, though it be new
(But sooth to sayen th' earths motion is of tri'd
Antiquitie, as I above did shew :
In Philolaus and in Heraclide
Those subtile thoughts of old did close reside)
Yet reason ought to bear away the bell.
But irefull ignorance cannot abide
To be outtopd, reprochfully she 'll yell,
Call's mad, when her own self doth with foul furie swell.

7

But let them bark like band-dogs at the Moon,
That mindlesse passeth on in silencie :
I'll take my flight above this outward sunne,
Regardlesse of such fond malignitie,

Lift my self up in the Theologie
Of heavenly Plato. There I'll contemplate
The *Archtype* of this sunne, that bright *Idee*
Of steddie *Good*, that doth his beams dilate
Through all the worlds, all lives and beings propagate.

8

But yet in words to trifle I will deigne
A while : They may our mind fitly prepare
For higher flight ; we larger breath may gain
By a low hovering. These words they are
All found in that old Oracle of Clare.
That heavenly power which Iao hight
The highest of all the Gods thou mayst declare,
In spring named Zeus, in summer Helios bright,
In autumn call'd Jao, Aides in brumall night.

9

These names do plainly denotate the sunne,
In Spring call'd *Zeus*, from life or kindly heat ;
In winter, 'cause the day's so quickly done,
He *Aides* hight, he is not long in sight ;
In Summer, 'cause he strongly doth us smite
With his hot darts, then *Helios* we him name
From *Eloim* or *Eloah* so hight ;
In Autumn *Jao, Jehovah* is the same :
So is the word deprav'd by an uncertain fame.

10

So great similitude twixt Phœbus light
And God, that God himself the Nations deem
The sunne. The learnèd Seventy 've boldly pight
A tent therein for the true Eloim ;
The sensible Deity you'll reckon him,
If Hermes words bear with you any sway ;
Or if you Christian Clerks do ought esteem,
In Davids odes they make Gods Christ a day ;
His father's then the sunne from whence this light doth
ray.

11

Then by all the wide worlds acknowledgement,
The sunne's a type of that eternall light
Which we call God, a fair delineament
Of that which *Good* in Plato's school is hight
His *Tagathon* with beauteous rayes bedight.
Let's now consult with their Theologie,
And that *Idea* with our inward sight
Behold, casheering sensibility
Then in clear reason view this correspondency.

12

One steddy *Good*, centre of essencies,
Unmovèd *Monad*, that *Apollo* hight,
The *Intellectuall* sunne whose energies
Are all things that appear in vitall light,
Whose brightnesse passeth every creatures sight,
Yet round about him stird with gentle fire
All things do dance ; their being, action, might,
They thither do direct with strong desire,
To embosome him with close embracements they aspire.

13

Unseen, incomprehensible He moves
About himself each seeking entity
That never yet shall find that which it loves.
No finite thing shall reach infinity,
No thing dispers'd comprehend that Unity,
Yet in their ranks they seemly foot it round,
Trip it with joy at the worlds harmony
Struck with the pleasure of an amorous stound,
So dance they with fair flowers from unknown root
ycrownd.

14

Still falling short they never fail to seek,
Nor find they nothing by their diligence ;
They find repast, their lively longings eek
Rekindled still, by timely influence.
Thus all things in distinct *circumference*
Move about Him that satisfies them all.
Nor be they thus stird up by wary sense
Or foresight, or election rationall,
But blindly reel about the heart of Lives *centrall*.

15

So doth the Earth one of the erring Seven
Wheel round the fixèd sunne, that is the shade
Of steddy Good, shining in this *Out-heaven*
With the rest of those starres that God hath made
Of baser matter, all which be array'd
With his far-shining light. They sing for joy,
They frisque about in circlings unstay'd,
Dance through the liquid air, and nimbly toy
While Sol keeps clear their sprite, consumes what may
accloy.

16

Better the indigent be mov'd, then he
That wanteth nought : He fills all things with light
And kindly heat : through his fecundity
Peoples the world ; by his exciting sprite
Wakens the plants, calls them out of deep night.
They thrust themselves into his fostring rayes,
Stretch themselves forth, stird by his quickning might.
And all the while their merry roundelayes
(As lightsome phansies deem) each Planet spritely playes.

17

But sooth to say that sound so subtile is
Made by percussion of th' ethereall fire
Against our air (if it be not transmisse
By its exility,) that none ought admire
That we no'te hear what well we mought desire
Heavens harmony. 'Cording to others lear
The sound's so big that it cannot retire
Into the windings of a mortall ear ;
No more than Egypt can Niles Catadupa bear.

18

There ought to be certain proportion
Betwixt the object and the outward sense.

Rash man that doth inferre negation
From thy dead ear, or non-experience.
Then let them dance and sing, raise influence
From lively motion, that preserves their sprite
From foul corruption: motion's the best sense
To keep off filth in children of cold *Night*,
Whose life is in dull matter; but the sunne's all Light.

19

Therefore full safely he may steddy stond,
Unmov'd, at least not remov'd out of place:
I'll not deny but that he may turn round
On his own centre. So the steps we'll trace
Of *Essence*, Plato's *On*, which steddy stayes
And moves at once, that same *Iao* hight
In that old Clarian Oracle, that sayes
It is the sunne. This answer will aright
To Jove or Plato's *On* as done those schools descry't.

20

That same first *Being, Beauty, Intellect,*
Turns to his father (of whom he was born)
In a brief instant. But who can detect
Such hidden mysteries? back mine eyes I'll turn,
Lest in this light like fluttering moth I burn.
Enough is shown of correspondency
Twixt this worlds sunne and *centre of hid Morn,*
The radiant light of the deep Deity.
Thus have I fairly prov'd the sunnes stability.

21

Then must the earth turn round, or we want day,
Or never be in night. Now I'll descend
Cloth'd with this truth. As wrathfull dogs do bay
At spectres solemn Cynthia doth send:
So now I backward to the senses wend:
They'll bark at th' shape of my disguisèd mind,
As stranger wights, they wrathfully will rend
This uncouth habit. They no such thing find
'Mongst their domestick forms, to whom they are more
kind.

22

And weaker reason which they wont misguide
Will deem all this nothing mysterious,
But my strong-wingèd Muse feeble to slide
Into false thoughts and dreams vertiginous,
And plainly judge us woxen furious,
Thus in our rage to shake the stable earth,
Whirling her round with turns prodigious;
For she doth stedfast stand as it appear'th
From the unshaken buildings she so safely bear'th.

23

If she should move about, then would she sling
From her self those fair extructed loads
Of carvèd stone: The air aloud would sing
With brushing trees; Beasts in their dark aboads
Would brainèd be by their own caves; th' earth strow'd

With strange destruction. All would shatter'd lie
In broken shivers. What mad frantick mood
Doth thus invade wary Philosophy,
That it so dotes on such a furious falsitie?

24

But still more subt'ly this cause to pursue.
The clouds would alwayes seem to rise from th' East.
Which sense and oft-experience proves untrue:
They rise from all the quarters, South, North, West.
From every part, as Æolus thinketh best.
Again the Earths sad stupid gravity
Unfit for motion, shows her quiet rest:
Lastly an arrow shot unto the sky
Would not return unto his foot that let it fly.

25

Adde unto these that contrariety
Of motion, whenas the self same things
At the same time do back and forward hie:
As when for speed the rider fiercely dings
His horse with iron heel, layes the loose strings
Upon his neck, westward they swiftly scoure,
Whenas the Earth, finishing her dayly rings,
Doth Eastward make with all her might and power,
She quite hath run her stage at end of twice twelve houres.

26

These and like phansies do so strongly tye
The slower mind to agèd Ptolemee,
That shamefull madnesse 't were for to deny
So plain a truth as they deem this to be.
But yet, alas! if they could standen free
From prejudice, and heavie swaying sense
That dims our reason that it cannot see
What's the pure truth, enough in just defense
Of Pythagore we find though with small diligence.

27

One single truth concerning unity
Of sprights and bodies, and how one Form may
Inact a various Corporeity,
Keep't up together, and her might display
Through all the parts, make't constantly obey
The powerfull dictates of its *centrall* spright,
Which being one can variously play:
This lore if we but once had learnd aright,
All what was brought afore would vanish at first sight.

28

For that Magnetick might doth so combine
Earth, Water, Air, into one animate,
Whose soul or life so sweetly 't doth incline,
So surely, easly, as none can relate
But he that's exercis'd in every state
Of moving life. What? Can the *plastick* spright
So variously his branching stock dilate
Downward to hell, upward to heaven bright,
And strangely figur'd leaves and flowers send into sight?

29

Can one poore single *Centre* do all this
In a base weed that suddenly decayes?
And shall not the earths life that is transmisse
Through sea and air, and with its potent rayes
Informs all this (all this on that life stayes)
Shall't not obtain the like variety
Of inward ruling motion? Your minds raise,
O sluggish men! single *centrality*
You'l find shall do, whatere's admit by phantasie.

30

Now see if this clear apprehension
Will not with ease repell each argument
Which we rehears'd with an intention
For to refute. The earths swift movement,
Because 'tis naturall not violent,
Will never shatter buildings. With straight line
It binds down strongly each partic'larment
Of every edifice. All stones incline
Unto that Centre; this doth stoutly all combine.

31

Nor is lesse naturall than circular motion,
Then this which each part to the centre drives:
So every stone on earth with one commotion
Goes round, and yet withall right stifly strives
To reach the centre, though it never dives
So deep. Who then so blind but plainly sees
How for our safety Nature well contrives,
Binding all close with down-propensities?
But now we'll answer make to the loud-singing trees.

32

Walls, towers, trees, would stir up a strange noise,
If th' air stood still, while the earth is hurled round
As doth the switch oft shak'd by idle boyes
That please themselves in varying of the sound.
But this objection we with reason sound
Have well prevented, while we plainly taught
Earth, Water, Air, in one to be fast bound
By one *spermatick* spright, which easly raught
To each part: Earth, Sea, Air so powerfully hath it
    caught.

33

All these as one round entire body move
Upon their common Poles; that difficulty
Of stirring sounds, so clearly we remove.
That of the clouds with like facility
We straight shall chace away. In th' air they ly
And whirl about with it, and when some wind
With violence afore him makes them fly,
Then in them double motion we find,
Eastward they move, and whither by these blasts they're
    inclin'd.

34

What they pretend of the Earths gravity,
Is nought but a long taken up conceit:

A stone that downward to the earth doth ly
Is not more heavie then dry straws that jet
Up to a ring, made of black shining jeat.
Each thing doth tend to the loud-calling might
Of sympathy. So 'tis a misconceit
That deems the earth the onely heavie weight:
They ken not the strange power of the strong centrall
    spright.

35

Were there a shiver cut from off the Moon
And cast quite off from that round entire masse,
Would't fall into our mouths? No, it would soon
Make back to th' centre from whence forc'd it was:
The same in Mars and Sol would come to passe,
And all the stars that have their proper centre.
So gravity is nought but close to presse
Unto one Magick point, there near to enter;
Each sympathetick part doth boldly it adventure.

36

Thus in each starry globe all parts may tend
Unto one point, and meantime turn around;
Nor doth that sway its circling ought offend:
These motions do not at all confound
One th' others course. The Earth's not heavie found.
But from that strong down-pulling *centrall* sway,
Which hinders not but that it may turn round,
Sith that it moves not a contrary way;
Which answer I will bend against the fifth assay.

37

An arrow shot into the empty air,
Which straight returning to the bowmans foot,
The Earths stability must proven clear.
Thus these bad archers do at random shoot,
Whose easie errour I do thus confute.
The arrow hath one spirit with this sphere,
Forc'd upward turns with it, mov'd by the root
Of naturall motion. So when back't doth bear
It self, still Eastward turns with motions circular.

38

So 'tis no wonder when it hath descended
It falleth back to th' place from whence it flew,
Sith all this while its circular course hath bended
Toward the East, and in proportion due
That arcuall Eastern motion did pursue:
Nearer the earth the slower it must go;
These Arks be lesse, but in the heavens blew
Those Arks increase, it must not be so slow,
Thus must it needs return unto its idle bow.

39

Nor ought we wonder that it doth conform
Its motions to the circles of the aire,
Sith water in a wooden bucket born
Doth fit itself unto each periphere,
By hight or depth, as you shall change the sphere.
So lowly set more water 't will contain,

'Cause its round tumour higher then doth bear
It self up from the brims.   So may't be sayen
The lowlier man the larger graces doth obtain.

40

But now to answer to the last objection,
Tis not impossible one thing to move
Contrary wayes, which by a fit retection
I strongly will evince and clearly prove.
Take but the pains higher for to remove
A clock with hanging plummet.   It goes down
At that same time you heave it high above
Its former place.   Thus fairly have we won
The field 'gainst stupid sense, that reason fain would
    drown.

41

Now let's go on (we have well-cleard the way)
More plainly prove this seeming paradox
And make this truth shine brighter then midday,
Neglect dull sconses mowes and idle mocks.
O constant hearts, as stark as Thracian rocks,
Well-grounded in grave ignorance, that scorn
Reasons sly force, its light slight subtile strokes.
Sing we to these wast hills, dern, deaf, forlorn,
Or to the cheerfull children of the quick-ey'd *Morn* ?

42

To you we sing that live in purer light,
Escap'd the thraldome of down-drooping sense,
Whose nimble spirit and clear piercing sight
Can easly judge of every conference
Withouten prejudice, with patience
Can weigh the moments of each reason brought ;
While others in tempestuous vehemence
Blow all away with bitter blasts.   Untought
In subtilties they shew themselves in jangling stout.

43

I have the barking of bold sense confuted,
Its clamorous tongue thus being consopite,
With reasons easie shall I be well-suited,
To show that Pythagore's position's right.
Copernicks, or whosever dogma't hight.
The first is that that's wisely signifi'd
By Moses Maymons son, a learnèd wight,
Who saith each good Astronomer is ty'd
To lessen the heavens motions vainly multiply'd,

44

And the foul botches of false feignèd Orbs :
Whose uselesse number reason must restrain,
That oft the loose luxuriant phansie curbs,
And in just bounds doth warily contain :
To use more means then needs is all in vain.
Why then, O busie sonnes of Ptolemee !
Do you that vast star-bearing sphere constrain
To hurl about with such celerity,
When th' earth may move without such strange velocity ?

45

What needlesse phansy's this that that huge sphere
In one short moment must thus whirl around,
That it must fly six hundred thousand sheere
Of Germane miles.   If that will not confound,
For pomp adde fourty thousand more, that 'bound :
Three thousand more if it were requisite,
You might annex, and more if they have found
The measure right ; whenas the earth's slow flight
One sixteenth of a mile her scarcely doth transmit.

46

But if this All be liquid, pervious,
One fine Ethereall (which reason right
Will soon admit : for 'tis ridiculous
Thus for to stud the heaven with nails bright,
The stars in fluid sky will standen tight,
As men to feigne the earth in the soft aire
To be unmov'd) How will proportion fit ?
So vast a difference there doth appear
Of motions in those stars that the same bignesse bear.

47

Besides that difficulty will remain
Of unconceivable swift motion
In the equinoctiall stars, where some contain
This earthy globes mighty dimension,
Ten thousand times twise told.   They hurry on
With the same swiftnesse I set down before,
And with more pains.   A globes extension,
The bigger that it grows, groweth still more
Nigh to a flat fac'd figure, and finds resistance sore.

48

But now that all the heavens be liquid, hence
I'll fetch an argument.   Those higher stars
They may as well in water hang suspense
As do the Planets.   Venus orb debars
Not Mars, nor enters he with knocks and jars ;
The soft fine yielding Æther gives admission :
So gentle Venus to Mercurius dares
Descend, and finds an easie intromission,
Casts ope that azur curtain by a swift discission.

49

That famous star nail'd down in Cassiopee,
How was it hammer'd in your solid sky?
What pinsers pull'd it out again, that we
Nor longer see it, whither did it fly?
Astronomers say 'twas least as high
As the eighth sphere.   It gave no parallax,
No more then those light lamps that there we spy.
But prejudice before herself she'll tax
Of holy writ and the heavens she'll make a nose of wax.

50

What man will now that's not vertiginous
Hurrie about his head these severall lights
So mighty vast, with so voracious
And rapid course whirling them day and night

About the earth, when the earths motion might
Save that so monstrous labour, with lesse pains,
Even infinitely lesse? But thoughts empight
Once in the mind do so possesse the brains,
That hard it is to wash out those deep ancient stains.

51

Two things there be whose reason's nothing clear :
Those cool continuall breathings of East wind
Under the line ; the next high Comets are,
In which Philosophers three motions find?
Concerning which men hitherto are blind,
That have not mov'd the earth unto their aid ;
Diurnall and an annuall course they have mind,
Like to the sunnes, beside, by what they're sway'd
To North or South. This myst'ry's easly thus display'd.

52

The Ecliptick course, and that diurnall moving,
Is but apparent as the sunnes, not true :
But that the earth doth move, that still wants proving,
You'll say. Then if you will, these Comets shew
One proof for her two motions. Whence issue
Those meteors turnings? what shall hale them on,
And guide their steps, that in proportion due
They dance Sols measures? what occasion
Or fruit can be of that strange double motion ?

53

Nought but the Earths circumvolution
Doth cause this sight, and but in outward show
This sight of double Sunlike motion,
Seen in the Comets. For the winds that blow
Under the Æquinoctiall, who doth know
Any other cause, that still they breathe from th' East ?
That constant feat from whence else can it flow,
Save from the Earths swift hurrying from the West ?
Mid part is strongliest rouz'd, the Poles do sleep in rest.

54

Wherefore men under th' Æquinoctiall,
Where the earths course most rapid is and swift,
Sensibly 're dash'd 'gainst that Aereall
Pure liquid essence. That clear aire is left
Not snatch'd away so fast, not quite bereft
Of its own Nature, nor like th' other skie
Unmovèd quite ; but slow-pac'd is ycleft
And driven close together ; sensibly
So feel we that fine aire that seems from East to flie.

55

Those parts be in farre greater puritie
Devoid of earthy vapours. Thence it is
They're not so easly turn'd by sympathie,
The air there having lesse of earthinesse ;
So that they move not with one speedinesse,
The earth and it. Yet curious men have fun
Something like this, even in the mid-land Seas
Ships foure times sooner the same stages run,
When Westward they do flie, then when they there
  begun.

56

But that disgracement of Philosophie,
From flux and reflux of the Ocean main
Their monethly and yearly change ; this Theorie
Might take't away and shew the causes plain.
Some parts of th' Earth do much more switnesse gain.
Whenas their course goes whirling on one way
With th' annuall motion, which must needs constrain
The fluid Sea with unexpected sway :
Long time it were this mystery fully to display.

57

Wherefore I'll let it passe, my self betake
Unto some reasons Astronomicall,
To which if't please the nimble mind t' awake
And shake off prejudice, that wont forestall
The ablest wit, I fear not but he'll fall
Into the same opinion, magnifie
That subtile spirit that hath made this All,
And hath half-hid his work from mortall eye,
To sport and play with souls in sweet philosophie.

58

But with crabb'd mind wisdome will nere consort,
Make her abode with a sowr ingenie ;
That harmlesse spright her self will nere disport
With bloudy zeal, currish malignitie,
With wrathfull ignorance, grave hypocrisie.
Mirth, and Free-mindednesse, Simplicitie,
Patience, Discretnesse, and Benignitie,
Faithfulnesse, [and] heart-struck Teneritie;
These be the lovely play-mates of pure veritie.

59

The Eternall Son of God, who *Logos* hight,
Made all things in a fit proportion ;
Wherefore, I wote, no man that judgeth right
In Heaven will make such a confusion,
That courses of unlike extension,
Vastly unlike, in like time shall be run
By the flight stars. Such huge distension
Of place, shews that their time is not all one ;
Saturn his ring no'te finish as quick as the moon.

60

Yet if the earth stand stupid and unmov'd,
This needs must come to passe. For they go round
In every twice twelve hours, as is prov'd
By dayly experience. But it would confound
The worlds right order, if't were surely found
A reall motion. Wherefore let it be
In them but seeming, but a reall round
In th' Earth it self. The world so's setten free
From that untoward disproportionalitie.

61

For so the courses of the erring Seven
With their own orbs will fitly well agree ;
Their Annuall periods in the liquid Heaven
They onely finish then : which as they be

19   L

Or lesse or greater, so the time they flie
In their own circlings hath its difference.
The Moon a moneth, Saturn years ten times three ;
Those have the least and bigg'st circumference :
So all their times and orbs have mutuall reference.

62

Next light's, the Planets dark opacitie,
Which long time hath been found in the low Moon :
Hills, Valleys, and such like asperitie
Through optick glasses thence have plainly shone :
By the same trick it hath been clearly shown
That Venus Moon-like grows corniculate
What time her face with flusher light is blown :
Some such like things others have contemplate
In Mercurie ; about the Sunne both circulate.

63

When Venus is the furthest off from us,
Then is she in her full.   When in her full,
She seemeth least ; which proves she's exterous
Beyond the Sunne, and further off doth roll.
But when her circling nearer down doth pull,
Then 'gins she swell, and waxen bug with horn,
But loose her light, parts clad with darknesse dull
She shows to us, She and Mercury ne're born
Farre from the Sunne, proves that about him both do
        turn.

64

They both opake, as also is the Moon
That turns about the earth (so turn those foure
'Bout Jupiter, tend him as he doth run
His annuall course).   That *Tellus* so may scoure
Th' Ethereall Plain, and have the self-same power
To run her circuits in the liquid skie
About the Sunne, the mind that doth not lour,
Drooping in earthy dregs, will not deny,
Sith we so well have prov'd the starres opacitie.

65

About the great the lesser lamps do dance,
The Medicean foure reel about Jove ;
Two round old Saturn without Nominance,
Luna about the earth doth nimbly move :
Then all as it doth seemly well behove,
About the bigg'st of all great Phœbus hight
With joy and jollitie needs round must rove,
Tickled with pleasure of his heat and light :
What tumbling tricks they play in his farre-piercing
        sight !

66

Next argument (could I it well expresse
With Poets pen) it hath so mighty force,
That an ingenious man 'twould stoutly presse,
To give assent unto the Annuall course
Of this our earth.   But prejudice the nurse
Of ignorance, stoppeth all free confession,

Als keeps the way that souls have not recourse
To purer reason, chok'd with that oppression :
This argument is drawn from the stars retrocession.

67

Planets go back, stand still, and forward flie
With unexpected swiftnesse : What's the cause
That they thus stagger in the plain-pav'd skie ?
Or stupid stand, as if some dull repose
Did numb their spirits and their sinews lose ?
Here 'gins the wheelwork of the Epicycle :
Thus patch they 'Heaven more botch'dly then old
        cloths.
This pretty sport doth make my heart to tickle
With laughter, and mine eyes with merry tears to trickle.

68

O daring phansie ! that dost thus compile
The Heavens from hasty thoughts, such as fall next ;
Wary Philosophers cannot but smile
At such feat gear, as thy rude rash context.
An heap of Orbs disorderly perplext,
Thrust in on every hint of motion,
Must be the wondrous art of Nature, next
Here working under God.   Thus, thus vain man
Intitles alwayes God to his opinion ;

69

Thinks every thing is done as he conceives ;
Would bind all men to his religion ;
All the world else of freedome he bereaves,
He and his God must have Dominion,
The truth must have her propagation :
That is his thought, which he hath made a God,
That furious hot inust impression
Doth so disturb his veins, that all abroad
With rage he roves, and all gainsayers down hath trod.

70

But to return from whence my Muse hath flown,
All this disordred superfluity
Of Epicycles, or what else is shown
To salve the strange absurd enormity
Of staggering motions in the azure skie ;
Both Epicycles and those turns enorm
Would all prove nought, if you would but let flie
The earth in the Ecliptick line yborn,
As I could well describe in Mathematick form.

71

So could I (that's another argument)
From this same principle most clearly prove
In regresse and in progress different
Of the free Planets : Why Saturn should rove
With shorter startings, give back lesse then Jove ;
Jove lesse then Mars ; why Venus flincheth out
More then Mercurius ; why Saturn moves
Ofter in those back jets then Jove doth shoot ;
But Mercury more oft then Venus and Mars stout,

72

And why the Sunne escap'd an Epicycle,
Whenas th' old prodigall Astronomie
On th' other six bestowed that needlesse cycle ;
Why Saturn, Jove, and Mars be very nigh
Unto the Earth, show bigger in our eye
At Eventide when they rise Acronicall ;
Why far remov'd with so vast distancy
When they go down with setting Cronicall :
All these will plain appear from th' earths course Annuall.

73

Many other reasons from those heauenly motions
Might well be drawn, but with exility
Of subtile Mathematicks obscure notions,
A Poets pen so fitly no'te agree ;

And curious men will judge't a vagrancy
To start thus from my scope. My pitchèd end
Was for to prove the immortality
Of humane souls : But if you well attend,
My ship to the right port by this bow'd course did bend.

74

For I have clearly show'd that stout resistence
Of the pure soul against the *Mundane* spright
And body, that's the lower mans consistence ;
How it doth quell by force of reason right
Those grosse impressions which our outward sight
Seald in our lower life : From whence we see
That we have proper independent might,
In our own mind, behold our own Idee,   ￢
Which needs must prove the souls sure immortality.

The *Argument of*

PSYCHATHANASIA,

Or,

The Immortality of the Soul.

BOOK III. CANT. 4.

Justice, true faith in the first good,
Our best perswasion
Of blest eternity unmov'd,
The earths conflagration.

I

T doth me good to think what things will
follow
That well-prov'd thesis in my former song ;
How we in liquid heavens more swift then
swallow
Do sail on *Tellus* lap, that doth among
The other starres of right not rudely throng,
We have what highest thoughts of man desire :
But highest thoughts of man are vain and wrong.
In outward heaven we burn with hellish fire,
Hate, envie, couetise, revenge, lust, pride and ire.

2

In the eighth sphear Andromeda from chains
Is not releast ; fearfull Orion flies
The dreadfull Scorpion. Alas ! what gains
Then is't to live in the bright starry skies ?
It no man can exeem from miseries.
All you that seek for true felicity
Rend your own hearts : There God himself descries
Himself ; there dwels his beautious Majesty ;
There shines the sun of righteousnesse in goodly glee.

3

And you who boldly all Gods providence
Confine to this small ball, that *Tellus* hight,
And dream not of a mutuall influence,
And how that she may shine with beames bright
At a farre distance clad with Sols lent light,
As Venus and the Moon ; O you that make

This earth Gods onely darling dear delight,
All th' other orbs merely for this orbs sake
So swiftly for to run, with labour never slack,

4

To dance attendance on their Princesse *Earth*
In their quick circuits, and with anger keen
Would bite him, that or serious or in mirth
Doubts the prerogative of your great Queen !
Best use of that your Theory, I ween,
Is this ; that as your selves monopolize
All the whole world, so your selves back again
You wholly give to God. Who can devise
A better way ? Mans soul to God this closely tyes.

5

But if the Earth doth thankfully reflect
Both light and influence to other starres,
As well as they to it, where's the defect ?
That sweet subordination it mars ;
Gods love to us then not so plain appears :
For then the starres be mutually made
One for another : Each all the good then bears
Of th' Universe, for 'tis single labour paid
With the joint pains of all that in the heavens wade.

6

Rare reason I why I then God would be too good.
What judgeth so but envie, and vain pride,
And base contract self-love ? which that free floud
Of bounty hath so confidently tied
Unto itself alone. Large hearts deride
This pent hypocrisie. Is he good to me ?
That grace I would not ere should be deny'd
Unto my fellow : My felicity
Is multiply'd, when others I like happy see.

7

But if the rolling starres with mutuall rayes
Serve one another ; sweet fraternity
And humble love, with such like lore we'll raise,
While we do see Gods great benignity
Thus mutually reflected in the skie,
And these round-moving worlds communicate
One with another by spread sympathy :
This all things friendly will concatenate :
But let more hardy wits that truth determinate.

8

It me behoves t' hold forward on my way,
Leaving this uncouth strange Philosophy,
In which my lightsome pen too long did play,
As rigid men in sad scuerity
May deem ; but we right carelesse leave that free
Unto their censure. Now more weighty thought
Doth sway our mind, thinking how all doth flee
Whatever we have painfully ytaught ;
So little fruits remain of all my skill hath wraught.

9

O th' emptinesse of vain Philosophy ;
When thin-spun reason and exile discourse
Make the soul creep through a straight Theory,
Whither the blunter mind can never force
Her self ; yet oft, alas ! the case is worse
Of this so subtile wight, when dangers deep
Approch his life, then his who learnings sourse
Did never drink of, nere his lips did steep
In Plato's springs, nor with low gown the dust did sweep.

10

Certes such knowledge is a vanity,
And hath no strength t' abide a stormy stour ;
Such thin slight clothing, will not keep us dry
When the grim heavens, all black and sadly soure
With rage and tempest, plenteously down shower
Great flouds of rain. Dispread exility
Of slyer reasons fails : Some greater power
Found in a lively vigorous Unity
With God, must free the soul from this perplexity.

11

Say now the dagger touch'd thy trembling breast,
Couldst thou recall the reasons I have shown
To prove th' immortall state of men deceast ?
Evolvèd reason cannot stand at one
Stoutly to guard thy soul from passion.
They passe successively like sand i' th' glasse ;
While thou look'st upon this the other's gone.
But there's a plight of soul such virtue has
Which reasons weak assistance strangely doth surpasse.

12

The just and constant man, a multitude
Set upon mischief cannot him constrain
To do amisse by all their uprores rude ;
Not for a tyrants threat will he ere stain
His inward honour. The rough Adrian
Tost with unquiet winds doth nothing move
His steddy heart. Much pleasure he doth gain
To see the glory of his Master Jove,
When his drad darts with hurrying light through all do
rove.

13

If Heaven and Earth should rush with a great noise,
He fearlesse stands ; he knows whom he doth trust,
Is confident of his souls after joyes,
Though this vain bulk were grinded into dust.
Strange strength resideth in the soul that's just,
She feels her power how't commands the sprite
Of the low man, vigorously finds she must
Be independent of such feeble might,
Whose motions dare not 'pear before her awfull sight.

14

But yet my Muse, still take a higher flight,
Sing of Platonick Faith in the first Good,

That Faith that doth our souls to God unite
So strongly, tightly, that the rapid floud
Of this swift flux of things, nor with foul mud
Can stain, nor strike us off from th' unity,
Wherein we stedfast stand, unshak'd, unmov'd,
Engrafted by a deep vitality :
The prop and stay of things is Gods benignity.

15

Als is the rule of his Oeconomie :
No other cause the creature brought to light
But the first *Goods* pregnant fecundity :
He to himself is perfect full delight ;
He wanteth nought, with his own beams bedight
He glory has enough. O blasphemy !
That envy gives to God or soure despight !
Harsh hearts ! that feign in God a tyranny,
Under pretense t' encrease his sovereign Majesty.

16

When nothing can to Gods own self accrew,
Who's infinitely happy ; sure the end
Of this creation simply was to shew
His flowing goodnesse, which he doth out-send
Not for himself ; for nought can him amend ;
But to his creature doth his good impart,
This infinite *Good* through all the world doth wend
To fill with heavenly blisse each willing heart :
So the free Sunne doth 'light and 'liven every part.

17

This is the measure of Gods providence,
The key of knowledge, the first fair Idee,
The eye of truth, the spring of living sense,
Whence sprout Gods secrets, the sweet mystery
Of lasting life, eternall charity.
But you O bitter men and soure of sprite !
Which brand Gods name with such foul infamy
As though poor humane race he did or slight,
Or curiously view to do them some despight,

18

And all to shew his mighty excellency,
His uncontrolled strength : fond men ! areed,
Is't not as great an act from misery
To keep the feeble, as his life to speed
With fatall stroke? The weak shak'd whisling reed
Shows Boreas wondrous strong ! but ignorance
And false conceit is the foul spirits meed ;
Gods lovely life hath there no enterance ;
Hence their fond thoughts for truth they vainly do
    advance.

19

If God do all things simply at his pleasure
Because he will, and not because its good,
So that his actions will have no set measure ;
Is't possible it should be understood
What he intends? I feel that he is lov'd
Of my dear soul, and know that I have born

Much for his sake ; yet is it not hence prov'd
That I shall live, though I do sigh and mourn
To find his face ; his creatures wish he'll slight and scorn.

20

When I breathe out my utmost vitall breath,
And my dear spirit to my God commend,
Yet some foul feigne close lurking underneath
My serious humble soul from me may rend :
So to the lower shades down we shall wend,
Though I in hearts simplicity expected
A better doom ; sith I my steps did bend
Toward the will of God, and had detected
Strong hope of lasting life, but now I am rejected.

21

Nor of well-being, nor subsistency
Of our poor souls, when they do hence depart,
Can any be assur'd, if liberty
We give to such odde thoughts, that thus pervert
The laws of God, and rashly do assert
That will rules God, but *Good* rules not Gods will.
Whatere from right, love, equity, doth start,
For ought we know then God may act that ill,
Onely to show his might, and his free mind fulfill.

22

O belch of hell ! O horrid blasphemy !
That Heavens unblemish'd beauty thus dost stain
And brand Gods nature with such infamy :
Can *Wise, Just, Good,* do ought that's harsh or vain?
All what he doth is for the creatures gain,
Not seeking ought from us for his content :
What is a drop unto the Ocean main?
All he intends is our accomplishment,
His being is self-full, self-joy'd, self-excellent.

23

He his fair beams through all has freely sent :
Purge but thy soul that thou mayst take them in.
With froward hypocrite he never went,
That finds pretexts to keep his darling sinne.
Through all the Earth this Sprite takes pains to winne
Unto himself such as be simply true,
And with malignant pride resist not him,
But strive to do what he for right doth shew ;
So still a greater light he brings into their view.

24

All Lives in severall circumference
Look up unto him and expect their food ;
He opes his hand, showrs down their sustinence :
So all things be yfild with their wish'd good,
All drink, are satisfi'd from this free floud.
But circling life that yet unsettled is
Grows straight, as it is further still remov'd
From the first simple *Good,* obtains lesse blisse,
Sustains sharp pains inflicted by just *Nemesis.*

25

But why do I my soul loose and disperse
With mouldring reason, that like sand doth flow.
Life close united with that *Good*, a verse
Cannot declare, nor its strange virtue show.
That's it holds up the soul in all her wo,
That death, nor hell, nor any change doth fray.
Who walks in light knows whither he doth go ;
Our God is light, we children of the day.
God is our strength and hope, what can us then dismay?

26

Goodnesse itself will do to us this good,
That godly souls may dwell with him for aye.
Will God forsake what of himself 's belov'd ?
What ever Lives may shrink into cold clay ;
Yet good mens souls deaths hests shall not obey.
Where there's no incompossibility
Of things, Gods goodnesse needs must bear the sway.
You virtuous brood take't for sure verity,
Your souls shall not fall short of blest eternity.

26

But yet bold men with much perplexity
Will here object against this principle,
Heaping up reasons (strange fecundity
Of ignorance I) that goodly might to quell
Of my left argument, so fairly well
Set down, right strongly the unsettled spright
To have confirmèd at my last far-well :
But contrair forces they bring into sight,
And proudly do provoke me with that rout to fight.

27

Whence was't, say they, that God the creature made
No sooner? why did infinite delay
Precede his work? should God his goodnesse staid
So long a time? why did he not display
From infinite years this *out-created ray ?*
The mighty starres why not inhabited,
When God may souls proportion to their clay
As well as to this earth? why not dispred
The world withouten bounds, endlesse uncompassèd?

28

Poore souls ! why were they put into this cave
Of misery, if they can well exist
Without the body? Why will not God save
All mankind? His great wisdome if it list
Could so contrive that they'd at last desist
From sinning, fallen into some providence
That sternly might rebuke them that have mist
Their way, and work in them true penitence :
Thus might they turn to God with double diligence.

29

Why be not damnèd souls devoyd of sense,
If nothing can from wickednesse reclaime,
Rather then fry in pain and vehemence
Of searching agony? or why not frame

Another form, so with new shape and name
Again to turn to life? One centrall spright
Why may't not many forms in it contain,
Which may be wak'd by some magnetick might,
'Cording as is the matter upon which they light?

30

For when two severall kinds by Venus knit
Do cause a birth, from both the soul doth take
A tincture ; but if free it were transmit
Uncloth'd with th' others seed, then it would make
One simple form ; for then they could not slake
One th' others working. Why is the World still
Stark nought, through malice, or through blind mistake?
Why had the first-made man such a loose will,
That his innumerous of-spring he should fouly spill.

31

Why was not this unlucky world dissolv'd
As soon as that unhappy Adam fell?
I itch till of this knot I be resolv'd :
So many myriads tumble down to hell,
Although partakers of Gods holy spell.
Beside, tis said, they that do not partake
Of Christian lore, for ever they must dwell
With cursèd fiends, and burn in brimstone lake :
Such drery drad designes do make my heart to quake.

32

One of a multitude of myriads
Shall not be sav'd but broyl in scorching wo?
Innumerous mischiefs then to mischiefs addes
This worlds continuance if that be so :
Ill infinitely more then good doth grow.
So God would show much more benignity
If he the ribs of heaven about would strow,
Powder the earth ; choke all vitality,
Call back the creature to its ancient nullity.

33

But thou whoere thou art that thus doth strive
With fierce assault my groundwork to subvert,
And boldly dost into Gods secrets dive,
Base fear my manly face no'te make m' avert.
In that odde question which thou first didst stert
I'll plainly prove thine incapacity,
And force thy feeble feet back to revert,
That cannot climb so high a mystery :
I'll shew thee strange perplexèd inconsistency.

34

Why was this world from all infinity
Not made? say'st thou : why? could it be so made
Say I? For well observe the sequency :
If this Out-world continually hath wade
Through a long long-spun-time that never had
Beginning, then there as few circulings
Have been in the quick Moon as Saturn sad ;
And still more plainly this clear truth to sing,
As many years as dayes or fleeting houres have been.

35

For things that we conceive are infinite,
One th' other no'te surpasse in quantity.
So I have prov'd with clear convincing light,
This world could never from infinity
Been made. Certain deficiency
Doth alwayes follow evolution :
Nought's infinite but tight eternity,
Close thrust into itself : extension
That's infinite implies a contradiction.

36

So then for ought we know this world was made
So soon as such a Nature could exist ;
And though that it continue, never fade,
Yet never will it be that that long twist
Of time prove infinite, though nere desist
From running still. But we may safely say
Time past compar'd with this long future list,
Doth show as if the world but yesterday
Were made, and in due time Gods glory out may ray.

37

Then this short night and ignorant dull ages
Will quite be swallowed in oblivion ;
And though this hope by many surly Sages
Be now derided, yet they'll all be gone
In a short time, like Bats and Owls yflone
At dayes approch. This will hap certainly
At this worlds shining conflagration.
Fayes, Satyrs, Goblins the night merrily
May spend, but ruddy Sol shall make them all to fly.

38

The roaring Lions and drad beasts of prey
Rule in the dark with pitious cruelty ;
But harmlesse man is maister of the day,
Which doth his work in pure simplicity :
God blesse his honest usefull industry.
But pride and covetize, ambition,
Riot, revenge, self love, hypocrisie,
Contempt of goodnesse, forc'd opinion ;
These and such like do breed the worlds confusion.

39

But sooth to say though my triumphant Muse
Seemeth to vaunt as in got victory,
And with puissant stroke the head to bruize
Of her stiffe foe, and daze his phantasie,
Captive his reason, dead each faculty :
Yet in her self so strong a force withstands
That of her self afraid, she'll not aby,
Nor keep the field. She'll fall by her own hand
As *Ajax* once laid *Ajax* dead upon the strand.

40

For thus her self by her own self's oppos'd ;
The Heavens, the Earth, the universall Frame
Of living Nature, God so soon disclos'd
As he could do, or she receive the same.
All times delay since that must turn to blame,
And what cannot he do that can be done?
And what might let but by th' all-powerfull Name
Or Word of God, the Worlds Creation
More suddenly were made then mans swift thought can
runne.

41

Wherefore that Heavenly Power or is as young
As this Worlds date ; or else some needlesse space
Of time was spent, before the earth did clung
So close unto her self and seas embrace
Her hollow breast ; and if that time surpasse
A finite number, then infinity
Of years before this Worlds Creation passe.
So that the durance of the Deity
We must contract, or strait his full Benignity.

42

But for the cradle of the *Cretian Jove*,
And guardians of his vagient Infancie
What sober man but sagely will reprove?
Or drown the noise of the fond *Dactyli*
By laughter loud ? Dated Divinitie
Certes is but the dream of a drie brain :
God maim'd in goodnesse, inconsistencie ;
Wherefore my troubled mind is now in pain
Of a new birth, which this one Canto'll not contain.

Nihil tamen frequentius inter Autores occurrit, quàm ut omnia adeò ex modulo ferè sensuum suorum æstimant, ut ea quæ insuper infinitis rerum spatiis extare possunt, sive superbè sive imprudenter rejiciant ; quin & ea omnia in usum suum fabricata fuisse glorientur, perinde facientes ac si pediculi humanum caput, aut pulices sinum muliebrem propter se solos condita existimarent, edque demum ex gradibus saltibúsque suis metirentur. The Lord Herbert in his De Causis Errorum.

De generali totius hujus mundi aspectabilis constructione ut rectè Philosophemur duo sunt imprimis observanda : Unum ut attendentes ad infinitam Dei potentiam & bonitatem, nè vereamur nimis ampla & pulchra & absoluta ejus opera imaginari : sed è contra caveamus, nè si quos fortè limites nobis non certò cognitos, in ipsis supponamus, non satis magnificè de creatoris potentia sentire videamur.

Alterum, ut etiam caveamus, nè nimis superbè de nobis ipsis sentiamus. Quod fieret non modò, si quos limites nobis nullâ cognitos ratione, nec divinâ revelatione, mundo vellemus affingere, tanquam si vis nostra cogitationis, ultra id quod à Deo revera factum est ferri posset ; sed etiam maximè, si res omnes propter nos solos, ab illo creatas esse fingeremus. Renatus Des Cartes in his Princip. Philosoph. the third part.

Democritus Platoniſſans,

OR

AN ESSAY

upon the

INFINITY OF WORLDS

out of

Platonick Principles.

Annexed

To this ſecond part of the Song

of the

SOUL,

as an *Appendix* thereunto.

Ἀγαθὸς ἦν τὺ πᾶν τόδε ὁ συνιστὰς, ἀγαθῷ δὲ οὐδεὶς περὶ οὐδενὸς οὐδέποτε ἐγγίνεται φθόνος.
Τούτου δ' ἐκτὸς ὢν πάντα ὅτι μάλιστα ἐβουλήθη γενέσθαι παραπλήσια αὐτῷ.   Plat.

Pythagoras Terram Planetam quendam esse censuit qui circa solem in centro mundi defixum conver-
tetur.   Pythagoram secuti sunt Philolaus, Seleucus, Cleanthes, &c. imò PLATO jam senex,
ut narrat Theophrastus.   Libert. Fromond. de Orbe terræ immobili.

CAMBRIDGE,
Printed by *Roger Daniel,* Printer to the
Univerſitie. 1647.

M

To the Reader.

Reader,

PRESENT to thee here in its proper place what I have heretofore offered to thee upon lesse advantage, but upon so little, no where (I conceive) as that I should despair of thy acceptance, if the overstrangenesse of the Argument prove no hinderance. *INFINITIE of WORLDS!* A thing monstrous if assented to, and to be startled at, especially by them, whose thoughts this one have alwayes so engaged, that they can find no leisure to think of any thing else. But I onely make a bare proposall to more acute judgements, of what my sportfull phancie, with pleasure hath suggested: following my old designe of furnishing mens minds with variety of apprehensions concerning the most weighty points of Philosophie, that they may not seem rashly to have settled in the truth, though it be the truth: a thing as ill beseeming Philosophers, as hastie prejudicative sentence Politicall Judges. But if I had relinquished here my wonted self, in proving Dogmaticall, I should have found very noble Patronage for the cause among the ancients, Epicurus, Democritus, Lucretius, &c. Or if justice may reach the dead do them the right, as to shew, that though they be hooted at, by the Rout of the learned, as men of monstrous conceits, they were either very wise or exceeding fortunate to light on so probable and specious an opinion, in which notwithstanding there is so much difficulty and seeming inconsistencie.

Nay and that sublime and subtill Mechanick too, Des-Chartes, though he seem to mince it, must hold infinitude of worlds, or which is as harsh, one infinite one. For what is his mundus indefinitè extensus, but extensus infinitè? Else it sounds onely infinitus quoad nos, but simpliciter finitus. But if any space be left out unstuff'd with Atoms, it will hazard the dissipation of the whole frame of Nature into disjoynted dust; as may be proved by the Principles of his own Philosophie. And that there is space wherever God is, or any actuall and self-subsistent Being, seems to me no plainer then one of their κοιναὶ ἔννοιαι.

For mine own part, I must confesse these apprehensions do plainly oppose what heretofore I have conceived; but I have sworn more faithfull friendship with Truth then with my self. And therefore without all remorse lay battery against mine own edifice: not sparing to shew how weak that is my self now deems not impregnably strong. I have at the latter end of the last Canto of Psychathanasia, not without triumph concluded, that the world hath not continued ab æterno from this ground:

—— Extension
That's infinite implies a contradiction.

And this is in answer to an objection against my last argument of the souls Immortalitie, viz. divine goodnesse. Which I there make the measure of his providence. That ground limits the Essence of the world as well as its duration, and satisfies the curiosity of the Opposer, by shewing the incompossibilitie in the Creature, not want of goodnesse in the Creatour to have staid the framing of the Vniverse. But now roused up by a new Philosophick furie, I answer that difficultie by taking away the Hypothesis of either the world or time being finite: defending the infinitude of both. Which though I had done with a great deal of vigour and life, and semblance of assent, it would have agreed well enough with the free heat of Poesie, and might have passed for a pleasant flourish: but the severity of my own judgement and sad Genius, hath cast in many correctives and coolers into the Canto it self: so that it cannot amount to more then a discussion. And discussion is no prejudice but an honour to the truth: for then and never but then is she victorious. And what a glorious Trophee shall the finite world erect when it hath vanquished the Infinite; a Pygmee a Giant!

H. M.

The *Argument of*
Democritus Platoniſſans,
Or
The Infinitie of Worlds.

'Gainst boundlesse time th' objections made,
And wast infinity
Of worlds, are with new reasons weigh'd ;
Mens judgements are left free.

1

Ence, hence unhallowed ears and hearts more
  hard
  Then winter clods last froze with Northern⎫
  wind.⎬
But most of all, foul tongue I thee discard
That blamest all that thy dark strait'ned mind,
Cannot conceive : But that no blame thou find ;
Whate're my pregnant Muse brings forth to light,
She'll not acknowledge to be of her kind,
Till Eagle-like she turn them to the sight
Of the eternall Word, all deckt with glory bright.

2

Strange sights do straggle in my restlesse thoughts,
And lively forms with orient colours clad
Walk in my boundlesse mind, as men ybrought
Into some spacious room, who when they've had
A turn or two, go out, although unbad.
All these I see and know, but entertain
None to my friend but who's most sober sad ;
Although, the time my roof doth them contain
Their presence doth possesse me till they out again.

3

And thus possest, in silver trump I sound
Their guise, their shape, their gesture and array,
But as in silver trumpet nought is found
When once the piercing sound is past away,
(Though while the mighty blast therein did stay,
Its tearing noise so terribly did shrill,
That it the heavens did shake, and earth dismay)
As empty I of what my flowing quill
In heedlesse hast elswhere, or here, may hap to spill.

4

For 'tis of force and not of a set will ;
Ne dare my wary mind afford assent
To what is plac'd above all mortall skill.
But yet our various thoughts to represent

Each gentle wight will deem of good intent.
Wherefore with leave th' infinitie I'll sing
Of Time, of Space : or without leave ; I'm brent
With eager rage, my heart for joy doth spring,
And all my spirits move with pleasant trembeling.

5

An inward triumph doth my soul up-heave
And spread abroad through endlesse 'spersèd air.
My nimble mind this clammie clod doth leave,
And lightly stepping on from starre to starre
Swifter then lightning, passeth wide and farre,
Measuring th' unbounded Heavens and wastfull skie ;
Ne ought she finds her passage to debarre,
For still the azure Orb as she draws nigh
Gives back, new stars appear, the worlds walls 'fore her
  flie !

6

For what can stand that is so badly staid ?
Well may that fall whose ground-work is unsure.
And what hath wall'd the world but thoughts un-
  weigh'd
In freer reason ? That antiquate, secure,
And easie dull conceit of corporature,
Of matter, quantitie, and such like gear
Hath made this needlesse, thanklesse inclosure,
Which I in full disdain quite up will tear
And lay all ope, that as things are they may appear.

7

For other they appear from what they are,
By reason that their Circulation
Cannot well represent entire from farre,
Each portion of the *Cuspis* of the Cone
(Whose nature is elsewhere more clearly shone)
I mean each globe, whether of glaring light
Or else opake, of which the earth is one.
If circulation could them well transmit
Numbers infinite of each would strike our 'stonishd
  sight ;

8

All in just bignesse and right colours dight :
But totall presence without all defect

'Longs onely to that Trinity by right,
Ahad, Æon, Psyche with all graces deckt,
Whose nature well this riddle will detect ;
A circle whose circumference no where
Is circumscrib'd, whose Centre's each where set,
But the low Cusp's a figure circular,
Whose compasse is ybound, but centre's every where.

9

Wherefore who'll judge the limits of the world
By what appears unto our failing sight
Appeals to sense, reason down headlong hurld
Out of her throne by giddie vulgar might.
But here base senses dictates they will dight
With specious title of Philosophie,
And stiffly will contend their cause is right.
From rotten rolls of school antiquity,
Who constantly denie corporall Infinitie.

10

But who can prove their corporalitie,
Since matter which thereto's essentiall
If rightly sifted's but a phantasie.
And quantitie who's deem'd Originall
Is matter, must with matter likewise fall.
Whatever is, is Life and Energie
From God, who is th' Originall of all ;
Who being every where doth multiplie
His own broad shade that endlesse throughout all doth
lie.

11

He from the last projection of light
Ycleep'd *Shamajim*, which is liquid fire
(It *Æther* eke and centrall *Tasis* hight)
Hath made each shining globe and clumperd mire
Of dimmer Orbs. For Nature doth inspire
Spermatick life, but of a different kind.
Hence those congenit splendour doth attire
And lively heat, these darknesse dead doth bind,
And without borrowed rayes they be both cold and
blind.

12

All these be knots of the universall stole
Of sacred *Psyche ;* which at first was fine,
Pure, thin, and pervious till hid powers did pull
Together in severall points and did encline
The nearer parts in one clod to combine.
Those centrall spirits that the parts did draw
The measure of each globe did then define,
Made things impenetrable here below,
Gave colour, figure, motion, and each usuall law.

13

And what is done in this Terrestrial starre
The same is done in every Orb beside.
Each flaming Circle that we see from farre
Is but a knot in *Psyches* garment tide.
From that lax shadow cast throughout the wide
And endlesse world, that low'st projection

Of universall life each thing's deriv'd
Whater'e appeareth in corporeall fashion ;
For body's but this spirit, fixt, grosse by conspissation.

14

And that which doth conspissate active is ;
Wherefore not matter but some living sprite
Of nimble nature which this lower mist
And immense field of Atoms doth excite,
And wake into such life as best doth fit
With his own self. As we change phantasies,
The essence of our soul not chang'd a whit ;
So do these Atomes change their energies,
Themselves unchanged, into new Centreities.

15

And as our soul's not superficially
Coloured by phantasms, nor doth them reflect
As doth a looking-glasse such imag'rie
As it to the beholder doth detect :
No more are these lightly or smear'd or deckt
With form or motion which in them we see,
But from their inmost Centre they project
Their vitall rayes ; not merely passive be,
But by occasion wak'd, rouse up themselves on high.

16

So that they're life, form, sprite, not matter pure,
For matter pure is a pure nullitie ;
What nought can act is nothing, I am sure,
And if all act, that is they'll not denie
But all that is is form : so easily
By what is true, and by what they embrace
For truth, their feignèd Corporalitie
Will vanish into smoke : But on I'll passe,
More fully we have sung this in another place.

17

Wherefore more boldly now to represent
The nature of the world, how first things were,
How now they are : This endlesse large Extent
Of lowest life (which I styled whileere
The *Cuspis* of the *Cone* that's every where)
Was first all dark, till in this spacious Hall
Hideous through silent horrour, torches clear
And lamping lights bright shining over all,
Were set up in due distances proportionall.

18

Innumerable numbers of fair Lamps
Were rightly rangèd in this hollow hole,
To warm the world and chace the shady damps
Of immense darknesse, rend her pitchie stole
Into short rags more dustie dimme then coal.
Which pieces then in severall were cast
(Abhorrèd relicks of that vesture foul)
Upon the Globes that round those torches trac'd,
Which still fast on them stick for all they run so fast.

19

Such an one is that which mortall men call Night,
A little shred of that unbounded shade.

And such a globe is that which earth is hight ;
By witlesse Wizzards the sole centre made
Of all the world, and on strong pillars staid.
And such a lamp or light is this our Sun,
Whose fiery beams the scorchèd Earth invade.
But infinite such as he, in heaven won,
And more then infinite Earths about those Suns do run ;

20

And to speak out ; though I detest the sect
Of *Epicurus* for their manners vile,
Yet what is true I may not well reject.
Truth's incorruptible, ne can the style
Of vitious pen her sacred worth defile.
If we no more of truth should deign t' embrace
Then what unworthy mouths did never soyle,
No truths at all 'mongst men would finden place,
But make them speedy wings and back to Heaven apace.

21

I will not say our world is infinite,
But that infinity of worlds there be ;
The Centre of our world's the lively light
Of the warm sunne, the visible Deity
Of this externall Temple. *Mercurie*
Next plac'd and warm'd more throughly by his rayes,
Right nimbly 'bout his golden head doth fly ;
Then *Venus* nothing slow about him strayes,
And next our *Earth* though seeming sad full sprightly
    playes.

22

And after her *Mars* rangeth in a round
With fiery locks and angry flaming eye,
And next to him mild *Jupiter* is found,
But *Saturn* cold wons in our outmost sky.
The skirts of his large Kingdome surely ly
Near to the confines of some other worlds
Whose Centres are the fixèd starres on high,
'Bout which as their own proper Suns are hurld
Joves, Earths, and *Saturns* : round on their own axes
    twurld.

23

Little or nothing are those starres to us
Which in the azure Evening gay appear
(I mean for influence) but judicious
Nature and carefull Providence her dear
And matchlesse work did so contrive whileere,
That th' Hearts or Centres in the wide world pight
Should such a distance each to other bear,
That the dull Planets with collated light
By neighbour suns might chearèd be in dampish night.

24

And as the Planets in our world (of which
The sun's the heart and kernal) do receive
Their nightly light from suns that do enrich
Their sable mantle with bright gemmes, and give
A goodly splendour, and sad men relieve
With their fair twinkling rayes, so our worlds sunne

Becomes a starre elsewhere, and doth derive
Joynt light with others, cheareth all that won
In those dim duskish Orbs round other suns that run.

25

This is the parergon of each noble fire
Of neighbour worlds to be the nightly starre,
But their main work is vitall heat t' inspire
Into the frigid spheres that 'bout them fare ;
Which of themselves quite dead and barren are,
But by the wakening warmth of kindly dayes,
And the sweet dewie nights, they well declare
Their seminall virtue, in due courses raise
Long hidden shapes and life, to their great Makers
    praise.

26

These with their suns I severall worlds do call,
Whereof the number I deem infinite :
Else infinite darknesse were in this great Hall
Of th' endlesse Universe ; For nothing finite
Could put that immense shadow into flight.
But if that infinite Suns we shall admit,
Then infinite worlds follow in reason right,
For every Sun with Planets must be fit,
And have some mark for his farre-shining shafts to hit.

27

But if he shine all solitarie, alone,
What mark is left ? what aimèd scope or end
Of his existence ? wherefore every one
Hath a due number of dim Orbs that wend
Around their centrall fire. But wrath will rend
This strange composure back'd with reason stout.
And rather tongues right speedily will spend
Their forward censure, that my wits run out
On wool-gathering, through infinite spaces all about.

28

What sober man will dare once to avouch
An infinite number of dispersèd starres?
This one absurdity will make him crouch
And eat his words : Division nought impairs
The former whole, nor he augments that spares.
Strike every tenth out, that which doth remain,
An equall number with the former shares,
And let the tenth alone, th' whole nought doth gain,
For infinite to infinite is ever the same.

29

The tenth is infinite as the other nine,
Or else, nor they, nor all the ten entire
Are infinite. Thus one infinite doth adjoyn
Others unto it and still riseth higher.
And if those single lights hither aspire,
This strange prodigious inconsistency
Groweth still stranger, if each fixèd fire
(I mean each starre) prove Suns and Planets flie
About their flaming heads amid the throngèd skie.

30

For whatsoever that there number be
Whether by seavens, or eights, or fives, or nines,
They round each fixèd lamp ; Infinity
Will be redoubled thus by many times.
Besides each greater Planet th' attendance finds
Of lesser ; Our *Earths* handmaid is the Moon,
Which to her darkned side right duly shines,
And *Jove* hath foure, as hath been said aboven,
And *Saturn* more then foure if the plain truth were
    known :

31

And if these globes be regions of life
And severall kinds of plants therein do grow,
Grasse, flowers, hearbs, trees, which the impartiall knife
Of all consuming Time still down doth mow,
And new again doth in succession show ;
Which also's done in flies, birds, men and beasts ;
Adde sand, pearls, pebbles, that the ground do strow,
Leaves, quills, hairs, thorns, blooms ; you may think
    the rest
Their kinds by mortall penne cannot be well exprest.

32

And if their kinds no man may reckon well,
The summe of successive particulars
No mind conceive nor tongue can ever tell.
And yet this mist of numbers (as appears)
Belongs to one of these opacous sphears,
Suppose this *Earth ;* what then will all those Rounds
Produce ? No *Atlas* such a load upbears.
In this huge endlesse heap o'rewhelmed, drown'd,
Choak'd, stifled, lo ! I lie, breathlesse, even quite con-
    found.

33

Yet give me space a while but to respire,
And I my self shall fairly well out-wind ;
Keep this position true, unhurt, entire,
That you no greater difficulty find
In this new old opinion here defin'd
Of infinite worlds, then one world doth imply.
For if we do with steddy patience mind,
All is resolv'd int' one absurdity,
The grant of something greater then infinitie.

34

That God is infinite all men confesse,
And that the Creature is some realtie
Besides Gods self, though infinitely lesse.
Joyn now the world unto the Deity.
What ? is there added no more entity
By this conjunction, then there was before ?
Is the broad-breasted earth ? the spacious skie
Spangled with silver light, and burning Ore ?
And the wide bellowing Seas, whose boyling billows roar,

35

Are all these nothing ? But you will reply ;
As is the question so we ought restrain

Our answer unto Corporeity.
But that that phantasie of the body's vain
I did before unto you maken plain.
But that no man depart unsatisfi'd
A while this Universe here will we feign
Corporeall, till we have gainly tride,
If ought that's bodily may infinite abide.

36

What makes a body, saving quantity ?
What quantitie unlesse extension ?
Extension if t' admit infinity
Bodies admit boundlesse dimension.
That some extension forward on doth run
Withouten limits, endlesse, infinite,
Is plain from Space, that ever paceth on
Unstop'd, unstaid, till it have fillèd quite
That immense infinite Orb where God himself doth sit.

37

But yet more sensibly this truth to show,
If space be ended set upon that end
Some strong arm'd Archer with his Parthian bow,
That from that place with speedy force may send
His fleeter shafts, and so still forward wend.
Where ? When shall we want room his strength to trie ?
But here perversly subtill you'l contend
Nothing can move in mere vacuity,
And space is nought, so not extended properly :

38

To solve these knots I must call down from high
Some heavenly help, feather with Angels wing
The sluggish arrow ; If it will not flie,
Sent out from bow stiff-bent with even string,
Let Angels on their backs it thither bring
Where your free mind appointed had before,
And then hold on, till in your travelling
You be well wearied, finding ever more
Free passage for their flight, and what they flying bore

39

Now to that shift that sayes Vacuity
Is nought, and therefore not at all extent
We answer thus : There is a distancy
In empty space, though we be well content
To balk that question (for we never meant
Such needlesse niceties) whether that it be
A reall being ; yet that there's parts distent
One from another, no mans phantasie
Can e're reject if well he weigh't and warily.

40

For now conceive the air and azure skie
All swept away from Saturn to the Sunne,
Which eath is to be wrought by him on high.
Then in this place let all the Planets runne
(As erst they did before this feat was done)
If not by nature, yet by divine power,
Ne one hairsbreadth their former circuite shun :
And still for fuller proof, th' Astronomer
Observe their hights as in the empty heavens they scoure.

41

Will then their Parallaxes prove all one
Or none, or different still as before ;
If so, their distances by mortall men
Must be acknowledg'd such as were of yore,
Measur'd by leagues, miles, stades, nor lesse nor more
From circuit unto circuit shal be found
Then was before the sweeping of the floor.
That distance therefore hath most certain ground
In emptinesse, we may conclude with reason sound.

42

If distance now so certainly attend
All emptinesse (as also mensuration
Attendeth distance) distance without end
Is wide disperst above imagination
(For emptinesse is void of limitation)
And this unbounded voidnesse doth admit
The least and greatest measures application ;
The number thus of th' greatest that doth fit
This infinite void space is likewise infinite.

43

But whatsoe're that infinite number be,
A lesser measure will a number give
So farre exceeding in infinity
That number as this measure we conceive
To fall short of the other. But I'll leave
This present way and a new course will trie,
Which at the same mark doth as fully drive
And with a great deal more facility ;
Look on this endlesse Space as one whole quantity.

44

Which in your mind in't equall parts divide,
Tens, hundreds, thousands, or what pleaseth best.
Each part denominate doth still abide
An infinite portion, else not all the rest
Makes one infinitude.
For if one thousandth part may be defin'd
By finite measures eas'ly well exprest,
A myriad suppose of miles assign'd
Then to a thousand myriads is the whole confin'd.

45

Wherefore this wide and wast Vacuity,
Which endlesse is outstretched thorough all.
And lies even equall with the Deity,
Nor is a thing meerly imaginall,
(For it doth farre mens phantasies forestall
Nothing beholden to our devicefull thought)
This inf'nite voidnesse as much our mind doth gall,
And has as great perplexities ybrought
As if this empty space with bodies were yfraught.

46

Nor have we yet the face once to deny
But that it is, although we mind it not ;
For all once minded such perplexity
It doth create to puzzled reason, that
She sayes and unsayes, do's she knows not what.
Why then should we the worlds infinity

Misdoubt, because whenas we contemplate
Its nature, such strange inconsistency
And unexpected sequels, we therein descry ?

47

Who dare gainsay but God is every where
Unbounded, measurelesse, all Infinite ;
Yet the same difficulties meet us here
Which erst us met and did so sore affright
With their strange vizards. This will follow right,
Whereever we admit Infinity
Every denominated part proves streight
A portion infinite, which if it be,
One infinite will into myriads multiply.

48

But with new argument to draw more near
Our purpos'd end. If God's omnipotent
And this omnipotent God be every where,
Where're he is then can he eas'ly vent
His mighty virtue thorough all extent.
What then shall hinder but a roscid air
With gentle heat eachwhere be 'sperst and sprent
Unlesse omnipotent power we will empair,
And say that empty space his working can debarre.

49

Where now this one supposèd world is pight
Was not that space at first all vain and void ?
Nor ought said ; no, when he said, *Let 't be light.*
Was this one space better then all beside,
And more obedient to what God decreed ?
Or would not all that endlesse Emptinesse
Gladly embrac'd (if he had ever tride)
His just command ? and what might come to passe
Implies no contradictious inconsistentnesse.

50

Wherefore this precious sweet Ethereall dew
For ought we know, God each where did distill,
And thorough all that hollow Voidnesse threw,
And the wide gaping drought therewith did fill,
His endlesse overflowing goodnesse spill
In every place ; which streight he did contrive
Int' infinite severall worlds, as his best skill
Did him direct and creatures could receive :
For matter infinite needs infinite worlds must give.

51

The Centre of each severall world's a Sunne
With shining beams and kindly warming heat,
About whose radiant crown the Planets runne,
Like reeling moths around a candle light ;
These all together, one world I conceit.
And that even infinite such worlds there be,
That inexhausted Good that God is hight,
A full sufficient reason is to me,
Who simple Goodnesse make the highest Deity.

52

Als make himself the key of all his works
And eke the measure of his providence ;

The piercing eye of truth to whom nought lurks
But lies wide ope unbar'd of all pretence.
But frozen hearts ! away ! flie farre from hence,
Unlesse you'l thaw at this celestiall fire
And melt into one mind and holy sense,
With Him that doth all heavenly hearts inspire,
So may you with my soul in one assent conspire.

53

But what's within, uneath is to convey
To narrow vessels that are full afore.
And yet this truth as wisely as I may
I will insinuate, from senses store
Borrowing a little aid.   Tell me therefore
When you behold with your admiring eyes
Heavens Canopie all to be spangled o're
With sprinkled stars, what can you well devize
Which causen may such carelesse order in the skies ?

54

A peck of peasen rudely pour'd out
On plaister flore, from hasty heedlesse hond
Which lie all carelesse scatterèd about,
To sight do in as seemly order stond,
As those fair glistering lights in heaven are found.
If onely for this world they were intended,
Nature would have adorn'd this azure Round
With better Art, and easily have mended
This harsh disord'red order, and more beauty lended.

55

But though these lights do seem so rudely throwen
And scattered throughout the spacious sky,
Yet each most seemly sits in his own Throne
In distance due and comely Majesty ;
And round their lordly seats their servants high
Keeping a well-proportionated space
One from another, doing chearfully
Their daily task. No blemish may deface
The worlds in severall deckt with all art and grace :

56

But the appearance of the nightly starres
Is but the by-work of each neighbour sun ;
Wherefore lesse marvell if it lightly shares
Of neater Art ; and what proportion
Were fittest for to distance one from one
(Each world I mean from other) is not clear.
Wherefore it must remain as yet unknown
Why such perplexèd distances appear
Mongst the dispersèd lights in Heaven thrown here and
there.

57

Again that eminent similitude
Betwixt the starres and Phœbus fixèd light,
They being both with steddinesse indu'd,
No whit removing whence they first were pight ;
No serious man will count a reason slight
To prove them both, both fixèd suns and stars

And Centres all of severall worlds by right ;
For right it is that none a sun debarre
Of Planets, which his just and due retinue are.

58

If starrs be merely starres, not centrall lights,
Why swell they into so huge bignesses ?
For many (as Astronomers do write)
Our sun in bignesse many times surpasse.
If both their number and their bulks were lesse
Yet lower placèd, light and influence
Would flow as powerfully, & the bosome presse
Of the impregnèd Earth, that fruit from hence
As fully would arise, and lordly affluence.

59

Wherefore these fixèd Fires mainly attend
Their proper charge in their own Universe,
And onely by the by of court'sie lend
Light to our world, as our world doth reverse
His thankfull rayes so far as he can pierce
Back unto other worlds. But farre aboven,
Further then furthest thought of man can traverse,
Still are new worlds aboven and still aboven,
In th' endlesse hollow Heaven, and each world hath his
Sun.

60

An hint of this we have in winter-nights,
When reason may see clearer then our eye,
Small subtil starres appear unto our sights
As thick as pin-dust scatterèd in the skie.
Here we accuse our seeing facultie
Of weaknesse, and our sense of foul deceit,
We do accuse and yet we know not why.
But the plain truth is, from a vaster hight
The numerous upper worlds amaze our dazzled sight.

61

Now sith so farre as sense can ever try
We find new worlds, that still new worlds there be,
And round about in infinite numbers lie,
Further then reach of mans weak phantasie
(Without suspition of temerity)
We may conclude ; as well as men conclude
That there is air farre 'bove the mountains high,
Or that th' Earth a sad substance doth include
Even to the Centre with like qualities indu'd.

62

For who did ever the Earths Centre pierce,
And felt or sand or gravell with his spade
At such a depth ? what Histories rehearse
That ever wight did dare for to invade
Her bowels but one mile in dampish shade ?   ꞌ
Yet I'll be bold to say that few or none
But deem this globe even to the bottome made
Of solid earth, and that her nature's one
Throughout, though plain experience hath it never shown.

63

But sith sad earth so farre as they have gone
They still descry, eas'ly they do inferre

Without all check of reason, were they down
Never so deep, like substance would appear,
Ne dream of any hollow horrour there.
My mind with like uncurb'd facility
Concludes from what by sight is seen so clear :
That ther's no barren wast vacuity
Above the worlds we see, but still new worlds there ly,

64

And still and still even to infinity :
Which point, since I so fitly have propos'd,
Abating well the inconsistency
Of harsh infinitude therein suppos'd
And prov'd by reasons never to be loos'd,
That infinite space and infinite worlds there be ;
This load laid down, I'm freely now dispos'd
A while to sing of times infinity :
May infinite Time afford me but his smallest fee.

65

For smallest fee of time will serve my turn
This part for to dispatch, sith endlesse space
(Whose perplext nature well mans brains might turn,
And weary wits disorder and misplace)
I have already passèd : for like case
Is in them both. He that can well untie
The knots that in those infinite worlds found place,
May easily answer each perplexity
Of these worlds infinite matters endlesse durancie.

66

The *Cuspis* and the *Basis* of the *Cone*
Were both at once dispersèd every where ;
But the pure *Basis* that is God alone :
Else would remotest sights as big appear
Unto our eyes as if we stood them near.
And if an Harper harpèd in the Moon,
His silvered sound would touch our tickled ear :
Or if one hollowed from highest Heaven aboven,
In sweet still Evening-tide, his voice would hither roame.

67

This all would be if the *Cuspe* of the *Cone*
Were very God. Wherefore I rightly 't deem
Onely a Creaturall projection,
Which flowing yet from God hath ever been,
Fill'd the vast empty space with its large streem.
But yet it is not totall every where
As was even now by reason rightly seen :
Wherefore not God, whose nature doth appear
Entirely omnipresent, weigh'd with judgement clear.

68

A reall infinite matter, distinct
And yet proceeding from the Deitie,
Although with different form as then untinct,
Has ever been from all Eternity.
Now what delay can we suppose to be,
Since matter alway was at hand prepar'd
Before the filling of the boundlesse sky
With framèd Worlds ; for nought at all debar'd,
Nor was His strength ungrown, nor was His strength
empair'd.

19

69

How long would God be forming of a fly ?
Or the small wandring moats that play in th' sun ?
Least moment well will serve none can deny,
His *Fiat* spoke and streight the thing is done,
And cannot He make all the World as soon ?
For in each Atom of the matter wide
The totall Deity doth entirely won,
His infinite presence doth therein reside,
And in this presence infinite powers do ever abide.

70

Wherefore at once from all eternity
The infinite number of these Worlds He made,
And will conserve to all infinitie,
And still drive on their ever-moving trade,
And steddy hold whatever must be staid ;
Ne must one mite be minish'd of the summe,
Ne must the smallest atom ever fade,
But still remain though it may change its room ;
This truth abideth strong from everlasting doom.

71

Ne fear I what hard sequel after-wit
Will draw upon me ; that the number's one
Of years, moneths, dayes, houres, and of minutes flee :
Which from eternitie have still run on.
I plainly did confesse awhile agone
That be it what it will that's infinite,
More infinites will follow thereupon,
But that all infinites do justly fit
And equall be, my reason did not yet admit.

72

But as my emboldened mind, I know not how,
In empty Space and pregnant Deitie
Endlesse infinitude dares to allow,
Though it begets the like perplexitie :
So now my soul drunk with Diuinitie,
And born away above her usuall bounds
With confidence concludes infinitie
Of Time of Worlds, of firie flaming Rounds ;
Which sight in sober mood my spirits quite confounds :

73

And now I do awhile but interspire,
A torrent of objections 'gainst me beat,
My boldnesse to represse and strength to tire.
But I will wipe them off like summer sweat,
And make their streams streight back again retreat.
If that these worlds, say they, were ever made
From infinite time, how comes't to passe that yet
Art is not perfected, nor metalls fade,
Nor mines of grimie coal low-hid in griesly shade.

74

But the remembrance of the ancient Floud
With ease will wash such arguments away.
Wherefore with greater might I am withstood :
The strongest stroke wherewith they can assay

N

To vanquish me is this ; The Date or Day
Of the created World, which all admit ;
Nor may my modest Muse this truth gainsay
In holy Oracles so plainly writ :
Wherefore the Worlds continuance is not infinite.

75

Now lend me, *Origen !* a little wit
This sturdy stroke right fairly to avoid,
Lest that my rasher rhymes, while they ill fit
With *Moses* pen, men justly may deride
And well accuse of ignorance or pride.
But thou, O holy Sage ! with piercing sight
Who readst those sacred rolls, and hast well tride
With searching eye thereto what fitteth right,
Thy self of former Worlds right learnedly dost write :

76

To weet that long ago there Earths have been
Peopled with men and beasts before this Earth,
And after this shall others be again
And other beasts and other humane birth.
Which once admit, no strength that reason bear'th
Of this worlds Date and Adams efformation ;
Another Adam once received breath
And still another in endlesse repedation,
And this must perish once by finall conflagration.

77

Witnesse ye Heavens if what I say's not true,
Ye flaming Comets wandering on high,
And new fixt starres found in that Circle blue,
The one espide in glittering *Cassiopie,*
The other near to *Ophiucbus* thigh.
Both bigger then the biggest starres that are,
And yet as farre remov'd from mortall eye
As are the furthest, so those Arts declare
Unto whose reaching sight Heavens mysteries lie bare.

78

Wherefore these new-seen lights were greater once
By many thousand times then this our sphear
Wherein we live, 'twixt good and evil chance.
Which to my musing mind doth strange appear
If those large bodies then first shapèd were.
For should so goodly things so soon decay?
Neither did last the full space of two year.
Wherefore I cannot deem that their first day
Of being, when to us they sent out shining ray.

79

But that they were created both of old,
And each in his due time did fair display
Themselves in radiant locks more bright then gold,
Or silver sheen purg'd from all drossie clay,
But how they could themselves in this array
Expose to humane sight who did before
Lie hid, is that which well amazen may
The wisest man and puzzle evermore :
Yet my unwearied thoughts this search could not give
    o're.

80

Which when I'd exercis'd in long pursuit
To finden out what might the best agree
With wary reason, at last I did conclude
That there's no better probability
Can be produc'd of that strange prodigie,
But that some mighty Planet that doth run
About some fixèd starre in *Cassiopie*
As *Saturn* paceth round about our Sun,
Unusuall light and bignesse by strange fate had wonne.

81

Which I conceive no gainer way is done
Then by the seazing of devouring fire
On that dark Orb, which 'fore but dimly shone
With borrowed light, not lightenèd entire,
But halfèd like the Moon.
And while the busie flame did siez throughout,
And search the bowels of the lowest mire
Of that *Saturnian* Earth ; a mist broke out,
And immense mounting smoke arose all round about.

82

Which being gilded with the piercing rayes
Of its own sun and every neighbour starre,
It soon appear'd with shining-silver blaze,
And then gan first be seen of men from farre.
Besides that firie flame that was so narre
The Planets self, which greedily did eat
The wasting mold, did contribute a share
Unto this brightnesse ; and what I conceit
Of this starre, doth with that of *Ophiuchus* fit.

83

And like I would adventure to pronounce
Of all the Comets that above the Moon,
Amidst the higher Planets rudely dance
In course perplex, but that from this rash doom
I'm bet off by their beards and tails farre strown
Along the skie, pointing still opposite
Unto the sunne, however they may roam ;
Wherefore a cluster of small starres unite
These Meteors some do deem, perhaps with judgement
    right.

84

And that their tayls are streams of the suns light
Breaking through their near bodies as through clouds.
Besides the Optick glasse has shown to sight
The dissolution of these starrie crouds.
Which thing if't once be granted and allow'd,
I think without all contradiction
They may conclude these Meteors are routs
Of wandering starres, which though they one by one
Cannot be seen, yet joyn'd, cause this strange vision.

85

And yet methinks, in my devicefull mind
Some reasons that may happily represse
These arguments it's not uneath to find.
For how can the suns rayes that be transmisse
Through these loose knots in Comets, well expresse
Their beards or curld tayls utmost incurvation ?

Beside, the conflux and congeries
Of lesser lights a double augmentation
Implies, and 'twixt them both a lessening coarctation.

86

For when as once these starres are come so nigh
As to seem one, the Comet must appear
In biggest show, because more loose they lie
Somewhat spread out, but as they draw more near
The compasse of his head away must wear,
Till he be brought to his least magnitude ;
And then they passing crosse he doth repair
Himself, and still from his last losse renew'd
Grows, till he reach the measure which we first had
  view'd.

87

And then farre-distanc'd they bid quite adiew,
Each holding on in solitude his way.
Ne any footsteps in the empty Blew
Is to be found of that farre-shining ray.
Which processe sith no man did yet bewray,
It seems unlikely that the Comets be
Synods of starres that in wide Heaven stray :
Their smallnesse eke and numerositie
Encreaseth doubt and lessens probabilitie.

88

A cluster of them makes not half a Moon,
What should such tennis-balls do in the skie?
And few'll not figure out the fashion
Of those round firie Meteors on high.
Ne ought their beards much move us, that do lie
Ever cast forward from the Morning sunne
Nor back-cast tayls turn'd to our Evening-eye,
That fair appear whenas the day is done :
This matter may lie hid in the starres shadowed Cone.

89

For in these Planets conflagration,
Although the smoke mount up exactly round,
Yet by the suns irradiation
Made thin and subtil no where else its found
By sight, save in the dim and duskish bound
Of the projected Pyramid opake ;
Opake with darknesse, smoke and mists unsound
Yet gilded like a foggie cloud doth make
Reflexion of fair light that doth our senses take.

90

This is the reason of that constant site
Of Comets tayls and beards : and that there show's
Not pure Pyramidall, nor their ends seem streight
But bow'd like brooms, is from the winds that blow,
I mean Ethereall winds, such as below,
Men finden under th' Equinoctiall line.
Their widend beards this aire so broad doth strow
Incurvate, and or more or lesse decline :
If not let sharper wits more subtly here divine.

91

But that experiment of the Optick glasse
The greatest argument of all I deem,

Ne can I well encounter nor let passe
So strong a reason if I may esteem
The feat withonten fallacie to been,
Nor judge these little sparks and subtile lights
Some ancient fixèd starres though now first seen,
That near the ruin'd Comets place were pight,
On which that Optick instrument by chance did light.

92

Nor finally an uncouth after-sport
Of th' immense vapours that the searching fire
Had boylèd out, which now themselves consort
In severall parts and closely do conspire,
Clumper'd in balls of clouds and globes entire
Of crudled smoke and heavy-clunging mists?
Which when they've stayed a while at last expire ;
But while they stay any may see that lists
So be that Optick Art his naturall sight assists.

93

If none of these wayes I may well decline
The urging weight of this hard argument,
Worst is but parting stakes and thus define :
Some Comets be but single Planets brent,
Others a synod joyn'd in due consent :
And that no new-found Meteors they are,
Ne further may my wary mind assent
From one single experience solitaire,
Till all-discovering Time shall further truth declare.

94

But for the new-fixt starres there's no pretence,
Nor beard nor tail to take occasion by,
To bring in that unluckie inference
Which weaken might this new built mysterie :
Certes in raging fire they both did frie.
A signe whereof you rightly may aread
Their colours changeable varietie,
First clear and white, then yellow, after red,
Then blewly pale, then duller still, till perfect dead.

95

And as the order of these colours went,
So still decreas'd that Cassiopean starre,
Till at the length to sight it was quite spent :
Which observations strong reasons are,
Consuming fire its body did empare
And turn to ashes. And the like will be
In all the darksome Planets wide and farre.
Ne can our Earth from this state standen free,
A Planet as the rest, and Planets fate must trie.

96

Ne let the tender heart too harshly deem
Of this rude sentence : for what rigour more
Is in consuming fire then drowning stream
Of Noahs floud which all creatures chok'd of yore,
Saving those few that were kept safe in store
In that well-builded ship? All else beside
Men, birds, and beasts, the lion, buck, and bore
Dogs, kine, sheep, horses all that did abide
Upon the spacious Earth, perish'd in waters wide.

97

Nor let the slow and misbelieving wight
Doubt how the fire on the hard earth may seize ;
No more then how those waters earst did light
Upon the sinfull world.   For as the seas
Boyling with swelling waves aloft did rise,
And met with mighty showers and pouring rain
From Heavens spouts, so the broad-flashing skies
With brimstone thick and clouds of fiery bain,
Shall meet with raging Etna's and Vesuvius flame.

98

The burning bowels of this wasting ball
Shall gullop up great flakes of rolling fire,
And belch out pitchie flames, till over all
Having long rag'd, Vulcan himself shall tire
And (th' earth an ashcap made) shall then expire :
Here Nature laid asleep in her own Urn
With gentle rest right easily will respire,
Till to her pristine task she do return
As fresh as Phenix young under th' Arabian Morn.

99

O happy they that then the first are born,
While yet the world is in her vernall pride :
For old corruption quite away is worn
As metall pure so is her mold well-tride.
Sweet dews, cool breathing airs, and spaces wide
Of precious spicery wafted with soft wind :
Fair comely bodies, goodly beautifi'd,
Snow-limb'd, rose-cheek'd, ruby-lip'd, pearl-teeth'd,
    star-eyn'd :
Their parts, each fair, in fit proportion all combin'd.

100

For all the while her purgèd ashes rest,
These relicks dry suck in the heavenly dew,
And roscid Manna rains upon her breast,
And fills with sacred milk, sweet, fresh, and new,
Where all take life, and doth the world renew ;
And then renew'd with pleasure be yfed.
A green soft mantle doth her bosome strew
With fragrant herbs and flowers embellishèd,
Where without fault or shame all living creatures bed.

101

Ne ought we doubt how nature may recover
In her own ashes long time buried.
For nought can e'er consume that centrall power
Of hid spermatick life, which lies not dead
In that rude heap, but safely coverèd ;
And doth by secret force suck from above
Sweet heavenly juice, and therewith nourishèd
Till her just bulk, she doth her life emprove :
Made mother of much children that about her move.

102

Witnesse that uncouth bird of Arabie
Which out of her own ruines doth revive
With all th' exploits of skilfull Chymistrie,
Such as no vulgar wit can well believe.

Let universall Nature witnesse give
That what I sing's no feignèd forgerie.
A needlesse task new fables to contrive,
But what I sing is seemly verity,
Well-suting with right reason and Philosophie.

103

But the fit time of this mutation
No man can finden out with all his pains.
For the small sphears of humane reason run
Too swift within his narrow-compast brains.
But that vast Orb of Providence contains
A wider period ; turneth still and slow.
Yet at the last his aimèd end he gains,
And sure at last a fire will overflow
The agèd Earth, and all must into ashes go.

104

Then all the stately works and monuments
Built on this bottome, shall to ruine fall.
And all those goodly Statues shall be brent
Which were erect to the memoriall
Of Kings, and Kæsars, ne may better 'fall
The boastfull works of brave Poetick pride
That promise life and fame perpetuall ;
Ne better fate may these poore lines abide.
Betide what will to what may live no lenger tide

105

This is the course that never-dying Nature
Might ever hold, from all Eternitie
Renuing still the faint decayèd creature,
Which would grow stark and drie as agèd tree,
Unlesse by wise-preventing Destinie
She were at certain periods of years
Reducèd back unto her Infancie,
Which well-fram'd argument (as plainly appears)
My ship from those hard rocks and shelves right safely
    stears.

106

Lo ! now my faithfull muse hath represented
Both frames of Providence to open view,
And hath each point in orient colours painted,
Not to deceive the sight with seeming shew
But earnest to give either part their due ;
Now urging th' uncouth strange perplexitie
Of infinite worlds and Time, then of anew
Softening that harsher inconsistency
To fit the immense goodnesse of the Deity.

107

And here by curious men 't may be expected
That I this knot with judgement grave decide,
And then proceed to what else was objected.
But, ah ! What mortall wit may dare t' areed
Heavens counsels in eternall horrour hid ?
And Cynthius pulls me by my tender ear,
Such signes I must observe with wary heed :
Wherefore my restlesse Muse at length forbear,
Thy silver-sounded Lute hang up in silence here.

                FINIS.

ANTIPSYCHOPANNYCHIA

OR

The third Book of the fong of the

S O U L :

Containing a Confutation of the sleep of the SOUL after death.

By *H. M.* Master of Arts, and Fellow of Christs
Colledge in *Cambridge*.

Τὸ μὲν τῆς αἰσθήσεως, ψυχῆς ἐστιν εὐδούσης. Ὅσον γὰρ ἐν σώματι
ψυχῆς, τοῦτο εὕδει, ἡ δὲ ἀληθινὴ ἐγρήγορσις, ἀληθινὴ ἀπὸ σώματος, οὐ μετὰ σώματος ἀνάστασις.
Plotin. Ennead. 3.

Ἐγώ εἰμι ἡ ἀνάστασις καὶ ἡ ζωή. Ὁ πιστεύων εἰς ἐμὲ κἂν ἀποθάνῃ
ζήσεται, καὶ πᾶς ὁ ζῶν καὶ πιστεύων εἰς ἐμὲ, οὐ μὴ ἀποθάνῃ εἰς τὸν
αἰῶνα.
John 11.

CAMBRIDGE
Printed by *Roger Daniel,* Printer to the
Univerfitie. 1647.

The Preface to the Reader.

O preface much concerning these little after-pieces of Poetry, I hold needlesse, having spoke my mind so fully before. The motives that drew me to adde them to the former are exprest in the Poems themselves. My drift is one in them all : which is to raise a certain number of well-ordered Phantasms, fitly shaped out and warily contrived, which I set to skirmish and conflict with all the furious phansies of Epicurisme and Atheisme. But here's my disadvantage, that victory will be no victory, unlesse the adversary acknowledge himselfe overcome. None can acknowledge himself overcome, unlesse he perceive the strength, and feel the stroke of the more powerfull arguments. But the exility and subtilty of many, and that not of the meanest, is such (nor can they be otherwise) that they will (as that kind of thunder which the Poets do commonly call ἀργής, from its over-quick and penetrating energie) go through their more *porous* and spongy minds without any sensible impression.

Sure I am that sensuality is alwayes an enemy to subtilty of reason, which hath its rise from subtilty of phansie : so that the life of the body, being vigorous and radiant in the soul, hinders us of the sight of more attenuate phantasmes ; but that being supprest or very much castigate and kept under, our inward apprehension grows clearer and larger. Few men can imagine any thing so clearly awake, as they did when they were asleep : And what's the reason, but that the sense of the body is then bound up or dead in a manner?

The dark glasse-windows will afford us a further illustration for this purpose. Why is it that we see our own faces there by night? What can reflect the species (as they phrase it) when the glasse is pervious and transparent? Surely reflexion in the ordinary apprehension is but a conceit. The darknesse behind the glasse is enough to exhibit visibly the forms of things within, by hiding stronger objects from the eye, which would bury these weak idola in their more orient lustre.

The starres shine and fill the air with their species by day, but are to be seen onely in a deep pit, which may fence the Suns light from striking our sight so strongly. Every contemptible candle conquers the beams of the Moon, by the same advantage that the Suns doth the Starrs, viz. propinquitie. But put out the candle, and you will presently find the moon-light in the room ; exclude the moon, and then the feeblest of all species will step out into energy, we shall behold the night.

All this is but to shew, how the stronger or nearer αἴσθημα doth obscure the weaker or further off ; and how that one being removed, the energie of the other will easily appear.

Now that our comparison may be the fitter, let us consider what Aristotle saith of phansie, that it is αἴσθησίς τις ἀσθενής. Thus much I will take of him, that Phansie is sense ; and adde to it that φάντασμα is also αἴσθημα, and αἴσθημα, φάντασμα· and what I have intimated in some passages of these Poems, that the soul doth alwayes feel it self, its own actuall Idea, by its omniform centrall self. So that the immediate sense of the soul is nothing else but to perceive its own energie.

Now sith that, that which we call outward sense, is indeed the very energie of the soul, and inward sense which is phansie can be no other, there seems to be no reall and intrinsecall difference betwixt the φάντασμα and αἴσθημα of any form ; no more then there is betwixt a frog born by the Sunne and mere slime, and one born by copulation : For these are but extrinsecall relations. Wherefore φάντασμα and αἴσθημα in the soul it self is all one.

But now sith it is the same nature, why is not there the same degrees in both? I say there is, as appears plainly in sleep, where we find all as clear and energetical as when we wake.

But here these αἰσθήματα or φαντάσματα (for I have prov'd them all one) do as greater and lesser lights dim one another ; or that which is nearest worketh strongliest. Hence it is that the light or life of this low spirit or body of ours, stirring up the soul into a perpetuall sensuall energie, if we foster this and unite our minds, will, and animadversion with it, will by its close nearenesse with the soul dim and obscure those more subtil and exile phantasms or αἰσθήματα risen from the soul it self, or occasioned by other mens writings. For they will be in the flaring light or life of the body as the starres in the beams of the Sunne scarce to be seen, unlesse we withdraw our selves out of the flush vigour of that light, into the profoundity of our own souls, as into some deep pit.

Wherefore men of the most tam'd and castigate spirits are of the best and most profound judgement, because they can so easily withdraw themselves from the life and impulse of the lower spirit of this body,

Thus being quit of passion, they have upon any occasion a clear though still and quiet representation of every thing in their minds, upon which pure bright sydereall phantasms unprejudiced reason may safely work, and clearly discern what is true or probable.

If my writings fall into the hands of men otherwise qualified, I shall gain the lesse approbation. But if they will endeavour to compose themselves as near as they can to this temper ; though they were of another opinion then what my writings intend to prove, I doubt not but they will have the happinesse to be overcome, and to prove gainers by my victory.

To say anything more particularly concerning these last I hold it needlesse. Onely let me excuse my self, if any chance to blame me for my Ἀντιμονοψυχία, as confuting that which no man will assert. For it hath been asserted by some ; as those Mauri whom Ficinus speaks of ; and the question is also discussed by Plotinus in his fourth Ennead, where he distinguisheth of, *all souls being one*, after this manner, Ἆρα γὰρ ὡς ἀπὸ μιᾶς ἢ μία αἱ πᾶσαι. The latter member is that, which my arguments conclude against, though they were ἀπὸ μιᾶς yet were we safe enough ; as safe as the beams of the Sun the Sun existing. But the similitude of Praxiteles broken glasse is brought in, according to the apprehension of such, as make the image to vanish into nothing, the glasse being taken away : and that as there is but one face, though there be the appearances of many ; so though there be the appearances of many souls, by reason of that ones working in divers bodies, yet there is but one soul ; and understanding sense and motion to be the acts of this one soul informing severall bodies.

This is that which both Plotinus and I endeavour to destroy, which is of great moment : For if one onely soul act in every body, what ever we are now, surely this body laid in the dust we shall be nothing.

As for the Oracles answer to Amelius, if any vulgar conceited man think it came from a devil with Bats wings and a long tail, the Seventies translation of the eight verse of the 32. chapter of Deuteronomy may make it at least doubtfull. *When the most High divided to the nations their inheritance, when he separated the sonnes of Adam he set the bounds of the people,* κατ' ἀριθμὸν ἀγγέλων Θεοῦ. He did not then deliver them into the hand and jurisdiction of devils, nor to be instructed and taught by them.

But if Apollo who gave so good a testimony of Socrates while he was living, and of Plotinus after his death, was some foul fiend, yet tis no prejudice to their esteem, since our Saviour Christ was acknowledged by the devil.

But I have broke my word, by not breaking off before this. Reader, tis time now to leave thee to the perusall of my writings, which if they chance to please thee, I repent me not of my pains : if they chance not to please, that shall not displease me much, for I consider that I also with small content and pleasure have read the writings of other men.

Yours *H. M.*

The Argument of

ANTIPSYCHOPANNYCHIA

Or

The confutation of the fleep of the Soul.

CANT. I.

Adams long sleep, will, mind compar'd
With low vitality,
The fondnesse plainly have unbar'd
Of Psychopannychie.

1

He souls ever durancy I sung before,
  Ystruck with mighty rage. A powerful fire
Held up my lively Muse and made her soar
So high that mortall wit, I fear, she'll tire

To trace her. Then a while I did respire.
But now my beating veins new force again
Invades, and holy fury doth inspire.
Thus stirrèd up, I'll adde a second strain,
Lest, what afore was said may seem all spoke in vain.

2

For sure in vain do humane souls exist
After this life, if lull'd in listlesse sleep
They senselesse lie, wrapt in eternal mist,
Bound up in foggy clouds, that ever weep

Benumming tears, and the souls centre steep
With deading liquor, that she never minds
Or feeleth ought.   Thus drench'd in *Lethe* deep,
Nor misseth she her self, nor seeks nor finds
Her self.   This mirksome state all the souls actions
    binds.

3

Desire, fear, love, joy, sorrow, pleasure, pain,
Sense, phancy, wit, forecasting providence,
Delight in God, and what with sleepy brain
Might sute, slight dreams, all banish'd farre from
    hence.
Nor pricking nor applauding conscience
Can wake the soul from this dull Lethargie :
That 'twixt this sleepy state small difference
You'll find and that men call Mortality :
Plain death's as good as such a *Psychopannychie.*

4

What profiteth this bare existency,
If I perceive not that I do exist?
Nought 'longs to such, nor mirth nor misery.
Such stupid beings write into one list
With stocks and stones.   But they do not persist,
You'll say, in this dull dead condition ;
But must revive, shake off this drowsie mist
At that last shrill loud-sounding clarion
Which cleaves the trembling earth, rives monuments of
    stone.

5

Has then old Adam snorted all this time
Under some senselesse sod with sleep ydead?
And have those flames, that steep Olympus climbe
Right nimbly wheelèd or'e his heedlesse head
So oft, in heaps of years low burièd :
And yet can ken himself when he shall rise
Wakenèd by piercing trump, that farre doth shed
Its searching sound?   If we our memories
And wit do lose by sicknesse, falls, sloth, lethargies :

6

If all our childhood quite be waste away
With its impressions, so that we forget
What once we were, so soon as age doth sway
Our bowèd backs, sure when base worms have eat
His mouldring brains, and spirits have retreat
From whence they came, spread in the common fire,
And many thousand sloping sunnes have set
Since his last fall into his ancient mire,
How he will ken himself now may well admire :

7

For he must know himself by some impression
Left in his ancient body unwash'd out ;
Which seemeth strange ; for can so long succession
Of sliding years that great Colosses mought
Well moulder into dust, spare things ywrought
So slightly as light phantasms in our brain,

Which oft one yeare or moneth have wrenched out
And left no footsteps of that former stain,
No more then's of a cloud quite melted into rain?

8

And shall not such long series of time,
When Nature hath dispread our vitall spright
And turn'd our body to its ancient slime,
Quite wash away whatever was empight
In that our spirit?   If flesh and soul unite
Lose such impressions, as were once deep seald
And fairly glisterèd like to comets bright
In our blew *Chaos,* if the soul congeald
With her own body lose these forms as I reveald,

9

Then so long time of their disjunction
(The body being into dust confract,
The spright diffusèd, spread by dispersion)
And such *Lethean* sleep that doth contract
The souls hid rayes that it did nothing act,
Must certainly wipe all these forms away
That sense or phansie ever had impact.
So that old Adam will in vain assay
To find who here he was ; he'll have no memory.

10

Nor can he tell that ere he was before :
And if not tell, he's as if then first born.
If as first born, his former life's no store.
Yet when men wake they find themselves at morn,
But if their memory away were worn
With one nights sleep, as much as doth respect
Themselves, these men they never were beforn,
This day's their birth day : they can not conject
They ever liv'd till now, much lesse the same detect.

11

So when a man goes hence, thus may he say,
As much as me concerns I die now quite.
Adiew, good self ! for now thou goest away,
Nor can I possibly thee ever meet
Again, nor ken thy face, nor kindly greet.
Sleep and dispersion spoyls our memory.
So my dear self henceforth I cannot weet.
Wherefore to me its perfectly to die,
Though subtiler Wits do call't but *Psychopannychie.*

12

Go now you *Psychopannychites !* perswade
To comely virtues and pure piety
From hope of ioy, or fear of penance sad.
Men promptly may make answer, Who shall try
That pain or pleasure?   When death my dim eye
Shall close, I sleep not sensible of ought :
And tract of time at least all memory
Will quite debarre, that reacquainten mought
My self with mine own self, if so my self I sought.

13

But I shall neither seek my selfe, nor find
My self unsought : Therefore not deprehend

My self in joy or wo.   Men ought to mind
What 'longs unto them.   But when once an end
Is put unto this life, and fate doth rend
Our retinence ; what follows nought at all
Belongs to us : what need I to contend,
And my frail spright with present pain to gall
For what I nere shall judge my self did ere befall ;

14

This is the uncouth state of sleeping soul,
Thus weak of her own self without the prop
Of the base body, that she no'te out-roll
Her vitall raies : those raies Death down doth lop,
And all her goodly beauty quite doth crop
With his black claws.   Wisdome, love, piety,
Are straight dried up : Death doth their fountain stop,
This is those sleepers dull Philosophy,
Which fairly men invites to foul impiety.

15

But if we grant, which in my former song
I plainly prov'd, that the souls energie
'Pends not on this base corse, but that self-strong
She by her self can work, then when we fly
The bodies commerce, no man can deny
But that there is no interruption
Of life ; where will puts on, there doth she hie
Or if she's carried by coaction,
That force yet she observes by presse adversion.

16

And with most lively touch doth feel and find
Her self.   For either what she most doth love
She then obtains ; or else with crosse, unkind
Contrary life since her decease sh' hath strove,
That keeps her wake, and with like might doth move
To think upon her self, and in what plight
She's fallen.   And nothing able to remove
Deep searching vengeance, groans in this sad Night,
And rores, and raves, and storms, and with her self doth
fight.

17

But hearty love of that great vitall spright,
The sacred fount of holy sympathy ;
Prepares the soul with its deep quickning might
To leave the bodies vain mortality.
Away she flies into Eternity,
Finds full accomplishment of her desire ;
Each thing would reach its own centrality :
So Earth with Earth, and Moon with Moon conspire.
Our selves live most, when most we feed our *Centrall* fire.

18

Thus is the soul continually in life
Withouten interruption, if that she
Can operate after the fatall knife
Hath cut the cords of lower sympathy :
Which she can do, if that some energie
She exercise (immur'd in this base clay)

Which on frail flesh hath no dependency,
For then the like she'll do, that done away.
These independent acts, 'tis time now to display.

19

All comprehending *Will*, proportionate
To whatsoever shall fall by Gods decree
Or prudent sufferance, sweetly spread, dilate,
Stretch'd out t' embrace each act or entity
That creep from hidden cause that none can see
With outward eyes.   Next *Intellect*, whose hight
Of working's then, whenas it stands most free
From sense and grosser phansie, deep empight
In this vild corse, which to purg'd minds yields small
delight.

20

Both Will and Intellect then worketh best,
When Sense and Appetite be consopite,
And grosser phansie lull'd in silent rest :
Then Will grown full with a mild heavenly light
Shines forth with goodly mentall rayes bedight,
And finds and feels such things as never pen
Can setten down, so that unexpert wight
May reade and understand.   Experienc'd men
Do onely know who like impressions sustain :

21

So far's the Soul from a dependency
(In these high actions) on the body base.
And further signe is want of memory
Of these impressions wrought in heavenly place,
I mean the holy *Intellect :* they passe
Leaving no footsteps of their former light,
Whenas the soul from thence descended has,
Which is a signe those forms be not empight
In our low proper *Chaos* or *Corporeall spright.*

22

For then when we our mind do downward bend
Like things we here should find : but all is gone
Soon as our flagging souls so low descend
As that straight spright.   Like torch that droppeth
down
From some high tower, held steddy, clearly shone,
But in its fall leaves all its light behind,
Lies now in darknesse on the grail, or stone,
Or dirty earth : That erst so fully shin'd,
Within a glowing coal hath now its light confin'd.

23

So doth the soul when from high *Intellect*
To groveling sense she takes her stooping flight,
Falling into her body, quite neglect,
Forget, forgo her former glorious sight.
Grosse glowing fire for that wide-shining light ;
For purest love, foul fury and base passion ;
For clearest knowledge, fell contentious fight
Sprong from some scorching false inust impression
Which she'll call truth, she gains. O witlesse Commu-
tation !

24

But still more clear her independent might
In understanding and pure subtile will
To prove : I will assay t' explain aright
The difference ('ccording to my best skill)
'Twixt these and those base faculties that well
From union with the low consistency
Of this *Out-world*, that when my curious quill,
Hath well describ'd their great disparity,
To th' highest we may give an independency.

25

The faculties we deem corporeall,
And bound unto this earthy instrument
(So bound that they no'te operate at all
Without the body there immerse and meint)
Be hearing, feeling, tasting, sight, and sent.
Adde lower phansie, *Mundane* memory :
Those powers be all or more or lesse ypent
In this grosse life : We'll first their property
Set down, and then the others contrariety.

26

This might perceives not its own instrument.
The taste discovers not the spungy tongue ;
Nor is the *Mundane* spright (through all extent)
From whence are sense and lower phansie sprong
Perceivèd by the best of all among
These learnèd *Five*, nor yet by phantasie :
Nor doth or this or those so nearly throng
Unto themselves as by propinquity
To apprehend themselves. They no'te themselves descry ;

27

Nor e're learn what their own impressions be.
The mind held somewhere else in open sight,
Whatever lies, unknown unto the eye
It lies, though there its image be empight,
Till that our soul look on that image right.
Wherefore themselves the senses do not know,
Nor doth our phansie ; for each furious wight
Hath phansie full enough, so full 't doth show
As sense ; nor he, nor 's phansie doth that phansie know.

28

Age, potent objects, too long exercise
Do weaken, hurt, and much debilitate
Those lower faculties. The Sun our eyes
Confounds with dazeling beams of light, so that
For a good while we cannot contemplate
Ought visible : thus thunder deafs the eare,
And age hurts both, that doth quite ruinate
Our sense and phansie : so if *long* we heare
Or see, 't sounds not so sweet, nor can we see so clear.

29

Lastly, the Senses reach but to one kind
Of things. The eye sees colours, so the eare

Hears sounds, the nostrills snuff perfumèd wind ;
What grosse impressions the out-senses bear
The phansie represents ; sometimes it dare
Make unseen shapes, with uncouth transformation,
Such things as never in true Nature are,
But all this while the phansies operation
To laws bodily is bound : such is her figuration.

30

This is the nature of those faculties
That of the lower *Mundane* spright depend.
But in our *Intellect* farre otherwise
We'st see it, if we pressely will attend
And trace the parallels unto the end.
There's no self-knowledge. Here the soul doth find
Her self. If so, then without instrument.
For what more fit to show our inward mind
Then our own mind ? But if 't be otherwise defin'd ;

31

Then tell me, Knows she that fit instrument ?
If she kens not that instrument, how can
She judge, whether truely it doth represent
Her self ? there may be foul delusion.
But if she kens this Organ ; straight upon
This grant, I'll ask how kens she this same tole ?
What ? by another ? by what that ? so go on
Till to infinity you forward roll,
An horrid monster count in Philosophick school.

32

The soul then works by 't self, and is self-liv'd,
Sith that it acts without an instrument :
Free motions from her own self deriv'd
Flow round. But to go on. The eyes yblent
Do blink, even blind with objects vehement,
So that till they themselves do well recure
Lesse matters they no'te see. But rayes down sent
From higher sourse the mind doth maken pure,
Do clear, do subtilize, do fix, do settle sure.

33

That if so be she list to bend her will
To lesser matters, she would it perform
More excellently with more art and skill :
Nor by long exercise her strength is worn ;
Witnesse wise Socrates, from morn to morn
That stood as stiff as any trunck of tree :
What eye could bear in contemplation
So long a fix'dnesse? none so long could see,
Its watery tears would wail its frail infirmity.

34

Nor feeble eld, sure harbinger of death,
Doth hinder the free work of th' *Intellect*.
When th' eye growes dim and dark that it unneath
Can see through age, the mind then close collect
Into her self, such mysteries doth detect
By her far-piercing beams, that youthfull heat

Doth count them folly and with scorn neglect ;
His ignorance concludes them but deceit ;
He hears not that still voyce, his pulse so loud doth beat.

35

Lastly sense, phansie, though they be confin'd
To certain objects, which to severall
Belong ; yet sure the Intellect or mind
Apprehends all objects, both corporeall,
As colours, sounds ; and incorporeall,
As virtue, wisdome, and the higher spright,
Gods love and beauty intellectuall ;
So that its plain that she is higher pight
Then in all acts to 'pend on any earthly might :

36

If will and appetite we list compare,
Like difference we easly there discover,
This pent, contract, yfraught with furious jar
And fierce antipathy. It boyleth over
With fell revenge ; or if new chance to cover
The former passion ; suppose lust or fear :
Yet all are tumults, but the will doth hover,
No whit enslav'd to what she findeth here,
But in a free suspence her self doth nimbly bear.

37

Mild, gentle, calm, quick, large, subtill, serene,
These be her properties which do increase
The more that vigour in the bodies vein
Doth waste and waxen faint. Desires decrease
When age the *Mundane* spright doth more release
From this straight mansion. But the will doth flower
And fairly spread, near to our last decease
Embraceth God with much more life and power
Then ever she could do in her fresh vernall hower.

38

Wherefore I think we safely may conclude
That Will and Intellect do not rely
Upon the body, sith they are indew'd
With such apparent contrariety
Of qualities to sense and phantasie,
Which plainly on the body do depend :
So that departed souls may phantasms free
Full well exert, when they have made an end
Of this vain life, nor need to *Lethe Lake* descend.

The Argument of

ANTIPSYCHOPANNYCHIA

Or,

The Confutation of the Sleep of the Soul.

CANT. II.

Bondage and freedom's here set out
By an inverted Cone :
The self-form'd soul may work without
Incorporation.

1

Fountain of beings ! the vast deep abysse
Of Life and Love and penetrating Will,
That breaks through narrow *Night*, & so
   transmiss
At last doth find it self ! What mortall skill

Can reach this mystery? my trembling quill
Much lesse may set it forth ; yet as I may
I must attempt this task for to fulfill,
He guide my pen while I this work assay
Who *All*, through all himself doth infinitely display.

2

My end's loose largenesse and full liberty
To finden out ; Most precious thing I ween.
When *centrall* life her outgone energy
Doth spreaden forth, unsnecp'd by foe-man keen,

And like unclouded Sunne doth freely shine ;
This is right Liberty, whose first Idee
And measure is that holy root divine
Of all free life, hight *Abad, Unitie:*
In all things He at once is present totally.

3

Each totall presence must be infinite :
So is He infinite infinity,
Those infinites you must not disunite ;
So is He one all-spreaden Unity,
Nor must you so outspread this Deitie,
But that infinitie so infinite
Must be in every infinite : so we
Must multiply this infinite single sight
Above all apprehension of a mortall wit.

4

What is not infinitely infinite,
It is not simply infinite and free :
For straitnesse (if you do conceive aright)
Is the true daughter of deficiency.
But sith there's no defect in *Unity,*
Or *Abad,* (*Abad* this first centre hight :
In Poetry as yet to vulgar eye
Unpublish'd). Him first freedome infinite
We may well style. And next is that eternall Light ;

5

Sonne unto *Abad, Æon* we him name
(In that same Poem) like his father free,
Even infinitely free I him proclaim
Everywhere all at once. And so is she
Which *Psyche* hight : for perfect *Unity*
Makes all those one. So hitherto we have
Unmeasurable freedome, *Semele*
Is next, whom though fair fluttering forms embrave,
Yet motion and defect her liberty deprave.

6

Imagination 's not infinite,
Yet freer farre than *sense ;* and *sense* more free
Then vegetation or *spermatick* spright.
Even absent things be seen by phantasie ;
By sense things present at a distancie ;
But that *spermatick* spright is close confin'd
Within the compasse of a stupid tree,
Imprison'd quite in the hard rugged rind,
Yet their defective *Replication* we find :

7

Farre more defective then in phantasie
Or sense ; yet freer is the *plastick* spright
Then quantity, or single quality,
Like quantity itself out-stretchèd right
Devoid of all *reduplicative* might :
If any such like qualities there were
So dull, so dead, so all devoid of light
As no communicative rayes to bear ;
If there be such, to *Hyle* they do verge most near.

8

But *Hyle's* self is perfect penurie,
And infinite straitnesse : here we finden nought,
Nor can do ought. If curiously we prie
Into this mirksome corner quite distraught
From our own life and being, we have brought
Our selves to nothing. Or the sooth to sayen
The subtilest soul her self hath never wrought
Into so strait a place, could nere constrain
Herself to enter, or that Hagge to entertain.

9

Lo ! here's the figure of that mighty Cone,
From the strait Cuspis to the wide-spread Base
Which is even all in comprehension.
What's infinitely nothing here hath place ;
What's infinitely all things steddy stayes
At the wide Basis of this Cone inverse,
Yet its own essence doth it swiftly chace,
Oretakes at once ; so swiftly doth it pierce
That motion here's no motion.

10

Suppose the Sunne so much to mend his pace,
That in a moment he did round the skie,
The nimble Night how swiftly would he chace
About the earth ? so swift that scarce thine eye
Could ought but light discern. But let him hie
So fast, that swiftnesse hath grown infinite,
In a pure point of time so must he flie
Around this ball, and the vast shade of Night
Quite swallow up, ever steddy stand in open sight.

11

For that which from its place is not away
One point of time, how can you say it moves?
Wherefore the Sunne doth alwayes steddy stay
In our Meridian, as this reason proves.
And sith that in an instant round he roves,
The same doth hap in each Meridian line ;
For in his instantaneous removes
He in them all at once doth fairely shine.
Nor that large stretchen space his freenesse can confine.

12

The Sun himself at once stands in each point
Of his diurnall circle : Thus we see
That rest and motion cannot be disjoynt,
When motion's swift even to infinity.
Here contrarieties do well agree,
Eternall shade and everlasting light
With one another here do well comply ;
Instant returns of Night make one long Night.
Wherefore infinity is freedome infinite.

13

No hinderance to ought that doth arrive
To this free camp of fair *Elysium,*
But nearer that to *Hyle* things do dive,
They are more pent, and find much lesser room.

Thus sensuall souls do find their righteous doom
Which *Nemesis* inflicts, when they descend
From heavenly thoughts that from above do come
To lower life, which wrath and grief attend,
And scorching lust, that do the souls high honour blend.

14

Wherefore the soul cut off from lowly sense
By harmlesse fate, farre greater liberty
Must gain : for when it hath departed hence
(As all things else) should it not backward hie
From whence it came? but such divinity
Is in our souls that nothing lesse then God
Could send them forth (as Plato's schools descry)
Wherefore when they retreat, a free abode
They'll find, unlesse kept off by *Nemesis* just rod.

15

But if kept off from thence, where is she then?
She dwells in her own self ; there doth reside,
Is her own world, and more or lesse doth pen
Her self, as more or lesse she erst did side
With sense and vice, while here she did abide.
Steril defect and nere-obtain'd desire
Create a Cone, whose Cusp is not more wide
Then this worlds Cone. Here close-contracted fire
Doth vex, doth burn, doth scorch with searching heat
and ire.

16

Nor easly can she here fall fast asleep
To slake her anguish and tormenting pain :
What drisling mists may here her senses steep?
What foggie fumes benumb her moistned brain?
The flitten soul no sense doth then retain.
And sleep ariseth from a sympathie
With these low sprights that in this flesh remain.
But when from these the soul is setten free,
What sleep may bind her from continuall energie?

17

Here they'll reply, It is not a grosse sleep
That binds the soul from operation.
But sith that death all phantasms clean doth wipe
Out of the soul, she no occasion
Can have of Will or Intellection.
The corpse doth rot, the spirit wide is spread,
And with the *Mundane* life fallen into one :
So then the soul from these quite being fled,
Unmov'd of ought must lie, sunk in deep drowsihead.

18

Nought then she hath whereon to contemplate,
Her ancient phantasms melt and glide away,
Her spright suck'd back by all-devouring fate
And spread abroad, those forms must needs decay
That were therein imprinted. If they stay,
Yet sith the soul from them is disunite,
Into her knowledge they can never ray.
So wants she objects the mind to excite :
Wherefore asleep she lies wrapt in eternall Night.

19

To which I answer, though she corporate
With no world yet, by a just *Nemesis*
Kept off from all ; yet she thus separate
May oft be struck with potent rayes transmisse
From divers worlds, that with such mockeries
Kindling an hungry fire and eager will,
They do the wretched soul but Tantalize,
And with fierce choking flames and fury fill,
So vext, that if she could, in rage herself she'd kill.

20

If any doubt of this perplexitie,
And think so subtil thing can suffer nought :
What's gnawing conscience from impietie
By highest parts of humane soul ywrought?
For so our very soul with pain is fraught,
The body being in an easie plight.
Through all the senses when you've pressly sought,
In none of them you'll find this sting empight :
So may we deem this dart the soul it self to hit.

21

Again, when all the senses be ybound
In sluggish sloth, the soul doth oft create
So mighty pain, so cruelly doth wound
Herself with tearing tortures, as that state
No man awake could ever tolerate.
Which must be in herself : for once return'd
Unto her body new resuscitate
From sleep, remembring well how erst she mourn'd,
Marvels how all so soon to peace and ease is turn'd.

22

Wherefore the soul itself receiveth pain
From her own self, withouten sympathie
With something else, whose misery must constrain
To deep compassion. So if struck she be
With secret ray, or some strong energie
Of any world, or Lives that there remain,
She's kept awake. Besides fecunditie
Of her own nature surely doth contain
Innate *Idees;* This truth more fully I'll explain.

23

Strong forward-bearing will or appetite,
A never-wearied importunitie,
Is the first life of this deep centrall spright :
Thus thrusts she forth before her some *Idee*
Whereby herself now actuall she doth see.
Her mighty *Fiat* doth command each form
T' appear : As did that ancient Majestie
This world of old by his drad Word efform,
And made the soul of man thus divine *Deiform*.

24

Thus in a manner th' humane soul creates
The image of her will, when from her centre

Her pregnant mind she fairly explicates
By actuall forms, and so doth safely enter
To knowledge of her self.
Flush light she sendeth forth, and live *Idees* :
Those be the glasse whereby the soul doth paint her.
Sweet centrall love sends out such forms as please ;
But centrall hate or fear foul shapes with evil ease.

25

The manner of her life on earth may cause
Diversity of those eruptions,
For will, desire, or custome do dispose
The soul to such like figurations :
Propension brings imaginations,
Unto their birth.   And oft the soul lets flie
Such unexpected eructations,
That she her self cannot devisen why,
Unlesse she do ascribe it to her pregnancy.

26

It is an argument of her forms innate
Which blazen out, perchance when none descry.
This light is lost, sense doth so radiate
With *Mundane* life, till this poor carcase die.
As when a lamp, that men do sitten by,
In some wide hall in a clear winter night,
Being blown out or wasted utterly,
Unwares they find a sly still silver light ;
The moon the wall or pavement with mild rayes hath
         dight.

27

So when the oyl of this low life is spent,
Which like a burning lamp doth waste away ;
Or if blown out by fate more violent ;
The soul may find an unexpected ray
Of light ; not from full-faced Cynthia,
But her own fulnesse and quick pregnancy :
Unthought of life her Nature may display
Unto her self ; not by forc'd industry,
But naturally it sprouts from her fecundity.

28

Now sith adversion is a property
So deeply essentiall to the rationall soul,
This light or life from her doth not so fly,
But she goes with it as it out doth roll.
All spirits that around them live, extoll
Possesse each point of their circumference
Presentially.   Wherefore the soul so full
Of life, when it raies out, with presse presence
Oretakes each outgone beam ; apprends it by advertence.

29

Thus plainly we perceive th' activity
Of the departed soul ; if we could find
Strong reason to confirm th' innate *idee*,
Essentiall forms created with the mind.
But things obscure no'te easly be defin'd.
Yet some few reasons I will venture at,

To show that God's so liberall and kind
As, when an humane soul he doth create,
To fill it with hid forms and deep *idees* innate.

30

Well sang the wise Empedocles of old,
That earth by earth, and sea by sea we see,
And heaven by heaven, and fire more bright than gold
By flaming fire ; so gentle love descry
By love, and hate by hate.   And all agree
That like is known by like.   Hence they confesse
That some externall species strikes the eye
Like to its object, in the self-same dresse :
But my first argument hence I'll begin to presse.

31

If like be known by like, then must the mind
Innate *idolums* in it self contain,
To judge the forms she doth imprinted find
Upon occasions.   If she doth not ken
These shapes that flow from distant objects, then
How can she know those objects? a dead glasse
(That light and various forms do gaily stain)
Set out in open streets, shapes as they passe
As well may see ; Lutes hear each soaming diapase.

32

But if she know those species out-sent
From distant objects ; tell me how she knows
Those species.   By some other?   You nere ment
To answer so.   For straight the question goes
Unto another, and still forward flows
Even to infinity.   Doth th' object serve
Its image to the mind for to disclose?
This answer hath as little sense or nerve :
Now reel you in a circle if you well observe.

33

Wherefore no ascititious form alone
Can make us see or hear ; but when this spright
That is one with the *Mundane's* hit upon
(Sith all forms in our soul be counite
And *centrally* lie there) she doth beget
Like shapes in her own self ; that energie
By her own centrall self who forth It let,
Is view'd.   Her *centrall omniformity*
Thus easily keepeth off needlesse infinity.

34

For the quick soul by 't self doth all things know.
And sith withouten apt similitude
Nought's known, upon her we must needs bestow
Essentiall centrall forms, that thus endew'd
With universall likenesse ever transmew'd
Into a representing energie
Of this or that, she may have each thing view'd
By her own *centrall self-vitality*
Which is her *self-essentiall omniformity*.

35

If plantall souls in their own selves contain
That vitall formative fecundity,
That they a tree with different colour stain,
And divers shapes, smoothnesse, asperity,
Straightnesse, acutenesse, and rotundity,
A golden yellow, or a crimson red,
A varnish'd green with such like gallantry :
How dull then is the sensitive? how dead,
If forms from its own centre it can never spread?

36

Again, an Universall notion,
What object ever did that form impresse
Upon the soul? What makes us venture on
So rash a matter, as ere to confesse
Ought generally true? when neverthelesse
We cannot e're runne through all singulars.
Wherefore in our own souls we do possesse
Free forms and immateriall characters.
Hence 'tis the soul so boldly generall truth declares.

37

What man that is not dull or mad would doubt
Whether that truth (for which Pythagoras,
When he by subtile study found it out,
Unto the Muses for their helping grace
An Hecatomb did sacrifice) may passe
In all such figures wheresoever they be?
Yet all Rectangle Triangles none has
Viewed, as yet, none all shall ever see.
Wherefore this free assent is from th' *innate Idee.*

38

Adde unto these incorporeity
Apprehended by the soul, when sense nere saw
Ought incorporeall. Wherefore must she
From her own self such subtile *Idols* draw.
Again, this truth more clearly still to know,
Let's turn again to our Geometry.
What body ever yet could figure show
Perfectly perfect, as rotundity
Exactly round, or blamelesse angularity?

39

Yet doth the soul of such like forms discourse,
And finden fault at this deficiency,
And rightly term this better and that worse ;
Wherefore the measure is our own *Idee,*
Which th' humane soul in her own self doth see.
And sooth to sayen when ever she doth strive
To find pure truth, her own profundity
She enters, in her self doth deeply dive ;
From thence attempts each essence rightly to descrive.

40

Last argument, which yet is not the least.
Wise Socrates dispute with Theætete
Concerning learning fitly doth suggest.
A midwifes sonne ycleeped Phenarete,
He calls himself : Then makes a quaint conceit,
That he his mothers trade did exercise.
All witlesse his own self yet well did weet
By his fit questions to make others wise ;
A midwife that no'te bear, anothers birth unties.

41

Thus jestingly he flung out what was true,
That humane souls be swoln with pregnancy
Of hidden knowledge ; if with usage due
They were well handled, they each verity
Would bringen forth from their fecunditie ;
Wise-framèd questions would facilitate
This precious birth, stirre up th' inward *Idee,*
And make it streme with light from forms innate.
Thus may a skilfull man hid truth elicitate.

42

What doth the teacher in his action
But put slight hints into his scholars mind?
Which breed a solemn contemplation
Whether such things be so; but he doth find
The truth himself. But if truth be not sign'd
In his own Soul before, and the right measure
Of things propos'd, in vain the youth doth wind
Into himself, and all that anxious leasure
In answering proves uselesse without that hid treasure.

43

Nor is his masters knowledge from him flit
Into his scholars head : for so his brain
In time would be exhaust and void of wit,
So would the sory man but little gain
Though richly paid. Nor is't more safe to sain
As fire breeds fire, art art doth generate,
The soul with Corporeity 't would stain :
Such qualities outwardly operate,
The soul within ; her acts there closely circulate.

44

Wherefore the soul it self by her *Idee,*
Which is her self, doth every thing discover ;
By her own *Centrall Omniformity*
Brings forth in her own self when ought doth move
    her ;
Till mov'd a dark indifferency doth hover.
But fierce desire, and a strong piercing will
Makes her those hidden characters uncover.
Wherefore when death this lower life shall spill,
Or fear or love the soul with actuall forms shall fill.

The *Argument of*

ANTIPSYCHOPANNYCHIA

Or,

The Confutation of the Sleep of the Soul.

CANT. III.

Departed souls by living Night
Suckt in, for pinching wo
No'te sleep ; or if with God unite,
For joyes with which they flow.

1

MY hardest task is gone, which was to prove
That when the soul by death's cut off from all,
Yet she within her self might live and move,
Be her own world, by life *imaginall*.
But sooth to sain, 't seems not so naturall.
For though a starre, part of the *Mundane* spright,
Shine out with rayes circumferentiall
So long as with this world it is unite ;
Yet what t' would do cut off, so well we cannot weet.

2

But sith our soul with God himself may meet,
Inacted by His life, I cannot see
What scruple then remains that moven might
Least doubt, but that she wakes with open eye,
When Fate her from this body doth untie.
Wherefore her choisest forms do then arise,
Rowz'd up by union and large sympathy
With Gods own spright ; she plainly then descries
Such plentitude of life, as she could nere devise.

3

If God even on this body operate,
And shakes this Temple when he doth descend,
Or with sweet vigour doth irradiate,
And lovely light and heavenly beauty lend.
Such rayes from Moses face did once extend
Themselves on Sinai hill, where he did get
Those laws from Gods own mouth, mans life to mend ;
And from Messias on mount Saron set
Farre greater beauty shone in his disciples sight.

4

Als Socrates, when (his large *Intellect*
Being fill'd with streaming light from God above)
To that fair sight his soul did close collect,
That inward lustre through the body drove
Bright beams of beauty. These examples prove
That our low being the great Deity
Invades, and powerfully doth change and move.
Which if you grant, the souls divinity
More fitly doth receive so high a Majesty.

5

And that God doth illuminate the mind,
Is well-approv'd by all antiquity ;
With them Philosophers and Priests we find
All one : or else at least Philosophy
Link'd with Gods worship and pure piety :
Witnesse Pythagoras, Aglaophemus,
Zoroaster, thrice-mighty Mercury,
Wise Socrates, nothing injurious,
Religious Plato, and vice-taming Orpheus.

6

All these, addicted to religion,
Acknowledg'd God the fount of verity,
From whence flows out illumination
Upon purg'd souls. But now, O misery !
To seek to God is held a phantasie,
But men hug close their lovèd lust and vice,
And deem that thraldome a sweet liberty ;
Wherefore reproch and shame they do devise
Against the braver souls that better things emprise.

7

But lo ! a proof more strong and manifest :
Few men but will confesse that prophesie
Proceeds from God, when as our soul's possest
By his All-seeing spright ; als ecstasie

Wherein the soul snatch'd by the Deity.
And for a time into high heaven hent
Doth contemplate that blest Divinity
So Paul and John that into Patmos went,
Heard and saw things inestimably excellent.

8

Such things as these, men joyntly do confesse
To spring from Gods own spirit immediately :
But if that God ought on the soul impresse
Before it be at perfect liberty,
Quite rent from this base body ; when that she
Is utterly releast, she'll be more fit
To be inform'd by that divine *Idee*
Hight *Logos*, that doth every man enlight
That enters into life, as speaks the sacred Writ.

9

Behold a fit resemblance of this truth,
The Sun begetteth both colours and sight,
Each living thing with life his heat indew'th,
He kindles into act each plastick spright :
Thus he the world with various forms doth dight
And when his vigour hath fram'd out an eye
In any living wight, he fills with light
That Organ, which can plainly then descry
The forms that under his far-shining beams do ly.

10

Even so it is with th' *intellectuall* sunne,
Fountain of life, and all-discovering light,
He frames our souls by his creation,
Als he indews them with internall sight,
Then shines into them by his lucid spright.
But corporall life doth so obnubilate
Our inward eyes that they be nothing bright ;
While in this muddy world incarcerate
They lie, and with blind passions be intoxicate.

11

Fear, anger, hope, fierce vengeance, and swoln hate,
Tumultuous joy, envie and discontent,
Self-love, vain-glory, strife and fell debate,
Unsatiate covetise, desire impotent,
Low-sinking griefe, pleasure, lust violent,
Fond emulation, all these dim the mind
That with foul filth the inward eye yblent,
That light that is so near it cannot find.
So shines the Sunne unseen on a trees rugged rind.

12

But the clean soul by virtue purifi'd
Collecting her own self from the foul steem
Of earthly life, is often dignifi'd
With that pure pleasure that from God doth streem,
Often's enlightn'd by that radiant beam,
That issues forth from his divinity,
Then feelingly immortall she doth deem
Her self, conjoynd by so near unity
With God, and nothing doubts of her eternitie.

19

13

Nor death, nor sleep nor any dismall shade
Of low contracting life she then doth fear,
No troubled thoughts her settled mind invade,
Th' immortall root of life she seeth clear,
Wisheth she were for ever grafted here :
No cloud, no darknesse, no deficiency
In this high heavenly life doth ere appear ;
Redundant fulnesse, and free liberty,
Easie-flowing knowledge, never weary energy,

14

Broad open sight, eternall wakefulnesse,
Withouten labour or consuming pain :
The soul all these in God must needs possesse
When there deep-rooted life she doth obtain,
As I in a few words shall maken plain.
This bodies life by powerfull sympathy
The soul to sleep and labour doth constrain,
To grief, to wearinesse and anxiety,
In fine, to hideous sense of dread mortality.

15

But sith no such things in the Deity
Are to be found ; Shee once incorporate
With that quick essence, she is setten free
From ought that may her life obnubilate,
What then can her contract or maken strait ?
For ever mov'd by lively sympathy
With Gods own spright, an ever-waking state
She doth obtain. Doth heavens bright blazing eye
Ever close, ywrapt in sleep and dead obscurity ?

16

But now how full and strong a sympathy
Is caused by the souls conjunction
With the high God, I'll to you thus descry.
All men will grant that spread dispersion
Must be some hinderance to close union :
Als must confesse that closer unity
More certainly doth breed compassion ;
Not that there's passion in the Deity,
But something like to what all men call Sympathy.

17

Now sith the soul is of such subtlety,
And close collectednesse, indispersion,
Full by her *centrall omniformity*,
Pregnant and big without distension ;
She once drawn in by strong attraction,
Should be more perfectly there counite
In this her high and holy union
Then with the body, where dispersion's pight :
(But such hard things I leave to some more learnèd
wight)

18

The first pure *Being's* perfect *Unity*,
And therefore must all things more strongly bind
Then Lives corporeall, which dispersèd be.
He also the first *Goodnesse* is defin'd

P

Wherefore the soul most powerfully's inclin'd
And strongly drawn to God. But life that's here,
When into it the soul doth closely wind,
Is often sneep'd by anguish and by fear,
With vexing pain and rage that she no'te easly bear.

19

Farre otherwise it fares in that pure life
That doth result in the souls Unity
With God: For there the faster she doth strive
To tie her selfe, the greater liberty
And freer welcome, brighter purity
She finds, and more enlargement, joy and pleasure
O'reflowing, yet without satietie,
Sight without end, and love withouten measure:
This needs must close unite the heart to that hid
    treasure.

20

This plainly's seen in that mysterious Cone
Which I above did fairly well descrive:
Their freenesse and incarceration
Were plainly setten forth. What down doth dive
Into the straitnèd Cuspis needs must strive
With stringent bitternesse, vexation,
Anxious unrest; in this ill plight they live:
But they that do ascend to th' top yflown
Be free, yet fast unite to that fair vision.

21

Thus purgèd souls be close conjoyn'd to God,
And closer union surer sympathy;
Wherefore so long as they make their abode
In Him, incorp'rate by due Unitie
They liven in eternall energie.
For Israels God nor slumbers, nor doth sleep;
Nor Israel lost in dull lethargie
Must listlesse ly, while numbing streams do steep.
His heavy head, overwhelmèd in oblivion deep.

22

But here more curious men will straight enquire,
Whither after death the wicked soul doth go,
That long hath wallowed in the sinfull mire.
Before this question I shall answer to,
Again the nature of the soul I'll show.
She all things in her self doth centrally
Contain; whatever she doth feel or know,
She feels or knows it by th' innate *Idee*:
She's all proportion'd by her *omniformity*.

23

God, heaven, this middle world, deep glimmering hell
With all the lives and shapes that there remain,
The forms of all in humane souls do dwell:
She likewise all proportions doth contain
That fits her for all sprights. So they constrain
By a strong-pulling sympathy to come,
And straight possesse that fitting vitall vein
That 'longs unto her, so her proper room
She takes as mighty *Nemesis* doth give the doom.

24

Now (which I would you presly should observe)
Though oft I have with tongue balbutient
Prattled to th' weaker ear (lest I should sterve
My stile with too much subtilty) I nere ment
To grant that there's any such thing existent
As a mere body: For all's life, all spright,
Though lives and sprights be very different.
Three generall sprights there be, *Eternall Light*
Is one, the next *our World*, the last *Infernall Night.*

25

This last lies next unto old *Nothingnesse*
Hight *Hyle*, whom I term'd point of the Cone:
Her daughter *Night* is full of bitternesse,
And strait constraint, and pent privation:
Her sturdy ray's scarce conquer'd by the moon.
The earths great shade breaks out from this hid
    spright,
And active is; so soon the Sun is gone,
Doth repossesse the aire shotten forth right
From its hid centrall life, ycleep'd *Infernall Night.*

26

In this drad world is scorching *Phlegethon;*
Hot without flame, burning the vexèd sense;
There hatefull *Styx* and sad *Cocytus* run,
And silent *Acheron*. All drink from hence,
From this damn'd spright receiven influence,
That in our world or poyson do outspue,
Or have an ugly shape and foule presence:
That deadly poison and that direfull hue
From this *Nocturnall* spright these ugly creatures drew.

27

This is the seat of Gods eternall ire,
When unmixt vengeance he doth fully powre
Upon foul souls, fit for consuming fire:
Fierce storms and tempests strongly doth he showre
Upon their heads: His rage doth still devoure
The never-dying soul. Here *Satanas*
Hath his full swing to torture every houre
The grisly ghosts of men; when they have passe
From this mid world to that most direfull dismall place.

28

Did Nature but compile one mighty sphere
Of this dark *Stygian* spright, and close collect
Its scatter'd being, that it might appear
Aloft in the wide heaven, it would project
Dark powerfull beams, that solar life ycheckt
With these dull choking rayes, all things would die.
Infernall poyson the earth would infect,
Incessant showrs of pitchie shafts let flie
Against the Sun with darknesse would involve the skie.

29

Nor is my Muse wox mad, that thus gives life
To Night or Darknesse, sith all things do live.
But Night is nothing (straight I'll end that strife)
Doth no impressions to the sense derive?

If without prejudice you'll deigne to dive
Into the matter, as much realty
To darknesse as to coldnesse you will give.
Certes both night and coldnesse active be,
Both strike the sense, they both have reall entity.

30

Again, 'tis plain that that nocturnall spright
Sends forth black eben-beams and mirksome rayes,
Because her darknesse as the Sunne his light
More clearly doth reflect on solid place,
As when a wall, a shade empighten has
Upon it, sure that shade farre darker is
Then is the aire that lies in the mid space.
What is the reason? but that rayes emisse
From *centrall Night* the walls reflexion multiplies.

31

The light's more light that strikes upon the wall,
And much more strongly there affects the eye,
Then what's spread in the space aereall :
So 'tis with shadows that amid do lie
In the slight air ; there scarce we them descrie,
But when they fall upon the wall or ground,
They gain a perfect sensibilitie.
Scarce ought in outgone light is to be found
But this Nocturnall ray's with like indowments crown'd.

32

But why doth my half-wearied mind pursue
Dim sculking darknesse, a fleet nimble shade?
If Moses and wise Solomon speak true,
What we assert may safely well be said.
Did not a palpable thick Night invade
The Land of Egypt, such as men might feel
And handle with their hands? That darknesse ray'd
From nether *Hell*, and silently did steal
On th' enemies of God, as Scripture doth reveal.

33

The womb of *Night* then fully flowrèd out :
For that all-swaying endlesse Majestie
Which penetrateth those wide worlds throughout,
This thin spread darknesse that dispers'd doth lie
Summon'd by his drad voice, and strong decree.
Much therefore of that spirit close unite
Into one place did strike the troubled eye
With horrid blacknesse, and the hand did smite
With a clam pitchie ray shot from that *Centrall Night*.

34

This *Centrall Night* or Universall spright
Of wo, of want, of balefull bitternesse,
Of hatred, envy, wrath, and fell despight,
Of lust, of care, wasting disquietnesse,
Of warre, contention, and bloud-thirstinesse,
Of zeal, of vengeance, of suspicion
Of hovering horrour, and sad pensivenesse ;
This *Stygian* stream through all the world doth run,
And many wicked souls unto it self hath wonne.

35

Lo ! here's the portion of the Hypocrite,
That serveth God but in an outward show.
But his drad doom must passe upon his sprite,
Where it propends there surely must he go.
Due vengeance neither sleepeth nor is slow.
Hell will suck in by a strong sympathie
What's like unto it self : So down they flow,
Devouring anguish and anxietie
Do vex their souls, in piteous pains, alas ! they lie.

36

Thus with live *Hell* be they concorporate,
United close with that self-gnawing sprite :
And this I wot will breed no sleeping state.
Who here descends finds one long restlesse Night.
May this the dreaming *Psychopannychite*
Awake, and make him seriously prepare
And purge his heart, lest this infernall might
Suck in his soul 'fore he be well aware.
Kill but the seeds of sinne then are you past this fear.

37

Thus have I prov'd by the souls union
With heaven and hell, that she will be awake
When she from this mid Nature is ygone.
But still more curious task to undertake ;
And spenden time to speak of Lethe lake,
And whether at least some souls fall not asleep.
(Which if they do of *Hell* they do partake)
Whether who liv'd like plant or grazing sheep,
Who of nought else but sloth and growth doth taken
    keep :

38

Whose drooping phansie never flowred out,
Who relish'd nought but this grosse bodies food,
Who never entertain'd an active thought,
But like down-looking beasts was onely mov'd
To feed themselves, whither this drousie mood
So drench the lowring soul and inly steep
That she lies senselese drownd in Lethe floud ;
Who will let dive into this mysterie deep :
Into such narrow subtilties I list not creep.

39

But well I wote that wicked crueltie,
Hate, envie, malice, and ambition,
Bloud-sucking zeal, and lawlesse tyrannie,
In that *Nocturnall* sprite shall have their wonne,
Which like this world admits distinction.
But like will like unto it strongly draw :
So every soul shall have a righteous doom.
According to our deeds God will bestow
Rewards : Unto the cruell he'll no mercy show.

40

Where's Nimrod now, and dreadfull Hannibal ?
Where's that ambitious pert Pellean lad,
Whose pride sweld bigger then this earthly ball ?
Where's cruell Nero, with the rest that had

Command, and vex'd the world with usage bad?
They're all sunk down into this nether hell;
Who erst upon the Nations stoutly strad
Are now the Devils footstool. His drad spell
Those vassals doth command, though they with fury
     swell.

41

Consuming anguish, styptick bitternesse,
Doth now so strangle their imperious will,
That in perpetuall disquietnesse
They roll and rave, and roar and rage their fill,
Like a mad bull that the slie hunters skill
Hath caught in a strong net. But more they strive
The more they kindle that tormenting ill.
Wo's me! in what great miserie they live!
Yet wote I not what may these wretched thralls relieve.

42

The safest way for us that still survive
Is this, even our own lust to mortifie;
So Gods own Will will certainly revive.
Thus shall we gain a perfect libertie,
And everlasting life. But if so be
We seek our selves with ardent hot desire,
From that *Infernall Night* we are not free;
But living *Hell* will kindle a fierce fire.
And with uncessant pains our vexèd soul will tire.

43

Then the wild phansie from her horrid wombe
Will senden forth foul shapes. O dreadfull sight!
Overgrown toads fierce serpents thence will come,
Red-scalèd Dragons with deep burning light
In their hollow eye-pits: With these she must fight;
Then thinks her self ill-wounded, sorely stung.
Old fulsome Hags with scabs and skurf bedight,
Foul tarry spittle tumbling with their tongue
On their raw lether lips, these near will to her clung,

44

And lovingly salute against her will,
Closely embrace, and make her mad with wo:
She'd lever thousand times they did her kill,
Then force her such vile basenesse undergo.
Anon some Giant his huge self will show,
Gaping with mouth as vast as any Cave,
With stony staring eyes, and footing slow:
She surely deems him her live-walking grave,
From that dern hollow pit knows not her self to save.

45

After a while, tost on the Ocean main
A boundlesse sea she finds of misery;
The fiery snorts of the Leviathan
(That makes the boyling waves before him flie)
She hears, she sees his blazing morn-bright eye:
If here she scape, deep gulfs and threatning rocks

Her frighted self do straightway terrifie;
Steel-coloured clouds with rattling thunder knocks,
With these she is amaz'd, and thousand such like mocks.

46

All which afflict her even like perfect sense:
For waxen mad with her sore searching pain
She cannot easly find the difference,
But toils and tears and tugs, but all in vain;
Her self from her own self she cannot strain.
Nocturnall life hath now let ope th' *Idee*
Of innate darknesse, from this fulsome vein
The soul is fill'd with all deformity.
But *Night* doth stirre her up to this dread energie.

47

But here some man more curious then wise
Perhaps will aske, where *Night* or *Hell* may be:
For he by his own self cannot devise,
Sith chearfull light doth fill the open sky.
And what's the earth to the souls subtilty?
Such men I'd carry to some standing pool,
Down to the water bid them bend their eye,
They then shall see the earth possest and full
Of heaven, dight with the sunne or starrs that there do
     roll.

48

Or to an hill where's some deep hollow Cave
Dreadfull for darknesse; let them take a glasse,
When to the pitchy hole they turned have
Their instrument, that darknesse will find place
Even in the open sunne-beams, at a space
Which measures twice the glasses distancy
From the Caves mouth. This well discoverèd has
How *Hell* and *Heaven* may both together lie,
Sith darknesse safely raies even in the sunny skie.

49

But further yet the mind to satisfie
That various apprehensions bearen down,
And to hold up with like variety
Of well-fram'd phantasms, lest she sink and drown
Laden with heavie thoughts sprong from the ground,
And miry clods of this accursèd earth;
Whose dull suffusions make her often sown,
Orecome with cold, till nimble Reason bear'th
Unto her timely aid and on her feet her rear'th:

50

I will adjoyn to those three former wayes
To weet, of the Souls self-activity
Of Union with Hell, and Gods high rayes
A fourth contrivement, which all souls doth ty
To their wing'd Chariots, wherein swift they fly.
The fiery and airy Vehicles they hight
In Plato's school known universally.
But so large matter can not well be writ
In a few lines for a fresh Canticle more fit.

THE

PRÆEXISTENCY

OF THE

SOUL,

Added as an Appendix to this third part of
the Song of the Soul.

By *H. M.* Mafter of Arts, and Fellow of Chrifts
Colledge in *Cambridge.*

Τίς οἶδεν εἰ τὸ ζῆν μέν ἐστι κατθανεῖν,
Τὸ κατθανεῖν δὲ ζῆν.   Euripid.

CAMBRIDGE
Printed by *Roger Daniel*, Printer to the
Univerfitie.   1647.

The Preface to the Reader.

ALthough the opinion of the Præexistency of the Soul be made so probable and passable in the Canto itself, that none can sleight and contemn it, that do not ordinarily approve themselves men by Derision more then by Reason; yet so heavie prejudice lying upon us both from Naturall diffidence in so high Points, and from our common Education, I thought it fit, for securing my self, from suspicion of overmuch lightnesse, to premize thus much: That that which I have taken the pains and boldnesse to present to the free judgement of others, hath been already judged of old, very sound and orthodox, by the wisest and most learned of preceding ages.

Which *R. Menassch Ben-Israel*, doth abundantly attest in his 15. *Problem. De Creatione;* avouching that it is the common Opinion of all the Hebrews, and that it was never called into controversie, but approved of, by the common consent and suffrage of all wise men.

And himself doth by severall places out of the Old Testament (as pat for his purpose, I think, as any can be brought against it) endeavour to make it good; but might I confesse, have been more fitly furnished, could his Religion have reached into the New. For *Philip.* 2. *v.* 6, 7, 8. *John* 9. *v.* 1, 2, 3. *John* 17. *v.* 4, 5. *Mark* 8. *v.* 27, 28. all those places do seem so naturally to favour this Probability, that if it had pleas'd the Church to have concluded it for a standing Truth; He that would not have been fully convinc'd upon the evidence of these passages of Scripture, would undoubtedly, have been held a man of a very timorous & Scepticall constitution, if not something worse.

Nor is the feeblenesse and miserable ineptnesse of Infancy any greater damp to the belief of this Preexistency then the dotage and debility of old Age, to the hope of the Souls future subsistency after death.

Nor, if we would fetch an argument from Theologie, is Gods Justice, and the divine Nemesis lesse set out, by supposing that the Souls of men, thorough their own revolting from God before they came into the body, have thus in severall measures engaged themselves in the sad, dangerous, and almost fatall entanglements of this Corporeall World; then it is, by conceiving that they must needs survive the Body, that the judgement of the Almighty may passe upon them, for what they have committed in the flesh.

Nor lastly, is it harder to phansie, how these Præexistent Souls insinuate into seed, Embryos, or Infants, then how Created ones are insinuated; nor yet so hard, to determine of their condition if they depart in Infancy, as of the condition of these.

But mistake me not, Reader; I do not contend (in thus arguing) that this opinion of the Præexistency of the Soul, is true, but that it is not such a self-condemned Falsity, but that I might without justly incurring the censure of any Vainnesse or Levity, deem it worthy the canvase and discussion of sober and considerate men.

Yours *H. M.*

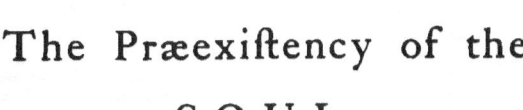

The Præexiftency of the
S O U L.

The Argument:

Of the Souls Præexistency
Her Orb of Fire and Aire,
Of Ghosts, of Goblins, of Sorcery,
This Canto doth declare.

1

Ise then *Aristo's* son ! assist my Muse
  Let that hie spright which did inrich thy
     brains
    With choice conceits, some worthy thoughts
     infuse
Worthy thy title and the Readers pains.
And thou, O *Lycian* Sage ! whose pen contains
Treasures of heavenly light with gentle fire,
Give leave a while to warm me at thy flames
That I may also kindle sweet desire
In holy minds that unto highest things aspire.

2

For I would sing the Præexistency
  Of humane souls, and live once ore again
  By recollection and quick memory
  All what is past since first we all began.
  But all too shallow be my wits to scan
So deep a point and mind too dull to clear
So dark a matter ; but Thou, O more then man !
Aread thou sacred Soul of *Plotin* deare
Tell what we mortalls are, tell what of old we were.

3

A spark or ray of the Divinity
  Clouded in earthy fogs, yclad in clay,
  A precious drop sunk from Æternitie,
  Spilt on the ground, or rather slunk away,
  For then we fell when we gan first t'assay
By stealth, of our own selves something to been,
Uncentring our selves from our great stay.
Which fondly we new liberty did ween
And from that prank right jolly wights our selves did
  deem.

4

For then forthwith some thing beside our God
  We did conceive our parted selves to be,
  And loosenèd, first from that simple Good,
  Then from great *Æon*, then from *Psyche* free,
  We after fell into low phantasie,
  And after that into corporeall sense,
  And after sense embarkd as in a tree,
  (First sown in earthly slime, then sprung from thence)
A fading life we lead in deadly influence.

5

Thus groping after our own Centres near
  And proper substance, we grew dark, contract,
  Swallow'd up of earthly life, ne what we were
  Of old, through ignorance can we detect.
  Like noble babe by fate or friends neglect
  Left to the care of sorry salvage wight,
  Grown up to manly years cannot conject
His own true parentage, nor read aright
What Father him begot, what womb him brought to
  light :

6

So we as stranger Infants elsewhere born
  Can not divine from what spring we did flow
  Ne dare these base alliances to scorn,
  Nor lift our selves a whit from hence below,
  Ne strive our Parentage again to know ;
  Ne dream we once of any other stock,
  Since foster'd upon *Rheas* knees we grow,
In Satyres arms with many a mow and mock
Oft danc'd, and hairy *Pan* our cradle oft hath rock'd.

7

But *Pan* nor *Rhea* be our Parentage
  We been the Of-spring of all-seeing *Jove*
  Though now, whether through our own miscariage
  Or secret force of fate, that all doth move
  We be cast low ; for why ? the sportfull love
  Of our great Maker (like as mothers dear
  In pleasance from them do their children shove
That back again they may recoyl more near)
Shoves of our souls a while, the more them to endear.

8

Or whether Justice and due Equity
Expects the truth of our affection,
And therefore sets us 'twixt the Deitie
And the created world, that thereupon
We may with a free resignation
Give up our selves to him deserves us best.
That love is none that's by coaction :
Hence he our souls from his own self releast
And left us free to follow what the most us pleas'd.

9

And for this purpose did enrich our choice
By framing of the outward Universe.
The framing of this world a meet devise
Whereby Gods wisedome thorough all may pierce,
From hight to depth.   In depth is vengeance fierce,
Whereby transgressing souls are sorely scourged
And back again are forced to reverse
By *Nemesis* deep-biting whips well urged,
And in sad sorrows bath well drench'd and soundly
purged.

10

Thus nothing's lost of Gods fecundity.
But stretching out himself in all degrees
His wisedome, goodnesse and due equity
Are rightly rank'd, in all the soul them sees.
O holy lamps of God ! O sacred eyes
Filled with love and wonder every where !
Ye wandring tapers to whom God descryes
His secret paths, great *Psyches* darlings dear !
Behold her works, but see your hearts close not too near.

11

But they so soon as vitall Orbs were made
That rolled round about each starry fire
Forth-with pursue, and strive them to invade :
Like evening flies that busily conspire
Following a Jade that travail long doth tire,
To seize his nodding head and suck his sweat.
But they suck'd in into the vitall mire
First died and then again reviv'd by heat,
Did people all the Orbs by this audacious feat.

12

But infinite Myriads undipt as yet
Did still attend each vitall moveing sphear,
And wait their turnes for generation fit
In airy bodies wafted here and there,
As sight and sympathy away did bear.
These corporate with bloud, but the first flight
Of fallen souls, ymeint with slimy gear
Rose from their earth, breaking their filmes slight :
As Storyes say, *Nile* living shapes sends forth to sight.

13

Here their third chariot cleep'd terrestiall
Great *Psyches* brood did enter ; for before
They rode more light ; first in cœlestiall
Or fiery chariots, wherein with *Uranore*

The care and thought of all the world they bore.
This is the Orb of pure quick life and sense
Which the thrice mighty *Mercury* of yore
Ascending, held with Angels conference,
And of their comely shapes had perfect cognoscence.

14

In this the famous *Tyanean* swain,
Lifted above the deadly charming might
Of the dull Carkasse could discover plain
From seven-hill'd *Rome* with speedy piercing sight
What they in *Egypt* did as Stories write.
This is that nimble quick vivacious Orb
All ear, all eye, with rayes round shining bright ;
Sphear of pure sense which noe perpessions curb
Nor uncouth shapen Spectres ever can disturb.

15

Next this is that light Vehicle of air,
Where likewise all sense is in each part pight.
This is more grosse subject to grief and fear
And most what soil'd with bodily delight ;
Sometimes with vengeance, envie, anger, spight.
This Orb is ever passive in sensation.
But the third wagon of the soul that hight
The terrene Vehicle, beside this passion
Hath organized sense, distinct by limitation.

16

These last be but the souls live sepulchres
Where least of all she acts, but afterward
Rose from this tomb, she free and lively fares
And upward goes if she be not debar'd
By *Adrastias* law nor strength empar'd
By too long bondage, in this Cave below.
The purged souls ascent nought may retard ;
But earthly-mindednesse may eath foreslow
Their flight, then near the ground in airy weeds they go ;

17

Awak'd to life more ample then before,
If they their fortune good could then pursue.
But sith unwillingly they were ytore
From their dear carkasses their fate they rue,
And terrene thoughts their troubled minds embue :
So that in languishment they linger near
Their wonted homes and oft themselves they shew ;
Sometimes on purpose, sometimes unaware
That wak'd by hasty call they streightway disappear.

18

For men that wont to wander in their sleep
By the fixt light of inward phantasie,
Though a short fit of death fast bounden keep
Their outward sense and all their Organes tye ;
Yet forth they fare steared right steddily
By that internall guide : even so the ghosts
Of men deceas'd bedewed with the sky
And nights cold influence, in sleep yclos'd
Awake within, and walk in their forewonted coast.

19

In shape they walk much like to what they bore
Upon the earth : For that light Orb of air
Which they inact must yielden evermore
To phansies beck, so when the souls appear
To their own selves alive as once they were,
So cloath'd and conversant in such a place,
The inward eyes of phansie thither stear
Their gliding vehicle, that bears the face
Of him that liv'd, that men may reade what wight it was.

20

And often ask'd what would they, they descry
Some secret wealth, or hidden injury.
That first they broach that over oft doth ly
Within their minds : but vanish suddenly
Disturb'd by bold mans importunity.
But those that on set purpose do appear
To holden talk with frail mortality
Make longer stay. So that there is no fear
That when we leave this earthly husk we perish clear.

21

Or what is like to perfect perishing,
That inert deadlinesse our souls shall seize,
That neither sense nor phansies fountains spring,
But ever close in dull unactive ease,
For though that Death our spirits doth release
From this distinguish'd organizate sense,
Yet we may hear and see, what, where we please,
And walk at large when we are gone from hence
And with both men and ghosts hold friendly conference ;

22

And all in virtue of that airy Waine
In which we ride when that of earth is gone,
Unlesse no terrene tinctures do us stein,
For then forthwith to heaven we be yflone,
In our swift fiery chariot thither drawn.
But least men deem me airy notions feigne :
All stories this sure truth do seem to own.
Wherefore my Muse ! some few do not disdain,
Of many, to relate, more firm assent to gain.

23

But first lay out the treasures of the Air
That immense womb from whence all bodies spring ;
And then the force of Phantasie declare.
Of Witches wonnes a while then maist thou sing,
Their Stygian rites, and nightly revelling.
Then to the wishèd port to draw more near
Als tell of the untimely wandering
Of the sad ghosts of men that oft appear,
All which to the hard search of truth, joynt light do bear ;

24

Shew fitly how the præexistent soul
Inacts and enters bodies here below,
And then entire, unhurt, can leave this moul
And thence her airy Vehicle can draw,

In which by sense and motion they may know
Better then we what things transacted be
Upon the Earth ; and when they list, may show
Themselves to friend or foe, their phantasie
Moulding their airy Orb to grosse consistency.

25

For sooth to sayn, all things of Air consist
And easly back again return to air.
Witnesse the carkases of man and beast
Which wast though teeth of Wolves them never tear,
Nor Crow nor Vulture do their flesh empare,
Yet all is wast and gone, no reliques seen
Of former shape, saving the bones bare,
And the bare bones by Time and Art, I ween,
First into liquour melt to air ychangèd been.

26

Besides experience doth maken plain
How clouds be but the crudling of the air.
Take a round glasse let 't nought but air contain,
Close it with Hermes seal, then cover it over
With cinders warm, onely the top discover,
The gentle fire hard at the bottome pight
Thins the low air, which got above doth hover
Like a white fume embodying in the hight
With cooler parts, then turns to drops all crystall bright.

27

Not much unlike to the experiment
That learnèd Leech professes to have seen
Amongst the *Alps*, where the wind violent
Hammered out clouds with his strong blustring, keen
'Gainst a steep rock, which streight themselves did teem
Upon the Earth and wet the verdant Plain,
Dissolvèd by the sight of Phœbus sheen.
But sometimes clouds afford, not onely rain
But bloud, stones, milk, corn, frogs, fire, earth and all
    contain.

28

Wherefore all bodies be of air compos'd
Great Natures all-complying Mercury,
Unto ten thousand shapes and forms dispos'd :
Like nimble quick-silver that doth agree
With gold with brasse or with what ere it be
Amalgamate, but brought unto the fire
Into an airy fume it all doth flie,
Though you before might turn to earth and mire
What into ancient air so quickly doth retire.

29

Wherefore the soul possest of matter meet
If she hath power to operate thereon
Can eath transform this Vehicle to sight,
Dight with due colour, figuration ;
Can speak, can walk, and then dispear anon
Spreading her self in the dispersèd air ;
Then if she please recall again what's gone.
Those th' uncouth mysteries of phansie are
Then thunder farre more strong, more quick then light-
    ning far.

30

Some heavings toward this strange activity
We may observe even in this mortall state.
Here health and sicknesse of the phantasie
Often proceed, which working minds create,
And pox and pestilence do malleate,
Their thoughts still beating on those objects ill,
Which doth the masterèd bloud contaminate,
And with foul poysonous impressions fill
And last, the precious life with deadly dolour kill.

31

And if't be true that learnèd Clerks do sayen
His phantasie whom a mad dog hath bit ,
With shapes of dogs doth all his Urine stain.
Women with child, if in their longing fit
They be differ'd, their eager appetite
So sharply edges the quick phantasie
That it the Signature doth carve and write
Of what she long'd for, on the Infants body,
Imprinting it so plain that all the world may see.

32

Those streakèd rods plac'd by that *Syrian* swain
Before the sheep when they receiv'd the ramme,
(Whence the best part of *Labans* flock became
All spotted or'e, whereby his shepheard wan
The greater wages,) show what phansie can.
And boyes ore night when they went to their rest
By dreams grown up to th' stature of a man ;
And bony shapes in mens sad hearts exprest
Dear image of their love, and wrought by loves unrest :

33

Things farre more wonderfull then *Cippus* horn
Who in the field with so much earnestnesse
Viewing the fight of bulls rose in the Morn
With forkèd front : for though the fight did cease
Amongst th' enragèd heards, yet ne're the lesse
His working phansie did the war revive.
Which on the bloud did make so strong impresse
In dewy sleep, that humours did arrive
His knobby head and a fair pair of horns contrive :

34

All these declare the force of phantasie
Though working here upon this stubborn clay.
But th' airy Vehicle yields more easily,
Unto her beck more nimbly doth obey.
Which truth the joynt confessions bewray
Of damnèd Hags and Masters of bold skill,
Whose hellish mysteries fully to display
With pitchy darknesse would the Heavens fill,
The earth would grone, trees sigh, and horrour all ore
   spill.

35

But he that out of darkness giveth light
He guide my steps in this so uncouth way,
And ill done deeds by children of the Night
Convert to good, while I shall thence assay

The noble souls conditions ope to lay,
And show her empyre on her ayry sphear
By what of sprights and specters Stories say.
For sprights and spectres that by night appear
Be or all one with souls or of a nature near.

36

Up then renownèd Wizard, Hermite sage !
That twice ten years didst in the desert wonne,
Convers'dst with sprights in thy hid Hermitage
Since thou of mortals didst the commerce shun,
Well seen in these bad arts that have foredone
Many a bold wit ; Up *Marcus !* tell again
That story of thy *Thrax*, who has thee wonne,
To Christian faith, the guise and haunts explain
Of all air-trampling ghosts that in the world remain.

37

There be six sorts of sprights. *Leturion*
Is the first kind, the next are nam'd from Air ;
The first aloft, yet farre beneath the Moon,
The other in this lower region fare.
The third Terrestriall, the fourth Watery are,
The fift be Subterranean, the last
And worst, Light-hating ghosts more cruel farre
Then Bear or Wolf with hunger hard opprest,
But doltish yet and dull like an unweildy beast.

38

If this sort once possesse the arteries
Of forlorn man : Madnesse and stupor seize
His salvag'd heart, and death dwels in his eyes.
Ne is there remedy for this sad disease.
For that unworthy guest so senselesse is
And deaf, no Exorcist can make him hear,
But would in vain with Magick words chastise.
Others the thundering threats of *Tartar* fear,
And the drad names of Angels that this office bear.

39

For they been all subject to passion.
Some been so grosse they hunger after food,
And send out seed of which worms spring anon,
And love to liggen warm in living bloud,
Whence they into the veins do often crowd
Of beasts as well as men ; wherein they bathe
Themselves, and sponge-like suck that vitall flood,
As they done also in their aery path
Drink in each unctuous steam, which their dire thirst
   allayth.

40

Such be the four last kinds, foul, dull, impure
Whose inward life and phansy's more inert
And therefore usually in one shape endure.
But those of aire can easily convert
Into new forms and then again revert ;
One while a man, after a comely maid,
And then all suddenly to make the stert,
Like leaping Leopard he'll thee invade,
Then made a man again he'll comfort thee afraid.

41

Then straight more quick then thought or cast of eye
A snarling Dog, or brisled Boar he'll be ;
Anon a jugge of milk if thou be dry,
So easily's turned that aire-consistency
Through inward sport and power of phantasie.
For all things virtually are containd in aire.
And like the sunne, that fiery spirit free
Th' internall soul, at once the seed doth rear
Waken and ripe at once as if full ag'd they were.

42

Cameleon-like thus they their colour change
And size contract, and then dilate again :
Like the soft earthworm hurt by heedlesse chance
Shrinks in her self to shun or ease her pain.
Nor done they onely thus themselves constrain
Into lesse bulk, but if with courage bold
And flaming brond thou strike these shades in twain,
A sudden smart they feel that cannot hold,
Close quick as cloven aire.   So sang that Wizzard old.

43

And truth he said whatever he has told,
As even this present Age may verifie,
If any lists its stories to unfold
Of Hags, of Hobgoblings, of Incubi,
Abhorrèd dugs by devils sucken dry,
Of leaping lamps and of fierce-flying stones,
Of living wool, and such like witchery,
Or prov'd by sight or self confessions,
Which things much credence gain to past traditions.

44

Wherefore with boldnesse we will now relate
Some few in breif, as of th' *Astorgan* lad,
Whose peevish mother in fell ire and hate
Quite drunk with passion, through quick cholar mad
With execrations bold the devil bad,
Take him alive, which mood the boy no'te bear
But quits the room, walks out with spirit sad
Into the court, where, Lo ! by night appear
Tall Giants with grim looks, rough limbs, black grizely
hair.

45

These in a moment hoist him into th' air,
Away him bear more swift then bird can fly,
Straight to the destin'd place arrivèd are
Mongst craggy rocks, and bushy Mountains high,
Where up and down they drag the sorry boy ;
His tender skin and goary flesh they tear
Till he gan on his Maker call and cry.
Which forc'd the villains home again him bear,
Where he the story told, restor'd by Parents care.

46

The walking Skeleton in *Bolonia*
Laden with rattling chains, that showd his grave
To th' watchfull Student, who without dismay
Bid tell his wants, and speak what he would have :

Thus clearèd he the house by courage brave.
Nor may I passe the fair *Cerdinian* maid
Whose love a jolly swain did kindly crave,
And oft with mutuall solace with her stay'd ;
Yet was no jolly swain but a deceitful shade.

47

More harmlesse mirth may that mad spright commend
Who in an honest widows house did won
At *Salamanca*, who whole showers would send
Of stones that swifter then a whirlwind come
And yet whereere they bit no hurt is done.
But cursèd cruell be those wicked Hags
Whom poysonous spight, envy and hate have won
T' abhorrèd sorcery, whose writhled bags
Fould feinds oft suck and nestle in their loathsome rags.

48

Such as the Devil woes in homely form
Of swarthy man, or some black shaggy Curre,
Or vermine base, and in sad case forlorn
Them male-content to evil motions stirre ;
Proffer their service, adding a quick spurre
To meditated vengance, and fell teen,
Whose hellish voice they beare without demur,
Abjure God and his Sonne, who did redeem
The world, give up themselves to Satan and foul sinne.

49

Thus 'bodyed into that *Stygian* crue
Of damnèd wights made fast by their own bloud
To their bad Master, do his service due,
Frequent the assemblies, dance as they were wood
Around an huge black Goat, in loansome wood
By shady night, farre from or house or town,
And kisse with driveling lips in frantick mood
His sacred breech.   Catch that catch may anon
Each Feind has got his Hag for copulation.

50

O loathsome law ! O filthy fond embrace !
The other root of cursèd sorcery.
For if the streams of this bad art we trace
They lead to two foul springs, th' one Veneriè
And coarsest Lust, the other near doth lie
And is ycleepèd Vengeance, Malice, Hate,
Or restlesse Envy that would all destroy.
But both but from one seed do germinate
Hight uncurb'd Will, or strong Desire inordinate.

51

Wherefore I needs must humbly here adore
Him whose chaste soul enwombd in Virgin chast,
As chast a body amongst mortals wore,
Who never woman knew, ne once did taste
Of Hymens pleasures while this life did last.
Ah ! my dear Lord ! dread Sovereigne of souls
Who with thy life and lore so warmèd hast
My wounded heart, that when thy Storie's told,
Sweet Love, methinks, in 's silver wings me all infolds.

52

How do I hang upon thy sacred lips
More sweet then Manna or the hony-dew !
Thy speech, like rosie drops doth cool my wits
And calme my fierce affections untrue,
And winne my heart unto obeisance due.
Blest O thrice blessèd be that holy hill
Whereon thou did'st instruct thy faithfull crue
In wayes of peace, of patience and good-will
Forbidding base self-love, revenge and speeches ill.

53

Meek Lambe of God ! the worlds both scourge and
    scorn !
How done th' infernall feinds thy face envy !
Thou light, they darknesse, they Night, thou the Morn !
Mild chariot of Gods lovely Majesty !
Exalted Throne of the Divinitie !
As thou with thine mak'st through the yielding aire
How do thy frighted foes before thee fly !
And grin and gnash their teeth for spight and fear
To see such awfull strength quite to themselves con-
    traire.

54

Ho ! you vain men that follow filthy lust
And swallow down revenge like pleasant wine,
Base earthly spirits ! fly this sinfull dust.
See with what hellish Comrades you combine,
Als see whose lovely friendship you decline.
Even his whose love to you more strong then death
Did death abide, foul shame and evil tine ;
But if sweet love your hearts may move uneath
Think how one fatall flame, shall burn all underneath.

55

Pans pipe shall then be mute, and Satyrs heel
Shall cease to dance ybrent in scorching fire ;
For pleasure then each earthly spright shall feel
Deep searching pain ; Revenge and base desire
Shall bear due vengeance, reap their worthy hire ;
From thee, great Prince of souls ! shall be their
    doome.
Then thou and thy dear Saints ascending higher
Shalt fly the fate, and quit this stinking room
With smouldry smoak, fierce fire, and loathsome stench
    o'rerun.

56

Go now you cursèd Hags, salute your Goat
Whether with driveling lips or taper end,
Whereby at last you fire his hispide coat,
And then the deadly dust on mischief spend
As your Liege Lord these ashes doth commend
For wicked use, thundring this precept drad,
Revenge, revenge, or I shall on you send
Due vengeance : Thus dismist th' Assembly bad
Hoyst up into the Air, fly home through clammy shade.

57

Which stories all to us do plainly prove
That airy sprights both speak, and hear, and see.
Why do not then the souls of mortalls move
In airy Chariots but stupid lie
Lock'd up in sloth and senselesse Lethargie.
Certes our soul's as well proportionate
To this aeriall weed as spirits free :
For neither can our souls incorporate
With naked Earth, the Air must ever mediate.

58

Which that bold Art which Necromancy hight
Doth know too well, and therefore doth prepare
A vap'rous vehicle for th' intended spright,
With reek of oyl, meal, milk, and such like gear,
Wine, water, hony ; Thus souls fitted are
A grosser Carkas for to reassume.
And though *Thessalian* Hags their pains do spare
Sometimes they enter without Magick fume ;
Witnesse ye *Cretick* wives, who felt their fruitlesse
    spume.

59

And therefore to prevent such hellish lust
They did by laws Municipall provide
That he that dar'd to rise out of his dust
And thus infest his wife, a stake should gride
His stubborn heart and 's body burn beside ;
Hereto belongs that story of the spright
Of fell Asuitus noted far and wide,
And of his faithfull comrade Asmund hight ;
Twixt whom this law was made, as Danish Records
    write :

60

Which of them two the other did survive
Must be intomb'd with 's fellow in one grave.
Dead *Asuit* therefore with his friend alive
His dog and horse all in one mighty Cave
Be shut together, yet this care they have,
That faithfull Asmund, be not lost for meat :
Wherefore he was well stor'd his life to save
And liv'd sometime in that infernall seat,
Till *Errick* King of Sweads the door did open break.

61

For well he ween'd there was some treasure hid
Which might enrich himself, or 's Army pay.
But when he had broke ope the brasen lid
Nought but a sory wight they finden may,
Whom out of darknesse brought to open day
The King beheld ; dight with most deadly hue,
His cheek all gore, his ear quite bit away.
Then gan the King command the cause to shew,
To which Asmundus answers, as doth here ensue :

62

Why gaze you thus on my sad squalid face,
Th' alive needs languish must amongst the dead,

But this sore wound that further doth deface
My wasted looks, Asuitus (who first fed
On 's horse and dog. and then with courage dred,
At me let fly), *Asuit* this wound me gave,
But well I quit my self, took off his head
With this same blade, his heart nayl'd to the Cave :
Thus I my self by force did from the monster save.

63

The soul of *Naboth* lies to *Ahab* told,
As done the learnèd Hebrew Doctours write,
His foe in mischief thereby to infold.
Go up to *Ramoth Gilead* and fight,
Go up and prosper, said the lying spright,
The angry ghost of *Naboth* whom he slew
Unjustly, and possest his ancient right.
Hence his revengefull soul with speech untrue
Sat on his Prophets lips, and did with lies embue.

64

Ne may I passe that story sad of *Saul*
And *Samuels* ghost, whom he in great distresse
Consulted, was foretold his finall fall
By that old man, whom *Endors* sorceresse
Awak'd from pleasant vision and sweet ease,
Straitning a while his wonted liberty
By clammy air more close and thick compresse ;
Then gan the mantled Sage *Sauls* destiny
To reade, and thine with his, dear *Jonathan* ! to tye.

65

That lovely lasse *Pausanias* did kill
Through ill surmise she ment him treachery ;
How did her angry spirit haunt him still
That he could no where rest, nor quiet ly :
Her wrongèd ghost was ever in his eye.
And he that in his anger slew his wife,
And was exempt by Law from penalty,
Poore sorry man he led a weary life
Each night the Shrow him beat with buffes and boxes
rife.

66

And love as well as hate the dead doth reach,
As may be seen by what *Albumaron*
Did once befall, that learnd *Arabian* Leach.
He of a late-deceas'd Physition
Upon his bed by dream or vision
Receiv'd a soveraign salve for his sore eye,
And just *Simonides* compassion
Unto the dead that did unburied ly
On washèd shore, him sav'd from jaws of destinie.

67

For he had perish'd in th' unruly waves,
And sudden storm, but lo ! the thankfull spright
Of the interr'd by timely counsell saves,
Warning him of the danger he would meet

In his intended voyage,
Simonides desists by 's counsell won :
The rest for want of faith or due foresight,
A prey to the devouring Seas become,
Their dashèd bodies welter in the weedy scum.

68

In Artick Climes, an Isle that *Thule* hight
Famous for snowy monts, whose hoary head's
Sure signe of cold, yet from their fiery feet
They strike out burning stones with thunders dread,
And all the Land with smoak, and ashes spread :
Here wandring Ghosts themselves have often shown,
As if it were the region of the dead,
And men departed met with whom they've known,
In seemly sort shake hands, and ancient friendship own.

69

A world of wonders hither might be thrown,
Of Sprights and spectres, as that frequent noise
Oft heard upon the Plane of *Marathon*,
Of neighing horses and of Martiall boyes.
The Greek, the Persian, nightly here destroyes
In hot assault, embroyl'd in a long war,
Foure hundred years did last these dreadfull toyes,
As doth by *Attick* Records plain appear,
The seeds of hate, by death so little slakèd are.

70

Nor lists me speak of *Remus* Lemures,
Nor haunted house of slain *Caligula*,
Nor *Julius* stern Ghost, who will, with ease
May for himself of old or new purvey.
Thousand such stories in mens mouths do stray,
But sith it much perplexeth slower minds
To think our souls unhurt can passe away
From their dear corps, so close thereto confin'd ;
From this unweildy thought let's now their wits unbind.

71

For if that spirits can possesse our veins
And arteries (as usuall stories tell)
Use all our Organes, act our nerves and brains,
And by our tongue can future things foretell,
And safely yet keep close in this warme cell
For many years, and not themselves impare
Nor lose ymeint with the bloud where they dwel,
But come out clever when they conjured are,
And nimbly passe away soft-gliding through the air :

72

Why scape not then the souls of men as clear
Since to this body they 're no better joyn'd
Then thorough it to feel, to see, to hear
And to impart the passions of the mind ?
All which done by th' usurping spright we find.
As witnesse may that maid in *Saxony*,
Who meanly born of rude unlearnèd kind,
Not taught to reade, yet Greek and Latine she
Could roundly speak and in those tongues did prophesie.

73

Timotheus sister down in childbed laid
Disturb, all-phrantick thorough deadly pain
Tearing the clothes, which much her friends dismai'd,
Mumbling strange words as confus'd as her brain
At last was prov'd to speak *Armenian.*
For an old man that was by chance in town
And from his native soyle *Armenia* came,
The woman having heard of his renown
Sent to this agèd Sire to this sick wight to come.

74

Lo! now has entred the *Armenian* Sage
With scalp all bald, and skin all brown and brent,
The number of his wrinkles told his age:
A naked sword in his dry hand he hent.
Thus standing near her bed strong threats he sent
In his own language, and her fiercely chid.
But she well understanding what he meant
Unto his threats did bold defiance bid;
Ne could his vaunts as yet the sturdy spirit rid.

75

Then gan he sternely speak and heave his hond
And feign'd himself enrag'd with hasty ire
As ready for to strike with flaming brond,
But she for fear shrunk back and did retire
Into her bed and gently did respire,
Muttering few easie words in sleepy wise.
So now whom erst tumultuous thoughts did tire
Compos'd to rest doth sweetly close her eyes,
Then wak'd, what her befell, in sober mood descryes.

76

Now, *Thrax!* thy Story adde of *Alytas*
Who got his freind into a Mountain high
Where he with him the loansome night did passe
In Stygian rites and hellish mystery.
First twiches up an herb that grew thereby,
Gives him to taste, then doth his eyes besmear
With uncouth salves, wherewith all suddenly
Legions of spirits flying here and there
Around their cursèd heads do visibly appear.

77

Lastly into his mouth with filthy spaul
He spot, which done, a spirit like a Daw
His mouth did enter, and possessèd all
His inward parts. From that time he gan know
Many secret things, and could events foreshow.
This was his guerdon this his wicked wage
From the inwoning of that Stygian Crow.
But who can think this bird did so engage
With flesh that he no'te scape the ruin of the cage.

78

No more do souls of men. For stories sayen
Well known 'mongst countrey folk, our spirits fly,
From twixt our lips, and thither back again,
Sometimes like Doves, sometime like to a Bee,
And sometime in their bodyes shape they be;
But all this while their carkase lyes asleep
Drownd in dull rest, son of mortality;
At last these shapes return'd do slily creep
Into their mouth, then the dead clouds away they wipe.

79

Nor been these stories all but Countrey fictions,
For such like things even learnèd Clerks do write,
Of brasen sleep and bodi's derelictions,
That *Proconnesian* Sage that *Atheus* hight
Did oft himself of this dull body quit,
His soul then wandring in the easie aire.
But as to smoking lamp but lately light
The flame catch'd by the reek descends from farre,
So would his soul at last to his warm blood repair.

80

And *Hermotime* the *Clazomenian*
Would in like sort his body leave alone,
And view with naked soul both Hill and Plain
And secret Groves and every Region,
That he could tell what far and near was done:
But his curs'd foes the fell *Cantharidæ*
Assault his house when he was far from home,
Burn down to ashes his forsaken clay:
So may his wandring ghost for ever freely stray.

81

And 'tis an art well known to Wizards old
And wily Hags, who oft for fear and shame
Of the coarse halter, do themselves with-hold
From bodily assisting their night game:
Wherefore their carkasses at home retain,
But with their soules at those bad feasts they are,
And see their friends and call them by their name,
And dance around the Goat and sing, har, har,
And kisse the Devils breech, and taste his deadly chear.

82

A many stories to this purpose might
Be brought of men that in this Ecstacy
So senselesse ly, that coales laid to their feet
Nor nips nor whips can make them ope their eye.
Then of a sudden when this fit's gone by,
They up and with great confidence declare
What things they heard and saw both far and nie,
Professing that their soules unbodied were,
And roam'd about the earth in Countries here and there.

83

And to confirm the truth of this strange flight
They oft bring home a letter or a ring
At their return, from some far distant wight
Well known to friends that have the ordering
Of their forsaken corps, that no live thing
Do tread or touch't, so safely may their spright
Spend three whole dayes in airy wandering.
A feat that's often done through Magick might,
By the *Norvegian* Hags as learnèd Authors write.

84

But now well-wearied with our too long stay
In these Cimmerian fogs and hatefull mists
Of Ghosts, of Goblins, and drad sorcery,
From nicer allegations we'll desist.
Enough is said to prove that souls dismist
From these grosse bodies may be cloth'd in air,
Scape free (although they did not præexist,)
And in these airy orbs feel, see, and hear
And moven as they list as did by proof appear.

85

But that in some sort souls do præexist
Seems to right reason nothing dissonant,
Sith all souls both of trees, of men and beast
Been indivisible ; and all do grant
Of humane souls though not of beast and plant :
But I elsewhere, I think, do gainly prove
That souls of beasts, by reasons nothing scant,
Be individuous, ne care to move
This question of a new, mens patiences to prove.

86

But if mens souls be individuous,
How can they ought from their own substance shed ?
In generation there's nought flows from us
Saving grosse sperm yspent in Nuptiall bed
Drain'd from all parts throughout the body spred,
And well concocted where me list not name.
But no conveyances there be that lead
To the souls substance, whereby her they drain
Of loosened parts, a young babe-soul from thence to gain.

87

Wherefore who thinks from souls new souls to bring
The same let presse the Sunne beams in his fist
And squeez out drops of light, or strongly wring
The Rainbow, till it die his hands, well-prest.
Or with uncessant industry persist
Th' intentionall species to mash and bray
In marble morter, till he has exprest
A sovereigne eye-salve to discern a Fay :
As easily as the first all these effect you may.

88

Ne may queint similies this fury damp
Which say that our souls propagation
Is as when lamp we lighten from a lamp.
Which done withouten diminution
Of the first light, shows how the soul of man
Though indivisible may another rear,
Imparting life. But if we rightly scan
This argument, it cometh nothing near :
To light the lamp's to kindle the sulphurious gear.

89

No substance new that act doth then produce
Onely the oyly atomes 't doth excite
And wake into a flame, but no such use
There is of humane sperm. For our free sprite

Is not the kindled seed, but substance quite
Distinct therefrom. If not, then bodies may
So changèd be by nature and stiff fight
Of hungry stomacks, that what erst was clay
Then herbs, in time itself in sense may well display.

90

For then our soul can nothing be but bloud
Or nerves or brains, or body modifide.
Whence it will follow that cold stopping crud,
Hard moldy cheese, dry nuts, when they have rid
Due circuits through the heart, at last shall speed
Of life and sense, look thorough our thin eyes
And view the Close wherein the Cow did feed
Whence they were milk'd ; grosse Pie-crust will grow wise,
And pickled Cucumbers sans doubt Philosophize.

91

This all will follow if the soul be nought
But the live body. For mens bodies feed
Of such grosse meat, and if more fine be brought,
Suppose Snipes heads, Larks heels for Ladies meet,
The broth of Barly, or that oily Sweet
Of th' unctious Grape, yet all men must confesse
These be as little capable of wit
And sense, nor can be so transform'd, I wisse :
Therefore no soul of man from seed traducted is.

92

Ne been they by th' high God then first create
When in this earthly mansion they appear.
For why should he so soon contaminate
So unspotted beauties as mens spirits are,
Flinging them naked into dunghills here ?
Soyl them with guilt and foul contagion ?
Whenas in his own hand they spotlesse were,
Till by an uncouth strange infusion
He plung'd them in the deep of Malediction.

93

Besides unworthily he doth surmise
Of Gods pure being and bright Majesty,
Who unto such base offices him ties,
That He must wait on lawlesse Venery ;
Not onely by that large Causality
Of generall influence (for Creation
More speciall concourse all men deem to be)
But on set purpose He must come anon,
And ratifie the act which oft men wish undone.

94

Which is a rash and shamelesse bad conceit,
So might they name the brat *Adeodatus*,
Whatever they in lawlesse love beget.
Again, what's still far more prodigious
When men are stung with fury poysonous
And burn with flames of lust toward brute beasts,

And overcome into conjunction rush,
He then from that foul act is not releast,
Creates a soul, misplacing the unhappy guest.

95

Wherefore mans soul's not by Creation,
Nor is it generate, as I prov'd before.
Wherefore let 't be by emanation
(If fully it did not præexist of yore)
By flowing forth from that eternall store
Of Lives and souls ycleep'd the World of life,
Which was, and shall endure for evermore.
Hence done all bodies vitall fire derive
And matter never lost catch life and still revive.

96

And what has once sprout out doth never cease
If it enjoy itself, a spray to be
Distinct and actuall, though if God please
He can command it into th' ancient tree.
This immense Orb of wast vitality
With all its Lives and Souls is everywhere,
And do's, where matter right-prepar'd doth lie,
Impart a soul, as done the sunne beams clear
Insinuate themselves, where filth doth not debarre.

97

Thus may the souls in long succession
Leap out into distinct activity :
But sooth to say though this opinion
May seem right fair and plausible to be
Yet toils it under an hard difficulty.
Each where this Orb of life's with every soul ;
Which doth imply the souls ubiquity.
Or if the whole Extent of Nature's full
Of severall souls thick set, what may the furthest pull ?

98

What may engage them to descend so low,
Remov'd farre from the steam of earthly mire ?
My wits been here too scant and faith too slow,
Ne longer lists my wearied thoughts to tire.
Let bolder spirits to such hight aspire,
But well I wote, if there admitted were
A præexistency of souls entire,
And due Returns in courses circular,
This course all difficulties with ease away would bear.

99

For then suppose they wore an airy sphear
Which choice or *Nemesis* suck'd lower down,
Thus without doubt they 'll leave their carcase clear ;
Like dispossessèd spright when death doth come
And by rude exorcisme bids quit the room.
Ne let these intricacies perplex our mind,
That we forget that ere we saw the sunne
Before this life. For who can call to mind
Where first he here saw sunne or felt the gentle wind.

100

Besides what wonder is 't, when fierce disease
Can so empair the strongest memory,
That so full change should make our spirits leese
What 'fore they had impress'd in phantasie.
Nor doth it follow thence that when we die
We nought retain of what pass'd in these dayes,
For Birth is Death, Death Life and Liberty.
The soul's not thence contract but there displayes
Her loosened self, doth higher all her powers raise.

101

Like to a light fast-lock'd in lanthorn dark,
Whereby, by night our wary steps we guide
In slabby streets, and dirty channels mark,
Some weaker rayes through the black top do glide,
And flusher streams perhaps from horny side.
But when we 've past the perill of the way
Arriv'd at home, and laid that case aside,
The naked light how clearly doth it ray
And spread its joyfull beams as bright as Summers day.

102

Even so the soul in this contracted state
Confin'd to these strait instruments of sense
More dull and narrowly doth operate.
At this hole hears, the sight must ray from thence,
Here tasts, there smels ; But when she's gone from hence,
Like naked lamp she is one shining sphear.
And round about has perfect cognoscence
Whatere in her Horizon doth appear :
She is one Orb of sense, all eye, all airy ear.

103

Now have I well establish'd the fourth way
The souls of men from stupid sleep to save,
First Light, next Night, the third the soules Self-ray,
Fourth the souls Chariot we namèd have
Whether moist air or fire all-sparkling brave
Or temper mixt. Now how these foure agree,
And how the soul herself may dip and lave
In each by turns ; how no redundancy
Ther's in them, might we tell, nor scant deficiency.

104

But cease my restlesse Muse be not too free,
Thy chiefest end thou hast accomplishèd
Long since, shak'd of the *Psychopannychie*
And rouz'd the soul from her dull drowsiehed.
So nothing now in death is to be dred
Of him that wakes to truth and righteousnesse.
The corps lies here, the soul aloft is fled
Unto the fount of perfect happinesse :
Full freedome, joy and peace, she lively doth possesse.

ANTIMONOPSYCHIA

Or

The fourth part of the Song

OF THE

SOUL,

Containing

A confutation of the Unity of Souls.

Whereunto is annexed a Paraphrase upon Apollos
answer concerning Plotinus his Soul
departed this life.

By *H. M.* Master of Arts, and Fellow of Christs
Colledge in *Cambridge.*

Χαίρετ', ἐγὼ δ' ὑμῖν θεὸς ἄμβροτος οὐκ
ἔτι θνητός.

CAMBRIDGE
Printed by *Roger Daniel*, Printer to the
Univerfitie. 1647.

K

The all-devouring Unitie
Of Souls I here disprove;
Show how they bear their memorie
With them when they remove.

1

Ho yields himself to learning and the Muse,
Is like a man that leaves the steddy shore,
And skims the Sea. He nought then can
refuse
Whatever is design'd by Neptunes power,
Is fiercely drove in every stormy stoure,
Slave to the water and the whistling wind :
Even so am I, that whylom meant recover
The wishèd land, but now against my mind
Am driven fiercely back, and so new work do find.

2

What though the Rationall soul immortall be,
And safely doth exist, this body gone,
And lies broad wake in her existency ;
If all souls that exist do prove but one.
Or, though a number, if oblivion
Of all things past, put them in such a state
That they can no-wise guesse that ere upon
This earth they trode ; even this seems to abate
Their happinesse. They'll deem themselves then first
create.

3

Wherefore to ease us of this double doubt,
With mighty force great Phœbus doth inspire
My raving mind. He'll bear me strongly out,
Till I have perfected his own desire ;

Nor will he suffer me once to respire
Till I have brought this song unto an end.
O may it be but short though a quick fire !
Such rage and rapture makes the body bend,
Doth waste its fading strength and fainting spirits spend.

4

Now comes the story of Praxiteles
Into my mind, whom looking in a glasse,
With surly countenance, it did much displease,
That any should so sourely him outface ;
Yet whom he saw his doggèd self it was :
Tho he with angry fist struck his own shade.
Thus he the harmlesse mirior shatterèd has
To many shivers ; the same shapes invade
Each piece, so numbers he of surly vizards made.

5

These shapes appeard from the division
Of the broke glasse : so rasher phansies deem
That Rationall souls (whom they suppose but one)
By the divided matter many seem :
Bodies disjoind, broke glasses they esteem :
Which if they did into one substance flow,
One single soul in that one glasse would shine :
If that one substance also were ygo,
One onely soul is left, the rest were but a show.

6

Well is their mind by this similitude
Explaind. But now lets sift the verity
Of this opinion, and with reason rude
Rub, crush, touse, rifle this fine phantasie,

As light and thin as cobwebs that do fly
In the blew air, caus'd by th' Autumnall sun,
That boils the dew that on the earth doth lie.
May seem this whitish rag then is the scum,
Unlesse that wiser men make 't the field-spiders loom.

7

But such deep secrets willingly I leave
To grand Philosophers. I'll forward go
In my proposèd way. If they conceive
There's but one soul (though many seem in show)
Which in these living bodies here below
Doth operate (some such opinion
That learnèd Arab held, hight Aven-Roe)
How comes't to passe that she's so seldome known
In her own self? In few she thinks her self but one.

8

Seems not this Soul or Intellect very dull,
That in so few she can her self discover
To be but one in all, though all be full
Of her alone? Besides, no soul doth love her
Because she sucks up all: but what should move her
Thus to detest her self, if so that she's
But one in all? right reason surely drove her
Thus to condemne this lonesome Unitie
Of soul: which reasons her own operations be.

9

Thoughts good and bad that Universall mind
Must take upon itself; and every ill,
That is committed by all humane kind,
They are that souls. Alas, we have no will,
No free election, nor yet any skill,
But are a number of dull stalking trees
That th' universall Intellect doth fill
With its own life and motion: what it please
That there it acts. What strange absurdities are these?

10

All plotted mischief that sly reason wrought,
All subtill falsities that nimbly fly
About the world, that soul them all hath brought;
Then upon better thoughts with penalty
Doth sore afflict her self, doth laugh and cry
At the same time. Here *Aristophanes*
Doth maken sport with some spruse Comedy;
There with some Tragick strain sad *Sophocles*
Strikes the Spectatours hearts, makes many weeping
eyes.

11

Such grief this soul must in her self conceive
And pleasure at one time. But nere you'll say
We ought not griefe or pleasure for to give
Unto the soul. To what then? This live clay?
It feels no grief if she were gone away:
Therefore the soul at once doth laugh and cry.
But in this Argument I'll no longer stay,
But forward on with swifter course will hie,
And finden out some grosser incongruity.

12

Let now two men conceiven any form
Within their selves, suppose of flaming fire;
If but one soul doth both their corpse inform,
There's but one onely species intire.
For what should make it two? The Idee of fire
That is but one, the subject is but one,
One onely soul that all men doth inspire.
Let one man quench that form he thought upon,
That form is now extinct and utterly ygone;

13

So that the other man can think no longer,
Which all experience doth prove untrue.
But yet I'll further urge with reason stronger,
And still more clearly this fond falshood shew.
Can contraries the same subject imbew?
Yes; black and white, heat, cold may both possesse
The mind at once; but they a nature new
Do there obtain, they're not grosse qualities,
But subtill sprights that mutually themselves no'te
presse.

14

But contradiction, can that have place
In any soul? *Plato* affirms Idees;
But *Aristotle* with his pugnacious race
As idle figments stifly them denies.
One soul in both doth thus Philosophise,
Concludes at once contradictoriously
To her own self. What man can here devise
A fit escape, if (what's sure verity)
He grant but the souls indivisibility?

15

Which stifly is maintaind in that same song
Which is ycleepèd *Psychathanasie*,
And safely well confirm'd by reasons strong:
Wherefore I list not here the truth to try,
But wish the Reader to turn back his eye,
And view what there was faithfully displaid.
Now if there be but one centrality
Of th' Universall soul which doth invade
All humane shapes; how come these contradictions
made?

16

For that one soul is judge of every thing,
And heareth all Philosophers dispute;
Herself disputes in all that jangling,
In reasoning fiercely doth her self confute,
And contradictions confidently conclude:
That is so monstrous that no man can think
To have least shew of truth. So this pursuit
I well might now leave off: what need I swink
To prove whats clearly true, and force out needlesse ink.

17

Again, she would the same thing will and nill
At the same time. Besides, all men would have

The self-same knowledge, art, experience, skill ;
The frugall parent might his money save,
The Pedagoge his pains : If he engrave
His Grammer precepts but in one boyes mind,
Or decent manners : He doth thus embrace
With single labour all the youth you'll find
Under the hollow Heavens, they'll be alike inclin'd.

18

And every man is skill'd in every trade,
And every silent thought that up doth spring
In one mans brest, doth every man invade ;
No counsel-keeper, nor no secret thing
Will then be found ; They'll need no whispering
Nor louder voice. Let Orators be dumb,
Nor need the eager auditours make a ring ;
Though every one keep himself close at home,
The silent Preachers thoughts through all the world will
    roam.

19

Find each man out, and in a moment hit
With unavoided force : Or sooth to sain
They all begin at once to think what's fit,
And all at once anon leave off again.
A thousand such incongruities vain
Will follow from the first absurdity,
Which doth all souls into one centre strain,
And make them void of self-centrality.
Strange soul from whence first sprong so uncouth falsity.

20

Now all the arguments that I have brought
For to disprove the souls strange solitude,
That there is not one onely soul, well mought
Be urg'd (and will with equall strength conclude)
To prove that God his creature hath indew'd
With a *self-centrall* essence, which from his
Doth issue forth, with proper raies embew'd,
And that not all the very Godhead is :
For that would straight beget the like absurdities.

21

For he is indivisibly one being,
At once in every place and knoweth all ;
He is omnipotent, infinite in seeing ;
Wherefore if Creatures intellectuall
(And in that order humane souls will fall)
Were God himself, they would be alike wise,
Know one anothers thoughts imaginall,
Which no man doth : such falshoods would arise
With many more, which an idiot might well despise.

22

Nor will mens souls that now be different
Be God himself hereafter, and all one :
For thus they were quite lost ; their life ylent
And subtill being quite away are flone.

This is a perfect contradiction,
They are all one with God, and yet they are.
If they be one with God, then they alone
Did make themselves, and every rolling starre :
For God alone made these, and God himself they are.

23

Before the Sun and all the host of heaven,
The earth, the sea, and mans deep centrall spright ;
Before all these were made, was not God even
With his own self? what then him moven might
To waste his words and say, *Let there be light*.
If the accomplishment of all things be,
That all be God himself. This is not right.
No more perfection, no more Entity
There's then, then was in that eternall *Silency*.

24

Or will you say, that God himself delights
To do and undo ? But how can this stand
With self-sufficiency ? There's nought that might
Adde to his happinesse (if I understand
His nature right.) But He with open hand
Doth easly feed the Creature that he made
As easly. Wherefore if the truth be scand
This Goodnesse would that nought should be decay'd ;
His mind is all should liue ; no life he would should fade.

25

But if the finall consummation
Of all things make the Creature *Deiform*,
As Plato's school doth phrase it ; there is non
That thence need fear to come to any harm :
For God himself will then inact, inform,
And quicken humane souls at the last day ;
And though the Devil rore, and rage, and storm,
Yet Deaths drad power shall be done away,
Nor living *Night* on men her poysonous beams shall ray.

26

He hasten it that makes that glorious day !
For certainly it is no fearfull thing
But unto pride, and love of this base clay :
Its their destruction, but the perfecting
Of the just souls. It unto them doth bring
Their full desire, to be more close unite
With God, and utter cleans'd from all their sin.
Long was the world involv'd in cloudy *Night*,
But at the last will shine the perfect Christian light.

27

Thus the souls numerous plurality
I've prov'd, and shew'd she is not very God ;
But yet a decent *Deiformity*
Have given her : thus in the middle trod
I safely went, and fairly well have row'd
As yet. Part of my voyage is to come,
Which is to prove that the souls new aboad
In heaven or hell (what ever is her doom)
Nought hinders but past forms even there again may
    bloom.

28

Which if they did not, she could never tell
Why she were thus rewarded, wherefore ill
Or good she doth enjoy, whether ill or well
She livèd here.   Remembrance death did spill.
But otherwise it fares ; as was her will
And inclination of her thirsty spright,
Impressions of like nature then doth fill
Her lively mind, whether with sad affright
Disturb'd, which she long fear'd ; or in hop'd-for delight.

29

The life that here most strongly kindled was
(Sith she awakes in death) must needs betray
The soul to what nearest affinity has
With her own self, and likenesses do sway
The mind to think of what ever did play
In her own self with a like shape or form :
And contraries do help the memory :
So if the soul be left in case forlorn,
Remembrance of past joy makes her more deeply mourn.

30

'Tis also worth our observation,
That higher life doth ever comprehend
The lower vitall acts : sensation
The soul some fitten hint doth promptly lend
To find out plantall life ; sense is retaind
In subtiller manner in the phantasie ;
Als reason phantasies doth well perpend :
Then must the souls highest capacity
Contain all under life.   Thus is their Memory.

31

This faculty is very intimate
And near the Centre, very large and free,
Extends itself to whatsoever that
The soul peracts.   There is no subtilty
Of Intellect, of Will, nor Phantasie,
No Sense, nor uncouth strange impression
From damnèd Night, or the blest Deity,
But of all these she hath retention,
And at their fresh approach their former shapes can own.

32

This memorie the very bond of life
You may well deem.   If it were cut away
Our being truly then you might contrive
Into a point of time.   The former day
Were nought at all to us : when once we lay
Our selves to sleep, we should not know at morn
That e're we were before ; nor could we say
A whit of sense ; so soon as off we turn
One word, that's quite forgot.   Coherence thus is torn.

33

Now sith it is of such necessitie,
And is the bundle of the souls duration,
The watchman of the soul, lest she should flie
Or steal from her own self, a sure fixation

And Centrall depth it hath, and free dilation,
That it takes notice of each energie
Of Phansie, Sense, or any Cogitation.
Wherefore this virtue no dependencie
Hath of this body, must be safe when it doth die.

34

But if dispersèd lifes collection,
Which is our memory, safely survive
(Which well it may, sith it depends not on
The *Mundane* spirit) what can fitly drive
It into action.   In heaven she doth live
So full of one great light, she hath no time
To such low trifles, as past sights, to dive,
Such as she gatherèd up in earthly slime :
Foreknowledge of herself is lost in light divine.

35

But can she here forget our radiant Sunne ?
Of which its maker is the bright *Idee*,
This is His shadow ; or what she hath done
Now she's rewarded with the Deitie ?
Suppose it : Yet her hid *Centralitie*
So sprightly's quickned with near Union
With God, that now lifes wishèd liberty
Is so encreas'd, that infinitely sh' has fun
Herself, her deep'st desire unspeakably hath wonne.

36

And deep desire is the deepest act,
The most profound and centrall energie,
The very selfnesse of the soul, which backt
With piercing might, she breaks out, forth doth flie
From dark contracting death, and doth descry
Herself unto herself ; so thus unfold
That actuall life she straightwayes saith, is I.
Thus while she in the body was infold,
Of this low life, as of herself oft tales she told.

37

In dangerous sicknesse often saith, I die ;
When nought doth die but the low plantall man.
That falls asleep : and while Nature doth tie
The soul unto the body ; she nere can
Avoid it, but must feel the self-same pain,
The same decay, if hereto she her mind
Do bend.   When stupid cold her corse oreran,
She felt that cold ; but when death quite doth bind
The sense, then she herself doth dead and senselesse find.

38

Or else at least just at the entrance
Of death she feels that slie privation,
How now it spreads ore all : so living sense
Perceives how sleep creeps on, till quite o'recome
With drousinesse, animadversion
Doth cease : but (lower sense then fast ybound)
The soul bestoweth her adversion
On something else : So oft strange things hath found
In sleep, from this dull carcase while she was unbound.

39

So though the soul, the time she doth advert
The bodies passions takes her self to die :
Yet death now finish'd, she can well convert
Herself to other thoughts.   And if the eye
Of her adversion were fast fixt on high,
In midst of death 'twere no more fear or pain,
Then 'twas unto Elias to let flie
His uselesse mantle to that Hebrew Swain,
While he rode up to heaven in a bright fiery wain.

40

Thus have I stoutly rescued the soul
From centrall death or pure mortalitie,
And from the listlesse flouds of Lethe dull,
And from the swallow of drad Unitie.
And from an all-consuming Deitie.
What now remains, but since we are so sure
Of endlesse life, that to true pietie
We bend our minds, and make our conscience pure,
Lest living Night in bitter darknesse us immure.

FINIS.

THE ORACLE

O R,

A Paraphrasticall Interpretation of the
answer of *Apollo*, when he was consulted by *Amelius* whither *Plotinus*
soul went when he de-
parted this life.

 Tune my strings to sing some sacred verse
Of my dear friend ; in an immortall strain
His mighty praise I loudly will rehearse
With hony-dewèd words : some golden vein
The strucken chords right sweetly shall resound.
Come, blessèd Muses, let's with one joynt noise,
With strong impulse, and full harmonious sound,
Speak out his excellent worth.   Advance your voice,
As once you did for great Æacides,
Rapt with an heavenly rage, in decent dance,
Mov'd at the measures of Meonides.
Go to, you holy Quire, let's all at once
Begin, and to the end hold up the song,
Into one heavenly harmony conspire ;
I Phœbus with my lovely locks ymong
The midst of you shall sit, and life inspire.
    Divine Plotinus I yet now more divine
Then when thy noble soul so stoutly strove
In that dark prison, where strong chains confine,
Keep down the active mind it cannot move

To what it loveth most.   Those fleshly bands
Thou now hast loos'd, broke from Necessitie.
From bodies storms, and frothie working sands
Of this low restlesse life now setten free,
Thy feet do safely stand upon a shore,
Which foaming waves beat not in swelling rage,
Nor angry seas do threat with fell uprore ;
Well hast thou swommen out, and left that stage
Of wicked Actours, that tumultuous rout
Of ignorant men.   Now thy pure steps thou stay'st
In that high path, where Gods light shines about,
And perfect Right its beauteous beams displayes.
How oft, when bitter wave of troubled flesh,
And whirl-pool-turnings of the lower spright,
Thou stoutly strov'st with, Heaven did thee refresh,
Held out a mark to guide thy wandring flight !
While thou in tumbling seas didst strongly toyl
To reach the steddie Land, struckst with thy arms
The deafing surges, that with rage do boyl ;
Stear'd by that signe thou shunn'st those common harms.

How oft when rasher cast of thy souls eye
Had thee misguided into crooked wayes,
Wast thou directed by the Deitie?
They held out to thee their bright lamping rayes:
Dispers'd the mistie darknesse, safely set
Thy feeble feet in the right path again.
Nor easie sleep so closely ere beset
Thy eyelids, nor did dimnesse ere so stain
Thy radiant sight, but thou such things didst see
Even in that tumult, that few can arrive
Of all are namèd from Philosophie
To that high pitch, or to such secrets dive.
   But sith this body thy pure soul divine
Hath left, quite risen from her rotten grave,
Thou now among those heavenly wights dost shine,
Whose wonne this glorious lustre doth embrave:
There lovely Friendship, mild smiling Cupid's there,
With lively looks and amorous suavitie,
Full of pure pleasure, and fresh flowring chear;
Ambrosian streams sprung from the Deitie
Do frankly flow, and soft love-kindling winds
Do strike with a delicious sympathie
Those tender spirits, and fill up their minds
With satisfying joy.   The puritie
Of holy fire their heart doth then invade,
And sweet Perswasion, meek Tranquillitie,

The gentle-breathing Air, the Heavens nought sad,
Do maken up this great felicitie.
Here Rhadamanthus, and just Æacus,
Here Minos wonnes, with those that liv'd of yore
I' th' golden age, here Plato vigorous
In holy virtue, and fair Pythagore.
These been the goodly Off-spring of Great Jove,
And liven here, and whoso fill'd the Quire
And sweet assembly of immortall Love,
Purging their spirits with refining fire;
These with the happy Angels live in blisse,
Full fraught with joy, and lasting pure delight,
In friendly feasts, and life-outfetching kisse.
But, ah! dear Plotin what smart did thy sprite
Indure, before thou reach'st this high degree
Of happinesse? what agonies, what pains
Thou underwent'st to set thy soul so free
From baser life? She now in heaven remains
Mongst the pure Angels.   O thrice-happy wight!
That now art got into the Land of Life,
Fast plac'd in view of that Eternall Light,
And sitt'st secure from the foul bodies strife.
   But now, you comely virgins, make an end,
Break off this musick, and deft seemly Round,
Leave off your dance: For Plotin my dear friend
Thus much I meant my golden harp should sound.

Notes upon *Pſychozoia*.

CANT. I.

He fittest station to take a right view of the *Song of the Soul*, is *Psyche*, or the soul of the Universe. For whatsoever is handled in *Psychozoia*, and the three other parts of this song hath a meet relation to *Psyche* as the subject of the whole Poem. For the whole Poem is spent either in her Parentage, Marriage, Clothing or Of-spring.

The three first are dispatched in the first Canto of *Psychozoia*, the last in the two latter Cantoes and three following parts of the Poem. For in the second Canto the manner of the production of Souls is set out till the 24 Stanza. Then all the residue of that and the whole Canto following in the description of their habitation. But their habitation being the Land of life, that is, the severall states of the Soul in good and evill, for this cause chiefly, as also in part, for the description in the first Canto of that life deriv'd from *Ahad* and *Æon* to *Psyche*, and that which flows from her καθ' ὑποστολὴν to the lowest skirts of the Universe, do I call this first part of the Song of the Soul, *Psychozoia*.

Vers. 7. *O life of time and all Alterity!*

For when is time but the perseverance of the motion of the soul of the world, while she by her restlesse power brings forth these things in succession, that Eternity hath at once altogether. For such is the nature of *Æon* or Eternity, viz. A life exhibiting all things at once, and in one. Διάστασις οὖν ζωῆς χρόνον εἶχεν, but distance of life makes time, and the prorogation of life continueth time, the præterition of life is the præterition of time, but *Psyche* is the fountain of this evolved life, whence she is also the very life of time.

And all Alterity.

It may be thus shadowed out. The seed of a plant hath all the whole tree, branches, leaves, and fruit at once, in one point after a manner closed up, but potentially. Eternity hath all the world in an indivisible indistant way at once, and that actually.

Psyche or the Soul of the world, when she begins this world, begets a grosser kind of Alterity, and dispersed diversity ὥσπερ ἐκ σπέρματος ἡσύχου ἐξελίττων αὐτὸν λόγος, &c. as the seminall forme spreads out it self, and the body it inacts into distant branches from the quiet and silent seed, making that actuall in time and succession which could not be here below in bodies at once. See *Plotin. Ennead.* 3. *lib.* 7. *cap.* 10. where the nature of time is more fully described.

Vers. 8. *The life of lives.*

Viz. God himself.

Νόος ἐσσι νόου ⎫ Of minds thou art the Mind.
Ψυχῶν Ψυχὰ ⎬ The Soul of souls.
Φύσις εἶ φυσίων ⎭ And Nature of each natures kind.
Synes. Hymn. 4.

STANZ. 5. Vers. 9. *That same that Above hight.*

The deepest Centre of all things, and first root of all beings; the Platonists call τ' ἀγαθὸν & τὸ ἓν, that is, the Good, and the One. See *Plot. Ennead.* 1. *lib.* 7. *cap.* 1. *Mercur. Trismeg. Serm. Univers. ad Æsculap.* This is the simple and naked essence of God, utterly devoid of division and plurality, and therefore not to be known by reason or Intellect, but νόου ἄνθει, as the Oracle speaks, by the flower, or the summity of the Intellect.

Ἔστι δὲ δή τι νοητὸν ὃ χρή σε νοεῖν νόου ἄνθει,

that is, ἑνιαίᾳ δυνάμει as *Mich. Psellus* expounds it, by the unitive power of the Intellect, or by a certain simple and tactuall Energie of the soul when it is roused into act.

For so is the expression of *Plotinus, Ennead.* 6. *l.* 9. *c.* 7. ἀλλ' ἔστι τῷδ' δυναμένῳ θιγεῖν παρὸν, τῷδ' καὶ ἀδωνατοῦντι οὐ πάρεστι. For he is present to him that can touch him, but to him that cannot, he is not present: and in the 9. Cap., describing more lively the state of our union with *Above*, or the eminent absolute Good, Καὶ τὸ ἐνταῦθα, &c. And there lyeth our happinesse, saith he, and to be removed from hence, is but to partake lesse of being. Here is the rest of the soul, set out of the reach of all evils, ascended into a place devoid of all danger and mischief. Here she becomes intellectuall, Here she is impassible, Here she truly lives indeed. But this life that we live disjoyned from God is but a shadow, and umbratil imitation of that. But that ἐνέργεια μὲν νόου, intellectuall energie, an energie that begets Gods ἐν ἡσύχῳ τῇ πρὸς ἐκεῖνο ἐπαφῇ in that still and silent tactuall conjunction with this Universall Good. It begets beauty, it begets righteousnesse, it begets valour ; for these doth the soul bring forth, being once impregned of God, and fil'd as it were with his sacred seed. And in the 10. Chap. describing further this Union, he saith, that God and the soul doth as it were *κέντρον κέντρῳ συνάψαι,* joyne centres, and centres do wholly swallow up one another, so that this union is even more then touch.

This tactuall conjunction of the soul with God surely in the Christian phrase is no more then divine love, as *S. John* speaks. God is love, and he that is in love is in God, and God in him. And *Plotinus* doth plainly acknowledge it, when as he saith, Every soul is a Venus and hath her Cupid born with her, an heavenly Cupid with an heavenly Venus, till she be defiled with earthly love, *πάνδημος γενομένη καὶ οἷον ἐταιρισθεῖσα,* made common and as it were become an Harlot : but that the soul in the purity of her own nature, loves God and desireth to be joyned with him, as a beautifull virgin to a beautifull man, *ὥσπερ παρθένος καλὴ πρὸς καλὸν ἄνδρα,* for so I think the text is to be read, and not *παρθένος καλοῦ πρὸς καλὸν ἔρωτα.* See the whole ninth book of the sixth *Ennead.* For the nature of *Atove* or *Ahad* and the manner of the conjunction of the soul with him is there exquisitely set out.

STANZA 6, 7. *Now can I not,* &c.

It being acknowledged both in the purest Philosophy and in Christianity, that the root of all things is goodnesse it self, the most genuine consequence of this is, That his providence being measured by himself, goodnesse it self is the measure thereof : so that all Melancholick and dismall dreams of idly affrighted men, may well vanish in the clearnesse of this light and truth ; as also the envious, malicious, and bloudy minded man may here consider, how far he hath wandred from the will of God, and the root of his own being.

STANZA 8. *This Ahad of himself the Æon fair,* &c.

This *Æon* is all things essentially and truly as *Ahad* or *Atove* above all things. It is the very intellectuall world, Eternall life, united ever with the father that brought him forth. The Λόγος ἐνδιάθετος of God, his understanding, or explicit inward comprehension of all things *ab æterno,* infinite and every where, differing onely from his fountain in this, that he is one simple Unity, this one ever-actuall omniformity,

νοεραῖς στράπτουσα τομαῖσιν.

as the Oracle speaks, being the very Essence or Idea of all things, at once, not successively or in part. See *Plotin. Ennead.* 3. *lib.* 7. where he doth acknowledge *Æon* and On all one : at the fourth Chapter.

STANZ. 9. *This is the ancient Eidos omniform Fount of all beauty,* &c.

The description of *Æon,* which is the first form also or pulchritude, is largely set out : *Ennead.* 5. *lib.* 8. περὶ τοῦ νοητοῦ κάλλους, where the condition of that

Eternall life is thus delineated. Καὶ γὰρ τὸ ῥεῖα ζώειν ἐκεῖ, καὶ ἀλήθεια δὲ αὐτοῖς καὶ γεννέτειρα καὶ τροφὸς. καὶ οὐσία καὶ τροφή· καὶ ὁρῶσι τὰ πάντα, οὐκ οἷς γένεσις πρόσεστιν ἀλλ' οἷς οὐσία, καὶ ἑαυτοὺς ἐν ἄλλοις· διαφανῆ γὰρ πάντα καὶ σκοτεινὸν οὐδὲ ἀντίτυπον οὐδέν. ἀλλὰ πᾶς παντὶ φανερὸς εἰς τὸ εἴσω καὶ πάντα· φῶς γὰρ φωτί. καὶ γὰρ ἔχει πᾶς πάντα ἐν ἑαυτῷ, καὶ αὖ ὁρᾷ ἐν ἄλλῳ πάντα· ὅτι πανταχοῦ πάντα, καὶ πᾶν, πᾶν, καὶ ἕκαστον πᾶν, καὶ ἄπειρος ἡ αἴγλη, ἕκαστον γὰρ αὐτῶν μέγα. ἐπεὶ καὶ τὸ μικρὸν μέγα. καὶ ἥλιος ἐκεῖ πάντα ἄστρα, καὶ ἕκαστον ἥλιος αὖ, καὶ πάντα. Ἐξέχει δὲ ἐν ἑκάστῳ ἄλλο, ἐμφαίνει δὲ καὶ πᾶν πάντα &c. that is, It is an easie life they live there, for truth is their mother, nurce, substance, and nourishment, and they see all things (not in which generation is but essence) and themselves in others. For all's pellucid, nothing dark or impervious, but every one to every one is perspicuous, and all to every one as light to light. For every one hath in him all things, and again sees all things in others. So that all things are every where, and all is all, and every thing all, and the splendour infinite. For every thing there is great, with what is little must be also great : the Sun there is all the starres, and again every starre the Sun, and all things : but every thing is more eminently some one thing, and yet all things fairly shine in every thing. &c. See *Plotin. Ennead.* 5. *lib.* 8. cap. 4.

STANZ. 13. *Far otherwise it fares in Æons realms.*

This is in reference to *Narcissus* story, Stanz. 12. that sets out the hazard of loving earthly beauty, and of the desire of conjunction with it : but there is no such danger in *Æon* land, for the objects there are perfective and not destructive, better then the soul, not baser : and chiefly *Abinoam* or *Ahad* which is as it were the Sun of that world, which *Æon* doth alwayes behold steddy and unmoved, and with him all they that arrive thither. *Æons* self is also an unspeakable plenitude of life, and it is an unexpresseable perfection of the mind to be joyned with him, so that there is plainly no danger or hurt to desire earnestly the enjoyment of these divine forms, though union with corporeall features may deface the soul.

STANZ. 14. *For Æon land which men Idea call Is nought but life,* &c.

So *Plotin.* Ἡ τοῦ νοῦ καὶ ὄντος φύσις κόσμος ἐστὶν ὁ ἀληθὼς καὶ πρῶτος, οὐ διαστὰς ἀφ' ἑαυτοῦ, οὐδὲ ἀσθενὴς τῷ μερισμῷ οὐδὲ ἐλλειπής, ἀλλὰ ἡ πᾶσα ζωὴ αὐτοῦ καὶ πᾶς νοῦς ἐν ἑνὶ ζῶα καὶ νοοῦντα ὁμοῦ. Καὶ τὸ μέρος παρέχεται ὅλον, καὶ πᾶν αὐτῷ φίλον, οὐ χωρισθὲν ἄλλο ἀπ' ἄλλου οὐδὲ ἕτερον γεγενημένον μόνον καὶ τῶν ἄλλων ἀπεξενωμένον. Ὅθεν οὐδ' ἀδικεῖ ἄλλο, ἄλλο, οὐδ' ἂν ᾖ ἐναντίον· πανταχοῦ δε ὂν ἓν καὶ τέλειον ὁπουοῦν, ἕστηκέ τε καὶ ἀλλοίωσιν οὐκ ἔχει. That is, The nature of *Intellect* and *On* is the true and first world not distant from it self, not weak by division or dispersion, nothing defective. But all of it is life, and all intellect living in one and at once understanding. A part exhibits the whole, and the whole is friendly to it self, not separated one part from another, nor become another alone ; and estrang'd from others. Whence one part is not injurious to another nor contrary. Wherefore every where being one and perfect every where, it stands unmoved and admits no alteration. See *Ennead.* 3. *lib. 2. cap.* 1.

STANZ. 15.   *That Virgin wife of Æon Vranore.*

Vranore or *Psyche* the wife of *Æon*, the daughter of *Ahad.* For indeed all things come from him, but *καθ' ὑποστολὴν* ; First *τὸ ἓν* or *Ahad*, that is a simple unity : then *Æon*, that's *ἓν πάντα* an actuall vnmoveable Omniformity : Lastly, *ἓν καὶ πάντα*, that's *Vranore*, or *Psyche,* viz. capable of that stable Omniformity, that Fulnesse of life even all things, and of him that is above all things : but it is not of her Essence to be all things actually and steddily. See *Plotin.* περὶ τῶν ἀρχιχῶν ὑποστάσεων. *Ennead.* 5. *lib.* 1. *cap.* 8. But nothing can be more plain than what he hath written, *Ennead.* 5. *lib.* 6. *cap.* 4. where speaking of *Ahad*, *Æon*, and *Psyche* Καὶ οὖν ἀπεικαστέον (saith he) τὸ μὲν φωτί, τὸ δὲ ἐφεξῆς ἡλίῳ, τὸ δὲ τρίτον τῷ σελήνῃ ἄστρῳ κομιζομένῳ τὸ φῶς παρ' ἡλίου. ψυχὴ μὲν γὰρ ἐπακτὸν νοῦν ἔχει ἐπιχρωννύντα αὐτὴν νοερὰν οὖσαν. νοῦς δὲ ἐν αὐτῷ οἰκεῖον ἔχει, οὐ φῶς ὢν μόνον, ἀλλ' ὅ ἐστι πεφωτισμένον ἐν τῇ αὐτοῦ οὐσίᾳ. τὸ δὲ παράχον τοῦτο τὸ φῶς οὐκ ἄλλο ὄν, φῶς ἐστιν ἀπλοῦν, παρέχον τὴν δύναμιν ἐκείνῳ τοῦ εἶναι ὅ ἐστιν. That is, And we may resemble the first, viz. *Ahad*, to lux or light, the next to the Sunne ; the third, viz. *Psyche*, to the Moon, borrowing her light of the Sunne. For *Psyche* hath but an adventitious Intellect, which doth as it were colour her, made Intellectual. But *Intellect* or *Æon* hath in himself proper Intellectuall life, not being that light onely, but that which is in his essence illuminated by *Ahad :* but that which imparts this light, viz. *Ahad*, is light alone, and nothing else beside, exhibiting a power to him to be what he is.

Vers. 4. 5.   *Because the fire*
                   Of Æthers essence, &c.

That the Intellect in man is clothed with the soul, the soul with fire or spirit ; and that through that instrument it governs and orders this grosse body, is the Opinion of *Trismeg.* in his Clavis ; and the like instrument he ascribes to the Maker of the whole World Δημιουργὸς γὰρ ἁπάντων τῶν οὐρανῶν τῷ πυρὶ πρὸς τὴν δημιουργίαν χρῆται. The Maker of the Heavens useth fire to his work. But I conceive indeed that the pure Heavens or *Æther*, which is from αἴθω to burn, is nothing else but attenuate fire בינּ׳, a subtill fiery liquor or liquid fire ; as I have else where intimated.

Vers. 6. 7.   *And inward unseen golden hew doth dight,*
             And life of Sense, &c.

I cannot better declare this matter then the Philosopher hath already, *Ennead.* 5. *lib.* 1. *cap.* 2.

Let any particular soul, saith he, quietly by her self conceive the whole Universe devoid of life, form, and motion ; let the Earth be still and stupid, the Sea, the Aire, and the Heaven : anon an universall soul flow into this torpent masse, inwardly infus'd, penetrating throughout, and illuminating all, as the beams of the Sunne doth some Cloud χρυσοειδῆ ὄψιν ποιοῦσαι, making a golden show by their gilding light. Such is the entrance of *Psyche* into the body of the Vniverse, kindling and exciting the dead mist, the utmost projection of her own life into an Æthereall vivacity, and working in this, by her plasmaticall Spirits or Archei, all the whole world into order and shape, fitting this sacred Animal for perfect sense, establishing that in being, which before was next to nothing.

Vers. 8.   *Æther's the vehicle of touch, smell, sight :*
            Of taste, &c.

This is true in the Microcosme as well as in the Macrocosme above described, *viz.* that the more subtill, fiery and attenuate spirits in mans body, are the medium whereby the soul is joyned to and doth work in the body.

STANZ. 16.——*May reach that vast profundity.*

Synesius also calleth it βυθὸν πατρῶον, the paternall depth. *Hymn.* 2.

STANZ. 18.   *Now rise, my Muse,* &c.

From this Stanza to the 33. is contained a description of the visible World.

Vers. 2.   *Th' outward vest.*

To make all this visible World the garment of *Psyche* is no forc'd or new fancy ; sith the Sibyll hath apparrelled God therewith, *Sibyll. Orac. lib.* 1.

Εἰμὶ δ' ἐγὼ ὁ ἐὼν (σὺ δ' ἐνὶ φρεσὶ σῇσι νόησον)
Οὐρανὸν ἐνδέδυμαι, περὶ βέβλημαι δὲ θάλασσαν,
Γαῖα δέ μοι στήρεγμα ποδῶν περὶ σῶμα κέχυται,
Ἀὴρ δ' ἠδ' ἄστρων με χορὸς περιδέδρομε πάντη.

That is,

I am JEHOVAH, *well my words perpend,*
Clad with the frory Sea, all mantled over
With the blew Heavens, shod with the Earth I wend,
The Starres around me dance, th' Air doth me cover.

Moses also (if we will believe *Philo* the Jew) made *Aarons* garment a symboll of the visible World, and it agrees well with this of the Sibylls. For first upon the top, on his Mitre was the τετραγράμματον JEHOVAH ; The shoulder-pieces mought represent the Heavens ; The two Precious-stones there, the two Hemispheres ; The twelve names engraven, the twelve signes of the Zodiack ; The blew Robe, the Air ; τὰ ἀνθινὰ or the flowry work at the hemme of the garment, the earth ; οἱ ῥοΐσκοι, the Pomegranèts (with an allusion to ῥέω *fluo*) the water ; οἱ κώδωνες the Bells, the harmony, that is, the mixture of earth and water for generation. But as for ἀνθινὰ there is nothing answereth to it in the Hebrew Text, and why should ῥοΐσκοι be Emblems of the water, and not rather of the whole Globe of the Earth and Water, it being a round fruit, and representing the seminall fullnesse of the Earth, by its scissure in the side, full of kernells or seeds ? Peradventure had *Philo* been as well instructed in Pythagorisme, as in Platonisme, and had mist the Septuagint's ἀνθινὰ & ῥοΐσκοι, he would hit of another harmony, then the mixture of Water and Earth doth make ; I mean the noise of those Balls mentioned Stanza 30. And so the order of having every Bell joyned with a Pomegranet, would have signified the many and numerous Globes at the severall depths of the World, with their concomitant sounds in their motion, or at the least proportionable velocities, and consequently *Pythagoras* harmony would have been ratified from *Aarons* robe : but I hold not this Argument apodicticall. *Phil. de vita Mosis.*

Vers. 7. *The many Plicatures.*
Every particular body is esteemed but a knot or close folding of that one intire Out-garment of *Psyche.*

STANZ. 19. vers. 9. *The garment round,* &c.
It is too too probable the world is round if it be not infinite, the reasons be obvious ; but to conclude it finite or infinite is but guesse, mans imagination being unable to represent Infinity to Reason to judge on.

STANZ. 30, 31. *But yet one thing I saw,* &c.
At the low hem, &c.
A glance at *Copernicus* opinion, as at theirs also that make the fixt starres so many Sunnes, and all the Planets to be inhabited : for by their inhabitants they will be deemed the lowest part of this visible world, be it *Saturn, Mars, Jupiter,* or what Planet soever else discovered, or, as yet not discovered : wherefore according to this conceit, it is said,
At the low hem of this large garment-gay.
That is, at the places that seem low, and these are all inhabited Planets supposing there be any inhabited.

STANZ. 33, 34. *Did tie them twain,* &c.
Æon and *Psyche* here become one, not as though they were one and the same essence, but nearer after that kind of manner that the body and soul become one man. For *Æon* is the Entelechia of *Psyche,* as I may say, but closer unite then any form or soul to any body, and never to be separate. Because the universall soul of the world finds all things in *Æon,* and knows also exactly inferiour things. For her animadversion is not fixed or determined to one, as mans soul is, but free, every where at once, above and below, so that she cannot possibly leave off this state, but is one, ever firmly united with *Æon.*

STANZ. 36. *To thee each knee,* &c.
A Christian mystery wrapt up in a Platonicall covering, the reduction of the world to conformity with the Eternall Intellect, and the soul of the world. For these move still, to this very day, to win men to be governed by them, and not by their own perverse and dark will. Or rather to speak in the Christian Idiom, the Sonne of God, and the Holy Ghost do thus stirre men up, and invite them to true and lively obedience to the eternall will of God, and to forsake their own selves, and their blind way, and to walk all in one everlasting way of light and saving health.

STANZ. 39. *Ahad these three in one,* &c.
Here we see *Ahad, Æon,* and *Psyche* all one, which is to be understood not of Essence, but Person (as I may so speak) and that they move and act upon the creature, as one man.

STANZ. 41. *We Physis name.*
Physis is nothing else but the vegetable World, the Universall comprehension of Spermaticall life dispersed throughout. This seminall World is neither the very Intellect it self, though it be stored with all forms, nor any kind of pure soul, though depending of both, οἶον ἐκλαμψις ἐξ ἀμφοῖν νοῦ, καὶ ψυχῆς, A kind of life eradiating and resulting both from Intellect and *Psyche.*
This enters and raiseth up into life and beauty, the whole corporeall world, orders the lowest projection of life, *viz.* the reall Cuspis of the Cone infinitely multiplied, awaking that immense mist of Atoms into severall energies, into fiery, watery and earthly ; and placing her Magick attractive points, sucks hither and thither to every centre a due proportion, and rightly disposed number of those Cuspidal particles, knedding them into Suns, Moons, Earths, &c. and then with a more curious artifice, the particular Archei frame out in every one such inhabitants and ornaments, as the divine Understanding hath thought fit. For *Physis* (as I said) is not the divine Understanding it self, but is as if you should conceive, an Artificers imagination separate from the Artificer, and left alone to work by it self without animadversion. Hence *Physis* or Nature is sometimes puzzeld and bungells in ill disposed matter, because its power is not absolute and omnipotent. See *Plot. Ennead.* 3. *lib.* 2.

STANZ. 59. *In midst of this fine web doth Haphe sit.*
Every sence to be a kind of touch, was the opinion of the ancient Philosophers, as you may see in *Theophrastus περὶ αἰσθήσεως.* Every sense in *Psyche* is plainly and perfectly Touch, or more then Touch rather, I mean, a nearer union. But this present Stanza respects more properly the nature of sense in particular Animals (so farre had my pen started aside) where Touch is the centre as it were from whence the soul discerns in the circumference all manner of Forms and Motions,
She is the centre from whence all the light
Dispreads, and goodly glorious forms do flit
Hither and thither.
Thus : for there is first a tactuall conjunction as it were of the representative rayes of every thing, with our sensorium before we know the things themselves, which rayes we really feeling, perceive those things at distance by this communication. For these rayes always convey the distance or place, as well as the colour. Hence do we discern figure, *viz.* the ray of every Atom of the object representing the site of its Atom. For figure is nothing else but the order or disposition of those Atoms : Thus have we all figures, colours, and shapes in a whole Horison conveighed to our sight by a centrall Touch of those rayes of the objects round about us.

STANZ. 49. *But Haphes Mother hight all-spread community.*

As is plain in the communication of rayes. For I cannot think that union simply with this sensible world, of it self can make us know things at distance, though *Plotinus* seem inclinable to that Opinion. See *Psychathan., lib.* 3, *Cant.* 1.

STANZ. 55. *All Sense doth in proportion consist.*

Some things are so light that the weight is indiscernable to some, as the Flie that sat upon the Bulls horns and apologized for her self, as having wearied him, as it is in the *Arabian* fable, some smells too weak to strike the nostrills of others, and some objects too obscure to be seen of the eyes of othersome. But *Arachne* is proportioned to all whatsoever is any way sensible to any ; because *Psyche* doth inact this All or Universe as a particular Soul doth the body.

Vers. 9. *All life of Sense is in great Haphes list.*

It must needs be so. For no living soul is sensible of ought in this out-World, but by being joyned in a living manner to it. Therefore *Psyche* being joyned to it all, must needs perceive all forms and motions in it, that are presented to any particular soul. For these representations be made in some particular body, which is but a part of the whole, a knot as it were of *Psyches* outward stole, but the universall body of the World, is one undivided peece, wherefore nor Owl, nor Bat, nor Cat, nor any thing else can possibly see, but *Psyche* seeth *ipso facto*, for 'tis part of her body that hath those representations in it ; wherefore man is transfixt through and through by the rayes of the divine Light, besides that more incomprehensible way of omnisciency in God.

STANZ. 5, 6. *Sense and Consent, &c.*

As *Psyche* sees all natural things, so she doth allow of them. For contrariety of Spirits is onely betwixt particulars, and uglinesse, and ill-favourednesse are but such to some kinds, nor is poyson poyson to all, else would the Spider be her own death, and all venomous monsters would save man the labour of encounter.

STANZ. 57. *Rich Semele display,*

Till we come to *Psyches* self, motion and mutabilitie have place ; But in *Æon* and *Ahad* is steddy and unalterable rest, τὰ ὡσαύτως ἔχοντα. And there hath *Psyche* the one eye plac'd as well as the other below, beholding all things, and that which is above all things, as also the shadows and projections of all things without distraction, at once, as easily as our eyes discern many colours at once in one thing.

STANZ. 59. *The mother of each Semele.*

How she is the mother of them, see the second Canto of this book at the 23. Stanz.

Vers. 3. *But she grasps all.*

The Mundane spirit (of which every body hath its part) inacted by *Psyche*, if any particular soul exert any imaginative act, needs must for a time at least be coloured as it were or stained with that impression, so that *Psyche* must needs perceive it, sith it affects her own

spirit. See *Psychath. lib.* 3. *Cant.* 2. *Stanz.* 46, 47. Besides this, euery particular soul as all things else depending so intimately on *Psyche* as being effluxes from her, it is inconceivable that the least motions of the mind, or stillest thought should escape her.

But if any man be puzled how the phantasie of a mans soul should make an impression upon any part of the universall spirit of the world, and *Semele* should not, let him consider, that the imaginative operations of *Psyche* are more high, more hovering and suspense from immersion into the grosser spirits of this body, which is little or nothing conscious of whats done so farre above, and so not receiving the impresse of so high acts, it ordinarily happens (even in the exaltation of our own phansie) that memory fails. And besides this, as the vigour of sense debilitates or quite extinguisheth the ordinary iminaginations of the soul, so doth her ordinary imaginations, or sense, or both, hinder the animadversion of the impresses of *Semele*. But particular imaginations and the vigour of sense weakened or extinct in sleep, or near death, the energies of the soul of the world are then more perceptible, probably, even in the very spirit of our body, as well as in the naked soul : hence come prophetick dreams and true predictions before death.

But to go back to the apprehensions of *Psyche*. Every sensible object and every sensitive and imaginative act appear before her, and whatsoever is in her sight, is also in the sight of *Æon*. Because the union betwixt *Æon* and *Psyche* is much more near then between *Psyche* and the Mundane spirit. And whatsoever is represented in *Æon* is also clearly in the view of *Ahad ;* by reason of the unexpresseable close unity of these two ; so that *Ahad* knowes every individuall thing and motion, as clearly, nay more clearly then any mortall eye can view any one thing, let it look never so steddily on it.

Thus the thoughts of all mens minds and motions of heart arise up into the sight and presence of the all-comprehending Divinity, as necessarily and naturally as reek or fume of frankincense rouls up into the open air. For the spirit of the Lord fills all the world, and that which conteineth all things hath knowledge of the voyce, yea of the outward shape, gestures, and thoughts too. *Wisd.* 1. 7.

Nor is *Eternity* changed or obscured by the projection of these low shadows. For infinite animadversion can discern all things unmixtly and undisturbedly, not at all loosing it self, though gaining nothing by the sight of inferiour things. Nor can I assent to that passage in *Plotin.* taken in one sense, nor is it (I think) necessary to take it in that sense, the words are these, "Ὅτι δ' ἡ τοιαύτη νεῦσις αὐτοῦ πρὸς αὐτὸν, οἷον ἐνέργεια οὖσα αὐτοῦ καὶ μονὴ ἐν αὐτῷ τὸ εἶναι ὅ ἐστι ποιεῖ, μαρτυρεῖ ὑποτεθὲν τοὐναντίον, ὅτι εἰ πρὸς τὸ ἔξω νεύσειεν αὐτοῦ, ἀπολεῖ τὸ εἶναι ὅπερ ἐστίν, that is, But that such a kind of inclining himself to himself, being as it were his energie and abode in himself, makes him to be what he is, the contrary supposed doth argue. For if he should incline to that which is without him, he would lose that being which he is. But this is to be considered, that God being infinitely infinite, without stooping or inclining, can produce all things, and view alwayes his work, keeping his own seat that is himself: for so saith the Philosopher in another place, Καὶ ἐστὶ πρώτη ἐνέργεια ἐκείνου καὶ πρώτη οὐσία, ἐκείνου μένοντος ἐν ἑαυτῷ, that is, That *Intellect* or *On*, or the Intellectuall world, is the first energie of God, is the first substance from him, he abiding in himself. See *Plotin. Ennead.* 6. *lib.* 8. *cap.* 16. also *Ennead.* 1. *lib.* 8. *c.* 2.

But now to take a short view of what I have runne through in my notes on this Canto. *Ahad*, *Æon*, *Psyche*, the Platonick Triad, is rather the τὸ θεῖον then θεὸς, the Divinity rather then the Deity. For God is but one indivisible unmovable self-born Unity, and his first-born creature is Wisdome, Intellect, *Æon*, *On*, or *Autocalon*, or in a word, the Intellectuall world, whose measure himself is, that is simple and perfect Goodnesse. Τὸ δὲ ἐστιν ἀνενδεὲς, ἱκανὸν ἑαυτῷ, μηδενὸς δεόμενον, μέτρον πάντων καὶ πέρας, δοὺς ἐξ αὐτοῦ νοῦν καὶ οὐσίαν καὶ ψυχήν. That is, For he is without need, self-sufficient, wanting nothing, the measure and term of all things, yielding out of himself Intellect or *On*, and *Psyche*.

And speaking of Intellect, Ἐνεργεῖ μέντοι περὶ ἐκεῖνον, οἷον περὶ ἐκεῖνον ζῶν. That intellect is taken up about him, imployed in a kind of vitall operation about him, living in him.

But of *Psyche*, Ἡ δὲ ἔξωθεν περὶ τοῦτον χορεύσασα ψυχή, περὶ αὐτὸν βλέπουσα καὶ εἴσω αὐτοῦ θεωμένη, τὸν θεὸν δι' αὐτοῦ βλέπει. But *Psyche* something removed and without, danceth about the Intellect, busily beholding it, and looking into it, seeth God through it. So that *Ahad* is the vitall perfection of *Æon* or *Intellect*, and *Æon* and *Ahad* the happinesse of *Psyche* and her vitall accomplishment. *Ennead.* 1. *lib.* 8. And both *Æon* and *Psyche*, and all things else are from *Ahad*, καθ' ὑποστολήν, that is with abatement, and farthest off from the fountain the weaker and darker, as is more fully set forth in the next Canto. Stanz. 7, 8. &c.

And that the world is inacted by *Psyche*, and so is (which *Trismegist* and *Plato* are not nice to grant) one intire Animal, and that therefore nothing can scape the knowledge of that universall soul, no more then any sensation, imagination, or motion of man can be hid from the soul of man, if she be at leasure to observe it. That *Psyche* is at leasure being uncapable of distraction, as whose animadversion is infinite, entirely omnipresent, and every where at once.

And now I have taken the pains so accurately to describe the Deity, me thinks, I have made myself obnoxious to almost a just censure of too much boldnesse and curiosity.

But give me leave to answer, that I have not taken upon me so much to set out the absolute nature of God, as those Notions that *Plato's* School have framed of Him, Which I hold neither my self nor any man else engaged to embrace for Oracles, though they were true, till such time as they appear to him to be so. But how ever, I think all men are to interpret both *Plato* and all

men else at the best, and rather mark what of undoubted truth they aime at, then quarrell and entangle themselves in disputes about the manner of expressing that which no man can reach unto. As for example, I had rather fill my mind with that unquestionable truth exhibited in their Triad, *viz.* that God is as fully Goodnesse, Wisedome, and powerfull Love, as if there were three such distinct Hypostases in the Deity, and then that he is as surely one with himself as if there were but one onely Hypostasis, then to perplex my mind with troublesome questions of Three and One, and One and three, &c.

For the mind of man being so unable to conceive any thing of the naked being of God, those more grosse and figurate representations of Him, so be they be sutable to & expressive of His unquestionable Attributes, are not onely passable but convenient for created understandings, to lead them on in the contemplation of God in easie Love and Triumph. Whereas by endeavouring more Magisterially and determinately to comprehend and conclude that which is so unconcludible and incomprehensible to the understanding of man, we work our selves into anxietie and subtile distemper and dry up the more precious outflowings of the Divinity in our souls, by this hellish thirst and importunate desire of dealing with the very naked essence of God. But let every modest Philosopher but read that Inscription in *Isis* Temple, a notable monument of the great wisedome of the Ancients: Ἐγὼ εἰμι πᾶν τὸ γεγονὸς, καὶ ὂν καὶ ἐσόμενον, καὶ τὸν ἐμὸν πέπλον οὐδείς πω θνητὸς ἀπεκάλυψεν, and then pronounce whether there be not roome enough in the Deity for every man to speak diversely one from another, in the representation thereof, and yet no man nor all men together to set out accurately and adequately the nature of God.

CANTO II.

STANZ. 6. *Its he that made us.*

Et not excluding *Ahad*. See what's written upon the 23. Stanza of this Canto.

STANZ. 9. *The last extreme, the fardest of from light*

Plotinus Ennead. 4. *lib.* 3. *cap.* 9 : describes the production of the corporeall world after this manner, *Psyche* cannot issue out into any externall vivificative act, unlesse you suppose a body, for thats her place properly, and naturally. Wherefore if she will have place for and vitall act, she must produce her self a body. So she keeping steddily her own station, οἷον πολὺ φῶς ἐκλάμψαν ἐπ' ἄκροις τοῖς ἐσχάτοις τοῦ πύρος, σκότος ἐγένετο, or rather ἐγείνατο, like a plentifull flame shining out in the extreme margins of the fire begot a fuliginous darknesse : which she seeing streightway actuated with life and form, γενόμενος δὲ οἷον οἰκός τις καλὸς καὶ ποικίλος οὐκ ἀπετμήθη τοῦ πεποιηκότος, so that darknesse becoming a variously adorned ædifice is not disjoyned from its builder, but dependeth thence as being the genuine and true energie of the soul of the World. This I conceive is the sense of the Philosopher, whose conceit I have improved and made use of, as here in this Canto for many Stanzas together, so also else where in *Psychathanasia.*

Vers. 2. Hyles *cell.*

What I understand by *Hyle,* see the *Interpret. Gen.* It's lower then this shadow that *Plotinus* speaketh of, and which maketh the body of the World. For I conceive the body of the World to be nothing else but the reall Cuspis of the Cone even infinitely multiplied and reiterated. *Hyle* to be nothing else but potentiality: that to be an actuall Centrality, though as low as next to nothing. But what inconvenience is in *Tasis,* or the corporeall sensible nature, to spring from *Hyle,* or the scant capacity, or incompossibility of the creature.

STANZ. 10. *Dependance of this All hence doth*
appear. (to the 17. Stanza.

The production of the World being by way of energy, or emanation, hath drawn strange expressions from some of the Ancients, as *Trismeg. cap.* 11. *Mens ad Mercur.* Αὐτουργὸς γὰρ ὢν, ἀεί ἐστιν ἐν τῷ ἔργῳ, αὐτὸς ὢν ὃ ποιεῖ, that is, For God being the sole Artificer, is alwayes in his work, being indeed that which he maketh. According to this tenour is that also in *Orpheus.*

Ζεὺς πρῶτος γένετο, Ζεὺς ὕστατος, ἀρχικέραυνος
Ζεὺς κεφαλὴ, Ζεὺς μέσσα, Διὸς δ' ἐκ πάντα τέτυκται
Ζεὺς πυθμὴν γαίης τε καὶ οὐρανοῦ ἀστερόεντος.
Ζεὺς ἄρσην γένετο, Ζεὺς ἄμβροτος ἔπλετο νύμφη.
Ζεὺς πνοιὴ πάντων, Ζεὺς ἀκαμάτου πυρὸς ὁρμή.
Ζεὺς πόντου ῥίζα, Ζεὺς ἥλιος ἠδὲ σελήνη.
Ζεὺς βασιλεὺς, Ζεὺς ἀρχὸς ἁπάντων ἀρχικέραυνος.
Πάντας γὰρ κρύψας, αὖθις φάος ἐς πολυγηθὲς
Ἐξ ἱερῆς κραδίης ἀνενέγκατο, μέρμερα ῥέζων.

That is,

Jov's first, Jov's last, drad Thunderer on high.
Jov's head, Jov's navell, Out of Jove all's made.
Jov's the depth of the Earth, and starry Skie.
Jove is a man, Jov's an immortall Maide.
Jove is the breath of all, Jove's restlesse fire,
Jov's the Seas root, Jove is both Sun and Moon,
Jov's King, Jov's Prince of all and awfull Sire:
For having all hid in himself, anon
He from his sacred heart them out doth bring
To chearfull light, working each wondrous thing.
Aristot. De Mundo, cap. 7.

And this Hyperbolicall expression of the close dependance that all things have on God, is not mis-beseeming Poetry. But *Trismeg.* is as punctuall in this excesse as the Poet, *Ad Tat. cap.* 5. Διὰ τί δὲ ὑμνήσω σε; ὡς ἐμαυτοῦ ὤν; ὡς ἔχων τι ἴδιον; ὡς ἄλλος ὤν; σὺ γὰρ εἶ ὃ ἐὰν ὦ, σὺ εἶ ὃ ἐὰν λέγω, σὺ γὰρ πάντα εἶ, τὸ ἄλλο οὐδέν ἐστιν ὃ σοῦ μή ἐστι σὺ εἶ πᾶν τὸ γενόμενον, σὺ τὸ μοῦ γενόμενον, νοῦς μὲν νοούμενος, πατὴρ δὲ δημιουργῶν, θεὸς δὲ ἐνεργῶν, ἀγαθὸς δὲ καὶ πάντα ποιῶν· ὕλης μὲν

γὰρ τὸ λεπτομερέστατον ἀήρ, ἀέρος δὲ ψυχή, ψυχῆς δὲ νοῦς, νοῦ δὲ ὁ θεός.

Hence is the strange opinion of God being all, and that there is nothing but God. But it is not at all strange that all things are the mere energie of God, and do as purely depend on him, as the Sun-beams of the Sunne. So that so farre forth as we may say the body, *lux & lumen* of the Sunne, all put together is the Sunne; so farre at least we may be bold to say that God is all things, and that there is nothing but God. And that all this may not seem to be said for nothing, the apprehension of what hath been writ on this 1. verse of the 10 Stanza will also clear well the 6, 7, and 8 verses of the 15 Stanza, where the whole *Universe* is exhibited to the mind as one vitall Orb, whose centre is God himself, or *Ahad.*

Vers. the 9. *In every Atom-ball.*

That is, *Ahad* and *Æon* are in every Cuspiall particle of the world.

STANZ. 12. *Why may'st not,* &c.

By differentiall profundity is understood the different kinds of things descending καθ' ὑποστολὴν or abatement from the first cause of all things. But by latitude is understood the multitude of each kind in *Individuo,* which whether they be not infinite in spirituall beings where there is no ἀντιτυπία or justling for elbow-room I know not, unlesse you will say there will be then more infinites then one. But those are numbers, and not one. I but those numbers put together are equall to that One. But yet that One may be infinitely better then all: For who will not say that Space or Vacuum is infinitely worse, then any reall thing, and yet its extension is infinite, as *Lucretius* stoutly proves in his first Book, *De natura rerum.*

STANZ. 15. *Throughly possest of lifes community.*

That the World or Universe is indewed with life, though it be denied of some, who prove themselves men more by their risibility, then by their reason, yet very worthy and sober Philosophers have asserted it. As *M. Anton.* τῶν εἰς ἑαυτὸν, *lib.* 10. where he calls this Universe τὸ τέλειον ζῶον, τὸ ἀγαθὸν, τὸ δίκαιον, καὶ καλὸν, a compleat Animal, good, just, and beautifull. And *Trismeg. cap.* 12. *de Commun. Intellectu. ad Tat.* Ὁ δὲ σύμπας κόσμος οὗτος ὁ μέγας θεὸς καὶ τοῦ μείζονος εἰκὼν, καὶ ἡνωμένος ἐκείνῳ καὶ συσσώζων τὴν τάξιν καὶ βούλησιν τοῦ πατρὸς, πλήρωμά ἐστι τῆς ζωῆς, &c. This Universe a great Deity (which I conceive he speaks in reference to *Psyche,* upon whom such divine excellency is derived) and the image of a greater, united also to him, and keeping the will and ordinances of his Father, is one entire fullnesse of life. νεκρὸν γὰρ οὐδὲ ἐν οὔτε γέγονεν, οὔτε ἐστὶν, οὔτε ἔσται, ἐν τῷ κόσμῳ. For there neither was, nor is, nor shall be any thing in the World devoid of life. And *Plotin. Ennead.* 4. *lib.* 3. *cap.* 10. shews how *Psyche* by her vitall power, full of form and vigour, shapes, and adorns, and actuates the World, οἷα καὶ οἱ ἐν σπέρματι λόγοι πλάττουσι καὶ μορφοῦσι τὰ ζῶα οἷον μικροὺς τινας κόσμους, as the seminall forms or Archei form and shape out particular Animals, as so many little Worlds.

Vers. 9. *And all the Vests be Seats,* &c. i.e. *Degrees.*

STANZ. 16. *That particular creature throng.*

In contradistinction to the Universall creature *Æon, Psyche, Physis, Tasis,* the centre as it were, and more firm essence of the particular creatures. For I must call these universall Orders of life, creatures too, as well as those, and onely one God, from whence is both the sensible and Intellectuall All, and every particular in them both, or from them both.

STANZ. 23. *Each life a severall ray is from that Sphere,*
Arachne, Semel, &c.

Not as if there were so many souls joyned together, and made one soul, but there is a participation of the virtue at least of all the life that is in the universall Orb of life, at the Creation of Mans soul, of which this place is meant, whence man may well be tearmed a Microcosme, or Compendium of the whole World.

STANZ. 24. *Great Psychany.*

The abode of the body is this Earth, but the habitation of the soul her own energy, which is exceeding vast, at least in some. Every man hath a proper World, or particular Horizon to himself, enlarged or contracted according to the capacity of his mind. But even Sence can reach the starres; what then can exalted phansie do, or boundlesse Intellect? But if starres be all inhabited, which Writers no way contemptible do assert, how vast their habitation is, is obvious to any phansie. Beside some inhabit God himself, who is unspeakably infinite.

STANZ. 25. *Two mighty Kingdomes,* &c.

Let *Psychanie* be as big or little as it will, *Autæsthesia,* and *Theoprepia,* be the main parts of it, and exhaust the whole. Let souls be in the body or out of the body, or where they will, if they be but alive, they are alive to God, or themselves, and so are either *Theoprepians,* or *Autæsthesians.*

Vers. 4. *Autæsthesie's divided into tway.*

Now they that are alive unto themselves, are either wholly alive unto themselves, or the life of God hath also taken hold upon them; they that are wholly alive to themselves, their abode is named *Adamah,* which signifieth the corrupt naturall life, the old *Adam,* or *Beirah,* because this *Adam* is but a brute, compared to that which *Plotinus* calleth the true Man, whose form, and shape, and life, is wisdome, and righteousnesse: That which is above, is, saith he, ὁ ἄνθρωπος ὁ ἀληθὴς σχεδὸν, ἐκεῖνα δὲ· τὸ λεοντῶδες καὶ τὸ ποικίλον ὅλως θηρίαν. but that low life in the body is but a Leonine or rather a mixture of all brutish lives together, and is the seat or sink of wickednesse. Ἡ γὰρ κακία, σύμφυτος τοῖς θηρίοις, as *Trismegist.* speaks. For vice is congenit or connaturall to beasts. See *Plotin. Ennead.* 1. *cap.* 1. whence it is manifest why we call one thing by these two names of *Adamah,* and *Beirah.* · · ..

The other part of *Autæsthesia* is *Dizoia,* their condition is as this present Stanza declares, mungrill, betwixt Man and Beast, Light and Darknesse, God and the Devill, *Jacob* and *Esau* struggle in them.

STANZ. 26. *Great* Michael *ruleth,* &c.

Theoprepia, is a condition of the soul, whereby she doth that which would become God himself to do in the like cases, whether in the body, or out of the body. *Michael* ruleth here, that is, the Image or likenesse of God, the true Man, the Lord from Heaven. For the true man indeed, *viz.* the second *Adam,* is nothing else but the Image of the God of Heaven. This is He of whom the soul will say when He cometh to abide in her, and when He is known of her כאל מי who is like unto God, for either beautie, or power? who so comely or strong as He?

Vers. 5. *His name is* Dæmon.

Dæmon the Prince of *Autæsthesie,* i.e. of self-sensednesse, it is the very image of the Devil, or the Devil himself, or worse if ought can be worse: it is a life dictating self-seeking, and bottoming a mans self upon himself, a will divided from the will of God, and centred in its self.

Vers. 7. *From his dividing force,* &c.

All divisions both betwixt God and Man, and Man and Man, are from this self-seeking life.

STANZ. 28. *Autophilus the one ycleeped is.*

Autophilus, is the souls more subtill and close embracements of her self in spirituall arrogancy, as *Philosomatus,* the love of her body; wherefore the one ruleth most in *Dizoia,* the other in *Beirah.*

Vers. 8. *Born of the slime of* Autæsthesia.

Dæmon, that is, the authour of division of man from God, born of self-sensednesse. See *Plotin. Ennead.* 5. *lib.* 1. *cap.* 1. where he saith, the first cause of evil to the soul was, τὸ βουληθῆναι ἑαυτῶν εἶναι, that they would be their own or of themselves. So delighted with this liberty, they were more and more estranged, till at last like children taken away young from their parents, they in processe of time grew ignorant both of themselves and of their parents.

STANZ. 29. *Duessa first invented Magick lore.*

Duessa is the naturall life of the body, or the naturall spirit, that, whereby we are lyable to Magick assaults, which are but the sympathies and antipathies of nature, such as are in the spirit of the world, Ἡ γὰρ ἀληθινὴ μαγεία ἡ ἐν τῷ παντὶ φιλία καὶ νεῖκος αὖ, καὶ ὁ γόης πρῶτος καὶ ὁ φαρμακεὺς οὗτός ἐστι. The true Magick (saith he) is nothing else but the concord and discord in the Universe, and he, *viz.* the world, is the first Magician and Enchanter, others do but learn of him by imitation: wherefore they that are established in a principle above the world, and are strong in God, which are the true and perfect Israel, are exempt from the danger of this Enchantment, οὐδεὶς γὰρ οὐδὲν δύναται οὔτε δαιμόνων οὔτε θεῶν πρὸς μίαν ἀκτῖνα τοῦ θεοῦ. For neither Astrall spirit nor Angel can prevail against one ray of the Deity ; as *Æsculapius* writes to King *Ammon.* *Plotinus* soul was come to that high and noble temper, that he did not onely keep off Magicall assaults from himself, but retorted them upon his enemy *Olympius*, which *Olympius* himself, who practised against him, did confesse to be from the exalted power of his soul, *Porphyr. de Vita Plot.*

STANZ. 30.   *Ten times ten times ten.*

The number of ten among the ancients called παντέλεια, is an emblem of perfection : for it comprehends all numbers, sith we are fain to come back again to one, two, &c. when we are past it.   So that ten may go for perfection of parts in the holy life : but the raising of it into a cube by multiplication, perfection of degrees in a solid, and unshaken manner.

STANZ. 33.   *Amoritish ground.*

'Αμορραῖοι *Philo* interprets λαλοῦντες and it is indeed from דִּבֵּר *dixit*, the Land of talkers.

STANZ. 34.   *Psittacusa land, id est*, the land of talkers or Parots.   See *Don Psittaco, Interpret. Gen.*

STANZ. 65.   *Ther's no Society*, &c.

This Stanza briefly sets out the *Beironites* condition as concerning their Society and friendship, the bond whereof and exercise, is either feasting and tippling ; or a complacency in the well-favourednesse of this mortall body, or some astrall concordance or hidden harmony of spirits, which also often knits in wedlock those that are farre enough from beauty.

Vers. 2.   *But beastlike grazing*, &c.

Aristotle defines very well and like a Philosopher the genuine society that should be among men, *viz.* in the communication of reason and discourse.   οὕτω γὰρ ἂν δόξειεν τὸ σνζῆν λέγεσθαι ἐπὶ τῶν ἀνθρώπων, καὶ οὐκ ὥσπερ ἐπὶ τῶν βοσκημάτων τὸ ἐν τῷ αὐτῷ νέμεσθαι. For that in men is right society, and not as in beasts, to graze in the same pasture.   *Moral, Nicom. lib.* 9. *cap.* 8.

How unlike to these *Beironites* was the divine communialty of *Pythagoras* followers (as *Iamblicus* describes it, *de vita Pythag. lib.* 1. *cap.* 33.) not onely supplying friendly one another in the necessities of life, but mutually cherishing in one another the divine life of the soul, and maintaining an inviolable concord in the best things.   Παρήγγελον γὰρ θάμα ἀλλήλους μὴ διασπᾶν τὸν ἐν ἑαυτοῖς θεόν.   Οὐκοῦν εἰς θεοκρασίαν τινὰ, καὶ τὴν πρὸς θεὸν ἕνωσιν καὶ τὴν τοῦ νοῦ κοινωνίαν καὶ τὴν τῆς θείας ψυχῆς, ἀπέβλεπεν αὐτοῖς ἡ πᾶσα τῆς φιλίας σπουδὴ δ' ἔργων τε καὶ λόγων.   For they often admonished one another not to dissipate the Deity in them : Wherefore their friendship wholly in words and works seemed to aim at a kind of commixtion and union with God, and communion with the divine Intellect and Soul.

STANZ. 136.   *The swelling hatefull toad.*

This Stanza sets out the nature of each *Beironite* singly considered by himself, which is referable to some bird or beast, who are sometime lightly shadowed out even in their very countenances.

STANZ. 137.   *None in Beiron virtuously do live.*

True virtue I make account is founded in true knowledge of God, in obedience and self-deniall, without which, those seeming virtuous dispositions, are but mock-virtues, no other then are found in some measure among the brutes.

Vers. 9.   *If outward form you pierce.*

For as *Cicero* from *Plato*, saith, *Mens cujusque is est quisque*, The soul is the man, not the outward shape. If she live therefore but the life of a Brute, if her vitall operation, her vigorous will, and complacency be that which a Beast likes, I cannot see that she is any more then a living Brute, or a dead Man, or a Beast clad in mans cloths.   See the 48 Stanza of this Canto.

STANZ. 138, 139.   From the 34. Stanza to the 138 are the Religion, Polity, Freindship, or familiar Society and single natures of the *Beironites* set out.   Here now begins the discovery of the way of escape from this bruitish condition, which is by obedience.   Now obedience consists in these two : Self-deniall (*Autaparnes*), and Patience (*Hypomone*).   Obedience discovers to us the doore of passage out of this pure brutality, *viz.* Humility.   For it is self-conceit and high presumption that we are all well, and wise already, that keeps us in this base condition.

STANZ. 144.   *The young mans speech caus'd sad perplexity*, etc.

That a man in *confuso*, or in generall, is more easily drawn to entertain obedience, but when it is more punctually discovered to him in self-denyall and patience, it is nothing so welcome.

STANZ. 146.   For understanding of this Stanza, see *Autaparnes* in the *Interpr. Gen.* as also in the 64, 65, 66, 67. Stanzas of the third Canto of this book.

STANZ. 147.   *Into Atuvus life doth melt.*

Ice, so long as it is, is a thing distinct, suppose, from the Ocean, but once melt by the warmth of the Sunne it becomes one with the rest of the sea, so that no man can say, at least, not perceive it is different from the sea.   This state of union with God *Plotinus* (as all things else) describes excellently well.   Τότε μὲν οὖν οὔτε ὁρᾷ, οὔτε διακρίνει ὁρῶν οὔτε φαντάζεται ὄψω, ἀλλ' οἷον ἄλλος γενόμενος καὶ οὐκ αὐτὸς, οὐθ' ἑαυτοῦ συντελεῖ ἐκεῖ, κακείνου γενόμενος, ἕν ἐστιν, ὥσπερ κέντρον κέντρῳ συνάψας.   Wherefore then the mind neither sees, nor seeing discerns, nor phansies too, but as it were become another, not her self nor her own, is there, and becoming His is one with Him, as it were joyning centre with centre.   *Ennead.* 6. *lib.* 9. *cap.* 10.   And that this may not seem a *Chimara*, I will annex what the noble Philosopher writes of his own experience, *Ennead.* 4. *lib.* 8. *cap.* 1.   Πολλάκις ἐγειρόμενος εἰς ἐμαυτὸν ἐκ τοῦ σώματος καὶ γενόμενος τῶν μὲν ἄλλων ἔξω, ἐμαυτοῦ δὲ εἴσω, θαυμαστὸν ἡλίκον ὁρῶν κάλλος, etc.   I often awaking out of the body into my self, and being without all things but within my self, do then behold an admirable beauty, and become confident of my better condition, having then so excellent a life, and being made one with the Deity: in which I being placed do set my self above all other Intellectuall beings. But after this my station and rest in God, descending out of Intellect into reason, I am perplext to think both how I now descend, and how at first my soul entred this body, she being such as she appeared to be by her self, although being in the body. Such an union as this that *Plotinus* professeth himself to have been acquainted with, though it be the thing chiefly aimed at in this Stanza, yet I do not confine my *Theoprepia* to it ; nor think I the soul of man disjoyned from God, that is not in that sort united to him. But if a man have lost his self-will, and self-love, being wholly dead to himself, and alive to God, though that life exert it self in successive acts, if a man I say, be but affected as God himself, if he were in the flesh, would be affected, he is also truly and really in *Theoprepia.*

CANTO III.

STANZA I. *Shafts which Uriel,* vers. 5. and vers. 7. *No other help we had for Gabriel.*

Riel, אוריאל *ignis Dei, Angelus Meridionalis,* He that rules in the power of the Meridian Sunne. *Quatuor Angeli præsidentes cardinibus Cæli, Michael, Raphael, Gabriel, Uriel.* For *Gabriel* in this place bears onely a naturall notion, elsewhere it is the strength of the Lord revealed in the soul. But as for those terms it was rather chance then choice that cast me upon them ; being nothing solicitous whether there be any such Presidents or no. I conceive they be some old Rabbinical inventions or traditions, by the grosse mistake in them.

For when as they assign to *Michael* the East, and the West to *Raphael,* they seem never to have dreamed of any East or West but what belonged to their own Horizon, when as, where ever East is, West is also to some Inhabitants, so that both these Angels will have the same province, *Cornel. Agrip. de Occult. Philos. lib.* 2. *cap.* 7.

STANZ. 3, 4, 5.

The first estate of man, when he begins to make conscience of the law of God, which I call *Diana,* which is the Moon, as not affording life and vigour though some small light. Small I deem it in comparison of the daystarre, the Sunne of righteousnesse himself. This estate is set out in these 4 Stanzas.

STANZ. 6, 7, 8, 9.

The penitent, perplext, and passionate estate of one that hath the true sight and sense of his sinne, and corruption, but is not rid of them.

STANZ. 10. *Me thought the Sunne it self,* etc.

The condition of him whose spirits indeed are unpurged, though the fire hath got hold on them, and burns, and glows, as in fowl rubbish. This estate is set

out by the appearance of the sunne from *Ida* hill, the description whereof follows in the next Stanz.

STANZ. 11. *But Phœbus form,* &c.

A sad image of bitter zeal and præcipitant wrath against all those that are not in the same sad condition with our selves, that is, that are either better or worse in life, and different in opinion.

Vers. 8. *Small things they will prize,* &c.

Such men scarce got into the spirit of Elias ; yet esteem their temper above the meeknesse of Christs own spirit, because they never yet had experience of it.

STANZ. 18. *All sects besides his own doth execrate.*

This was the disease of the Gnosticks in *Plotinus* time, who contemned all beside their own sect, to whom the incomparable Philosopher, gravely and more like a Christian, then those that call themselves by that name, writes to this sense, That if they were so much better then all the world, they ought to be so much the more mild and modest, and not so full of ferocity and rudenesse, and to think that there may be room with God for others also. Τοῖς δὲ ἄλλοις νομίζειν εἶναι χώραν παρὰ τῷ θεῷ καὶ μὴ αὐτοὺς μόνους μετ᾽ ἐκεῖνον τάξαντας ὥσπερ ὀνείροις πέτεσθαι. And not in placing themselves onely next to God, to sore as it were in a dream, to flie in their sleep.

STANZ. 35. *Whom with cruel spear.*

The difficulty here is how the eternall Sonne of God may suffer, he being everlasting and immortall life it self, and not contradict what was written, *Canto.* 1. *Stanz.* 9. 14, 35, 36, 37. For to the impassible eternall being is the inheritance of the world there promised, but here to that which is possible and mortall. I answer, that the eternal and immortall sonne of God is to take possession of the world by that which after a manner is mortall and extinguishable, which is the energie of himself, exerted upon the souls of men, or a kind of life diffused in mans heart and soul, whereby God doth inact us, and is our ἐντελέχεια, as the soul is the ἐντελέχεια of the body and governs and guides it. And if Æon as he is the sonne of *Ahad* or *Atove* (to speak Platonically) that is, the simple and free good, or in brief as he is the sonne of God, who is the simple good without all self-nesse or straitnesse, even pure and perfect Light it self (for this Æon contains in him also the whole creature and is the essence or Idea of all things) I say if he as he is the sonne of God be in us by his imparted life, he then takes possession of the world, and God by him. But he hath not yet enquickened men generally with this Deiform life, but it hath lyen dead to them or they to it, that influx being rather suspended then absolutely destroyed, but as the soul to its body, or any part of her body that is numb and dead. But when that life shall flow into them, as the vitall rayes of the soul into this mortall body, He shall then as truly govern, rule, and possesse the world as any soul doth her body.

And that there is an eternall sonne of God, immortall impassible, and not onely in the souls of men, but that fills the whole universe, the Evangelist I think will confirm. For he ascribes the creation of all things to him, yea and calls him God, which makes me wonder that the Turks have so high an esteem of this Gospel of S. John, unlesse they will interpret, Καὶ θεὸς ἦν ὁ λόγος according to the same tenour that Καὶ ὁ λόγος σὰρξ ἐγένετο is to be interpreted, neither place then signifying, unity or identity, but union onely and conjunction.

But to prove the thing in hand (John the 1. vers. 10.) *He was in the world and the world was made by him, and the world knew him not.*

By world must be understood either the whole universe, or men inhabiting it, and they either the godly or the wicked.

If the Universe, he is then the eternall principle whereby God made the whole creation. If the godly onely (as he may be said in some more speciall manner to be their maker) how came they not to know him, when he was in them and alive in them ; τὸ ὅμοιον γὰρ τῷ ὁμοίῳ γινώσκεται. If the wicked onely, he made them not wicked, so that if he made them at all, he made their naturall being, soul and body, and if them why not all the world ? whence a man may reasonably conclude, that the λόγος, that is the Word is eternall and immortall, and invulnerable. And if any Authority will now be worth looking after (*S. Johns* testimony being so plain) *Philo* the Jew speaks out to this purpose, Δῆλον δὲ ὅτι καὶ ἡ ἀρχέτυπος σφραγὶς, ἣν φαμεν εἶναι κόσμον νοητὸν, αὐτὸς ἂν εἴη τὸ ἀρχετυπον παράδειγμα, ἰδέα τῶν ἰδεῶν, ὁ θεοῦ λόγος. Περὶ κοσμοπ. p. 3. It is manifest that the Archetypal seal, which we call the intellectuall world, is the very word of God, the Archetypall Paradigme, the Idea of Ideas, or Form of Forms. And in his περὶ γεωργίας He plainly ascribes the government of the Universe, Heavens, Starres, Earth, Elements, and all the creatures in them, to that which he tearms τὸν ὀρθὸν θεοῦ λόγον πρωτόγονον υἱον, that is, the upright word of God, his first-born son. Which is pure Platonisme, and may for ought I know go for right Christianisme, so long as the first chapter of S. John for Gospel.

> Vers. 2, 3,   *True crucified Sonne*
>   *Of the true God.*

For the life that is in him and should flow into us, is hindred in its vitall operation. But if any man make it a light matter that God himself or the Word himself is not hurt, let him consider that he that can find of his heart to destroy the deleble image of God, would, if it lay in his power, destroy God himself, so that the crime is as high and as much to be lamented.

STANZ. 38. *Earth-groveling Aptery.*

From *Beirons* wall to *Pantheothen* dwell the *Apterites*, that is, such as have souls without wings, or ψυχὰς πτεροῤῥυούσας, as the Platonick phrase is, souls that have their feathers moult off of them, and so are fain to flag among the dirty desires of the world, though sometime full of sorrow and vexation for their grosse vices, but yet in a kind of Hypocritical humility, acknowledging that to be their destin'd condition, and that it is worse then that condition, to believe that a man by the help of God may get out of it.

STANZ. 44, 45, 46. *Hight Pteroessa.*

The land betwixt *Pantheothen* and the valley of *Ain*, is *Pteroessa*, because the Inhabitants have wings whereby they raise themselves above the mire and dirt of the corrupt body. One of the wings is Faith in the power of God against the forces of the Prince of darknesse. The other Love and desire of appearing before God. See the 8. verse of 45. Stanza and the 5, 6, 7. verses of the 46. Stanza.

STANZ. 47. *And Gabriel sware, &c.*

Gabriel is the strength of God, which will certainly assist them that walk in the precepts of God with simplicity of heart.

STANZ. 49. *But I observed well, &c.*

And it is well worth our observation that the main danger of *Pteroessa* is the making too much haste, or a slubbering speed, promoving our selves into a greater liberty, or gaping after higher contemplations than we are fitted for, or we can reap profit from, or are rightly capable to conceive.

STANZ. 50. *And Autaparnes face, &c.*

See Interpr. Gen.

STANZ. 51. Vers. 9. *Back to retreat, &c.*

That is, to reassume that more punctuall and vigilant care over our wayes in thought, word, and deed, with a kind of austerenesse of life, crossing our own desires many times even in things indifferent, and to reattempt a perfect mortification of the old man throughout, giving no unseasonable liberty to our deceitfull body. For is it not Hypocrisy or partiality to avoid that our selves, which we often impose upon our young children, whom we oft abridge of things, that are not hurtfull of themselves, to break them off their stubborn wills ? And believe it ; a grown mans body is but a boy or brute, and must be kept under severely by the lash of reason and holy discipline.

STANZ. 57. *The Jasper, enemy to spirits won.*

This kind of stone the Caspian sea affords, as *Dionysius Afer* writes, who ascribes this virtue to it.

> Φύει μὲν κρύσταλλον ἰδ' ἡερόεσσαν Ἰασπιν
> Ἐχθρὴν ἐμπούσῃσι καὶ ἄλλοις εἰδώλοισιν.
> *It sends forth Crystall and the Jasper green*
> *Foe to Empusa's and all spectres seen.*

And this stone is none of the meanest jewels in the Platonick Diadem. Certainly the purging of our naturall spirits and raising our soul to her due hight of purity, weaning her from the love of this body, and too tender a sympathy with the frail flesh, begets that courage and Majesty of mind in a man, that both inward and outward fiends will tremble at his presence, and fly before him as darknesse at lights approch. For the soul hath then ascended her fiery vehicle, and it is noon to her at midnight, be she but awake into her self.

STANZ. 59. *Both love of man, &c.*

Those virtues there recited are refulgently conspicuous in Platonisme, Pythagorisme, and Stoicisme. Where's then the defect ? But I'll first set out their virtues, *Plo-*

tinus, Ennead. i. *lib.* 2. περὶ ἀρετῆς, raiseth virtue to her hight by these 4. degrees. The first are *Virtutes politicæ*, the second *Purgatoriæ*, the third *Animi jam purgati*, the fourth and last *Paradigmaticæ*.

Now for the better understanding of those degrees, we are to take notice of the first and second motions that be in us.

The first are such as surprise our body or living beast (as I may so call it) by some outward objects represented to sense and naturall imagination before reason hath consulted of them, or it may be phansie clearly apprehended them. Such are present frights and pleasant provocations.

The second consist in the pursuit or declining of these objects represented after the animadversion of our supernall phansie and consultation of reason. *Mars. Ficin.* upon *Plotin.*

Now those virtues that do onely amputate, prune, and more handsomely proportionate these second motions in us, are called Politicall, because a common citizen, or vulgar man ordinarily exerciseth this degree of virtue, perhaps for his credit, profit, or safety-sake.

But those virtues that do not onely prune but quite pluck up those second enormous motions of the mind are called Purgative.

Thirdly those that do both extirpate the second irregular motions, and also tame the first in some good measure, are the virtues of the soul already purged.

Fourthly and lastly, those virtues that put away quite and extinguish the first motions, are Paradigmaticall, that is, virtues that make us answer to the Paradigme or Idea of virtues exactly, *viz.*, the Intellect or God.

These foure degrees of virtues make so many degrees of men, if I may call them all men.

᾽Αρεταὶ	Πολιτικαὶ Καθαρτικαὶ Αἱ ἐν τῷ κεκαθάρθαι Παραδειγματικαὶ	῎Ανθρωπον. Θεάνθρωπον. Θεοδαίμονα. Θεὸν.
Virtues	*Politicall* *Purgative* *Animi jam purgati* *Paradigmaticall*	*Man.* *God-man.* *Angel-god.* *God.*

And this he doth plainly confesse, acknowledging that the motions or passions of the mind are not sins, if guided, directed and subjected to reason, ἀλλ᾽ ἡ σπουδὴ οὐκ ἔξω ἁμαρτίας εἶναι ἀλλὰ Θεὸν εἶναι. But our endeavour must be not onely to be without sin, but to become God, that is, impassible, immateriall, quit of all sympathy with the body, drawn up wholly into the intellect, and plainly devoid of all perturbation. And who would not be thus at ease? who would not crowd himself into this safe castle for his own security? I can not quite excuse the old man of self-love for that round elegancie Κρεῖττον δὲ τὸν παῖδα κακὸν εἶναι ἢ σὲ κακοδαίμονα. It doth not run so well in plain English. It is better thy sonne be wicked then thou miserable, that is, passionate, *Epictet, Enchirid. cap.* 16. Yet to speak the truth, Stoicisme, Platonisme, and Pythagorisme are gallant lights, and a

noble spirit moves in those Philosophers vains, and so near Christianisme, if a man will look on them favourably, that one would think they are baptized already not onely with water, but the holy Ghost. But I not seeing humility and self-denyall and acknowledgement of their own unworthinesse of such things as they aimed at, nor mortification, not of the body (for that's sufficiently insisted upon) but of the more spiritual arrogative life of the soul, that subtill ascribing that to our selves that is Gods, for all is Gods ; I say, I not seeing those things so frequently, and of purpose inculcated in their writings, thought I might fitly make their Philosophy, or rather the life that it doth point at (for that's the subject of this Poem) a Type of that life which is very near to perfection, but as yet imperfect, having still a smack of arrogation, and self-seeking. But believe it, a man shall often meet with frequent Testimonies of their charity and universall love, of meeknesse and tranquillity of mind, of common care of men, of hearty forgivenesse of offences. Temperance, Justice, and contempt of death, are obvious and triviall ; also their Prayer to God, and belief that he helps, both in finding out of Truth, and improvement of Virtue. So that I reserve as the true and adequate Character of Christianisme, the most profound and spirituall humility, that any man can have experience of, and a perfect self-deadnesse, which is the begetter indeed of the former. For where selfenesse is extinguished, all manner of arrogation must of necessity be extinct ; and this is the passage through the valley of *Ain.* So that it must be acknowledged, that though there have been many brave and generous lights risen upon the Earth, yet none so plainly perfect, so purely amiable and lovely, as that sweet life of the Messias, to whom the possession of the world is promised.

STANZ. 59. Vers. 7, 8, 9.
True fortitude that truest foes doth awe,
Justice and abstinence from sweetest ill,
And Wisedome like the Sunne doth all with light
ore-spill

This ravishing beauty and love, is lively set out by *Plotinus, lib.* 6. *cap.* 5. *Ennead.* 1. ᾽Εαυτοὺς δὲ ἰδόντες τὰ ἔνδον καλοὺς, τί πάσχετε ; καὶ πῶς ἀναβαχχεύεσθε καὶ ἀνακινεῖσθε, καὶ ἑαυτοῖς συνεῖναι ποθεῖτε συλλεξάμενοι ἀπὸ σωμάτων ; πάσχουσι μὲν γὰρ ταῦτα οἱ ὄντως ἐρωτικοί, ὅταν ἤ ἐν αὐτοῖς ἴδωσιν ἤ καὶ ἐν ἄλλῳ θεάσωνται μέγεθος ψυχῆς, καὶ ἦθος δίκαιον, καὶ σωφροσύνην καθαρὰν, καὶ ἀνδρίαν βλοσυρὸν ἔχουσαν πρόσωπον, καὶ σεμνότητα, καὶ αἰδὼ ἐπιθέουσαν ἐν ἀτρεμεῖ καὶ ἀκύμονι καὶ ἀπαθεῖ διαθέσει, ἐπὶ πᾶσι δὲ τούτοις τὸν θεοειδῆ νοῦν ἐπιλάμποντα. And when you behold your selves beautifull within, How are you affected? How are you moved and ravished? and gathering your selves from your bodies, desire more nearly and closely to embrace your naked selves? For thus are they affected that are truely amorous, when they either contemplate in themselves, or behold in others that gallantry and greatnesse of soul, that constant garb of Justice, pure and undefiled Temperance, manly, and awfull-eyed Fortitude, Gravity and Modesty gently mooving in all peaceable stillnesse and steddy Tranquillity and a god-like Understanding, watering and varnishing all these Virtues, as it were with golden showers of lustre and light.

STANZ. 63. *But Autaparnes wox more wan, and wo, &c. See Autaparn. Interpr. Gen.*

STANZ. 66. *This dale hight Ain, &c.*

This valley of *Ain* is nothing else but self deadnesse, or rather self-nothingnesse : wherefore the fume rising thence must needs be *Anautesthesie,* that is self-senslesnesse, no more feeling or relishing a mans self, as concerning himself, then if he were not at all.

STANZ. 67. *Here* Autaparnes, &c. See *Autaparn. Interpr. Gen.*

Notes upon *Psychathanasia.*

LIB. I. CANTO I.

STANZ. 10. *Like men new made contriv'd into a Cave.*

SEE *Jamblich, Protrept. cap.* 15.
STANZ. 12. Vers. 4. *Calling thin shaddows,* &c.

Πάντα τῷ ὀφθαλμῷ ὑποπίπτοντα εἴδωλά, ἐστι καὶ ὥσπερ σκιογραφίαι. *Merc. Trismeg.* 6.

STANZ. 16. *This Errors den.*

The condition of the soul in this life is so disadvantagious to her, that the Philosopher in the 3. Chapter of the 8. Book of his 4. *Ennead.* falleth into these expressions, ἦ καὶ δεσμὸς τὸ σῶμα καὶ τάφος, καὶ ὁ κόσμος αὐτῇ σπήλαιον καὶ ἄντρον. That the body is but a prison and sepulchre to the soul, and this World a Den and Cave.

Vers. 6. *As deep as Hyles Hell.*

The *Materia prima;* such as the schools ordinarily describe. Else where *Hyle* signifieth mere potentiality.

STANZ. 17. *That loves the body,* &c.

Ἑκάστη ἡδονὴ καὶ λύπη ὥσπερ ἧλον ἔχουσα προσηλοῖ τὴν ψυχὴν πρὸς τὸ σῶμα καὶ ποιεῖ σωματοειδῆ, δοξάζουσαν ταῦτα ἀληθῆ εἶναι ἅπερ ἂν καὶ τὸ σῶμα φῇ. Ἐκ γὰρ τοῦ ὁμοδοξεῖν τῷ σώματι καὶ τοῖς αὐτοῖς χαίρειν, ἀναγκάζεται, οἶμαι, ὁμότροπός τε καὶ ὁμότροφος γίγνεσθαι. *Jamblich. Protrept. cap.* 3. *pag.* 80. Also *Plat. Phæd.*

STANZ. 18. *Th' unthankefull Stagirite.*

There is notorious testimony of *Aristotles* pride, conceitednesse, and unthankfulnesse towards *Plato. Ælian. Var. Histor. lib.* 3. *cap.* 19. as also *lib.* 4. *cap.* 9. The Title of that Chapter is, Περὶ Πλάτωνος ἀτυφίας καὶ Ἀριστοτέλους ἀχαριστίας. Of *Plato's* humility, and *Aristotles* ingratitude.

Vers. 3. *Most men prefer 'fore holy* Pythagore.

See *Jamblich. De Vita Pythag.* where the purity and holinesse of his spirit is sufficiently evidenced from the Character of his manners, *cap.* 2. *pag.* 30. where it is

said that what ever he did or spake, he did it, εὐδίᾳ καὶ ἀμιμήτῳ τινὶ γαλήνῃ, μήτε ὀργῇ ποτὲ, μήτε γέλωτι, μήτε ζήλῳ, μήτε φιλονεικείᾳ, μήτε ἄλλῃ ταραχῇ ἢ προπετείᾳ ἁλισκόμενος, with inimitable serenity, and sedatenesse of mind, never surpriz'd with anger, laughter, zeal, contention, or any other precipitancy or perturbation.

STANZ. 21. *Love of the Carcas.*

Ἐὰν μὴ πρῶτον τὸ σῶμά σου μισήσῃς ὦ τέκνον, σεαυτὸν φιλῆσαι οὐ δύνασαι, φιλήσας δὲ σεαυτὸν, νοῦν ἕξεις, καὶ τὸν νοῦν ἔχων καὶ τῆς ἐπιστήμης μεταλήψῃ, Wherefore the love of Mortality, is the Mother of Ignorance, especially, in divine things, for we cannot cleave to both ; τὸ δὲ ἕτερον ἐλαττωθὲν τὴν τοῦ ἑτέρου ἐφανέρωσεν ἐνέργειαν. *Mercur. Trismeg.* 4. *pag.* 21.

Vers. 9. *Here will true wisedome lodge.*

Παραγίνομαι ἐγὼ ὁ νοῦς τοῖς ὁσίοις καὶ ἀγαθοῖς καὶ καθαροῖς, &c. *Pœmandr. pag.* 7.

CANTO II.

STANZ. 5. *Or like a Lamp,* &c.
See *Plotin. Ennead.* 4. *lib.* 1. *cap.* 8. *& 12.*

STANZ. 24. *Withouten body having energie.*

'Tis the opinion of *Plotinus.* Ἐν τῷ κόσμῳ τῷ νοητῷ ἡ ἀληθινὴ οὐσία, νοῦς τὸ ἄριστον αὐτοῦ, ψυχαὶ δὲ κἀκεῖ, ἐκεῖθεν καὶ ἐνταῦθα. κἀκεῖνος ὁ κόσμος ψυχὰς ἀνθ' σωμάτων ἔχει. *Ennead.* 4. *lib.* 1.

STANZ. 57. *But if 't consist of points, then a Scalene I'll prove all one with an Isosceles,* &c.

If quantity consists of Indivisibles or Atoms, it will follow that a *Scalenum* is all one with an *Isosceles,* &c.

Before I prove this and the following conclusions, it will be necessary to set down some few *Axioms* and *Definitions :*

Axioms.

I.

That a Line hath but two ends.

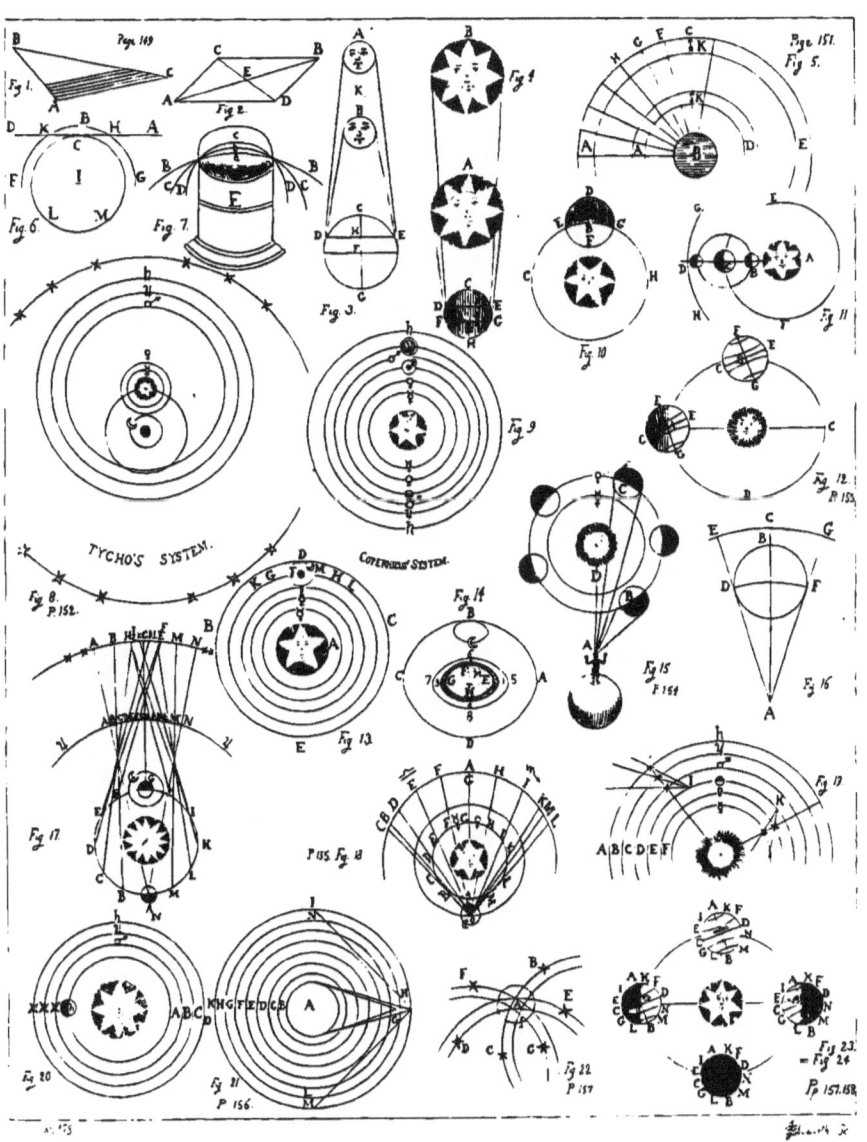

2.

That Lines that consist of an equall number of Atoms, are equall.

3.

That it is indifferent where we pitch upon the first Line in a superficies, so that we fill the whole *Area*, with Lines parallell to what first we choose.

4.

That no Motion goeth on lesse, then an Atom at a time, or the breadth of a Mathematicall Line.

Definitions.

1.

An *Isosceles*, is a Triangle having two equall sides.

2.

A *Scalenum*, is a Triangle having all sides unequall.

Theorem. 1.

That a *Scalenum*, and an *Isosceles*, be all one.

[See the Plate containing all the diagrams of these Notes.]

Let A B C be a *Scalenum;* The same A B C is also an *Isosceles.* For fill the whole *Area* A B C with lines parrallell to A C by the 3. *Axiom.* There is then as many points in B A as in B C by the 1. *Axiom;* and therefore by the second, B A is equall to B C, and consequently by the 1. *Definition,* A B C is an *Isosceles.*

Appendices.

The same reason will prove. 1. That every Triangle is an *Isopleuron* or *equilaterall* Triangle. 2. That the Diametre of a Quadrangle is equall to any of its sides. 3. That the Chord of a segment of a Circle, is equall to the Ark, &c.

Vers. 4. *That the crosse Lines of a Rhomboides,*
That from their meeting to all corners presse,
Be of one length.

Theorem. 2.

That the diagoniall Lines of a *Rhomboids* be equall.

[See plate as before.]

Let A C B D be a *Rhomboides,* and A B stretch'd out in *infinitum,* after the infinite productions of C B and A D. I say, that D C will be equall to A B. For E C is equall to E A, and E D to E B, by the precedent *Theorem.* Wherefore D C and A B are equall.

The same is also as briefly prov'd by the first or second *Appendix* of the precedent *Theorem.*

STANZ. 58. *And with her grasping rayes,* &c.

Theorem. 3. ;

That the Moon sometimes enlightens the whole Earth, and the Sunne sometimes enlightens not the Earth at all.

To prove this, I must set down some received Propositions in *Opticks* and *Astronomie.*

Propositions *Opticall.*

1.

S*Phæriodes luminosum minus si propinquius est opaco, minorem portionem illustrat quam si remotius existat.*

2.

Sphæroides luminosum majus è propinquo ampliorem partem opaci irradiat quam è remoto. Aguilon. lib. 5.

Propositions *Astronom.*

1.

T*He greatest distance of the Full or New Moon, from the Centre of the Earth, is 64. semi-diameters of the Earth.*

2.

The least distance of the Moon New or Full, from the Centre of the Earth, is 54. semidiameters of the Earth : so that there is five Diameters difference.

3.

The Sun in his Apogee, is distant from the Centre of the Earth 1550 semidiameters of the Earth, but in his Perigee 1446. So there is 52. Diameters difference.

[See plate as before.]

Now let B be the Moons Perigee, A her Apogee, C E G D, the Earth enlightned so farre as D E, by the Moon at B. Let the Moon be now removed from B into A. By this removall into A, the Earth C E G D will be more enlightned by the first propositions Opticall. But I say C E G D is enlightned all over by the Moon in A, for the distance A B is five times bigger then the Diameter C G from the Consect. of the first and second propositions Astronomicall. But H G is but part of C G, so that A B will be above five times bigger then G H, to which also E G is but equall by the first and second Axiom, or the third appendix of the first Theorem. Wherefore there is above five times as many Atoms in A B as in E G. But in every Atom remove from B toward A, the light, has gaind an Atom in E G by the fourth Axiom. Therefore the Moon at B has enlightned the Earth C D G D even unto the utmost point G, long before it be removed to A : so that C D G D when the Moon has got to A will be swallowed over and over again into the Moons rayes.

But now for the second part of the Theorem. That the Sunne sometimes enlightens not the earth at all.

[See plate as before.]

Let the Sunne be in his Perigee A, enlightening the Earth C E H D so farre as F G. Remove him from A to his Apogee B. In his recession to B the Earth C E H D is lesse and lesse enlightned by the second Opticall Proposition, I say, it is not enlightned at all.

For suppose he had gone back but the length of I G, then had F C G been devoyd of light, because that C G hath no more points in it then I C hath, by the first and second Axiom, or third Appendix of the first Theorem. And the light cannot go off lesse then an Atom a time by the fourth Axiom. Much more destitute therefore is the Earth C H E D of light, the Sunne being in B, when as the distance of Λ B will measure above fifty times C H (which yet is bigger then I C) by the Consect. of the third proposition Astronomicall, so that day will hang in the sky many thousand miles off from us, fastiginted into one conicall point, and we become utterly destitute of light.

A man might as well with placing the Sunne in B first prove him to enlighten all the Earth at once, and make perfect day.

As also the Moon if you place her in her Apogee first, that she enlightens not the least particle of the Earth though in her full.

Lastly, if you place them in K you might prove they do enlighten every part and never a part of the Earth at once, so that a perfect Universall darknesse and light would possesse the World at the same time, which is little better then a pure contradiction. The matter is very plain at the first sight.

STANZ. 28. *In every place*, &c.

Γῆ μὲν δὴ πᾶσα ζῴων ποικίλων πλήρης καὶ μέχρις οὐρανοῦ μεστὰ πάντα. *Ennead* 2. *lib.* 9. *cap.* 7.

LIB. II. CANTO I.

STANZ. 10. *This is that strange fram'd statue*, &c.

REad *Plotin. Ennead.* 6. *lib.* 4, *cap.* 14. And *cap.* 15. Ἀλλὰ πῶς προσελήλυθε τὸ προσεληλυθός; ἢ ἐπειδὴ ἐπιτηδειότης αὐτῷ παρῆν, ἔχε πρὸς ὃ τῷ ἐπιτήδειον, &c. And a little after he saith, that the corporeall substance being thus prepared, catches life and soul from the *Mundus vitæ*, as *Ficinus* calls it. Οἶον γειτονείᾳ καρπωσαμένου τι ἔχνος ψυχῆς οὐκ ἐκείνου μέρους, ἀλλ᾽ οἶον θερμασίας τινὸς ἢ ἐλλάμψεως ἐλθούσης, γένεσις ἐπιθυμιῶν καὶ ἡδονῶν καὶ ἀλγηδόνων ἐν αὐτῷ ἐξέφυ. Reade the 14. and 15. chap. of that fourth Book.

CANTO II.

STANZ. 12. *The naked essence of the body's this.*
See Body, *Interpr. Gener.*

STANZ. 26. *But like a Centre that around doth shoot*, &c.

Δεῖ τοίνυν τοῦτο ὥσπερ κέντρον εἶναι, *Ennead.* 4. *lib.* 7. *cap.* 6.

CANTO III.

STANZ. 3. *Knowledge of God.*
Εὐσέβεια δέ ἐστι θεοῦ γνῶσις, *Merc. Trismeg.* 9. *p.* 37.

LIB. III. CANTO I.

STANZ. 14. *Three Centres hath mans soul*, &c.

PLotinus. Ψυχῆι δὲ ἡμῶν τὸ μὲν ἀεὶ πρὸς ἐκείνοις (τῷ ἀγαθῷ δηλονότι, τῷ νόῳ, καὶ τῇ ψυχῇ) τὸ δὲ πρὸς ταῦτα ἔχειν τὸ δὲ ἐν μέσῳ τούτων, φύσεως γὰρ οὔσης μιᾶς ἐν δυνάμεσι πλείοσιν, ὁτὲ μὲν τὴν πᾶσαν συμφέρεσθαι τῷ ἀρίστῳ αὐτῆς καὶ τοῦ ὄντος, ὁτὲ δὲ τὸ

χεῖρον αὐτῆς καθελκυθὲν συνελκύσασθαι τὸ μέσον, τὸ γὰρ πᾶν αὐτῆς οὐκ ἦν θέμις καθελκύσαι. The opinion of the Philosopher is here, methinks, something perplext. Nor can we easly gather, whether he makes three essences, or onely three generall faculties. If three essences, why sayes he φύσεως μιᾶς δυνάμεσι πλείοσιν one nature in many faculties? If but one essence and three faculties, how comes that supernall facultie to be ever employed in intellectuall and divine speculations, and we seldome or never perceive it? See *Ennead* 2. *lib.* 9. *cap.* 2.

STANZ. 22. *Shee sees more clear*, &c.

Sith God moves all things, and all things immediately depend of him, or if you will is all things, it cannot be but he must have the sense of all things in the nearest and most immediate manner; as you may see more at large in *Merc. Trismeg.* in his περὶ νοήσεως καὶ αἰσθήσεως 9. *pag.* 39. 40.

CANTO II.

STANZ. *By his own plastick point, or else deep Night Drawn on*, &c.

PLotinus mentions also a middle way. That the great soul of the World does at least inchoate, and rudely delineate the fabrick of our body at first. The particular soul afterward accomplishes. Τί γὰρ κωλύει τὴν μὲν δύναμιν τῆς τοῦ παντὸς ψυχῆς προΰπο γράφειν ἅτε λόγου πάντα οὖσαν πρὶν καὶ παρ᾽ αὐτῆς (τῆς ἐν μέρει ψυχῆς) ἥκειν τὰς ψυκιχὰς δυνάμεις καὶ τὴν προΰπογραφήν, οἶον προδρόμους ἐλλάμψεις εἰς τὴν ὕλην εἶναι, &c. See *Ennead.* 6. *lib.* 7. *cap.* 7. He seems also in his second Ennead to intimate that our bodies are made by the soul of the World. Δεῖ δὲ μένειν μὲν ἐν οἴκοις σῶμα ἔχοντας, κατασκευασθεῖσιν ὑπὸ ψυχῆς ἀδελφῆς ἀγαθῆς πολλὴν δύναμιν εἰς τὸ δημιουργεῖν ἀπόνως ἐχούσης. *lib.* 9. *cap.* 18.

STANZ. 5. *By what the soul in her self feels and tryes*, &c.

Plotinus professes himself to have frequent experience of this, *Ennead* 4. *lib.* 8. *cap.* 1.

STANZ. 16. *Then like to flowing stream*, &c.

This seems to be the opinion of that learned Knight in his Book of Bodies. But I cannot satisfie my self in some difficulties it is entangled with. How it can be possible that any fiery Atom or thin particle should be capable of so strong an impetus impressed on it, as to carry it so many thousand miles, and not to cease from motion or be extinct. Nor can the particles that follow drive on the former. For there is still the same difficulty that was afore. Besides our sense shall then discover onely those particles of light that are in our eye, so that the Sunne will seem to have neither distance nor due figure. There's the same reason in colours.

Monsieur des Chartes his gentle ἀντέρεισμα or *renixus* of the Æthereall Vortices against the Organ of sight, is far more solid and ingenuous, agreeing exactly with all the properties of light. The contending in this and the following stanzes for the received way of species is but a πάρεργον. These rayes are here used for illustration rather then proof.

STANZ. 20. *Yet nought at all is lost.*
See *Merc. Trismeg.* πρὸς τάτ. 8.

STANZ. 21. *When that compounded nature is dissolv'd,*
Each Centre's safe.

Θάνατος δὲ οὐκ ἀπώλεια τῶν συναχθέντων, διάλυσις δὲ τῆς ἑνώσεώς ἐστι. Νοῦς πρὸς Ἑρμῆν, 11. p. 57.

CANTO III.

STANZA. 12. *One steddy good centre of Essences.*
See *Trismeg. pag.* 41, 52, 68, 69. *Edit. Turneb.*

STANZ. 38. *Nearer the Earth the slower it must go,*
These Arks be lesse, but in the Heavens blew
Those Arks increase. it must not be so slow.
Thus must it needs return unto its idle Bow.

An Arrow shot up into the sky, the higher it goes, the faster it circuleth toward the East because the Arches it there moves in are larger, as plainly appears out of the following figure.

[See plate as before.]

Where let B be the earth. A the East. Let an arrow fly in the line B C, let D E be severall hights of the air. Let the arrow K keep in B C the same line of the air or earthly magnetick spirit. So that B F, B G, B H &c. are not new lines of the air but of immovable imaginary space, which spaces let be æquall one with another. Now let the arrow K moving upward or downward in B C make also toward the East A in a circular motion. I say then it goes faster in E then in D. For the ark D A is divided into parts of the same proportion to the whole D A that the parts of E A to the whole E A. Now E A is far greater then D A, and therefore must the parts of E A be far greater then the parts of D A. And yet in the same time doth the arrow K passe thorough the portion of E A that it doth of D A, otherwise it would not keep in the line B C which is contrary to our hypothesis, and indeed to ordinary experience. For our eye finds the arrow come down in the same line it went up. Therefore it must needs go faster in E A then D A.

But this may seem strange and uncouth that the arrow should thus moderate it self in its motion, and proportion its swiftnesse to the ark it is in. But I conceive it is no more wonderfull then that water should figure it self according to the variety of its situations in hight and depth.

STANZ. 39. *Nor ought we wonder that it doth conform*
Its motions to the circles of the aire,
Sith water in a wooden bucket born,
Doth fit itself unto each Periphere, &c.

The truth and sense of this stanza will appear thus. Water is a heavie body, and therefore will get so near the centre as it can. That all the parts may get as near as they can, they must of necessity cast themselves into a sphæricall figure. For any other figure though it may happily let some parts nearer then they be in a sphear, yet it necessarily bears others further off from the Centre

then the furthest would be, were they all cast into a sphericall, as plainly appears in the following Scheme.

[See plate as before.]

Where let D A be a proportion of water casting it self into a rectilinear figure. F G the same proportion casting it self into a sphæricall. 'Tis plain that though D A be nearer the Centre at the point C and thereabout then F G at B or any where else, yet the highest point in the surface of F G is not so high, or so far remov'd from the centre I, as any betwixt D K or H A, wherefore all the particles of the proportion of water D A are not brought to the nearest position to the centre I, till they conform with the circle C L M, which we suppose the same proportion of water F G to have done, wherefore the lubricous particles of the water D A, will never cease tumbling, as being plac'd in an undue hight, till the surface thereof be concentricall with I.

[See plate as before.]

This being premised, let E be a vessel of water in severall situations of hight. The first and highest situation of this vessel let be B A B which is plainly the biggest circle. Let C B C be the next, a lesse circle then B A B. The tumour at B is bigger then, then at A, let *B C* B be the third, lesser then any of the former, the tumour at G is then highest of all, and so on still. There will ever be a new conformation of the surface of the water, according to the distance from the Centre of the earth, as is plain from the præmized Theorem.

STANZ. 48. *Venus Orb debars not Mars, &c.*

That the Planets get into one anothers supposed Orbs, is plain from their greatest & laste distances from the centre of the Earth,

Mars his least distance	556	
Venus greatest distance	2598	Semidiam.
Venus least distance	399	
Mercuries greatest distance	2176	

Now they that make solid Orbs, must of necessity make the Orb of the Planet as high or as low as the Planet it self is at least. Wherefore the lowest distance of an high Planet being much lower then the highest distance of a lower Planet, as appears out of *Landsbergius* his calculation in his *Vranometria*, it must needs be that their supposed solid orbs will runne one into another. But you'll say it is foul play to appeal to *Landsbergius* his Calculation, sith he is a party. But I see no man distrust his conclusions, though they mislike his Hypothesis.

How ever that this objection may be taken away. The fluidnesse of the Planetary heavens is acknowledged even by them that are against the motion of the Earth. As by *Tycho* that famous Astronomer who hath made such a System of the world, even the earth standing still, as may well agree with the conclusions of *Landsbergius* about the distances of the Planets from the Centre of the earth. For there *Mars* his least distance must needs be lower then *Venus* greatest distance, and *Venus* least distance must needs be lower then *Mercuries* greatest distance. As you may see in the *Paradigme.* Where it is very plain that *Venus* sometime is nearer the earth then

Mercury, that *Mars* is sometime nearer the earth then *Venus*, which cannot be without penetration of dimensions in solid Orbs.

[See plate as before.]

But what an untoward broken system of the world this of *Tycho's* is in comparison of that of *Copernicus* will appear even at first sight, if we do but look upon them both.

I have set down this scheme of *Copernicus* because it is usefull also for the better understanding of some following passages.

[See plate as before.]

It is plain to any man that is not prejudic'd that this System of the world is more naturall & genuine then that of *Tycho's*. No enterfaring or cutting of circles as in *Tycho's*, where the course of the Sunne cuts Mars his circuit. No such vast eccentricity as there, nor disproportionatednesse of Orbs and motions. But I'll leave these things rather for the beholder to spy out then to spend needlesse words in an easie matter.

STANZ. 56. *But that disgracement of Philosophy*
From Flux and Reflux of the Ocean main
Their mouethly and yearly change, &c.

How the Flux and Reflux of the sea depends on the motion of the earth I shall endeavour to explain as follows.

[See plate as before.]

About the Centre A, describe the circumference of the Earths annuall course H B C from West to East. In the point B describe the globe of the earth, D E F G running also from West to East in its diurnall course; that is, from G to D, from D to E, and so on till it come to G again. Here we may observe that every part of the earth at severall times hath a contrary motion.

As for example. Those parts at D tending toward E have a contrary motion to what they have when they come to F and ascend toward G. So the parts twixt G D as they go on toward E, move contrary to the motion they are moved betwixt E F going on toward G. But the parts about D move one way with the annuall motion, so that the swiftnesse of the motion of those parts of the earth is increased, the annuall and diurnall motion going in one, and tending Eastward. But the parts about F go Westward toward G, so that much of the annuall swiftnesse is taken of by the diurnall motion in these parts, they going a contrary way to the annuall.

The parts about E and G go not either Westward or Eastward, but are inconsiderable in the annuall motion.

Now, saith *Galilæus*, the sea being in his channell as water in a movable vessell the acceleration or retardation of the motion of the Earth will make the sea fluctuate or swill, like water in a shaken vessel, which must needs come to passe twice in every foure and twenty houres because of the great swiftnesse at D and extraordinary slownesse at F.

What the cause is of the dayly flux and reflux of the sea according to *Galilæos* mind is now conspicuous, *viz.* The addition or subduction of the Earths diurnall motion from the annuall, which according to that Authours compute is thrice swifter then the diurnall.

Now as the dayly Flux and Reflux consists in this addition and subduction, so the monethly and yearly changes and variations of this Flux and Reflux consist in the variation or change of proportion in those additions and subductions: they bearing sometime lesse, sometime greater proportion to the annuall motion.

Finally, this variation of proportions ariseth either from a new swiftnesse or slownesse in the annuall motion of the Earth; or else, from the various position of the Axis thereof; it sometimes conspiring more fully with the annuall motion then other sometimes. Whence it comes to passe that the compound motion is not alwayes of the same swiftnesse or slownesse. But we shall better understand this by applying our selves to a figure. And first of the monethly variation at full and new Moon.

Let A be the Sunne. C the earth. C E F G the annuall circle of the Earth. B the Moon in conjunction. D in opposition or full Moon. Now we will suppose that which *Galilæo* proves in his fourth dialogue. That in circular motion the same impetus being in the moveable,

[See plate as before.]

the movable will move swifter if it be reduced to a lesser circle, as is plain in Pendents, and in the balance of a clock. For the nearer you place the lead to the centre the swifter the balance moves. Again he considers the moon peculiarly and inseparably joyned with the Earth and so necessarily to move together. And that the position of the moon in D lengthens out the semidiametre of the *Orbis magnus* of the earth which is then H F. The position of the moon in B shortens it, that reacheth but to C. And the Moon in B is as the weight laid nearer to the Centre in the balance of the clock. Therefore the whole B C must move much swifter, then C D, the Moon being in D : there being in both places the same *impetus* of motion, or inward moving principle.

But here I must professe it seems to me very hard, how the swiftnesse of the Moon in B, or her slownesse in the Ark H D G should engage the Earth in C, in the like slownesse and swiftnesse, there being no such solid and stiff continuation from A to D as there is in a balance of a clock.

Again supposing this conceit to hold good. How will it answer to the history of the Flux aud Reflux of the sea. Which is increased much, as well when the Moon is in B as when she is in D. That the Flux should be greater the Moon being in D is reasonable, because C being then much retarded in the annuall motion, the subduction and addition of the diurnall will bear a greater proportion to the annuall, and so consequently cause a greater alteration in the Flux and Reflux. But when as the Moon being in B makes the annuall motion of C swifter, the subduction and addition of the diurnall will bear a lesse proportion to the annuall, and so the Flux and Reflux shall be rather diminished then increased, which is against experience and the history of the Flux and Reflux of the sea.

But now in the third place, to find out the reason why

at certain points of the years period the Flux and Reflux should be increased. We must observe that this is according to the severall positions of the Axis of the Earth, not but that it is alwayes parallel to it self, but in reference to the Ecliptick. For such is its position in the Solstitiall points that there the diurnall motion added or subducted bears a greater proportion to the annuall then elsewhere. In the Equinoctiall points a lesse. As will appear in the following scheme.

[See plate as before.]

Let A D C B be the Ecliptick, Let the circles G C F E cut A D C B to right angles. Let the annuall motion of the Earth be from C to B, from B to A, &c. the diurnall C A E C and C B E C. The Earth at A in her Solstitiall point : at B in her Equinoctiall. It is plain at first sight that C A E C complies much more with the motion B A D, then C B E doth with C B A. It is not worth more curious proposall and proof : since the truth thereof is so farre from giving a reason of the yearly alteration in the Flux and Reflux, that it is quite repugnant with the history thereof. For according to this device of *Galilæo* the greatest Flux and Reflux should be in the Solstices, But according to the observation of Writers it is in the Æquinoxes.

But however it was a witty attempt of *Galilæo*, though not altogether so solid. Mounsieur *Des Chartes* in my judgement is far more successfull in his Hypothesis, who renders the causes of all these φαινόμενα after the manner following.

For your more fully understanding of what I am now about to premise, I must refer to you *Des Chartes* his *Principia Philosophiæ*. Mean while peruse this present Scheme.

[See plate as before.]

Where C D B E is that great Vortex, in which, and by which the Planets are carried from West to East, according to the order of C D B E. Let A be the Sun, the Centre of this great Vortex, about which all the liquid matter of our Heaven is carried about, as grosse water in a whirlepooll ; and with it the Planets like corks or strawes. Let F be the Planet we are in, *viz.* the Earth, which is the Centre of a lesser Vortex H D G I. Let M be the Moon carried about the earths Vortex in her monethly course. This Vortex of the earth is not perfect sphericall, but cometh nearer the figure of an Ellipsis.

Because as *Chartesius* giveth you to understand, that part of the Vortex, which is the Circuit K L is more like the matter of the Vortex H D G I, then that matter which is above or below at D and I ; and therefore D H I G, giveth out more easily and naturally toward K and L.

Perhaps this reason may be added : That all the parts of the Vortex C D B E endeavouring through their circular Motion to recede from their Centre A, and thereby to widen one from another ; I mean the parts of any one Circle ; suppose K L : and yet all the Circles urging one another ἀθρόως, from A, to C D B E, they will easily give place in their Circles, as in K L, and the rest, but rather presse close in the Diametre, as in D I.

So that the Diametre of the Vortex of the Earth D I, shall be lesser then its Diametre G H. In so much that when the Moon M, is in D, or I, she will straiten the stream of the Vortex a great deal more, then when she is in G or H, which will make it run more swiftly, and bear down the Air and Water of the Sea more strongly.

But now that we may come more nearly to our businesse in hand, and apply our selves wholly to the Earths Vortex, in which the mystery of the Flux and Reflux of the Sea is to be discovered.

Let therefore this Vortex of the earth be A B C D. The Earth her self E F G H. 1234. the surface of the sea, wherewith for greater perspicuity, let the whole Earth be covered : Let 5678. be the surface of the Air, encompassing the Sea.

[See plate as before.]

And now let us consider, that if there were no Moon in this Vortex, the point T, which is the Centre of the earth, would be in the point M the Centre of the Vortex ; but the Moon being at B, this Centre T must be betwixt M and D : because seeing that the ethereall matter of this Vortex is something swiftlier moved, then the Moon or Earth which it bears along with it, unlesse the point T, be somewhat more distant from B then D, the Moons being there would hinder the ethereal matter from flowing so freely betwixt B and T, as betwixt T and D. Wherefore the position of the Earth in this Vortex not being determined, but from the equality of force of the ethereall matter that flows about it, it is manifest that she must come somewhat nearer toward D.

And after the same manner when the Moon is in C, the Centre of the Earth must be betwixt M and A ; and thus alwayes will the Earth recede somewhat from the Moon. Furthermore, because that from the Moons being in B, not only that space which is betwixt B & T but also that betwixt T and D is made narrower ; hence cometh it to passe that the ethereall matter floweth swiftlier in those places, and therefore presseth harder both upon the surface of the Air, in 6. and 8. as also upon the waters surface in 2. and 4. then if the Moon were not in the Diametre B D. And sithence the bodies of Air and Water be fluid, and easily yielding to that pressure, they must needs abate more in their height upon the parts of Earth, at F H ; then if the Moon were out of the Diametre B D. But contrary wise, they must become higher at G and E, in so much that the surface of Water 1. 3. and of Air 5. 7. will be there protuberant.

But now because that part of the Earth, which at this moment is in F (over against B) where the Sea is at the lowest, will after six houres be in G (over against the point C) where it is at the highest, and after other six houres in H over against D, and so on, Or rather, because the Moon her self also in the interim, maketh some little progresse from B towards C, as finishing her whole Circle A B C D in the space of a moneth ; that part of the Earth which is now in F over against the body of the Moon, after six houres and about 12. minutes, will have reached the point G in a Diametre of the Vortex A B C D which cuts that Diametre B D in which the Moon then

19

is, to right angles, and then will the water be at highest there, *viz.* at F. And after other six houres and twelve minutes, F will have reached the point H, where the water will be at lowest ebb, &c. Whence we may clearly understand, that the water of the sea must in the same place ebb and flow every twelve houres and 24 minutes.

Furthermore it is to be noted that this Vortex A B C D is not exactly round, but that diametre of it in which the Moon is at full and change to be shorter then that which is cut by it to right angles, as is above demonstrated. Whence it follows that the Flux & Reflux of the sea ought to be greater at new and full Moon then in the intermediate seasons.

We may also note, that whereas the Moon is alwayes in a Plain near to the Plain of the Eclipstick, and the earth is in her diurnall motion, turn'd according to the Plane of the Æquatour, which Planes intersect one another in the Æquinoxes, but are they also most distant from one another in the Solstices, that the greatest Flux and Reflux will be about the beginning of Spring and Autumne.

And these principles of *Mons. des Chartes* as they are plain and perspicuous in themselves, so are they also exactly agreeable with the φαινόμενα of Nature. So that though I was mistaken with *Galilæo* in the manner, yet in the main I am not mistaken : The cause of the Flux and Reflux of the sea lying in the motion of the earth.

STANZ. 62. *That Venus Moon-like*, &c.

This ensuing Diagram will explain all what is said of Venus in this and the following stanza.

First, that she increaseth and decreaseth like the Moon (it being suppos'd that she is opake, which is discovered also by the optick glasse) is plainly shown in this figure. For in B she is not halflighted, in C she is even in the full.

Secondly, that when she is farthest of she is in her full, as appeareth by the line A C.

[See plate as before.]

Thirdly, that she then seemeth lesse though in her full, because she is so much removed from us, even further then the Sun himself, as appeares by the said line A C.

Fourthly, that she must appear bigger when she least is enlightned, because she is then so very near us, in respect of that remotenesse in her full, as also appears plainly if you compare A B and A C together.

Lastly, here is set forth how she rounds the Sun in her circuits continually, as also doth Mercurius, which is confirmed by their never being far from the Sun. Hence it is that Venus is the Morning and Evening starre. Either to rise not long before the Sun, and so to prœnunciate the Day, or to set not long after him and so to lead on the Night.

STANZ. 65. *The Medicean foure reel about Jove.*
See *Copernic.* System. at Stanz. 48.

STANZ. 67. and 70.
    Planets go back, stand still, and forward flie
    With unexpected swiftnesse, &c.
Before we can well understand the sense of these stanzas we must have a right apprehension of the epicycle,

and the station, direction, and retrogradation of Planets, And all these depend one of another.

Let B D H F be an Epicycle. The order of the signes G C E. The line touching the Eastern side A D E.

Now the line of the true motion of a Planet is twofold. One is refer'd to the centre of the Epicycle, the other to the body of the Planet. According to the latter sense are the following descriptions.

A Planet is direct when the line of true motion goes on with the order of the Signes.

Retrograde when it goes contrary to the order of the Signes.

Stationary, when this line seems not to move either backward or forward.

[See plate as before.]

The line of true motion of the Epicycle which is A C alwayes goes with the order of the Signes. But the line that strikes through the Planet it self goes in the upper part of the Epicycle F B D with the order of the signes, but in the lower part D H F contrary to that order. This is the nature of the Epicycle and of retrogradation and station of Planets. Which superfluous motions or stands, as needlesse botchings *Copernicus* his System admits not of ; the motion of the Earth so fitly salving all such φαινόμενα, as the following figure will make plain.

[See plate as before.]

Let the circuit of the earth be A G A about the Sunne standing still at the Centre Z. Let A N be a twelfth part of Jupiters circle that he moves in about the Sunne. For Jupiter finisheth his course but in twelve years. Divide the circuit of the earth A G A into twelve equall parts. By that time the earth hath gone through all these, Jupiter will have gone the twelfth part of his own circuit, *viz.* A N. Divide A N into twelve equall parts, according to the number of parts in the Earths circuit before describ'd. That while the Earth passeth thorough one twelfth of her whole circle A G A, Jupiter may also dispatch a twelfth of the ark A N. Let both these twelves be signed with the same letters, A B C D E F G H I K L M N.

Now place the Earth at the point A. Let it go forward till it come to B. Jupiter hath also gone forward in his circuit and appears in the starry firmament at B, going forward on his way suppose with the order of the signes : Let the Earth proceed to C, then is Jupiter also come to C, and appears yet direct in the highest C, so he doth in D and in E, but in F he appears Stationary betwixt F E. Let the Earth proceed to G. Here Jupiter has skip'd back in appearance as far as from F to G. Let the earth go on to H, in appearance he has gone back as far as from G to H. Let her still move forward till she reach I, there Jupiter becomes Stationary again in I H. Put her on further to K, then he is again direct. So is he in L and M and N which is the entire finishing of the Earths annuall course.

Thus according to *Copernicus* his supposition, is the station and repedation of the Planets, at least the three highest, Saturn, Jupiter, and Mars, plainly discovered to be an appearance onely ; & that the Heavens are not guilty of any such reall irregularity of motion. Which concinnity, nor *Ptolemees*, nor *Tycho's* Hypothesis can afford us.

But lest any mistrust that the same seeming irregularity, will not fall out in Mercury, and Venus, which are betwixt the Sunne and our Earth ; The following scheme will show how there is a station and repedation in them too, according to this Hypothesis of *Copernicus*.

[See plate as before.]

Set the earth at some certain point of its annuall circle, *viz.* at O. Let A B C D E F G H I K L M divide the circle of Venus or Mercury into equall parts. Mercury and Venus will be in all these sites in respect of the Earth before they can be in conjunction with the Earth again, though the Earth be not fixt in the point O. Now draw a line from the point O into every section, you shall find direction, station, and repedation in these Planets as well as in the other higher Planets. For supposing the order of the Signes to go according to ♎♏ : place Venus first in A, then let her Proceed to B. She has taken a long journey backward contrary to the series of the Signes, and recoyled from A in the starry firmament to B. Let her go on to C. She has given another skip back into C, but a very little one. In D E F G H I K L she is direct ; but then at M she goes backward again, and in A B C, till she come at D again. This for the Retrogradation, and direction. As for the station of this Planet, it is betwixt B and D, and M and K, as the figure plainly discovers. What hath been said of Venus is also appliable to Mercury, as was intimated at first.

STANZ. 71.   *Why Saturn should rove*
With shorter startings, give back lesse then Jove ;
Jove lesse then Mars ; why Venus flincheth out
More then Mercurius.

[See Plate as before.]

Let A B C D E F be the circles of Saturn, Jupiter, Mars, Tellus, Venus, Mercurie, Saturn, Jupiter, Mars let them all ly in one line G H. The Earth be at the point I. It is plain that the nearest the Earth flyeth of the widest, and so in order. The same happeneth in Venus and Mercury, supposing the Earth at the point K. This matter is very plain even at the first sight.

STANZ. 72. *Why Saturn, Jove, and Mars be very nigh*
Unto the Earth, show bigger in our eye
At Eventide, &c.

Why Saturn Jupiter and Mars, when they rise Acronychall, that is, at the beginning of the night seem bigger and be indeed nearer us, then when they follow the Sunne close, and set Acronychall. The reason of this is very evident in *Copernicus* his Hypothesis, as you may see in this Diagram.

[See plate as before.]

Mars when he riseth Acronychall is distant from the Earth, but the space of A B. But when he setteth Acronychall he is distant the space of H B. So Jupiter, when he riseth Acronychall, is distant but A C from the Earth, but when he setteth he is distant the space of H C, the like is in Saturn.

CANTO IV.

STANZ. 13. *Is confident of his souls after joyes.*

THe condition of the bad and good soul in reference to their estate after death *Plotinus* has very Philosophically set out as follows. Τὴν οὖν αὐτοῦ τις κακίαν συνάψας ἐγνώθητε ὅς ἐστι, καὶ μετὰ τὴν αὐτοῦ φύσιν ὤσθη εἰς ὃ ἔχει καὶ ἐνταῦθα, καὶ ἐντεῦθεν ἀπαλλαγεὶς εἰς ἄλλον τοιοῦτον τόπον, φύσεως ὁλκαῖς. Τῷ δὲ ἀγαθῷ αἴτε λήψεις, αἴτε δόσεις, καὶ αἱ μεταθέσεις ἄλλαι, ὥσπερ ἐκ μηρίνθων ὁλκαῖς τισι φύσεως μετατιθεμένων. Οὕτω θαυμαστῶς ἔχει δυνάμεως καὶ τάξεως τόδε τὸ πᾶν, γινομένων ἁπάντων ἀψόφῳ κελεύθῳ μετὰ δίκην ἣν οὐκ ἔστι φυγεῖν οὐδενί· ἧς ἐπαίει μὲν ὁ φαῦλος οὐδὲν, ἄγεται δὲ οὐκ εἰδὼς οἷ δεῖ ἐν τῷ παντὶ φέρεσθαι· ὁ δὲ ἀγαθὸς καὶ οἶδε, καὶ οἷ δεῖ ἄπεισι, καὶ γινώσει πρὶν ἀπιέναι οὗ ἀνάγκη αὐτῷ ἐλθόντι οἰκεῖν, καὶ εὐελπίς ἐστιν ὡς μετὰ Θεῶν ἔσοιτο. *Ennead.* 4. *lib.* 4. *cap.* 45.

Notes upon
The Infinity of Worlds.

A Circle whose Circumference no where
Is circumscrib'd, &c.
The Cuspis *and the Basis of the Cone*
Were both at once, &c.

Hen I speak of God this Mathematicall way,
(which is no new thing ; for the Ancients
also have defined Him to be a Circle whose
Centre is everywhere and Circumference no
where. And *Synesius* calls him κέντρων κέντρον, the
Centre of Centres,) I say when I speak thus of God, I
then set out that modification of his Being which
answers to quantity in Bodies. But God is so perfect
that no one appellation or resemblance can exhaust
that Treasure of Attributes in him, He being so fully all
things in himself. So that if we will venture to call
Him all that He eminently contains, we must be forc'd
upon at least seeming inconsistencies.

And now we endeavour to set out that which answers
in God to Quantity, we fall into disagreeing terms of
Centre, and Basis of a Cone. But why we adumbrate
the divine *Entity* by this representation you shall compendiously conceive in the following figure : and see in
what respect he is a Centre, and in what the Basis of a
Cone, as also what that is we call the Cuspis of the
Cone.

[See plate as before.]

Let K I H K be the whole Orb of beings. The
Centre A. *Ahad* or *Atove,* B C D E F G H *Æon, Psyche,*
Semele, Arachne, Physis, Tasis, Hyla. I say that
Ahad in respect of those subsequent Effluxes B C D, &c.
is fitly termed a Centre, and is as the Sunne in respect
of the Light and Rainbow. But now all things flowing
from him καθ' ὑποστολὴν with abatement as is most dis-
cernable in the Extremes (for the point A is in every point
of the whole Orb K I H K, and so is as large as the whole
Orb. *As for example,* The point A is at the point G
and every where else as well as at A ; but the point G is
onely at G, or if it be at L it is onely then at L, and not
at G nor any where else) therefore A though in respect
of the Universall orders of Beings which flow from him
may be the Centre of a Circle, yet in respect that these
orders fall short of his large Ubiquity (some of them at
least, all of his perfection and excellency) and the last
reall efflux is contracted after a manner to a mere

mathematicall point, for such is the nature of the Orb
G, or corporeall substance, as I have intimated. For
this reason I say, may A rightly be called the largest
Basis of the Cone, whose Diametre is I M, or N L, as
the descent of these Degrees and Beings from *Ahad* or
Atove may fitly resemble a Conicall figure whose Cuspis
is G.

And here I may seasonably appeal unto the apprehensions of men, whether the divine fecundity A flow'd
out *per saltum,* and produced onely the Orb G, or
whether there being a possibility of more excellent intermediate Orbs, (I will not stand upon this number I have
assigned) he did not produce B C D, &c. And if he
produced G onely, whether that Orb G be not either an
arbitrarious or naturall efflux from A. *i.e.* dependeth on
him as closely and intimately, as a Ray doth on the
Sun. And if so, why the nature of *Atove* should be
lesse fruitfull then the imaginations of men, who can in
reason, and distinct notion place severall Orbs betwixt
A and G. Or why the free will of *Atove* or *Ahad* should
be lesse bountifull then the minds of well meaning men,
who if it were in their power as it is in the arbitrarious
power of *Ahad,* (it clashing with no other good attri-
bute) would fill up that empty gulf betwixt A and G.
Wherefore as farre as free reason and authority of
Platonisme will reach, the mystery of the Cone will
hold good, though my drift at this time was rather to
explaine it, then confirm it.

But if any should be so adventrous as to deny such
an Ubiquity as I have described, yet in some sort this
adumbration of the Cone, will still hold good. For
there will be a latitude and contraction of power, if not
of presence. And this will be ground enough for this
expression.

But it is to be noted, that if we forsake this apprehension of the omnipotency of *Ahad,* God and all things
else will prove mere bodies. And then must God, if he
can, make himself up in severall parcells and pieces.
And God administring the affairs of the Earth, will
scarce know what God doth in *Saturn,* or at least many
millions of miles distant, which conceit seems to me
farre below the light of Nature and improv'd Reason.
But to conceive God not onely a body, but a body
devoid of life, sense, and understanding, is so dark and
melancholick a phansie, that I professe, I think I could

with far lesse pain and reluctancy, suffer my body to be buried alive in the cold Earth, then so stark and stupid conceit to entombe my soul.

STANZ. 85.

*Beside, the Conflux and Congeries
Of lesser lights a double augmentation
Implies, and 'twixt them both a lessening coarctation.*

The difficulty that their opinion is entangled with that hold the Comets to be nothing but a conflux of lesser stars, is this. That they must then seem first bigger, then lesser ; then bigger again, which will evidently appear in the following Scheme.

[See plate as before.]

Where let the closest meeting of the Stars, D F B E G C be at A. I say before they come to A, they will make the show of a broad light ; suppose, when come all to the Circle I. But afterward this light will be lesse and lesse, till they come to the Centre A, where it will be least of all, they coming there closest of all one to another. But then they holding on stil in their severall Arks, they will passe by one another, and the Comet will grow bigger, and bigger, till they have reached the Circle I again, where the Comet is as big as at the biggest before. But then disjoyning themselves more wide one from another, their severall Circles so carrying them, they cease to be seen of us.

This would be the φαινόμενον of a Comet, if it did consist of a conflux of Starres. But sith there is no such thing observed in Comets it is very probable they arise not from this cause.

Notes upon
The Philosophers Devotion.

*Nimbly they hold on their way
Shaping out their Night and Day,
Summer, Winter, Autumn, Spring,
Their inclined Axes bring.*

TO shew how Day and Night, Winter and Summer arise from *Copernicus* his Hypothesis, will not onely explane these verses but exceedingly set out the fitnesse and genuinenesse of the Hypothesis it self. Which I will therefore do out of *Galilæo* for the satisfaction of the unprejudiced and ingenuous Reader.

Let the Circle ♑ ♎ ♋ ♈ be the Ecliptick, where, by the way, we may take notice that when the Earth is in the sign ♑, the Sun will appear in the opposite sign ♋, when in ♈, in ♎ &c. And so while the earth doth really passe through the Signes, the sunne seems to passe through the Signs opposite to those the Earth is really passing through ; whence this annuall motion through the Zodiack has been ascribed unto him.

Let now the centre of the Earth be plac'd in the point, of ♑. Let the Poles and Axis of the Earth be A B,

inclining upon the Diametre of Capricorn and Cancer 23 degrees and an half. We must also suppose this inclination immutable ; the upper pole A, to be the North pole, the South pole, B.

Now imagine the Earth turned round on her Axis in 24 hours from West to East : then will every point in the semicircle A D B describe a parallel Circle. We'll for the present take notice onely of that great circle C D, and two other furthermost circles 23. gr. viz. E F. and G N, the one above, the other below, and lastly two other furthermost circles I K and L M equidistant from the Poles A B.

Furthermore we are to understand that while the Earth moves on, that her Axis keeps not onely the same inclination upon the Plane of the Ecliptick, but also one constant direction toward the same part of the Universe or Firmament, remaining alway parallel to it self.

Now this immutability of inclination and steddy direction of her Axis presupposed, place the Earth also in the first points of Aries Cancer and Libra, according as you see in the present Scheme.

We will go thorough all the foure figures, and first that in Capricorn. In which, beenuse the Axis A B declines from a perpendicular, upon the Diametre of Capricorne and Cancer, 23. grad. and an half, towards the Sun O, and the Ark A I, is 23. grad. and an half, (the Sun enlightening an Hemisphere of the Earth divided from the dark Hemisphere by the Circle K L which *Galilæo* calls *Terminator lucis*) this *Terminator lucis* K L must divide C D as being a great circle, into equall parts, but all the other as being lesser circles into unequall ; because K L passeth not through A B the poles of all these Circles. And the parallel I K with all the parallels described within I K even to the pole A will be wholly in the enlightned part of the Earth, as all the opposite parallels from L M to the pole B, wholly in the dark. Furthermore whereas the Ark A K is equall to the Ark E C, and the Ark A E common : these two, K I E and A E C will be equall, and each of them make a quadrant. And because the whole Ark K E L is a Semicircle, the Ark L E will be a quadrant and equall to the other E K, and therefore the Sun O shall in this posture of the Earth be verticall at Noon to all them that live in the parallel E F which is the Tropick of Cancer described by the Earths turning upon her own Axis in that posture. And thus ariseth the height of Summer to all them that dwell on this side of the Tropick of Cancer.

Moreover we see plainly, that of all the parallel circles we may imagine drawn betwixt I K and L M. C D is onely divided into equall parts by the circle of light K L : in such sort that the diurnall arks of the parallels above C D are bigger then the Nocturnall, but under C D, lesser.

[See plate as before.]

Also that the differences of the arks grow bigger and bigger by how much nearer and nearer they come to the Poles, till I K be wholly taken in to the enlightned part of the Earth and make day there, of 24 houres long, and contrariwise, the parallel L M be wholly covered in the dark part, and make night of 24 houres long. So that from hence we may see how the true differences of the lowest and shortest dayes and nights are caused to the Inhabitants of severall parallels of the Earth.

Lets now consider the third figure the centre of the earth plac'd in ♋ from whence the sun will appear in the first point of Capricorn. Now it is manifest, being that the inclination and direction of the Earths Axis A B is utterly the same it was before, it remaining parallel to it self that the situation of the Earth is the same, saving that that Hemisphere which was before enlightened is now in the dark, and that which was in the dark before, is now in the light, and so the differences of dayes and nights are quite contrary to what they were. In what parallel was the longest day before is now the shortest, and in what the shortest now the longest, as is plain to sight. For now I K is wholly in the dark which before was in the light wholly, and L M in the light that was before in the dark &c. And the Sun is now verticall to the Inhabitants of G N as before it was to them of E F. And as it was the height of Summer before to E F and to all on this side E F : so it is now the depth of winter to them and to all on this side of them. For the Sun seems to have descended, or is removed from them, or they from it by the whole arch F D N that is 47. degrees.

All which mutation proceeds from the immutable posture of the axis of the Earth, remaining still in the same inclination to the Plane of the Ecliptick and continuing ever parallel to it self. For so it must needs decline as much from the Sun O in the point ♑ as it inclin'd to him in the point ♑. For as, if the *Axis* A B were supposed parallel to the *Axis* of the Plane of the Ecliptick the Sunne will be verticall to D and to C. So I A the inclination of the *Axis* toward the Sunne, will make the Sunne verticall at E in the point ♑, and the declination of the said *Axis* from the Sunne at the point ♋ will make the Sun verticall to N.

But now if we consider the Earth plac'd in the point ♎ the Sun O will appear in the beginning of ♈. And whereas the Axis of the Earth which is in the first figure at ♑ stands inclined upon the Diametre of *Capricorn* and *Cancer*, and therefore understood to be in a Plane which cutteth the Plane of the Ecliptick along the Diametre of *Capricorn* and *Cancer*, being erected perpendicularly to the said Plane of the *Ecliptick :* This *Axis* kept still parallel to it self, will also here be in a Plane, erected perpendicular to the Plane of the *Eclip-*

tick, and parallel to the forenamed Plane which cut the Plane of the *Ecliptick* to right angles along the Diametre of *Cancer* and *Capricorn*. And therefore a Line going from the Centre of the Sunne to the Centre of the Earth, such as the line O tending to ♎ *Libra*, will be perpendicular to the *Axis* A B. But a Line drawn from the Suns Centre, to the Centre of the Earth is alwayes perpendicular to the Circle of illumination ; therefore shall the Circle of Illumination, or the *Terminator Lucis* passe through the Poles A B in this Figure, and the *Axis* A B shall be in the Plane of this Circle. But a great Circle passing through the Poles of the parallels will divide them all into equall parts. Therefore I K, E F, C D, G N, L M, the diurnall Arches be all semicircles, and dayes and nights be of equall length to all the Inhabitants of the Earth.

Lastly, seeing that a Line drawn from the Centre of the Sunne, to the Centre of the Earth is perpendicular to the *Axis* A B, to which the greatest of the parallel Circles C D is also perpendicular ; this Line thus drawn will necessarily passe along the Plane of the parallel C D, and cut its circumference in the midst of the diurnall Arch of that Circle C D. And therefore the Sunne will here be verticall to them that live in the parallel C D.

[See plate as before.]

And what hath been said of the Earth at this point of *Libra* ♎, will agree exactly to her placed in the point ♈. There is no difference, saving that the dark side turned from the Sunne is represented in this last posture as the light side in the former. The nocturnall semicircles here, as there the Diurnall. And so we see how Spring and Autumn cometh about as well as how Winter and Summer.

Finally, whereas the Earth being in the Solstitial points the Polar Circles I K, L M, one of them is in the Light, the other in the dark ; but being in the Equinoctial points, the halfs onely of the Polar Circles be in the light or dark : 'tis easie to understand how the Earth passing, suppose from *Cancer* (where the parallell I K is wholly in the dark) to *Leo* ♌, one part of the parallell I K toward the point K begins to enter into the light, and the Circle of Illumination to bear back toward the Pole A, and more inward toward the Pole B, cutting the Circle A C B D no longer in K I., but in two other points betwixt A K & L B, whence the Inhabitants of the Circle I K begin to enjoy the light, and the Inhabitants of L M, to be conveyed into Night.

The Interpretation Generall.

I F any man conceive I have done amisse in using such obscure words in my writings, I answer, That it is sometime fit for Poeticall pomp sake, as in my Psychozoia : Otbersome time necessitie requires it,

Propter egestatem linguæ, & rerum novitatem,

as Lucretius pleads for himself in like case. Again, there is that significancie in some of the barbarous words (for the Greeks are Barbarians to us) that, although not out of superstition, yet upon due reason I was easily drawn to follow the Counsel of the Chaldee Oracle, Ὀνόματα βάρβαρα μή ποτ' ἀλλάξῃς, Not to change those barbarous terms into our English tongue. Lastly, if I have offended in using such hard names or words, I shall make amends now by interpreting them.

A

A Binoam אבינעם *Pater amœnitatis,* Father of delight.

Acronychall. See Cronychall.

Adamah. אדמה Earth, The earthly or naturall mans abode.

Adonai. אדוני The Lord, or the sustainer of all things, from יד the Basis or foot of a pillar.

Aelpou. Ἀέλπων, not hoping, or without hope.

Æon. Αἰών, Eternity.

Æther. Αἰθήρ, from αἴθω, to burn. The fluid fiery nature of heaven, the same that שמים which signifies as much, *viz.* a fiery fluour, or fluid fire.

Africk Rock. See Pompon. *Mel. lib.* 1. *cap.* 8. Rom. 9. 33. 1. Cor. 10.4. 1. Pet. 2. 5, Revel. 5. 10. Psal. 105. 15.

Ahad. אחד Τὸ ἕν. One, or The One. The Platonists call the first Originall of all things, Τὸ ἕν and Τἀγαθὸν, for these reasons : Τὸ ἕν, or One, because the multitude or plurality of Beings is from this One, as all numbers from an unit : Τἀγαθὸν, or The Good, παρὰ τοῦ ἄγειν, or ἄγαν θέειν, because all things are driven, drawn, or make haste to partake of it. Διότι μὲν ἐξ αὐτοῦ τὸ πλῆθος ὑπέστη, τήν τοῦ ἑνὸς αὐτῷ προσηγορίαν ἐπάγομεν· Διότι δὲ πρὸς αὐτὸ πάντα καὶ μέχρι τῶν ἀμυδροτάτων ἐπιστρέφεται, τὸ ἀγαθὸν αὐτὸ προσονομάζομεν, *Procl. Theolog. Plat. lib.* 2. *cap.* 4.

Aides. Ἀΐδης, It ordinarily signifies Orcus or Pluto : here the Winter Sunne : the etymon fits both, παρὰ τοῦ μή ἰδεῖν· Hell is dark, and the Sunne in Winter leaves us to long nights.

Ain. Not to be, To be nothing ; from יִן *Non, nihil,* or *nemo.*

Alethea-land, That is, the land of truth, τὸ πεδίον τῆς ἀληθείας, as the Platonists call it.

Alopecopolis, Ἀλωπεκόπολις. The foxes city, or politie.

Ananke. Ἀνάγκη. The same that Hyle is. But the proper signification of the word is Necessity. See Hyle.

Anautæsthetus, Ἀναυταίσθητος, One that feels not himself, or at least relisheth not himself.

Anautæsthesie, Ἀναυταισθησία, Without self-sensedness, or relishing ones self.

Animadversall. That lively inward animadversall. It is the soul it self, for I cannot conceive the body doth animadvert ; When as objects plainly exposed to the sight are not discovered till the soul takes notice of them.

Anthropion, The same with Adamah : Onely Adamah signifies earthlinesse ; *Anthropion* from ἄνω ἀθρεῖν, uprightnesse of body or looking up.

Apathie, Ἀπάθεια. To be without passion.

Apogee, Ἀπόγειον, is that *absis* or ark of the circle of a Planet, in which the Planet is further off from the earth, as the word it self intimates.

Apterie, Ἀπτερία, from *a,* negative, and πτέρον a wing. It signifies the want of wings.

Arachnea bath its name from ἀράχνη, a spider.

Atom-lives. The same that Centrall-lives. Both the terms denote the indivisibity of the inmost essence it self ; the pure essentiall form I mean, of plant, beast, or man, yea of angels themselves, good, or bad.

Atove. See *Hattove.*

Autaparnes, Αὐταπαρνης from αὐτὸς and ἀπαρνέομαι. Simon, Autaparnes & Hypomone are but the soul, thrice told over. Autaparnes is the soul denying it self : Hypomone the soul bearing the anguish of this deniall of it self : From these two, results Simon, the soul obedient to the spirit of Christ. Now there is no self-deniall where there is no corrupt or evill life to be supprest and satisfied ; nor any Patience or Hypomone, where there is no agony from the vexation of self-deniall. So that the soul as long as it is *Autaparnes* or *Hypomone,* is a thing complex or concrete, necessarily including the corruption of that evill life or spirit, which is the souls self for a time. Hence is that riddle easily opened ; How the strength of *Autaparnes* is the weakning of *Simon* and the destruction of him and *Hypomone* in the valley of *Ain Simons* consummation and perfection, or rather his translation, or ἀποθέωσις.

Autæsthesia, Αὐταισθησία, Self-sensednesse.

Autokineticall, Αὐτοκίνητος, That which moves it self.

Autopathia, Αὐτοπάθεια, Denotates the being self-strucken, to be sensible of what harms us, rather then what is absolutely evill.

Autophilus, Αὐτόφιλος, A lover of himself.

B

BAcha, Weeping, *Bacha* Vale is the Valley of tears; from בכה *Flevit.*

Beirah, or *Beiron,* The brutish life, from בעיר *brutum.*
Body. The ancient Philosophers have defined it Τὸ τριχῆ διάστατον μετ' ἀντιτυπίας. *Sext. Emperic. Pyrrhon. Hypotyp. lib.* 3, *cap.* 5. Near to this is that description, *Psychathan. Cant.* 2. *Stanz.* 12. *lib.* 2. *Matter extent in three dimensions:* But for that ἀντιτυπία, simple trinall distension doth not imply it, wherefore I declin'd it. But took in matter according to their conceit that phansic a *Materia prima,* I acknowledge none; and consequently no such *corpus naturale* as our Physiologist make the subject of that science. That τριχῆ διάστατον ἀντίτυπον is nothing but a fixt spirit, the conspissation or coagulation of the cuspidall particles of the Cone, which are indeed the Centrall Tasis, or inward essence of the sensible world. These be an infinite number of vitall Atoms that may be wakened into divers tinctures, or energies, into Fiery, Watery, Earthy, &c. And one divine *Fiat* can unloose them all into an universall mist, or turn them out of that sweat, into a drie and pure Ethereall temper. These be the last projections of life from the soul of the world; and are act or form though debil and indifferent; like that which they call the first matter. But they are not merely passive, but meet their information half way, as I may so speak; are radiant *ab intimo,* and awake into this or the other operation, by the powerfull appulse of some superadvenient form. That which change of phantasmes is to the soul, that is alteration of rayes to them. For their rayes are *ab intrinseco,* as the phantasmes of the soul. These be the reall matter of which all supposed bodies are compounded, and this matter (as I said) is form and life, so that all is life and form what ever is in the world, as I have somewhere intimated in *Antipsychopan.* But how ever I use the term *Body* ordinarily in the usuall and vulgar acception. And for that sense of the Ancients, nearest to which I have defined it in the place first above mentioned, that I seem not to choose that same as most easie to proceed against in disproving the corporeity of the soul, the Arguments do as necessarily conclude against such a naturall body as is ordinarily described in *Physiologie* (as you may plainly discern if you list to observe) as also against this body composed of the Cuspidall particles of the Cone. For though they be Centrall lives, yet are they neither Plasticall, Sensitive, or Rationall; so farre are they from proving to be the humane soul, whose nature is there discust.

C

CEntre, *Centrall, Centrality.* When they are used out of their ordinary sense, they signifie the depth, or inmost Being of any thing, from whence its Acts and Energies flow forth. See *Atom-lives.*

Chaos, In our blew Chaos, that is, In our corporeall spirit: for that is the matter that the soul raiseth her phantasmaticall forms in, as the life of the World, doth bodily shapes in the Heavens or Air.

Circulation. The term is taken from a toyish observation, *viz.* the circling of water, when a stone is cast into a standing pool. The motion drives on circularly, the first rings are thickest, but the further they go, they grow the thinner, till they vanish into nothing. Such is the diffusion of the Species audible in the strucken Air, as also the visible Species. In breif, any thing is said to circulate that diffuseth its Image or Species in a round. It might have been more significantly called orbiculation, seeing this circumfusion makes not onely a Circle, but fills a Sphere, which may be called the Sphere of activity: Yet Circulation more fitly sets out the diminution of activity, from those rings in the water, which as they grow in compasse, abate in force and thicknesse. But sometimes I use Circulate in an ordinary sense to turn round, or return in a Circle.

Clare, Claros, a Citie of *Ionia,* famous for *Apollo's* Temple, and answers, amongst which was this, which I have interpreted in *Psychathanasia.*

> Φράζεο τὸν πάντων ὕπατον θεὸν ἔμμεν' Ἰαώ,
> Χείματι μὲν τ' Ἀΐδην, Δία δ' εἴαρος ἀρχομένοιο,
> Ἠέλιον δὲ θέρους, μεταπώρου δ' ἀβρὸν Ἰαώ.
> *Macrob. Saturnal. lib.* 1. *cap.* 18.

Cone; Is a solid figure made by the turning of a rectangular Triangle, about; one of the sides that include the right angle resting, which will be then the *Axis* of the compleated *Cone.* But I take it sometimes for the comprehension of all things, God himself not left out, whom I tearm the Basis of the *Cone* or Universe. And because all from him descends, καθ' ὑποστολὴν, with abatement or contraction, I give the name of *Cone* to the Universe. And of *Cone* rather then *Pyramid,* because of the roundnesse of the figure; which the effluxes of all things imitate.

Cronychall, or *Acronychall,* that is, ἀκρόνυχος, vespertine, or at the beginning of night. So a starre is said to rise or set *Acronychall,* when it riseth or setteth at the Sunne-setting; For then is the beginning of Night.

Cuspis of the Cone. The multiplide *Cuspis* of the *Cone* is nothing but the last projection of life from *Psyche,* which is a liquid fire, or fire and water, which are the corporeall or materiall principles of all things, changed or disgregated (if they be centrally distinguishable) and again mingled by the virtue of *Physis* or Spermaticall life of the World; of these are the Sunne and all the Planets, they being kned together, and fixt by the centrall power of each Planet and Sunne. The volatile Æther is also the same, and all the bodies of Plants, Beasts and Men. These are they which we handle and touch, a sufficient number compact together. For neither is the noise of those little flies in a Summer-evening audible severally: but a full Quire of them strike the eare with a pretty kind of buzzing. Strong and tumultuous pleasure, and scorching pain reside in these, they being essentiall and centrall, but sight and hearing are onely *of the Images* of these. See *Body.*

D

DÆmon, Any particular life, any divided spirit ; or rather the power ruling in these. This is Δαίμων, *a* δαίω *divido.*

Dæmoniake, That which is according to that divided life or particular spirit that rules for it self.

Deuteropathie, Δευτεροπάθεια, is a being affected at second rebound, as I may so say. We see the Sunne not so properly by sympathy, as deuteropathie. As the mundane spirit is affected where the Sunne is, so am I in some manner ; but not presently, because it is so affected, but because in my eye the Sunne is vigorously represented. Otherwise a man might without question see the Sunne if he had but a body of thin Aire.

Diana, The Moon, by which is set out the dead light, or letter of the Law.

Dicaosyne, Δικαιοσύνη, Justice or Morall righteousnesse.

Dizoia, Διςωΐα, Double livednesse.

Duessa, Division, or duality.

E

EIdos, Εΐδος, Form or Beauty.

Eloim or *Eloah,* אלה signifie properly the strong God.

Energie, it is a peculiar Platonicall term, I have elsewhere expounded it, *Operation, Efflux, Activity ;* None of those words bear the full sense of it. The examples there are fit, *viz.* the light of the Sun, the phantasmes of the soul. We may collect the genuine sense of the word, by comparing severall places of the Philosopher. Έχει γὰρ ἕκαστον τῶν ὄντων ἐνέργειαν, ἥ ἐστιν ὁμοίωμα αὐτοῦ, ὥστε αὐτοῦ ὄντος κἀκεῖνο εἶναι, καὶ μένοντος φθάνειν εἰς τὸ πόῤῥω, τὸ μὲν ἐπὶ πλεῖον τὸ δὲ εἰς ἔλαττον. καὶ αἱ μὲν ἀσθενεῖς καὶ ἀμυδραὶ, αἱ δὲ καὶ λανθάνουσαι, τῶν δέ εἰσι μείζους καὶ εἰς τὸ πόῤῥω. For every being hath its *Energie,* which is the image of it self, so that it existing that *Energie* doth also exist, and standing still is projected forward more or lesse. And some of those *Energies,* are weak and obscure, others hid or undiscernable, other some greater and of a larger projection, *Plotin.* Ennead. 4. *lib.* 5. *cap.* 7. And again, *Ennead.* 3. *lib.* 4. Καὶ μένομεν τῷ μὲν νοητῷ ἄνω· τῷ δὲ ἐσχάτῳ αὐτοῦ, πεπεδήμεθα τῷ κάτω, οἷον ἀπόῤῥοιαν ἀπ' ἐκείνου διδόντες εἰς τὸ κάτω, μᾶλλον δὲ ἐνέργειαν, ἐκείνου οὐκ ἐλαττουμένου. And we remain above by the Intellectuall man, but by the extreme part of him we are held below, as it were yielding an efflux from him to that which is below, or rather an *Energie,* he being not at all lessened. This curiosity *Antoninus* also observes (*lib.* 8. *Meditat.*) in the nature of the Sun-beams, where although he admits of χύσις, yet he doth not of ἀπόῤῥοια which is ἔκχυσις. Ὁ ἥλιος κατακεχύσθαι δοκεῖ, καὶ πάντη γε κέχυται οὐ μὲν δὲ ἐκκέχυται. ἡ γὰρ χύσις αὐτοῦ τάσις ἐστίν, ἀκτῖνες γοῦν αἱ αὔγαι αὐτοῦ ἀπὸ τοῦ ἐκτείνεσθαι

λέγονται. The Sun, saith he, is diffused, and his fusion is every where but without effusion, &c. I will onely adde one place more out of *Plotinus, Ennead.* 3. *lib.* 6. Ἐκάστου δὲ μορίου ἡ ἐνέργεια ἡ μετὰ φύσιν ζωὴ οὐκ ἐξιστᾶσα. The naturall *Energie* of each power of the soul is life not parted from the soul though gone out of the soul, *viz.* into act.

Comparing of all these places together, I cannot better explain this Platonick term, *Energie,* then by calling it the rayes of an essence, or the beams of a vitall Centre. For essence is the Centre as it were, of that which is truly called *Energie,* and *Energie* the beams and rayes of an essence. And as the Radii of a circle leave not the Centre by touching the Circumference, no more doth that which is the pure *Energie* of an essence, leave the essence by being called out into act, but is ἐνέργεια a working in the essence, though it flow out into act. So that *Energie* depends alwayes on essence, as *Lumen* on *Lux,* or the creature on God ; Whom therefore *Synesius* in his Hymnes calls the Centre of all things.

Entelechia, Ἐντελέχεια : It is nothing else but *forma,* or *actus,* and belongs even to the most contemptible forms, as for example to Motion, which is defined by *Arist.* in the third of his physicks, ἡ τοῦ δυνατοῦ, ᾐ δυνατὸν, ἐντελέχεια. *Scaliger* in his 309 exercitation against *Cardan,* descants very curiously upon this word : *Cùm igitur formam dixeris* (that is ἐντελέχειαν) *intelliges immaterialitatem, simplicitatem, potestatem, perfectionem, informationem. Hoc enim est* ἐν : *quod innuit maximus Poetarum, Totásque infusa per artus. Hoc est* τέλος : *quia est ultima forma sub cœlestibus, & princeps inferiorum, finis & perfectio. Hoc est* ἔχειν, *posse.* This goodly mysterie and fit significancy seems plainly forced or fictitious, if you compare it with what was cited out of *Arist.* about Motion. So that when we have made the best of ἐντελέχεια, it is but the form of any thing in an ordinary and usuall sense. If we stood much upon words, ἐνδελέχεια would prove more significant of the nature of the Soul, even according to *Scaligers* own *Etymon,* from ἐν, διέων, ἐλᾶν, and ἔχειν : from its permeation, & colligation or keeping together the body from defluxion into its ancient principles, which properties be included in ἐν and δέων : ἐλᾶν moves forward the body thus kept together : ἔχειν intimates the possession or retention of the body thus moved, that it is rather promov'd by the Soul, than mov'd from the Soul. But of these words enough, or rather too much.

Eternitie is the steddy comprehension of all things at once. See *Æon* described in my Notes upon *Psychozoia.*

Euphrona, Εὐφρόνη, The night.

F

FAith. Platonick faith in the first Good. This faith is excellently described in *Proclus,* where it is set above all ratiocination, nay, Intellect it self. Πρὸς δὲ αὐτὸ ἀγαθὸν οὐ γνώσεως ἔτι καὶ συνεργείας δεῖ τοῖς συναφθῆναι σπεύδουσιν, ἀλλ' ἱδρύσεως καὶ μονίμου

19

καταστάσεως καὶ ἠρεμίας. But to them that endeavour to be joyned with the first Good, there is no need of knowledge or multifarious cooperation, but of settlednesse, steddinesse and rest, *lib.* 1. *cap.* 24. *Theolog. Platon.* And in the next chapter, Δεῖ γὰρ οὐ γνωστικῶς οὐ δ' ἀτελῶς τὸ ἀγαθὸν ἐπιζητεῖν, ἀλλ' ἐπιδόντας ἑαυτοὺς τῷ θείῳ φωτὶ καὶ μύσαντας, οὕτως ἐνιδρύεσθαι τῇ ἀγνώστῳ καὶ κρυφίῳ τῶν ὄντων ἑνάδι.

For we must not seek after that absolute or first good cognoscitively or imperfectly, but giving our selves up to the divine light, and winking (that is shutting our eyes of reason and understanding) so to place ourselves steddily in that hidden Unity of all things: After he preferres this faith before the clear and present assent to the Κοινὰ ἔννοιαι, yea and the νοερὰ ἁπλότης, so that he will not that any intellectuall operation should come in comparison with it. Πολυειδὴς γὰρ αὕτη καὶ δι' ἑτερότητος χωριζομένη τῶν νοουμένων, καὶ ὅλως κίνησίς ἐστι νοερὰ περὶ τὸ νοητόν. Δεῖ δὲ τὴν θείαν πίστιν ἑνοειδῆ καὶ ἤρεμον ὑπάρχειν ἐν τῷ τῆς ἀγαθότητος ὅρμῳ τελείως ἱδρυθεῖσαν. For the operation of the Intellect is multiform, and by diversity separate from her objects, and is in a word, intellectuall motion about the object intelligible. But the divine faith must be simple and uniform, quiet and steddily resting in the haven of goodnesse. And at last he summarily concludes, Εἷς οὖν οὗτος ὅρμος ἀσφαλὴς τῶν ὄντων ἁπάντων. See *Procl. Theolog. Platonic. lib.* 1. *cap.* 25.

G

Gabriel, The strength of God, from גבר and אל.
Glaucis, Glaux, γλαὺξ, an Owle.

H

Haphe. Ἁφή, The touch.
Har-Eloim, הר־אלהים The mount of Angels, Genii, or particular spirits.
Hattove, הטוב τἀγαθόν, the Good, or that eminent Good, or first Good from whence all good is derived. See *Ahad.*
Helios, Ἥλιος, The Sunne.
Heterogeneall, is that which consists of parts of a diverse nature, or form : as for example, a man's body, of flesh, bones, nerves, &c.
Homogeneall, That whose nature is of one kind.
Hyle, Materia prima, or that dark fluid potentiality of the creature, the straitnesse, repugnancy, and incapacity of the creature : as when its being this, destroyes or debilitates the capacity of being something else, or after some other manner. This is all that any wary Platonist will understand by Ἀνάγκη πολλὰ τῷ θεῷ δυσμαχοῦσα καὶ ἀφηνιάζουσα, *in Plutarch's ψυχογονία.*
Hypomone, Ὑπομονή, Patience. See *Autaparnes.*

I

IAo, A corruption of the *Tetragrammaton.* Greek writers have strangely mash'd this word יהוה, some calling it Ιωβά, others Ιαώ, some Ινεώ. It is very likely that from this Ιευώ came *Bacchus* his apellation Εὔιος, and the Mœnades acclamations εὐοί in his Orgia.

Which sutes well with the Clarian Oracle, which saith that in Autumne, the Sun is called Ιαώ, which is the time of vintage.
μεταπώρου δ' ἁβρὸν Ιαώ. See Fuller's Miscel.
Ida. See *Pompon. Mel. lib.* 1. *cap.* 17.
Ideas, or *Idees,* sometimes they are forms in the Intellectuall world, *viz.* in Æon, or On ; other sometimes, phantasmes or representations in the soul. Innate *Idees* are the soul's nature it self, her uniform essence, able by her *Fiat* to produce this or that phantasme into act.
Idea Lond. The Intellectuall world.
Idiopathie, ἰδιοπάθεια, is one's proper peculiar πάθος, my or thy, being affected thus or so, upon this or that occasion ; as ἰδιοσυγκρασία, is this or that mans proper temper. But this propriety of affection may also belong unto kinds. As an Elephant hath his idiopathy, and a man his, at the hearing of a pipe ; a Cat and an Eagle at the sight of the Sunne ; a Dogge and a Circopithecus at the sight of the Moon, &c.
Idothea, The fleet passage of fading forms ; from εἶδος, *Forma,* and θέω, *curro.*
Intellect. Sometimes it is to be interpreted Soul. Sometimes the intellectuall faculty of the Soul. Sometimes Intellect is an absolute essence shining into the Soul : whose nature is this. A substance purely immateriall, impeccable, actually omniform, or comprehending all things at once : which the soul doth also being perfectly joyned with the Intellect. Ἔχομεν οὖν καὶ τὰ εἴδη διχῶς ἐν μὲν ψυχῇ οἷον μὲν ἀνειλιγμένα καὶ οἷον κεχωρισμένα, ἐν δὲ τῷ νῷ ὁμοῦ τὰ πάντα. *Plot. Ennead.* 1. *lib.* 1. *cap.* 8.
Isosceles, A triangle with two sides equall.

L

Lampropronæa, The bright *side of* Providence.
Leturion, Nocturnall fire, from ליל and אור.
Leontopolis, Λεοντόπολις, The Lion's citie or Politie.
Life. The vitall operation of any soul. Sometimes it is the Soul it self, be it sensitive, vegetative, or rationall.
Logos, Λόγος, The appellation of the Sonne of God. It is ordinarily translated the *Word,* but hath an ample signification. It signifieth Reason, Proportion, Form, Essence, any inward single thought, or apprehension ; is any thing but matter, and matter is nothing.
Lower man, The lower man is our enquickned body, into which our soul comes, it being fully prepared for the receiving of such a guest. The manner of the production of souls, or rather their non-production is admirably well set down in *Plotinus,* See *Ennead.* 6. *l.* 4. *c.* 14, 15.
Lypon, from Λύπη, sorrow.

M

Magicall, that is, attractive, or commanding by force of sympathy with the life of this naturall world.
Melampronæa, the black *side of* Providence.

Memory. Mundane memory. Is that memory that is seated in the Mundane spirit of man, by a strong impression, or inustion of any phantasme, or outward sensible object, upon that spirit. But there is a memory more subtill and abstract in the soul it self, without the help of this spirit, which she also carries away with her having left the body.

Michael, who like unto God? from ‫מי‬ *quis,* & ‫כ‬ *similitudinis,* & ‫אל‬ *Deus.*

Moment. Sometimes signifies an instant, as indivisible, as κίνημα, which in motion answers to an instant in time, or a point in a line, *Arist. Phys.* In this sense I use it, *Psychathan. lib. 3. cant. 2. stanz.* 16: " But in a moment Sol doth ray." But *Cant.* 3. *stanz.* 45, *vers.* 2, I understand, as also doth *Lansbergius,* by a moment one second of a minute. In *Antipsych. Cant.* 2. *stanz.* 10. *vers.* 2, by a moment I understand a minute, or indefinitely any small time.

Monad, Μονάς, is *Unitas,* the principle of all numbers, an embleme of the Deity : And the *Pythagoreans* call it Θεὸς, God. It is from μένειν, because it is μόνιμος, stable and immovable, a firme Cube of it self, One time one time one remains still one, See *Ahad.*

Monocordia, Μονοκαρδία, from μόνος and καρδία, Single-heartednesse.

Mundane, Mundane spirit, is that which is the spirit of the world, or Universe. I mean by it not an Intellectuall spirit, but a fine unfixt, attenuate, subtill, ethereall substance, the immediate vehicle of plasticall or sensitive life.

Myrmecopolis, Μυρμηκόπολις, the city or polity of Pismires.

N

N Eurospast, νευρόσπαστον, a Puppet or any Machina that's mov'd by an unseen string or nerve.

O

O Gdoas, 'Ογδοὰς, *numerus octonarius,* the number of eight.

Omniformity, the omniformity of the soul is the having in her nature all forms, latent at least, and power of awaking them into act, upon occasion.

On, τὸ ὄν. The being.

Orb. Orb Intellectuall is nothing else but Æon or the Intellectuall world. The Orbs generall mentioned, *Psychathan. lib.* 1. *cant.* 3. *stanz.* 23. *vers.* 2, I understand by them but so many universall orders of being, if I may so terme them all ; for Hyle hath little or nothing of being.

Out-World, and *Out Heaven.* The sensible World, the visible Heaven.

P

P Andemoniothen, Πᾶν-δαιμονιοθεν, all from the devill ; *viz.* all false perswasions, and ill effects from them.

Panoply, Πανοπλία, Armour for the whole body.

Pantheothen, Πᾶν-θεόθεν, All from God. Which is true in one sense, false in another. You'll easily discern the sense in the place you find the word. This passage of Pantheothen contains a very savory and hearty reproof of all, be they what they will, that do make use of that intricate mystery of fate and infirmity ; safely to guard themselves from the due reprehensions and just expostulations of the earnest messengers of God, who would rouse them out of this sleep of sin, and stir them up seriously to seek after the might and spirit of Christ, that may work wonderfully in their souls to a glorious conquest and triumph against the devill, death and corruption.

Parallax, παράλλαξις, is the difference betwixt the true and seeming place of a star ; proceeding from the sensible difference of the centre, and the height of the superficies of the earth in reference to the star, and from the stars declining from the Zenith.

Parelies, Παρήλια, are rorid clouds which bear the image of the Sunne.

Parturient. See *Vaticinant.*

Penia, Πενία, Want or poverty.

Perigee, Περίγειον, is that absis or ark of a Planet's circle, in which it comes nearer to the earth.

Periphere, Peripheria, it is the line that terminates a circle.

Phantasie, Lower phantasie, is that which resides in the Mundane spirit of a man. See *Memory.*

Phantasme, φάντασμα, any thing that the soul conceives in it self, without any present externall object.

Philosomatus, Φιλοσώματος, a lover of his body.

Phobon, from φόβος, fear.

Phrenition, anger, impatiency, fury ; from φρενῖτις, phrensie or madnesse. *Ira furor brevis est.*

Physis, Φύσις, Nature vegetative.

Pithecus, Πίθηκος, an Ape.

Pithecusa, the land of Apes.

Plastick, δύναμις πλαστική, is that efformative might in the seed that shapes the body in its growth.

Protopathy, πρωτοπάθεια. It is a suffering or being affected at first, that is, without circulation. If any man strike me, I feel immediately ; because my soul is united with this body that is struck : and this is protopathy. If the air be struck aloof of, I am sensible also of that, but by circulation or propagation of that impression into my eare ; and this is deuteropathy. See *Deuteropathy.*

Proteus, Vertumnus, changeablenesse.

Psittaco. Don Psittaco, from *Psittacus* a Parot, a bird that speaks significant words, whose sense notwithstanding it self is ignorant of. The Dialogue betwixt this Parot and Mnemon sets out the vanity of superficiall conceited Theologasters, that have but the surface and thin imagination of divinity, but truly devoid of the spirit and inward power of Christ, the living well-spring of knowledge and virtue, and yet do pride themselves in prattling and discoursing of the most hidden and abstruse mysteries of God, and take all occasions to shew forth their goodly skill and wonderfull insight into holy truth, when as they have indeed scarce licked the outside of the glasse wherein it lies.

Psittacusa, the land of Parots.

Psychania, the land of Souls.

Psyche, Ψυχή, Soul, or spirit.

Psychicall, Though Ψυχή be a generall name and belongs to the souls of beasts and plants, yet I understand by life Psychicall, such centrall life as is capable of Æon, and Ahad.

Pteroessa, Πτερόεσσα, the land of winged souls ; from πτέρον, a wing.

Q

QUadrate. A figure with foure equall sides, and foure right angles. The rightnesse of the angles, is a plain embleme of erectnesse or uprightnesse of mind. The number of the sides, as also of the angles, being *pariter par,* that is, equall divisible to the utmost unities (τὸ δὲ ἴσον δίκαιον, as it is in *Aristotle*) intimates equity or justice. The sides are equall one with another, and so are the angles ; and the number of the sides and angles equall one with another. Both the numbers put together are a number *pariter par* again, and constitute the first cube which is eight : That adds steddinesse and persevererance in true justice and uprightnesse toward God and man. *Hypomone* bears all this, that is, all that dolour and vexation that comes from the keeping our perverse heart to so strait and streight a rule.

Quantitative. Forms quantitative, are such sensible energies as arise from the complexion of many natures together, at whose discretion they vanish. That's the seventh orb of things, though broken and not filling all as the other do. But if you take it for the whole sensible world, it is intire and is the same that *Tasis* in *Psychozoia.* But the centre of *Tasis, viz.* the multiplication of the reall Cuspis of the Cone (for Hyle that is set for the most contract point of the Cuspis is scarce to be reckoned among realities) that immense diffusion of atoms, is to be referred to Psyche, as an internall vegetative act, and so belongs to Physis the lowest order of life. For as that warmth that the soul doth afford the body, is not rationall, sensitive or imaginative, but vegetative ; So this, שמים that is, liquid fire, which Psyche sends out, and is the outmost, last, and lowest operation from her self, is also vegetative.

R

RAyes. The rayes of an essence is its energie. See *Energie.*

Reason. I understand by Reason, the deduction of one thing from another, which I conceive proceeds from a kind of continuity of phantasmes ; and is something like the moveing of a cord at one end ; the parts next it rise with it. And by this concatenation of phantasms I conceive, that both brutes and men are moved in reasonable wayes and methods in their ordinary externall actions.

Reduplicative. That is reduplicative, which is not onely in this point, but also in another, having a kind of circumscribed ubiquity, *viz.* in its own sphear. And this is either by being in that sphear omnipresent it self, as the soul is said to be in the body *tota in toto & tota*

in qualibet parte; or else at least by propagation of rayes, which is the image of it self ; and so are divers sensible objects *Reduplicative,* as light, colours, sounds. And I make account either of these wayes justly denominate any thing spirituall. Though the former is most properly, at least more eminently spirituall. And whether any thing be after that way spirituall saving the Divinity, there is reason to doubt. For what is intirely omnipresent in a sphear, whose diametre is but three foot, I see not, why (that in the circumference being as fresh and intire as that in the centre) it should stop there and not proceed, even *in infuitum,* if the circumference be still as fresh and entire as the centre. But I define nothing.

Rhomboides, is a parallelogrammicall figure with unequall sides and oblique angles.

S

SCalen, a triangle with all sides unequall.

Self reduplicative. See *Reduplicative.*

Semele, Imagination ; from צמל *imago.*

Simon, intimates obedience, from שמע *obedivit.*

Solyma, or *Salem,* from שלום Peace.

Soul, when I speak of man's soul, I understand that which Moses saith was inspired into the body, (fitted out and made of Earth) by God, Gen. 2. which is not that impeccable spirit that cannot sinne ; but the very same that the Platonists call ψυχή, a middle essence betwixt that which they call νοῦς (and we would in the Christian language call πνεῦμα) and the life of the body which is εἴδωλον ψυχῆς, a kind of an umbratil vitalitie that the soul imparts to the body in the enlivening of it : That and the body together, we Christians call σάρξ, and the suggestions of it, especially in its corrupt estate, φρόνημα σαρκός. And that that which God inspired into Adam was no more then ψυχή, the soul, not the spirit, though it be called נשמת חיים *Spiraculum vitae;* is plain out of the text ; because it made man but become a living soul, נפש חיה. But you will say, he was a dead soul before, and this was the spirit of life, ye the spirit of God, the life of the soul that was breathed into him.

But if חיה imply such a life and spirit, you must acknowledge the same to be also in the most stupid of all living creatures, even the fishes (whose soul is as but salt to keep them from stinking, as *Philo* speaks) for they are said to be נפש חיה chap. 1. v. 20, 21. See 1. Cor. chap. 15. v. 45, 46. In brief therefore, that which in Platonisme is νοῦς ; is in Scripture πνεῦμα ; what σάρξ in one, τὸ θηρίον, the brute or beast in the other, ψυχή the same in both.

Sperm. It signifies ordinarily seed. I put it for the λόγος σπερματικὸς, the *ratio seminalis,* or the invisible plasticall form that shapes every visible creature.

Spermaticall. It belongs properly to Plants, but is transferred also to the Plasticall power in Animalls, I enlarge it to all magnetick power whatsoever that doth immediately rule and actuate any body. For all mag-netick power is founded in *Physis*, and in reference to her, this world is but one Plant, one λόγος σπερματικὸς giving it shape and corporeall life) as in reference to *Psyche*, one happy and holy Animall.

Spirit. Sometimes it signifieth the soul, othersome-time, the naturall spirits in a man's body, which are *Vinculum animae & corporis*, and the souls vehicle : Sometimes life. See *Reduplicative.*

T

TAgathon, τἀγαθὸν, The Good ; the same with *Hattove.*

Tasis, τάσις, extension.

Tricentreity. Centre is put for essence, so *Tricen-treity* must imply a Trinity of essence. See *Centre* and *Energie.*

V

VAticinant. The soul is said to be in a *vaticinant,* or *parturient* condition, when she hath some kind of sense, and hovering knowledge of a thing, but yet cannot distinctly and fully, and commandingly represent it to herself, cannot plainly apprehend, much lesse com prehend the matter. The phrase is borrowed of *Proclus,* who describing the incomprehensiblenesse of God, and the desire of all things toward him, speaks thus ; "Ἀγνω-στον γὰρ ὃν ποθεῖ τὰ ὄντα τὸ ἐφετὸν τοῦτο καὶ ἄληπτον, μήτε οὖν γνῶναι μήτε ἑλεῖν ὃ ποθεῖ, δυνάμενα, περὶ αὐτὸ πάντα χορεύει καὶ ὠδίνει μὲν αὐτὸ καὶ οἶον ἀπομαντεύεται. *Theolog. Platon. lib.* 1. *cap.* 21. See *Psychathan. lib.* 3. *cant.* 3. *stanz.* 12. & 14.

Vranore. The light or beauty of heaven, from οὐρανὸς, and אוֹר *lux,* or ὥρα *pulchritudo.*

Z

ZAphon, Aquilo. The North.

Zeus, Ζεὺς, Jupiter, from ζέω, *ferveo,* or ζάω, *vivo.*

THus have I run through the more obscure terms in the preceding Poems. But for the many points a man may meet withall therein, though I did hereto-fore make some sleight promise of speaking more deter-minately of them, I hope I may without offence decline the performance as yet, till I abound more with leasure and judgement. For as I am certain I have little enough of the one, so I can not but doubt (Nature having lavished so much upon all men else, even to the infallible Determining of mutuall contradictions) whether I have got any share at all of the other. But yet I hope, without breach of modesty, I may presume to under-stand the purpose of my own writings. Which, as I have heretofore signified, was no other then this, to stirre men up to take into their thoughts these two main considerations. The heartie good will of God to mankind, even in the life of this world, made of the commixture of light and darknesse, that he will through his power rescue those souls, that are faithfull in this their triall, and preferre the light before the dark ; that he will, I say, deliver them from the power of living

Death, and Hell, by that strong arm of their salvation, Jesus Christ, the living God enthron'd in the heart of man, to whom all the Genii of the Universe, be they never so goodly and glorious shall serve. They and all their curious devices and inventions shall be a spoil, prey, and a possession to Him that is most just, and shall govern the nations in righteousnesse and equity. And that, beside this happinesse on earth, every holy soul hereafter shall enjoy a never-fading felicity in the invisible and eternall Heaven, the Intellectuall world. Which if it be not true, I must needs confesse, it seems almost indifferent whether any creature be or no. For what is it to have lived, suppose 70 years, wherein we have been dead or worse above two third parts of them ? Sleep, youth, age and diseases, with a number of poor and contemptible employments, swallow up at least so great a portion : that as good, if not better, is he that never was, then he is, that hath but such a glance or glimpse of passing life to mock him.

And although the succession of righteousnesse upon earth may rightly seem a goodly great and full spread thing, and a matter that may beare an ample corre-spondencie even to the larger thoughts of a good and upright man ; yet to say the truth, no man is capable of any large inheritance, whose life and existence is so scant that he shall not be able so much as to dream of the least happinesse once seised on by death.

But there are continually on earth such numbers of men alive, that if they liv'd well it would be an Heaven or Paradise. But still a scant one to every particular man, whose dayes are even as nothing. So that the work of God seems not considerable, in the making of this world, if humane souls be extinguished when they go out of it. You will say that those small particles of time that is thus scattered and lost among men in their successions, are comprehended and collected in God who is a continuall witnesse of all things.

But, alas ! what doth the perpetuall repetition of the same life or deiform Image throughout all ages adde to Him, that is at once infinitely himself, viz. good, and happy?

So that there is nothing considerable in the creation, if the rationall creature be mortall. For neither is God at all profited by it, nor man considerably. And were not the Angels a great deal better employed in the be-holding the worth of their Creatour, then to deminish their own happinesse, by attending those, whom nothing can make happy? looking on this troubled passing stream of the perishing generations of men, to as little purpose almost, as idle boyes do on dancing blebs and bubbles in the water.

What designe therefore can there be in God in the making of this world that will prove θεοπρεπὲς, worthy of so excellent a goodnesse and wisdome ; but the triall of the immortall spirit of man? It seems the deepest reach of his counsell in the creation ; and the life of this world but a prelude to one of longer durance and larger circumference hereafter. And surely it is nothing else but the heavy load of this body, that keeps down our mind from the reaching to those so high hopes, that I may not say from a certain sense and feeling of that undisturbd state of immortality.

And thus much I have ventured to speak boldly without *Scepticisme* in Faith and Sense, that the first Principle of all things is living Goodnesse, armd with Wisdome & all-powerfull Love. But if a man's soul be once sunk by evil fate or desert from the sense of this high and heavenly truth, into that cold conceit ; that the Originall of things doth lie either in shuffling Chance, or in that stark root of unknowing Nature and brute Necessity ; all the subtile cords of Reason, without the timely recovery of that divine touch within the hidden spirit of man, will never be able to pull him back, out of that abhorred pit of Atheisme and Infidelity. So much better is Innocency and Piety then subtile Argument, and earnest and sincere Devotion then curious Dispute.

II.—MINOR POEMS.

NOTE.

The ' Minor Poems ' formed pp. 297-334 of the volume of 1647. They are reproduced with the same fidelity to the Author's own text as in the ' Philosophical Poems.' The modest original title-page is given opposite.-- G.

AN

ADDITION

of ſome few ſmaller

POEMS,

BY

HENRY MORE:

Master of Arts, and Fellow of

CHRISTS COLLEDGE in

CAMBRIDGE.

CAMBRIDGE,
Printed by *Roger Daniel*, Printer to the
Universitie. 1647.

MINOR POEMS.

Cupids Conflict.

Mela. Cleanthes.

Cl. **M**Ela my dear ! why been thy looks so sad
As if thy gentle heart were sunk with
care ?
     Impart thy case ; for be it good or bad
Friendship in either will bear equall share.
  Mel. Not so ; *Cleanthes*, for if bad it be
My self must bleed afresh by wounding thee :

But what it is, my slow, uncertain wit
Cannot well judge. But thou shalt sentence give
How manfully of late my self I quit,
When with that lordly lad by chance I strive.
    Cl. Of friendship *Mela !* let's that story hear.
    Mel. Sit down *Cleanthes* then, and lend thine ear.

Upon a day as best did please my mind
Walking abroad amidst the verdant field
Scattering my carefull thoughts i' th' wanton wind
The pleasure of my path so farre had till'd
    My feeble feet that without timely rest
    Uneath it were to reach my wonted nest.

In secret shade farre moved from mortalls sight
In lowly dale my wandring limbs I laid
On the cool grasse where Natures pregnant wit
A goodly Bower of thickest trees had made.
    Amongst the leaves the chearfull Birds did fare
    And sweetly carol'd to the echoing Air.

Hard at my feet ran down a crystall spring
Which did the cumbrous pebbles hoarsly chide
For standing in the way. . Though murmuring
The broken stream his course did rightly guide
    And strongly pressing forward with disdain
    The grassie flore divided into twain.

The place a while did feed my foolish eye
As being new, and eke mine idle ear
Did listen oft to that wild harmonie
And oft my curious phansie would compare
    How well agreed the Brooks low muttering Base,
    With the birds trebbles pearch'd on higher place.

But senses objects soon do glut the soul,
Or rather weary with their emptinesse ;

So I, all heedlesse how the waters roll
And mindlesse of the mirth the birds expresse,
    Into my self 'gin softly to retire
    After hid heavenly pleasures to enquire.

While I this enterprize do entertain ;
Lo ! on the other side in thickest bushes
A mighty noise ! with that a naked swain
With blew and purple wings streight rudely rushes
    He leaps down light upon the flowry green,
    Like sight before mine eyes had never seen.

At's snowy back the boy a quiver wore
Right fairly wrought and gilded all with gold :
A silver bow in his left hand he bore,
And in his right a ready shaft did hold.
    Thus armed stood he, and betwixt us tway
    The labouring brook did break its toilsome way.

The wanton lad whose sport is others pain
Did charge his bended bow with deadly dart,
And drawing to the head with might and main,
With fell intent he aim'd to hit my heart.
    But ever as he shot his arrows still
    In their mid course dropt down into the rill.

Of wondrous virtues that in waters been
Is needlesse to rehearse, all books do ring
Of those strange rarities. But ne're was seen
Such virtue as resided in this spring.
    The noveltie did make me much admire
    But stirr'd the hasty youth to ragefull ire.

As heedlesse fowls that take their per'lous flight
Over that bane of birds, *Averno lake,*
Do drop down dead : so dead his shafts did light
Amid the stream, which presently did slake
    Their fiery points, and all their feathers wet
    Which made the youngster Godling inly fret.

Thus lustfull Love (this was that love I ween)
Was wholly changed to consuming ire.
And eath it was, sith they're so near a kin
They be both born of one rebellious fire.
    But he supprest his wrath and by and by
    For feathered darts, he wingèd words let flie.

Vain man ! said he, and would thou wer'st not vain
That hid'st thy self in solitary shade

And spil'st thy precious youth in sad disdain
Hating this lifes delight ! Hath God thee made
Part of this world, and wilt not thou partake
Of this worlds pleasure for its makers sake?

Unthankfull wretch ! Gods gifts thus to reject
And maken nought of Natures goodly dower.
That milders still away through thy neglect
And dying fades like unregarded flower.
   This life is good, what's good thou must improve,
   The highest improvement of this life is love.

Had I (but O that envious Destinie,
Or Stygian vow, or thrice accursèd charm
Should in this place free passage thus denie
Unto my shafts as messengers of harm !)
   Had I but once transfixt thy froward breast,
   How would'st thou then —— I staid not for the rest ;

But thus half angry to the boy replide :
How would'st thou then my soule of sense bereave !
I blinded, thee more blind should choose my guide !
How would'st thou then my muddied mind deceive
   With fading shows, that in my errour vile,
   Base lust, I love should tearm ; vice, virtue stile.

How should my wicked rhymes then idolize
Thy wretched power, and with impious wit
Impute thy base born passions to the skies,
And my souls sicknesse count an heavenly fit,
   My weaknesse strength, my wisdome to be caught,
   My bane my blisse, mine ease to be o'rewraught.

How often through my fondly feigning mind
And frantick phansie, in my Mistris eye
Should I a thousand fluttering *Cupids* find
Bathing their busie wings ? How oft espie
   Under the shadow of her eye-brows fair
   Ten thousand Graces sit all naked bare?

Thus haunted should I be with such feat fiends,
A pretty madnesse were my portion due.
Foolish my self I would not hear my friends.
Should deem the true for false, the false for true.
   My way all dark more slippery then ice
   My attendants, anger, pride, and jealousies.

Unthankfull then to God I should neglect
All the whole world for one poore sorry wight,
Whose pestilent eye into my heart project
Would burn like poysonous Comet in my spright.
   Aye me ! how dismall then would prove that day
   Whose onely light sprang from so fatall ray.

Who seeks for pleasure in this mortall life
By diving deep into the body base
Shall loose true pleasure : But who gainly strive
Their sinking soul above this bulk to place
   Enlarg'd delight they certainly shall find,
   Unbounded joyes to fill their boundlesse mind.

When I my self from mine own self do quit
And each thing else ; then an all spreaden love
To the vast Universe my soul doth fit,
Makes me half equall to All-seeing Jove.
   My mightie wings high stretch'd then clapping light
   I brush the starres and make them shine more bright.

Then all the works of God with close embrace
I dearly hug in my enlargèd arms,
All the hid paths of heavenly Love I trace
And boldly listen to his secret charms,
   Then clearly view I where true light doth rise,
   And where eternall Night low-pressèd lies.

Thus lose I not by leaving small delight
But gain more joy, while I my self suspend
From this and that ; for then with all unite
I all enjoy, and love that love commends,
   That all is more then loves the partiall soul
   Whose petty love the impartiall fates controll.

Ah son ! said he, (and laughèd very loud)
That trickst thy tongue with uncouth strange disguize,
Extolling highly that with speeches proud
To mortall men that humane state denies,
   And rashly blaming what thou never knew ;
   Let men experienc'd speak, if they'll speak true.

Had I once lanc'd thy froward flinty heart
And cruddled bloud had thawn with living fire
And prickt thy drousie sprite with gentle smart
How wouldst thou wake to kindle sweet desire !
   Thy soul fill'd up with overflowing pleasures
   Would dew thy lips with honey dropping measures.

Then would thou caroll loud and sweetly sing
In honour of my sacred Deity
That all the woods and hollow hills would ring
Reechoning thy heavenly harmony.
   And eke the hardy rocks with full rebounds
   Would faithfully return thy silver sounds.

Next unto me would be thy Mistresse fair,
Whom thou might setten out with goodly skill
Her peerlesse beauty and her virtues rare,
That all would wonder at thy gracefull quill.
   And lastly in us both thy self shouldst raise
   And crown thy temples with immortall bayes.

But now thy riddles all men do neglect,
Thy rugged lines of all do ly forlorn.
Unwelcome rhymes that rudely do detect
The Readers ignorance. Men holden scorn
   To be so often non-plus'd or to spell,
   And on one stanza a whole age to dwell.

Besides this harsh and hard obscurity
Of the hid sense, thy words are barbarous
And strangely new, and yet too frequently
Return, as usuall plain and obvious,
   So that the show of the new thick-set patch
   Marres all the old with which it ill doth match.

But if thy haughty mind, forsooth would deign
To stoop so low as t' hearken to my lore,
Then wouldst thou with trim lovers not disdeign
To adorn th' outside, set the best before.
   Nor rub nor wrinkle would thy verses spoil,
   Thy rhymes should run as glib and smooth as oyl.

If that be all, said I, thy reasons slight
Can never move my well establish'd mind.
Full well I wote alwayes the present sprite,
Or life that doth possesse the soul, doth blind,
   Shutting the windows 'gainst broad open day
   Lest fairer sights its uglinesse bewray.

The soul then loves that disposition best
Because no better comes unto her view.
The drunkard drunkennesse, the sluggard rest,
Th' Ambitious honour and obeysance due.
   So all the rest do love their vices base
   'Cause virtues beauty comes not into place.

And looser love 'gainst Chastity divine
Would shut the door that he might sit alone.
Then wholly should my mind to him incline,
And woxen strait, (since larger love was gone)
   That paultry spirit of low contracting lust
   Would fit my soul as if 't were made for 't just.

Then should I with my fellow bird or brute
So strangely metamorphiz'd, either ney
Or bellow loud : or if't may better sute
Chirp out my joy pearch'd upon higher spray.
   My passions fond with impudence rehearse,
   Immortalize my madnesse in a verse.

This is the summe of thy deceiving boast
That I vain ludenesse highly should admire,
When I the sense of better things have lost
And chang'd my heavenly heat for hellish fire.
   Passion is blind : but virtues piercing eye
   Approaching danger can from farre espie.

And what thou dost Pedantickly object
Concerning my rude rugged uncouth style,
As childish toy I manfully neglect,
And at thy hidden snares do inly smile.
   How ill alas ! with wisdome it accords
   To sell my living sense for livelesse words.

My thought's the fittest measure of my tongue,
Wherefore I'll use what's most significant,
And rather then my inward meaning wrong
Or my full-shining notion trimly skant,
   I'll conjure up old words out of their grave,
   Or call fresh forrein force in if need crave.

And these attending on my moving mind
Shall duly usher in the fitting sense.
As oft as meet occasion I find.
Unusuall words oft used give lesse offence ;
   Nor will the old contexture dim or marre,
   For often us'd they're next to old, thred-bare.

And if the old seem in too rusty hew,
Then frequent rubbing makes them shine like gold.
And glister all with colour gayly new.
Wherefore to use them both we will be bold.
   Thus lifts me fondly with fond folk to toy,
   And answer fools with equall foolery.

The meaner mind works with more nicetie
As Spiders wont to weave their idle web,
But braver spirits do all things gallantly
Of lesser failings nought at all affred :
   So Natures carelesse pencill dipt in light
   With sprinkled starres hath spattered the Night.

And if my notions clear though rudely thrown
And loosely scattered in my poesie,
May lend men light till the dead Night be gone,
And Morning fresh with roses strew the sky :
   It is enough, I meant no trimmer frame
   Nor by nice needle-work to seek a name.

Vain man ! that seekest name 'mongst earthly men
Devoid of God and all good virtuous lere ;
Who groping in the dark do nothing ken ;
But mad, with griping care their souls do tear,
   Or Burst with hatred or with envie pine,
   Or burn with rage or melt out at their eyne.

Thrice happy he whose name is writ above,
And doeth good though gaining infamy ;
Requiteth evil turns with hearty love,
And recks not what befalls him outwardly :
   Whose worth is in himself, and onely blisse
   In his pure conscience that doth nought amisse.

Who placeth pleasure in his purgèd soul
And virtuous life his treasure doth esteem ;
Who can his passions master and controll,
And that true lordly manlinesse doth deem,
   Who from this world himself hath clearly quit,
   Counts nought his own but what lives in his sprite.

So when his spright from this vain world shall flit
It bears all with it whatsoever was dear
Unto it self, passing in easie fit,
As kindly ripen'd corn comes out of th' ear.
   Thus mindlesse of what idle men will say
   He takes his own and stilly goes his way.

But the Retinue of proud Lucifer,
Those blustering Poets that fly after fame
And deck themselves like the bright Morning-starre,
Alas ! it is but all a crackling flame.
   For death will strip them of that glorious plume,
   That airie blisse will vanish into fume.

For can their carefull ghosts from *Limbo Lake*
Return, or listen from the bowed skie
To heare how well their learnèd lines do take ?
Or if they could ; is Heavens felicitie
   So small as by mans praise to be encreas'd,
   Hells pain no greater then hence to be eas'd ?

Therefore once dead in vain shall I transmit
My shadow to gazing Posterity ;
Cast Tarre behind me I shall never see't,
On Heavens fair Sunne having fast fixt mine eye.
    Nor while I live, heed I what man doth praise
    Or underprize mine unaffected layes.

What moves thee then, said he, to take the pains
And spenden time if thou contemn'st the fruit ?
Sweet fruit of fame, that fills the Poets brains
With high conceit and feeds his fainting wit.
    How pleasant 'tis in honour here to live
    And dead, thy name for ever to survive !

Or is thy abject mind so basely bent
As of thy Muse to maken Merchandize ?
(And well I wote this is no strange intent.)
The hopefull glimps of gold from chattering Pies,
    From Daws and Crows, and Parots oft hath wrung
    An unexpected Pegaseian song.

Foul shame on him, quoth I, that shamefull thought
Doth entertain within his dunghill breast,
Both God and Nature hath my spirits wrought
To better temper and of old hath blest
    My loftie soul with more divine aspires,
    Then to be touched with such vile low desires.

I hate and highly scorn that Kestrell kind
Of bastard scholars that subordinate
The precious choice induements of the mind
To wealth or worldly good. Adulterate
    And cursèd brood I Your wit and will are born
    Of th' earth and circling thither do return.

Profit and honour be those measures scant
Of your slight studies and endeavours vain,
And when you once have got what you did want
You leave your learning to enjoy your gain.
    Your brains grow low, your bellies swell up high,
    Foul sluggish fat ditts up your dullèd eye.

Thus what the earth did breed, to th' earth is gone,
Like fading hearb or feeble drooping flower,
By feet of men and beast quite trodden down,
The muck-sprung learning cannot long endure,
    Back she returns lost in her filthy source,
    Drown'd, chok'd or slocken by her cruell nurse.

True virtue to her self's the best reward,
Rich with her own and full of lively spirit,
Nothing cast down for want of due regard,
Or 'cause rude men acknowledge not her merit.
    She knows her worth and stock from whence she
        sprung,
    Spreads fair without the warmth of earthly dung.

Dew'd with the drops of Heaven shall flourish long ;
As long as day and night do share the skie,
And though that day and night should fail yet strong,
And steddie, fixed on Eternitie
    Shall bloom for ever. So the soul shall speed
    That loveth virtue for no worldly meed.

Though sooth to say, the worldly meed is due
To her more then to all the world beside.
Men ought do homage with affections true
And offer gifts, for God doth there reside.
    The wise and virtuous soul is his own seat
    To such what's given God himself doth get.

But earthly minds whose sight's seal'd up with mud
Discern not this flesh-clouded Deity,
Ne do acknowledge any other good
Then what their mole-warp bands can feel and trie
    By groping touch ; (thus worth of them unseen)
    Of nothing worthy that true worth they ween.

Wherefore the prudent Law-givers of old
Even in all Nations, with right sage foresight
Discovering from farre how clums and cold
The vulgar wight would be to yield what's right
    To virtuous learning, did by law designe
    Great wealth and honour to that worth divine.

But nought's by law to Poesie due said he,
Ne doth the solemn Statesmans head take care
Of those that such impertinent pieces be
Of common-weals. Thou'd better then to spare
    Thy uselesse vein. Or tell else, what may move
    Thy busie Muse such fruitlesse pains to prove.

No pains but pleasure to do th' dictates dear
Of inward living nature. What doth move
The Nightingail to sing so sweet and clear
The Thrush, or Lark that mounting high above
    Chants her shrill notes to heedlesse ears of corn
    Heavily hanging in the dewy Morn.

When Life can speak, it cannot well withold
T' expresse its own impressions and hid life.
Or joy or greif that smoothered lie untold
Do vex the heart and wring with restlesse strife,
    Then are my labours no true pains but ease
    My souls unrest they gently do appease.

Besides, that is not fruitlesse that no gains
Brings to my self. I others profit deem
Mine own : and if at these my heavenly flames
Others receiven light, right well I ween
    My time's not lost. Art thou now satisfide
    Said I : to which the scoffing boy replide :

Great hope indeed thy rhymes should men enlight,
That be with clouds and darkness all o'recast,
Harsh style and harder sense void of delight
The Readers wearied eye in vain do wast.
    And when men win thy meaning with much pain,
    Thy uncouth sense they coldly entertain.

For wotst thou not that all the world is dead
Unto that Genius that moves in thy vein
Of poetrie ! But like by like is fed.
Sing of my Trophees in triumphant strein,
    Then correspondent life, thy powerfull verse
    Shall strongly strike and with quick passion pierce.

The tender frie of lads and lasses young
With thirstie care thee compassing about,
Thy Nectar-dropping Muse, thy sugar'd song
Will swallow down with eager hearty draught :
   Relishing truly what thy rhymes convey,
   And highly praising thy soul-smiting lay.

The mincing maid her mind will then bewray,
Her heart-bloud flaming up into her face,
Grave matrons will wax wanton and betray
Their unresolv'dnesse in their wonted grace ;
   Young boyes and girls would feel a forward spring,
   And former youth to eld thou back wouldst bring.

All Sexes, Ages, Orders, Occupations
Would listen to thee with attentive ear,
And eas'ly moved with thy sweet perswasions,
Thy pipe would follow with full merry chear.
   While thou thy lively voice didst loud advance
   Their tickled bloud for joy would inly dance.

But now, alas ! poore solitarie man !
In lonesome desert thou dost wander wide
To seek and serve thy disappearing Pan,
Whom no man living in the world hath cyde :
   For Pan, is dead but I am still alive,
   And live in men who honour to me give :

They honour also those that honour me
With sacred songs.   But thou now singst to trees
To rocks, to Hills, to Caves that senselesse be
And mindlesse quite of thy hid mysteries,
   In the void air thy idle voice is spread,
   Thy Muse is musick to the deaf or dead.

Now out alas ! said I, and wele away
The tale thou tellest I confesse too true.
Fond man so doteth on this living clay
His carcase dear, and doth its joyes pursue,
   That of his precious soul he takes no keep
   Heavens love and reasons light lie fast asleep.

This bodies life vain shadow of the soul
With full desire they closely do embrace,
In fleshly mud like swine they wallow and roll,
The loftiest mind is proud but of the face
   Or outward person ; if men but adore
   That walking sepulchre, cares for no more.

This is the measure of mans industry
To wexen some body and gotten grace
To's outward presence ; though true majestie
Crown'd with that heavenly light and lively rayes
   Of holy wisdome and Seraphick love,
   From his deformed soul he farre remove.

Slight knowledge and lesse virtue serves his turn
For this designe.   If he hath trod the ring
Of pedling arts ; in usuall pack-horse form
Keeping the rode ; O ! then 't's a learned thing.
   If any chanc'd to write or speak what he
   Conceives not, 'twere a foul discourtesie.

To cleanse the soule from sinn, and still diffide
Whether our reasons eye be clear enough
To intromit true light, that fain would glide
Into purg'd hearts, this way's too harsh and rough :
   Therefore the clearest truths may well seem dark
   When sloathfull men have eyes so dimme and stark.

These be our times.   But if my minds presage
Bear any moment, they can ne're last long,
A three branch'd Flame will soon sweep clean the stage
Of this old dirty drosse and all wex young.
   My words into this frozen air I throw
   Will then grow vocall at that generall thaw.

Nay, now thou'rt perfect mad, said he, with scorn,
And full of foul derision quit the place.
The skie did rattle with his wings ytorn
Like to rent silk.   But I in the mean space
   Sent after him this message by the wind
   Be't so I'm mad, yet sure I am thou'rt blind.

By this the out-stretch'd shadows of the trees
Pointed me home-ward, and with one consent
Foretold the dayes descent.   So straight I rise
Gathering my limbs from off the green pavement
   Behind me leaving then the slooping Light.
   Cl. And now let's up, *Vesper* brings on the Night.

Fides Fluctuans.

O Deus æterno lucis qui absconditus Orbe
   Humanos fugis aspectus ! da cernere verum,
Da magnum spectare diem non mobilis Ævi.
Da contemplari nullius in infera noctis
Lapsurum solem.   Spissas caliginis umbras
Adventu dispelle tuo.   Pernicibus alis,
Ocyus advolitans, animam tu siste solutam
Mobilitate sua ; rapidæ quam cursus aquai
Deturbat secum atque in cæco gurgite condit.
Sed tamen ex fluxu hoc rerum miseroque tumultu
En ! vultus attollo meos ; tu porrige dextram,
Exime ut excelso figam vestigia saxo.
O Deus ! O centrum rerum ! te percita motu
Arcano circumvolitant cuncta atque requirunt
Nequicquam, quoniam æterna te contegis umbra.
Attamen insano exerces mea pectora amore,
Et suspirantem volupe est tibi ludere mentem
Ignibus occultis.   Non talibus æstuat *Ætna*,
Intima cùm accensas eructet flamma favillas
Pleniùs, & lato spargat sua viscera campo.
   Omnia solicita mecum quæ mente revolvi
Somnia sunt? stultéque animi satagentis inane
Figmentum? spes nostra perit radicitùs omnis?
Expectata diu vacuas vita exit in auras?
   Hei mihi ! quam immensæ involvor caligine noctis !
Subsido, pereo, repeto jam material
Infensas tenebras & ahenæ vincula mortis.
   Quæ me intemperies agitat ! Rescindito cœlos
Summe Deûm, tantósque animi componito fluctus.

Resolution.

Where's now the objects of thy fears :
 Needlesse sighs and fruitlesse tears?
They be all gone like idle dream
Suggested from the bodies steam.
O Cave of horrour black as pitch !
Dark Den of Spectres that bewitch
The weakned phansy sore affright
With the grim shades of grisely Night.
What's Plague and Prison? Losse of friends?
Warre, Dearth and Death that all things ends?
Mere Bug-bears for the childish mind
Pure Panick terrours of the blind.
 Collect thy soul into one sphear
Of light and 'bove the earth it rear.
Those wild scattered thoughts that erst
Lay losely in the World disperst
Call in : thy spirit thus knit in one
Fair lucid orb ; those fears be gone
Like vain impostures of the Night
That fly before the Morning bright.
Then with pure eyes thou shalt behold
How the first Goodnesse doth infold
All things in loving tender armes :
That deemed mischiefs are no harms
But sovereign salves ; and skilfull cures
Of greater woes the world endures ;
That mans stout soul may win a state
Far rais'd above the reach of fate.
 Then wilt thou say, *God rules the World*,
Though mountain over mountain hurl'd
Be pitch'd amid the foaming Maine
Which busie winds to wrath constrain.
His fall doth make the billowes start
And backwark skip from every part.
Quite sunk, then over his senselesse side
The waves in triumph proudly ride.
Though inward tempests fiercely rock
The tottering Earth, that with the shock
High spires and heavie rocks fall down
With their own weight drove into ground ;
Though pitchy blasts from Hell up-born
Stop the outgoings of the Morn,
And Nature play her fiery games
In this forc'd Night, with fulgurant flames,
Baring by fits for more affright
The pale dead visages, ghastly sight
Of men astonish'd at the stoure
Of Heavens great rage, the rattling showers
Of hail, the hoarse bellowing of thunder
Their own loud shreeks made mad with wonder :
All this confusion cannot move
The purgèd mind freed from the love
Of commerce with her body dear
Cell of sad thoughts, sole spring of fear.
 What ere I feel or heare or see
Threats but these parts that mortall be.

Nought can the honest heart dismay
Unlesse the love of living clay
And long acquaintance with the light
Of this Outworld and what to sight
Those too officious beams discover
Of forms that round about us hover.
 Power, Wisedome, Goodnesse sure did
 frame
This Universe and still guide the same.
But thoughts from passions sprung, deceive
Vain mortals. No man can contrive
A better course then what's been run
Since the first circuit of the Sun.
 He that beholds all from on high
Knowes better what to do then I.
I'm not mine own, should I repine
If he dispose of what's not mine.
Purge but thy soul of blind self-will
Thou streight shalt see God doth no ill.
The world He fills with the bright rayes
Of his free goodnesse. He displayes
Himself throughout. Like common aire
That spirit of life through all doth fare
Suck'd in by them as vitall breath
That willingly embrace not death.
But those that with that living Law
Be unacquainted, cares do gnaw ;
Mistrust of Gods good providence
Doth daily vex their wearied sense.
 Now place me on the *Libyan* soil,
With scorching sun and sands to toil,
Far from the view of spring or tree,
Where neither man nor house I see.
Place me by the fabulous streams
Of *Hydaspes ;* In the Realms
Where *Caucasus* his lofty back
Doth raise in wreaths and endlesse tract.
Commit me at my next remove
To icy *Hyperborean Jove.*
Confine me to the *Arctick* Pole
Where the numbd heavens do slowly roll ;
To lands, where cold raw heavie mist
Sols kindly warmth and light resists.
Where louring clouds full fraught with snow
Do sternly scoul, where winds do blow
With bitter blasts, and pierce the skin
Forcing the vitall spirits in ;
Which leave the body thus ill bested
In this chill plight at least half dead :
Yet by an Antiperistasis
My inward heat more kindled is :
And while this flesh her breath expires
My spirit shall suck celestiall fires
By deep-fetchd sighs and pure devotion.
Thus waxen hot with holy motion,
At once I'll break forth in a flame ;
Above this world and worthlesse fame
I'll take my flight, carelesse that men
Know not, how, where I die or when.

Yea ! though the Soul should mortall prove
So be Gods life but in me move
To my last breath : I'm satisfide
A lonesome mortall God t' have dide.

Devotion.

GOod God ! when thou thy inward grace dost shower
      Into my brest,
How full of light and lively power
      Is then my soul !
      How am I blest
How can I then all difficulties devour !
        Thy might
        Thy spright
With ease my combrous enemy controll.

If thou once turn away thy face and hide
      Thy chearfull look,
My feeble flesh may not abide
      That dreadfull stound,
      I cannot brook
Thy absence.   My heart with care and grief then gride
        Doth fail,
        Doth quail,
My life steals from me, at that hidden wound.

My phansie's then a burden to my mind,
      Mine anxious thought
Betrayes my reason, makes me blind :
      Near dangers drad
      Make me distraught.
Surpriz'd with fear, my senses all I find.
        In hell
        I dwell
Opprest with horrour, pain and sorrow sad.

My former Resolutions all are fled,
      Slip't over my tongue,
My Faith, my Hope, and Joy, are dead.
      Assist my heart
      Rather then my song
My God ! my Saviour ! when I'm ill bested
        Stand by,
        And I
Shall bear with courage, undeserved smart.

Aphroditus.

Synes. hymn. 2 & 3. *Macrob. Saturnal.*
lib. 3. cap. 8.

SUmme Pater ! rerum fixa inconcussáque Sedes !
   Omnia qui fulcis mundo non fictus Adonis.
Fundamen cœlorum ! immobile Sustentamen
Telluris ! magnûmque quies secura Deorum !
Omniparens Amor ! In dias tu luminis oras
Omnia producis vastus quæ continet orbis :
Innumera tu prole tua terrasque feraces,
Aerá que immensum comples camposque natantes.
Sæclorum Pater es, Mater pia, sedula Nutrix.
Te circum quoniam ludunt humana propago,

Quos nisi tu sistis, nutricis more, patenti
In gremio, & circumjectis tutare lacertis,
Protinus heu ! pereunt, priscas repetendo tenebras,
Submersosque suo claudit *Styx* lurida, fundo.
Lurida *Styx,* summi quam oderunt tangere *Olympi*
Incolæ, inextinctum spirantes semper amorem ;
Hujus enim horrendas nemo quisquam petet umbras
Fluminis, accensus lucenti pectora ab igni.
Nos tamen intereà charis dum amplecteris ulnis
Materno sistisque genu, te cernere contrà
Vix cupimus, blandosve tuos advertere vultus.
Sed veluti lactens infantulus ubera matris
Quæritat, & cunctas complet vagitibus ædeis
Ni sedet & mollem sibi nudam veste mamillam
Exhibet : Hæc igitur properat, sævumque tyrannum
Demulcet dictis, atque oscula dulcia figit.
Ille autem non dicta moratur, nec pia matris
Oscula, non hilares oculos vultumque serenum
Attendit, pulchros neque, amantum rete, capillos.
Nulla mora est, quò cæca fames vocat, instat, in uber
Involat, & niveum sitienti fauce liquorem
Haurit, & alterno jactans sua cruscula motu
Maternum refricat gremium, dulcedine sensûs
Exultans, tenerum succo feriente palatum.
Sic nos, magna Parens ! quorum provectior ætas,
Sic tua sic avidis premimus sacra ubera labris,
Sed formam vultumve tuum quis conspicit ? Omneis
Cæcus amor quò tractat & expectata voluptas
Auferimur, plenoque unà devolvimur alveo.
    Verùm ego si possim ! neque enim deprendere possum
Divinam speciem ; nimio tua pignora lusu
Namque soles lassare & gratam avertere formam.
At cùm conatu longo defessus ocellos
Adduco & facilis vincit mea tempora somnus ;
Tu tamen intereà vigilas & membra sopore
Dulci extensa vides & amico lumine mulces.
    Hæc *Venus* alma ! animus, nebulas, noctemque malignam
Somniat obfusus, neque enim poti' cernere quicquam est ;
Sed furit & cæco rerum perculsus amore
Evomit insanum turbato pectore carmen.

Out of the Anthologie a Distick.

Εἰ τὸ φέρον σε φέρει φέρε καὶ φέρου, εἰ δ' ἀγανακτεῖς
Καὶ σαυτὸν λυπέεις, καὶ τὸ φέρον σέ φέρει.

In English thus :

WHen the strong Fates with Gigantean force,
    Bear thee in iron arms without remorse
Bear and be born. But if with pievish struggle
Thou writhe and wrest thy corse, thou dost but double
Thy present pain, and spend thy restlesse spright,
Nor thou more heavie art, nor they more light.

Or thus :

If Chance thee change, be chang'd and change thou it
To better, by thy well complying wit.

If thou repine, thou dost but pain and grieve
Thy self, and Chance will change thee without leeve.

R Ight well I wot, my rhymes seem rudely drest
In the nice judgement of thy shallow mind
That mark'st expressions more then what's exprest,
Busily billing the rough outward rinde,
But reaching not the pith. Such surface skill's
Unmeet to measure the profounder quill.

Yea I alas ! my self too often feel
Thy indispos'dnesse ; when my weakened soul
Unstedfast, into this Outworld doth reel,
And lyes immerse in my low vitall mold.
For then my mind, from th' inward spright estrang'd,
My Muse into an uncouth hew hath chang'd.

A rude confusèd heap of ashes dead
My verses seem, when that cælestiall flame
That sacred spirit of life's extinguishèd
In my cold brest. Then gin I rashly blame
My rugged lines : This word is obsolete ;
That boldly coynd, a third too oft doth beat

Mine humourous ears. Thus fondly curious
Is the faint Reader, that doth want that fire
And inward vigour heavenly furious
That made my enrag'd spirit in strong desire
Break through such tender cob-web niceties,
That oft intangle these blind buzzing flies.

Possest with living sense I inly rave,
Carelesse how outward words do from me flow,
So be the image of my mind they have
Truly exprest, and do my visage show ;
As doth each river deckt with Phebus beams
Fairly reflect the viewer of his streams.

Who can discern the Moons asperity
From of this earth, or could this earths discover
If from the earth he raisèd were on high
Among the starrs and in the sky did hover ?
The Hills and Valleyes would together flow
And the rough Earth, one smooth-fac'd Round would
show.

Nor can the lofty soul snatch'd into Heven
Busied above in th' Intellectuall world
At such a distance see my lines uneven,
At such a distance was my spirit hurld,
And to my trembling quill thence did endite,
What he from thence must reade, who would read
right.

Fair Fields and rich Enclosures, shady Woods,
Large populous Towns, with strong and stately Towers,
Long crawling Rivers, far distended Flouds,
What ever's great, its shape these eyes of ours
And due proportions from high distance see
The best ; And *Paro !* such my Rhyme's to thee.

Thy groveling mind and moping poreblind eye,
That to move up unmeet, this to see farre,

19

The worth or weaknesse never can descry
Of my large wingèd Muse. But not to spare
Till thou canst well disprove, proves well enough
Thou art rash and rude how ere my rhymes are rough.

Necessitas Triumphata.

Seu,

Humanam voluntatem ad unum *necessariò
non determinari.*

O Dea ! quæ clavum manibus cuneúmque superbis
Gestas, & stricta liquidi compagine plumbi
Cuncta premis, duramque soles imponere legem,
Usque adeone tuo indulges, sævissima rerum !
Imperio, astringas tristi tibi ut omnia nodo?
Terra tua est & quos sub verno tempore flores
Proruit, & quicquid tenebrosa in viscera condit.
Amnes quò tu cunque vocas salsæque lacunæ
Pergunt, & lati palantia sydera mundi.
Aer sub ditione tua est, nimbique ruentes,
Quæque boant rauco metuenda tontitrua cælo.
Et nimis angustum si forte bæc omnia regnum
Infernas moderare umbras, sedesque silentûm,
Horrificosque suis ructantem è faucibus æstus
Tartaron. His addas brutum genus omne animantûm
Innumeras pecorum species atque Altivolantûm.
Mancipium Natura tuum est ; seu tristior illa
Quam Nox ima premit cæca in caligine, sive
Quam matutinis radiis fovet Ætherius Sol.
Omnibus his dare jura potes, durasque catenas
Nectere, & ad rigidum nodis mordentibus *Unum*
Stringere. At hac stupida non torpent cætera lege.
Liberum enim est genus humanum, veluti innuba virgo
Quæ nondum ullius thalamis addicta mariti est.
Multi hanc ergo viri precibus blandisque loquelis
Facundos quos fecit amor noctisque cupido
Solicitant. Nostras alios ita manibus imis
E mediis alios, alios è sedibus altis
Impugnasse procos animas sentimus, & ipsum
Descendisse Jovem casto in præcordia lusu, ut
Virtutem inspiret sanctumque accendat amorem.
Scilicet hæc fiunt quoniam mens libera nostra est
Legibus æterni fati *Uniusque* severi.
Quod si animæ motus solido Dea ferrea clavo
Præfixos jam olim, determinet ; illius omnes
Fictitii assensus, libertas nil nisi inane
Commentum : quod qui est ausus fabricare, necesse est
Æstuet implicitus nodis quos consulit ipse,
Et Chrysippeum sudet volvendo cylindrum.

Exorcismus.

W Hat's this that in my brest thus grieves and groanes
Rives my close-straitned heart, distends my sides
With deep fetch'd sighs, while th' other in fell pride
Resists and choaks? O hear the dreadfull moanes
Of thy dear son, if so him cleep I may.
If there be any sense 'twixt Heven and Earth,

Z

If any mutuall feeling sure this birth
May challenge speed, and break off all delay.
You Wingèd people of the unseen sky
That bear that living Name in your pure brest,
Chariots of God in whom the Lord of rest
Doth sit triumphant, can not you espy
The self same Being in such jeopardy?
Make haste make haste if you Gods army been,
Rescue his son, wreak your revengefull teen
      On his fast holding Enemy.
      Hath Nature onely sympathy?

What? may I deem you self-exulting sprights
Lock'd up in your own selves, whose inward life
Is self-contenting joy, withouten strife
Of doing good and helping wofull wights.
Then were you empty carres and not the throne
Of that thrice-beautious sun the god of love
The Soul of souls and heart of highest Jove,
If you to others good were not most prone.
Open thou Earth; unclose thou fast-bound ball
Of smoring darknesse! The black jawes of Hell
Shall issue forth their dead, that direfull cell
Of miscreant Lives that strive still to enthrall,
Shall let him go at last, and before all
Shall triumph. Then the gladsome Progeny
Of the bright Morning star shining on high,
      Shall fill the Round ætheriall
      With sound of voices musicall.

Nor yet this breath's quite spent. Swift flight of wing
Hath shot my soul from th'hight to th'depth again
And from the depth to th' height. The glistring Main
Of flowing light and darknesse curs'd spring
I've mov'd with sacred words: (the extreme worlds
In holy rage assaulted with my spell)
I'll at the middle Movable as well
As those, and powerfull magick gainst it hurle.
   You waving aires! and you more boistrous winds!
Dark *Zaphons* sons, who with your swelling blasts
Thrust out the ribs of heaven, and that orepast
Leave Nature languid to her wont confind,
Suppresse your spright and be at his command
Who on the troubled *Galilean* lake
Did wind and storm to him obedient make.
      Let still serenity the land
      Inclose about with steddy hand.

And you heaven-threatening rocks, whose tops be
    crown'd
With wreaths of woolly clouds, fall into dust.
And thou, O *Ida* hill! thy glory must
Consume, and thou lye equall with the ground.
O're quick-ey'd *Ida!* thou which seest the Sun
Before day spring? those Eastern spatterd lights
And broad spread shinings purpling the gay Night,
And that swoln-glowing ball; they'll all be gone.
You summer neezings when the Sun is set
That fill the air with a quick fading fire,
Cease from your flashings, and thou Self-desire

The worst of meteors, curs'd Voraginet!
The wind of God shall rend thee into nought
And thou shalt vanish into empty air,
Nor shall thy rending out leave any scarre.
   Thy place shall not be found though sought
   So perish shall all humane thought.

Deliquium.

Vires deficiunt abítque vita.
   Virtutem revoca, O Deus! fugacem.
O sol justitiæ, atque origo vitæ!
Vitæ, qua reficis tuos alumnos,
Inspira, obsecro, spiritum suavem
Venis languidulis, meósque ocellos
Lucis vivifica novo vigore,
Perculsum saliat novóque amore
Pectus, compositas agat choreas
Lætum cor, cupidis premátque in ulnis
Quæ tu cunque facis, Pater Deorum!
Immensíque opifex perite mundi!
Cuncta exosculer ambitu benigno &
Injectis teneam fovens lacertis.
Nam jucunda cluent, cluent amœna
Ni nubes animum gravent acerbum
Atque urat dolor intimus medullam.
   Ergo magnanimam piámque mentem
Sedatam, facilémque, callidámque
Concedas quæ hominum sciat ferátque
Mores omnimodos bonos malósque.
Nec cor concutiant superbiarum
Fluctus turgidulum; furor dolórque
Vitæ ne obsideant vias misellæ
Soffocéntque suis feris catenis.
   Mentem præbe humilem at simul serenam,
Mentem præbe hilarem at simul severam,
Te circum choreas leves agentem,
Pulsantem citharam at tibi canentem.

Insomnium Philosophicum.

It was the time when all things quiet lay
   In silent rest; and Night her rusty Carre
Drawn with black teem had drove above half way.
Her curbed steeds foaming out lavering tarre
   And finely trampling the soft misty air
With proner course toward the West did fare.

I with the rest of weak mortality
For natures due relief lay stretch'd on bed.
My weary body lay out-stretch'd, not I.
For I, alas! from that dead corse had fled,
   Had left that slough, as erst I doft my clothes,
   For kindly rest that very Evening close.

Free as in open Heaven more swift then thought
In endlesse spaces up and down I flie,
Not carryèd on wings, or as well taught
To row with mine own arms in liquid skie:

As oft men do in their deceiving sleep
Hovering over Waters, Woods, and Valleys steep :

But born on the actuall efflux of my will
Without resistence thither easly glide
Whither my busie mind did breathe untill.
All-suddenly an uncouth sight I spide,
  Which meanly as I may I will propound
  To wiser men to weigh with judgement sound.

Behold a mighty Orb right well compil'd
And kned together of opacous mould.
That neither curse of God nor man defil'd,
Though wicked wights as shall anon be told
  Did curse the ill condition of the place,
  And with foul speech this goodly work disgrace.

But vain complaints may weary the ill tongue
And evil speeches the blasphemer stain,
But words Gods sacred works can never wrong,
Nor wrongfull deeming work dame Natures bane.
  Who misconceives, conceives but his own ill,
  Brings forth a falshood, shows his want of skill.

This globe in all things punctually did seem
Like to our earth saving in magnitude :
For it of so great vastnesse was, I ween,
That if that all the Planets were transmewd
  Into one Ball, they'd not exceed this Round
  Nor yet fall short though close together bound.

At a farre distance from this sphear was pight
(More then the journey of ten thousand year
An hundred times told over, that swiftest flight
Of bird should mete, that distance did appear)
  There was there pight a massie Orb of light
  Æquall with this dark Orb in bignesse right.

Half therefore just of this dark Orb was dight
With goodly glistre and fair golden rayes,
And ever half was hid in horrid Night.
A duskish Cylindre through infinite space
  It did project, which still unmovèd staid,
  Strange sight it was to see so endlesse shade.

Th' Diametre of that Nocturnall Roll
Was the right Axis of this opake sphear.
On which eternally it round did roll.
In Æquinoctiall posture 't did appear,
  So as when Libra weighs out in just weight
  An equall share to men of Day and Night.

Thus turning round by turns all came in view
What ever did that massie Ball adorn.
Hills, Valleys, Woods, themselves did plainly shew,
Towns, Towers, and holy Spires to Heaven born,
  Long winding Rivers, and broad foaming Seas.
  Fair Chrystall springs fierce scorching thirst t' ap-
    pease.

And all bespread were the huge Mountains green
With Fleecy flocks and eke with hairy goats.

Great fields of Corn and Knee-deep grasse were seen,
Swine, Oxen, Horses, Carriages, Sheep-cotes,
  What ere the Countrey or the wallèd town
  Can show with us, the like things there were shown.

And look what ever that Half-sphear of light
Did bear upon it (the Ball turning round)
The same into the Hemisphear of Night
Were carried. And look what things were found
  In that dark Hemisphear, were brought anon
  To th' Hemisphear the light did shine upon.

For sooth to say, they both make up one Ball.
The self same parts now dipt in deepest Night
Anon recovered from their former fall
Do shine all glorious deckt with gladsome light.
  And oft PANGAION as it turn'd, I red
  In mighty characters decypherèd.

Th' inhabitants of this big swollen sphear
Were of two kinds, well answering unto
The diverse nature of each Hemisphear.
One foul, deform'd, and ghastly sad in show,
  The other fair and full of lively mirth,
  These two possess this Universall Earth.

They both had wings : The foul much like a Bat
Or forgèd Fiend and of a pitchy hew,
And ovall eyes like to a blinking Cat.
The fair had silver wings all-glistering new
  With golden feathers set, shap'd like a Doves
  Or lovely Swans, that in *Meander* moves.

In other parts most like to spotlesse man
Made out in comely due proportion.
Both with their wings uncessantly did fan
The agil air, but never light upon
  The moving Orb, but in suspense they hovered.
  Therefore Light these, eternall Night those covered.

For though the Globe doth move, it moves them not ;
Passing as water underneath a brig.
Yet what thus passeth by, they deem their lot,
Both of their deemèd lots together lig,
  To wit, that Sphear with all its ornaments,
  Nor yet that sphear them both alike contents.

For they on the dim side with fell uprore
Do hideously houl and Nature blame
For her ill works. Enrag'd with fury sore
Oft God himself they curse ; blaspheme his Name.
  And all his creatures, as they passen by
  In goodly pomp, they view with scornfull eye.

Instead of hymnes they bold invectives make
Against the Maker of that Universe.
My quivering quill, and palsied hand do quake
Now I recall to mind the wicked verse
  Which those bad men had fram'd in fell despight,
  And foul detraction to the God of light.

And while with hollow howlings they did chaunt
That hellish Ode. Ravens more black then pitch

And fatall Owles, Dragons, and what so wont
To do or token mischeif ; every such
   Came flying round about t' encrease the sound,
   Such sound as would with madnesse man confound.

When they had made an end of this ill ditty,
As execrable thing they would forsake
This work of God, and out of dear self-pitty
Fly from the creatures, and themselves betake
   To higher region : but their labour's vain
   Fly never so high, Night doth them still contain.

For the projection of that endlesse Roll
Cast to unmeasurèd infinity,
Wearies to death their ill-deceivèd soul :
For nought but darknesse and obscurity
   They finden out by their high tedious flight,
   But now I'd turn'd me to the land of Light.

There might I see with lovely pleasant look
And mild aspect, the people all things view,
Interpreting right what ever seemèd crook.
Crooked for crook'd is right ; and evil hew
   For evil shapèd mind, that fear may breed.
   Good oft doth spring from evil-seeming seed.

Viewing the works of God they ever smil'd
As seeing some resemblance of that face
That they so dearly lov'd, that undefil'd
And spotlesse beauty, that sweet awfull Grace
   Where Love and Majesty do alway sit
   And with eternall joy the viewer greet.

Ravisht with heavenly mirth and pure delight
They sing a sacred song with chearfull voice.
It kindles holy pleasure within my spright
As oft I think on that Angelick noise.
   The living Spring of blisse they loudly praise
   Blesse all His creatures in their pious layes.

And while the creatures goodnesse they descry
From their fair glimps they move themselves up higher
Not through contempt or hate they from them fly
Nor leave by flying, but while they aspire
   To reach their fountain, them with sight more clear
   They see.   As newly varnish'd all appear.

This is the mystery of that mighty Ball
With different sides.   That side where grisly Night
Doth sit bold men *Melampronæa* call,
The other side *Lampropronæa* hight,
   Logos that Orb of light, but *Foolishnesse*
   (To speak plane English) the Roll doth expresse.

These words I read or heard, I know not whether :
Or thought, or thought I thought.   It was a dream.
But yet from dreams wise men sound truth may gather
And some ripe scatterings of high knowledge glean.
   But where, or heavy passions cloud the eyes,
   Or prejudice, there's nothing can make wise.

Monocardia.

QUæ vis nunc agitat meas medullas?
   Et cor, molliculo ferire motu
Ceptat? percutiunt novi furores
Mentem, concipio novos amores.
Ah ! nunc me fluidos abire in igneis
Totum sentio.   Flamma mollis artus
Dulcis, vivida, permeavit omneis,
Jucundúmque ciet calore sensum
Toto corpore spiritúque toto.
Bellam hic laude suam efferat Fabullam
Formosam ille suam canat Corinnam.
Me leni Monocardia urit igni
Et sacrum instituit suum poetam.
Pulchra O Simplicitas ! beata virgo !
Tu vincis radios nitore Phœbes,
Tu stellas superas decore cunctas.
Nam quis pectora? quis sinus apertos?
Candorísve tui potest tueri
Thesauros niveos eburneósve?
Quin Luna imbrifera tepentis Austri
Nube obscurior, atque sydus omne
Sit nigrum magis ac imago noctis
Et Hyles tenebris, nives cbúrque.
Quod si orbes hilares amabilésque
Lucentésque tuor faces, amorum
Blandas illecebras, ruit statim Sol
Et lati species perit Diei
Submersa in tenebris Meridianis.
O princeps Charitum ! Dea O Dearum !
Cœli splendor ! & unica O voluptas
Humani generis ! catena nodis
Auratis, homines ligans Deósque !
Te circumvolitant leves *Olympi*
Alati juvenes, tuósque gressus
Sustentant manibus suis tenellos,
Et firmant tua crura mollicella,
Dulcis cura Deûm Venúsque cœli !
O fons lætitiæ pífque lusus !
O ter pulchra puella ! blanda virgo !
Nostris mollûter insidens medullis
Cœlestómque animo fovens amorem
In cœtu superûm locas Deorum.

The Philosophers Devotion.

SIng aloud His praise rehearse
   Who hath made the Universe.
He the boundlesse Heavens has spread
All the vitall orbs has kned ;
He that on *Olympus* high
Tends his flocks with watchfull eye,
And this eye has multiplide
Midst each flock for to reside.
Thus as round about they stray
Toucheth each with out-stretch'd ray,
Nimble they hold on their way,
Shaping out their Night and Day.

Summer, Winter, Autumne, Spring,
Their inclinèd Axes bring.
Never slack they ; none respires,
Dancing round their Centrall fires.
   In due order as they move
Echo's sweet be gently drove
Thorough Heavens vast Hollownesse,
Which unto all corners presse :
Musick that the heart of *Jove*
Moves to joy and sportfull love ;
Fills the listning saylers eares
Riding on the wandring Sphears. '
Neither Speech nor Language is
Where their voice is not transmisse.
   God is good, is Wise, is Strong,
Witnesse all the creature-throng,
Is confess'd by every Tongue.
All things back from whence they sprong.
As the thankfull Rivers pay
What they borrowed of the Sea.
   Now my self I do resigne,
Take me whole I all am thine.
Save me, God ! from Self-desire,
Deaths pit, dark Hells raging fire,
Envy, Hatred, Vengeance, Ire.
Let not Lust my soul bemire.
   Quit from these thy praise I'll sing,
Loudly sweep the trembling string.
Bear a part, O Wisdomes sonnes !
Free'd from vain Religions.
Lo ! from farre I you salute,
Sweetly warbling on my Lute.
Indie, Egypt, Arabie,
Asia, Greece, and *Tartarie,*
Carmel-tracts, and *Lebanon*
With the *Mountains* of the *Moon,*
From whence muddie *Nile* doth runne
Or where ever else you wonne ;
Breathing in one vitall air,
One we are though distant farre.
   Rise at once let's sacrifice
Odours sweet perfume the skies.
See how Heavenly lightning fires
Hearts inflam'd with high aspires !
All the substance of our souls
Up in clouds of Incense rolls.
Leave we nothing to our selves
Save a voice, what need we els !
Or an hand to wear and tire
On the thankfull Lute or Lyre.
   Sing aloud His praise rehearse
Who hath made the Universe.

Charitie and Humilitie.

FArre have I clambred in my mind
   But nought so great as love I find :
Deep-searching wit, mount-moving might
Are nought compar'd to that good spright.

Life of delight and soul of blisse !
Sure source of lasting happinesse !
Higher then Heaven ! lower then hell
What is thy tent ? where maist thou dwell ?
   My mansion hight humilitie,
Heavens vastest capabilitie.
The further it doth downward tend
The higher up it doth ascend ;
If it go down to utmost nought
It shall return with that it sought.
   Lord stretch thy tent in my strait breast,
Enlarge it downward, that sure rest
May there be pight ; for that pure fire
Wherewith thou wontest to inspire
All self-dead souls. My life is gone,
Sad solitude 's my irksome wonne.
Cut off from men and all this world
In Lethes lonesome ditch I'm hurld.
Nor might nor sight doth ought me move,
Nor do I care to be above.
O feeble rayes of mentall light !
That best be seen in this dark night,
What are you ? what is any strength
If it be not laid in one length
With pride or love ? I nought desire
But a new life or quite t' expire.
Could I demolish with mine eye
Strong towers, stop the fleet stars in skie,
Bring down to earth the pale-fac'd Moon,
Or turn black midnight to bright Noon :
Though all things were put in my hand,
As parch'd as dry as th' Libyan sand
Would be my life if Charity
Were wanting. But Humility
Is more then my poore soul durst crave
That lies intombd in lowly grave.
But if 't were lawfull up to send
My voice to Heaven, this should it rend.
   Lord thrust me deeper into dust
That thou maist raise me with the just.

THE TRIUMPH,
OR

A Paraphrase upon the ninth Hymn of
Synesius, written in honour of Jesus,
the Son of *Mary,* the SAVIOUR
of the World.

O Lovely Child, with Glory great arraid !
   Sweet Of-spring of the *Solymcian* Maid !
Thee would I sing, and thy renownèd Acts :
For thou didst rid the boundlesse flowry tracts
Of thy dear Fathers Garden from the spoyles
Of the false Serpent, and his treacherous toyles :
When thou hadst once descended to this earth
A stranger wight 'mongst us of humane birth ;

After some stay new voyage thou didst take
Crossing cold *Lethe* and the *Stygian* Lake,
Arriv'st at the low fields of *Tartara*
There where innumerable flocks do stray
Of captive souls, whom pale-fac'd Death doth feed
Forc'd under his stiff Rod, and churlish Reed.
Streight at thy sight how did that surly Sire
Old *Orcus* quake, and greedy Dogg retire
From's usuall watch ! whiles thou from slavish chain
Whole swarms of souls, to freedome dost regain.
Then 'ginst thou with thy immortall Quire to praise
Thy Father, and his strength to Heaven to raise.
Ascending thus with joy, as thou dost fare
Through the thin Sky, the Legions of the Aire
Accursèd Fiends, do tremble at thy sight,
And starry Troops wax pale at thy pure light.
But *Æther* master of queint Harmonies
With smiling look on's Musick doth devise,
Tunes his seven-corded Harp, more trimly strung ;
Then strikes up loudly thy Triumphall song.
Lucifer laughs bright Nuncio of the Day,
And golden *Hesperus*, to hear him play.
The Moon begins a dance, great Queen of Night,
Her hollow horns fill'd up with flusher light.
Titan his streaming locks along doth strow
Under thy sacred feet more soft to go,
Doth homage to thee as to Gods dear Son,
And to the Spring whence his own light doth run.
Then thou, drad Victour ! thy quick wings didst shake
And suddenly ascend'st above the back

Of the blew Skie.   In th' Intellectuall sphears
Dispreadst thy self : Where the still Fount appears
Of inexhausted Good, and silent Heaven
Smiles without wrinckle, ever constant, even.
Unwearied Time this mansion cannot seize
Nor *Hyles* worm, importunate Disease.
Here *Æon* wons that cannot wexen old,
Though of his years the numbers no'te be told.
Youthfull and ag'd at once here doth he live,
And to the Gods, unmov'd duration give.

Ἀπορία.

Οὐκ ἔγνων πόθεν εἰμὶ ὁ δύσμορος, οὐδὲ τίς εἰμι,
   Ὦ τῆς ἀφροσύνης, οὐδὲ πῇ ἐρχόμενος.
Ἀλλ' ὀδύνης τε γόου τε πολυγνάμπτοις ὀνύχεσσι,
   Ζώω, ἔμοιγε δοκεῖ πανταχοῖ ἑλκόμενος.
Ἴσα ἐγρηγόρσεις καὶ ὀνείρατα, ὦ πάτερ, ὦ Ζεῦ,
   Ὡς σεμνὸν· χ' ἡμεῖς ζώομεν ἐν νεφέλαις.
Ψεύδεα, φαντασίη, κενότης, τερετίσματ', ἀνάγκη.
   Τἆλλα μὲν ἀγνώσας τὸν βίον οἶδα μόνον.

Εὐπορία.

Οὐρανόθεν γέγονα προθορὼν, θεοῦ ἄμβροτος ἀκτίς,
   Κ', ὦ τῆς εὐφροσύνης, πρὸς θεὸν εἰμι πάλιν.
Νῦν δὲ τ' ἔρως με πτέροισι θεόσσυτος ἐξυπερείδει,
   Ζῶ δ' ἐπ' ἀληθείᾳ, πάντοτε τερπόμενος.
Νὺξ ἀπέβη μὲν ὄναρ τε.   Πάτερ θεοδερκέος αὐγῆς.
   Ἀΐδιον χ' ἡμᾶς ἀμφικάλυψε φάος.
Πίστις καὶ σοφίη, θεότης, χαρά, εὔπτερος ἀλκή.
   Ταῦτα ζωή, ᾅδης τἆλλα καὶ οὐδενία.

III.—DIVINE HYMNS.

NOTE.

On these ' Divine Hymns ' see our Memorial-Introduction.—G.

DIVINE HYMNS.

AN HYMN

Upon the *Nativity of CHRIST.*

HE Holy Son of God most high,[1]
For Love of *Adam's* lapsèd Race,
Quit the sweet Pleasure of the Sky,
To bring us to that happy Place.

His Robes of Light he laid aside,
Which did his Majesty adorn,
And the frail State of Mortals try'd,
In human Flesh and Figure born.

Down from above this Day-Star slid,
Himself in living Earth t' entomb,
And all his heav'nly Glory hid
In a pure lowly Virgin's Womb.

Whole Quires of Angels loudly sing
The Mystery of his sacred Birth,
And the blest News to Shepherds bring,
Filling their watchful Souls with Mirth.

The Son of God thus Man became,[2]
That Men the Sons of God might be,
And by their second Birth regain
A likeness to his Deity.

Lord, give us *humble* and *pure* Minds,
And fill us with thy heav'nly Love,
That *Christ* thus in our Hearts enshrin'd
We all may be born from above.

And being thus regenerate,
Into a Life and Sense divine
We all Ungodliness may hate,
And to thy living Word encline.

That nourish'd by that heav'nly Food,
To manly stature we may grow,
And stedfastly pursue what's good,
That all our high Descent may know.

Grant we, thy Seed, may never yield
Our Souls to soil with any Blot,
But still stand Conqu'rors in the Field,
To shew his Pow'r who us begot.

[1] The Historical Narration.
[2] The Application to the Improvement of Life.

That after this our Warfare's done,
And Travails of a toilsom Stage,
We may in Heav'n, with *Christ* thy Son,
Enjoy our promis'd Heritage. *Amen.*

AN HYMN

Upon the Passion *of CHRIST.*

THE faithful Shepherd from on high,[1]
Came down to seek his strayèd Sheep,
Which in this earthly Dale did lie,
Of Grief and Death the Region deep.
Those Glories and those Joys above
'Twas much to quit for Sinners sake :
But yet behold far greater Love,
Such Pains and Toils to undertake.

An abject Life, which all despise,
The Lord of Glory underwent,
And with the Wicked's worldly guize
His righteous Soul for Grief was rent.
His Innocence Contempt attends,
His Wisdom and his Wonders great ;
Envy on these her Poison spends,
And Pharisaick Rage their Threats.

At last their Malice boil'd so high
As Witnesses false to suborn,
The Lord of Life to cause to die,
His Body first with Scourges torn.
With royal Robes in scorn th' him dight,
And with a Wreath of Thorns him crown :
A Scepter-Reed in farther spight,
They add unto his Purple Gown.

Then scoffingly they bend the Knee,
And spit upon his sacred Face ;
And after hang him on a Tree
Betwixt two Thieves, for more Disgrace.
With Nails they pierc'd his Hands and Feet,
The Blood thence trickled to the Ground :
The Pangs of Death his Countenance sweet
And lovely Eyes with Night confound.

Thus laden with our Weight of Sin,
This spotless Lamb himself bemoans,

[1] The Historical Narration.

And while for us he Life doth win,
Quits his own Breath with deep-fetch'd Groans.
Affrighted Nature shrinketh back,
To see so direful dismal sight ;
The Earth doth quake, the Mountains crack
Th' abashèd Sun withdraws his Light.

Then can we, Men, so senseless be,[1]
As not to melt in flowing Tears,
Who Cause were of his Agony,
Who suffered thus to cease our Fears :
To reconcile us to our God
By this his precious Sacrifice,
And shield us from his wrathful Rod,
Wherewith he Sinners doth chastise?

O wicked Sin to be abhorr'd,
That God's own Son thus forc'd to die !
O Love profound to be ador'd ;
That found so potent Remedy !
O Love more strong than Pain and Death,
To be repaid by nought but Love,
Whereby we vow our Life and Breath
Entire to serve our God above !

For who for shame durst now complain
Of dolorous dying unto Sin,
While he recounts the hideous Pain
His Saviour felt our Souls to win?
Or who can harbour Anger fell,
Envy, revengeful Spight or Hate,
If he but once consider well
Our Saviour lov'd at such a rate?

Wherefore, Lord, since thy Son most just,
His natural Life for us did spill ;
Grant we our *sinful* Lives and Lusts
May sacrifice unto his Will.
That to our selves we being dead
Henceforth to him may wholly live,
Who us to free from Danger's dread,
Himself a Sacrifice did give.

Grant that the Sense of so great Love
Our Souls to him may firmly tie,
And forcibly us all may move
To live in mutual Amity.
That no pretence to Hate or Strife
May rise from any Injury,
Since thy dear Son, the Lord of Life,
For Love of us (when Foes) did die.

AN HYMN
Upon the Resurrection of *CHRIST.*

WHo's this we see from *Edom* come,[2]
  With *bloody Robes* from *Bosrah* Town
He whom false *Jews* to Death did doom,
And Heav'n's fierce Anger had cast down.

---

[1] The Application to the Improvement of Life.
[2] The Historical Narration.

His righteous Soul alone was fain
The Wine-press of God's Wrath to tread,[1]
And all his Garments to distain,
And sprinkled Cloaths to die blood-red.

'Gainst Hell and Death he stoutly fought,
Who captive held him for three Days :
But straight he his own Freedom wrought,
And from the Dead himself did raise.

The brazen Gates of Death he brake,
Triumphing over Sin and Hell,
And made th' Infernal Kingdoms quake,
With all that in those Shades do dwell.

His murthered Body he resum'd
Maugre the Grave's close Grasp and Strife,
And all these Regions thence perfum'd
With the sweet Hopes of lasting Life.

O mighty Son of God most high,[2]
That conquer'dst thus Hell, Death and Sin,
Give us a glorious Victory
Over our deadly Sins to win.

Go on, and *Edom*[3] still subdue,
And quite cut off his wicked Race :
And raise in us thine Image true,
Which sinfull *Edom*[4] doth deface.

Teach us our Lusts to mortifie,
In virtue of thy precious Death :
That while to Sin all dead we lie,
Thou mayst infuse thy heav'nly Breath.

To Righteousness our Spirits raise,
And quick'n us with thy Life and Love ;
That we may walk here to thy Praise,
And after live in Heav'n above.

Grant we in Glory may appear,
Clad with our *Resurrection Vest,*
When thou shalt lead thy Flock most dear
Up to the Mansions of the Blest.

AN HYMN
Upon CHRIST'S Ascension.

GOD is ascended up on high[5]
  With merry noise of Trumpet's sound,
And princely seated in the Sky,
Rules over all the World around.

The Tabernacle did of old
His Presence to the *Jews* restrain :

---

[1] Isa. 63. 3.
[2] The Application to the Improvement of Life.
[3] 'O γηΐνος Ἐδώμ, *Phil. Jud.* Flesh and Blood in the moral Sense.
[4] The old Adam, Rom. 6. 6.
[5] The Historical Narration.

But after in our Flesh enfold,
A larger Empire he did gain.

For suffering in human Flesh
For all, he rich Redemption wrought,
And will with lasting Life refresh
His Heritage so dearly bought.

Sing Praises then, sing Praises loud
Unto our Universal King :
He who ascended on a Cloud,[1]
To him all Laud and Praises sing.

Captivity he Captive led,
Triumphing o're the Powers of Hell,
And struck their Eyes with Glory dread
Who in the airy Regions dwell.

In human Flesh and Shape he went,
Adorn'd with his Passion Scars ;
Which in Heaven's sight he did present
More glorious than the glittering Stars.

O happy Pledge of Pardon sure,[2]
And of an endless blisful State,
Since human Nature once made pure
For Heaven becomes so fit a Mate !

Lord raise our sinking Minds therefore
Up to our proper Country dear,
And purifie us evermore,
To fit us for those Regions clear.

Let our Converse be still above,
Where *Christ* at thy right Hand doth sit ;
And quench in us all worldly Love,
That with thy self our Souls may knit.

Make us all earthly things despise,
And freely part with this World's good,
That we may win that heav'nly Prize
Which *Christ* has purchas'd with his Blood.

That when he shall return again
In Clouds of Glory[3] as he went,
Our Souls no foulness may retain,
But be found pure and innocent.

And so may mount to his bright Hosts
On Eagles Wings up to the Sky,
And be conducted to the Coasts
Of everlasting Bliss and Joy.

AN HYMN

Upon the Descent of the Holy Ghost at the Day of Pentecost.

WHEN *Christ* his Body up had born[4]
To Heav'n, from his Disciples sight,
Then they like Orphans all forlorn
Spent their sad Days in mournful plight.

But he ascended up on high,
More sacred Gifts for to receive
And freely show'r them from the Sky
On those which he behind did leave.

He for the Presence of his Flesh
To them the Holy Spirit imparts,
And doth with living Springs refresh
Their thirsty Souls and fainting Hearts.

While with one Mind, and in one Place
Devoutly they themselves retire,
In rushing Wind the promis'd Grace
Descends, and cloven Tongues of Fire.

The House th' Almighty's Spirit fills,
Which doth the feeble Fabrick shake ;
But on their Tongue such Power instils,[1]
That makes the amazèd Hearer quake.

The Spirit of holy Zeal and Love,[2]
And of discerning, give us, Lord ;
The Spirit of Power from above,
Of Unity and good Accord :

The Spirit of convincing Speech,
Such as will every Conscience smite,
And to the Heart of each Man reach,[3]
And Sin and Error put to flight :

The Spirit of refining Fire,
Searching the inmost of the Mind,
To purge all foul and fell Desire,
And kindle Life more pure and kind.

The Spirit of Faith in this thy Day
Of Power against the force of Sin,
That through this Faith we ever may
Against our Lusts the Conquests win.

Pour down thy Spirit of inward Life,
Which in our Hearts thy Laws may write,
That without any Pain or Strife
We naturally may do what's right.

On all the Earth thy Spirit pour,
In Righteousness it to renew :
That Satan's Kingdom 't may o'repow'r,
And to *Christ's* Sceptre may subdue.

Like mighty Wind or Torrent fierce,
Let it Withstanders all o'rerun,
And every wicked Law reverse,
That Faith and Love may make all one.

Let Peace and Joy in each place spring,
And Righteousness, the Spirit's Fruits,
With Meekness, Friendship, and each thing
That with the Christian Spirit suits.

Grant this, O holy God and true,
Who th' ancient Prophets did inspire :
Haste to perform thy Promise due,
As all thy Servants thee desire.

---

[1] Acts 1. 9.
[2] The Application to the Improvement of Life.
[3] Acts 1. 11.   [4] The Narration.

[1] Acts 2.   [2] The Application.   [4] Acts 2. 37

AN HYMN

Upon the Creation *of the World.*

WHEN God the first Foundations laid [1]
　Of the well-framèd Universe,
And through the darksome Chaos ray'd ;
　The Angels did his Praise rehearse.

The Sons of God then sweetly sung,[2]
　At first Appearance of his Light,
When the Creation-Morning sprung
　To deck the World with Beauty bright.

Within six Days he finish'd all
　Whate're Heaven, Earth, or Sea contain,
And sanctify'd the seventh withal,
　To celebrate his Holy Name.

Then with the Sons of God let's sing
　Our bountiful Creator's Praise,
Who out of nothing all did bring,
　And by his Word the World did raise.

O holy God, how wonderful
　Art thou in all thy Works of might,
Astonishing our Senses dull
　With what thou daily bring'st in sight.

The fit Returns of Night and Day,
　The grateful Seasons of the Year,
Which constantly Man's Pains repay,
　With wholsome Fruit his Heart to chear :

The Shape and Number of the Stars,
　The Moon's set Course thou dost define,
And Matter's wild distracting Jars
　Composest by thy Word divine.

The Parts of th' Earth thou holdest close
　Together by this sweet Constraint :
Thou round'st the Drops that do disclose
　The Rainbow in his glorious Paint.

The Clouds drop Fatness on the Earth,
　Thou mak'st the Grass and Flow'rs to spring :
Thou cloath'st the Woods, wherein with Mirth
　The chearful Birds do sit and sing.

Thou fill'st the Fields with Beasts and Sheep,
　Thy Rivers run along the Plains :
With scaly Fish thou stor'st the Deep,
　Thy Bounty all the World maintains.

All these and all things else th' hast made [3]
　Subject to Man by thy Decree ;
That thou by Man might'st be obey'd
　As duly subject unto thee.

Wherefore, O Lord, in us create
　Clean Hearts, and a right Spirit renew :
That we regaining that just State,
　May ever pay thee what is due.

That as we wholly from thee are,
　Both Gifts of Mind and Body's Frame ;
So by them both we may declare
　The Glory of thy Holy Name.

AN HYMN

Upon the Redemption *of the World through* CHRIST *in his Reintroduction of the New Creature.*

THE Lord both Heaven and Earth hath made,[1]
　His Word did all things frame,
And Laws to every Creature gave,
　Who still observe the same.
The faithful Sun doth still return
　The Seasons of the Year,
And at just times the various Moon
　Now round, now horn'd appears.

The Plants retain their Virtue still,
　Their Verdure and their Form :
Nor do the Birds or Beasts their Guize
　Once Change, or Shape transform.
'Tis only Man, alas ! that brake
　Betimes thy sacred Law,
And from that Image heav'nly, pure,
　To beastly Shape did grow.

He headstrong left thy holy Will,
　His own Lusts to pursue ;
Whence the true Manly Form did fail
　And Brutishness ensue.
But thou, O God, who by thy Word
　Didst frame all things of Nought,
By the same Word made Flesh, for Man
　Hast rich Redemption wrought.

Thy choice Creation-piece thus marr'd,
　Thou dost again create,
And by th' incarnate Word restor'st
　Unto his pristine State.
The Glory of which Work raying forth,
　Whiles *Christ* from Death doth rise,
These two Creations, one Seventh Day
　By right doth solemnize.

God, who commanded first the Light [2]
　Out of the Dark to shine,
Enliven and enlight our Hearts
　By his pure Word Divine :
That when this New-creation Work
　In us is finish'd clear,
The bright and glorious Face of *Christ*
　May in our Souls appear.

That we thus once redeem'd from Sin,
　From our own Works may cease,[3]
And rest in God's eternal Love,
　The Spirit's Joy and Peace ;
And quit from this Earth's Toil, at last
　May sing among the Blest
In that long-lasting Sabbath-day,
　That Jubilee of Rest.

Amen.

FINIS.

---

[1] The Narration.　　[2] Job 38. 7.　　[3] The Application.

[1] The Narration.　　[2] The Application.　2 Cor. 4. 6.
[3] Heb. 4. 10.

IV.—FROM PROSE WORKS.

FROM PROSE WORKS.

Some VERSES *taken out of the* AUTHOR'S Philofophical Writings.

In the Antidote against Atheism, *Book* 3., Ch. 4.

LIKE to a *Light* fast lock'd in *Lanthorn dark,*
  Whereby, by Night, our wary Steps we guide
In slabby streets, and dirty Channels mark,
Some weaker rayes through the black top do glide,
And flusher streames perhaps from horny side :
But when we've past the peril of the way,
Arriv'd at home, and laid that case aside,
The naked light, how clearly doth it ray,
And spread its joyful beams as bright as Summers day.

Even so the *Soul,* in this contracted state,
Confin'd to these strait *instruments of Sense,*
More dull and narrowly doth operate :
At this hole hears, the Sight must ray from thence ;
Here tasts, there smells : But when she's gone from hence,
Like naked lamp, she is one shining sphear,
And round about has perfect cognoscence
Whate're in her *Horizon* doth appear ;
She is one Orb of Sense, all Eye, all airy Ear.

In the defence of the Moral Cabbala, *Chap.* 3.

A harder lesson to learn continence
In joyous pleasure than in grievous pain :
For sweetness doth allure the weaker sense
So strongly, that uneathes it can refrain
From that which feeble Nature covets fain ;
But grief and wrath that be our enemies,
And foes of life she better can restrain ;
Yet Vertue vaunts in both her Victories,
And *Guyon* in them all shews goodly Masteries.

IN THE DIVINE DIALOGUES.

The Song of Hylobaris *concerning Divine Providence,* Dialog. 2. Sect. 28.

Where's now the objects of thy fears ;
Needless sighs and fruitless tears?

They be all gone like idle dream
Suggested from the Body's steam.
O Cave of horrour, black as pitch !
Dark Den of Spectres that bewitch
The weakned phansy sore affright
With the grim shades of grisely Night.
What's Plague and Prison? Loss of friends?
War, Dearth and Death, that all things ends?
Mear Bug-bears for the childish mind,
Pure Panick terrours of the blind.
  Collect thy Soul into one sphear
Of light, and 'bove the Earth it rear.
Those wild scattered thoughts that erst
Lay loosely in the World disperst
Call in : thy Spirit thus knit in one
Fair lucid orb ; those fears be gone
Like vain impostures of the Night
That fly before the Morning bright.
Then with pure Eyes thou shalt behold
How the first Goodness doth infold
All things in loving tender arms :
That deemèd mischiefs are no harms
But sovereign salves ; and skilful cures
Of greater woes the World endures ;
That man's stout Soul may win a state
Far rais'd above the reach of fate.
  Power, Wisdom, Goodness sure did frame
This Universe, and still guide the same.
But thoughts from passions sprung, deceive
Vain Mortals. No man can contrive
A better course then what's been run
Since the first circuit of the Sun.
  He that beholds all from on high
Knows better what to do than I,
I'm not my own, should I repine
If he dispose of what's not mine.
Purge but thy Soul of blind self-will,
Thou streight shalt see God doth no ill.
The World he fills with the bright rayes
Of his free Goodness. He displays
Himself throughout. Like common air,
That Spirit of life through all doth fare,
Suck'd in by them as vital breath,
That willingly embrace not death.

But those that with that living Law
Be unacquainted, cares do gnaw ;
Mistrust of God's good Providence
Doth daily vex their wearied sense.

The Song of Bathynous, *Dialog.* 3. Sect. 37.

Sing aloud, His praise rehearse
Who hath made the Universe.
He the boundless Heavens has spread,
All the vital Orbs has kned ;
He that on *Olympus* high
Tends his flocks with wachful eye,
And this eye has multiply'd
Midst each Flock for to reside.
Thus as round about they stray
Toucheth each with out-stretch'd ray,
Nimble they hold on their way,
Shaping out their Night and Day.
Summer, Winter, Autumn, Spring,
Their inclinèd Axes bring.
Never slack they : none respires,
Dancing round their Central fires.
In due order as they move
Echos sweet be gently drove
Thorough Heavens vast Hollowness,
Which unto all corners press :
Musick that the heart of *Jove*
Moves to joy and sportful love ;
Fills the listning Saylors ears
Riding on the wandring Sphears.
Neither Speech nor Language is
Where their voice is not transmiss.
God is Good, is Wise, is Strong,
Witness all the creature-throng,
Is confess'd by every Tongue.
All things back from whence they sprung,
As the thankful Rivers pay
What they borrowed of the Sea.
Now my self I do resign,
Take me whole, I all am thine.
Save me, God ! from *Self-desire*,
Death's pit, dark Hell's *raging fire*,
Envy, Hatred, Vengeance, Ire.
Let not Lust my Soul bemire.
Quit from these, thy praise I'll sing.
Loudly sweep the trembling string.
Bear a part, O Wisdom's sonnes !
Free'd from vain Religions.
Lo ! from far I you salute,
Sweetly warbling on my Lute,
Indie, Egypt, Arabie,
Asia, Greece, and *Tartarie,*
*Carmel-*tracts and *Lebanon,*
With the *Mountains* of the *Moon,*
From whence muddy *Nile* doth run,
Or where ever else you wonne
Breathing in one vital air,
One we are, though distant far.

Rise at once let's sacrifice,
Odours sweet perfume the skies.
See how Heavenly lightning fires
Hearts inflam'd with high Aspires !
All the substance of our Souls
Up in clouds of Incense rolls.
Leave we nothing to our selves
Save a voice, what need we else !
Or an hand to wear and tire
On the thankful Lute or Lyre.
Sing aloud His praise rehearse
Who hath made the Universe.

The Song of Sophron *sung by* Bathinous, Dialog. 4. Sect. 39.

Great and marvellous are
Thy works, Lord God of Might ;
Thou Sovereign of Saints,
Thy ways are just and right.
Who shall not fear thee, Lord,
And glorifie thy Name?
Thou only Holy art :
Thine Acts no tongue can stain.
All Nations shall adore
Thy Judgments manifest,
Thy holy Name implore,
And in thy Truth shall rest.

* The Song of Philotheus, Dialog. 5. Sect. 41.

Thou who art enthron'd above,
Thou by whom we live and move,
O how sweet ! how excellent
Is't with Tongue and Heart's consent,
Thankful Hearts and joyful Tongues,
To renown thy Name in Songs :
When the Morning paints the Skies,
When the sparkling Stars arise,
Thy high Favours to reherse,
Thy firm Faith in gratful verse !
Take the Lute and Violin,
Let the solemn Harp begin,
Instruments strung with ten strings,
While the silver Cymbal rings.
From thy Works my Joy proceeds :
How I triumph in thy Deeds !
Who thy Wonders can express?
All thy Thoughts are fathomless,
Hid from men in Knowledge blind,
Hid from Fools to Vice inclin'd.
Tell mankind Jehovah reigns ;
He shall bind the World in chains,
So as it shall never slide,
And with sacred Justice guide.
Let the smiling Heavens rejoice,
Joyful Earth exalt her voice :
Let the dancing Billows roar,
Echos answer from the shoar,

Fields their flowry mantles shake :
All shall in their Joy partake ;
While the Wood-Musicians sing
To the ever-youthful Spring.

Fill his Courts with sacred Mirth.
He, He comes to judge the Earth.
Justly He the World shall sway,
And His Truth to men display.

CARMINA

Quædam in Scriptis Philosophicis *Anglice* occurrentia.

IN DIVINIS DIALOGIS

Hylobaris Cantilena de *Divina Providentia,*
Dialog. 2. Sect. 28.

BI nunc objecta tui sunt
Luctûs Gemitûsque Metûsque?
Abiêre ut somnia vana
E fumis corporis orta.
Piceum ô Formidinis antrum !
Lemurum tenebrosa Caverna !
Animam quæ Noctis amaræ
Tetris perterritat *Umbris.*
Quid Pestis? Carcer? Amicûm
Jactura, ac Bella Famésque
Quid Mors quæ cuncta resorbet ?
Nil sunt nisi *Mormolycæa*
Mentis ratione carentis,
Cæcorum & *Panicus* horror.
   Unum te collige in Orbem
Lucis, terrámque relinque,
Animæ vaga sensa coërce
Latum peragrantia mundum ;
Sphæram sic mens tua in unam
Lucentem pacta, Timores
(Ut *Noctis* inania *Spectra*
Surgens *Aurora*) fugabit.
   Clarè tunc cernere possis
Teneris ut cuncta lacertis
Bonitas complectitur *alma,*
Quódque hæc non sunt mala vera,
Mala quæ vulgò esse putantur,
Verùm opportuna medela ac
Majorum cura malorum ;
Anima ut mortalia cuncta
Sublími transvolet alâ ;
Talem repetâtque statum quo
Pedibus Fata omnia calcet.
   Vis certò secula Mundi
Quædam *Divina* creavit,
Sapientérque atque benignè
Etiamnum cuncta gubernat :
Sed nostra *Inscitia* casus
Temerè causatur iniquos,
Cùm nemo fingere possit
Meliori tramite cursum

Primo quàm qui extitit usque
Decurso Solis ab Orbe.
   Summi de vertice Cœli
Qui conspicit omnia, novit
Meliùs quàm ego quid sit agendum.
Nec, cùm meus ipse ego non sim,
Mea si fortè ille reposcit,
Ægrè id reputo esse ferendum.
   Cæcis tua pectora curis
Propriâque cupidine purga,
Mala nulla Deo esse profecta
Clarâ tunc luce videbis.
Totum rutilantibus Orbem
Radiis *Bonitatis* hic implet,
Seséque per omnia fundit.
Cuncta *hic*, seu Lumen & Aura,
Pertransit *Spiritus*, illis
Vitalis ut Halitus haustus,
Sibi queis non turpiter ultrò
Volupe est consciscere mortem.
   Verùm quos occupat hujus
Vivæ Ignorantia *Legis*,
Hos semper solicitudo
Rerum de casibus angit,
Miseris perplexáque rodunt
Tristes præcordia Curæ.

Bathynoi *Cantilena, Dialog.* 3. *Sect.* 37.

Clarè hujus pangite laudes
Mundum qui condidit altum,
Cœlos sine fine tetendit,
Vivósque hic pinsuit Orbes.
Hic celsi in vertice *Olympi*
Oculo vigili agmina pascit ;
Oculúmque hunc multiplicavit,
Medio ut quóque agmine præsit.
Radio sic singula recto
Circumcurrentia tangit.
Agili motu illa rotata
Formant Noctémque Diémque
Æstas, Autumnus, Hyémsque
Prono horum inducitur Axe.
Nunquam circa *Ignea Centra*
Cessant agitare Choreas.
   Dum pulchro hoc ordine pergunt,

Jucundam motibus Echo
Vasti per inania Cœli
Penetrantem molliter urgent.
Melos ! quod *Jovis* imum
Læto cor mulcet amore,
Vagulis delinit & aures
In sphæris velificantûm.
Non sermo, Lingua nec ulla,
Quò vox non ivit eorum.
    Deus est sapiénsque Bonúsque
Testatur tota creata
Vis, Linguáque quæque fatetur.
Unde orta, hunc cuncta recurrent,
Ut grata flumina, Ponto,
Hinc quod sumpsére, rependunt.
    Totum nunc me, ecce, resigno,
Tuus omnis sum, accipe me omnem.
Propriâ Deus eripe *flammâ*,
Vera hæc *Mors*, vera *Gehenna*.
Odium atrox, *Livor* & *Ira*
Gravis & *Vindicta* facessat,
Pia nec præcordia tentet
Quævis male sana *Cupido*.
    Liber, tua facta canendo,
Tremulus tunc pectine chordas
Feriam ictu vividiori.
    O proles sancta *Sophiæ*
Vanas qui Relligiones
Ritè excussistis, adeste,
Cantúsque adjungite vestros.
Vos de procul, ecce, saluto
Citharâ mihi dulcè vibrissans.
    Seu vos *Ægyptia* Tellus,
Seu *Graeca*, *Asiatica*, sive
Juga *Carmeli* Libantve,
Montísve cacumina *Lunæ*,
(Pinguis nivea ubera *Nili*)
Aliúsve locus teneat, Nos
Omnes sumus unus & idem,
Quamquam loca dissita habemus,
Dum omnes communiter unâ
Vitali vescimur Aurâ.
    Unâ vice surgite, sacra
Unâ faciamus, odores
Tingant suavi Æthera fumo.
    O, quàm bene molliter urit
Cœlestis fulgetra mentem
Mysteria ad ardua anhelam !
Substantia tota Anima !
In nubes Thuris odoras
Cœlum scandit resoluta :
    Scandat cœlósque ita tota,
Nostri ut pars nulla supersit
Præter vocémve manúmve
(Neq; enim his est pluribus usus)
Operâ quas porrò teramus
Gratæ Citharæve Lyræve.
    Clarò hujus pangite laudes
Mundum qui condidit altum.

Sophronis Cantilena à Bathynoo *cantata,*
Dialog. 4. *Sect.* 39.

O Deus omnipotens ! equidem magna atque stupenda
    Tua sunt opera edita Mundo.
Est ratióque viarum justa ac vera tuarum,
    Sanctorum ô inclyte Princeps !
Quis poterit quin te timeat, Domine, atque verendum
    Submissé nomen honoret ?
Quippe quòd es sanctus solus, tuáque omnia Facta
    Puro candore renident ;
Omnis adoratum veniet Gens quum innotuére
    Tua Judicia æqua per Orbem :
Vota tibi sanctè facient, & lumine cuncti
    Sub Evangelico requiescent.

Cantilena Philothei,
Dialog. 5. *Sect.* 41.

O tu quem in sede superna
Residentem gloria cingit,
Quo vivimus atque movemur !
O quàm dulce atque decorum est
Consensu Cordis & Oris,
Hilari corde oréque grato
Nomen celebrare tuum, cùm
Rosea Aurora Æthera pingit !
Cùm fulgida Sydera surgunt,
Memorare fidem atque favores
Ingentes, carmine læto !
    Citharam cape Barbitulúmque
Quin incipiat Lyra dulcis,
Instrumenta & decachorda,
Cúmque his argentea jungant
Tinnitus Cymbala acutos.
    Animum ut recreant tua Facta !
Quantos ago ego indé Triumphos !
Tua quis miracula narret !
Tua Consilia alta ut Abyssus,
Cæcis abscondita homullis,
Stultis abscondita quorum
Vitium corda obtenebravit.
    Humanæ dicite Genti
Regnum occepisse *Jehovam*,
Arctis Populúmque catenis
Ad justum astringere & æquum.
Ridentes plaudite Cœli !
Vocem effer lætaque Tellus !
Fluctus saltate Marini
Atque augustum edite murmur,
Littúsque reverberet Echo.
Tunicas vibrate virentes
Ornati floribus Agri ;
Lætentur cunctáque, Veri
Æterno dulcè reflectunt
Avium dum cantica Sylvæ.
    Reboënt sacro atria plausu,
Venit, en ! venit ille superbum
Juste qui temperet Orbem,
Populo qui jura det æqua,
Mysteria veráque pandat.

V.—QUOTATIONS FROM THE CLASSICS.

QUOTATIONS FROM THE CLASSICS

IN

'An Explanation of the Grand Myſtery of Godliness.'

1. Lucretius (lib. 2. de Rerum Natura.)

Jamque adeo fracta est Ætas, effætaque Tellus,
Vix animalia parva creat, quæ cuncta creavit
Secla, deditque ferarum ingentia corpora partu.

The Earth who of her self at first brought forth
Huge Lusty Men of Stature big and bold,
And large-limb'd Beasts, she grown effete and old
Hardly bears small ones now, and little worth.

(B. II. C. VI.)

---

2. Virgil (Georgicks, Lib 1.)

Sæpe etiam steriles incendere profuit agros,
Atque levem stipulam crepitantibus urere flammis:
Sive inde occultas vires ac pabula terræ
Pinguia concipiunt; sive illis omne per ignem
Excoquitur vitium, atque exudat inutilis humor.

The fruitless Field with its dry standing Straw
'Tis fit sometimes to burn with crackling Fire:
For whether hence the Earth did Virtue draw
And oyly moisture, or she doth perspire
And sweat out all Corruption; by this Law
The bettered Soil answer's the Swain's Desire. (Ibid.)

---

3. Lucretius (lib. 5).

Tres Species tam dissimiles, tria talia Texta,
Una dies dabit exitio; multosque per annos
Sustentata ruet moles & machina mundi.

Three Species of things so different,
Three such contextures, shall one fatal day
Ruin at once; and the world's Machina
Vpheld so long rush into Atomes rent. (B. II. C. VII.)

4. Hymns of Orpheus.

Κέκλυθι τηλεπόρου δίνης ἑλικαύγεα κύκλον
Οὐρανίαις στροφάλιγξι περίδρομον αἰὲν ἑλίσσων.
Ἀγλαὲ Ζεῦ, Διόνυσε, πάτερ πόντου, πάτερ αἴης,
Ἥλιε παγγενέτορ, παναίολε, χρυσεοφεγγές.

Thou that dost guide the ever-winding Gyre
And wide Rotations of th' Æthereal Fire,
O Sol, great Sire of Sea and Land, give ear.
Omniparent Sol with golden Visage clear,
All-various Godhead, Bacchus, *glorious* Jove,
Or what e're else thou'rt styl'd, my Vows approve.

(B. III. C. I.)

---

5. Homer.

Ὤρνυθ' ἵν' Ἀθανάτοισι φόως φέροι ἠδὲ Βροτοῖσι.

He rose to shine to Gods as well as Men. (Ibid.)

---

6. Virgil.

Diique Deæque omnes, studium quibus arva tueri.

---

7. Oracle.

Εἰμὶ θεὸς τοιόσδε μαθεῖν οἷον κέγὼ εἴπω·
Οὐράνιος Κόσμος κεφαλὴ, γαστὴρ δὲ θάλασσα,
Γαῖα δέ μοι πόδες εἰσὶ, τάδ' οὔατ' ἐν αἰθέρι κεῖται,
Ὄμμα τε τηλαυγὲς λαμπρὸν φάος ἠελίοιο.

Such is my Godhead as to thee I tell:
The Heaven's my Head, the Seas my Belly swell;
The Earth's my Feet, my Ears lie in the Air,
My piercing Eye's the Lamp of Phœbus fair.

(Ibid. C. II.)

8. Homer.

'Ὃς ᾔδη τά τ' ἐόντα, τά τ' ἐσσόμενα, πρὸ τ' ἐόντα.

Who knew what was, what is, and what's to come.
(B. III. C. IV.)

---

9. Life a Stage.

Σκηνὴ πᾶς ὁ βίος, καὶ παίγνιον ἢ μαθὲ παίζειν
Τὴν σπουδὴν μεταθείς, ἢ φέρε τὰς ὀδύνας.

This Life's a Scene of Fools, a sportful Stage,
Where Grief attends him that is over-sage.   (*Ibid.*)

---

10. The god Sylvanus.

Veste Deus lusus fallentes lumina Vestes
Non amat, & nudos ad sua sacra vocat.

The God abus'd by Cloths that hinder sight,
Unto his Feasts the naked doth invite.
(*Ibid.* C. XI.)

---

11. Claudian (lib. 1).

Jam mihi cernuntur trepidis delubra moveri
Sedibus, & clarum dispergere culmina lumen,
Adventum testata Dei : jam magnus ab imis
Auditur fremitus terris, Templumque remugit
CECROPIDUM——

Now do I see the trembling Temple move
From the Foundation, and the Roof all bright
To send down sudden day shot from above,
Sign of the God's approach ; Now strange affrights
Of bellowing murmurs echoing under ground
Fill the CECROPIAN structure with their sound.
(*Ibid.* C. XII.)

---

12. Papinius Statius.

Lustralemne feris ego te, puer improbe, Thebis
Devotumque caput, vilis ceu mater, alebam ?

Have I, O wicked Child, thee nourishèd
Like Mother poor, for cruel Thebes to be
A lustral Wretch, a vile devoted Head ?
(*Ibid.* C. XVI.)

Ζεὺς κύκνος, ταῦρος, σάτυρος, χρυσός, δι' ἔρωτα
Ληδης, Εὐρώπης, 'Αντιόπης, Δανάης.

---

13. Virgil (Georg. lib. 3).

Ore omnes versæ in Zephyrum stant rupibus altis,
Exceptántque leves auras ; & sæpe sine ullis
Conjugiis, vento gravidæ (mirabile dictu !)
Saxa per & scopulos fugiunt——

All standing on high Crags with turnèd Face
To gentle Zephyr, the light Air they draw ;
And oft (O Wonder !) without Venus Law,
Quick with the Wind o're Hills and Rocks they trace.
(*Ibid.* C. XVIII.)

---

14. Cato.

Cum sis ipse nocens, moritur cur victima pro te ?
    Since thou thy self art guilty, why
    Does then thy Sacrifice for thee die ? (B. IV. C. XIV.)

---

15. Plautus.

Men' piaculum oportet fieri propter stultitiam tuam
Vt meum tergum stultitiæ tuæ subdas succedaneum ?

---

16. Virgil (Georg. lib. 1).

Ille etiam extincto miseratus Cæsare Romam,
Cum caput obscurâ nitidum ferrugine texit,
Impidque æternam timuerunt secula noctem.

At Cæsar's Death he Rome compassionèd,
In rusty hue hiding his shining Head,
And put the guilty World into a fright
They were surpris'd with an eternal Night.
(*Ibid.* CXV.)

---

17. Ovid (Met. lib. 15.)

. . . Solis quoque tristis imago
Lurida sollicitis præbebat lumina terris.

The Sun's sad Image Cæsar's fate to moan
With lurid light to anxious Mortals shone. (*Ibid.*)

---

18. Virgil (Georgic. lib. 1.)

Armorum sonitum toto Germania cœlo
Audiit——

All o're the Heavens the Noise of Arms was heard
In Germany.—(B. VI. C. 2.)

---

19. Ovid.

Arma ferunt inter nigras crepitantia nubes
Terribilesque tubas auditaque cornua cælo.

Clashing of Arms amidst black pitchy Clouds
Was heard, with Trumpets hoarse and Cornets loud.
(*Ibid.*)

20. Virgil (Geor.).

Sæpe etiam stellas vento impendente videbis
Præcipites cælo labi, noctisque per umbram
Flammarum longos à tergo albescere tractus.

Oft mayst thou see upon approaching Wind
Stars slide from Heaven, and through the Night's
great shade
Long Tracts of flaming white to draw behind.
(B. VI. C. VIII.)

21. Lucretius.

Quæ facile insinuantur, & insinuata repente
Dissolvunt nodos omnes, & vincla relaxant.

Which easily pierce, and piercing straightway loose
All Knots, and suddenly break every Noose. (*Ibid.*)

22. Prophecy of Daphilus the Tragedian.

῞Εσται γὰρ, ἔσται καινὸς αἰώνων χρόνος,
'Οτ' ἂν πυρὸς γέμοντα θησαυρὸν σχάση
Χρυσωπὸς αἰθήρ, ἡ δὲ βοσκηθεῖσα φλοξ

῞Απαντα ταπίγεια καὶ μετάρσια
Φλέξει μανεῖσα.

The time will come when as the golden Sky
His hidden fiery Treasures shall let fly,
And raging Flames burn up all and consume,
Filling both Earth and Air with noisome Fume.
(*Ibid.* C. IX.)

23. Virgil.

Candidus auratis aperit cum Cornibus annum
Taurus—

When the white Bull opens with Golden Horns
The early Year. (B. VII. C. 19.)

24. Imprecation (from the Greek).

Ζεῦ κύδιστε, μέγιστε, καὶ ἀθάνατοι θεοὶ ἄλλοι,
῾Οππότεροι πρότεροι ὑπὲρ ὅρκια πημήνειαν,
῟Ωδε σφ' ἐγκέφαλος χαμάδις ῥέοι ὡς ὅδε οἶνος.

Thrice great and Glorious Jove, and ye the Gods
His Heavenly Senators, which of these twain
First break this solemn League and fall at odds;
As doth this Wine, so may their scattered Brain
Pash'd from their cursèd Sculls the Pavement stain.
(B. IX. C. VIII.)

VI.—OCCASIONAL POEMS.

1632-46.

2 C

NOTE.

ONE can never be certain of having discovered all the 'Occasional Poems' of an old Writer, such as Dr. Henry More. To his own neglect of them—not having included them in any of his volumes—there is the additional difficulty of a life extending from 1614 to 1687. But I have had willing fellow-workers in consulting the numerous University Collections and other likely sources ; so that, if not absolutely complete, the following eleven separate poems may be accepted as sufficiently representative. On these see our Introduction.—G.

Occasional Poems.

I.—From 'Anthologia in Regia Exanthemata.'
1632.

'ΕΥΧΑΡΙΣΤΙΚΟΝ ΕΙΣ ΤΗΝ ΤΟΥ
ΚΑΡΟΛΟΥ
ὑγίειαν ἀναληφθεῖσαν.

'Εκβαλεν εἰς Κάρολον βέλος ἀργυρέοιο βιοῖο
Φοῖβος. ὀδυρόμεναι δάκρυον αἱ χάριτες·
Τίπτε, φάσαν, βλάπτεις ἱερὸν χρόα σοῖσι βέλεσσιν
"Ω ἄνα ; Εἶτα γελῶν θήκατο κῆλα θεός·
'Αμβροσίης δὲ χέλιν χερσὶν λάβε, καὶ τάδ' ἔειπε,
Παίειν, καὶ παύειν τάς γε νόσους δύναμαι.

Hen. More, Colleg. Christ.

II.—From 'Rex Redux.' 1633.

Τοῦ Καρόλου μέγα χαῖρ' ἄρμα τριπόθητον, ἀταρπῶν
"Αξιον εἶ χθονίων, ἄξιον οὐρανίων.
Οὐράνιος, χθόνιός τε πέλει Καρόλοιο ἄμαξα.
Εἰ δὲ μὴ, οὐράνιος χ' ἢ χθόνιος γένετο.
'Αλλὰ σὺ μὴ λίην σπεύδοις ὁδὸν Οὐλύμποιο,
Κάρρολε, θεσπεσίην τοῖσι τροχοῖσι μετρεῖν.
Καὶ γὰρ ἂν ἐν θνητοῖσιν ἔμεν μερόπεσσι δύνηαι
'Οππότερον βούλει, ἄστρον ἢ ἠέλιος·
'Αστέρος ἐν Σκοτίη, ἐν δ' 'Αλβίον' ἠελίοιο
Τοὔνομά σοι γ' ἱκανὸν χῶρον ἀμειβομένῳ.
Εἰ δὲ μικρὴν ἄστρον κλῆσιν πολύκλειτος ἀναίνῃ,
'Εσσεαι, ὡς εἰκός, πανταχοῦ ἠέλιος.
Τοῦ γὰρ ὑπὲρ γαῖαν λαμπρῶν ἐπιτελλομενάων
'Ακτίνων, ἔρση ἄζεται ἐν βοτάναις.
Καὶ σέο ἐμπελάσαντος ἐν ἀλγεωῆσι παρειαῖς
'Αζάνεται ταχέως δακρυόεσσα δρόσος.
Κλαυθμὸς ἀπών, μέγα χάρμα παρῶν ὁκόσοισι φαάνθης,
"Ηλιον ἐκμιμῇ, καὶ γὰρ ὅγ' ἐστὶ γέλως.

Ζεὺς ποτὶ Αἰθιοπῆας ἔβη μετὰ δαῖτα καέντας.
"Ωρά γε πάντα ἰδὼν οὐκ ἴδεν Αἰθιόπων ;
'Ημέτερος Κρονίδης, Ζεὺς ἥλιός ἐστιν. ἵκανεν
Οὐ ποτὶ Αἰθίοπας, πρὸς δ' ἄπυρον Σκοτίην.
Νῦν δ' ἀνέβη ὃς ἔβη. "Αμφω ἄρα, ΧΑΙΡ' ἱερὸν φῶς,
Εἰπὲ σὺ 'Αγγλίη, εἰπέ τε σὺ Σκοτίη.

Hen. More, Coll. Christ.

III.—From 'Rex Redux.' 1633.

Jam densus aër pulvere concito
Candet : superbus jam sonipes fremit ;
  Audimus hinnitus equorum.
    Ecce ! suum Carolus revisit
Regnum relictum.   Desine, desine
Sperare quod jam, lætior Anglia,
  Parcæ dederunt mitiores :
    Desine, quod renuunt, timere.
Non bellicoso vociferantium
Nostra exprimantur gaudia militum
  Ritu : decus nostrum recedens
    Pace abiit, rediitque pace.
Phœbus corona pocula nectare
(Namque oppidorum plurima inania
  Donare præfecti) manúque
    Porrige Castalios liquores.
At tu profundis carceribus Dea
Carnem remorde vipeream, videns
  Nostram salutem : nil habebis
    Hinc quo avidos repleas hiatus.
Rex quippe noster, Rex Carolus sibi
Junxit decoram connubio Themin ;
  Compressa quæ nobis gemellas
    Eunomiam tulit atque Pacem.

Idem.

IV.—From 'Musarum Cantabrigiensium Σινῳδία.'
1637.

Τὸ πάρος μέλαινα φόρμιγξ,
'Επὶ νυκτίοις στεναγμοῖς,
Στυγερὸν Κρόνῳ πρόσωπον
Φθονερόν τε δαῖμον' ᾄδες·
"Ετι δὲ τρέμει βαρεῖαν
'Υπάτη φοβοῖσα πληγάν.
'Ετέραν δὲ, κεῖν' ἀφεῖσαν,
Κελαδεῖν πρέπει σὲ μολπάν.
Μέθες, ὦ λίγεια φόρμιγξ.
Μέθες ἀστέρων ἀπειλὰς,
Μέθες ἀστέρων μέδοντος
Κότον, ἀστραφεὺς τε "Ηρας.

Ἐθέλω λέγειν τὶ καλὸν,
Ἐθέλω λέγειν τὶ τερπνὸν,
Τὰ δὲ Κύπριδος μὲν οὐχί.
Ἐθέλω λέγειν ἔρωτα,
Τὸ δὲ παιδίον Κυθήρης
Καὶ ἀφρὸν μεθεὶς θαλάσσης.
Λέγε μοι λίγεια φόρμιγξ,
Τὸν Ἔρωτα τὸν γέροντα,
Τὸν ἀειθαλῆ γέροντα,
Τὸν ἁλός τε γᾶς τ' ἄνακτα,
῝Ος ἅπασι τοῖς θεοῖσιν
Ἐπέταξε τὰς θέμιστας,
Ὃς ἅπαντα τόνδε κόσμον
Ἱεροῖς λόγοις ἔδησε.
Τὸ δὲ πλεῖστον ὃς δαμάσδει
Ἐπίβουλον ἔχθος ὕλας.
Ἀτὰρ ἂν τι πλημμελήσῃ,
Σμικρὰ δὲ βροτὼς κακώσῃ,
Ἐθέλει τι μεῖζον αὐτοῖς
Ἀγαθόν ποτ' ἀντιδοῦναι.
Λέγε ὦν λίγεια φόρμιγξ,
Ἐνιαυσίαν μετ' ἄταν,
Πολέων μετ' οἶτον ἀνδρῶν,
Περίφρων τί κάρρον ἄμμιν
Ὁ Ἔρως τανῦν ἔδωκεν;
Ἀνέφυσε καλὸν ἔρνος,
Βασιλήϊον τὸ ἔρνος,
Θεοείκελον τὸ ἔρνος.
Τόδε ἔν σοι ἀντὶ πολλῶν
Δέδοται, μάκαιρα νᾶσε,
Ἀπολωλότων Βρεταννῶν.
Ἄφες Ἀλβίων ὀδυρμὼς,
Ἐπέφυ τὸ καλὸν ἔρνος·
Ἄφες Ἀλβίων γέλωτα,
Ἔτ' ἐπ' ἦρι φύλλα ῥίπτει.
Κακὰ ξὺν καλοῖσι· τάνδε
Φύσις ἁρμογὰν συνῆψεν.
Ὄφελον τὸ ἄμμα θυμῶς
Ἀεσίφρονας πεδῆσαι
Ποτὶ Δωρίως ἀοιδάς.

      Ἑρρῖκος ὁ Μοροῦ, ἐκ τοῦ Χριστοῦ.

V.—From 'Juxta Edovardo King naufrago—Cantab.' 1638.

Τὴν τῆς φθορᾶς πηγὴν ἐναντιότητά μοι
Ἐκ πολλοῦ ἤδη ἔδειξεν ὁ φιλόσοφος λόγος,
Ὥστ' αἰτίαν εἰδότα σαφῶς τῆς δυστυχίας
Οὐδέν με ἐκπλῆξαι τὸ γεγονὸς οὐδαμῶς.
Τί γὰρ τὸ θαῦμα, εἴ ποτ' ἐμπεσὼν πυρὶ
Λύχνου φεραυγεῖ ἀφάνισε τὸ χαροπὸν φάος
Ὑγρὸς σταλαγμός; νῦν δὲ τὴν ἱερὰν φλόγα,
Τηλοπὸν αἴγλην τῆς Ἀθηνῶν λαμπάδος,
Ἔσβεσσεν, ἀφάνισε τὰ πολύθροα κύματα
Ἅλμης Ἱερνίδος. Ὤλεσεν τὸ νεανίον
Τὸ ἀμενὲς πόντου ἀμείλιχος ἀγριότης,
Νέκταρ σταλάζειν χειλέα ποτ' εἰωθότα

Στύφει θαλάσσης ἁλμυρὸν, καὶ πικρὸν ὕδωρ
Ἁγνὸν μιαίνει σῶμα. Τῆς Κυπρίδος θεᾶς
Πατὴρ βδελυκτὸς τῆς ἀγαιομένης ἁλὸς
Ἀφρὸς ὁ ἀπόπτυστος, ἰδοὺ ὡς χειμάζεται
Ψυχῆς βεβαίας ἄρτι ὁ ζάθεος νεώς.
Ἀρετὰς τοῦ ἀνδρὸς ἐξαριθμεῖν προυθέμην·
Βύζει δὲ στόμα τοῦ πράγματος τὸ ὑπερφυὲς,
Ὡσανεὶ ἄπειρος ἐπικυλινδόμενος ῥόος
Ὀγκώδεος πελάγους. Ὅμως δ' οὐ δυσφορῶ,
Τῷ τεθνεῶτι ταυτὰ πως κ' αὐτὸς παθών.

                  H. More.

VI.—From 'Voces Votivae.' 1640.

In Serenissimam Reginam Mariam parturientem

Praeceps ruenti quò feror impetu?
Quem saltum & in quos conjicior specus
     Veloce motu? quò rapis me, ò
         Magne Jovis Semelésque fili?

Nil vile mecum cogito, nescio
Quid grande jam nunc mens mea parturit.
     O me beatum, qui suaves
         Condidici sobolis dolores!

Nunc Musa primùm (mittimus ordinem)
Parit. Ferenda audacia, quae tuum,
     Regina, partum promptiori
         Praevenit officio salutans.

O sacra proles, quem parit integra
Maria! Gentem restitues piam,
     Quem nulla contra fors valebit
         Mórsve nigro metuenda curru.

Seu tu Dicaeus, sive vocabere
Dicaea, mentes sola feras potes
     Sedare, monstro viperinum ab-
         scindere Hyperboreo capillum

Serpente multo complicitum. O decus,
Solamen, & spes unica gentium!
     Vitam satis longam benignus
         Juppiter & celeres sorores

Cedant mihi, insignem ut videam tuum
Vivus triumphum, ut facta celebria
     Solenniter testudine inter
         Pacificos referam Britannos.

Haec ipse mecum montibus avilis
Dum canto, quas non inficiunt virûm
     Mortalium corrupti ocelli,
         Monticolae mihi dulcè nymphae

Rident; & hi quos urbis anhelitus
Et caetuum sudor malè olentium
     Nunquam inquinaverunt, resultant
         Capripedes Satyri atque Fauni.

VII.—*Ibid.*

In Principem sub finem solennis Jejunii natum.

Rectè augurabar, nec mihi spiritu
Vano intumebant pectora. Quis pium,
Justúmve quis non nominarit,
Quem peperere preces puellum

Famésque sancta? scilicet abstinens
Mens vilioris pura cibi, sacrum
Nectar capit seménque Divûm,
Magnificam paritura prolem.

Hic te juvabit rebus in arduis,
Pacémque virésque hic dabit, Anglia :
Non Gallum, Iberum non timebis,
Non rigidûm rabiem Scotorum.

VIII.—*Ibid.*

Εἰs τὸν αὐτόν.

Λαγνείην μέτα, καὶ ὕβριν, δεῦρ' εἰπέ, Ἐρινύs,
Καὶ οἰνοφλυγίην, ποῖα νέμεις Νέμεσις ;
Λιμὸν ὁμοῦ καὶ λοιμὸν, ἔριν τ', ἀνδροκτασίην τε·
Οἴμοι. Θερμὸν ἀρ' οὖν πρᾶγμα καὶ ἀργαλέον.
Ἀλλ' εὐχὴν μέτα, καὶ νῆστιν, καὶ πένθεα λυγρά,
Ἀγνὴ, ποῖα Θεόs ; εἰπέ μοι, Εὐφροσύνη.
Ἄσμα, χορὸν, κιθάρην, θαλίην· συνελόντι δὲ εἰπεῖν,
Βρῶμα πόσιν τε θεῶν, νέκταρ ἰδ' ἀμβροσίην.
Ὦ ἄρτου ζαθέου· ὦ ῥοῆς πνεύματος· ὦ τῆς
Παρθενικῆς ἐρατὸν παιδαρίου Μαρίης.

H. More, A.M. è Christi.

IX.—From '*Irenodia Cantabrigiensis.*' 1641.

Εἰς τὰν ποττὼς Σκότως συγγραφθεῖσαν εἰράναν ἐπιδη-
μοῦντος τὸ μεταξὺ παρὰ τοῖς Ἄγγλοις
τῷ λοιμῷ.

Εἰράνα τὸν Ἄρηα κατειργάσατ', ἀλλάγε λοιμὸν
Εἴπατε ὤνθρωποι πῶς διαφράξομεθα ;
Καὶ γὰρ ἀποφάντες τὰ βροτῆϊα ὅπλα, τί σεμνὸν,
Ὄφρα βελεσσιχαρεῖ δαίμονι συμπέσομεν ;
Ἀλλὰ δὴ ἐντί τις εἰράνα, ἂν οὐ δύναταί τις
Δαίμων ὀχλᾶσαι, οὐδ' ἐθέλει ὁ Θεός.
Ἄδε λόγον ψυχᾶς ποτ' ἀλαθέα ἁρμονὰ ἐντι
Ἅνικα νῶ εἴκει ἄσμενα πάντα πάθη.
Τοίαν οὐδὲν πῆμα ἐπισκιάσαιτο γελάναν,
Ἄσβεστον καθαρᾶς χάρμα δικαιοσύνας.

Ἑῤῥῖκος ὁ Μοροῦ, ἐκ τοῦ Χριστοῦ.

X.—From '*Horae Vacivae*' of John Hall of Cambridge. 1646.

ΠΡΟ῾Σ ΤΟ῾Ν Ἐ῾ΥΦΥΕ῾
στατον νεανίσκον γράψαντα μὲν καλῶs
καὶ παρ' ἡλικίαν, ἅμα δὲ τοὺs ἀμφὶ
Πυθάγοραν διασκώψαντα,
Ἐξάστιχον.

Τοῖα γράφειν δύνασαι παῖs ὤν, φίλε, μηκέτι δοιδs
Εὖν χθονὶ ἀντλήσαις τῶν ἐτέαν δεκάδαs ;

Οὐ μὰ τὸν ἀλλὰ πάλαι προμαθὼν πότε καὶ προβίωσας,
Πολλά τε καὶ καλ' ἐρεῖς ὡς ἀναμνησάμενος.
Εἰ δὲ σὺ καὶ τὰ σὰ ἔργα παλαίτερα ἐστι σεαυτοῦ,
Τίπτε σοφὼν σκώπτεις, φίλτατε, Πυθάγοραν.

Ἑῤῥῖκος ὁ Μοροῦ
ἐκ τοῦ Χριστοῦ.

XI.—From '*Poems by John Hall, Cambridge.*' 1646.

To the young Authour upon his incomparable veine in Satyre and Love-sonnets.

Young Monster ! born with teeth ! that thus canst bite
So deep, canst wound all sorts at ten and eight,
Fierce *Scythian* Brat ! young *Tamerlan!* the Gods
Great scourge, that kickst all men like skulls and clods !
Rough creature, born for terrour ! whose stern look
Few strings and muscles mov'd is a whole book
Of biting Satyrs ! who did thee beget ?
Or with what pictures was the curtains set ?
John of the Wildernesse ? the hayry child ?
The hispid *Thisbite?* or what Satyr wild
That thou thus satyrizest ? Storm of wit
That fall'st on all thou meetst, and all dost meet !
Singest like lightening the Reverend furre
Of ancient Sages. Mak'st a fearfull stirre
With my young Maister and his Pædagog,
And pull'st by th' eares the Lads beloved Dog.
Then hast thy finger in Potato pies
That make the dull Grammarian to rise.
Anon advancing thy Satyrick Flail
Sweepst down the Wine-glasses and cups of ale.
Nor yet art spent. Thy manly rage affords
New coyle against young wenches and old words,
Gainst *Jos.* and *Tycho* that flings down the spheares,
Like *Will* with th' wisp sitst on moyst Asses eares.
And now stept in, most quick and dexterous,
Boldly by th' elbow jogst *Maurolycus,*
Causing him in his curious numbrings loose
Himself. Tak'st *Galilæo* by the nose.
Another stroke makes the dry bones, O sinne !
Of lean Geometry rattle in her skinne,
New rage transforms thee to a Pig, that roots
In *Jury-land* or crumps *Arabick* roots.
Or els made Corn cutter, Thou loutest low
And tak'st old Madam *Eva* by the toe.
Anon thy officious phansie at randon sent
Becomes a Chamberlain, waits on *Wood* of *Kent.*
S' much good do't you, then the table throws
Into his mouth his stomacks mouth to close.
Another while the well drench'd smoaky *Jew,*
That stands in his own spaul above the shooe,
She twitcheth by the Cloak and thred bare plush,
Nor heats his moist black beard into a blush.
  Mad soul ! Tyrannick wit ! that thus dost scourge
All Mortalls and with their own follies urge.
Thou'rt young ; therefore as Infant, Innocent,
Without regret of conscience all are rent

By thy rough knotted whip. But if such blows
Thy younger years can give ; when Age bestows
Much firmer strength, sure thy Satyrick rods
May awe the Heavens and discipline the gods.
    And now, I ween, we wisely well have shown
What Hatred, Wrath, and Indignation
Can do in thy great parts. How melting Love
That other youthfull heat thou dost improve
With phansies queint and gay expressions pat,
More florid then a Lanspresado's hat ;
That province to some fresher pens we leave
Dear Lad I and kindly now we take our leave.
Onely one word. Sith we so highly raise
Thy wrathfull wit ; take this compendious praise.
    Thy Love and Wrath seem equall good to me,
For both thy Wrath and Love right Satyrs be.

Thus may we twitch thee now, young Whelp I but when
Thy paw's be grown who'll dare to touch thee then ?

H. More
Fell. of Chr. Coll.

[On the following Latin epitaph—see our Memorial-
Introduction :—]

EFFARE MARMOR.

Cuja sunt hæc duo quæ sustentas capita ;
Duorum Amicissimorum, quibus Cor erat unum unaque
    Anima,
D. IOANNIS FINCHII et D. THOMÆ BAINESII
    Equitum Auratorum,
Virorum omnimodâ Sapientiâ Aristotelicâ, Platonicâ,
    Hippocraticâ,
Rerumq. adeo gerundarum Peritiâ Plane summorum
Atq. hisce nominibus et ob Praeclarum immortalis
    amicitiæ exemplum
Sub amantissimi Tutoris HENRICI MORI auspicijs
    hoc ipso in Collegio initæ   ·
Per totum terrarum orbem celebratissimorum.
Hi mores, hæc studia, hic successus, genus vero
    si quæris et necessitudines
Horum alter D. HENEAGII FINCHII Equitis Aurati
    Filius erat
HENEAGII vero FINCHII Comitis Nottingamiensis
    Frater,
Non magis Iuris quam Iustitiæ consulti,
Regiæ Majestati a consiliis secretioribus summiq.
    Angliæ Cancellarij,
    Viri prudentissimi, religiosissimi,
        eloquentissimi, integerrimi,
Principi, Patriæ, atq. Ecclesiæ Anglicanæ Charissimi,
Ingeniosâ, numerosâ, prosperaq. Prole prae cæteris
    mortalibus, felicissimi :
Alter D. IOANNIS FINCHII, viri omni laude
    majoris Amicus intimus,
Perpetuusq. per triginta plus minus annos
Fortunarum ac Consiliorum Particeps
Longarumq. in exteras Nationes Itinerationum
    individuus comes ;
Hic igitur peregrè apud Turcas vitâ functus
    est, nec prius tamen quam alter

A serenissimo Rege Angliæ per Decennium Legatus
    præclare suo functus esset munere,
Tunc demum dilectissimus BAINESIUS suam et Amici
    FINCHII simul Animam Byzantii efflavit,
Die V. Septembris H. III. P.M. A.D. MDCLXXXI
    Ætatis suæ LIX
Quid igitur fecerit alterum hoc corpus animâ cassum
    rogas,
Ruit ; sed in amplexus alterius indoluit, ingemuit,
    ubertim flevit
Totum in lacrymas, nisi nescio quæ Communis utriq.
    Animæ
        Reliquiæ cohibuissent, Diffluxurum.

Nec tamen totus dolori sic indulsit nobilissimus
    FINCHIUS
Quin ipsi quæ incumberent solerter gesserit
    confeceritq. negotia,
Et postquam ad Amici pollincturam quæ spectarent
    curaverat
Visceraq. telluri Byzantinæ, addito marmore eleganter
    a se pieq. Inscripto, commiserat
Cunctasq. res suas sedulo paraverat ad reditum in
    optatam Patriam,
Corpus etiam defuncti Amici a Constantinopoli usq.
(Triste sed pium officium I) per longos Maris tractus
Novam subinde salo e lacrymis suis admiscens salsedinem
    ad Sacellum hoc deduxit :
Ubi funebri ipsum oratione adhibitâ mœstisq. sed
    dulcisonis Threnodiis,
In Hypogæum tandem sub proxima Areâ situm
Commune utriq. paratum Hospitium solenniter honori-
    ficeq. condidit.
Hæc pia FINCHIUS officia defuncto Amico præstitit,
    porroq., cum eo, in usus pios
Quater mille libras Anglicanas huic Christi collegio
    donavit
Ad duos socios totidemq. scholares in Collegio alendos
Et ad augendum libris quinquagenis redditum
    Magistri annuum.
Cui rei ministrandæ riteq. finiendæ Londini
    dum incumberet
Paucos post menses in morbum incidit Febriq. ac
    Pleuritide
Maxime vero Amici BAINESII desiderio adfectus et
    afflictus
Inter lacrymas luctus et amplexus charissimorum
    diem objit
Speq. beatæ immortalitatis plenus piè ac placidè in
    Domino obdormivit
Die XVIII Novembris H. II. P.M. A.D. MDCLXXXII
    Ætatis suæ LVI
Londinoq. huc delatus ab illustrissimo Domino D.
    FINCHIO
HENEAGII Comitis Nottingamiensis filio Primo-
    genito
Aliisq. ejùs filiis ac Necessariis Comitantibus
Eodem in sepulchro quo ejus Amicissimus heic conditus
    jacet ;
Ut studia, Fortunas, consilia, immo Animas vivi qui
    miscuerant
Iidem suos defuncti sacros tandem miscerent Cineres.

GLOSSARIAL INDEX

AND

NOTES AND ILLUSTRATIONS.

NOTE.

The references in this Glossarial Index are as follow :—

> 30/125 = Page 30, st. 125.
> 136/23a = Page 136, line 23, column 1—column 2 being
> similarly marked *b*, as 7/42 (*b*).

It has been my aim to register every noticeable word. Occasionally now familiar words are entered, because, while they do not call for explanation or annotation, (1) They illustrate the growth of the language and usage, and (2) the variations of orthography. Merely technical terms must be sought for in the Author's own special Indices and Notes. Classical commonplaces of names and allusions are left unannotated. All words or things calling for illustration or explanation will be found less or more annotated. Only those who have undertaken work of this sort can appreciate the labour spent on this Glossarial Index. As with those to Davies of Hereford, Nicolas Breton, and the other Worthies of our Series, I hope this Glossarial Index will add to the materials so largely accumulating, for that urgent *desideratum*—an adequate Dictionary of our magnificent language.—A. B. G.

Glossarial Index and Notes and Illustrations.

A

Aboad = abode, 71/8, 132/27.

Aboven = above, with suffix 'en,' and so nearer the root-form, 23/40, 94/30, 96/59, 97/66.

Abusive = offensive, injurious, 30/125.

Aby = abide, or tarry, 87/39. In Mid. N. Dr. III. 2, 175, 335, 'aby' of Q¹ and 'abie' of Q² are in the folio (1623) 'abide,' also in l. 175 in Q², as thus—

> 'Disparage not the faith thou dost not know,
> Lest to thy peril thou *abide* it deare.'

and

> 'For if thou dost intend
> Neuer so little shew of loue to her,
> Thou shalt *abide* it.' (l. 175.)

Schmidt and others, *s.v.*, = atone, seems too strong, though in the Anglo-Saxon root it denoted this.

Acception = acceptation, 160/41 (*a*).

Accloy'd, accloyes = satiated, satiates or surfeits, 44/12, 63/3, 75/54, 77/15.

Accord, 16/35, 32/142.

Accoyes = daunts, 44/11. Spenser, Shep. Cal. Feb., l. 47, and Peele (Eclogue 1589)—'How soon may heere thy courage be accoyed.' (Dyce, p. 562.)

Acronychall or acronicall, 83/72, 155/10 (*b*) = in astronomy signifies the rising of a star when the sun sets, or the setting of a star when the sun rises; in which cases the star is said either to rise or set achronically; which is one of the three poetical risings or settings. Harris (Bailey, *s.v.*). Latin *achronicus*, of a priv., and χρονος, time = being out of, or without time.

Actualities, 70/5.

Adamantine = pertaining to or made of a diamond—inflexible, indestructible, 29/114.

Adeodatus = given by God, 127/94.

Admire, 104/6.

Adrian = Adriatic, 84/12.

Adulterate = contaminated—as by adultery, 10/10 (*b*).

Adumbrate = to shadow out (imperfectly), 156/21 (*a*).

Adumbration = imperfect representation, 156/31 (*b*).

Adventitious, 138/29 (*a*).

Adversion, 50/45, 71/7, 74/45, 75/54, 105/15, 110/28, 133/38, 134/39.

Advert = take heed, 57/1, 134/39.

Advertence = attention, 110/28.

Advisement = information, 14/17.

Advisen = advise, with suffix 'en,' 31/127.

Aestimant—misprint for 'aestiment,' page 87, col. 1, l. 2 (Latin).

Aethiopian [hell] = black or dark, 16/36.

Afeard = afraid, 34/14.

Affred = afraid, 172/11.

Afore = before, 62/31, 75/56, 78/27, 96/53, 103/1.

After-advertisements, 4/17.

After-sport, 99/92.

After-wit = cunning (or wit) which comes too late, 97/71.

Aggrize = astonish—usually spelled with one 'g,' 16/30.

Agguize,—from 'guise,' *i.e.* to adorn, as in Spenser, F. Q. II. i. 31, and M. Hubb. Tale, l. 665, 15/23, 17/43, 38/56.

Agill = agile, 61/20.

Aglaophemus,—unknown to the Editor—cannot be 'Aglaopheme' of the Sirens, 112/5.

Agone = ago, past, since, 97/71.

Aieric, 51/51.

Air-trampling, 122/36.

Aire-consistency, 103/41.

All-approved, 10/19 (*b*).

All-complying, 121/28.

All-discovering, 113/10.

All-phrantick = frantic, 126/73.

All-potencye, 51/54.

All-sparkling, 128/103.

All-spreaden, 108/3.

Allayeth = quench or mitigate, 122/39.

Als = also, 85/15, 95/52, 112/7, 113/10, 113/16, 124/54, 133/50.

Alterity, a word found in Coleridge (Lit. Remains, vol. iii. p. 2)—perhaps a reminiscence of More, or a re-coinage?—13/1, 136/23 (*a*), 136/34 (*a*).

Amain = vigorously, vehemently, 19/5, 37/43.

Amalgamate, 121/28.

A many, 126/82. So Ben Jonson—'We see before a many of books' (Underwoods—Epistle to Selden), and 'she was in one a many parts of life' (*Ibid.* Elegy on . . . Lady Venetia Digby).

Amazen = amaze, with suffix 'en,' 98/79.

Amid, 115/31.

Amounds = amounts? 21/24.

Amoved, 49/36, 62/36.

Anautæsthet—see the Author's Interpretation-General, *s.v.*, 39/67.

Anautæsthesie, 39/68.

Anchor'd, *adj.* = anchor-shaped, forked, 49/29.

Ancienter, 22/34.

Anew, 127/85.

Angularity, 111/38.

Animadversall, 62/35.

Animadvert, 50/45.

Animadversion, 42/36 (*a*), 50/45, 75/52, 102/29 (*b*), 133/38, *et alibi*.

Animadversive = reflecting, considering, judging, 48/26 —'The soul is the only *animadversive* principle.' Glanville (Bailey, *s.v.*).

Animate (*sb.*), 78/28.

Antiquate (*adj.*), 91/6.

Apaid = satisfied, 46/2.

Apall, 33/2.

Apish = imitative, 4/4.

Apodicticall = demonstration or convincing proof, 139/11 (*a*).

Apogeon = apogæon, apogæ or apogæum—that part in the orbit of the sun or a planet which is farthest from the earth, 46/6, 51/58.

Apparitions = appearances, 7/42 (*b*). See Bailey, *s.v.*, for excellent illustrations.

Apprends = apprehends, 110/28.

Approchen = approach, with suffix 'en,' 35/27.

Appulse and appulses (*sb.*) = act of striking against, 47/13, 54/27, 74/46, 160/32 (*a*). (Latin, *appulsus*.)

Apterites, 146/10 (*a*—from bottom).

Arbitrarious = arbitrary, 156/15 (*b*).

Arcades = Arcadians, 22/34.

Archei=plasmaticall spirits, 138/8 (*b*), 139/23 (*b*), 143/1 (*a*).

Archetypall = pertaining to the Supreme Original, 146/29 (*a*).   Archtype, 77/7.

Arcuall = arcuate (Latin, *arcuatus*), curved like a bow, 79/38.

Aread, areed = declare or explain, 15/19, 23/49, 25/65, 85/18, 99/94, 100/107, 119/2. Cf. Spenser, Daphn. l. 182, *et alibi*.

Aristo = Ariosto, 119/1.

Arrogation = over-proud claim by an individual for himself, 147/15 (*b*).

Arrogative, 147/8 (*b*).

Ascititious = adventitious, 65/25, 110/33.

Asheap = ash-heap, 100/98.

Asperitie, 82/62, 111/35.

Aspine, 17/41.

Aspires, 173/4, 181/44.

Assayes, 52/5.

Assistencie, 75/57.

Astrall = belonging to the stars, 143/ last line (*b*), 144/26 (*a*). Even Dryden uses it.

Asuitus—unknown to the Editor, 124/59.

Attent, *adj.*, 47/15.

Attenuate, *adj.*, 102/24 (*a*), 138/48 (*a*), 138/16 (*b*).

Atuvean, 14/16.

Atuvus, 16/33.

Audibles (*sb.*), 59/4.

Autocal = a fancy-being and name, 14/16.

Autokineticall = self-moving? 48/25, l. 1, 48/26, 48/27.

Autority = authority, 26/81.

Aven-roe = Averroes or Ibn Roschid : died Decr. 12, 1198, 131/7.

Avert, 86/33.

Avise = advise, 33/6.

Awfull-eyed, 147/ last line (*b*).

Awhit = a whit, *i.e.* in the least, 31/134.

Awide = wide, with prefix 'a,' 58/14.

Azur = azure, 15/24, 80/48.

B

BABE-SOUL, 127/86.

Back-cast = cast back, 99/88.

Bad = bade, 53/18.

Bags = breasts, 123/47.

Bain = bane (*sb.*), 100/97.

Balbutient—query = ebullient, boiling over, 114/24.

Bale = sorrow, 34/9, 54/22. Cf. Spenser, Daphn. l. 320, 'Let now your bliss be turned to *bale*.'

Baleful, 115/34.

Balk, 94/39.

Band = bond, 73/39.

Band-dogs = bound-dogs—kept for baiting bears, etc., 76/7. Marston and Heywood spell as More does, not 'ban-dogs.'

Beach = beech, 33/1, 39/70.

Bearen = bear, with suffix 'en,' 116/49.

Beaten, 20/7.

Beck = salutation by bowing, 49/35, 57/2, 121/19, 122/34.

Bedight = bedeck, 18/54, 22/31, 47/7, 54/21, 77/11, 85/15, 105/20, 116/43.

Bedrencht, 45/19.

Been = have been, were, 17/50, 22/37, 35/20, 99/91, *et frequenter*.

Beforn = before, 49/35, 104/10. Cf. Spenser, Shep. Cal. May, l. 103, 'Ought may happen that hath been *beforn*.'

Beholden = under obligation, 95/45.

Belate, 16/31.

Belch, 44/7, 85/22.

Believen, 27/93.

Bemire, 181/26 (*a*).

Bet = beaten, 26/76, 98/83.

Bever = hat, 22/38.

Biformity = double-form, 39/70.

Bignesse, 51/54.

Billing = tapping with the bill or beak, 177/2.

Blazen = blazon, 110/26.

Blebs = blobs? 165/10 (*b*—from bottom).

Blend = pollute, 109/13.

Blent = mixed, blended, 52/6.

Blew-glimmering, 68/22.

Blewly, 99/94.

Blin = cease, 33/6.

Blith, 22/31.

Bolonia (walking skeleton) = of Bologna, 123/46.

Bookish = book-loving (Bibliomania), 4/20.

Botch'd, *adj.*, 75/60.

Botchdly, 82/67.

Botcher = butcher, 80/44.

Bougen = bulge? 17/46.

Bounden = bound, with suffix 'en,' 120/18.

Bout, 82/64, 93/21, 93/25.

Bowed, *adj.*, 172/18.

Bow'd = curved, indirect, 83/74.

Boxes, 125/65.

Brat, 58/15.

Bravest, 6/9 (*a*).

Braving, *adj.* = brave, defiant? 76/1.

Bray = ass's sound, 45/21.

Breadthlesse, 59/6.

Breaken, 62/37.

Cold-pated, 6/19 (*a*).
Collated, *adj.*, 93/23.
Collect, 106/34.
Collection, 8/17 (*a*—to Reader), 12/11 (*a*).
Collectednesse, 113/17.
Colligation = keeping together, 161/42 (*b*).
Combrous, 176/14 (*a*).
Commination, 49/39.
Conmixtion, 144/8 (*a*—from bottom).
Commixture, 165/4 (*a*—from bottom).
Common sense, 61/27, 61/28, 62/31.
Common spright, 74/47.
Communialty, 144/38 (*a*).
Community, 16/38, 17/49.
Companied, *v.*, 66/2.
Compassion (*sb.*) = sympathy, 113/16.
Compear, 61/28.
Compile, 82/68.
Complement = interchange compliments, 4/3.
Complexion = temperament, 6/22 (*b*).
Complishment, 37/46.
Compost, 72/20.
Compositall (*sb.*), 56/9.
Composures, 55/3.
Compresse, 15/28, 125/64.
Comprize, 36/38.
Concatenate, 84/7.
Conceit, *v.*, 95/51, 98/82.
Conceiven, 36/32, 131/12.
Concinnity, 155/2 (*a*), *et alibi*.
Concomitant (*sb.*) = companion, 32/142.
Concorporate, 115/36.
Concorporation, 69/26.
Conducibienesse, 7/32 (*a*).
Conductour = conductor, 7/36 (*b*).
Conference, 80/42.
Conflictation, 71/17.
Confound = confounded, 94/32.
Confract, *v.* = broken ? 104/9.
Confusely = confusedly, 64/11.
Congenit, *adj.* = connatural, 92/11, 143/4 (*a*—from bottom).
Congied, 25/63.
Conique, 15/25.
Conject, *v.* = conjecture, 104/10, 119/5.
Connaturall, 143/3 (*a*—from bottom).
Consopite, *v.* = calm, compose, 73/37, 80/43, 105/20.
Consort, 44/9, 81/58.
Conspire, *v.*, 99/92, 105/17, 134/ l. 14 (Oracle).
Conspiring, *adj.*, 29/109.
Conspissate, *v.* = thicken, 92/14, *et alibi*.
Conspissation, 92/13, *et alibi*.
Constipated, 15/28.
Context, 82/68.
Contract, *adj.*, 84/6, 119/5.
Contract, *v.*, 60/8, 67/8, 70/5, 119/5.
Contradictariously, 131/14.
Contradictious, 95/49.
Contrair, *adj.*, 18/56, 24/51, *et frequenter*.

Contrair, *v.*, 23/50.
Contrary, *v.*, 22/37.
Contrary'd, 22/37.
Contrive, *v.*, 44/10, 133/32.
Contrivement, 116/50.
Convert, *v. intr.*, 122/40.
Convert, *v. tr.*, 134/39.
Coppell'd, *adj.* = high-topped, 15/25. *See* Nares, *s.v.*, ' copped ' and cognates.
'Cording = according, 36/32, 44/8, *et frequenter*.
Corniculate = horned, 82/62.
Corporalitie, 66/29, 74/44, 92/10, 92/16.
Corporate, *v.*, 109/19.
Corporative, 91/6.
Corporeals (*sb.*), 58/14, 59/1, 59/6, 65/19.
Corporeitie, and *pl.*, 50/46, 58/13, 60/15, *et frequenter*.
Corps = body, 23/45, *et frequenter*.
Corse, 49/29, 105/19.
Cosmopolite, 30/122.
Counite, *v.*, 16/39, 74/44, 110/33, 113/17.
Count = accounted, 23/49.
Coursie = corrosive, 24/52.
Courtship = courtliness, 14/2.
Covetise, covetize, 29/116, 83/1, 87/38, 113/11.
Coyle = noise, tumult, 205/ l. 22 (on Hall).
Crabb'd, 81/58.
Cragg'd, 8/2, 68/25.
Crank, *adj.* = brisk, lively, 30/121.
Crasie, 38/51, 67/4, 73/29.
Creaturall, 48/25, 97/67.
Credulous = believing, 4/16.
Cretian = of Crete ? 87/42.
Cretick = Cretan ? 124/58.
Cring'd, 25/63.
Cronicall, cronychall, 83/72, 160/39 (*b*). (*See* under ' A-cronychall.')
Crook, *adj.* = crooked, 180/4.
Crud = curd, 127/90.
Crudled, cruddled, 15/25, 99/92, 171/14.
Crudling (*sb.*), 121/26.
Crumenall = purse, 35/19. Nares, *s.v.*, very oddly quotes Spenser (Shep. Cal. September, l. 118),
    ' The fat oxe that wont to lig in the stall,
    Is now fast stalled in her *crumenal.*'
This is his only example.
Crumpled, 37/50.
Cumbrous, 170/5.
Curiosity, 6/29 (*a*).
Currish, 81/58.
Cur'sy = courtesy, 61/21.
Cushionet, 26/76. *See* Nares, *s.v.*
Cuspis, 91/7.
Cylindre, 179/8.
Cynocephals = monster-headed beings ? 39/71.

D

Dactyli, 87/42.
Dampish, 93/23, 96/62.
Dart-holding, 39/68.

Daze, 87/39.
Dead, *v.* = deaden, 72/20, 87/39.
Deading, *adj.*, 104/2.
Deaf, *v.* = deafening, 106/28.
Deafing = deafening, 134/19 (*b*).
Dear, 8/9 (*b*—to Reader).
Death-shadowed, 35/21.
Debil = weak, feeble, 160/28 (*a*).
Decent =fit or suitable and comely, 132/27, 134/10 (*a*).
Deemed, *adj.*, 63/2, 175/24 (*a*), 79/16.
Deeming (*sb.*), 179/4.
Deep-biting, 120/9.
Defluxion, 161/43 (*b*).
Deform, *adj.* = deformed, 14/9, 74/41, 109/23.
Deft, 135/24 (*b*).
Deiform, 50/47, 69/30, 71/7, 132/25, 165/39 (*b*).
Deiformity, 132/37.
Deieble = capable of being blotted out, 146/45 (*a*).
Delice = delight or deliciousness, 36/32.
Delineament, 77/11.
Demeanance = demeanour, 27/87.
Denominate, 95/44.
Denotate, *v.* = denote, 77/9, 159/25 (*b*).
Depaint, depeint, 13/3, 16/29, 53/9.
Deprave, *v.*, 47/9, 108/5.
Deprehend = discover? 104/13.
Derelictions = forsaking, abandonment, 126/79.
Derivative, 54/26.
Dern = dark, solitary, sad, 44/10, 68/22, 80/41, 116/44.
Descry=describe or show (also 'descrys'), 113/16, 120/10, 133/36.
Descrive = describe, 111/39, 114/20.
Detect, 22/36.
Determ, *v.* = determine, 51/59.
Determinate, 84/7.
Determinations, 6/41 (*b*).
Deuteropathie = sympathetic affection, 68/24.
Devest, 50/44, 65/18.
Devicefull, 94/45, 98/85.
Devisen, 110/25.
Diametre, 12/38 (*a*).
Diametrall = diametrical, 17/47.
Diapase = diapason (in music the octave), 20/15, 110/31.
Diapason, 18/56.
Diffide = distrust (' fide ' from *fides*), 62/37, 174/10.
Dight, *v.* = deck, adorn, 14/15, 15/25, 24/61, *et frequenter.*
Dilation = dilatation, *i.e.* expansion, 133/33.
Ding, *v.* = dash down—in living use in Scotland, 78/25.
Discided, 21/27.
Discission = opening ? 80/48.
Discoloured, 13/3, 16/30, 20/8.
Discriminance, 61/24.
Disease = uneasiness, distress, 35/20.
Disgrace, *v.*, 179/3.
Disgracement, 81/56.
Disgregate = separate, 65/25, 160/11 (*b*—from bottom).
Disimagine, 7/18 (*b*).
Disjoynt, 108/12.

Dispeared =disappeared, 18/51, 48/22, 54/18, 56/5, 121/29.
Disport = amuse, 81/58.
Dispread, dispred, 15/26, 17/43, 17/49, 35/27, 57/3, *et frequenter.*
Disproportionalitie, 81/60.
Disproportionatedness, 152/17 (*a*).
Disquietall = disquietful, 48/21.
Dissolvable, 8/4 (*b*).
Dissonant, 127/85.
Dissunder, 35/25.
Distain, 186/1 (*b*).
Distancie, distancy = distance, 50/42, 71/14, 72/24, 76/4, 83/72, 94/39, 108/6, 116/48.
Distent = spread, 51/56, 65/19, 94/39.
Distention, 81/59.
Disterminate = separate by bounds, 20/10.
Distraught = distracted, 22/35, 38/58, 108/8, 176/3 (Devotion).
Distrought = distracted, 60/10, 61/26.
Ditts, *v.* = closes up.
Divides, 11/50 (*a*).
Docible, 23/41.
Dogged, 130/4.
Dolour = grief, 122/30.
Doltish, 122/37.
Done = to do, 124/53, 128/95, 128/96.
Doom = judgment, sentence, 20/13, 97/70, 98/83, 115/39, *et alibi.*
Double-livednesse = two-fold life, 161/22 (*a*).
Down-drooping, 80/42.
Down-looking, 115/38.
Down-propensies, 79/31.
Down-sliding, 33/7.
Drad=dread, 8/21 (*a*), 29/110, 33 l. 4 (motto), 33/4. 39/65. 39/66, 39/67, 44/8, 57/2, *et frequenter.*
Drawable, 70/2.
Drearyhood, dreryhed = dreariness, 56/6.
Dred = dreaded, 128/104.
Drery = dreary, 35/21.
Droop (*sb.*), 35/25.
Drossie, 98/79.
Drousihead, drowsihead, 59/2, 67/9, 109/17, 128/104.
Drown = drowned, 68/20.
Dry (essence) = simple essence, or essence *per se*, 7/6 (*a*).
Ducks (*sb.*), 25/70.
Dunghill, *adj.* = base, vile, 36/38, 173/4.
Durance = duration, 50/46, 56/10, 57/1, 165/3 (*b*—from bottom).
Durancie, durancy = duration, 50/47, 97/65, 103/1.
Duskish, 20/8, 39/64, 46/6, 93/24, 99/89, 179/7.
Duskishnesse, 15/22, 44/12.

E

EARTHILY = earthly, 26/77.
Earth-groveling, 36/38.
Easily = easily, 132/24.
Eath = easy, 94/40, 170/13, 121/29, *et alibi.*
Eben = ebony, 35/20.

Eben-beams = ivory ? 115/29.
Eben-box = ebony or ivory, 17/45.
Efform = shape or form, 16/37, 109/23.
Efformation, 70/3, 98/76.
Efformative, 163/35 (*b*).
Effund = shed, pour out, 32/146.
Eftsoons = immediately, 47/13.
Egs = urges, 36/32.
Egre = eager, 34/15.
Eke = also, 32/146, 38/59, 43/1, *et frequenter*.
Eld = old age, 32/143, 32/148, 47/15, 106/34, 174/2.
Eldship = eldership, *i.e.* seniority, 22/31.
Elicitate, *v.* = draw out, 111/41.
Embark'd = enclosed in bark of tree, 119/4.
Embosome, 42/23 (*b*), 77/12, 132/17, *et alibi*.
Embracement, 77/12.
Embrave = embellish, 108/5, 132/17, 135/16 (*a*).
Embue, 125/63.
Emisse = sent out, 115/30.
Empare = impare, 50/48.
Empassion, *v.*
Empierced, 33/5.
Empight and empighten = fix (see under 'pight'), 74/45,
     81/50, 104/8, 105/19, 105/21, 106/29, 109/20, 115/30.
Emprise = enterprise (*sb.* and *v.*), 33/6, 112/6.
Empse = empty, uninhabited ? 16/36.
Enact, *v. tr.*, 23/45.
Encroch, 35/19.
Enfold, 187/1 (*a*).
Enforcing, 18/58.
Engins, 54/26.
Enlight, and enlights, 45/25, 51/58, 63/3, 113/8, 173/17,
     et alibi.
Enorm = enormous, 48/22, 82/70.
Enquickened, 145/12 (*b*—from bottom).
Ensuen, 55/3, 69/29.
Enterance, 85/28.
Enterfaring = interfering, 152/15 (*a*).
Entitle, 6/10 (*b*).
Entity, 94/34, 115/30, 132/23.
Entrall = entrance, 70/6.
Envassall, *v.* = subjugate, enslave, 45/23.
Enwomb'd, 123/51.
Equallize, 24/55.
Eradicating = springing from a root, *e radice*, 139/2.
Erring, *adj.* = wandering, 77/15, 81/61.
Eructations, 110/25.
Espide, 98/77.
Essencies, 77/12.
Etern = eternal, 24/52.
Ethercall (*pl.*), 80/46.
Ever-actuall, 137/1.
Evolved, *adj.*, 84/11.
Exeem, *v.* = exempt, 83/2.
Exert, *v.* = exerted, 16/39, 57/1.
Exile, *adj.*, 12/35 (*a*), 57/6, 84/9, 102/30 (*b*).
Exilitie, exility = slenderness, 59/2, 61/21, 67/13, 76/2,
     77/17, 83/73, 84/10, 102/14 (*a*).
Existencie, existency, 55/2, 104/4, 130/1.

Exotick, 42/21.
Expedite, 23/41.
Experientially, 12/9 (*a*).
Explendency, 71/14.
Explicate, 110/24.
Exprest = pressed out, 127/87.
Extense = extended ? 61/26, 65/20, 73/32.
Extent, 51/55, 51/58, 60/12, 60/18, 61/20, 65/19, 94/39,
     106/26.
Extentionall, *adj.*, 65/19, 65/20.
Exterous = exterior ? 82/63.
Extoll, 110/28.
Extrinsecally, 11/38 (*a*).
Extructed = constructed, 78/23.
Extruded, *adj.* = expelled, 78/23.
Eyen, eyne, 14/13, 17/40, 22/37, 26/74, *et frequenter*.

F

FACT (*sb.*) = deed, 74/42.
Fain = glad, 186/1 (*b*).
Fainly, 59/2.
Fairs = affairs, 23/50.
Falsitie, falsity, 75/61, 132/19.
Fardest = farthest, 141/40 (*b*).
Farre-piercing, 82/65.
Farre-shining, 93/26, 98/87.
Farst = farthest or farrest, 59/3.
Farwell, 86/26.
Fastigiated = tapered, 150/5 (*a*).
Fast-lock'd, 128/101.
Fat, *v.* = fatten, 74/41.
Fauster'd = fostered, 63/4.
Fayes, 87/37.
Feat (*sb.*), 81/53.
Feat, *adj.*, 82/68, 170/7.
Feeten = feet, 34/9.
Feigne = fiend, 85/20.
Fell = fierce, cruel, 56/6.
Felly = fiercely, 21/27.
Fend, *v.* = defend, 15/27.
Fet, *v.* = fetched, 39/67.
Few, 131/8.
Fiduciall = undoubting, 55/3.
Fierce-flying, 123/43.
Figurate, 141/15 (*b*).
Figuration, 106/29, 121/29.
Fimbling, *v.* = fumbling ? 26/83.
Fime (*sb.*) = mud, 53/2.
Finden, 47/12, 61/19, *et frequenter*.
Fire-eyed, 68/22.
Fit, *v.* = fitted, 93/26.
Fitten, 133/30.
Fixation, 133/33.
Flake, 18/60.
Flames, 18/58.
Flesh-clouded, 137/11.
Flet = fled? 39/67.
Flewest, 46/3.

Flight, *adj.*, 81/59.
Flit, 69/29, 111/43.
Flitten, 19/5, 62/38, 109/16.
Flittie = flitting, 44/11.
Flitting, *adj.*, 54/19, 65/26.
Flone = flown, 71/15.
Flore, 96/54.
Floting, 18/57.
Floud, 57/5.
Flouring, 18/57.
Flowred = flowered or blossomed, 115/38.
Flush = ripe, full, 110/24.
Flusher, 82/62, 128/101, 182/24 (*a*), *et alibi*.
Fond = foolish, 13/3, 14/17, *et frequenter*.
Fondling (*ib.*), 48/18.
Fondly, 25/67, 36/35, 53/15, 58/11, 119/3.
Fondnesse, 103 l. 3.
Foot, 77/13.
Fordone or foredone, 16/32, 36/34, 122/36.
Fore = before, 54/21, 57/2.
Fore, *v.* = fared, 15/26.
Fore-imprest, 75/60.
Foreslow, *v.*, 49/39, 100/16.
Fore-wonted, 120/18.
Forgerie, 100/102.
Forlorn, *v.* = forsaken, 13/6, 13/7, 45/20, 68/25.
Formlesse, 56/7.
Forrest-work, 17/41. In the East the finest and richest shawls are woven under trees in the open air.
Forthy = therefore, 48/28 : Spenser, F. Q., II. i. 14.
Foul = fowl, 179/14.
Frampared, frampar'd, *adj.* = frampold, rugged ? 37/40, 63/3.
Fraught = freighted, 109/20.
Fray, *v.* = frighten, 86/25.
Freez = frieze, 22/31.
Fridge = move hastily, 65/22.
Frie (*ib.*) = brood, 57/1, 174/1.
Frie, *v.*, 69/27, 99/94.
Frienge = fringe, 26/83.
Front = face, 23/49.
Fulgurant, 175/44 (*a*).
Fuliginous, 141/6 (*b*—from bottom).
Full-shining, 172/8.
Fulminant, 31/137.
Fulsome, = foul, 35/19, 55/31, 116/43.
Fulvid = fulvous, *i.e.* tawny, 13/3.
Fume = smoke, 172/17.
Fun, *v.* = found, 81/55, 133/35.
Furd = furred, thickened, 44/7.

G

Gainer, *adj.* = more advantageous, 98/81.
Gainly = readily, dexterously, 94/35, 127/85, 171/9.
Gan, 16/33, 35/22, *et frequenter*.
Gars, *v.* = makes (compulsion implied), 31/131.
Gate = gait, 53/10.
Gear = goods, 82/68, 91/6, 120/12, 124/58, 127/88.
Gent, *adj.* = gentle, well-born, 22/38, 23/41.

Gentle-breathing, 135/ l. 1 (*b*).
Getten, 174/8.
Ghesse, 23/48.
Gigantean = gigantic, 176/ l 1. (Anthologie).
'Gin, 33/1, 37/48, 46/1, 67/15, 71/11.
Ginst, 30/118.
Glaring = dazzling, 15/25. M'Cheyne in his fine hymn, 'When this passing world is done,' uses this word thus : ' When has sunk yon *glaring* sun.'
Glitterandly, 60/16.
Gloring = glorifying, transfiguring, 68/25. I too hastily concluded this was a misprint for ' glowing.' It ought to have been left ' gloring.' It is just possible that ' glaring' was intended, as in 15/25.
Godling = little god, 170/12.
Governance, 14/12.
Grail = broad open dish or snuffer-tray, 105/22.
Grammar-might, 23/49.
Gride, *v.* = cut, pricked, 48/28, 124/59, 176/20.
Grisell (*ib.*), 15/25.
Grisly, grissly, grizely, grisely, 33/6, 35/20, 97/73, 114/27, 123/44. Davies of Hereford so spells.
Grimic, 97/73.
Gulled, 29/111, 38/53.
Gullery, 6/30 (*b*).
Gullop, *v.* = gulp, 100/98.
Gulls, 24/51.
Gustables, 59/4.
Gyres = circles, 50/42.

H

Hale, 81/52.
Halfed, *v.*, 98/81.
Half-hid, *v.*, 81/57.
Half-nasty, 74/41.
Hap, *v.*, 15/24, 87/37.
Har, har = witches' cry, 126/81.
Heard = herd, 34/14.
Heart-bloud, 174/2.
Heart-striking, 31/134.
Heart-struck, 81/58.
Heaven, 58/13.
Heaven-threatening, 178/46 (*a*).
Heavy-clunging = clinging, 99/92.
Heddy = heady, 44/7.
Hent, *v.* = seize, take, 52/6, 76/4, 113/7, 126/74. Cf. Shakespeare :—
> ' Jog on, jog on, the footpath way,
> And merrily *hent* the stile-a.'
> *Winter's Tale*, iv. 2.

Hests, 17/46, 53/91, 86/26.
Heterogeneall, 48/24.
Heve = heave, 64/14.
Hew, hews, 17/45.
Hie, 119/1.
Hiew = hue, 15/20, 20/8, 20/11, 23/41.
High-gazing, 26/74.
Hight, *v.* = named, 13/5, 14/7, *et frequenter*.
Highs, 94/40.

Hispide = rough, 124/56, 205/ l. 10 (on Hall).
Histing, *v.* = calling me with 'hist,' 24/57.
Holden, 36/36, 76/5, 121/20, 171/17.
Hollowed, 97/66.
Holm = evergreen oak, 17/41.
Holp, *v.* = helped, 25/72.
Homogeneall, 12/13 (*b*), 73/31.
Hond = hand, 24/52, 52/6, 96/54, 126/75.
Honey-dewed, 134/4 (*a*).
Hoodwink, 44/10.
Hop'd-for, 133/28.
Hore = hoar, 14/15.
Hot-glowing, 67/12.
Hoyst, 124/56.
Humorous = given to humours, 6/29 (*a*).
Hydraes, 17/42.

I

I = ay, 142/29 (*b*).
Idea-Lond, 17/44.
Idiopathie, idiopathy = idiosyncrasy, 42/19 (*b*), 68/24, *et alibi.*
Idiot (*sb.*), idiots = ignorant, unlearned person, 7/25 (*b*), 23/49, 132/21.
Idiot (*adj.*), 24/55.
Idola, 102/38 (*a*).
Idole, 14/10.
Idols, 111/38.
Idolums, 110/31.
Idyllium, 7/38 (*a*).
Iim = wild beasts, 16/36. (See under 'Ziim.') Cf. Isaiah xiii. 22.
Imaginall, 14/16, 52/28, 55/4, *et frequenter.*
Imbew, 131/13.
Immerse, 6/21 (*a*), 106/25, 177/3.
Immersion, 7/54 (*a*).
Imminution = diminution, 14/9.
Immure, 67/7, 134/40.
Immur'd, 105/18.
Immutations, 15/23.
Impact, *v.* = to forcibly press, 104/9.
Impassible = incapable of suffering, 136/39 (*b*).
Impeccable = incapable of sinning, 164/26 (*a*).
Impregned, *adj.*, 18/58, 19/5, 96/58, 137/1.
Impresse, 18/58.
Imprest, 17/44.
Inact, *v.* = inactuate, *i.e.* put in action, 48/27, 112/2, *et frequenter.*
Inacted, 7/57 (*a*), 70/1, *et frequenter.*
Incarcerate, 113/10.
Inchoate, *v.*, 150/22 (*b*).
Incitation, 49/39.
Incivility = rudeness, 4/18.
Incompossibility = not being possible but by negation or destruction, 54/24, 86/26, 90/19 (*b*), *et alibi.*
Inconsistentnesse, 95/49.
Incorporate, 113/15, 124/57.
Incorporeitie, incorporeity, 59/1, 63 l. 1, 66/3, 111/38.
Incubi, 123/43.

Inculcate, *adj.*, 75/16.
Incurvate, *adj.*, 99/90.
Incurvation, 98/85.
Indentures, 37/47.
Independencies, 74/43.
Indewd, 27/84.
Indews, 113/10.
Indispers'd, indisperst, 60/9, 73/35.
Indispersial, 113/17.
Indistant, 136/39 (*a*).
Individuation, 72/19.
Individuous, 72/25, 127/85, 127/86.
Induements, 173/5.
Inebriate, 13/1.
Ineptnesse, 118/19.
Infold, *v.*, 133/36.
Informative, 48/24.
Ingenie, ingeny = genius, wit, 19 l. 3 (motto), 81/58.
Inly, 28/99, 54/18.
Inne, 18/61, 34/10.
Innumerous = innumerable, 86/30, 86/32.
Intellection = apprehension of ideas, 60/15, 64/9, 67/14, 109/17.
Intellective, 50/47.
Interfare = interfere, 25/71.
Insculption = inscription, 74/46.
Insert, *v.*, 72/24.
Insultations, 66/30.
Intended, 45/18.
Intentionall, 127/87.
Interpeal, *v.* = interpell, *i.e.* interrupt (by questioning), 36/31.
Interpellation, 23/44.
Interspire, *v.*, 97/73.
Intitle, *v.*, 82/68.
Intoxicate = intoxicated, 113/10.
Intromission, 80/48.
Intromit, 174/10.
Inust, 82/69, 105/23.
Inustion = branding, 163/3 (*a*).
Inwalling, *adj.*, 36/31.
Inwoning (*sb.*) = indwelling, 126/72.
Irefull, 76/6.
Irefulnesse, 63/4.
Irksome, 71/14.
Isosceles, 51/57.

J

JEAT = jet, 79/34.
Jejune, 67/13, 69/29.
Jet, *v.* = spring, leap, 79/34.
Jets, 18/52, 82/71.
Jollity, 28/100, 82/65.
Jot, 22/39.
Junctures, 49/35.

K

KAESARS, 100/104.
Karkas = carcase, 25/70.
Ken, 24/51, 64/15, 79/34, 104/5, 104/6, 106/31, 110/31.

Mete, 49/32.
Mickle, 45/25.
Microcosme = little world, 138/14 (*b*), *et alibi.* (*See* under Macrocosme.)
Milders, *v.* = turns to dust, 171/2.
Milk-white, 35/26.
Mimicall, 22/39.
Mince, 90/ l. 29 (*a*).
Mincing, 174/2.
Mindlesse = heedless, 76/7, 172/16.
Mind-mudding, 55/31.
Minish'd, 97/70.
Mirksome, 55/2, 60/17, 104/2, 108/8, 115/30.
Misconceit, 79/34.
Misfashion, 43/4.
Misgovernance, 53/16.
Moe, 29/116.
Moil'd = toiled, 75/56. *See* Nares, *s.v.*
Moistnesse, 56/8.
Mole-warp, 173/11.
Molten, 52/1.
Moment = momentum, 80/42, 174/11.
Monadicall, 54/23, 54/24.
Mongrill, 39/70.
Monts (*sb.*) = mounts, 125/68.
Moody, 16/37, 18/52, 36/41.
Moon-trampling, 36/29.
Morn-bright, 116/45.
Mornful, 53/13.
Mortalize, *v.*, 57/4.
Mostwhat, 42/54 (*a*), 120/15.
Mought, *v.* = might, 27/91, 29/109, 30/126, *et frequenter.*
Moul (*sb.*) = mould, earth, 69/29, 121/24.
Mount-moving, 181/ l. 3. (*Charitie.*)
Movable (*sb.*), 178/3.
Moven, 112/2, 127/84, 132/23.
Mow, mowes, 80/41, 119/6.
Muck-sprung, 173/7.
Muddy, 65/27.
Mungril, 21/25.
Musing, 54/28.
Mutings = dung-droppings, 30/119.

N

NARRE = near, 98/82.
Narrow-compast, 100/103.
Nathelesse, 15/28, 23/47, 33/2.
Navell, 24/59.
Nay = neigh, 172/5.
Ne = not, 14/8, 26/83, *et frequenter.*
Nearly, 8/4 (*a*—To Reader).
Neater, 96/56.
Nectar-droppings, 174/1.
Neezings, 178/54 (*a*).
Neurospast = a puppet or little moving figure, 49/34.
Never-shaken, 71/12.
Nicer, 127/84.
Nie, 35/27.
Night-trifling, 47/11.

Nill, *v.*, 131/17.
Nimble, 33/2.
Nominance, 82/65.
Non, 132/35.
Non-quantity, 59/7.
Non-replicate, 60/18.
No'te, 20/14, 30/116, *et frequenter.*
Nould = ne would, 16/38, 22/38, *et frequenter.*
Nullitie, 55/1.
Numbing, 114/21.
Numerositie, 99/87.
Numerous = metrical, 8/3 (*b*—To Reader).
Nummed, 49/29.
Nuncio = ambassador, 182/21 (*a*).

O

OBEDIENTIALL, 32/139.
Object, *v.* = to place or bring before, 52/2.
Obmurmurings, 60/10.
Obnubilate, *v.* = be-cloud, 113/10, 113/15.
Occasionate, *v.* = occasion, cause, 69/34.
Occasioned, 70/5.
Ocean main, 19/5.
Occident, 25/63.
Odde, 85/21, 86/33.
Oeconomie (economy), 6/23.
Officious, 7/43 (*b*).
Ogdoas = ὀγδοάς, *i.e.* the number eight, 20/15.
Oke = oak, 17/41
Omniform, 14/9, 102/7 (*b*), *et alibi.*
Omniformity, 110/33, 110/34, 111/44, 113/17, 114/22, *et alibi.*
Omnisciency, 140/32 (*a*).
Onyons = onions, 22/37.
Opacity, 71/14, 82/62, 82/64.
Opacous, 94/32, 179/3.
Opake, 33/2, 82/64, 91/7.
Opakeness, 49/31.
Ope-right = right open, 68/23.
Ophiucbus = Ophiuchus—one of the old northern constellations, 98/77.
Oppugne, 76/5.
Optick-glasses, 82/62.
Orbe, 51/52.
Orbiculation, 160/13 (*b*).
Ore = gold, 94/34.
Ore-crow, 27/87.
Ore-spill, 38/59, 122/34.
Orewraught, 171/5.
Organity, 48/24.
Organizate, *adj.*, 121/21.
Originall (*sb.*), 73/38.
Othersome, 140/14 (*a*), 159/4 (*a*).
Othersometime, 165/6 (*a*).
Out-created, 86/27.
Out-garment = outer-garment or visible, 139/14 (*u*).
Out-heaven, 77/15.
Out-ray'd, 72/22.
Out-roll, *v.*, 105/14.

Proven, 79/37.
Psychathanasie, 131/15.
Psychopannychie, 103 l. 4, 104/3, 104/11.
Psychopannychite, 104/12, 115/36, 128/104.
Psychycall, 54/23.
Pulchritude, 137/2 (a—from bottom).
Purvey, 125/70.
Putid = base, worthless, 43/6.
Py, pye, 17/41, 25/62.
Pythagore = Pythagoras, 13/4.

Q

QUADRATE, 32/143, 37/51, 37/52.
Quære, quere (sb.), 27/84, 51/53.
Queint, 27/88, 58/15, 127/88.
Quelme, v., 15/25.
Quenchen, 56/10.
Queres = queries, 27/84.
Queristers-wood, 24/60.
Querks, 37/46.
Quick, 60/9, 110/34, 120/13, 130/3.
Quick-eyd, 50/41, 178/50 (a).
Quire, v. = enquire, 23/45.

R

RAGEFULL, 43/5, 170/11.
Rascall, 66/3.
Raught, 22/35, 68/15, 79/32.
Raving, 130/3.
Ray, rays, rayd, raying, 71/16, 77/10, 87/36, 109/18, 110/28, 115/32, 116/48, 128/102, 132/25, 188/5 (a), 188/33 (b).
Reacquainten, 104/12.
Readen, 35/26.
Realtie, realty = reality, actuality, 61/22, 77/55, 94/34, 115/29.
Receiven, 114/26, 173/16.
Recomfort, 52/3.
Record, 13/1.
Recoyl = to return, 119/7.
Recure, 52/4, 54/20, 62/38, 106/32.
Redound, v. = to be redundant, 61/29.
Red-scaled, 116/43.
Reduceth, 11/22 (a), 12/3 (a).
Reduplicate, 62/36.
Reduplicative, 108/7.
Reechoning, 171/15.
Reek (sb.) = smoke, 126/79, 140/2.
Refert, v., 72/24.
Refract, 19/7.
Regiment = government, 34/16.
Reluctancy, 157/1 (a).
Remorse, 90/2.
Renown, v. tr., 192/1. 6. (Philotheus.)
Repast (sb.), 37/49.
Repeal, 61/23.
Repedation = stepping or going back, 98/76, 155/17 (a).
Repugnant, 7/14 (a).
Requere, 35/24.
Resect, v., 50/46.

Respired, 16/38.
Restauration, 53/9.
Restrain, 66/4.
Resty (adj.) = restive, 26/7.
Retection = act of disclosing, 20/7, 80/40.
Retent, v., 65/26.
Retention, 133/31.
Retinence, 105/13.
Retinue, 96/57. Even Dryden so accentuates.
Retractions, 49/34.
Retracts, 20/16.
Retreat, v., 104/6.
Retrocession, 82/66.
Retrogradation, 154/1 (b), 155/26 (a).
Retrude = thrust back, 59/6.
Reverse, v., 120/9.
Revert, 86/33, 122/40.
Rid, 19/2, 127/90.
Rine = rime frost, 22/31.
Risen, 135/14 (a).
Risibility = power of laughing, 142/38 (b).
Rives, 177/l. 2. (Exosc.)
Riving, 14/7.
Rode = road, 22/35.
Romboides, 51/57.
Rorid = ruddy, 163/16 (b).
Rose-cheek'd, 100/99.
Roul, 35/23.
Round and rounds, 16/30, 135/24 (b).
Rout and Routs, 34/13, 86/26, 90/23 (a), 98/84, 134/9 (b).
Rowling, 31/29.
Roxid = dewy, 53/18, 54/25, 95/48, 100/100.
Ruby-lip'd, 100/99.
Rue, 54/18.
Ruinate, v., 35/22, 53/15, 58/11, 74/43, 106/28.
Russet, 23/42.
Rusty = rust-coloured, 178/1 (Ins. Phil.), 198/23 (b).
Rythmes, 8/23 (To Reader b), 13/2.

S

SAD—sometimes ordinary sense, and in other cases = solid, 7/11 (b), 23/44, 78/24, 86/34, 90/28, 93/21 (= sorrowful), 96/61, 96/63.
Sadly, 13/2.
Sadducisme, 6/8 (b).
Salvage (sb.), 119/5.
Salvag'd (adj.) 122/38.
Salve, 82/70.
Sans = without (French), 47/17, 127/90.
Saron = Sharon? 112/3.
Satisfiable, 7/50 (b).
Saught, 38/58, 69/26.
Sayen, sayn, sain = say and also bless, 76/6, 80/39, 108/8, 111/39, et frequenter.
Scalene, 51/57.
Sciency, 21/26, 45/24, 51/54, 67/6.
Scissare = longitudinal opening, 138/l. 3 (b—from bottom).
Sconses, 80/41.

Scoure, 82/64, 94/40.
Seazing, 98/81.
Secesse, 8/11 (a—To Reader).
Secundary, 56/5.
Seemly, 36/37.
Self-centrality, 132/19.
Self-centrall, 132/20.
Self-deadnesse, 147/26 (b), 148/2 (b).
Self-desire, 178/ last line a.
Self-essentiall, 110/34.
Self-gnawing, 115/36.
Selfnesse, 133/36, et alibi.
Self-nothingnesse, 148/3 (b).
Self-ray, 128/103.
Self-reduplication, 62/33.
Self-sens'd, 38/60.
Self-sensednesse, 143/2, 159/18 (b).
Self-senselessnesse, 148/4 (b).
Self-strucken, 159/ last line (b).
Self-vitality, 110/34.
Self-vivacious, 50/45.
Senden, 62/36, 116/43.
Sense-sympathy, 17/49.
Sent, 7/12 (b), 59/4, 64/9.
Sequency, 86/34.
Setten, 45/23, 58/8, 58/14, 60/18, et frequenter.
Settlednesse, 162/3 (a).
Seven-corded, 182/19 (a).
Severall, 92/18, 96/55.
Shaken, 36/32.
Shapen, 120/14.
Shapen'd, 58/9.
Shapening, 58/9, 68/19.
Sheen, 53/11, 61/24, 68/22, 98/79, 121/27.
Shent = reproached, scolded—participle of 'shend,'
    34/16, 37/42. Shakespeare, Twelfth Night, iv. 2.
Shelves, 100/105.
Shift, 94/39.
Shining-silver, adj., 98/82.
Shiver = shive, or small slice, 79/35.
Shreeks, 29/110.
Shrill, v., 91/3.
Shone = shown, 91/7.
Shotten, 114/25.
Shrow = shrew, 125/65.
Siez = sieze, 98/81.
Sighen, 36/39.
Silency, 21/20, 39/65, 132/23.
Silken, 50/48, 53/12.
Silver-bowed, 50/42.
Silvered, 97/66.
Silver-sounded, 8/14 (b—To Reader), 100/107.
Siping = sipping or leaking, 35/24.
Site, 59/6, 65/22, 68/23.
Sith = since, 8/1, 12/1, et frequenter.
Sithence, 153/19 (b—from bottom).
Sitten, 56/9, 110/26.
Skonses, 34/13.
Sky-coloured, 15/26.

Slabby = viscuous, 128/101, 191/ l. 5 (a).
Slake, slaked = slacken, 86/30, 125/69, 170/12.
Slavering, 34/15.
Slick = sleek—in living use in United States of America,
    61/24.
Slocken = slaked, 173/7. (Still in use in Scotland.)
Slooping = sloping, 174/13.
Slouch (ib.), 34/8.
Slow-foot, 24/57.
Slow-footed, 32/148.
Slubbering, adj., 146/17 (b).
Smoreing, smoring = smothering, 36/38, 71, 15,
    178/21 (a).
Smouldry, 60/8, 124/55.
Sneep'd = sneaped, i.e. reproved abruptly, 114/18.
Sneezing, adj., 45/22.
Snorted, v., 104/5.
Snow-limb'd, 100/99.
Soaming—query--an imitative word? 110/31.
Soliditie, 50/42.
Solitaire, 99/93.
Solitude, 132/20.
Solyma, 15/27.
Sootie, 44/8.
Sore = soar, 145/24 (b).
Sory, 60/14.
Soul-smiting, 174/1.
Soure or sowr, 75/61, 81/58, 84/10, 85/15, 85/17.
Sourely, 130/4.
Sourse = source, 19/ l. 2, 32/147, 47/14, 53/17, et alici.
Souse = dip, 24/56.
Souses, 34/7.
Sown = to swoon, 116/49.
Spattered, adj., 172/11, 178/4 (a).
Spaul = spittle, 36/29, 126/77, 206/12.
Specious, 64/12.
Spectres, 78/21.
Speedinesse, 81/55.
Spell = gospel, 86/31.
Spenden, 115/37, 73/2.
Sperm, 48/25, 127/86.
Spermall, 58/9.
Spermaticall, 48/25, 48/27, et frequenter.
Spermatick, 79/32, 92/11, 100/101, 108/6.
Spersed, sperst, 91/5, 95/48.
Spight = spite, 120/15, 123/47, 124/53.
Spill = spoil, 43/5, 64/8, 86/30, 111/44, 133/28. So Ben
    Jonson,

    ' Nor look too kind on my desires,
      For then my hopes will *spill* me.'
                    (Underwoods : 11. Song)
    and,
    ' 'Twere better spare a butt [of wine] then *spill* his Muse '
                    (Ibid. lxxxvi)

Spirituall, 60/11, 62/36, 64/17.
Sportfull, 119/7.
Spot, v., = spat, 126/77.
Spreaden, 20/8, 43/3, et frequenter.
Spreed, 58/8.

Sprent, 95/48.
Spright = spirit, 8/9 (*a*—To Reader), 13/6, *et frequenter*.
Springen, 28/99, 62/35.
Spritely, *adv.*, 77/16, 133/35.
Sprong, 13/1, 13/5, 63/6, 65/20, *et frequenter*.
Spruse = spruce, 22/39, 131/10.
Spume = foam, 124/58.
Squalid, 124/62.
Stabilitates, 50/43.
Stades = stadia, *i.e.* paces, 95/41.
Stage, 19/5.
Stain, *v.*, 50/41, 179/4.
Stalking (trees) = trees behind which sportsmen conceal themselves in aiming, 131/9.
Standen, 54/20, 78/26, 80/46, 99/95.
Star-eynd, 100/99.
Star-like, 38/57.
Stayest, 50/43.
Steddy, 97/70.
Steel-coloured, 116/45.
Steem = esteem and steam, 31/134, 34/17, 43/6, 70/2, 113/12.
Steeple-cap = steeple-crown or high-crowned cap or hat, 15/25.
Stein = stain, 121/22.
Sterill, 51/52, 67/11.
Stert = start, 62/35, 122/40.
Sterve, 114/24.
Stiff-standers, 76/5.
Still-pac'd, 15/25.
Stilly, 172/16.
Stillest, 140/5 (*b*).
Stole, 92/2, 92/18.
Stond = stand, 96/54.
Stony, 116/44.
Stound, 31/134, 33/5, 52/6, 77/13, 176/18 (*a*).
Stouping, 67/4.
Stour, stowre = tumult, disturbance, 18/53, 37/43, 84/10, 130/1, 175/47 (*a*).
Strad, *v.* = strode, 31/132, 116/40.
Straight, streight, 61/22, 97/69, 97/73, 99/90.
Straighted, 23/42.
Stranger, 62/39.
Streak, 49/30.
Streem, 97/67.
Stretchen, 60/14, 108/11.
Strifefull, 56/6.
Strond, 17/44.
Strong-awing, 39/66.
Strong-winged, 78/22.
Strowd = strewed, 78/23.
'Stroy, 'stroy'd, 44/12, 56/6, 59/1, 65/23.
Strucken, 134/5 (*a*), 160/10 (*b*).
Style = stylus, 93/20.
Styptick, *adj.*, 116/41.
Subducted, 153/6 (*a*).
Subduction, 152/ last line (*a*), 152/2 (*b*).
Subordinance, 20/12.
Subservient, 10/15 (*b*).

Subsistencie, 51/59, 85/21.
Subtile, 65/18, 99/91.
Sucken = sucked, 123/43.
Suddenly = instantly, 6/2 (*a*).
Suing, 13/3.
Summitie, summity = height or top, 69/30, 75/57, *et alibi*.
Sun-bright, 13/3.
Sunday-cloths = best clothes, 15/20.
Superficiary, 12/37 (*b*).
Surceast, 54/18.
Surquedry = pride, pomp, 31/130.
Susception, 65/24.
Suspense, *adj.*, 140/10 (*b*).
Suspiration = sigh, 69/26.
Sustentacle = support, 54/25.
Swallow (*sb.*), 134/40.
Swapping, *adj.* = sweeping (noise implied), 44/11.
Swiftnesse—misprinted 'switnesse,' 81/56.
Swill, *v.* = drink (to excess implied), 152/7 (*a*—from bottom).
Swink = toil, labour, 37/48, 66/29, 131/16.
Swoln-glowing, 178/4 (*a*).
Swommen, 134/8 (*b*).
Swonk, 47/12. (See under 'Swink.')
Symtomes, 29/110.
Synods, 99/87, 99/93.

T

T'AGATHON = the good, 77/11.
Tactuall, 68/21, *et alibi*.
Taffity, 26/75.
Taken, 115/37.
Tantalize, 105/19.
Tarre = tar, 178/1. (Ins. Phil.)
Tarry, *adj.*, 116/43.
Teen = grief, and also rage, 22/37, 29/109, 123/48, 178/9 (*a*).
Temperate, *v.*, 50/43.
Tender, 64/15.
Teneritie, 81/58.
Terrene, 8/15 (*a*), 120/17, 121/22.
Testation = attestation, 73/29.
Theiv'd, *adj.*, 45/20, 45/23.
Then = than, 4/3, *et frequenter*.
Theologasters = empirics in Theology, 163/10 (*b*—from bottom).
Theosophicall, 76 l. 3 (motto).
Thick, *v.*, 15/27, 15/28.
Thickest = thickset, 170/8.
Thin-shot, 68/23.
Thin-spun, 84/9.
Tho' = then, 22/35, 130/4.
Thorough = through, 91/45, 93/36, 126/72, 126/73, 181/7.
Thorough-siping = through-sipping, leaking drop by drop or oozing, 35/24.
Thralls, 116/41.
Threatning, 49/29.
Throw (*sb.*), 53/10.
Throwen, 96/55.

Warranter, 7/5 (*a*).
Wast = waste, 91/45, 121/25, 128/96.
Wastefull, 8/8 (*b*—To Reader), 22/33, 91/5.
Wastning, *adj.*, 98/82.
Waxen, *v.*, 24/66, 47/15, *et frequenter.*
Wayment = lamentation, 53/9.
Weak, 26/80.
Weed, 19/2, 51/51, 124/57.
Weedery, 32/141.
Weeds, 18/61, 120/16.
Ween = think, imagine, 27/88, 35/27, *et frequenter.*
Weend, 23/45, 124/61.
Weet = wit, 32/145, 104/11, 111/40, 112/1, 116/50. (See under 'to-weet.')
Weetingly = wittingly, 53/15.
Welkin = sky, 19/7, 71/14.
Well away, 174/6.
Well-favorednesse, 144/25 (*a*).
Well-proportionated, 96/55.
Wex, 174/11.
Wexen, 13/3, 174/8.
Whenas, 47/14, 95/46.
Whereas, 38/55.
Whileare, whileere, 20/11, 46/6, 92/17, 93/23.
Whilome, whylom = formerly, 14/16, 21/28, 31/132, *et alibi.*
Whinneying, 44/13.
Whirl-pool-turnings, 134/14 (*b*).
Whisling, 85/18.
Wight, 14/8.
Wis, wisse = wish, wit, 22/32, 27/94, 67/10, 127/91.
Wise-preventing, 100/105.
Wist, 24/53.
Wistly = earnestly, 50/43, 61/25.
Withstond, 17/44.
Withouten, 15/24, 18/56, 20/12, 21/23, *et frequenter.*
Witlesse, 93/19.
Witty = wise, 29/107.
Wizard, wizzard = wise man, 47/10, 93/19, 122/36, 123/42, 126/81.
Woes = woos, 123/48.
Won, *v.* = went, 16/32.
Won, wonne, wonnes, *v.* = to dwell, 16/32, 16/36, *et frequenter.*
Won, wonne, wonnes (*sb.*) = dwelling, 17/50, 21/22, *et frequenter.*
Wood, *adj.* = mad, 18/59, 27/93. 53/15, 123/49.
Wool-gathering = vagrant idleness, 93/27.
Wool-lining, 123/43.
Worken, 38/55.
Wot, wote = wit, know, 8/9 (*a*—To Reader), 14/12, *et frequenter.*
Wot'st, 173/18.
Wox, 39/63, 39/64, 114/29.
Woxen, 23/44, 55/30, *et frequenter.*
Wraught = wrought, 84/8.
Wrigge, *v.* = wriggle, 62/37.
Wrimpled, *adj.* = query—wimpled? 17/47.
Writh = writhe, 32/143.

Writheld = withered, haggard, 123/47.
Writhen, 7/17 (*b*).

Y

Yblent, 24/56, 106/32, 113/11.
Yblown, 47/9.
Yborn = born, 21/28, 36/33, 56/5, 74/41.
Yborn = borne, 56/5, 68/25, 74/41, 82/70.
Ybound, 92/8, 109/21, 133/38.
Ybrent = burned, 14/17, 124/55.
Ybrought, 91/2, 95/45.
Ychanged, 58/8, 121/25.
Ycheckt, 114/28.
Yclad, 20/13, 22/31, 22/33, 38/56, 66/3. 119/3.
Ycleeped = named, 21/28, 25/67, *et frequenter.*
Ycleft, 81/54.
Yclos'd, 120/18.
Ycrown'd, 77/13.
Ydead, 104/5.
Ydrad = dread, 18/51.
Ydred, 48/19.
Ydrest, 38/56.
Yfed, 100/100.
Yfere = together, 32/144, 35/24. *See* Spenser, F. Q. I. ix. 1.

> 'O goodly chain, wherewith *yfere*
> The vertues linked are.'

Yfild = filled, 85/24.
Yflone, yflown, 34/47, 87/37, 114/20, 121/22.
Yfraught, 95/45, 107/36.
Ygo, 130/5.
Ygone, 37/43, 115/37, 131/12.
Yielden, 121/19.
Ylent, 59/4, 132/22.
Ylet, 53/12.
Ymeint = mixed, 120/12, 125/71.
Ymet, 33/2.
Ymong, 134/15 (*a*).
Yode = past tense of *yede*, to go,' 22/35, 22/38, 33/5. So Spenser, 'Before them *yode* on lustie tabrere' (Shep. Cal. May, l. 22).
Yongster, 22/38.
Ypent = enclosed or penned, 106/25.
Yrapt, 21/20.
Yrold, 15/18, 26/76.
Yspent, 127/86.
Ystruck, 103/1.
Ytaught, 84/8.
Ytore, 120/17.
Ytorn, 31/129, 68/25, 174/12.
Ytost, 19/4, 35/21, 71/8.
Ywrapt, 13/1, 21/20, 67/8, 113/15.
Ywrit, 35/26.
Ywrought, 104/7, 109/20.

Z

Ziim = wild beasts, 16/36. *See* Isaiah xiii. 21, and under 'Iim.'

FINIS.